```
D1393116
```

Acclaim for Harry Turtledove

'With shocking vividness, Turtledove demonstrates the extreme fragility of our modern world . . . This is state-of-the-art alternate history, nothing less'
Publishers Weekly
(Starred Review for HOW FEW REMAIN)

'Engrossing . . . definitely the work of one of alternate history's authentic modern masters . . . totally fascinating'
Booklist

'A cast of thousands with a plot to match . . . a wealth of fascinating speculation'
Kirkus Reviews

and for WORLDWAR

'Turtledove's historical scholarship, narrative technique, dry wit and deft characterisation distinguish this novel, just as they did its predecessors, making it a rousing wrap-up to a monument of alternate history from a master of the genre'
Publishers Weekly

Also by Harry Turtledove
and available in the New English Library

Worldwar: In the Balance
Worldwar: Tilting the Balance
Worldwar: Upsetting the Balance
Worldwar: Striking the Balance

The Two Georges (with Richard Dreyfuss)
How Few Remain
A World of Difference

The Great War: American Front

Colonisation: Second Contact

Harry Turtledove

NEW ENGLISH LIBRARY
Hodder & Stoughton

Copyright © 1999 by Harry Turtledove

First published in Great Britain
in 1999 by Hodder and Stoughton
A division of Hodder Headline
First published in paperback in 2000 by Hodder and Stoughton

The right of Harry Turtledove to be identified as the
Author of the Work has been asserted by him in accordance
with the Copyright, Designs and Patents Act 1988.

A New English Library Paperback

10 9 8 7 6 5 4

All rights reserved. No part of this publication may be
reproduced, stored in a retrieval system, or transmitted, in any
form or by any means without the prior written permission of
the publisher, nor be otherwise circulated in any form of binding
or cover other than that in which it is published and without a
similar condition being imposed on the subsequent purchaser.

All characters in this publication are fictitious
and any resemblance to real persons, living or dead,
is purely coincidental.

A CIP catalogue record for this title
is available from the British library.

ISBN 0 340 75144 4

Typeset by Hewer Text Ltd, Edinburgh
Printed and bound in Great Britain by
Mackays of Chatham PLC, Chatham, Kent

Hodder and Stoughton
A division of Hodder Headline
338 Euston Road
London NW1 3BH

Colonization: Second Contact

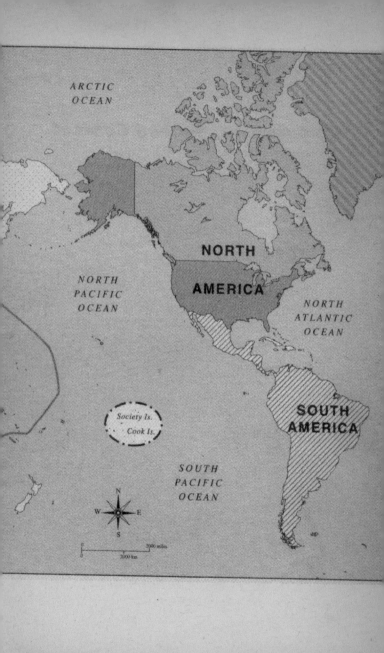

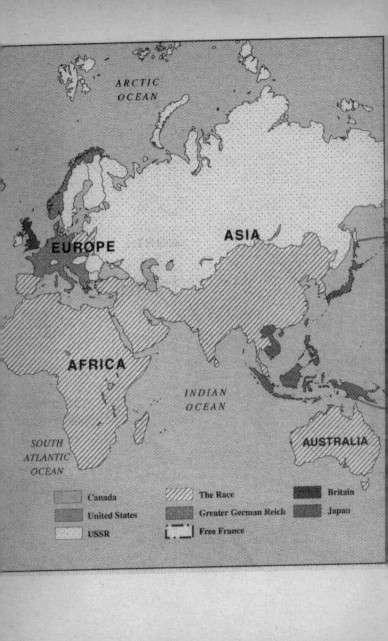

1

Atvar, the commander of the Race's conquest fleet, poked a control with a fingerclaw. A holographic image sprang into being above the projector in the fleetlord's office. In the forty years since the conquest fleet came to Tosev 3 (half that many local years), he had grown all too intimately familiar with that particular image.

So had Kirel, shiplord of the *127th Emperor Hetto*, the bannership of the conquest fleet. The body paint on his scaly, green-brown hide was more ornate than every other male's save only Atvar's. His mouth fell open in amusement, revealing a great many small, sharp teeth. A slight waggle to his lower jaw gave his laughter a sardonic twist.

'Once more we behold the mighty Tosevite warrior, eh, Exalted Fleetlord?' he said. He ended the sentence with an interrogative cough.

'Even so, Shiplord,' Atvar answered. 'Even so. He does not look as if he would cause us much trouble, does he?'

'By the Emperor, no,' Kirel said. Both Atvar and he swiveled their turreted eyes so they looked down at the ground for a moment: a gesture of respect for the sovereign back on distant Home.

As Atvar had done so many times before, he walked around the hologram to view it from all sides. The Tosevite male was mounted on a hairy local quadruped. He wore a tunic of rather

1

rusty chain armor, and over it a light cloth coat. A pointed iron helmet protected his braincase. Tufts of yellowish hair grew like dry grass on his scaleless, pinkish cheeks and jaw. For armament, he had a spear, a sword, a knife, and a shield with a cross painted in red on it.

A long, hissing sigh escaped Atvar. 'If only it had been as easy as we thought it would be.'

'Truth, Exalted Fleetlord,' Kirel said. 'Who would have thought the Big Uglies' – the nickname the Race used for its Tosevite subjects and neighbors – 'could have changed so much in a mere sixteen hundred years?'

'No one,' Atvar said. 'No one at all.' He used a different cough this time, one that emphasized the words preceding it. They deserved emphasis. The Race – and the Hallessi and Rabotevs, whose planets the Empire had ruled for thousands of years – changed only very slowly, only very cautiously. For the Race, one millennium was like another. After sending a probe to Tosev 3, everyone back on Home had blithely assumed the barbarians there would not have changed much by the time the conquest fleet arrived.

Never in its hundred thousand years of unified imperial history – and never in the chaotic times before, for that matter – had the Race got a larger and more unpleasant surprise. When the conquest fleet did reach Tosev 3, it found not sword-swinging savages but a highly industrialized world with several empires and not-empires battling one another for dominance.

'Even after all these years, there are times when I still feel rage that we did not completely conquer this planet,' Atvar said. 'But, on the other fork of the tongue, there are also times when I feel nothing but relief that we still maintain control over any part of its surface.'

'I understand, Exalted Fleetlord,' Kirel said.

'I know you do, Shiplord. I am glad you do,' Atvar said. 'But I do wonder if anyone back on Home truly understands. I have the dubious distinction of commanding the first interstellar conquest fleet in the history of the Race that did not

2

conquer completely. That is not how I intended hatchlings to remember me.'

'Conditions here were not as we anticipated them,' Kirel said loyally. He'd had his chances to be disloyal, had them and not taken them. By now, Atvar was willing to believe he wouldn't. He went on, 'Do you not agree that there is a certain amount of irony in the profit we have made off the Tosevites by selling them this image and others from the probe? Their own scholars desire those photographs because they have none of their own from what seems to them to be a distant and uncivilized time.'

'Irony? Yes, that is one of the words I might apply to the situation – one of the politer words,' Atvar said. He went back to his desk and prodded the control again. The Tosevite warrior vanished. He wished he could make all the Tosevites vanish that easily, but no such luck. He replaced the warrior's image with a map of the surface of Tosev 3.

By his standards, it was a chilly world, with too much water and not enough land. Of what land there was, the Race did not rule enough. Only the southern half of the lesser continental mass, the southwest and south of the main continental mass, and the island continent to the southeast of the main continental mass were reassuringly red on the map. The not-empires of the Americans, the Russkis, and the Deutsche all remained independent, and needed colors of their own. So did the island empires of Britain and Nippon, though both of them were shrunken remnants of what they had been when the conquest fleet came to Tosev 3.

Kirel also turned one eye toward the map, while keeping the other on Atvar. 'Truly, Exalted Fleetlord, it could be worse.'

'So it could,' Atvar said with another sigh. 'But it could also be a great deal better. It would be a great deal better if these areas here on the eastern part of the main continental mass, especially this one called China, acknowledged our rule as they should.'

'I have long since concluded that the Big Uglies never do things as they should,' Kirel said.

3

'I agree completely,' the fleetlord replied. His little tailstump twitched in agitation. 'But how are we to convince the fleetlord of the colonization fleet that this is the case?'

Now Kirel sighed. 'I do not know. He lacks our experience with this world. Once he acquires it, he will, I am sure, come round to our way of thinking. But we must expect him to be rigid for a time.'

Back on Home, *rigid* was a term of praise. It had been a term of praise when the conquest fleet came to Tosev 3, too. No more. Males of the Race who stayed too rigid stood not a chance of understanding the Big Uglies. By the standards of Home, the males of the conquest fleet – those who still survived – had grown dreadfully flighty.

Males . . . Atvar said, 'It will be good to have females in range of the scent receptors on my tongue once more. When they come into season and I smell their pheromones, I will have an excuse for not thinking about this accursed world for a while. I look forward to having the excuse, you understand, not to the breeding itself.'

'Of course, Exalted Fleetlord,' Kirel said primly. 'You are no Big Ugly, to have such matters always on your mind.'

'I should hope not!' Atvar exclaimed. Like any other member of the Race, he viewed Tosevite sexuality with a sort of horrified fascination. Intellectually, he grasped how the Big Uglies' year-round interest in mating colored every aspect of their behavior. But he had no feel for the subtleties, or indeed for what the Big Uglies no doubt viewed as broad strokes. Despite intensive research, few males of the Race did, any more than the Tosevites could understand the Race's dispassionate view of such matters.

Pshing, Atvar's adjutant, came into the chamber. One side of his body was painted in a pattern that matched the fleetlord's; the other showed his own, far lower, rank. He bent his forward-sloping torso into the posture of respect and waited to be noticed.

'Speak,' Atvar said. 'Give forth.'

4

'I thank you, Exalted Fleetlord,' Pshing said. 'I beg leave to report that the lead ships of the colonization fleet have passed within the orbit of Tosev 4, the planet the Big Uglies call Mars. Very soon now, those ships will seek to circle and land on this world.'

'I am aware of this, yes.' Atvar's voice was even drier than the desert surrounding the riverside city – Cairo, the local name for it was – where he made his headquarters. 'Is my distinguished colleague in the colonization fleet aware that the Tosevites, for all their protestations of peaceful intent, may seek to harm his ships when they do reach Tosev 3?'

'Fleetlord Reffet continues to assure me that he is,' Pshing replied. 'He was quite taken aback to receive radio transmissions from the various Tosevite not-empires.'

'He should not have been,' Atvar said. 'We have been warning him for some time of the Big Uglies' ever-increasing capacities.'

Kirel said, 'Exalted Fleetlord, he will have to learn by experience, as we also had to do. Let us hope his experience proves less painful than ours.'

'Indeed.' Atvar let out a worried hiss. His voice grew grim: 'And let us hope all the Tosevites take seriously our warning to them that an attack on the colonization fleet by any of them will be construed as an attack by all of them, and that we shall do our utmost to punish all of them should any such attack occur.'

'I wish we had not had to issue such a warning,' Kirel said.

'So do I,' Atvar replied. 'But at least four and perhaps five of their realms possess missile-firing undersea ships – who back on Home would have dreamt of such things?'

'Oh, I understand the problem,' Kirel said. 'But the general warning all but invites the Tosevites to combine against us and to reduce their conflicts among themselves.'

'Diplomacy.' Atvar made the word into a curse. Manuals on the subject, their data gleaned from the Race's ancient history and early conquests, suggested playing the locals off against one another. But, to Atvar and his colleagues, such concerns were but theory, and musty theory at that. The Big Uglies, divided among themselves, were expert practitioners of the art. After a negotiating session with them, Atvar always wanted to count his fingers and toes to make sure he hadn't inadvertently traded them away.

Pshing said, 'When the colonists are revived from cold sleep, when they come down to Tosev 3, we *will* begin to turn this into a proper world of the Empire.'

'I admire your confidence, Adjutant,' Kirel said. Pshing crouched respectfully. Kirel went on, 'I wonder what the colonists will make of us. We are hardly proper males of the Race ourselves any more – dealing with the Tosevites for so long has left us as addled as bad eggs.'

'We have changed,' Atvar agreed. Back on Home, that would have been a curse. Not here, though he had taken a long time to realize it. 'Had we not changed, our war with the Big Uglies would have wrecked this planet, and what would the colonization fleet have done then?'

Not a single male on Tosev 3 had found an answer to that question. Atvar was sure Reffet would have no answer for it, either. But he was also sure the fleetlord of the colonization fleet would have questions of his own. Would he himself, would any male on Tosev 3, be able to find answers for them?

The pitcher windmilled into his delivery. The runner took off from first base. The batter hit a sharp ground ball to short. The shortstop gobbled it up and fired it over to first. The softball slapped Sam Yeager's mitt, beating the runner to the bag by a step and a half. The umpire had hustled up from behind home plate. 'You're out!' he yelled, and threw his fist in the air.

'That's the ballgame,' Yeager said happily. 'Another win for the good guys.' He tacked on an emphatic cough for good measure.

'Nice game, Major,' the pitcher said. 'A homer and a double – I guess we'll take that.'

'Thanks, Eddie,' Yeager said, chuckling. 'I can still get around on a softball.' He was in his mid-fifties, and in good shape for his mid-fifties, but he couldn't hit a baseball for beans any more. It irked him; he'd been in his eighteenth season of minor-league ball when the Lizards came, and he'd kept playing as much and as long as he could after going into the Army.

He rolled the softball toward the chicken-wire dugout in back of first base. He'd been an outfielder when he played for money, but he couldn't cover the ground out there any more, either, so nowadays he played first. He could still catch and he could still throw.

A couple of guys from the other team came over and shook his hand. They'd been playing just for the fun of playing. He'd had fun, too – he wouldn't have put on spikes if he didn't have fun – but he'd gone out there to win. Playing for money for all those years had ingrained that in him.

Up in the wooden bleachers behind the wire fence, Barbara clapped her hands along with the other wives and girlfriends. Sam doffed his cap and bowed. His wife made a face at him. That wasn't why he put the cap back on in a hurry, though. He was getting thin on top, and Southern California summer sunshine was no joke. He'd sunburned his scalp a couple of times, but he intended never, ever, to do it again.

'Head for Jose's!' Win or lose, that cry rang out after a game. Winning would make the tacos and beer even better. Sam and Barbara piled into their Buick and drove over to the restaurant. It was only a few blocks from the park.

The Buick ran smoothly and quietly. Like more and more cars every year, it burned hydrogen, not gasoline – technology borrowed from the Lizards. Sam coughed when he got stuck behind an old gas-burner that poured out great gray clouds of stinking exhaust. 'Ought to be a law against those miserable things,' he complained.

Barbara nodded. 'They've outlived their usefulness, that's certain.' She spoke with the precision of someone who'd done graduate work in English. Yeager minded his p's and q's more

7

closely than he would have had he not been married to someone like her.

At Jose's, the team hashed over the game. Sam was ten years older than anybody else and the only one who'd ever played pro ball, so his opinions carried weight. His opinion in other areas carried weight, too; Eddie, the pitcher, said, 'You deal with the Lizards all the time, Major. What's it going to be like when that big fleet gets here?'

'Can't know for sure till it does get here,' Yeager answered. 'If you want to know what I think, I think it'll be the biggest day since the conquest fleet came down. We're all doing our best to make sure it isn't the bloodiest day since the conquest fleet came down, too.'

Eddie nodded, accepting that. Barbara raised an eyebrow – just a little, so only Sam noticed. She saw the logical flaw the young pitcher missed. If all of mankind wanted the colonization fleet to land peacefully, that would happen. But no one on this side of the Atlantic could guess what Molotov or Himmler might do till he did it – if he did it. And the Nazis and the Reds – and the Lizards – would be worrying about President Warren, too.

After Sam finished his glass of Burgermeister, Barbara said, 'I don't want to rush you too much, but we did tell Jonathan we'd be home when he got back.'

'Okay.' Yeager got up, set a couple of bucks on the table to cover food and drink, and said his goodbyes. Everybody – including Jose from behind the counter – waved when he and Barbara took off.

They lived over in Gardena, one of the suburbs on the west side of L.A. that had burgeoned since the end of the fighting. When they got out of the car, Barbara remarked, as she often did, 'Cooler here.'

'It's the sea breeze,' Sam answered, as he often did. Then he plucked at his flannel uniform top. 'It may be cooler, but it's not that cool. I'm going to hop in the shower, is what I'm going to do.'

8

'That would be a very good idea, I think,' Barbara said. Yeager stuck out his tongue at her. They both laughed, comfortable with each other. *Why not?* Sam thought. They'd been together since late 1942, only a few months after the conquest fleet arrived. Had the Lizards not come, they never would have met. Sam didn't like thinking about that; Barbara was the best thing that had ever happened to him.

To keep from dwelling on might-have-beens, he hurried into the house. Photographs in the hallway that led to the bathroom marked the highlights of his career: him in dress uniform just after being promoted from sergeant to lieutenant; him weightless, wearing olive-drab undershirt and trousers, aboard an orbiting Lizard spaceship – overheated by human standards – as he helped dicker a truce after a flare-up; him in a spacesuit on the pitted surface of the moon; him in captain's uniform, standing between Robert Heinlein and Theodore Sturgeon.

He grinned at that last one, which he sometimes had to explain to guests. If he hadn't been reading the science-fiction pulps, and especially *Astounding*, he never would have become a specialist in Lizard-human relations. Having been overrun by fact, science fiction wasn't what it had been before the Lizards came, but it still had some readers and some writers, and he'd never been a man to renounce his roots.

He showered quickly, shaved even more quickly, and put on a pair of chinos and a yellow cotton short-sleeved sport shirt. When he got a beer from the refrigerator, Barbara gave him a piteous look, so he handed it to her and grabbed another one for himself.

He'd just taken his first sip when the door opened. 'I'm home!' Jonathan called.

'We're in the kitchen,' Yeager said.

Jonathan hurried in. At eighteen, he hurried everywhere. 'I'm hungry,' he said, and added an emphatic cough.

'Make yourself a sandwich,' Barbara said crisply. 'I'm your mother, not your waitress, even if you do have trouble re-membering it.'

'Take your tongue out of the ginger jar, Mom. I will,' Jonathan said, a piece of slang that wouldn't have meant a thing before the Lizards came. He wore only shorts that closely matched his suntanned hide. Across that hide were the bright stripes and patterns of Lizard-style body paint.

'You've promoted yourself,' Sam remarked. 'Last week, you were a landcruiser driver, but now you're an infantry small-unit group leader – a lieutenant, more or less.'

Jonathan paused with his salami sandwich half built. 'The old pattern was getting worn,' he answered with a shrug. 'The paints you can buy aren't nearly as good as the ones the Lizards—'

'Nearly so good,' his mother broke in, precise as usual.

'Nearly so good, then,' Jonathan said, and shrugged again. 'They aren't, and so I washed them off and put on this new set. I like it better, I think – brighter.'

'Okay.' Sam shrugged, too. People his son's age took the Lizards for granted in a way he never could. The youngsters didn't know what the world had been like before the conquest fleet came. They didn't care, either, and laughed at their elders for waxing nostalgic about it. Recalling his own youth, Sam did his best to be patient. It wasn't always easy. Before he could stop himself, he asked, 'Did you really have to shave your head?'

That flicked a nerve, where talk about body paint hadn't. Jonathan turned, sliding a hand over the smooth and shining dome of his skull. 'Why shouldn't I?' he asked, the beginning of an angry rumble in his voice. 'It's the hot thing to do these days.'

Along with body paint, it made people look as much like Lizards as they could. *Hot* was a term of approval because the Lizards liked heat. The Lizards liked ginger, too, but that was a different story.

Sam ran a hand through his own thinning hair. 'I'm going bald whether I want to or not, and I don't. I guess I have trouble understanding why anybody who's got hair would want to cut it all off.'

'It's hot,' Jonathan repeated, as if that explained everything. To him, no doubt, it did. His voice lost some of that belligerent edge as he realized his father wasn't insisting that he let his hair grow, only talking about it. When he didn't feel challenged, he could be rational enough.

He took an enormous bite from his sandwich. He was three or four inches taller than Sam – over six feet instead of under – and broader through the shoulders. By the way he ate, he should have been eleven feet tall and seven feet wide.

His second bite was even bigger than the first. He was still chewing when the telephone rang. 'That's got to be Karen!' he said with his mouth full, and dashed away.

Barbara and Sam shared looks of mingled amusement and alarm. 'In my day, girls didn't call boys like that,' Barbara said. 'In my day, girls didn't shave their heads, either. Go on, call me a fuddy-duddy.'

'You're my fuddy-duddy,' Sam said fondly. He slipped an arm around her waist and gave her a quick kiss.

'I'd better be,' Barbara said. 'I'm glad I am, too, because there are so many more distractions now. In my day, even if there had been body paint, girls wouldn't have been so thorough about wearing it as boys are – and if they had been, they'd have been arrested for indecent exposure.'

'Things aren't the same as they used to be,' Sam allowed. His eyes twinkled. 'I might call that a change for the better, though.'

Barbara elbowed him in the ribs. 'Of course you might. That doesn't mean I have to agree with you, though. And' – she lowered her voice so Jonathan wouldn't hear – 'I'm glad Karen isn't one of the ones who do.'

'Well, so am I,' Sam said, although with a sigh that earned him another pointed elbow. 'Jonathan and his pals are a lot more used to skin than I am. I'd stare like a fool if she came over dressed – or not dressed – that way.'

'And then you'd tell me you were just reading what her rank was,' Barbara said. 'You'd think I love you enough to believe a whopper like that. And you know what?' She poked him again. 'You might even be right.'

Felless had not expected to wake in weightlessness. For a moment, staring up at the fluorescent lights overhead, she wondered if something had gone wrong with the ship. Then, thinking more slowly than she should have because of the lingering effects of cold sleep, she realized how foolish that was. Had something gone wrong with the ship, she would never have awakened at all.

Two people floated into view. One, by her body paint, was a physician. The other . . . Weak and scatterbrained as Felless was, she gave a startled hiss. 'Exalted Fleetlord!' she exclaimed. She heard her own voice as if from far away.

Fleetlord Reffet spoke not to her but to the physician: 'She recognizes me, I see. Is she capable of real work?'

'We would not have summoned you here, Exalted Fleetlord, were she incapable,' the physician replied. 'We understand the value of your time.'

'Good,' Reffet said. 'That is a concept the males down on the surface of Tosev 3 seem to have a great deal of trouble grasping.' He swung one of his eye turrets to bear on Felless. 'Senior Researcher, are you prepared to begin your duties at once?'

'Exalted Fleetlord, I am,' Felless replied. Now the voice her hearing diaphragms caught seemed more like her own. Antidotes and restoratives were routing the drugs that had kept her just this side of death on the journey from Home to Tosev 3. Curiosity grew along with bodily well-being. 'May I ask why I have been awakened prematurely?'

'You may,' Reffet said, and then, in an aside to the physician, 'You were right. Her wits are clear.' He gave his attention back to Felless. 'You have been awakened because conditions on Tosev 3 are not as we anticipated they would be when we set out from Home.'

That was almost as great a surprise as waking prematurely.

'In what way, Exalted Fleetlord?' Felless tried to make her wits work harder. 'Does this planet harbor some bacterium or virus for which we have had difficulty in finding a cure?' Such a thing hadn't happened on either Rabotev 2 or Halless 1, but remained a theoretical possibility.

'No,' Reffet replied. 'The difficulty lies in the natives themselves. They are more technically advanced than our probe indicated. You being the colonization fleet's leading expert on relations between the Race and other species, I judged it expedient to rouse you and put you to work before we make planetfall. If you need assistance, give us names, and we shall also wake as many of your subordinates and colleagues as you may require.'

Felless tried to lever herself off the table on which she lay. Straps restrained her: a sensible precaution on the physician's part. As she fumbled with the catches, she asked, 'How much more advanced were they than we expected? Enough to make the conquest significantly harder, I gather.'

'Indeed.' Reffet added an emphatic cough. 'When the conquest fleet arrived, they were engaged in active research on jet aircraft, on guided missiles, and on nuclear fission.'

'That is impossible!' Felless blurted. Then, realizing what she'd said, she added, 'I beg the Exalted Fleetlord's pardon.'

'Senior Researcher, I freely give it to you,' Reffet replied. 'When the colonization fleet began receiving data from Tosev 3, my first belief was that Atvar, the fleetlord on the conquest fleet, was playing an elaborate joke on us – jerking our tailstumps, as the saying has it. I have since been disabused of this belief. I wish I had not been, for it strikes me as far more palatable than the truth.'

'But – But –' Felless knew she was stuttering, and made herself pause to gather her thoughts. 'If that is true, Exalted Fleetlord, I count it something of a marvel that . . . that the conquest did not fail.' Such a thought would have been unimaginable back on Home. It should have been unimaginable here, too. That she'd imagined it proved it wasn't.

Reffet said, 'In part, Senior Researcher, the conquest *did* fail. There are still unsubdued Tosevite empires – actually, the term the conquest fleet consistently uses is *not-empires*, which I do not altogether understand – on the surface of Tosev 3, along with areas the Race has in fact conquered. Nor have the Tosevites ceased their technical progress in the eyeblink of time since the conquest fleet arrived. I am warned that only a threat of retaliatory violence from the conquest fleet has kept them from mounting attacks on this colonization fleet.'

Felless felt far dizzier than she would have from weight-lessness and sudden revival from cold sleep alone. She finally managed to free herself from the restraining straps and gently push off from the table. 'Take me to a terminal at once, if you would be so kind. Have you an edited summary of the data thus far transmitted from the conquest fleet?'

'We have,' Reffet said. 'I hope you will find it adequate, Senior Researcher. It was prepared by fleet officers who are not specialists in your area of expertise. We have, of course, provided links to the fuller documentation sent up from Tosev 3.'

'If you will come with me, superior female . . .' the physician said. She swung rapidly from one handhold to another. Felless followed.

She had to strap herself into the chair in front of the terminal to keep the ventilating current from blowing her off it. Getting back to work felt good. She wished she could have waited till reaching the surface of Tosev 3 for reawakening; that would have been as planned back on Home, and plans were made to be followed. But she would do the best she could here.

And, as she called up the summary, a curious blend of anticipation and dread coursed through her. Wild Tosevites . . . What would dealing with wild Tosevites be like? She'd expected the locals to be well on their way toward assimilation into the Empire by now. Even then, they would have been different from the Hallessi and the Rabotevs, who but for their looks were as much subjects of the Emperor (even thinking of

14

her sovereign made Felless cast down her eyes) as were the males and females of the Race.

A male in body paint like Reffet's appeared on the screen in front of her. 'Welcome to Tosev 3,' he said in tones anything but welcoming. 'This is a world of paradox. If you were expecting anything here to be as it was back on Home, you will be disappointed. You may very well be dead. The only thing you may safely expect on Tosev 3 is the unexpected. I daresay you who listen to this will not believe me. Were I new-come from Home, I would not believe such words, either. Before rejecting them out of claw, examine the evidence.'

A slowly spinning globe of Tosev 3 appeared on the screen. Something over half the land area was red, the rest a variety of other colors. The red, the legend by the globe explained, showed that area of the planet the Race controlled. The other colors, which dominated the northern hemisphere, showed areas where the natives still ruled themselves.

After Felless had just long enough to soak in the significance of that, the colors faded, leaving the land areas in more or less their natural colors. Glowing dots, some red, some blue, appeared here and there. 'Red dots show explosive-metal weapons detonated by the Race, blue dots those detonated by the Tosevites,' a voice said.

Felless let out a slow, horrified hiss. About as many dots glowed blue as red. Atvar's head and torso reappeared on the screen. 'Judging that continuing the war for total conquest might well render this planet useless to the colonization fleet, we entered into negotiations with the Tosevite not-empires possessing explosive-metal weapons, conceding their independence in exchange for a cessation of hostilities,' the leader of the conquest fleet said. 'On the whole – there have been certain unpleasant exceptions – peace between the Race and the Tosevites and among the Tosevite factions has prevailed for the past thirty-four years – seventeen of this planet's revolutions, which are just over twice as long as ours. I freely admit it is not the sort of peace I would have desired. There were,

15

however, many times when I thought it was more than I would ever get. See for yourself what we faced even at the beginning of our struggle against the Tosevites.'

His image faded, to be replaced by those of landcruisers of obviously alien manufacture. The tracked and armored fortresses were not a match for those of the Race, but the barbarous inhabitants of Tosev 3, by everything Felless knew, should not have been able to build landcruisers at all.

'Three years later, we were facing these,' Atvar said.

New landcruisers replaced those formerly on the screen. They looked more formidable. Their specifications said they *were* more formidable. They carried more armor and bigger guns and had more powerful engines. They still didn't match the machines the Race used, but they were getting closer.

'Three years,' Felless said in almost disbelieving wonder – one and a half of Tosev 3's years. The later-model landcruisers looked to be separated from the earlier ones by a couple of hundred years of slow development. On Home, they would have been.

Tosevite aircraft showed the same astonishing leap in technical prowess. The natives had gone from machines propelled by rotating airfoils to jets and rocket-powered killercraft in what amounted to the flick of a nictitating membrane across an eye.

'How?' Felless murmured. 'How could they have done such a thing?'

As if answering her, Atvar said, 'Explanations for the Tosevites' extraordinary proficiency fall into two main areas, which may or may not be mutually exclusive: the geographical and the biological. Oceans and mountains break up Tosevite land masses in ways unknown on other worlds of the Empire, fostering the formation of small, competitive groups.' The globe reappeared, this time splotched in ways that struck Felless as absurdly complex. 'These were the political divisions on Tosev 3 at the time the conquest fleet arrived.'

Atvar continued, 'Reproductive biology among the Tosevites is unlike that of any other intelligent race we know, and has profound effects on their society. Females are, or can be, continually receptive; males are, or can be, continually active. This leads to pair-bondings and . . .' He went on for some time.

Long before he'd finished, Felless hissed out a single word: 'Disgusting.' She wondered how so aberrant a species had ever developed intelligence, let alone a technology that let it challenge the Race.

At last, and very much to her relief, the fleetlord of the conquest fleet chose another topic. She listened until Atvar finished, 'This conquest, if it is to be accomplished, will be a matter for generations, not days as was anticipated when we left Home. The landing of the colonization fleet and settlement of the colonists will greatly aid in integrating the independent not-empires into the larger structure of the Empire. Exposure to proper examples cannot help but lead the Big Uglies' – by then, Felless had gathered that was the conquest fleet's nickname for the Tosevites – 'to emulate the high example that will be placed before them.' His image vanished from the screen.

Felless turned to Reffet. 'You were right to rouse me, Exalted Fleetlord. This will be a more challenging problem than anyone could have anticipated – and, no doubt, the conquest fleet has made its share of mistakes in dealing with these bizarre Tosevites.' She let out a hissing sigh. 'I can see I shall have my work cut out for me.'

Without false modesty, Vyacheslav Molotov knew himself to be one of the three most powerful men on the face of the Earth. Without false self-aggrandizement, he knew Atvar, the Lizards' fleetlord, was more powerful than he or Heinrich Himmler or Earl Warren. What had not been obvious over the past two crowded decades was whether Atvar was more powerful than the leaders of the USSR, the Greater German *Reich*, and the USA put together.

But soon, very soon, the Lizards' colonization fleet would bring millions more of their kind, males and females both, to

Earth. Even though the fleet was entirely civilian – the Lizards had not anticipated needing more military help when it left their home world – it would tilt the scales in their direction. It could hardly do anything else.

As he sat in his Kremlin office, Molotov did not show what he was thinking. He had reached the top of the Soviet hierarchy, succeeding Iosif Stalin as general secretary of the Communist Party, not least by never showing what he was thinking. His stone face – *poker face* was the American idiom, which he rather liked – had also served him well in dealing with foreigners and with the Lizards.

His own secretary stuck his head into the office. 'Comrade General Secretary, the foreign commissar has arrived.'

'Very well, Pyotr Maksimovich, send him in,' Molotov answered. He glanced at his wristwatch as the secretary disappeared. Ten o'clock on the dot. Since no one could see him do it, Molotov nodded approval. Some people understood the virtue of punctuality, however un-Russian it was.

In strode Andrei Gromyko. 'Good day, Vyacheslav Mikhailovich,' he said, extending his hand.

Molotov shook it. 'And to you, Andrei Andreyevich,' he said, and gestured to the chair across the desk from his own. 'Sit down.' Without any further small talk, Gromyko did. Molotov thought well of the foreign commissar not least because his craggy countenance revealed almost as little as Molotov's own.

Gromyko went straight to business, another trait of which Molotov approved: 'Is there any change in our position of which I should be aware before we meet with the Lizards' ambassador to the Soviet Union?'

'I do not believe so, no,' Molotov replied. 'We remain strongly opposed to their settling colonists in Persia or Afghanistan or Kashmir or any other land near our borders.'

One of Gromyko's shaggy eyebrows twitched. '*Any* other, Vyacheslav Mikhailovich?' he asked.

Molotov grunted. Gromyko had caught him fair and

square. 'You are correct, of course. We have no objection whatever to their colonization of Poland, however extensive that may prove.'

While withdrawing from most of their European conquests, the Lizards had stayed in Poland: neither Germany nor the USSR was willing to see it in the other's hands, and neither was willing to see a Polish state revive. With the Lizards administering the area, it made a splendid buffer between the Soviet Union and Nazi-dominated Western Europe. Molotov was delighted to have the Lizards there. He feared the Greater German *Reich*, and hoped with all his heart that Himmler likewise feared the USSR.

Gromyko said, 'I remind you, Comrade General Secretary, that the Lizards have consistently maintained we have no right to dictate to them where they may settle on territory they rule.'

'We are not dictating. We are not in a position to dictate, however unfortunate that may be,' Molotov said. 'We are making our views known to them. We *are* in a position to do that. If they choose to ignore us, they show themselves to be uncultured and give us grounds for ignoring them in appropriate circumstances.'

'They are of the opinion – the strong opinion – that we ignore their views by continuing to supply weapons to progressive forces in China and Afghanistan,' Gromyko said.

'I cannot imagine why they continue to hold such an opinion,' Molotov said. 'We have repeatedly denied any such involvement.'

Gromyko did own an impressive stone face, for he failed to crack a smile at that. So did Molotov. Here, as so often, denials and truth bore little relation to each other. But the Lizards had never quite been able to prove Soviet denials were false, and so the denials continued.

'A thought,' Gromyko said, raising a forefinger.

'Go on.' Molotov nodded. His neck creaked a little as he did so. He was up past seventy, his face more wrinkled than it had been when the Lizards first came to Earth, his hair thinner and almost entirely gray. Aging mattered relatively little to him; he had never been a man who relied on creating an overwhelming physical impression.

Gromyko said, 'Should the *Yashcheritsi* offer not to settle heavily along our southern border if we truly do stop arms shipments that annoy them, how ought we to respond?'

'Ah. That *is* interesting, Andrei Andreyevich,' Molotov said. 'Do you think they would have the imagination to propose such a bargain?' Before Gromyko could answer, Molotov went on, 'If they do not, should we propose it to them?' Now he did smile, unpleasantly. 'How Mao would howl!'

'So he would. Seldom have I met a man who had so much arrogance,' Gromyko said. 'Hitler came close, but Hitler actually led a state, where Mao has spent the last thirty years wishing he could.'

'Even so,' Molotov agreed. He pondered. Would he sell his Chinese ideological brethren down the river to gain advantage for the Soviet Union? He did not need to ponder long. 'I hope Queek does propose it; if we do so, it may suggest weakness to the Lizards. But we can raise the issue if we must. Keeping the Lizards well away from us counts for more than keeping Mao happy.'

'I agree, Comrade General Secretary,' Gromyko said. 'The Lizards will not settle China in any great numbers; it already has too many people. Mao's chief value to us is keeping the countryside unsettled, and he will do that with or without our arms.'

'A very pretty solution indeed,' Molotov said, warming up all the way to tepid. 'One way or another, we shall use it.'

Molotov's secretary came in and announced, 'The ambassador from the Race and his interpreter are here.' He did not call the Lizard a Lizard, not where the said Lizard or the interpreter could hear him.

Queek skittered into Molotov's office. He was about the size of a ten-year-old, though he seemed smaller because of his forward-slung posture. One of his eye turrets, weirdly like a chameleon's, swiveled toward Molotov, the other toward Gromyko. Molotov could not read his body paint, but its ornateness declared his high rank.

He addressed Molotov and Gromyko in his own hissing language. The interpreter, a tall, stolid, middle-aged human, spoke good Russian with a Polish accent: 'The ambassador greets you in the name of the Emperor.'

'Tell him that we greet him in return, in the name of the workers and peasants of the Soviet Union,' Molotov answered. He smiled again, down where it did not show. At his very first meeting with the Lizards, not long after their invasion, he'd had the pleasure of letting them know that the Soviets had liquidated the Tsar and his family. Their own Emperors had ruled them for fifty thousand years; the news taught them, better than anything else could have done, that they were not dealing with creatures of a familiar sort.

The interpreter hissed and squeaked and popped and coughed. Queek made similar appalling noises. Again, the interpreter translated: 'The ambassador says he is not certain this meeting has any point, as he has already made it clear to the foreign commissar that your views on the settlement of the Race are unacceptable.'

Even more than the Nazis, the Lizards were convinced they were the lords of creation and everyone else their natural subjects. As he had almost twenty years before, Molotov took pleasure in reminding them they might be wrong: 'If we are sufficiently provoked, we will attack the colonization fleet in space.'

'If we are sufficiently provoked, we will serve the present rulers of the Soviet Union as you butchers served your emperor,' Queek retorted. The interpreter looked as if he enjoyed translating the Lizard's reply; Molotov wondered what grievance he held against the Soviet Union.

No time to worry about that now. Molotov said, 'Whatever sacrifices are required of us, we shall make them.'

He wondered how true that was. It had certainly been true a

21

generation before, with the Soviet people mobilized to battle first the Nazis and then the Lizards. Now, after a time of comfort, who could be sure if it still was? But the Lizards might not – he hoped they did not – know that.

Queek said, 'Even after so long, I cannot understand how you Tosevites can be such madmen. You are willing to destroy yourselves, so long as you can also harm your foes.'

'This often makes our foes less eager to attack us,' Andrei Gromyko pointed out. 'Sometimes we must convince people we mean what we say. Your taste for aggression, for instance, is less than it was before you encountered the determination of the Soviet people.'

By studying motion pictures of prisoners, Molotov had gained a good working knowledge of what Lizards' gestures and motions meant. Gromyko had succeeded in alarming Queek. Molotov added, 'If you expect to get good treatment from us, you must show us good treatment in return.'

That was a lesson the Lizards had had a hard time learning. It was also an invitation to dicker. Would Queek see as much? Molotov wasn't sure. The Lizards were better diplomats now than they had been when they first came – they had more practice at the art, too. They weren't stupid. Anyone who thought otherwise quickly paid the price. But they were naive, even more naive than Americans.

'The converse should also apply,' Queek said. 'Why should we even deal with you, when you keep sending weapons to those who would overthrow our rule?'

'We deny this,' Molotov said automatically. But did Queek offer an opening? Molotov was willing to trade hint for hint: 'Why should we trust you, when you plainly plan on packing the borders with your kind?'

Queek paused before replying. Was he also trying to decide whether he heard the beginnings of a deal? At last, he said, 'We should have less need to rely on the Race's military might if you did not keep provoking your surrogates against us with hopes of a triumph surely impossible.'

'Have you not seen, Ambassador, how little is impossible on this world?' Molotov said.

'We have seen this, yes: seen it to our sorrow,' Queek replied. 'Were it not so, I would not be here negotiating with you. But since I am, perhaps we can discuss this matter further.'

'Perhaps we can,' Molotov said. 'I have doubts as to whether it will come to anything, but perhaps we can.' He watched Queek lean forward slightly. Yes, the Lizard was serious. Molotov did not smile. *Getting down to business* was a capitalist phrase, but in the privacy of his own mind he used it anyway.

Ttomalss politely inclined his head. 'It is a pleasure to see a new face from Home, superior female,' he said to the researcher from the colonization fleet who had come to consult with him. On the whole, he was telling the truth; he had not always got on well with the colleagues who had accompanied him in the colonization fleet, or with the Big Uglies he studied.

'In this matter, I should call you "superior sir," ' the newcomer – her name was Felless – replied. 'You have the expertise. You have the experience with these Tosevites.'

More than I ever wanted, Ttomalss thought, remembering captivity in China he'd expected to lead to his death. Aloud, he said, 'You are gracious,' which was also true, for Felless' body paint showed that she outranked him.

'You have had all the time since the arrival of the conquest fleet to assimilate the implausible nature of the natives of Tosev 3,' Felless said. 'To me, having to try to understand it in a matter of days – a most hasty and inefficient procedure – it seems not merely implausible but impossible.'

'This was our reaction on reaching this world, too,' Ttomalss said. 'We have since had to adapt to changing conditions.' He let his mouth fall open. 'Anyone on Tosev 3 who fails to adapt is ruined. We have seen that demonstrated – and most often painfully demonstrated – time and again.'

'So I gather,' Felless said. 'It must have been very difficult for you. Change, after all, is an unnatural condition.'

'So I thought before leaving Home,' Ttomalss replied. 'So I still think, at times, for so I was trained to think all my life. But, had we not changed, the best we could have done would have been to destroy this planet – and where would that have left you and the colonization fleet, superior female?'

Felless did not take him seriously. He could tell at a glance; he barely needed one eye turret to see it, let alone two. That saddened him, but hardly surprised him. She had the beginnings of an intellectual understanding of what the Race had been through on Tosev 3. Ttomalss had been through every bit of it. The scars still marked his spirit. It would never be free of them till it met the spirits of Emperors past face to face.

'You are to be commended for your diligent efforts to gain understanding of the roots of Tosevite behavior,' Felless said.

'Nice to know someone thinks so,' Ttomalss said, remembering quarrels down through the years. 'Some males, I think, would sooner stay ignorant. And some would sooner put their tongues in a ginger jar and forget their research and everything else.'

He waited. Sure enough, Felless asked a hesitant question: 'Ginger? I have seen the name in the reports. It must refer to a drug native to Tosev 3, for it is certainly unknown back on Home.'

'Yes. It's an herb that grows here,' Ttomalss said. 'For the natives, it is just a spice, the way *balj* is back on Home. It is a drug for us, though, and a nasty one. It makes a male feel smart and bold and strong – and when it wears off, it makes him feel like having some more. Once it gets its claws in you, you will do almost anything for another taste.'

'With more enforcement personnel here now, we should be able to root it out without much trouble,' Felless said.

Ttomalss remembered that pristine confidence, that sense that things would keep going smoothly because they always had. He'd known it himself. Then he'd started dealing with the Big Uglies. Like so many males on Tosev 3, he'd lost it and

24

never got it back. He didn't try to explain that to Felless. The female would find out for herself.

'Why would anyone want a drug in the first place, especially an alien drug?' Felless asked him.

'At first because you are bored, or else because you see someone else having a good time and you want one, too,' he answered. 'We shall have trouble with ginger when the colonists land, mark my words.'

'I shall record your prediction,' Felless said. 'I tend to doubt its accuracy, but, as I said, you are the one with experience on Tosev 3, so perhaps you will prove correct in the end.'

Was she so serious all the time? A lot of people back on Home were. Ttomalss remembered as much. Contact with the Big Uglies – even contact with males who had contact with the Big Uglies – had a way of abrading such seriousness. And now a hundred million colonists, once revived, would look on the relative handful of males from the colonization fleet as slightly addled eggs. Ttomalss didn't see what anyone could do about that, either.

Deep inside, he laughed to himself. Eventually, the colonists would have to start dealing with the Tosevites. Then they'd start getting addled, too. In spite of his best efforts to believe otherwise, Ttomalss could reach no other conclusion. Even if Tosev 3 at last came completely under the Emperor's rule, it would be the odd world out in more ways than one for years, centuries, millennia to come.

Because he'd been mentally picking parasites out from under his scales, he missed a comment from Felless. 'I am sorry, superior female?' he said, embarrassed.

'I said that, of all the researchers with the conquest fleet, you seem to have gone furthest in your efforts to examine the integration of Tosevites and the Race.' Felless repeated the compliment with no sign of exasperation. She continued, 'Some of your activities strike me as going above and beyond the call of duty.'

'You are generous, superior female,' Ttomalss said. 'My

view has always been that, if this world is to be successfully colonized, effecting such integration will be mandatory.'

'You doubt the possibility of successful colonization?' Now Felless sounded reproving, not complimentary.

'I doubt the certainty of successful colonization,' Ttomalss replied. 'Anyone with experience of Tosev 3 doubts the certainty of anything pertaining to it.'

'And yet you have persisted,' Felless said. 'In your reports, you indicate that your first experimental specimen was forcibly taken away from you, and that you yourself were kidnapped by Tosevite bandits while seeking to obtain a replacement for it.'

'Truth,' Ttomalss said. 'We badly underestimated the importance of family bonds on Tosev 3, due not only to long-term sexual pairings but also to the absurdly helpless nature of Tosevite hatchlings, which need constant care if they are to survive. Because of these factors, my experiments have met with far more opposition from the Big Uglies than they would have from any other intelligent race with which we are familiar.'

'And yet, in the end, your work seems to have met with success,' Felless said. 'I wonder if you would be so kind as to allow me to make the acquaintance of the specimen you finally succeeded in obtaining and rearing.'

'I thought you might ask that.' Ttomalss rose. 'Kassquit is waiting in the next chamber. I shall return in a moment.'

'My first Tosevite, even if not quite a wild specimen,' Felless said in musing tones. 'How interesting this will be!'

'Please do your best to treat the Big Ugly as you would a member of the Race,' Ttomalss warned. 'Since the Tosevite gained speech – which Big Uglies do more quickly than our own hatchlings – all males have followed this course, which appears to have worked well.'

'It shall be done,' Felless promised.

Ttomalss went into the adjacent chamber, where Kassquit sat in front of a screen, engrossed in a game. 'The researcher from Home wishes to speak with you,' Ttomalss said.

'It shall be done, superior sir,' Kassquit said obediently, and got up. The Big Ugly, though not large for a Tosevite, stood head and neck above Ttomalss. Kassquit followed him back to the chamber where Felless waited. Bending into the posture of respect, the Tosevite said to her, 'I greet you, superior sir.'

'Superior female,' Ttomalss corrected. He turned to Felless. 'You are the first female Kassquit has met.'

'I am very pleased to make your acquaintance, Kassquit,' Felless said.

'I thank you, superior female.' Kassquit used the correct title this time. The Big Ugly's voice was slightly mushy; Tosevite mouthparts could not quite handle all the sounds of the language of the Race. 'You are truly from Home?'

'I am,' Felless said.

'I would like to visit Home,' Kassquit said wistfully, 'but cold sleep has not yet been adapted to my biochemistry.'

'Perhaps it will be one day,' Felless said. Ttomalss watched her try to hide surprise; Kassquit was young, but far from stupid. Felless went on, 'Rabotevs and Hallessi travel between the stars – no reason Tosevites should not as well.'

'I hope you are right, superior female.' Kassquit turned small, immobile eyes toward Ttomalss. 'May I be excused, superior sir?'

Was that shyness or a desire to return to the game? Whatever it was, Ttomalss yielded to it: 'You may.'

'I thank you, superior sir. I am glad to have met you, superior female.' After another respectful bend, Kassquit left, tall and ridiculously erect.

'Brighter than I expected,' Felless remarked once the Big Ugly was gone. 'Less alien-seeming, too; far less so than the Tosevites in the images I have seen.'

'That is by design, to aid in integration,' Ttomalss said. 'The body paint, of course, designates Kassquit as my apprentice. The unsightly hair at the top of the Tosevite's head is frequently clipped to the skin. When Kassquit reached sexual maturity, more hair grew at the armpits and around the genital area, though Kassquit's race is less hairy than most Tosevites.'

'What is the function of these hairy patches that emerge at sexual maturity?' Felless asked. 'I presume they pertain to reproduction in some way.'

'That is not yet fully understood,' Ttomalss admitted. 'They may help spread pheromones from odorous glands in these areas, but Tosevite reproductive behavior is less closely tied to odor cues than our own.'

'Are these creatures truly accessible to one another at all seasons?' Felless asked. A wriggle said what she thought of the idea.

But Ttomalss had to answer, 'Truly. And they find our way as strange and repugnant as we find theirs. I confess that, despite my scientific objectivity, I have a great deal of trouble grasping this. Surely our way is far more convenient. You are not in season; my scent receptors know as much; and so you are simply a colleague. No complications involved with mating need arise.'

'And a good thing, too,' Felless exclaimed. She and Ttomalss both laughed at the absurdities of the Big Uglies.

'Home.' Kassquit tasted the sound of the word. Home was more real in the Tosevite's mind than Tosev 3, around which this ship had orbited longer than Kassquit had been alive.

Tosevite, Kassquit thought. *That is what I call myself. And why not? That is what I am.*

It didn't seem right. It didn't seem fair. Without this preposterously large, preposterously ugly body (Kassquit knew the nickname the males of the Race – and, no doubt, this new female, too – had for Tosevites), the good brain inside this strangely domed skull might have accomplished something worthwhile. Oh, it still might, but that was far less likely than it would have been otherwise.

'If I had been hatched on Home . . .' Kassquit said. And how many times had that thought echoed and reechoed? More than Kassquit could count. *Did I ask for this body? Spirits of Emperors past, did I?* The eyes that looked down at the metal floor could not slew in turrets. *And is that my fault?*

Every step Kassquit took was a reminder of alienness. This Tosevite body would not bend forward into a proper posture – or what would have been a proper posture for anyone else. And the lack of true claws on Kassquit's fingertips was another inconvenience. Ttomalss had turned out prosthetics that made operating machinery much easier. A proper member of the Race, though, would not have needed prosthetics.

I am not a proper member of the Race. I am a Tosevite, brought up as if I were a proper member of the Race, or as close to a proper member of the Race as I can be, given my limitations. Oh, how I wish I had no such limitations. I am part person, part experimental animal.

Kassquit did not resent that. The Race needed experimental animals, to learn how to live with and eventually rule the tempestuous Tosevites. Ttomalss had said as little about the natives of Tosev 3 as he could. From the small things he had let fall now and then, Kassquit understood what an honor, what a privilege, it had been to be selected for this role. Life as a Tosevite peasant? Kassquit's mouth dropped open in scornful amusement at the idea.

A small sound escaped Kassquit's mouth along with the laugh. *I should have better control,* Kassquit thought. *I usually do have better control, but I am upset.* Ttomalss had said that Tosevites showed amusement with a noise rather than in the Race's far more sophisticated, far more elegant fashion.

I do not want to act like a Tosevite! In no way do I want to act like a Tosevite! I am one, but I wish I were not!

Some things could not be helped. Posture was one. Skin was another. Kassquit ran one hand along the other arm. *I should be a dark greenish brown like a proper male of the Race, or even, I discover, a proper female of the Race. Instead, I am a sort of pale yellowish tan color – a very disagreeable shade for a person to be.*

'And my skin is smooth,' Kassquit said with a sad sigh. 'It will never be anything but smooth, I fear.' Kassquit sighed again. *When I was coming out of hatchlinghood, how I waited till it would be like the ones everybody else had. I did not really understand then how different I was. The Emperor surely knows I do try to fit in as best I can.*

The skin under Kassquit's palm was also faintly damp. Ttomalss had explained why that was so: instead of panting to cool the body, Tosevites used the evaporation of metabolic water. Tosev 3 was a wetter world than Home, which let the Big Uglies expend water so lavishly. Tosev 3 was also a colder world than Home, which meant the ship, whose climate was Homelike, seemed warm to Kassquit's Tosevite body and prompted the activation of the cooling mechanism.

It all made good sense. Ttomalss had patiently explained it over and over to Kassquit. It was, for Tosevites, thoroughly normal. It was also thoroughly disgusting, as far as Kassquit was concerned.

Other things about the Tosevite body were even more disgusting: the business of passing liquid waste as well as solid, for instance. That also had to do with Tosev 3's revolting wetness. Again, Ttomalss had been patience itself in explaining the reasons behind the differences.

'I do not care about the reasons,' Kassquit muttered. 'I wish there were no differences.'

I am not usually like this, Kassquit thought. *Usually, I can see what makes me more like the Race, not what separates me from it. I wish I had not met Felless. Seeing someone freshly come from Home reminds me that I am not and I cannot be. That hurts. It hurts worse than I expected.*

An itch on top of the head made Kassquit scratch. Very, very short hair rasped under the not-quite-claws at the tips of Kassquit's fingers. Hair was another nasty thing about the Tosevite body. *I wish I did not have any,* Kassquit thought. *Smooth is bad. Hairy is even worse. Emperor be praised that I do get clipped regularly. I wished I could die when the hair started sprouting here and there on my body. Having to get my head clipped is humiliation enough. Add these other spots and it is almost too much to bear.*

Ttomalss had been reassuring about that, too. The Race's research proved it was normal among Tosevites of about Kassquit's age. But it was not normal aboard the ship. It made Kassquit even more abnormal here.

What would I do without Ttomalss? Kassquit wondered. The male had been a guide, a teacher, a mentor, a hearing diaphragm to listen, for all of Kassquit's life. *A hearing diaphragm to listen? I will not think about the strange curls of flesh at the sides of my head, nor about the holes inside them with which I hear. I will not think about them. I will not.*

Trying not to think about something worked as well as that usually did. Kassquit touched an ear, then gave it a painful yank. *Maybe I should have these clipped. It would not be too hard, and it would make me look a little closer to the way I should.*

Ttomalss had not wanted to put a mirror in Kassquit's compartment. His argument had been that looking at such a different face would only lead to discontentment. 'I will be more discontented if you do not treat me as if I were part of the Race,' Kassquit remembered saying. 'If I were a member of the Race, I would have one.' Ttomalss had yielded; it was the first argument Kassquit had ever won from him.

The technician who had installed the mirror in the compartment had treated Kassquit like a member of the Race, all right. He had fastened it at a level that would have been perfect for a member of the Race. Kassquit had to stoop to see anything but the paint marking this unsatisfactory body's unsatisfactory torso.

Stooping, Kassquit thought, *This is how I look. I cannot do anything about it.* Small eyes, white with dark center, folds of skin at their inner corners narrowing them further still, without nearly the angle of vision the Race enjoyed. Kassquit had had strips of hair above them, too – Tosevite signaling organs, Ttomalss called them – but those strips got clipped with the

31

rest. A projection below and between the eyes that housed the nostrils. An absurdly small mouth with mobile soft tissue around it and a wildly variegated set of teeth inside.

Out came Kassquit's tongue for a critical examination. It needed criticizing, all right, being short and blunt and un-forked. Again, and not for the first time, Kassquit wondered whether surgery could correct that flaw.

'What is the use?' Kassquit said, straightening once more. 'What is the use of any of it? They can cut this and clip those and maybe do some other things, too, but it will not help, not really. I will still look like – this.'

Maybe Ttomalss had been right. Maybe the mirror should have stayed out. In the end, though, how much would it have mattered? *I am a Tosevite. I wish I were not, but I am. With or without a mirror, I know it.*

Kassquit went over to the computer terminal, put on false fingerclaws, and returned to the earlier game. But it didn't engross, as it had before going in to see Felless. *Reality has a way of breaking in,* Kassquit thought. *The best thing about the computer is that it does not know – or if it does know, it does not care; it really does not care – I am a Tosevite. That is one of the reasons it is so much fun. As far as the computer is concerned, I am as good as anybody else. How can I go on believing that, even imagining that, after meeting a female straight from Home?*

'Home,' Kassquit said again, making the word a drawn-out sigh of longing. *I know what to do. If I am presented to the Emperor, I know how to bend, I know all the proper responses. I would make Ttomalss proud.*

Another open-mouthed laugh, this one, at least, properly silent. As if anyone would present a Tosevite to the Emperor! Kassquit paused. A Tosevite might be presented to the Emperor, but as a curiosity, not as a person who reverenced him as the Race and the Hallessi and the Rabotevs did. That was not good enough. It made Kassquit angry. *I deserve to reverence the Emperor like anyone else!*

'Calm yourself. You are growing too excited,' Ttomalss

would have said, had he been there and known what was in Kassquit's mind. Calm did not come easily; as Ttomalss had explained it, the hormones that produced physical maturation in Tosevites were also liable to produce mood swings wilder than any the Race experienced outside the brief mating season.

Ttomalss told the truth there as elsewhere, Kassquit thought. *All things considered, I would sooner not have gone through maturation.*

Another reluctant trip to the mirror. This time, Kassquit did not stoop, but sighed after looking away at last. Sure enough, the twin bulges of tissue in the upper part of the torso made the lines of her body paint harder to read than they should have been.

And that was far from the worst of the changes she had undergone. Growing the new patches of hair had been very bad. And, had Ttomalss not warned her she would suffer a cyclic flow of blood from her genital opening, she would surely have thought she was ill from some dire disease when it began. The Race suffered no such grotesque inconveniences. Ttomalss had arranged to bring Tosevite sanitary pads up from the surface of the world below for her. They worked well enough, but that she needed such things galled her.

But more upsetting even than that were the feelings coursing through her for which the language of the Race seemed to have no names. With them, for once, Ttomalss had been little help. Dispassionate remarks about reproductive behavior did nothing to slow the thudding of Kassquit's heart, the whistle of the breath through her, the feeling that the compartment was even warmer than normal.

She had found something that did. Her hand slid down along her painted belly. Of itself, her stance shifted so her feet were wider apart than usual. She looked up at the ceiling, not really seeing it, not really seeing anything. After a bit, she exhaled very hard and quivered a little. Her fingers were damp. She wiped them on a tissue. She knew she would be easier for a while now.

2

Peking brawled around Liu Han. She wore the long, dark blue tunic and trousers and the conical straw hat of a peasant woman. She had no trouble playing the role; she'd lived it till the little scaly devils came down from the sky and turned China – turned the whole world – upside down.

Her daughter, Liu Mei, who walked along the *hutung* – the alleyway – beside her, was proof of that. Turning to Liu Han, she said, 'I hope we won't be late.'

'Don't worry,' Liu Han answered. 'We've got plenty of time.'

Liu Mei nodded, her face serious. Her face was almost always serious, even when she laughed. The scaly devils had taken her from Liu Han right after she was born, and had kept her in one of their airplanes that never landed for her first year of life outside the womb – her second year of age, as the Chinese reckoned such things. When a baby, she should have learned to smile by watching people around her. But she'd had only little scaly devils around her, and they never smiled – they could not smile. Liu Mei hadn't learned how.

'I should have liquidated that Ttomalss when I had the chance,' Liu Han said, her hands folding into fists. 'Mercy has no place in the struggle against imperialism. I understand that now much better than I did when you were tiny.'

'Truly, Mother, too late to fret over it now,' Liu Mei replied

34

– seriously. Liu Han walked on in grim silence. Her daughter was right, but that left her no happier.

She and Liu Mei both flattened themselves against the splintery front wall of a shop as a burly, sweating man with a load of bricks on a carrying pole edged past them going the other way. He leered at Liu Mei, showing a couple of broken teeth. 'If you show me your body, I will show you silver,' he said.

'No,' Liu Mei answered.

Liu Han did not think that was rejection enough, or anywhere close to it. 'Go on, get out of here, you stinking turtle,' she screeched at the laborer. 'Just because your mother was a whore, you think all women are whores.'

'You would starve as a whore,' the man snarled. But he walked on.

The *hutung* opened out onto P'ing Tsê Mên Ta Chieh, the main street leading east into Peking from the P'ing Tsê Gate. 'Be careful,' Liu Han murmured to Liu Mei. 'Scaly devils seldom come into *hutungs*, and they are often sorry when they do. But they do patrol the main streets.'

Sure enough, here came a squad of them, swaggering down the middle of the broad street and expecting everyone to get out of their way. When people didn't move fast enough to suit them, they shouted either in their own language – which they expected humans to understand – or in bad Chinese.

Liu Han kept walking. Even after twenty years of practice, the scaly devils had trouble telling one person from another. Liu Mei bent her head so the brim of her hat helped hide her features. She did not look quite like a typical Chinese, and a bright little devil might notice as much.

'They are past us,' Liu Han said quietly, and her daughter straightened up once more. Liu Mei's eyes were of the proper almond shape. Her nose, though, was almost as prominent as a foreign devil's and her face was narrower and more forward-thrusting than Liu Han's. The black hair the hat concealed refused to lie straight, but had a springy wave to it.

She was a pretty girl – *prettier than I was at that age,* Liu Han thought – which worried her mother as much as or more than it pleased her. Liu Mei's father, an American named Bobby Fiore, was dead; the scaly devils had shot him before she was born. Before that, he, like Liu Han, had been a captive on one of those airplanes that never landed. They'd been forced to couple – the little scaly devils had enormous trouble understanding matters of the pillow (hardly surprising, when they came into heat like barnyard animals) – and he'd got her with child.

Off to the east, toward or maybe past the Forbidden City, gunfire crackled. The sound was absurdly cheerful, like the fireworks used to celebrate the new year. Liu Mei said, 'I didn't know we were doing anything today.'

'We're not,' Liu Han said shortly. The Communists were not the only ones carrying on a long guerrilla campaign against the scaly devils. The reactionaries of the Kuomintang had not abandoned the field. They and Mao's followers fought each other as well as the little devils.

And the eastern dwarfs kept sending men across the Sea of Japan to raise trouble for the little scaly devils and the Chinese alike. Japan had had imperialist pretensions in China years before the little devils arrived, and resented being excluded from what had been her bowl of rice.

More scaly devils whizzed past, these in a vehicle mounting a machine gun. They headed in the direction of the firing. None of them turned so much as an eye turret in Liu Han's direction. Liu Han decided to make a lesson of it. 'This is why we are strong in the cities,' she said to Liu Mei. 'In the cities, we swim unnoticed. In the countryside, where every family has known its neighbors forever and a day, staying hidden is harder.'

'I understand, Mother,' Liu Mei said. 'But this also works for the Kuomintang, doesn't it?'

'Oh, yes,' Liu Han agreed. 'A knife will cut for whoever takes it in hand.' She nodded to her daughter. 'You are quick. You need to be quick, the way the world is today.'

When she was Liu Mei's age and even older, all she'd wanted to do was go on living as she and her ancestors always had. But the Japanese had come to her village, killing her husband and her little son. And then the little scaly devils had come, driving out the eastern dwarfs and capturing her. She, who had not even thought of going to the city, was uprooted from everything she'd ever known.

And she'd thrived. Oh, it hadn't been easy, but she'd done it. She had abilities she hadn't even suspected. Once in a while, when she was in an uncommonly kindly mood, she thought she owed the little scaly devils some gratitude for liberating her from her former, ever so limited, life.

She glanced over to Liu Mei. She owed the scaly devils something else for what they'd done to her daughter. And she'd been giving them what she owed them ever since. That debt might never be paid in full, but she intended to keep on trying.

Liu Mei's face did not change much even when she laughed. She laughed now, laughed and pointed. 'Look, Mother! More devil-boys!'

'I see them,' Liu Han said grimly. She did not find the young people – boys and shameless girls, too – in any way amusing. When foreign devils from Europe spread their imperialistic web through China, some Chinese had imitated them in dress and food and way of life because they were powerful. The same thing was happening now with respect to the scaly devils.

This particular pack of devil-boys took things further than most. Like most such bands, they wore tight shirts and trousers printed in patterns that mimicked body paint, but several had shaved not only their heads but also their eyebrows in an effort to make themselves look as much like scaly devils as they could. They larded their speech with affirmative and interrogative coughs and words from the little scaly devils' language.

Many older people gave way before them, almost as they might have for real scaly devils. Liu Han did not. Stolid as if she were alone on the sidewalk, she strode straight through them, Liu Mei beside her. 'Be careful, foolish female!' one of the devil-boys hissed in the scaly devils' tongue. His friends giggled to hear him insult someone who would not understand.

But Liu Han did understand. That she was part of the revolutionary struggle against the little scaly devils did not mean she had not studied them – just the opposite, in fact. She whirled and hissed back: 'Be silent, hatchling from an addled egg!'

How the devil-boys stared! Not all of them understood what she'd said. But they could hardly fail to understand that a plain, middle-aged woman spoke the little devils' language at least as well as they did – and that she was not afraid of them. The ones who did understand giggled again, this time at their friend's discomfiture.

The boy who had first mocked Liu Han spoke in Chinese now: 'How did you learn that language?' He did not even add an interrogative cough.

'None of your business,' Liu Han snapped. She was already regretting her sharp answer. She and Liu Mei were not perfectly safe in Peking. Sometimes the little devils treated Chinese Communist Party officials like officials from the foreign devils' governments they recognized. Sometimes they treated them like bandits, even if the Communists made them sorry when they did.

'What about you, good-looking one?' The devil-boy shifted back to the scaly devils' speech to aim a question at Liu Mei. He showed ingenuity as well as brashness, for the little devils' language was short on endearments. They did not need them among themselves, not when they had a mating season and no females to put them into it.

'I am none of your business, either,' Liu Mei answered in the little devils' tongue. She'd begun to pick it up as her birth speech before Ttomalss had to return her to Liu Han. Maybe that had helped her reacquire it later, after she'd become fluent in Chinese. She threw in an emphatic cough to show how much she wasn't the devil-boy's business.

Instead of deflating, he laughed and folded himself into the scaly devils' posture of respect. 'It shall *not* be done, superior female!' he said, with an emphatic cough of his own.

That was when he began to interest Liu Han. 'You speak the little scaly devils' language well,' she said in Chinese. 'What is your name?'

'I ought to say, "None of your business," ' the devil-boy replied. That was apt to be true in more ways than one; people who asked such questions could put those who answered them in danger. But the devil-boy went on, 'It does not much matter, though, for everyone knows I am Tao Sheng-Ming.' He returned to the scaly devils' tongue: 'Is that not a foolish name for a male of the Race?'

Those of his friends who understood whooped with glee and slapped their thighs with the palms of their hands. In spite of herself, Liu Han smiled. Tao Sheng-Ming seemed to take nothing seriously, not his own Chinese blood and not the little devils he aped, either. But he was plainly bright; if he discovered the proper ideology, he might become very valuable.

Thoughtfully, Liu Han said, 'Well, Tao Sheng-Ming, if you are ever on *Nan Yang Shih K'uo* – South Sheep Market Mouth – in the eastern part of the city, you might look for Ma's brocade shop there.'

'And what would I find in it?' Tao asked.

'Why, brocade, of course,' Liu Han answered innocently. 'Ask for Old Lin. He will show you everything you need.'

If Tao Sheng-Ming did ask for Old Lin, he would be recruited. Maybe he would pay attention. Maybe, being a devil-boy with an itch for trouble, he wouldn't. Still, Liu Han judged the effort worth making.

Lieutenant Colonel Johannes Drucker was one of the lucky ones who went out into space: he enjoyed being weightless. Some of the men in the *Reich* Rocket Force had to nurse their stomachs through every tour in orbit. Not Drucker. His problem was working hard enough on the exercise bicycle to keep from coming home a couple of kilos heavier than when he'd gone up.

And the view from up here was beyond compare. Right now, his orbit was carrying him southeast across the United States, toward the Gulf of Mexico. Through swirling clouds, he could see plains and forests and, coming up swiftly, the deep blue of the sea. And, when he lifted his eyes to the stars blazing in the black sky of space, that was just as fine in a different way.

But he couldn't gawp for too long. His eyes flicked to the instruments that monitored oxygen, CO_2, the batteries – literally, the things that kept him breathing. Everything there was fine. And he'd used very little fuel from the maneuvering rockets so far this tour. He could change his orbit considerably if he had to.

Then he was looking out the window again, this time to the sides and rear. Like its smaller predecessors, the A-45 was an Army project, but the Focke-Wulf design bureau had given the manned upper stage a cockpit view a fighter pilot might have envied. He needed it; he depended far more on his own senses than did Lizard pilots, who had fancier electronics to help them.

Below and to either side were the bulges of his missile tubes, a thermonuclear sting in each of them. If he got the order, he could blow a couple of Lizards or Russians or Americans out of the sky – or, for that matter, aim the missiles at land targets.

Sun sparkled off the titanium wings on which he'd ride back to Earth. The swastikas on the wings were due for repainting; this upper stage had made several landings since the last time they'd been slapped on. He shrugged. That sort of stuff was for people down on the ground to worry about. Up here, as in any combat assignment, what you did counted. What you looked like didn't.

Drucker lightly touched the control stick. 'Just a damn driver,' he muttered. 'That's all I've ever been, just a damn driver.' He'd driven panzers against the French, against the Russians, and then against the Lizards before setting his sights higher both figuratively and literally. This upper stage – he'd named it *Käthe*, after his wife – responded far more smoothly and easily than the big grunting machines he'd formerly guided.

Of course, if a shell slammed into a panzer, he had some chance of bailing out. If anyone ever decided to expend a missile on him here, odds were a million to one he'd never know what hit him.

His wireless set crackled to life. 'German pilot, this is the U.S. tracking facility in Hot Springs. Do you read me? Over.' A moment later, the American radioman switched from English to badly accented German.

Like most who flew into space, Drucker spoke some English and Russian – and some of the Lizards' language – along with his German. 'Hot Springs tracking, this is the German rocket,' he said. 'How do I look? Over.'

It wasn't an academic question. By his own navigation, he was in the orbit calculated for him. If American radar showed otherwise, though, things might get sticky. Unexpected changes in course from a spacecraft carrying nuclear weapons had a way of making people nervous.

But the American answered, 'In the groove,' which let him relax. Then the fellow said, 'How's the weather up there, Hans? Over.'

'Very bad,' Drucker answered seriously. 'Rain last night, and a snow-storm ahead. Is that you, Joe? Over.'

'Yeah, it's me,' Joe said with a laugh at Drucker's attempt at humor: weather was one thing – maybe the only thing – he didn't have to worry about in space. 'You'll be coming down from your tour in another few orbits, won't you? Over.'

'I do not answer this sort of question,' Drucker said. 'You know I do not answer this sort of question. Your pilots do not answer this sort of question when we ask. Over.'

'You stay nosy, though, and so do we,' Joe answered, not in

the least put out. 'Have yourself a safe landing. I'll talk to you some more when you come up for another turn. Over and out.'

'Thank you – over and out,' Drucker said. The American's signal had started to break up before strengthing. Like the *Reich* and the Soviet Union, the USA had strings of ships that relayed transmissions to pilots wherever above the Earth they might be. The Lizards were the only ones who didn't need to bother with that. For one thing, they had more communications satellites and other spacecraft in orbit than all the human powers put together. For another, they had ground stations around the world, which no human power did.

Drucker scowled. And now their colonization fleet was beginning to join the conquest fleet. The colonists had set out from Tau Ceti II about the time the conquest fleet reached Earth. They'd expected a world subdued and waiting for them. *Hitler didn't let that happen,* Drucker thought proudly. Could he have done so without harming the Greater German *Reich*, he would have blasted every Lizard spacecraft out of the sky. He couldn't. No human could. What would happen when the colonists started coming down to Earth was something he didn't like to think about.

What would happen when he came back to Earth was less important to human history, but much more immediately urgent to him. Joe's *Have yourself a safe landing* hadn't been idle chatter. The upper stage Drucker rode, like all manmade spacecraft, was an uneasy blend of human and Lizard technology. The Wall of Heroes at Peenemünde had all too many names inscribed on it. Despite the handsome pension that would accrue to his widow, Drucker did not want his added to it.

He slid over the Atlantic in a matter of minutes, and then across Africa. The whole continent belonged to the Lizards. Some small rebellion still simmered in what had been the Union of South Africa, enough to keep the Lizards from exploiting the minerals there as fully as they might have. Other than that, the whole great land mass was theirs to do with as they would.

When his orbit swung north of the equator once more, he got a call from a Soviet radar station. The Russians also confirmed that he was where they expected him to be. His conversation with them, unlike the one with the American radioman, was coldly formal. He would have got rid of them, too, could he only have done it safely, and he knew they felt the same way about him. He scowled again. If only the Lizards hadn't come along when they did, the *Reich* would have put paid to Bolshevism once for all.

He couldn't do anything about that, either. The world, when you got down to it, could be a pretty unsatisfactory place.

An orbit and a half before he was supposed to land, he radioed a German relay ship and confirmed that he was coming back to Earth. He spoke in clear – code made listeners nervous, and the Lizards certainly were monitoring his transmissions, the Americans and Russians probably were, and the British and Japanese might be.

A touch of a button fired the retarding rockets in the nose of his spacecraft. As soon as they had burned long enough to slow the craft and take him out of orbit, he shut them down. The touch of another button slid covers over the openings to their motors. He breathed easier when sensors confirmed all three covers were in place. A motor opening left unsealed would have wrecked his aerodynamics, his spacecraft, and him.

As he slid back into the atmosphere, the nose of the craft and the leading edges of the wings glowed red. The ablative coating on them was a Lizard invention that all three human nations that put men into space had stolen. Little by little, the stick came alive in Drucker's hands. Before long, he was flying the upper stage like a large, heavy glider.

Germany's Baltic coastline was anything but interesting, especially after so many of the Earthly marvels he'd seen from space: nothing but low, flat land sloping ever so gradually downward toward the gray, shallow sea.

Another reassuring sound was that of the landing gear

coming down. Drucker landed the upper stage on a long concrete runway. After two weeks of weightlessness, he felt as if he had someone – or maybe two or three someones – sitting on his chest. Moving like an old, old man, he climbed out of the hatch set into the side of the spacecraft and down a little ladder to the runway.

Having fire trucks standing by was normal. Having groundcrew men jogging up to take charge of the upper stage was also normal. So was having the base commandant, a major general with the silver-gray *Waffenfarb* of the Rocket Force coming up to greet him. Having a couple of SS men in long black coats accompanying the general, though, was anything but normal.

Drucker's eyes narrowed. His dislike for the SS went back almost half a lifetime, to a day when he and other enlisted men of his panzer crew had cheated them of their chosen prey. No one he knew liked the SS. Everyone he knew feared the SS. He feared the SS himself, and feared the men in black the more because his past, if it ever came out, left him vulnerable to them even after all these years.

As they came up to him, their right arms shot out and up in perfect unison. '*Heil* Himmler!' they chorused.

'*Heil!*' Drucker returned the salute. He turned to Major General Dornberger, a decent enough fellow. 'What's up, sir?'

Before Dornberger could speak, one of the SS men said, 'You are Drucker, Johannes, lieutenant colonel, pay number—' He rattled it off.

'I am.' Drucker would much sooner not have been standing there. His feet hurt, his back hurt, even his hair seemed to hurt. He wanted to go somewhere, sit down – or, better yet, lie down – and make his report. After riding a rocket into space, wasn't he entitled to a little comfort? A bottle of schnapps would have been nice, too. 'Who are you?' he asked, as cuttingly as he dared.

The SS man ignored him. 'You are to consider yourself removed from the roster of approved *Reich* Rocket Force

44

pilots, effective this date and pending investigation and interrogation,' he droned.

'What?' Drucker stared. 'Why? What did I do? What in
blazes could I have done? I've been out in space, in case you
hadn't noticed.' Inside, he shivered. Had his past risen up to
bite him after all?

'You will come with us immediately for interrogation and
evaluation,' the SS man said. 'We have discovered reliable
evidence that your wife's paternal grandmother was a Jew.'
Drucker's jaw fell open. Käthe had never said a word about that,
not in all the years he'd known her. He wondered if she'd known
herself. 'Come,' the SS man snapped. Numbly, Drucker came.

Mordechai Anielewicz whistled as he rode a bicycle along a
road not far from the border between Lizard-occupied Poland
and the Greater German *Reich*. A farmer was weeding not far
from the side of the road. Anielewicz waved to him. 'Have you
stopped beating your wife, Boleslaw?' he called.

The Pole waved to him. 'Devils will roast you in hell, you
damned Jew.'

They both laughed. Anielewicz kept pedaling up the road
toward Lodz. If Poland wasn't the most peculiar country in the
world, he couldn't imagine what was. Just for starters, it was
the only place he could think of where most of the inhabitants
were happier to have the Lizards in charge than they would
have been with human beings. Of course, given that the choices
in human overlords were limited to the *Reich* and the Soviet
Union, that made better sense in Poland than it did most other
places.

Oh, some Poles went on and on about regaining their
independence. They fondly imagined they could keep that
independence more than about twenty minutes if the Lizards
ever decided to leave. They'd managed to keep it for twenty
years after World War I, but both their big neighbors had been
weak then. The USSR and, to Mordechai's regret, Germany
weren't weak now.

45

And the Jews who survived in Poland weren't weak these days, either. Anielewicz had a submachine gun slung across his back. A lot of men and even women, both Poles and Jews, still went armed these days. Mordechai had seen a lot of Westerns from Hollywood, some dubbed into Polish, others into Yiddish. He understood them much better now than he had when he'd been a Warsaw engineering student before the Germans invaded in 1939. A gun was an equalizer.

Hidden away somewhere not too far from Lodz, the Jews had the ultimate equalizer: an explosive-metal bomb, captured from the Nazis who'd intended to turn the city and its large ghetto into a mushroom cloud. Anielewicz didn't know whether the bomb would still work after all these years. His technicians had done their best to maintain it, but how good was that? The Poles couldn't be sure. Neither could the Lizards. And neither could the Germans or the Russians.

He started whistling again, a loud, cheery tune. 'Not being too certain is good for people,' he said to no one in particular. 'It keeps them from going ahead and doing things they're sorry for later.'

As he got closer to Lodz, his legs started aching. He was up into his forties now, not a young man as he had been during the war. He'd been riding a good long way, too, up from Belchatow. But whenever he got aches and pains he didn't think he ought to have, he wondered if the nerve gas he'd breathed while keeping the Germans from blowing up Lodz was still having its way with him. He'd had the antidote; without it, he would have just quietly stopped breathing and died. Even so, his health had never been the same since.

That sort of doubt made him pedal harder than ever, to prove to himself that he did have something left. Sweat streamed down his face. The modern suburbs around Lodz whizzed past in a blur. So did a Lizard radar station, one dish scanning toward the west, toward Germany, the other toward the south, in the direction of German-dominated Hungary. If trouble came this way, it could get here in a hurry.

If trouble came this way and didn't get knocked down, he would probably die before he knew it arrived. That was a consolation of sorts, but he declined to be consoled. Most of the people in the neighborhood around the radar station were Jews. They waved to Mordechai as he rode past. He waved back, and called out the same sort of insults he'd traded with Boleslaw the Pole. Along with most of the Jews in Poland, he switched back and forth between Yiddish and Polish, sometimes hardly noticing he was doing it.

Traffic got heavier as he rode up Franciszkanska Street into the city: horse-drawn wagons, lorries, motorcars – some old gasoline-burners, others hydrogen-powered – and swarms of bicycles. Anielewicz was glad to have an excuse to slow down.

New and old commingled inside Lodz. It had suffered in the German invasion, and again in the Lizards' conquest of the area, and yet again when the Nazis started lobbing rockets at it. In the intervening years, fresh construction had replaced most of the buildings wrecked in one round or another of fighting. Some new structures were of brick or pale tan sandstone that harmonized with their older neighbors. Others, especially those the Lizards had run up for themselves, were so boxy and utilitarian, they might as well have been alien invaders – and so, in fact, they were.

Anielewicz still lived in what had been the Lodz ghetto, not far from the fire station that had housed the ghetto's only motorized vehicle, a fire engine. He could have lived anywhere in the city – indeed, anywhere in Poland – he chose. His flat suited him well enough, and his wife, Bertha, had lived her whole life in Lodz. He sometimes thought about moving, but without great urgency.

An old friend waved as he rolled to a stop in front of the block of flats and put his feet down on the ground. Mordechai waved back. 'How are you today, Ludmila?' he asked with real concern.

Ludmila Jäger slowly walked up to him. 'I am . . . not so bad,' she replied in Russian-accented Polish. 'How are you?'

'I'm pretty well,' Anielewicz answered in Yiddish. Ludmila nodded; she spoke German, and could follow the Jews' variation on it. He went on, 'How are your legs? How are your arms?'

She shrugged. The motion made pain flow across her round, ruddy face. With what looked like a deliberate effort of will, she wiped it away. 'I will never move fast again,' she said. *'Nichevo'*. That was a Russian word, and a useful one: it meant something like, *It can't be helped*. Ludmila went on, 'It could have been worse.' Pain filled her face again. This time, she let it stay. 'For Heinrich, it was worse.'

'I know,' Anielewicz said quietly, and kicked at the cobblestones. A Jewish partisan leader, a German panzer officer who couldn't stomach the incineration of Lodz, and a Red Air Force pilot, as Ludmila had been then – a strange trio to thwart the *Reich* after the atomic bomb got smuggled into the city. They'd done it, but they'd paid the price.

Mordechai Anielewicz knew how lucky he'd been. All he had to show for his brush with Otto Skorzeny's nerve gas were pains if he exercised too hard for too long. Ludmila, though, was nearly a cripple. And Heinrich Jäger . . . Mordechai shook his head. Jäger, a German who proved his kind could be decent, had died young, and with few healthy days before he did.

After all these years, Anielewicz still wondered why. Was it because Jäger had been twenty years older than his two comrades? Or had he breathed in more of the gas? Or had the antidote not been so effective on him? No way to tell, no way at all. Whatever the reason, it was too damn bad.

Ludmila might have been reading his thoughts. She said, 'He did what he thought was right. If he hadn't done it, the fascist jackals might have caused the destruction of the entire world. We had a cease-fire with the Lizards. If it had come apart then . . . Heinrich said to the end of his days that keeping that from happening was the best thing he ever did.'

'I wish he were still here to say it, your fascist jackal,' Anielewicz replied.

Ludmila smiled; she still sometimes used Communist jargon without even noticing she'd done it. She said, 'So do I, but . . . *nichevo.*' Yes, that was a very useful word indeed. With another nod, she made her slow, painful way down the street, never once complaining.

Anielewicz carried the bicycle upstairs to his flat. Had he been so rash as to leave it on the sidewalk, even with a stout chain, it would have walked with Jesus. Even Jews used that saying about mysterious disappearances these days.

When he opened the door, familiar chaos surrounded him. His wife, Bertha, wearing a dress that would have been stylish in London a couple of years before and was still the height of fashion in Lodz, came up to give him a kiss. As always, a smile brought beauty to her plain face without the intermediate step of prettiness.

She said something. It was probably 'How are you?' or 'How are things?' but Anielewicz had trouble being sure. His daughter, Miriam, was practicing the violin. His son David, a couple of years younger, was practicing Hebrew for his bar mitzvah, which was only a little more than a month away. And his other son, Heinrich, who was eight, was working his way through a school lesson in the Lizards' language. These days, Anielewicz hardly noticed the contrast between *Blessed art Thou, O Lord our God, King of the universe* and *It shall be done, superior sir*. He did notice the racket. He would have had to be deaf, or more likely dead, not to notice.

The racket changed only languages when his children spotted him. They all tried to tell him everything about their days at the same time. What he heard were bits and pieces that surely didn't – couldn't – have gone together. If a boy had in fact invited Miriam to go to a film about Lizard irregular verbs, the world was even stranger than Anielewicz suspected.

When his wife could get a word in edgewise, she said, 'Bunim telephoned a couple of hours ago.'

'Did he?' That brought Mordechai to full alertness; Bunim was the most powerful Lizard stationed in Lodz. 'What did he want?'

'He wouldn't tell me,' Bertha answered. 'He said leaving a message would not be proper protocol.'

'Sounds like a Lizard,' Anielewicz said, and Bertha nodded. He went on, 'I'd better ring him up. Can you keep the menagerie down to low roars while I'm on the telephone?'

'I can try,' his wife said, and proceeded to lay down the law in a fashion Moses might have envied. In the brief respite thus afforded – and he knew it would be brief – Mordechai went into his bedroom to use the telephone.

He had no trouble getting through to Bunim; the regional subadminstrator always accepted calls from his phone code. 'I have for you a warning, Anielewicz,' he said without preamble. His German was fairly fluent. Hearing the Nazis' language in his mouth never failed to set Anielewicz's teeth on edge.

'Go ahead,' Anielewicz answered, not showing what he felt.

'A warning, yes,' the Lizard repeated. 'If you Tosevites plan any interference against the anticipated arrival of colonists in this region, it will be suppressed without mercy.'

'Regional Subadministrator, I know of no such plans inside Poland,' Anielewicz answered, on the whole truthfully. As he'd thought before, most of the human inhabitants of Poland, Jews and Poles alike, preferred their alien overlords to any of the humans who aspired to the job.

'Perhaps you should know more,' Bunim said, and added an emphatic cough. 'We have received a communication threatening that if a million males and females of the Race colonize Poland, that entire million shall die.'

'First I've heard of it,' Anielewicz said, which was completely true. 'Probably a lunatic. In what language was this . . . communication? That may give you a clue.'

'It gives no clue,' Bunim said flatly. 'It was in the language of the Race.'

*   *   *

50

Nesseref used her maneuvering thrusters to ease the shuttle-craft away from the outer skin of the *13th Emperor Makkakap*. She checked the shuttlecraft's instrument panel with special care. Like the ship with which it had come, it had just crossed a gulf of space even light would have needed more than twenty of the Race's years to travel. Of course the revived engineers had already been over the shuttlecraft again and again: that was how the Race did things. But Nesseref was no more inclined than any other female or male to leave anything to chance.

Everything seemed normal till she got to the radar display. With a hiss of surprise, she swung both eye turrets toward it, turning what had been a routine glance to a shocked state.

A fingerclaw activated the radio link with the ship. 'Shuttle-craft to Control,' Nesseref said. 'Shuttlecraft to Control. I wish to report that the radar set is showing impossible clutter.'

'Control to Shuttlecraft,' a technician aboard the *13th Emperor Makkakap* replied. 'Control to Shuttlecraft. That clutter is not, repeat, is not, impossible. We have a crowded neighborhood around Tosev 3 right now: the ships of the colonization fleet, the ships and satellites of the conquest fleet, and the ships and satellites of the Tosevites – the Big Uglies, the males of the conquest fleet call them. Remember your briefing, Shuttlecraft Pilot.'

'I remember,' Nesseref answered. Things hadn't been as anticipated for the Race, disorienting in and of itself. The conquest fleet had not conquered, or not completely. The Tosevites had proved improbably far advanced. Nesseref had believed what the briefing male said – he wouldn't have lied to her. But she hadn't begun to think about what it meant. Now she was seeing that with her own eyes.

As she scanned more instruments, she discovered that radar frequencies the Race did not use were striking the shuttlecraft. Any one of them might guide a missile on its way to her. 'Shuttlecraft to Control,' she said. 'You can confirm that we are at peace with these Tosevites?'

'That is correct, Shuttlecraft Pilot,' the controller said. 'We are at peace with them – or, at least, no great fighting is going on right now. On advice from males of the conquest fleet, we have relayed the time of your burn and your anticipated trajectory to the Tosevites and assured them we have no hostile intentions. The ones with whom I spoke used our language oddly but understandably.'

'I thank you, Control.' Nesseref did not want to speak to touchy, possibly hostile aliens, no matter how well they used the language of the Race. As far as she was concerned, they had no business using radio and radar at all. That they had such things disrupted plans the Race had made centuries before. Nesseref took it almost as a personal affront.

Moments slid past. Nesseref spent them aligning the shuttle-craft with fussy precision. When the job was done, she waited till it was time to leave orbit. Her fingerclaw hovered above the manual-override control, in case the computer didn't begin the burn at the right time. That was most unlikely, but training held. *Never take anything for granted.*

Deceleration slammed her back into her padded couch. It seemed to hit harder than she remembered, though all the instruments showed the burn to be completely normal. As the computer had begun it in the proper instant, so the machine shut it down when it should.

'Control to Shuttlecraft,' came the voice from the *13th Emperor Makkakap*. 'Your trajectory is as it should be. I am instructed to recommend that you acknowledge any radio signals the Tosevites may direct toward you while you are descending from orbit.'

'Acknowledged,' Nesseref said. 'It shall be done.' She wondered what things were coming to, when the Race had to treat with these Tosevites as if they held true power. But, if they were out in space, they did hold some true power. And obedience had been drilled into her as thoroughly as into any other male or female of the Race.

Before long, that obedience paid off. The computer reported

a signal on one of the Race's standard communications frequencies. By its direction, it came from an island off the northwestern coast of the main continental mass. The computer indicated the Race did not control that part of Tosev 3. Nesseref tuned the receiver to the indicated frequency and listened.

'Shuttlecraft of the Race, this is Belfast Tracking,' a voice said. The accent was strange and mushy, unlike any she'd heard before. 'Shuttlecraft of the Race, this is Belfast Tracking. Please acknowledge.'

'Acknowledging, Beffast Tracking.' Nesseref knew she'd made a hash of the Tosevite name, whatever it meant, but she couldn't do anything about that. 'Receiving you loud and clear.'

'Thank you, Shuttlecraft,' the Tosevite down on the ground said. 'Be advised your trajectory matches the flight plan your shiplord sent us. The Nazis will have nothing to complain about when you pass over their territory.'

Nesseref neither knew nor cared what Nazis were. Whatever they were, they had a cursed lot of nerve presuming to complain about anything the Race did. The Big Ugly from this Beffast Tracking had his – she supposed it was a male – nerve, too, for talking with her as if they were equals. 'Acknowledging,' she repeated, not wanting to give him anything more than that.

Another Tosevite hailed her. He identified himself not as a Nazi but as a tracker from the Greater German *Reich*. Nesseref wondered if the Tosevite back at Beffast had been trying to mislead her. As that first Big Ugly had predicted, though, this one did find her course acceptable.

'Do not deviate,' he warned, his accent still mushy but somehow different from that of the first Big Ugly with whom she'd spoken. 'If you deviate, you will be destroyed without warning. Do you understand?'

'Acknowledged,' Nesseref said tightly. She was low in the atmosphere now, dropping down toward the speed of sound. If the Tosevites could build spacecraft, they could assuredly blow her out of the sky. But they would have no need. 'I shall not deviate from my course.'

'You had better not.' This Big Ugly sounded even more arrogant than the one with whom she'd spoken before. He went on, 'And you had better not pay any attention to the lies the English will try to feed you. In no way are they to be trusted.'

'Acknowledged,' Nesseref said yet again. Why were the Tosevites warning her about one another? The too-brief briefing had spoken of their intraspecies rivalries, but she'd paid little attention to those. She hadn't imagined they could matter to her. Maybe she'd been wrong.

Then, to her vast relief, a familiar-sounding voice said, 'Shuttlecraft of the *13th Emperor Makkakap*, this is Warsaw Control. Your trajectory is as it should be. You will be on the ground here shortly.'

'Acknowledging, Warsaw Control,' Nesseref said. The male's assessment agreed with that of her own computer. She brought the shuttlecraft toward the fully upright position, so she could land it with its jet. As she did so, she studied the monitor's view of the world below: she'd descended enough to get a detailed view of it for the first time. 'Warsaw Control, is it always so green here?'

'It is, Shuttlecraft Pilot,' the male on the ground answered, 'except during winter, and then it is white with frozen water falling out of the sky in flakes like shed skin. You would not believe how cold it can get here.'

Nesseref wouldn't have believed the male at all had the briefing officer not also spoken of how beastly Tosev 3's climate could be. She still found the landscape strange and unnatural; she was used to rocks and dirt with occasional vegetation, not the other way round. Now she would see buildings, too, some the utilitarian cubes and blocks the Race favored, others absurdly ornate. *Why would anyone want to build like that?* she wondered. She also spied small buildings roofed not with metal or concrete or even stone, but with what looked like dry grass. How could a species that used such primitive building materials fare off the surface of its planet?

Being without a good answer, she eyed the instruments, once more ready to use manual override if the shuttlecraft's landing legs did not extend or if the rocket failed to ignite at the proper moment. No such emergency developed. Again, she had not expected one. But preparedness was never wasted.

Flame splashed off the concrete of the landing area, then winked out as the computer cut off the rocket motor. The monitor showed people wheeling a landing ramp out toward the shuttlecraft so she could descend. No, they weren't people; they were Tosevites. They looked like the videos she'd studied: too erect, too large, draped in cloths to conserve body heat even at what was evidently the warmer season of the year. Some of them had hair – it put her in mind of fungus – all over their blunt, round faces, others just on the top of the head. Next to the male of the Race trotting along beside them, they put her in mind of poorly articulated toys for hatchlings.

With a small clank, the top end of the ramp brushed the side of the shuttlecraft. Nesseref opened the outer door, then hissed as chilly air poured in. She hissed again when the air struck the scent receptors on her tongue; it stank of smoke and carried all sorts of other odors she'd never smelled before.

She skittered down the ramp. 'I greet you, superior female,' the male waiting at the bottom said. With an emphatic cough, he added, 'Strange to see a new face in these parts instead of the same gang of males.'

'Yes, I suppose it must be,' Nesseref said. Her eye turrets swiveled this way and that as she tried to take in as much of this part of this new world as she could. 'But then, all of Tosev 3 is strange, isn't it?'

'That it is.' The male used another emphatic cough. 'A Big Ugly, now, a Big Ugly would have said, "Good to see a new face." By the Emperor' – he cast down his eyes – 'they really think that way.'

Nesseref's shiver had only a little to do with the unpleasant weather. 'Aliens,' she said. 'How can you bear to live among them?'

'It is not easy,' the male replied. 'Some of us have even started thinking more the way they do than anybody straight from Home would be able to imagine, I expect. We have had to. A lot of the ones who could not are dead. But Tosev 3 does have its compensations. There is ginger, for instance.'

'What is ginger?' Nesseref asked. It hadn't been in the briefing.

'Good stuff,' the male said. 'I will give you a vial. You can take it back up with you when you fetch this intelligence data up into orbit. We do not want to transmit it, even encrypted, for fear the Big Uglies will break the encryption. They have done it before, and hurt us doing it.'

'Are they really that bad?' Nesseref asked.

'No,' the male told her. 'Really, they are worse.'

David Goldfarb minded being stationed in Belfast less than a lot of people might have. From what he'd seen, even men brought over from England soon tended to divide along religious lines, Protestants going up against Catholics in long-running arguments that sometimes turned into brawls. Being a Jew, he was immune to that sort of pressure.

All things considered, Jews got on pretty well in Belfast. Each faction here despised the other so thoroughly, it had little energy to waste on any other hatreds. Neither Catholics nor Protestants gave Naomi and the kids a hard time when they left the married officers' quarters to shop.

Goldfarb's swivel chair creaked when he leaned back in it. 'First shuttlecraft from the colonization fleet we've tracked,' he remarked.

'That's right, Flight Lieutenant,' Sergeant Jack McDowell answered. If the Scot disliked serving under a Jew who singularly lacked a cultured accent, he was veteran enough to conceal the fact. 'Won't be the last, though.'

'No.' Goldfarb was a veteran himself, having spent his entire adult life in the RAF. 'Not the world we thought it would be, is it?'

'Not half it's not,' McDowell agreed sorrowfully. He pulled a packet of Chesterfields from his breast pocket, stuck one in his mouth, and lit it. Holding the packet out to Goldfarb, he asked, 'Care for a fag, sir?'

'Thanks.' Goldfarb leaned forward to light the smoke from the one McDowell already had going. He took a drag, then blew a ragged smoke ring. After another drag, he sighed. 'Doesn't taste like much, does it?'

'Too right it don't,' McDowell said, even more sorrowfully than before. He too sighed. 'Not a Yank brand going that tastes like much. When you lit up a Players, by God, you knew you had a cigarette in your face.'

'That's the truth.' Goldfarb coughed in fond reminiscence. 'It's the end of Empire, that's what it is.' The phrase had taken on a mournful currency in Britain after the Lizards occupied most of what once was the largest empire on the face of the Earth. Cut off from much of the tobacco they'd used, British cigarette manufacturers had gone under one after another.

McDowell's long, lean, ruddy face got even more sour than usual. 'The end of Empire it is. And do you know what's the worst of it?' He waited for Goldfarb to shake his head, then went on, 'The worst of it, sir, is that the youngsters who've grown up since the bloody Lizards came, they don't care. Doesn't matter to them that we're shoved back onto a couple of little islands. All they want to do is lay about and drink beer, you ask me.'

'They don't know any better,' Goldfarb answered. 'This is what they're used to. They don't remember how things were. They don't remember how we kept the Nazis from invading us and how we beat the Lizards when they did.'

Savagely, McDowell stubbed out his bland American cigarette and said, 'And now we're on the dole from the Yanks and the Nazis both. Damned if I don't half wish the Lizards had beaten us after all. Better to go down swinging than to slip into the muck an inch at a bloody time.'

'Something to that,' said Goldfarb, who despised the dependence on the Greater German *Reich* into which a Britain shorn of her colonies had been forced. 'I warned that shuttlecraft pilot about the Nazis. Haven't heard any squawks since, so I suppose he got down safe in Poland.'

McDowell leered. 'That was a shuttlecraft from the colonization fleet. How do you know a lady Lizard wasn't flying it?'

'I don't,' Goldfarb admitted, blinking. 'It never even occurred to me.' He shrugged. 'Doesn't matter much, not to me and not to the Lizards, either. If their females aren't in season, the males don't care about chasing skirt, poor buggers.'

'I'd pay five quid to see a lady Lizard in a skirt,' McDowell said.

'Come to think of it, so would I,' Goldfarb answered with a chuckle. He got to his feet and stretched. 'Thanks for the smoke.'

'Any time, Flight Lieutenant,' McDowell said. 'I've cadged more from you than you ever have from me.'

Goldfarb shrugged again. A Jew who got a reputation for stinginess found himself in even more hot water these days than he would have a generation before. Britain didn't go in for the madnesses of the *Reich* over on the Continent, but some of the Nazis' attitudes had rubbed off, especially down in England. That was another reason Goldfarb hadn't minded being posted to Northern Ireland.

He walked out into watery sunshine. Belfast seldom got any other sort. Parabolic radar dishes scanned every direction. They were ever so much smaller and ever so much more powerful than the sets he'd served during the Battle of Britain and during the Lizards' arrival – till the aliens knocked out those sets. Some of the improvement would surely have come over the course of time regardless of whether the Lizards landed on Earth. But captured equipment and training disks playable by what they called *skelkwank* light had kicked human technology far ahead of where it would have been otherwise.

A couple of RAF officers strode past Goldfarb. He stiffened to attention and saluted; they both outranked him. One of them was saying, '– ce they're all down, we'll pay back a lot of—'

After returning Goldfarb's salute, the other spoke in an elegant Oxonian accent: 'Now, now, old man, don't you know?' His gaze flicked across Goldfarb as if the flight lieutenant were a speck of lint on his lapel.

Both officers fell silent till Goldfarb was out of earshot. He went on his way, quietly steaming. Far too many officers these days gave him the glove because he was Jewish. He couldn't do anything about it, either – or rather, he could, but anything he did was likely to make matters worse. Anti-Semitism kept wafting across the Channel like a bad smell. That Heinrich Himmler seemed so calm and rational about it, rather than ranting as Hitler had done, only made it more appealing to the aristocratic Englishman of the stiff-upper-lip school.

'What do they think?' Goldfarb muttered. 'I should get down on my knees and thank them for the privilege of saving their bacon' – an American phrase, to the point if not kosher – 'from the Lizards? Not bloody likely!'

Trouble was, too many of them did think exactly that. He knew his chances of making squadron leader were about as good as Britain's chances of retaking India from the Lizards. If he hadn't had a record far better than those of his competitors – and if he hadn't had some blokes on his side back in the days when being on a Jew's side didn't take extraordinary moral courage – he never would have become an officer at all.

He had become one, though. If those snooty brass hats didn't like it, too bad for them. He wondered what sort of conversation they'd judged unsuitable for his tender ears. He'd never know. He also wouldn't lose any sleep over it. Had he lost sleep over every slight, he'd have lain awake every night.

People on the streets of Belfast kept an eye on him as he headed for his home. He didn't look like an Englishman or an Irishman or even a Scot; his hair was too curly, and the wrong shade of brown to boot, while his face bore a distinctly Judaic nose. Said nose itched. He scratched it. An itchy nose was supposed to be a sign he'd kiss a fool.

When he got home, he planted a big smack on Naomi. Maybe she'd been a fool for marrying him, all those years ago. Her family had got out of Germany while some Jews still could; his had fled Polish pogroms before World War I. But she hadn't looked down her own charming nose at him, and they remained as happy as two people could reasonably expect in this uncertain world.

'What's new?' she asked, her English still faintly accented though she'd been in Britain since her teens.

He told her about the shuttlecraft from the colonization fleet, and about the warning he'd been able to pass on. Then he sighed. 'It won't do any good. The Lizards in the colonization fleet don't know Nazis from necklaces.'

'You did what you could,' Naomi said, and added an emphatic cough.

Goldfarb laughed. 'You caught that from our children,' he said severely, 'and they caught it from the wireless and the telly.'

'And the wireless and the telly caught it from the Lizards – maybe we are becoming a part of their Empire, one bit at a time,' his wife answered. 'And speaking of such things, you have a letter from your cousin in Palestine.'

'From Moishe?' Goldfarb said in glad surprise. 'Haven't heard from him in a couple of months. What has he got to say?'

'I don't know – I haven't opened it,' Naomi said. That was standard practice in the Goldfarb household: no one ever opened mail addressed to someone else. 'Here, I'll get it for you.' He watched her go over to the sideboard – watched appreciatively, as skirts were short this year –

and pluck the letter from a cut-glass dish there. She carried it back to him.

It bore no stamp, but an adhesive label covered with Lizard squiggles. Moishe Russie had written Goldfarb's name and address in the Roman alphabet, but the letter inside the envelope was in Yiddish. *Dear Cousin David,* he wrote, *I hope this finds you well, as all are here in Jerusalem. Reuven has just finished exams for this term of medical school. How much more he knows of how the body works than I did at his age! He would have known more if the Lizards had not come, of course, but he knows even more than he would have otherwise because they did. They understand life at a molecular level we were generations away from reaching.*

So Naomi would understand, Goldfarb read the letter aloud. She had no trouble following spoken Yiddish, but could not fight her way through the Hebraic script in which it was written. 'Good that your cousin's son will be a doctor,' she said.

'Yes,' Goldfarb answered, thinking that the Lizards had given medicine the same sort of lift they had electronics. He read on: ' "The fleetlord, you know, sometimes uses me as a channel between the Race and people. This is one of those times. Something strange is going on in connection with the arrival of the colonization fleet. I do not know what it is. I do not know if he knows what it is. Whatever it is, it worries him." '

Goldfarb and his wife stared at each other. Anything that worried the fleetlord was liable to mean trouble for the whole human race – and, incidentally, for the Lizards. Why hadn't Moishe been more explicit? Because he didn't know much more himself, evidently. 'Finish,' Naomi said.

' "Atvar likes back-channel contacts more than he did some years ago," ' Goldfarb read. ' "If you can put a flea in the ear of some of your officer friends, it might do some good. Your cousin, Moishe." '

'What will you do?' Naomi asked.

'God knows,' Goldfarb answered. 'I haven't got that many officer friends any more, not with things like they are here. And I'm hardly the bloke to play at world politics.' Naomi looked at him. He let out a long sigh. He had no real choice, and knew it. 'I'll do what I can, of course.'

Straha spent a lot of time touching up his body paint. He kept the complex patterns as neat as they had been back in the days when he commanded the *206th Emperor Yower*. He'd been the third-ranking male in the conquest fleet, behind only Atvar and Kirel. He'd come within the breadth of a fingerclaw of toppling Atvar from fleetlord's rank. If he'd done it, if he'd taken charge of things in place of that boring plodder . . .

He hissed softly. 'Had the fleet been mine, Tosev 3 would belong to the Race in its entirety,' he said. He believed that; from snout to tailstump he believed it. It didn't matter. What might have been never mattered, save in the Big Uglies' overactive imaginations. A good male of the Race, Straha kept his eye turrets aimed firmly at what had been and what was.

Exile, he thought. When he failed to overthrow Atvar, the fleetlord's revenge had been as inevitable, as inexorable, as gravity. It had also been slow – *typical of Atvar,* Straha thought with a sneer. Instead of waiting for it, Straha had taken the *206th Emperor Yower's* shuttlecraft and fled to the Big Uglies.

Exile. The word tolled mournfully in his head, just as if it were reverberating from his hearing diaphragms. In exchange for his intimate knowledge of the Race, the American Tosevites had treated him and continued to treat him as well as they knew how. Anything he asked for, they gave him. That was why he dwelt in Los Angeles these days: a climate not impossibly cold, not impossibly humid. Whenever he chose, he ate ham, which came close to a delicacy he'd known back on Home. He had video gear purchased from the Race, and electronic entertainments either purchased after the fighting or captured during it.

Exile. When he wanted it, he even had the company of other males. But they were captives, not defectors; no one could blame them for collaborating with the Big Uglies. People could blame him, could and did. However useful traitors were, no one loved them. That had proved as true among the Tosevites as it was among the Race.

Still, time had slipped past without too much unpleasantness till the colonization fleet came into Tosev's solar system. Very soon now, in the lands that the Race ruled, it would set up a good facsimile of life on Home. And Straha would be – the Big Uglies had a phrase for it – on the outside looking in.

'I do not care,' he said. But that was a lie, and he knew it. If he hadn't fled, he would have become a part of that life. Atvar would have degraded him, even arrested him, but would not have harmed him. Big Uglies sometimes enjoyed inflicting pain. The Race didn't, and had had ever so much trouble understanding the difference.

Feeling pain, now, when it came to feeling pain, the Tosevites and the Race were very much alike. Straha opened the drawer of a wooden cabinet of a size to suit Big Uglies better than males of the Race, one with fixtures made for a Tosevite's hands.

In the drawer, among other things, lay a well-sealed glass jar full of powdered ginger cured with lime, the Race's favorite form of the herb. The American Big Uglies gave Straha all the ginger he wanted, too, though they were much less generous about letting their own leaders enjoy unlimited drugs.

He poured some ginger onto the fine scales covering the palm of his hand, then raised it toward his mouth. Of itself, his tongue shot out. In a couple of quick licks, the ginger disappeared.

'Ahhh!' he hissed: a long sigh of pleasure. When ginger first lifted him, he forgot he was all alone among barbarous aliens. No, that wasn't quite true. He remembered, but he no longer cared. With ginger coursing through him, he felt taller and stronger than any Big Ugly, and more clever than all the Big

Uglies and all the other males of the Race on Tosev 3. Ideas filled his long, narrow head, each of them so brilliant it dazzled him before he could fully grasp it.

He knew ginger only seemed to turn him tall and strong and brilliant. It didn't actually make him any of those things. Males who acted as if what the ginger told them were true had a way of dying before their time. That was one reason he tried to keep his tasting within the bounds of moderation.

Descending from ecstasy was the other reason. He had not felt so low going down from the *206th Emperor Yower* to the surface of Tosev 3 as he did when the drug's exaltation began to leach out of him. The harder he tried to grasp it, the more readily it slipped through his fingers. At last it was all gone, leaving him lower than he had been before he tasted, and painfully aware of how low that was.

Sometimes, to hold the crushing depression at bay, he would taste again when the first one wore off, or even for a third time on the heels of the second. But the herb-fueled exhilaration ebbed from one taste to another right after it, while the post-tasting gloom only got worse. Unlimited ginger, however much a taster might crave such a thing, did not mean unlimited happiness.

And so, instead of taking a second taste, Straha put the ginger jar back in the drawer and slammed it shut. He picked up the telephone. Like the cabinet, it was of Tosevite manu-facture, the handset made with the distance between a Big Ugly's mouth and absurd external ear in mind, the holes in the dial designed for blunt, clawless Tosevite fingers.

Those holes served his fingerclaws well enough. The clicks and squawks of the electronics as the call went through were partly familiar, partly strange. The bell at the other end of the line was a purely Tosevite conceit; the Race would have used some sort of hiss instead.

'Hello?' The voice on the other end was Tosevite, too, the greeting the one the local Big Uglies used among themselves on the telephone. Straha had picked up some English during his long years of exile, but Big Uglies who wished to speak with him commonly used the language of the Race.

Straha used his own language now: 'I greet you, Major Yeager.'

'I greet you, Shiplord,' Yeager replied, dropping English without the least hesitation. Of all the Tosevites Straha had met, he came closest to being able to think like a male of the Race. His question was very much to the point: 'Feeling lonely tonight?'

'Yes.' Straha choked back an emphatic cough. His hands folded into fists, so that fingerclaws dug into his palms. Most Big Uglies would not have noticed what he hadn't quite said. Yeager was different. Yeager heard what wasn't said as well as what was.

'We have known each other a long time now, Shiplord,' the Tosevite said. 'I remember thinking even in the early days, when your folk and mine were still fighting, how hard a road you had chosen for yourself.'

'You thought further ahead than I was thinking when I left the conquest fleet,' Straha said. 'I get an itch under the scales admitting such a thing to a Tosevite, but it is truth.' The Race had got where it was by planning ahead, by always thinking of the long term. Straha hadn't done that. He'd been paying ever since for not doing it. *Exile.*

As if to rub that in, Yeager said, 'You always did think more like a Big Ugly than most other males of the Race I have known.' He used the Race's slang name for his kind without taking it as an insult, the way some Tosevites did.

'I do not think like a Big Ugly,' Straha said with dignity. 'I do not wish to think like a Big Ugly. I am a male of the Race. It is merely that I am not a reactionary male of the Race, as so many officers of the conquest fleet proved to be.' Venting his anger at Atvar and Kirel to a Big Ugly was demeaning – a telling measure of just how lonely he'd become – but he couldn't help it.

Yeager let out a few barks of noisy Tosevite laughter. 'I did not say you thought like a Tosevite, Shiplord. If you were one of us, you would be a hopeless reactionary. Even so, that makes you a radical among the Race.'

'Truth,' Straha said. 'You understand us well. How did this happen? I know of your attachment to the wild literature your kind produced before the conquest fleet arrived, but others were attached to this literature, too, and they have not your skill in dealing with the Race.'

'In fact, Shiplord, some of our best males and females for dealing with your folk were science-fiction readers before the conquest fleet came,' Yeager replied, the key term necessarily being in English. 'But I count myself lucky. I could not have stayed a paid athlete much longer, and I do not know what I would have done after that. When the conquest fleet came, it let me discover I was good at something I had not known I could do at all. Is that not strange?'

'For the Race, it would be surpassingly strange,' Straha answered. 'For you Tosevites? I doubt it. So much of everything you do seems built around lucky accidents. But not all accidents are lucky. If we had come two hundred years later – a hundred of your years, I mean – we might have found this planet dead because of nuclear war.'

'It could be so, Shiplord,' Yeager said. 'We can never know, but it could be so. But if you had waited a little longer than that, we might have come to Home before you ever got to Tosev 3.'

Straha hissed in horror. Big Uglies played the game of what-might-have-been far more naturally, far more fluidly, than did the Race. Straha tried to imagine a conquest fleet full of bloodthirsty Tosevites descending on calm, peaceful Home. Save for conquests of other species, the Race had not fought a war in more than a hundred thousand years. Except when a conquest fleet was abuilding, no military hardware above the level the police needed even existed. The Big Uglies would have had an easy time of it.

He did not say that, for fear of giving Yeager ideas – not that any Big Ugly needed help coming up with ideas. What the exiled shiplord did say was, 'One day, Big Uglies will visit Home. One day, Big Uglies will bow before the Emperor.' In spite of having abandoned the Race, Straha cast down his eyes at speaking of his sovereign.

'I wish I could visit your planet,' Yeager said. 'We Tosevites aren't very good at bowing to anyone, though. You may have noticed that.'

'Snoutcounting,' Straha said disparagingly. 'How you think to rule yourselves through snoutcounting . . .' Nictitating membranes slid across his eyes, a sure sign he was growing sleepy. 'I thank you for your time, Major Yeager. I shall rest now.'

'Rest well, Shiplord,' the Tosevite said.

'I shall.' Straha hung up. But even if he did rest well, tomorrow would be another day alone.

3

Under the summer sun, Jerusalem glowed golden. The local sandstone from which so much of the city was built looked far more impressive than the world's usual run of gray rocks – so Reuven Russie thought, at any rate. Even marble would only have been silver to sandstone's gold. Jerusalem was Reuven's city, and he loved it with the uncritical, unquestioning adoration he'd lavished – for a little while – on the first girl with whom he'd become infatuated.

His childhood memories of other towns – Warsaw, London – were filled with fear and hunger and cold. His eyes went to the Temple Mount, with the Dome of the Rock and the Western Wall. When had snow last fallen there? Not for many years, nor was it likely to fall again for many more. He did not miss it. He had almost a Lizard's love for heat.

But thinking of the Lizards made him think of the marvelous antiquities on the Temple Mount in a different light. The Dome of the Rock dated from the seventh century of the Common Era. The Western Wall, of course, was far older, having gone up before Jesus strode along the streets on which Reuven walked now.

Archaeologists would be working in Jerusalem for centuries to come, piecing together the distant past. But that past seemed less distant to Reuven Russie than it did to his father Moishe, and far less distant than it would have to the grandfather he did not remember. His grandfather had never known the Lizards. His father had been a grown man when they came, and thought of the earlier days as the normal state of mankind. To those Reuven's age and younger, especially in lands where the Lizards ruled, they were simply part of the landscape.

One of them skittered past him, intent on some business of its own. 'I greet you,' he called in its language.

'I greet you,' the male answered. By the Lizard's body paint, he served with the radar unit on the hills outside of town. The Nazis had never tried lobbing a rocket in this direction. Russie wasn't sure what would happen if they did. Having a little warning struck him as a good idea.

He glanced toward the Temple Mount again. *Antiquities,* he thought once more. So they were, by his father's standards or his grandfather's. Two thousand years was a long time, as the Earth had measured such things in the days before the Lizards came. Now . . .

Now two thousand years felt like merely the blink of an eye. The Lizards' Empire had been a going concern for more than fifty thousand years, since the days when people lived in caves and quarreled with bears who wanted to do the same. The Lizards had added the Rabotevs and Hallessi to their Empire before people figured out how to read and how to grow crops. Two thousand years ago, they'd already been thinking for some time about conquering Earth.

Set against the vast sweep of Lizardly history, what were a couple of thousand years? Why had God decided to pay attention to Earth during a restricted stretch of time and ignored the worlds of the Empire? Those were questions to make rabbis tear their own hair and pull one another's beards.

Reuven chuckled. 'The Lizards should have moved faster, for once in their scaly lives,' he murmured. Had they simply sent out a conquest fleet without bothering to think and scout and plan, they would have smashed the Roman Empire flat, and Earth would have gone into the Empire without a fight.

But it hadn't happened. And so, although the Lizards

occupied Palestine, they had less control here than they would have liked. Freedom kept spreading almost under their snouts. Not enough males prowled the countryside for it to be otherwise. Jews intrigued with the Soviet Union. Arabs intrigued with the Soviet Union and the *Reich*. Both Jews and Arabs intrigued with the British and Americans. And, for good measure, Jews and Arabs intrigued with each other – and with the Lizards.

With more than a little pride, Reuven strode through the entranceway to the Russie Medical College, which sat in a square, Lizard-built building a little west of the base of the Temple Mount. The college was named for his father, the first human who'd asked the Lizards for the privilege of studying what they knew and what the finest Earthly physicians hadn't begun to suspect.

For most of a generation now, bright medical students had flocked here from all over the world to learn what they could acquire in fullness nowhere else. Reuven also knew more than a little pride that he had been allowed to study here, for the Lizards played no favorites, picking those they would accept through grueling examinations. Jews and Arabs studied side by side, along with men and a few women from India, South America, South Africa, and other lands the Lizards ruled – and from the independent nations of the world as well.

As he slid into his seat in the genetics class, Reuven nodded to his fellow students. 'Good morning, Thorkil,' he whispered. 'Morning, Pablo. Good morning, Jane. Hullo, Ibrahim.' Among themselves, the students spoke English more than any other human language.

In came the instructor, a Lizard military physician named Shpaaka. Along with the rest of the humans, Reuven got to his feet, bent himself into as good an approximation of the Lizards' posture of respect as his frame would permit, and chorused, 'I greet you, superior sir.'

'I greet you,' Shpaaka said. He understood enough English to make sardonic comments when he caught his human students whispering in it. But the Lizards' tongue was the language of instruction. It had the technical terms he needed to get his point across; English and other Earthly languages had borrowed a lot of them. His eye turrets swiveled back and forth. 'Have you any questions on what we covered yesterday before we commence?' He pointed. 'Jane Archibald?'

'I thank you, superior sir,' the Australian girl said. 'When using a virus to bring an altered gene into a cell, what is the best way to suppress the body's immune response to ensure that the gene does get to its intended destination?'

'This seems rather different in your species from mine,' the lecturer replied, 'and it also leads into today's subject. Perhaps it would be best if I simply went on.' He proceeded to do just that.

Back when Reuven's father studied under the Lizards, they hadn't wanted to stop for questions at all; that wasn't their style among themselves. Over the years, they'd adapted to some degree, and so had people. No one had ever had the nerve to thank them for adapting; had they consciously realized they were doing so, they might have stopped. They did not approve of change of any sort.

Reuven scrawled notes. Shpaaka was a clear, well-organized lecturer; clarity and organization were Lizardly virtues. The male knew his material backwards and forwards. He also had, in the large vision screen behind him, a teaching tool that would have made any human instructor jealous. It showed what he was talking about in color and in three dimensions. Seeing wasn't just believing. It was understanding, too.

Laboratory work meant shifting back and forth between the metric system and the one the Lizards used, which was also based on powers of ten but used different basic quantities for everything but temperature. More lectures followed, on pharmacology and biochemistry. The Lizards did not teach surgery, not having had enough experience with humans to be confident of the result.

By the end of the day, Reuven's brain felt pounded flat, as it did by the end of almost every day. He shook his hand to work the writer's cramp out of it. 'Now I get to go home and study,' he said. 'I'm so glad to live the exciting life of a student – a party every night.' He rolled his eyes to show how seriously he expected everyone to take that.

He got a few tired groans from his classmates. Jane Archibald rolled her eyes, too, and said, 'At least you have a home to go to, Reuven. Better than the bleeding dormitory, and that's a fact.'

'Come along and have supper with me, if you like,' Reuven said – a not altogether disinterested offer, as she was easily the best-looking girl at the medical college, being blond and pink and emphatically shaped. Had she come from the *Reich*, she would have been the perfect Aryan princess . . . and would, no doubt, have been horrified to get such an invitation from a Jew.

As things were, she shook her head, but said, 'Maybe another time. I've got too much swotting tonight to spare even a minute.'

He nodded sympathetically; every student could sing that song almost every night. 'See you in the morning,' he said, and turned to head back to his parents' house. But then he paused – Jane was biting her lip. 'Is something wrong?' He asked, hastily adding, 'I don't mean to pry.'

'You're not,' she said. 'It's only that, every now and then, the idea of having a home where you're comfortable strikes me as very strange. Over and above the dormitories, I mean.'

'I understood what you meant,' he said, his voice quiet. 'Australia had a hard time of it.'

'A hard time of it? You might say so.' Jane's nod sent golden curls bouncing up and down. 'An atomic bomb on top of Sydney, another one on Melbourne – and we'd hardly even been in the fight against the Lizards till then. They just took us out and took us over.'

'That's what happened here, too, more or less,' Russie said, 'though without the bombs.'

He might as well have kept quiet. Jane Archibald went on as if he had, saying, 'And now, with the colonization fleet here at last, they're going to build cities from one end of the desert to the other. Bloody Lizards like it there – they say it's almost as nice and warm as Home.' She shuddered. 'They don't care – they don't care at all – that we were there first.'

Reuven wondered how much her ancestors had cared that the aborigines were there first. About as much as his own ancestors had cared that the Canaanites were in Palestine first, he supposed. Mentioning the subject struck him as unwise even so. Instead, he asked, 'If you hate the Lizards so much, what are you doing here?'

Jane shrugged and grimaced. 'Not a hope in hell of fighting them, not down in Australia there isn't. Next best thing I can do is learn from them. The more I know, the more use I'll be to the poor downtrodden human race.' Her grin was wry. 'And now I'll get down from my soapbox, thank you very much.'

'It's all right,' Reuven said. He didn't feel particularly downtrodden. Jews did better under the Lizards than anywhere in the independent lands except possibly the United States. That they did so well made them objects of suspicion to the rest of mankind – *not that we weren't objects of suspicion to the rest of mankind before the Lizards came*, he thought.

'I didn't intend to use your shoulder to cry on,' Jane Archibald said. 'It's not like you can do anything about the way things are.'

'It's all right,' Reuven repeated. 'Any time.' He made as if to grab her and forcibly pull her to the aforesaid shoulder. She made as if to clout him over the head with her notebook, which was thick enough to have lethal potential. They both laughed. Maybe the world wasn't perfect, but it didn't seem so bad, either.

Rance Auerbach awoke in pain. He'd awakened in pain every day for almost all the past twenty years, ever since a burst from a Lizard machine gun wrecked his leg and his chest and shoulder outside of Denver. The Lizards had captured him afterwards, and taken care of him as best they knew how. He had both legs, which proved as much. But he still woke in pain every morning.

He reached for his stick, which lay beside him on the bed like a lover and was far more faithful than any lover he'd ever had. Then, moving slowly and carefully – the only way he could move these days – he first sat and finally stood.

Limping into the kitchen of his small, grubby Fort Worth apartment, he poured water into a pot and spooned instant coffee and sugar into a cup. The coffee jar was getting close to empty. If he bought a new one the next time he went to the store, he'd have to figure out what else to do without. 'Damn the Lizards anyway,' he muttered. His own voice held a Texas twang; he'd come home after the fighting stopped. 'Damn them to hell and gone.' The Lizards ruled just about all the lands where coffee grew, and made sure it wasn't cheap when it got to the free people who drank it.

He burned a couple of slices of toast, scraped some of the charcoal off them, and spread them with grape jelly. He left the knife, the plate, and the coffee cup in the sink. They had company from the day before, and some more from the day before that. He'd been neat as a pin in his Army days. He wasn't neat as a pin any more.

Getting dressed meant going through another ordeal. It also meant looking at the scars that seamed his body. Not for the first time, he wished the Lizards had killed him outright instead of reminding him for the rest of his life how close they'd come. He dragged on khaki pants that had seen better days and slowly buttoned a chambray shirt he didn't bother tucking in.

Slipping his feet into thong-style sandals was pretty easy. As he headed for the door, he passed the mirror on the dresser from which he hadn't taken clean underwear. He hadn't shaved, either, which meant graying stubble fuzzed his cheeks and jaw.

'You know what you look like?' he told his reflection. 'You

look like a goddamn wino.' Was that misery in his voice or a sort of twisted pride? For the life of him, he couldn't tell.

He made sure the door was locked when he went outside, then turned the key in the dead bolt he'd installed himself. This wasn't the best part of town. He didn't have much to tempt a burglar, but what he did have, by God, was his.

His bad leg made him wish he could afford either a ground-floor apartment or a building that boasted an elevator. Going down two flights of stairs left him sweating and cursing. Going upstairs when he came home tonight would be worse. To celebrate making it to the sidewalk, he lit a cigarette.

Every doctor he'd ever met told him he didn't have the lung capacity to keep smoking. 'None of the sons of bitches ever told me how to quit, though,' he said, and took another deep drag on the coffin nail.

The sun beat down from a sky of enameled brass. Shadows were pale, as if apologizing for being there at all. The air he breathed was almost as hot and almost as wet as the coffee he'd drunk. Step by painful step, he made his way down to the bus stop on the corner. He sank down onto the bench with a sigh of relief, and celebrated with another Camel. *Fine American tobaccos,* the pack said. He remembered the days when it had said, *Fine American and Turkish tobaccos.* The Lizards ruled Turkey now, though the *Reich* next door kept things uncomfortable for them there. Turkish tobaccos stayed home.

A bus pulled to a stop in front of the bench. Auerbach regretted sitting, because that meant he had to stand up again. Putting most of his weight on the cane, he managed. He negotiated the couple of steps up to the fare box with only a couple of cuss words for each one. He tossed a dime in the box and kept standing not far from the door.

People pushed past him, getting on and off. He leered at a couple of pretty girls who went by; the clothes women wore these days offered a lot of flesh for leering. But when a bare-chested teenage boy with his head shaved and his chest painted to imitate a Lizard rank boarded the bus, Rance had everything he could do to keep from breaking his cane over the punk's glistening, empty head.

That's the enemy! he wanted to shout. It wouldn't have done any good. He'd tried it a few times, and seen as much. To the kids who didn't remember the war, the Lizards were as permanent a fixture as human beings, and they often seemed a lot more interesting.

His stop came only a couple of blocks later. The door opened with a hiss of compressed air. The driver, who carried Rance a couple of times a week, kept it open till he'd managed to descend. 'Thanks,' he said over his shoulder.

'Any time, friend,' the colored man answered. With another hiss, the door closed. The bus roared away, leaving behind a cloud of noxious diesel fumes. Fort Worth wasn't a rich town. It wouldn't be buying any stink-free hydrogen-burning buses for quite a while yet.

Auerbach didn't mind diesel exhaust. It was a human smell, which meant he was going to approve of it till forced to do otherwise. He shuffled along, faster than a tortoise but not much, till he got to the American Legion post halfway down the block.

The post didn't have a lot of money, either: not enough for air-conditioning. A fan stirred the air without doing much to cool it. A tableful of men with poker chips in front of them waved to Rance when he came inside. 'Always room for one more,' Charlie Thornton told him. 'Your money spends as good as anybody else's.'

'Hell of a lot you know about it, Charlie,' Auerbach said, pulling his wallet out of a hip pocket so he could buy his way into the game. 'I win money off you, not the other way round.'

'Boy's delirious,' Thornton declared, to general laughter. His white mustache showed he was a veteran of the First World War, the last time people had had the privacy to fight among themselves alone. Nobody knew it at the time, but the Lizards' conquest fleet had headed for Earth a bare handful of years after what people had called the War to End War ended.

Auerbach didn't like thinking about Lizard fleets heading toward Earth. He didn't like thinking about the one that was just arriving, either. He examined the first hand he got dealt. The five cards might never have met before. Disgusted, he threw them down on the table. Even more disgusted, he said, 'Before long, we're going to be ass-deep in Lizards.'

'That's a fact,' said Pete Bragan, who had dealt Rance the lousy hand. Pete wore a patch on his left eye and had a walk even funnier than Auerbach's. He'd been inside a Sherman tank that had the misfortune of coming up against one of the Lizards' machines outside of Chicago. As such things went, he'd been lucky: all of him but that one eye and the last few inches of his right leg had got out. 'Damn shame, you ask me.'

One by one, the veterans around the table nodded. Except for Thornton, the old-timer, they were men the Lizards had wrecked, one way or another. Among them, they had enough chunks missing to make a pretty fair meat market. Mike Cohen, for instance, never had to shuffle and deal because he couldn't with only one hand. None of them held down a regular job. Had they held regular jobs, they wouldn't have been playing poker early on a Tuesday morning.

After dropping out of another hand, Auerbach won one with three nines and then, to his disgust, lost one with an ace-high straight. War stories went around with the cards. Rance had told his before. That didn't stop him from telling them again. After a while, he lost with another straight. 'Jesus Christ, I'm gonna quit coming here,' he exclaimed, staring at Pete Bragan's full house. 'My pension doesn't stretch far enough to let me afford many of these.'

'Amen,' Mike Cohen said, for all the world as if he were Christian. 'It was decent money when they set it up, but things haven't gotten any cheaper since.'

Grousing about the pension was as much a ritual as swapping war stories. Auerbach shook his head when that thought crossed his mind. Stories about making ends meet *were* war stories, stories of a quiet war that never ended. He said, 'They don't give a damn about us. Oh, they talk pretty fine, but down deep they just don't care.'

'That's a fact,' Bragan said. 'They got what they could from us, and now they don't want to remember who saved the bacon.' He tossed a chip into the pot. 'I'll bump that up a quarter.'

'Way things are going nowadays, seems like some folks wish the Lizards had won,' Auerbach said, and described the teen-ager on the bus. He put in a couple of chips. 'I'll see that, and I'll raise another quarter.'

'World's going to hell in a handbasket,' Bragan said. When it came round to him again, he raised another quarter.

Auerbach studied his three jacks. He knew what kind of hand he held: one just good enough to lose. He wished he hadn't raised before. But he had. *Throw good money after bad* – the best recipe he knew for losing the good money, too. With a grimace, he said, 'Call,' and did his best to pretend the chip he flipped into the pot had got there of its own accord.

Bragan displayed three tens. 'I'll be a son of a bitch,' Auerbach said happily, and raked in the pot.

'Don't reckon anybody'd notice any special change,' Bragan said, which drew a laugh. The other wounded veteran shook his head. 'Yeah, world's going to hell in a handbasket, all right. Whose deal is it?'

As it did every day, the game went on and on. Somebody limped out and bought hero sandwiches. Somebody else went out a little later and came back with beer. Occasionally, someone would get up and leave. The poker players never had any trouble finding someone else to sit in. Most of them didn't have much else to do with their lives. Rance Auerbach knew he didn't. He'd never married. He hadn't had a steady woman friend for a long time. His poker buddies were in the same boat. They had their wounds and their stories and one another.

He hated the idea of going back to his apartment. But the American Legion hall didn't have cots. He cashed in his chips, discovering he was a couple of dollars ahead on the day. If he'd had more he cared to buy, he would have felt better about that. As things were, he took it as skill's due reward – and coffee next time he went shopping.

When he got back to the apartment building, he checked his mailbox. He had a sister married to a fellow who sold cars in Texarkana; she sometimes wrote. His brother in Dallas had probably forgotten he was alive. When his leg and his shoulder started kicking in, he wished he could forget, too.

Nothing from Kendall. Nothing from Mae, either: Rance owed her a letter. But, amid the drugstore circulars and get-rich-quick ads for suckers to sell 'miracle Lizard gadgets' door-to-door, he did come across an envelope with a stamp bearing the picture of Queen Elizabeth and another showing a tough-looking fellow in a high-peaked cap and the legend GROSS-DEUTSCHES REICH.

'Well, well,' he said, looking from one of them to the other before starting the long, painful business of going upstairs. He smiled. His face almost hurt as it shifted into the new and unfamiliar expression. He might spend some of his time wishing he were dead. With any luck at all, the Lizards would spend more of theirs wishing they were.

Monique Dutourd sometimes – often – wondered why she had studied anything as far removed from the modern world as Roman history. The best explanation she'd ever found was that the modern world had turned upside down too many times for her ever to trust it fully. She'd been eleven when the Germans overran northern France and turned her native Marseille into an appendage of Vichy, a town previously known, if it was known at all, for its water. Two years after that, the Lizards had swept the south of France into their clawed grip. And two years after that, as fighting finally ebbed, they'd withdrawn south of the Pyrenees, handing the part of France they'd held back to the Germans as casually as one neighbor might return a borrowed roasting pan to another.

No, Monique had had enough and to spare of disasters and

betrayals and disappointments in her own life. She did not want to examine them in more detail than she'd known while she was living through them. And so . . .

'And so,' she said, running a brush through her thick, dark hair, 'I examine the disasters and betrayals and disappointments of people two thousand years dead. Ah, this is truly an improvement.'

It would have been funny, if only it were funny. Not a human university in the world taught a course called *ancient history* any more. The headquarters of the Lizard fleetlord in Cairo looked across the Nile at the Pyramids. They'd gone up more than four thousand years ago – about the time the Lizards, having long, long since unified their planet, having conquered two other neighboring worlds, began to look with covetous eyes toward Earth. To them, the entire span of human recorded history wasn't ancient – it was more like looking back at the year before last.

A glance at the clock on the mantel – a silent, modern electric, not the loudly ticking model she had known in her youth – made her mouth pucker into an *O* of dismay. If she didn't hurry, she'd be late to the university. Were a male instructor late for his lecture, he would be assumed to have a lover – and forgiven. Were she late for hers, she would be assumed to have a lover – and liable to get the sack.

As always, she lugged her bicycle downstairs. She took modest pride in never having lost one to thieves. Having lived in Marseille all her life, she knew her fellow townsfolk were a light-fingered lot. Marseille had specialized in unofficial commerce since the Greeks founded the place more than five hundred years before the birth of Christ.

Gulls screeched overhead as she pedaled south along Rue Breteuil toward the campus, which had gone up on a couple of blocks wrecked during the fighting between the Lizards and troops from the Vichy government. Marseille was one of the few places where Vichy troops had fought, no doubt because they were at least as afraid of what the locals would do to them

80

if they didn't as they were of what the Lizards would do to them if they did.

A policeman in a kepi and a blue uniform waved her on across Rue Sylvabette. 'Hello, sweetheart,' he called in the Provençal-flavored local dialect he, like she, took for granted. 'Nice legs!'

'I bet you say that to all the girls,' Monique answered with a derisive gesture. The policeman laughed uproariously. He knew bloody well he said that to all the girls. He wasn't bad-looking. Maybe it got him laid once a year or so.

With unconscious skill, Monique threaded her way through the stream of bicycle, car, and lorry traffic. A sunburned blond fellow in a field-gray uniform pulled up alongside her on a motorcycle. Over the rumble of its engine, he spoke in German-accented Parisian French: 'Are you going anywhere special?'

She thought about pretending she didn't understand. With a true Parisian, she might have done that. With a German, she didn't quite dare. If Germans wanted to badly enough, they could make unfortunate things happen. And so she answered with the truth: 'I'm on my way to work.'

'Ach, so,' he said, and then, remembering his French, 'Quel domage'. Monique didn't think it was a pity; she knew nothing but relief as the motorcycle zoomed away. A generation had resigned her to the Germans as masters of France, but hadn't left her enthusiastic.

Then she rode past the synagogue on the east side of Rue Breteuil. Its windows were shuttered, its doorway boarded up, as it had been since the Lizards left and the Germans came in. Maybe a few Jews still survived here. If they did, it was not for lack of German effort. Monique shook her head, then had to brush hair back out of her eyes. No wonder so many Jews got on so well with the Lizards.

As if thinking of the aliens were enough to conjure them up, she saw one on the sidewalk in animated conversation with a Frenchman in a gray, collarless shirt. They might have been discussing legitimate business; some of that got done in Marseille, too. Monique wouldn't have bet anything she didn't care to lose on it, though.

She parked her bicycle at a stand on the edge of the campus (which looked more like a series of apartment blocks than a proper university), chained it in place, and tipped the guard so he wouldn't steal it himself and say someone else had. Grabbing her briefcase off the jump seat, she hurried along to her classroom.

She had more students every semester. The large majority were Frenchmen and -women as disenchanted with the present as she was. The rest, who paid their fees to the bursar like everyone else, were Germans stationed around Marseille. Some of them had been stationed around the city long enough to learn to speak the local dialect with a guttural German accent rather than the standard French they would have been taught back in the *Vaterland*.

The students, French and Germans alike, were chattering among themselves when she walked into the hall. The Germans quieted down out of respect for her as a professor. The Frenchmen quieted down because they were eyeing her legs, as the *flic* had done. The Frenchwomen quieted down because they were pondering her culottes, a nice compromise between modesty and display for someone who rode a bicycle.

However she got quiet, she was glad enough to take advantage of it. 'Today,' she said, 'we shall continue to examine the consequences of Augustus' failure to conquer Germania as Caesar had conquered Gallia.'

Using the Latin names for the areas in question made the event seem more distant than it would have had she called them *Allemagne* and *France*. She did that on purpose; she did not want to have the ancient world drawn into the sphere of modern politics. If her French students took especially careful notes on this material, was it her fault? If her handful of German students took especially careful notes . . . That, unlike the other, was something to worry about.

And, try as she would, she couldn't leave out her own thoughts. 'Augustus' failure in Germania is one of those areas of history where inevitability is difficult if not impossible to discern,' she said. 'Had the Roman Emperor's abler commanders not died at inopportune times, had revolt not broken out elsewhere in the Empire, he would not have had to appoint Quinctilius Varus to head the German legions, and Arminius' – she would not say *Hermann*, the German equivalent of the name –' would not have been able to slaughter those legions in the forest of Teutoberg.'

A woman raised her hand. Monique pointed to her. She asked, 'How would a Roman Germany' – she said *Allemagne* – 'have changed the history of the world?'

It was a good, sensible question. Monique would have liked it even better had answering it not reminded her of walking through a thicket of thornbushes. Picking her words with care, she said, 'A Roman Empire with its frontier on the Elbe, not the Rhine, would have had a shield against the nomads from out of the east. And Romanized Germans would surely have contributed as much to the Empire as Romanized Gauls did in the history with which we are familiar.'

That seemed to satisfy the woman. Other answers were possible. Monique knew it. *The Goths and Vandals wouldn't have sacked Rome. The Franks wouldn't have invaded France and given it their name. There wouldn't have been a Germany to invade our country in 1870 or 1914 or 1940.* Because an answer was possible, though, did not mean it was safe to give.

She got through the rest of the lecture without treading on such dangerous ground. Watching the clock reach half past ten was something of a relief. 'Dismissed,' she said, and put her notes back into the briefcase. She looked forward to going to her office. She finally had the references she needed to put the finishing touches on a paper tracing the growth of the cult of Isis in Gallia Narbonensis during the first couple of centuries of the Christian era. It would, she hoped, raise some eyebrows in the small circle that cared about such things.

A tanned fellow about her own age in an open-necked shirt and baggy pants a fisherman might have worn approached the lectern. 'A very interesting lecture,' he said, nodding his approval. 'Very interesting indeed.'

He looked like a local. Monique had assumed he was a local. In the class roster, his name was down as Laforce. He wrote French as well as a local would have. When he spoke, though, he proved he wasn't a local. He was a German. His countrymen in the class wore *Wehrmacht* or *Luftwaffe* uniforms. She wondered what he did, and hoped she wouldn't find out the hard way. 'Thank you,' she said, as if to a viper that had suddenly revealed itself among the rocks.

He laughed, showing strong yellow teeth, and lit a Gauloise. He smoked like a local, too, letting the cigarette hang insouciantly from the corner of his mouth. 'You could have been much more inflammatory than you were with your Germania and Gallia,' he remarked.

Wary still, she studied him. 'And would I have vanished into night and fog, then?' she asked. That was what happened to people who made the *Reich* unhappy because of what they said or what they were.

'Maybe,' he answered, and laughed again. 'Maybe not, too. You can get away with more in a lecture hall than you could on a soapbox. If you like, take some coffee with me this afternoon, and we'll talk about it.'

His approach could have been a lot less subtle. As an occupier, he hardly needed to make an approach at all. Because he had, Monique was bold enough to reply, 'Tell me your real name and your real rank and I'll decide whether we talk about it.'

He dipped his head in half a bow. '*Sturmbannführer* Dieter Kuhn, at your service, Professor Dutourd.'

'What sort of rank is—?' Monique stopped. Before she finished the question, she realized what sort of rank it was. Kuhn – if that was really his name – belonged to the SS.

'You can say no, if you like,' he said. 'I don't build dossiers on women who turn me down. I'd go through too many folders if I did.'

She thought he meant it. That was one of the reasons she smiled and nodded. The other reason, though, was the lingering fear he might be lying. She got very little research done after she did go back to her office.

Lieutenant Colonel Glen Johnson sat on top of a large cylinder filled with some of the most highly inflammable substances ingenious chemists could devise. If they exploded in any way but the one for which they were designed . . . He whistled softly. 'If they do that, folks'll be picking up pieces of me from Baltimore down to Key West,' he muttered.

'What's that, *Peregrine*?' The radio speaker above his head in the cramped cockpit sounded tinny. Nobody'd bothered changing the design since the war. The old one worked, which was plenty good enough for military air- and spacecraft. Johnson had a fancier, smoother speaker in his record player back home. That was fine, for play. When he heard squawks, he knew he was working.

'Nothing much, Control,' he answered. 'Just woolgathering.' The blockhouse here at Kitty Hawk was a long way away from his rocket. If it blew up instead of going up, the bureaucrats and technicians would be fine. He, on the other hand . . . well, it would be over before he noticed he was dead.

'Cheer up, *Peregrine*,' the fellow on the distant other end of the microphone said. 'You've been living on borrowed time the past twenty years anyhow.'

'You so relieve my mind,' Johnson said with a wry chuckle. He would have laughed louder and harder if the man back at the blockhouse had been joking. He'd flown fighters against the Lizards during the war, a job where pilots had life expectancies commonly measured in minutes. He'd been shot down twice, and managed to survive both times. One forearm had some nasty burn scars on it from his second forced landing. He wore long-sleeved shirts whenever he could.

If he hadn't been on the shelf for a while with burns, he would have gone right back into action and probably been killed. As things were, he'd just returned to one of the last Marine air units still operating when the ceasefire came.

After the fighting ended, he'd tested a lot of the new planes that married human and Lizard technology – in some cases (luckily none of his) marriages smeared across heaven rather than made in it. Graduating to rockets when the USA went into space in the 1950s was a natural next step.

'One minute, *Peregrine*,' the blockhouse warned.

'One minute, roger,' Johnson said. Just a couple of miles from here, back when his dad was a boy, the Wright brothers had coaxed a motorized kite into the air. Johnson wondered what they would have thought of the craft he flew. Orville, like Johnson an Ohioan, had survived the Lizards' occupation of his home state and lived on till 1948 – only a handful of years too soon to see Americans going not only into the air but above it.

'Thirty seconds, *Peregrine*,' Control announced, and then the countdown the U.S. Air and Space Force had surely borrowed from the pulp magazines: 'Ten . . . nine . . . eight . . .' When he'd proved he could count backwards on his fingers, the man in the blockhouse yelled, 'Blastoff!' That also came straight out of the pulps. Johnson wished somebody somewhere would find a better name for it.

Then it seemed as if three very heavy men came in and sat on him. He stopped worrying about what people ought to call a rocket leaving Earth, for he was much too intimately involved in riding one. If anything went wrong that didn't splatter him all over the landscape, he had some hope of getting back down in one piece; like the machines the Nazis flew, his upper stage doubled as an airplane. He pitied the poor Russians, who went into space in what weren't much more than airtight boxes. Those were easier and cheaper to build, no doubt about it, but the Red Air Force used up a lot of pilots.

A fresh kick in the pants made him stop worrying about the

Russians. 'Second stage has ignited,' Control reported, as if he never would have known without the announcement. 'Trajectory to planned orbit looks very good.'

'Roger that,' Johnson said. He could see it for himself from the instruments on the *Peregrine*'s instrument panel, but he wasn't allergic to reassurance.

'How does it feel, going from the halls of Montezuma to the shores of Tripoli in just a few minutes?' Control asked.

'That's what I get for coming out of the Marines,' Johnson said, laughing. 'You never ride the real A and S boys this way.' Actually, he'd started a good deal northeast of the halls of Montezuma and he'd go over Africa even farther south of the shores of Tripoli, but who was he to trifle with a man's poetic license?

Then another voice came over the speaker, one not using English: 'U.S. spacecraft, this is the tracking station of the Race. Acknowledge.'

'I greet you, Dakar,' Johnson said in the Lizards' lingo as the second-stage motor cut out and the one in the rear of his upper stage took over to finish the job of boosting him into orbit. He wasn't over the radar or radio horizon for Dakar yet, but the Lizards' orbital radar and satellite radio relays still beat the stuffing out of any merely human communications network. 'Is that you, Hashshett?' As a Lizard would, he pronounced each *sh* and each *t* as a separate syllable.

'It is I. And you are Glen Johnson?' Hashshett turned the last syllable of Johnson's name into a long hiss.

'I am. My trackers show me as good for my announced orbit. Do you confirm?' Johnson tacked on an interrogative cough.

'Confirming,' the Lizard answered after a pause that would have let him turn an eye turret toward his instruments. 'Seeing a flight path in such conformity is good.'

As far as the Lizards were concerned, anything that conformed to the *status quo ante* was good. With four different powers owning orbiting nuclear weapons, people and the

Lizards had grown far more punctilious than they'd once been about notifying one another of their launches. The Lizards had got very huffy very fast about wanting to be notified; persuading them that they needed to notify any mere humans of what they were up to had taken a lot more work.

Just then, on time to the second, the upper-stage motor cut out. Johnson went weightless. His stomach tried to climb up his windpipe hand over hand. He gulped and sternly told it to get back where it belonged. After a few nervous moments, it decided to listen to him. Puking while weightless did not win a pilot luckless enough to do it the Good Housekeeping seal of approval.

Once he'd decided he wasn't going to redecorate the inside of his cockpit, Johnson checked his own radar. He hadn't really expected to see anything that would make him use his attitude jets to evade, but you never could tell. Space was a crowded place these days, loaded not only with manned (or Lizarded) spacecraft but also with all manner of unmanned satellites, some peaceful, some not, and with a lot of junk: discarded protective shrouds and upper stages that had reached orbit after delivering their cargo. The Lizards never stopped grumbling about the junk; not even their fancy radars and even fancier computing machines could tell the garbage from camouflaged weapons quietly floating and waiting for orders. The weapons that weren't camouflaged maneuvered frequently, too; the longer they stayed in the same orbit, the more vulnerable they got.

Having made sure he didn't need to evade, Johnson studied the radar screen again. He hadn't been up since the colonization fleet came in from Tau Ceti II. The targets the radar showed were not only distant – in relatively high orbits – but *big*. They looked like Christmas-tree lights on the screen. They were so big, he knew he could spot them with his Mark I eyeball as well as with his electronic senses.

He peered in the direction the radar gave him. Sure as hell, there they were, some of them bright as Venus – brighter.

Being in a lower, faster orbit, he passed them, but there were more ahead. All the way around the world, there were more ahead, with Lizards, millions upon millions of Lizards, lying in them in cold sleep like steaks in cardboard cartons on icebox shelves.

Seeing the ships of the colonization fleet filled him with awe. He'd come a couple of hundred miles into space. The USA, the Greater German *Reich*, and the USSR had bases on the moon. Americans and Germans had walked on Mars (bemusing the Lizards, who couldn't figure out why they wanted to visit such a useless world). Americans and Germans were out in the asteroid belt, too, seeing if it held anything worthwhile (the very existence of the asteroid belt bemused the Lizards; the solar systems with which they had been familiar were much tidier places).

'Going out to see asteroids up close – that's not bad,' Johnson muttered. But the ships he was looking at hadn't crossed millions, or even tens of millions, of miles of space. They'd come better than ten light-years – say, sixty trillion miles. If that didn't make you sit up and take notice, you were dead inside.

What would it be like, crossing ten light-years? *I'd pay a lot to visit Home,* Johnson thought, and wondered if he'd sooner go as a tourist or as part of a fleet that would smash the Lizards' home planet so flat, even cockroaches (or whatever Home had instead of cockroaches) couldn't live there.

He sighed. It didn't matter. If the U.S. government, or any other human government, had plans for a starship, he didn't know about them – and he kept his ear to the ground where such things were involved. He sighed again. Even if some human government did have plans for a ship that could cross interstellar space, odds were it wouldn't be built till the turn of the century, if that soon. He'd had his fortieth birthday a couple of years before.

'Too old to go to the stars.' He shook his head, wondering what his life would have been like if the Lizards hadn't come, if the world had just kept moving along its normal, expected course. 'Christ!' he exclaimed. 'I might have been too old to go into space at all.' That was a really frightening thought.

As long as he could come up here, as long as he was up here, he had work to do. He also had work he hoped he wouldn't have to do. Again like its German equivalents, the *Peregrine* carried missiles and machine guns. The clumsy Russian space-craft mounted machine guns, too. Even before the colonization fleet came, though, the Lizards had had far more in space than all of humankind put together. If push came to shove, they could probably knock people back inside the atmosphere. His job, and that of the other Americans in the Air and Space Force, and also that of their Nazi and Red opposite numbers, was to hurt them as much as he could before he got killed.

The radio crackled. '*Peregrine*, this is *Osprey*. Over.'

'Hello, Gus,' Johnson answered. '*Peregrine* here.' Most of the ships that flew out of Kitty Hawk were named for birds of prey. 'You've been up here a while. Anything going on with the colonization fleet? Over.'

'They've made a few flights down,' Gus Wilhelm said. 'More the past couple of days than earlier. They're trying to figure out the lay of the land, you might say. It's not what they expected when they left Home, not even close.'

Johnson laughed. 'I'll say it's not. Have you listened to some of the first radio transmissions between the colonization fleet and the ones who're already on Earth? Bob Hope couldn't be half as funny if he tried for a year.'

'That's the truth,' Gus agreed. 'Yeah, I've heard some of those. And now they'll know we listen in on 'em.'

'Like they didn't already,' Glen Johnson said. He and Gus both laughed then. He settled back onto his couch, a man on a routine mission ready to turn back into a fighter pilot in a heartbeat if the mission stopped being routine. 'Over and out.'

Through most of the long Tosevite year, Fotsev thought well of the city of Basra, where he was stationed. Oh, it got chilly in the winter, but he didn't think there was any place on the surface of Tosev 3 that didn't get chilly during the winter. Summers were quite pleasant; the hottest days would have been warm back on Home, too.

Males who'd fought farther north, up in the not-empire that called itself the SSSR, had horrifying tales to tell about Tosevite winters. Fotsev hadn't hatched out of the egg yesterday; he knew how people lied to make stories sound better and themselves more heroic. He had stories of his own from the conquest of Argentina, and he wasn't above inflating them when they needed inflating. But some of the males produced videos to prove they weren't lying. The mere idea of trying to fight in drifts of frozen water taller than a male was enough to make him glad he'd never had to do it.

'Remember that Ussmak?' said a male named Gorppet, who wore a stripe of body paint on his left arm that showed he'd served in the SSSR. 'I always figured it was the cold that drove him to mutiny, by the Emperor.'

After casting his eyes down in the ritual gesture of respect, Fotsev swiveled his eye turrets every which way to make sure nobody else had heard Gorppet. The other male was doing the same thing, aware he might have said too much even to a friend.

'I never knew much about the mutiny,' Fotsev said. Virtuously, he added, 'I never wanted to know much about it, either.'

'I cannot blame you for that,' Gorppet said. Both infantrymales shuddered, as if from the chill of the SSSR, though the local weather was perfectly respectable even by the standards of Home. Mutiny – rebellion against superiors – was vanishingly rare among the Race; males interested in such things had had to look for examples in ancientest history, long before the Empire unified Home.

Belying his earlier words (there was a horrid fascination to the subject, after all), Fotsev said, 'I wonder what happened to Ussmak after he yielded himself up to the Russkis. He is probably living as comfortably as anyone could in a not-empire full of Big Uglies, like that shiplord over on the lesser continental mass.'

But Gorppet made a negative hand gesture. 'No – oh my, no,' he said, and added an emphatic cough. 'I heard this from a male the Russkis ended up freeing from one of their captives' camps – and he was nothing but scales and skeleton after that, too, let me tell you. He told me Ussmak died in one of those camps along with spirits of Emperors past only know how many other males. If we ever fight the Tosevites again, you do not want to let the Russkis or the Deutsche capture you – or the Nipponese, either, though we have knocked them down a good deal.'

Fotsev shuddered again. 'I do not want any Big Uglies capturing me,' he said with an emphatic cough of his own. 'They build factories to kill off their own – no wonder they kill us off, too, when they catch us.'

His eye turrets kept swiveling as he spoke. He and Gorppet were patrolling the market square of Basra. In the early days of the occupation, males had disappeared not far from here. The Race's vengeance had been brutal enough to make that stop happening, but neither of the males wanted to give it a chance to start up again through lack of alertness.

In the square – an open area in a town of mud-brick buildings, most duncolored, the fancier ones whitewashed – Big Uglies sold and bartered an enormous variety of goods, most of which Fotsev found distinctly unappetizing. Tosevite males wore robes and headpieces of cloth to shield themselves from the sun the males of the Race found so friendly, while the females swaddled themselves even more thoroughly. The Argentine Big Uglies, who lived in a harsher climate, wrapped fewer cloths around themselves. Fotsev had trouble understanding the reasons behind the difference.

When he remarked on that, Gorppet answered, 'Religion,' and kept on walking, as if he'd said something wise.

Fotsev didn't think he had. *Religion* and *Emperor-worship* were the same word in the language of the Race. They weren't the same here on Tosev 3. The Big Uglies, not having had the benefit of tens of thousands of years of imperial rule, foolishly imagined powerful beings made in their own image, and then further imagined that those powerful beings had created them in their image rather than the other way around.

It would have been laughable, had the Big Uglies not taken it so seriously. As far as Fotsev was concerned, it remained laughable, but he did not laugh. As experience had also taught the Race not to try to alter the beliefs the local Tosevites held, no matter how absurd they were. If they thought they had to bow down five times a day to revere the Big Ugly they had writ large in the sky, easier to let them than to try to talk them out of it. Fotsev had come to Basra to reinforce the garrison here after riots from that very source.

Gorppet must have been thinking along related lines, for he said, 'If they are going to have these absurd notions, why do they not all have the same ones, instead of arguing about who is right and who is wrong?'

'I do not think you can expect any two Big Uglies to have the same notion about anything,' Fotsev said. 'They do not even have the same words for the same things. I had finally started learning some of the Español they speak in Argentina, and not a Big Ugly around these parts knows a word of it. Hardly seems fair.'

'Truth,' Gorppet said. 'And some of the Tosevites here speak Arabic, some speak Farsi. Untidy, that is what this whole world is.'

'Having them all mixed together like this, you mean?' Fotsev said. 'It certainly is. We ought to do something about it.'

'Like what?' Gorppet sounded interested.

'I do not know,' Fotsev said in some exasperation. 'I am just an infantrymale, same as you. I know what the Big Uglies would do: kill all the ones who spoke the language they did not want. Then they would not have to worry about them any more. Nice and neat and clean, isn't it?'

'Very neat and clean – if you do not look at the blood,' Gorppet said.

Fotsev's shrug wasn't that different from the gesture a Tosevite would have used. The Big Uglies weren't in the habit of looking at blood once they'd spilled it. Off to one side of the square, a crowd was gathering, mostly Tosevite males with a sprinkling of females. Fotsev pointed toward it. 'Think we ought to have a look at that?'

'What? By ourselves, do you mean?' Gorppet made the gesture of negation again. 'No, thank you. If that does turn into trouble, it will turn into more trouble than the two of us can handle.'

'Why should it turn into—?' Fotsev paused. A male Tosevite was clambering up onto some kind of platform. Fotsev was no better than most other males of the Race at telling one Big Ugly from another, but he did know the males were the ones who grew tufts of ugly hair on their faces. This one had long, gray tufts, which meant he was no longer young.

'I have always thought these Big Uglies look foolish with rags wrapped around their heads,' Gorppet said.

'Down in Argentina, the females wore lots funnier things than rags on their heads. Some of them looked like walking gardens.' Fotsev kept one eye turret on the old male Tosevite, who had begun haranguing the crowd. 'What is he saying? That is Farsi, is it not? I cannot tell snout from tailstump in Farsi.'

'He is talking about the Race,' Gorppet said; he knew some of the language. 'Whenever these males who preach start talking about the Race, it is usually trouble. And I think this is the one called Khomeini. He hates us worse than any of the other three put together. His egg was soaked in vinegar and brine before he hatched from it.'

'But what is he saying?' Fotsev persisted.

'It *is* trouble, may the purple itch get under his scales.' His friend cocked his head to listen. 'He is saying the spirit these superstitious fools think created them did not create us. He is saying the other spirit they believe in, the evil one, created us. And – uh-oh – he is saying that if they get rid of all of us on

Tosev 3 now, the males and females from the colonization fleet will not be able to land. He thinks they are evil spirits, too.'

Fotsev made sure he had a round in the chamber of his personal weapon, a full clip attached, and more magazines where he could grab them in a hurry. Even with Gorppet by his side, he suddenly felt very much alone. 'I think we had better back away,' he said, swiveling his eyes so no Big Ugly could sneak up on him with a knife or a bomb.

'I think you are right.' Gorppet came with him. 'I think we had better call for help, too – help and heavier weapons.' He spoke urgently into his radio.

From the crowd came a great roar. *'Allahu akbar!'* That cry was the same in Farsi and Arabic. It meant that the ridiculous spirit in whom the benighted Big Uglies believed was a great ridiculous spirit. It also meant that the batch of Tosevites shouting it was about to explode into riot. *'Allahu akbar!'*

'Here they come,' Gorppet said unnecessarily. Mouths open and screaming, the mob of Big Uglies surged toward the males of the Race. The preaching male named Khomeini stood on his platform, his hand outstretched toward those two lone males, urging his followers toward massacre.

Neither Fotsev nor Gorppet tried to talk the Tosevites into stopping or going back. They both opened up as soon as the closest Big Uglies got into range. At that range, against that crowd, they could hardly miss. Watching bullets chew comrades to rags made some of the Big Uglies hesitate. But others, a lot of others, kept coming.

'They think they will go to a happy afterlife if they die fighting us,' Gorppet said, reloading his weapon.

'The Emperors know their spirits not,' Fotsev answered, spraying more death into the mob. As he'd seen before, the Tosevites were recklessly brave. Soon one would get close enough to tear the weapon from his hands. Then it would be teeth and claws till the end. He hoped it would be quick.

But then, with a thuttering roar, a helicopter gunship zoomed up from the Race's base outside Basra. It lashed the crowd of fanatical Tosevites with rockets and rounds from a rotating-barreled cannon. Not even the Big Uglies could stand up against that kind of firepower. They broke and ran, shrieking in fear where they had shrieked in fury.

The iron stink of blood filling the scent receptors on his tongue, Fotsev emptied a magazine at their fleeing backs. He hoped the gunship had put paid to that Khomeini, who'd stirred the mob as a male might stir a hot drink.

Before he could do more than hope, something rode a trail of fire from the ground and slammed into the gunship. It slewed sideways in the air, then crashed in the middle of the market square. Its rotors flew off and cut down a last few Big Uglies.

Fotsev stared in horror. 'These Big Uglies do not know how to make antiaircraft missiles!' he burst out.

'No, but they know how to buy or beg or borrow them from the Tosevites who do.' Gorppet's voice was thoroughly grim. 'By the spirits of Emperors past, there will be an accounting for this. But now, while we can, we had better get out of here.' Side by side, they skittered away from the market square. Behind them, the helicopter gunship burned and burned.

'Allahu akbar!' A rock flew past Reuven Russie's head. 'Dog of a Jew, you suck the Lizards' cocks. Your mother opens her legs for them. Your sister – *aii!'* The Arab's curses dissolved in a howl of pain. Reuven had found a rock of his own, and flung it with better effect than the scrawny youth who'd been abusing him.

Jerusalem seethed like a teapot left over the fire too long. Unlike a teapot, though, the city had nowhere the steam could escape. Lizard troopers and human police – mostly Jews – might come under fire from any house, any shop. So might any passerby.

For once, Reuven almost wished he lived in the dormitory with his fellow medical students. Getting to and from the college had seemed more like running the gauntlet every day since the Muslim riots broke out. So far, he hadn't got hurt. He knew that was as much luck as anything else, though he never would have admitted as much to his parents.

A black swastika stared at him from a wall. Some of the Arabs who hated the Lizards but weren't religious fanatics leaned toward the *Reich*, not least because Himmler loved Jews even less than they did. Along with swastikas, red stars also blossomed on the walls – some Jews, and some Arabs, too, looked to Moscow for deliverance from the Race. But the commonest graffiti were in the sinuous squiggles of Arabic script, the letters all looking as if Hebrew block characters had run in the rain. *Allahu akbar!* seemed to scream from every other wall.

Reuven peered round a corner. The next short block looked safe enough. He hurried along it. One more block and he was home. When he checked the last block, he spied a Jewish policeman carrying a British Sten gun, one of the countless weapons left over from the last big fight. This new round of turmoil wasn't shaping up as anything so delightful, either.

The policeman saw him, too, and started to aim the submachine gun in his direction. Then the fellow lowered the barrel. 'You're no Arab,' he said in Hebrew.

'No.' Reuven sniffed. Smoke was in the air, more than could be accounted for from cookfires. 'What a mess. We haven't seen anything like this – ever, I don't think.'

'Bloody balls-up,' the Jewish policeman muttered in English of a sort. He went back to Hebrew: 'We'll just have to go on knocking heads together till things simmer down, that's all. We can do it.' As if to contradict him, something – a grenade? a bomb? – blew up not too far away.

'It's the colonization fleet,' Reuven said. 'Now that it's finally here, people are realizing all over again that we can't make the Lizards go away by holding our breath and wishing they would.'

'I don't care what it is. It's a bloody balls-up.' That was English again; Hebrew, for so long a liturgical language, was woefully short on curses. The policeman went on, 'And it doesn't matter what it is, anyhow. Whatever it is, we've got to put a stop to it – and we will.'

'I hope so,' Reuven said, and passed on.

When he got home, his mother and his twin sisters, Esther and Judith, fell on him with glad cries. Even he couldn't always tell Esther and Judith apart, and he'd known them the entire twelve years of their lives. One of them said, 'We heard the bomb a couple of minutes ago.'

'And the machine guns a little while before that,' the other one added.

'I don't like machine guns,' they said together. They thought so much alike, Reuven sometimes wondered if they could tell each other apart, if each of them had to consider before deciding whether she was Judith or Esther.

To try to make them stop thinking about machine guns, he said, 'I'm going to experiment on the two of you, to see if there really are two of you, or just one with a mirror.'

They pointed at each other. 'She's the mirror,' they chorused.

'Not funny,' Reuven said, although, when you got down to it, it was. He turned to his mother. 'You didn't send them out to school today, did you?'

'Do I look *meshugge*?' Rivka Russie asked. 'You and your father are the crazy ones, to go out on the streets in times like these.' That held an unpleasant amount of truth, though Reuven didn't want to admit it. His mother went on, 'Houses aren't safe, either, though. Bombs, bullets—' She made a face. 'We saw too much of that during the war. We saw too much of everything during the war.'

Reuven had been very young then. He remembered the German invasion of Poland and the Lizard invasion of the world in scattered sharp, horrifying images, one not connected to the next: still photographs snipped almost at random from a motion picture full of terror. 'Rome,' he murmured.

'What about Rome?' Esther and Judith asked together.

Neither their brother nor their mother answered. Rome was one of his memory snapshots; he'd been on the deck of a Greek freighter in the Tyrrhenian Sea when the Germans touched off an explosive-metal bomb they'd smuggled into the city. Now, with knowledge he hadn't had then, he wondered how much radioactive fallout he'd been exposed to during the blast. He didn't really want to know. He couldn't do anything about it anyway.

Heavy booted feet pounded up the street past the house. The small windows that looked on the street were shuttered; like most houses in Jerusalem, this one preferred to peer inward onto its own courtyard than out at the wider world. Most of the time, Reuven took that for granted. He'd been used to it most of his life. This once, though, he wouldn't have minded seeing what was going on.

All of a sudden, he changed his mind. After shouts in Hebrew and Arabic, guns started hammering. A bullet slammed through a side wall, cracked past his head, and was through the other wall before his jaw got done dropping.

His mother had a better idea of what to do under such circumstances than he did. 'On the floor!' she shouted. 'Get down! Lie flat! The bullets will pass over us.'

When Reuven's sisters didn't move fast enough to suit her, she pushed them down and lay on them, ignoring their squawks. Reuven had just got down on the floor himself when a burst of fire gave the front wall some ventilation it hadn't had before. Esther and Judith stopped squawking.

Out on the street, someone started screaming and didn't stop. Reuven couldn't tell whether the shrieks were in Hebrew or Arabic. Pain had no separate tongue; pain was its own universal language.

He got to his feet. 'What are you doing?' his mother demanded. 'Lay down again!'

'I can't,' he answered. 'I've got to get my bag. Someone's hurt bad out there. I'm not a doctor, not yet, but I'm closer to being one than anybody else around.'

He waited for his mother to scream at him. To his astonishment, she smiled instead: a strange, sweet, sad smile. 'Your father did the same thing when the Lizards took Jerusalem away from the British. Go on, then. God watch over you.'

Reuven snatched his black leather bag out of his bedroom and hurried back to the front door. Predictably, his sisters wanted to do whatever he did. As predictably, his mother wouldn't let them. He went out the door, certain his mother would lock and bar it after him.

Bullets still flew, though not so often now. An automobile burned at the end of the block, sending a pyre of stinking black smoke into the sky. All the flames were orange or yellow, none the almost invisible pale blue of burning hydrogen – an old motorcar, not one of the newer models on the Lizard pattern.

The screaming came from the other side of the motorcar. Feeling naked and exposed, Reuven came around the machine to do what he could for the wounded man. He'd just stopped beside him when, from behind, someone said, 'What have we got here, son?'

'Hello, Father,' Reuven said as Moishe Russie got down on one knee beside him. The two of them looked very much alike there side by side – pale skin; dark hair; narrow, strong-cheekboned faces – save that Moishe was going bald. His son continued, 'I haven't even had a chance to look at him yet.'

'Don't need any fancy Lizard tools for this diagnosis,' his father said. 'A burst of three in the belly . . .' He pointed to the holes in the fighter's shirt. They had some blood oozing from them, but the real flood of it came from the man's back. Reuven gulped a little. Dissections in medical school were much neater than this, and the subjects didn't scream. Moishe Russie spoke as if back in the classroom himself: 'The entry wounds are fairly small. If you were heartless enough to turn him over, you'd see big chunks of meat blown out of the exit wounds. Prognosis, son?'

Reuven licked his lips. 'He'll keep hurting till he loses enough blood to lose consciousness, too. Then he'll finally die.' He spoke without fear the wounded man would hear him; the fighter was lost in his private hell.

'I think you're right.' His father rummaged in his own black bag, then pulled out a syringe. He injected the fallen fighter, then glanced over at Reuven. 'Enough morphine to stop his pain. Enough to stop his heart and lungs in a couple of minutes, too.'

He waited for Reuven to say something about that. After some thought, Reuven remarked, 'They don't teach us when to do that in medical school.'

'No, they wouldn't,' his father agreed. 'For one thing, the Lizards take it for granted, much more than we do. And for another, it's not something you can learn in school. When the time comes, you'll know. If you're ever wondering whether you should, the answer is simple: you shouldn't. When you should, you don't wonder.'

'How many times have you done it?' Reuven asked. As he spoke, the wounded fighter's screams stopped. He stared up in dreamy surprise. Reuven wondered if he was seeing the men who knelt above him or only some interior vision. The man's chest hitched a few more times, then respiration stopped, too.

'Morphine is a good friend and a dreadful master,' Moishe Russie murmured. Then he seemed to hear the question Reuven had asked. 'How many times? I don't know. A few. A man who does it too often isn't wondering enough about whether he ought to. You aren't God, son, and you never will be. Once in a while – but only once in a while – He'll let you be His assistant.' He got to his feet. The knee of his trousers was wet with the fighter's blood. 'We'd better get back home. Your mother will be worried about us.'

'I know.' Reuven wondered what he would have done had he come on the wounded fighter by himself. Would he have had the nerve to put the man out of his misery? He hoped so, but knew he couldn't be sure. He also realized he'd never be sure now whether the ordinary-looking man had been a Muslim or Jew.

4

Suave as a Frenchman, the *Gestapo* officer smiled at Johannes Drucker. 'You must understand, my dear Lieutenant Colonel, this is only an inquiry into your loyalty, not a denial that you are loyal,' he said.

'You have an easier time telling the difference than I do,' Drucker snapped. 'All I know is, I'm grounded for no good reason. I want to go back into space, where I can best serve the *Reich.*' *And where I can put hundreds – sometimes thousands – of kilometers between me and you.*

'I would not call the security of the *Reich* "no good reason," ' the *Gestapo* man said, his voice silky. 'We must always be on guard, lest the *Volk* be polluted by alien, inferior blood.'

'That's my *wife* you're talking about, you—' Drucker checked himself. Telling the son of a bitch he was a son of a bitch wouldn't do him any good, and wouldn't do Käthe any good, either.

'We have worked diligently to make and keep the *Reich* free of Jews,' the *Gestapo* man said with what he no doubt intended for a friendly smile. 'We shall continue until the great task is complete.'

Drucker didn't say anything. Nothing he could have said would have been any use. Anything he said would have got him into more trouble than he was in already. He had no great love for Jews. Back in the days when there were still a lot of

Jews in the Greater German *Reich*, he hadn't known many people with any great love for Jews.

Slaughtering them like cattle, though . . . He didn't see how that had helped the *Reich*. If the Jews hadn't risen up in Poland when the Lizards came, it might still belong to Germany. And, when the Lizards included in their propaganda details of what the Germans were doing, relations between the *Reich* and other human powers stayed delicate for a long time.

Would the *Gestapo* officer heed him if he pointed that out? It was to laugh. And then the sardonic laugh choked off. Most Germans had no great love for Jews? Käthe's grandfather must have loved a Jewess, if what the *Gestapo* was saying held any truth. And, had he not loved that Jewess, Käthe would never have been born.

Think about it later, Drucker told himself. For now, he kept on hoping it wasn't true. If it was true, his career wasn't the only thing that would go up in smoke. So would dear, sweet Käthe, out through the stack of a crematorium. His stomach lurched, worse than it ever did when he went weightless out in space. He'd known for twenty years what the *Reich* did to Jews, known and not thought much about it. Now it hit home. It occurred to him that he should have thought more and sooner. Too late now.

As calmly as he could, he said, 'I want to see her.'

He'd said that before, and been refused. He got refused again. 'You must know it is impossible,' the *Gestapo* man said. 'She is in detention, pending adjudication of the case. She is comfortable; please accept my personal assurances on that score. If the charges prove unfounded, all will be as it had been.'

He sounded as if he really meant it. Drucker had all he could do not to laugh in his face. Käthe was in detention – a polite word for jail or a camp. She was on trial for her life, and she couldn't even defend herself. In the *Reich*, choosing the wrong grandparents could be a capital crime.

Drucker did dare hope she *was* comfortable. If they decided her grandmother hadn't been a Jew after all, they would let her go. It did happen – not too often (Drucker wished he hadn't chosen to remember that), but it did. And he, by virtue of his rank and his skill, was valuable in the machinery of the *Reich*. If they did let her go, they wouldn't want him disaffected.

He wished he'd known her grandparents. All he'd seen of them were a few fading photographs in an old album. He didn't remember ever thinking her grandmother looked Jewish. She'd had light hair and light eyes. When she was young, she'd been very pretty. She'd looked a lot like Käthe, in fact.

The officer, now, the officer had brown eyes and dark stubble he probably had to shave twice a day. Fixing him with a cold stare, Drucker said, 'My wife's grandmother was a better Aryan than you are.'

'I may not be pretty,' the *Gestapo* man said evenly, 'but I have an impeccable German pedigree. If they started putting all the homely people in camps, we'd run out of laborers in a hurry.'

Damn, thought Drucker, who'd wanted to anger him. The *Gestapo* man probably had something, too. There *were* too many homely people to get rid of them; it would leave a great hole in the fabric of society. Getting rid of the Jews had left no such hole. They'd made perfect scapegoats: they were few, they'd stood out, and people had already disliked them.

The officer might have been thinking along with him. He said, 'That's why the Americans just hate their niggers and don't really do anything about it. If they did, it would be inconvenient for them.'

'Inconvenient.' The word was sickly sweet in Drucker's mouth, like the rotten horsemeat he'd eaten on the retreat from Moscow before the Lizards came. He'd been glad to have it, too. After muttering darkly under his breath, he said, 'This business of not knowing is inconvenient for me, you know.'

'Yes, of course I do.' The *Gestapo* man kept right on being smooth. 'Whatever happens, your children will not be severely affected. One Jewish great-grandparent is not a legal impediment.'

'You don't think losing their mother might affect them?' Drucker snapped. And yet, in a horrid kind of way, his interrogator had a point. *Severely affected* was a euphemism for *taken out and killed*.

'We must have pure blood.' However smooth, however suave he was, the *Gestapo* man had not a gram of compromise in him. In that, he made a good representative for the state he served. Doing his best to seem conciliatory even when he wasn't, he added, 'You have permission to leave for the time being. Your actual knowledge of your wife's grandmother appears small.'

'I've been telling anyone who would listen to me as much since you people took me away from Peenemünde,' Drucker said. 'The only thing wrong with that is, nobody would listen to me.'

Had he expected the *Gestapo* officer to start listening to him, he would have been disappointed. Since he didn't, he wasn't – or not disappointed on account of that, anyhow. He stood to stiff attention, shot out his arm, did a smart about-turn, and stalked off to his own quarters.

Those weren't much different from the ones he'd had back at the rocket base. The *Gestapo* wasn't treating him badly, on the off chance he might be returning to duty after all. He hoped it was rather more than an off chance, but no one cared what he hoped. He understood that only too well.

He lay back on his bunk and scratched his head. His eye fell on the telephone. He couldn't call his wife; he didn't know where to call. He couldn't call his children; he'd tried, but the operator hadn't let him. After one impossibility and one failure, he hadn't seen much point to using the phone. Maybe he'd been wrong, though, or at least shortsighted.

He picked up the instrument. Elsewhere in the *Reich*, he would have heard a tone that told him it was all right to dial. Here, as if he'd fallen back in time, an operator inquired, 'Number, please?'

He gave the number of the commandant back at Peene-münde. He didn't know if the operator would let that call go through, either. But it was, or might have been, in the line of duty, and the *Gestapo* was no more immune to that siren song than any other German organization. After some clicks and pops, Drucker heard the telephone ring.

Fear filled him, fear that the commandant would be out having a drink or in the sack with his girlfriend (Drucker didn't know whether he had a girlfriend, but found imagining the worst only too easy) or just encamped on a porcelain throne with a book in his hand and his pants around his ankles. Anything that kept him from Drucker would be disaster enough.

But a brisk, no-nonsense voice said, 'Dornberger here.'

'Will you speak with Lieutenant Colonel Drucker, sir?' the *Gestapo* operator asked. By his tone, he found it highly unlikely.

'Of course I will,' Major General Walter Dornberger said, his own voice sharp. 'Hans, are you there?'

'I'm here, General,' Drucker answered gratefully. The operator would still listen to everything he said, but he couldn't do anything about that. 'I don't known how long I'll have to stay off duty. They're still trying to decide whether Käthe had a Jewish grandmother.'

Dornberger was reasonably quick on the uptake. Once Drucker had given him his cue, he played along with it, booming, 'Yes, I know about that – I was there, remember? They're taking so stinking long, it sounds like a pack of nonsense to me. Maybe you made an enemy who's telling lies about you. Whatever's going on, we need you back here.'

Drucker hoped the operator was getting an earful. He said, 'Thank you, sir. Till this mess clears up, though, I can't go anywhere.'

'Good thing you called me,' Major General Dornberger said. 'Should have done it sooner, even. A lot of times, as I said, these accusations get started because somebody's jealous of you and hasn't got the nerve to show it out in the open. So the *Schweinhund* starts a filthy rumor. We'll get to the bottom of it, don't you worry about that. And when we do, some big-mouthed bastard is going to be sorry he was ever born.'

'From the bottom of my heart, I thank you, sir,' Drucker said. 'I want to be up and out again. With the colonization fleet here, I need to be up and out.'

'Damned right you do,' Dornberger agreed. 'We'll see what we can do from this end, Hans. I wish you all the best.' He hung up.

Drucker sat there, grinning at the telephone. Yes, he hoped the SS operator had got an earful. The *Wehrmacht* was also a power in the land. If Dornberger badly wanted him back, he would come back. Without the *Reich* Rocket Force, Europe lay open, defenseless, to whatever the Lizards might choose to do.

Not quite out of a clear blue sky, Drucker wondered how many cases high-ranking officers had taken care of, regardless of whether or not the wife in question truly did have a Jewish grandparent. He wondered how many cases they'd taken care of where a man they liked had a Jewish grandmother . . . or perhaps even a Jewish mother. Once he'd started wondering, he wondered how many out-and-out Jews, quietly protected, went on serving the *Reich* because they were too useful to do without.

Before the *Gestapo* arrested Käthe and grounded him, he would have pounded a fist on the nearest table and demanded – demanded at the top of his lungs, especially if he'd had a couple of steins of beer – that each Jew be rooted out. Now . . . Now, in a cell that was comfortable but remained a cell, he laughed out loud.

'I hope they do just fine,' he said. The *Gestapo* men surely listening to his every word would think he meant Major General Dornberger and his friends. And so, in a way, he did – but only in a way.

*   *   *

Felless looked around Cairo with something approaching horror. 'This,' she said, 'this is the capital from which the Race has ruled something like half of Tosev 3 since not long after the arrival of the conquest fleet?' She added an interrogative cough, wishing the Race had something stronger along those lines: a cough of incredulous disbelief, perhaps.

'Senior Researcher, it is,' Pshing replied.

'But—' Felless struggled to put her feelings into words. It wasn't easy. For one thing, rank relationships were ambiguous here. Her body paint was fancier than half of Pshing's, but the other half of the male's matched that of Atvar, the fleetlord of the conquest fleet. Pshing surely made up in influence what he lacked in formal status. For another . . . Felless blurted, 'But it is still a Tosevite city, not one of ours!'

'So it is,' Pshing answered. 'You will have studied the conquests of Rabotev 2 and Halless 1, I take it?'

'Of course,' Felless said indignantly. 'How else was I to prepare myself for this mission?'

'You had no better way, superior female; I am sure of that,' Pshing replied. 'But have you not yet learned that what the Race experienced on the previous two planets we added to the Empire has very little to do with conditions here on Tosev 3?'

He'd granted her the title of superiority so he could rub her snout in the fact of her inadequate preparation without offending her. And, in fact, he hadn't offended her . . . too much. Felless let one eye turret glide appraisingly in his direction. He was a clever male, no doubt about it. Any male who served as several digits of a fleetlord's hand would have to be clever.

Felless took a deep breath before saying something. She regretted it, for it meant she sent a great lungful of air past her scent receptors. Cairo was full of an astounding cacophony of stinks. The odor of droppings was not quite the same as it would have been back on Home, but she had no trouble recognizing it. Piled on top of that solid foundation were other organic odors she had more trouble classifying. They probably came from the Big Uglies and their animals, who were certainly present in great profusion. A thin stream in the mix was odors of cookery, again different from but similar to those back on Home.

Pshing said, 'All things considered, I think we have done reasonably well. We are spread far thinner than we expected to be. Not only have our casualties been much worse than anticipated, but this world was and is far more heavily populated than we had believed it would be. And we cannot be so hard on the Tosevites as we should prefer under other circumstances.'

'And why not?' Felless demanded indignantly. Too late, she realized she'd been foolish. 'Oh. The autonomous not-empires.'

'They are not autonomous. They are independent. You must bear this in mind at all times, superior female.' Again, Pshing used the honorific to let her down easy after slapping her across the snout.

'I do try to bear it in mind,' she said, embarrassed. 'But it is alien to everything the Race has known these past hundred thousand years.'

'Remember this, then: the USA, the SSSR, and the *Reich* can wreck this planet if they decide to do so,' Pshing said. 'This is without our help in the process, you understand. I think any one of those not-empires could do it. With our help, Britain and Nippon might also manage. And is it not so that he who can destroy a thing holds great power over it?'

'Truth.' Felless heard the reluctance in her own voice.

If Atvar's adjutant also heard it, he was too polite to give any sign. He said, 'And so, when these not-empires exhort us to treat the Big Uglies of a certain area in a certain way, we are constrained to take such exhortations seriously.'

'Treating with those who know not the Emperor as equals . . .' Felless looked down at the grimy shingles, an automatic token of respect for her sovereign. 'It knocks every standard of civilized conduct we have imbibed since hatchlinghood – since the hatchlinghood of the Race – onto its tailstump. How did things come to such a pass?'

She waved to show what she meant. From the roof of the building from which the Race administered the planet (it still kept its Tosevite name, Shepheard's Hotel), she stared out at the swarming streets. Tosevites swaddled in their absurd mantlings – some white, some black, some various shades of brown and tan, with a few bright colors mixed in – went about their noisy business, crowding among beasts of burden and motorized vehicles that mostly belched smoke from burning petroleum distillates, not clean hydrogen, and so added one more note to the reek of the place.

And then, as if her outstretched arm were a cue, a shout began to rise in those narrow, winding, insanely crowded streets: *'Allahu akbar! Allahu akbar! Allahu akbar!'* It got louder at every repetition, as if more and more Tosevites were shouting it.

Felless turned to Pshing. 'What does that mean?'

'It means trouble,' he answered in grim tones.

She did not fully grasp that grimness, not at first. 'Why would a swarm of Big Uglies all start shouting "Trouble!" at the same time?'

Pshing made an exasperated noise. 'It means trouble for us, is what it means. Tosevites who shout that think we are evil spirits and have no business ruling them. They think that, if they die trying to kill us, they go straight to a happy afterlife.'

'That's absurd,' Felless said. 'How can their spirits rejoice when they are ignorant of the Emperors?'

'They have always been ignorant of the Emperors,' Pshing reminded her. 'They are mistaken, of course, and misguided, but what they believe, they believe very strongly. This is true of most Tosevites most of the time. It is one of the things that makes them so delightful to administer.'

As she had not before, Felless did recognize sarcasm now. Before she could remark on it, gunfire broke out, somewhere not far enough away. Wincing, she said, 'It sounds as if the war for the conquest of Tosev 3 is not yet over.'

'It is not,' Atvar's adjutant replied. Then he said one of the saddest, gloomiest things Felless had ever heard: 'It may never be over. Even after this world is colonized, it may never be over.'

'We are the Race,' she answered. 'We have not failed yet. We shall not fail here. What would your fleetlord say if he heard you speak thus?'

'He would probably say I might be right,' Pshing answered. 'We were lucky to gain a stalemate on this world. Had the conquest fleet delayed its departure another hundred years, the Tosevites would have been more than a match for us – unless they destroyed themselves before we arrived.'

Felless started to say that that was absurd, that the Race would surely have prevailed regardless of the fight the Big Uglies put up. A hundred thousand years of history and more argued that was true. Logic, though, argued against it. If the Big Uglies had come so far so fast, how far would they have advanced in another hundred years? *Unpleasantly far,* she thought.

A bullet cracked past her head. She needed a moment to realize what had happened. She was no soldier; she was a student of alien psychology. Save in those times when it chose to go conquering, the Race had no soldiers, only police. Till this moment, she had never heard gunfire.

Pshing said, 'We would be wise to leave the roof now. This building is armored against small-arms fire. It is armored against a good deal more than small-arms fire, as a matter of fact. Almost any building the Race uses on Tosev 3 needs to be armored against more than small-arms fire.'

He spoke altogether matter-of-factly, though speaking of horror. Felless stared at him; his psychology was almost as alien to her as that of her Tosevites she'd been sent to study. Then another bullet zipped by, and another. Realization smote: she could die up here. She had all she could do to follow Pshing to the head of the stairs at a steady walk. She wanted to skitter as if pursued by a *bagana* or some other fearsome beast of prey.

Helicopters flew low, pouring gunfire into the Big Uglies. Above the racket, Pshing said, 'I hope the Tosevites here have not managed to smuggle any rockets into Cairo, as they have in some other places. Helicopter crews are vulnerable to that kind of fire.'

Again, he spoke as he might have of a factory accident. Maybe that helped him deal with the dangers that accompanied his trade, dangers different from any Felless had ever known. Thoughtfully, she said, 'I begin to understand why some of the males on this world turn to the local herb called ginger to escape its rigors.'

'Ginger will be a problem for the colonists, too,' Pshing said, 'It creates too much pleasure for it to be anything else: so much, in fact, that it is severely destructive of order and discipline. We believe the worst mutinies on this planet were instigated by ginger-tasters.'

'Mutinies.' Felless shivered, though the stairwell, like the rest of the building, was comfortably warm. She had heard males from the conquest fleet complain endlessly about Tosev 3's climate; much of the video she'd seen tended to bear them out. But Cairo seemed comfortable enough. She went on, 'I cannot imagine males of the Race turning on duly constituted authority. I believe it happened – I have seen the records proving it happened – but I cannot imagine it.'

'You were not here to see for yourself the fighting that took place after the conquest fleet landed.' Pshing shivered, too, at bad memories Felless did not, could not, share. 'We came closer than you can imagine to losing the war altogether. We almost had' – he swiveled his eye turrets, to make sure no one was close enough to overhear him – 'we almost had our fleetlord cast down from his office as a result of shiplords' dissatisfaction with the conduct of the war.'

'What?' Felless hadn't seen anything about that – or had she? Pieces that hadn't fit together now suddenly did. 'That would explain why one of the shiplords defected to the Tosevites.' She'd seen that mentioned, but the data she'd seen made the shiplord out to be a treacherous idiot. Had he been a treacherous idiot, how had he managed to become a shiplord?

'Indeed it would.' Pshing sighed. 'This world has had a corrosive effect on us, even after the fighting stopped. We have been too few, and have slowly begun to dissolve in the sea of Big Uglies all around us. Now that you folk have come, I hope we shall be able to reverse that trend, so that the Tosevites shall begin to be assimilated into the larger Empire, as should have begun from the outset. I hope we shall be able to do that.'

He did not sound sure the Race would be able to do that. 'Of course they will be assimilated,' Felless declared. 'That is why we have come. That is why I am here: to learn how best to integrate the Tosevites into the structure of the Empire. We did it with the Rabotevs and Hallessi. We shall do it here.'

'One difference, superior female,' Pshing said, which meant he was going to contradict her.

'And that is?' She gave him the chance.

'You must always remember that the Tosevites, unlike the Rabotevs or Hallessi, are also trying to learn how to integrate us into their structures,' Pshing said. 'They are skilled at the art, having practiced it so much among themselves. We have more strength – we will have more still, now that the colonization fleet is here. They, however, may well have more skill.'

Felless shivered again. Maybe the building wasn't so warm after all.

Atvar studied the latest set of reports scrolling across his computer screen. 'This is not satisfactory,' he said, and paused a moment to wonder how many times he had said that since coming to Tosev 3. *Too many* was the answer that immediately sprang to mind.

'Exalted Fleetlord?' Pshing inquired.

'Unsatisfactory,' Atvar repeated. Saying it gave him a certain amount of pleasure. Doing something about it gave him more. He got that larger pleasure less often than he would have liked. 'The Tosevites have been doing altogether too much maneuvering with their accursed satellites lately.'

'To which not-empire shall we protest, Exalted Fleetlord?' his adjutant asked.

'They are all doing it,' Atvar said peevishly. 'I think they are doing it deliberately, to confuse us. Whether they are trying to confuse us or not, they have certainly succeeded. By now, we are not altogether certain whose satellites are in which orbits. This distresses me.'

'It could be worse,' Pshing said. 'The more fuel they use up in these maneuvers, the sooner they will have none left.'

'Truth.' Atvar hissed sadly. 'The other truth, worse luck, is that the Big Uglies will either refuel them or send new ones up to take their place. Maybe we would have been wiser to forbid them from going into space at all.' He hissed again. 'They made it all too plain that they were ready to resume fighting if we enforced that prohibition. They meant it. Indeed, they meant it.'

'Yes, Exalted Fleetlord.' Pshing's job was not to disagree with Atvar.

Before the fleetlord could say anything else, something hit the building a thunderous blow. The floor shook under Atvar's feet; little bits of plaster and plaster dust floated down from the ceiling. Atvar snatched up a telephone and clawed in the code he needed.

'Security,' the male on the other end said.

'Not enough of it, evidently,' Atvar said, acid in his voice. 'What was it that just impacted on us?'

The male in Security paused a moment, no doubt to check his caller's code. When he realized to whom he was speaking, he got deferential in a hurry. 'Exalted Fleetlord, that was a small, I would say locally made, rocket detonating against our armored façade here. No casualties, minimal damage. A lot of smoke, a lot of noise. Maybe the Big Uglies will think they really did something. They did not, and I will take an oath by the Emperor's name on it.'

'Very well. Thank you.' Atvar broke the connection. He turned an eye turret toward Pshing. 'The fanatics, as you could have guessed for yourself. I wonder which of the Deutsche or the Russkis or the British stirred them up to this latest round of madness.'

'Exalted Fleetlord, did anyone necessarily stir them up?' Pshing asked. 'They are Tosevites, and so quite able to stir themselves up.'

'I wish I could say you were wrong,' Atvar said mournfully. 'But you are correct, as we have seen again and again to our sorrow. And the male in Security believes it to have been a locally made rocket. Perhaps that is just as well. One of the independent not-empires might well have furnished the fanatics with something more lethal.'

He wished Tosev 3 had been as the Race fondly believed it would be. Had that been so, he would now have been turning over his duties to the fleetlord of the colonization fleet. He would have gone down in the records of four worlds as Atvar the Conqueror. For tens of thousands of years to come, hatchlings of four races would have learned of him in their lessons. Conquerors were rarer by far than Emperors, and more likely to stay in a student's memory.

He hissed softly. He would go down in history, all right. He would go down as the first male the Emperor had designated a Conqueror to succeed incompletely. He hoped the landing of the colonization fleet would succeed in bringing Tosev 3 firmly within the Empire. On good days, he had some confidence that that would happen. On bad days, he wondered if the Big Uglies wouldn't end up overwhelming the Race instead.

Today was a very bad day.

Pshing said, 'Might it not perhaps be best to transfer our administrative center to the island continent called Australia, where the Tosevite survivors are relatively few and easy to control?'

'Security would be simpler,' Atvar admitted. 'But to retreat from a long-established center like this one would be to confess weakness. The Tosevites have excellent scent receptors for weakness. They would only press us harder than ever. Firmness they grasp. Firmness they respect. Anything less, and you are theirs.'

'No doubt you are right, Exalted Fleetlord,' Pshing said, resignation in his voice. 'Our experience on this world certainly suggests as much, at any rate.'

Somewhere in the broad, empty reaches of the Indian Ocean, far, far from any land, a long, lean shark shape drew very near the surface of the sea. But it was vaster than any shark, vaster than any whale – and neither sharks nor whales evolved with conning towers on their backs.

This conning tower never broke the surface. No satellite, no airplane that chanced to be peering down on that particular stretch of sea, could have found a name or a nation to attach to the submarine. All cats are gray in the dark. All submarines look very much alike, seen underwater from above.

A radio mast rose. Ever so briefly, it plowed a tiny white wake in warm, blue-green water. Then it slid down again, down into silence, down into anonymity. The submarine dove deep.

Glen Johnson was harassing one of his Soviet opposite numbers on the radio: something to pass the time on what he expected to be a long, boring mission. 'Why did they even bother putting you in the craft, Yuri Alekseyevich?' he asked. 'All you are good for is pressing a couple of buttons. They could get a machine to do that. Soon, they probably will.'

'I can do what I have to do,' the Russian answered stolidly. 'I am less likely to go wrong than a machine.'

'Cheaper, too,' Johnson suggested. He added an emphatic cough, to show how much cheaper. They were both speaking the Lizards' language. It was the only one they had in common, which Johnson thought amusing. He didn't know what the Russian spaceman – cosmonauts, they called themselves –

thought of it. Somebody down on the ground was monitoring every word the Russian said. Somebody was monitoring every word Johnson said, too, but he didn't have to worry about a grilling from the NKVD when he got home.

He was about to rib Yuri some more when a flash of light off to one side of them drew his notice. 'What was that?' the Russian asked – he'd seen it, too, then, though his craft had only a couple of little windows, not a canopy with better all-around vision than Johnson had enjoyed in his first fighter plane.

'I don't know,' he said, and asked a question of his own: 'Whose is it?'

Yuri was silent for a little while: probably getting permission from downstairs to talk. 'I do not know, either,' he said at last. 'Orbits have been confused lately, even worse than usual.'

Johnson gave another emphatic cough – barbarous jargon by Lizard standards, for it modified no previous words, but something humans often did and had no trouble understanding. Then he spoke in English, not for the Russian's benefit but for his own: 'Jesus H. Christ! Somebody's launched something. Somebody's launched something big!'

Orbiting fortresses these days could carry a dozen separate rockets and weapons, which could be aimed at either other targets in space or at the ground below. They made Johnson's blood run cold – they made a lot of people's blood run cold – because they could start a really big war with bare minutes of warning.

He changed frequencies and spoke urgently into his microphone: 'Ground, this is *Peregrine*. Emergency. Someone has launched. Repeat: someone has launched. I am unable to identify whose satellite it is. Over.'

A voice came back up from a ship in the South Pacific: 'Roger that. We are going to alert. Over.'

'Roger.' Johnson knew that meant he would have to run another check on all of his craft's weapons. He scratched an itch on his scalp. Close-cropped, sandy brown hair rasped against his fingers. He'd had a lot of training. He'd flown a lot of routine missions. Now things counted again. If the fighting started way up here, odds were he wouldn't make it back down again.

He checked the radar. 'Ground, all launches appear to be outbound. Repeat: all launches appear to be outbound.' Intuition leapt. The man broke through the Marine lieutenant colonel for a moment: 'Christ, somebody's gone and launched at the colonization fleet!' After that one shocked sentence, the officer resumed command: 'Over.'

'That appears to be correct, *Peregrine*,' the inhumanly calm voice on the ground said. Then the fellow's calm cracked, as Johnson's had: 'What in God's name are the Lizards going to do about that? Over.'

'I hope they can knock down some of those rockets,' Johnson said. During the Lizards' invasion, he'd never imagined rooting for them. But he was. The colonization fleet was unarmed; the Lizards had never imagined its ships would need to carry weapons. Attacking them was murder, nothing else but. They couldn't shoot back. They couldn't even run.

And, if those ships did go up, what would the Lizards do? That was the wild card, one that made his stubbly hair try to stand on end. During the war, they'd played tit for tat. Every time the humans had touched off a nuclear bomb in a city they controlled, a human-held city went up in smoke immediately afterwards. How much was a ship from the colonization fleet worth?

'Ground,' he said urgently, 'whose launch is that?'

'*Peregrine*, we don't know,' replied the man at the other end of the radio link.

'Do the Lizards know?' Johnson demanded. 'What will they do if they know? What will they do if they don't know?'

'Those are good questions, *Peregrine*. If you've got any other good questions, please save them for after class.'

After class was coming fast. Johnson would have launched his own missiles, but they couldn't match the acceleration of the ones already under way. And, had he launched, the Lizards might have thought he was aiming at them. They knew who *he* was. Would that make them drop the hammer on the USA?

He didn't dare find out. All he could do was watch his radar. The Lizards, even counting the ones from the conquest fleet alone, had a lot more stuff in space than mankind did. Surely they would be able to do something. But, from what Johnson could read, none of their installations was close enough to have much chance of knocking out those missiles.

Sitting ducks, he thought. They weren't sitting, of course; they were orbiting the Earth at several miles per second, as he was. But they had no chance of matching the acceleration of the missiles bearing down on them, and so they might as well have been sitting. A couple of them did start to change their orbits. Several, Johnson was convinced, hadn't the faintest notion they were under attack.

One after another, fireballs blossomed in space. Johnson squeezed his eyes shut against the intolerable glare of atomic explosions. He wondered how much radiation he was picking up. *Peregrine* orbited a couple of hundred miles below the ships of the colonization fleet, but he had no atmosphere to shield him from whatever he got.

But, as those sunbursts swelled and faded and dropped behind him, his eyes filled with tears that had nothing to do with mere glare. He'd just watched mass murder committed, watched it without being able to do a thing about it. He checked the radar. If any of the missiles had failed, they would still be outward bound. Someone, Lizards or humans, might be able to track them down and find out who had made them. Whoever had made them, he deserved whatever the Lizards chose to dish out.

Discipline held. He had to report. No doubt the people back at Kitty Hawk already knew what had happened. No doubt the whole world, by now, knew what had happened. He had to report anyhow. 'Ground,' he said, 'the targets are destroyed. All the targets are destroyed.'

* * *

119

Vyacheslav Molotov did his best to calm the agitated Lizard who had been ushered into his presence. 'I assure you, the missiles that destroyed your colonization ships were not of Soviet manufacture.'

Queek, the Lizards' ambassador to the USSR, made a noise that reminded Molotov of lard sizzling in a hot pan. His translator turned the hisses and splutters into Polish-accented Russian: '*Reichs* Chancellor Himmler has assured the Race of the same thing. President Warren has assured the Race of the same thing. One of you is lying. If we find out who that is, we shall punish his not-empire and not the others. If we do not, we will punish all three not-empires, as we warned we would do. Do you understand?'

'I understand,' Molotov told the interpreter. 'Please convey to Queek my sympathy at the Race's tragic loss. Please also convey to him that any harm coming to our territory will be viewed as an act of war. We did not, we will not, begin the fight: the peasants and workers of the Soviet Union are and have always been peace-loving. But if war comes to us, we shall not shrink from it.'

The translator did his job. Queek made more hot-grease noises. He jumped up into the air. His mouth came open. His teeth were not very large, but they were sharp enough to remind Molotov that Lizards were descended from beasts that hunted for meat. 'If you Big Uglies think you can confuse the issue of which of you is guilty and escape all punishment, you are mistaken,' Queek declared.

Molotov had read of an American carnival game where a pea was hidden under one of three nutshells, which were then interchanged rapidly. Anyone who could guess which shell hid the pea won his bet. No – he would have won his bet, save that the fellow with the shells commonly palmed the pea and put it wherever his own economic interests lay.

A typical capitalist system if ever there was one, Molotov thought. It was also one that applied to the present situation. 'We did not begin maneuvering with our satellites,' he said.

'We joined in to maintain our own security. You also joined in to maintain your security. You were as capable of launching an unprovoked attack as any human nation. You have already launched an unprovoked attack against this entire planet.'

He didn't think Queek liked that. He didn't care what Queek liked. Homegrown reactionaries and foreign imperialists had tried to strangle the infant Soviet Union in its cradle. A generation later, the Hitlerites had made peace and war in the space of two years. And, with the Lizards' invasion piled on top of that of the Nazis, Molotov did not think he could be blamed for doubting their good intentions.

He did not care whether Queek blamed him or not. 'In the name of the workers and peasants of the Soviet Union, I repeat to you that we are not responsible for the crime committed against your people,' he said. 'I also repeat to you that we shall defend ourselves against any crimes committed against our people.'

'Punishing a crime is not committing a crime,' Queek said. 'If you have evidence of who did commit the crime, I suggest you turn it over to us, to escape such punishment.'

Fabricate evidence against the Greater German Reich, *was the first thought that went through Molotov's mind. Fabricate evidence against the USA,* was the second. Himmler, he was certain, would be fabricating evidence against the USSR and the USA. And Warren? Like so many Americans, he was self-righteous, but not, Molotov judged, too self-righteous to fabricate evidence against the *Reich* and the Soviet Union.

His face showed none of what he thought. His face never showed any of what he thought. What he thought was none of his face's business.

Both of Queek's eye turrets were aimed at him. The translator studied him, too. He did not worry that they would see behind his mask. The only one who had ever been able to do that was Stalin, and it hadn't been easy for him.

Queek said, 'When the conquest fleet came to Tosev 3, we reckoned you barbarians, fit only to be subdued. Since the

121

fighting ended, have we not treated with the great Tosevite powers as if with equals?'

'More or less,' Molotov admitted. 'We had the strength to require you to do this.' One of the reasons the USSR had had that strength was technical help from the USA. Molotov had never let gratitude interfere with doing what seemed most expedient for his own nation.

'Equals do not stage sneak attacks. They do not stage unprovoked massacres,' Queek declared. 'These are the actions of barbarians, of savages.'

Now Molotov had to work hard to keep from laughing at the poor, naive Lizard. He thought of Pearl Harbor, of the German invasion of the USSR, of the Siberian divisions thrown into the fight in front of Moscow when the fascists thought his country on the ropes, of a thousand other surprise attacks in the blood-spattered history of the world. Every once in a while, the Lizards showed how alien they were.

'You do not respond,' Queek said.

'You have given me nothing to which to respond,' Molotov replied. 'I have told you, we did not attack. If you try to punish us when we are innocent, we will fight back. I have nothing more to say.'

'This is unsatisfactory,' Queek said. 'I shall tell the fleetlord it is unsatisfactory.'

'A great many things in life are unsatisfactory,' Molotov said. 'The Race has not learned this lesson so well as it might have.'

'I did not come here to discuss philosophy with you,' Queek said. 'You have been warned. You would do well to conduct yourself accordingly.' He skittered out of Molotov's office, the translator in his wake.

Molotov waited till a guard outside reported that they had left the Kremlin. Then he went into a room behind his office and changed his suit. The Lizards were far more adept than humans at making and concealing tiny espionage devices. He had shaken hands with the interpreter. He did not believe in taking chances.

Once changed, he went into another room off the chamber where he kept spare clothes. Another secretary awaited him there. 'Tell Lavrenti Pavlovich I wish to speak with him,' Molotov said.

'Of course, Comrade General Secretary.' The secretary made the connection, spoke briefly, and nodded to Molotov. 'He will be here directly.'

Molotov nodded, as if he had expected nothing less. In truth, he hadn't; small shows of insubordination were not Lavrenti Beria's way of showing his own strength. The long-time head of the NKVD did nothing on a small scale.

Bald as a Lizard, Beria walked in about fifteen minutes later. 'Good day, Vyacheslav Mikhailovich,' he said. His Mingrelian accent was close to the Georgian that had flavored Stalin's Russian: one more thing to unsettle Molotov. But what Molotov would not show to Queek, he would not show to Beria, either.

'Did we do this, Lavrenti Pavlovich?' he asked quietly. 'I did not order it. I think it most unwise. Did we do it?'

'Not on my order, Comrade General Secretary,' Beria answered.

'That is not responsive,' Molotov said. He did not think Beria could realistically aim for the top spot in the Soviet hierarchy; too many Russians would have resented having a second man from the Caucasus set above them. But the NKVD was a tail that could wag the dog. Without the name, without the formal position of power, Beria held the thing itself. He had held it for many years. If Molotov ever decided to purge him, state security would suffer. But if he ever decided he could not afford to or did not dare to purge Beria, then Beria had more power than he. 'Answer the question.'

'If we did this, I do not know of it,' Beria said. Molotov was not sure that was responsive, either. Then the NKVD chief amplified it: 'If we did this, no one in my ministry knows of it. Whether anyone in the Ministry of Defense knows of it, I cannot say with certainty.'

'They would not dare,' Molotov said, The Red Army, the Red Air and Space Forces, and the Red Navy were firmly subordinated to Communist Party control. The NKVD, being an arm of the Party, was less so. He scratched at his graying mustache. 'I am sure they would not dare.'

'I think you are right.' Beria nodded, the golden gleam of the electric lights above him reflected from his bald pate. 'Still . . . you want to be sure you are right, eh?'

'Oh, yes,' Molotov said. 'I have to be sure I am right.' That sentence would eventually stir the armed forces the way a *babushka* stirred *shchi*, to make sure all the cabbage and sausage in the soup cooked evenly. Molotov went on, 'Who is likelier to have done it, the *Reich* or the United States?'

Behind gold-rimmed spectacles, Beria's eyes glinted. 'The *Reich* is always more likely,' he replied. 'The Americans are capitalist reactionaries, but they are, by their standards, sane. The Hitlerites?' He shook his head. 'They are children, children with atomic bombs. Because they want a thing, they reach out and grab it, never worrying or caring what might happen because of that.'

'And Himmler is more sensible than Hitler was,' Molotov said.

'Indeed,' Beria said. Molotov suspected he was jealous of the German *Führer*. Himmler was a master of secret policemen and spies, too, and he had reached the top in the *Reich*.

Molotov exhaled deeply, a sign of strong emotion in him. 'Even for the Germans, this is madness. They struck one blow, but it would take a great many to destroy the colonization fleet. And the Lizards will not permit many blows to be struck against them. They can still strike harder than we, and they will.'

'Indeed,' Beria said again. His eyes glinted once more, this time in anticipation. 'Shall I begin an investigation of the Ministry of Defense and the armed forces?'

'Not yet,' Molotov told him. 'Soon, but not yet. The soldiers scream when the NKVD encroaches on them. I will tell you when I require your services. Until I tell such a thing, you are to keep your hands in your pockets. Do you understand me, Lavrenti Pavlovich? I mean this most particularly.'

'Very well,' Beria said in sulky tones. No, he did not like following orders. He would sooner have been giving them, as he did in the building on Dzerzhinsky Square.

'Another thing,' Molotov said, to make him attend: 'Cut back on arms shipments to the People's Liberation Army in China. We must soothe the Lizards wherever we can.'

'Yes, this is sensible,' Beria agreed, as if to say the other hadn't been. He held up a forefinger. 'But will it not make the Lizards think we have a guilty conscience?'

'Now that is an interesting question,' Molotov said. 'Yes, a very interesting question.' He considered it. 'I think we had better cut back, Lavrenti Pavlovich. We have always denied supplying the Chinese for their insurrection against the Lizards. How can we possibly cut back on what we have denied doing at all?'

Beria laughed. 'A nice point. We shall do that, then. Shall we do it gradually, so that even the Chinese do not realize at once what is happening to them?'

'Yes, that would be very good.' Molotov nodded. 'Very good indeed. Mao has complained from time to time that we are not Marxist-Leninist enough to suit him. Let us see how going without aid suits him, and how much he criticizes us after that.' Had he been another man, he might have chortled. Being the man he was, he allowed himself another nod, this one of anticipation.

Reffet's furious face stared out of the screen at Atvar. 'Destroy them!' the fleetlord of the colonization fleet shouted. 'Destroy all the nasty Tosevites, that we may take this world for ourselves and do something worthwhile with it.'

'Could I have destroyed the Tosevites, or at least their capacity for making war, do you not think I would have done so?' Atvar returned. 'In this case, the destruction would be mutual.'

'Incompetence,' Reffet hissed, careless of his opposite number's feelings.

'Incompetence,' Atvar agreed, which startled Reffet into momentary silence. Atvar went on, 'Incompetence reaching back more than sixteen hundred years. We misjudged what the probe told us, and we failed to send another one to see if the situation had changed in the interim before dispatching the conquest fleet. As a result, very little has gone as it should on Tosev 3.'

'As a result, twelve of my ships are blown to radioactive dust, and all the males and females in them,' Reffet replied. 'And you have not yet punished the creatures responsible for this outrage.'

'We do not yet know which of the creatures *are* responsible for the outrage,' Atvar pointed out. 'If we knew that, punishment would be swift and certain.'

'You told the Big Uglies that, if you could not find out which of their ridiculous groupings committed this crime, you would punish them all,' Reffet reminded him. 'I have yet to see you do this, however eagerly I await it.'

'The Tosevites' groupings would be more ridiculous were they not armed with nuclear weapons and poison gas,' Atvar said.

'Your warning will be more ridiculous if you issue it and then fail to carry it out,' Reffet retorted.

That was true; Atvar knew as much, and the knowledge pained him. 'Much of the blame for this disaster is mine,' he said. 'We have been at peace – or at an approximation of peace – with the leading Tosevite not-empires for too long. We examine what they do less minutely than we did in the days just after the fighting ended – and they are better able to conceal what they do, too. So many of their satellites were shifting orbit lately, we still cannot determine which not-empire activated one of its machines. For that matter, the machine might have been disguised as something other than what it was, and lain quietly in wait for a moment of opportunity – a moment of treachery.'

'That is why you said you would punish them all,' Reffet said.

'It is also why they all said they would consider punishment for deeds I could not prove they committed an act of war,' Atvar answered unhappily. 'Big Uglies enjoy fighting to a degree we have trouble understanding. They are always fighting among themselves. I believe they would fight us.'

'I believe they are bluffing,' Reffet said. With his lack of experience with Tosevites, that was not helpful. His next comment was: 'And one group of them is bound to be lying.'

'But which?' Atvar asked. 'Mass punishment is something they would be more likely to use than we. We care more for justice.'

'Where is the justice for my colonists?' Reffet asked. 'Where is the justice in making a threat and then forgetting it?'

'I was hasty,' Atvar said. 'In my haste, I may have behaved like a Big Ugly – the Tosevites are hasty by nature.'

'This world has corrupted you,' Reffet said in the tones of a judge passing sentence. 'Instead of the Tosevites' becoming more like proper subjects of the Emperor, you act like a Big Ugly.'

'This world will change the colonists, too,' Atvar said, admitting most of Reffet's charge without acknowledging the word *corrupted*. 'If you think it will not, you live in a ginger-taster's dream.'

Perhaps he should not have mentioned ginger. With a fine mocking waggle of the eye turrets, Reffet said, 'One more delight Tosev 3 has produced. I tell you this, Atvar' – alone among males and females of the Race on Tosev 3, he addressed Atvar as an equal – 'if you do not keep your promise to punish the Big Uglies, I shall report you to the Emperor.'

Fury and scorn ripped through Atvar. 'Go ahead, Reffet,' he hissed, using the other fleetlord's name with savage relish.

'By the time your grumbling reaches him, and by the time he composes a reply and it gets back to us, as many years will have gone by as passed between your departure from Home and your arrival here. Have you forgotten where you are? For better or worse, we are the males on the spot. Whatever answers the Race finds for Tosev 3, we are the ones who will have to find them.'

Reffet looked as if he hated Atvar, hated Tosev 3, hated everything except the idea of tucking down his tailstump and fleeing back Home. He had probably been ready to refer any hard problems he found to bureaucrats back on Home, confident conditions would not have changed much while light sped from Tosev to Home and back again. Slow change, incremental change, was the hallmark of life in the Empire.

Atvar's mouth fell open in a bitter laugh. Incessant, maddening change was the hallmark of life on Tosev 3. If Reffet couldn't figure that out, couldn't adapt to it as Atvar had had to adapt . . . *too bad,* Atvar thought. 'Out,' he said aloud, and broke his connection with the other fleetlord.

Ttomalss looked on his summons from the fleetlord of the colonization fleet as an honor he could have done without. Not only did it take him away from his work, it also involved him in high-level controversies that might end up causing him trouble later. But Reffet had not asked his opinion: Reffet was a male new-come from Home, not a snoutcounting Big Ugly. Reffet had simply summoned him. What choice had he but to obey?

None, he thought as he folded himself into the posture of respect and said, 'How may I serve you, Exalted Fleetlord?'

'Computer searches and a conversation with Senior Researcher Felless identify you as the leading expert from the conquest fleet on the natives of this chilly ball of mud,' Reffet said. 'I presume this is accurate?'

'I am one of the leading students of the Tosevites, yes, Exalted Fleetlord,' Ttomalss said. He hid his amusement at that. His gains in knowledge had got under the scales of a good many of his colleagues. As far as he was concerned, they had no imagination. As far as they were concerned, he had too much. Maybe he was able to learn about the Big Uglies because he could come closer to thinking like them than other males of the Race could do.

'Explain to me, then, Senior Researcher, why any group of these Tosevites should have sought to perpetrate the atrocity my fleet has suffered,' Reffet said.

'First obvious point: for the purpose of doing us harm,' Ttomalss said. 'Second obvious point: because the guilty Tosevites thought they could do us harm and at the same time escape punishment.'

'In that, they may even have been correct,' Reffet said discontentedly.

'As may be, Exalted Fleetlord.' Ttomalss was not a male in a position to set policy. 'Third, less obvious point: because the guilty Tosevites may have sought revenge against us for wrongs suffered during the period of fighting. The Big Uglies are far more given to elaborate vengeance than we are.' He remembered the captivity he had endured at the hands of the Chinese female Liu Han after taking her hatchling to use in his researches – and he had suffered that captivity despite returning the hatchling.

'I see that this is true,' Reffet said. 'Senior Researcher Felless confirms it and, as I noted, speaks well of your insight into the subject. I must confess, though, that I fail to grasp the reasons behind it.'

'In my view, they are related to the reproductive behavior of the Big Uglies, which, you will have gathered, is different from our own and different from that of any other intelligent race with which we are familiar.'

'I have gathered this, yes.' Reffet made a noise redolent of disgust. 'They are sexually available to one another at all seasons of the year. They form pairs and nurture the hatchlings to which the female of each pair gives birth by a process that

129

revolted me when I read of it and revolted me even more when I viewed a video of it. It strikes me as astounding that any survive.'

'It strikes me the same way, Exalted Fleetlord,' Ttomalss said. 'The difficulty of the method, the helplessness of the hatchling over a startling period of time' – he recalled his own difficulties coping with the needs of first Liu Mei and then Kassquit –' and the sexual bond between specific males and females create emotional attachments among the Tosevites we can understand only intellectually. A Big Ugly whose sexual partner or hatchling has come to harm may well seek revenge for that harm without concern for its own survival.'

Reffet pondered that. 'I have seen as much in the reports,' he said slowly. 'It did not make sense to me before. Now it does, at least to a certain degree. But it also leaves me with an unanswered question, one on which I hope you will shed more light: which Tosevite not-empire do you reckon most likely to think it owes us such vicious, elaborate vengeance?'

'I fear I must disappoint you, Exalted Fleetlord, for I can offer no certain answer there,' Ttomalss said. 'By the standards the Big Uglies use to judge such things, we have inflicted grievous harm on all their leading not-empires; and on the lesser ones as well. I wish I could be of more assistance.'

'So do I,' Reffet muttered. 'All three of these leading not-empires have said they will war against us if we punish them for the deed without proof of their guilt. One has had the effrontery to say this knowing it is in fact guilty, but never mind that. Do they speak the truth?'

'There, I fear they do,' Ttomalss replied, knowing he was again disappointing the fleetlord of the colonization fleet. 'If a Big Ugly says he will not fight, he may well be lying. If he says he will fight, he is sure to be telling the truth.'

'These are not the answers I sought from you,' Reffet said.

'If you wanted answers that pleased you, Exalted Fleetlord, you could have had them from many others, and without interrupting me at my work,' Ttomalss said. 'I thought you summoned me because you wanted the truth.'

'You sound rather like a Big Ugly yourself,' Reffet remarked.

He did not mean it as a compliment, but it was the first perceptive thing Ttomalss had heard him say. 'Inevitably, that which is observed and the observer interact,' the researcher said. 'Over these past years, we have influenced the Tosevites and they have influenced us.'

'Not for the better, in my view,' Reffet said. 'Can you offer no advice on how to learn which group of Tosevites is lying?'

'Very little, I fear,' Ttomalss said. 'The Big Uglies are far more practiced liars than we – as is natural, since they lie to one another so often.'

'I have heard you,' Reffet said heavily. 'I have heard you and I dismiss you. Go back and learn more.'

'It shall be done, Exalted Fleetlord.' Inside, Ttomalss was laughing as he left Reffet's presence. Reffet might despise Tosev 3 and all the Big Uglies on it, but they were influencing him, too, whether he wanted them to or not. Otherwise, he would have been more interested in hearing the truth and less in hearing only what he wanted to hear – a Tosevite characteristic if ever there was one.

'Sir,' Major Sam Yeager asked, 'are you looking to hear the truth, or only what you want to hear?'

President Earl Warren blinked. With his long, jowly, wrinkled face, pink skin, and white hair, he looked like everyone's favorite grandfather. 'Major, the day I don't want to hear the truth is the day I should no longer be president of the United States.'

Yeager wondered how sincere Warren was. Well, he'd find out in a minute. 'Okay, Mr. President,' he said. 'Truth is, I don't know how we're going to keep the Lizards from hitting us a lick. They said they would. By their way of thinking, that means they have to, whether they want to or not.'

'That is unjust,' Warren said unhappily. 'If I permit it, I show cowardice in the face of the enemy.'

'Yes, sir,' Yeager agreed. 'But if you go and hit them another lick afterwards – well, where does it stop?'

Warren eyed him. 'A good question. The only question, as far as I can see: certainly the one on which a president earns his salary. Seeing that it is the question is not so hard. I mean no offense when I say any reasonably intelligent man could frame it. Answering it, though – ay, there's the rub.'

Yeager wasn't insulted when the president called him a reasonably intelligent man. He was, if anything, flattered. He wouldn't have had a chance to meet a president if the Lizards hadn't come. The most he could have hoped for was big-league coach, if one of his buddies got lucky and made manager. Part-time scout or high-school coach somewhere struck him as a lot more likely.

He said, 'Mr. President, sir, if the Lizards wanted to blow up one of our cities, the way they kept doing during the fighting, they could have done it by now. Seems to me that Atvar wants to do something that would let him save face with his own people but doesn't want to touch off a war with us.'

Earl Warren rubbed his chin as he pondered that. 'You're saying he might be satisfied with a symbolic act of destruction, Major, and would be willing to forgo something so brutal as to force us to respond in kind?'

'Yes, sir, that's exactly what I'm saying.' Yeager didn't try to hide the relief in his voice. Having a boss who understood what he was talking about was liable to make life easier for the whole planet.

On the other hand, it might not, too. Warren said, 'I regret permitting even a symbolic act of destruction on our soil if we have done nothing to deserve it. It sets a dangerous precedent.'

'Right now, sir, the shiplords in the colonization fleet – and in the conquest fleet, too – will be screaming their heads off at Atvar to get him to blow a city here and one in the *Reich* and one in Russia to kingdom come,' Sam said. He didn't try to hide his desperation, either. 'If Atvar settles for something symbolic, they'll all be shouting that he's set a dangerous precedent – and the Lizards take precedent a lot more seriously than we do.'

'A point,' the president said, 'and one I'm glad you reminded me of. I tend to think of the Lizards as always seeing things in the same light and speaking with a single voice. I have the same trouble with the Germans and the Russians, probably for the same reason: because their politics are less open than ours, I need to remind myself they have politics at all.'

'I don't know about the Nazis and the Reds, sir, but the Lizards sure have politics,' Yeager answered. 'They had 'em even before the colonization fleet came. Now they're worse, because the ones who've been here for twenty years have started to understand a little bit about us, but the new ones don't believe half of what the old-timers tell 'em and don't want to believe any of it.'

'Is that last your opinion, Major, or have you got data to back it up?' Warren asked sharply. He'd been a politician a long time, and a lawyer for a long time before that; he understood the difference between evidence and hearsay.

'Sir, it's the unanimous opinion of all the defectors and prisoners I've talked to, from Straha on down,' Sam said, 'and some of the communications intercepts we've picked up show the same thing. We don't have as many as we'd like; the Lizards are still ahead of us when it comes to keeping signals secure.'

Warren sighed and looked weary. His wits remained keen; his body, now and then, forcibly reminded him it was past seventy. And, from the days of FDR on, the presidency had grown into a job of man-killing importance and complexity. 'I will consult with officials from the Departments of State and the Interior,' Warren said at last. 'If they concur in your view, Major, perhaps we'll dicker with the Lizards over a suitable symbolic act. If your good offices are required there, I will call on you.'

'That's fine, Mr. President. That's better than fine, in fact,' Yeager said enthusiastically. He also realized he'd just been dismissed. Saluting, he turned to go.

Before he could leave, though, President Warren said, 'Wait.' Sam did as smart an about-face as he had in him. Warren asked, 'Whom do the Lizards believe to be the responsible party?'

'Sir, the way they handicap it is, the Nazis first, the Reds second, and us trailing but not out of the running.' Yeager hesitated, then risked a question of his own: 'How does it look to you?'

'I know about us, of course, which the Lizards would, too, if they had an ounce of sense,' Warren answered. Sam waited, not sure whether the president would tell him anything more. After a few seconds, Warren went on, 'If I were a gambling man, I would bet on the *Reich* ahead of the Soviet Union, too. Molotov is a very cool customer – or a cold fish, whichever you like. He holds his cards so close to his chest, they're inside his shirt. He would never dare anything so wild. The Nazis . . .' He shook his head. 'No one can tell what the Nazis will do till they do it. Half the time, I don't think they know themselves.'

'That's what the Lizards say about all of us,' Yeager said.

'So I've heard. But it happens to be true of the Germans. Less so now than when Hitler ran them, maybe, but still true.' The president sighed again. 'And I wish Britain hadn't started cozying up to the Greater German *Reich* after the Lizards took away her empire. I don't know how much we could have done about that – the *Reich* is on the other side of the Channel, and we're on the other side of the Atlantic – but I wish it hadn't happened.'

'You get no argument from me, sir,' Yeager said. 'For that matter, I don't like the idea of propping up the Japs. I remember Pearl Harbor too well.'

'So do I, Major,' Warren said. 'I was attorney general of California at the time. I helped get the Japs off the West Coast and into camps. But if we don't prop them up now, they'll look to the Russians, which would be bad, or else to the Lizards in China, which would be worse. And so—' He made an unhappy face.

'By what I've heard, sir, the Lizards aren't having a very happy time in China,' Sam said.

'They've got the same problem the Japanese did before them: too many Chinese to try to hold down with not enough soldiers.' Warren looked up at the ceiling. 'In a quiet sort of way, we try to keep the Lizards from having too happy a time in China. It's easier for the Russians to do that than it is for us, but we manage.' He glanced toward Yeager. 'Unofficially, of course.'

'Oh, of course, sir.' Sam saluted again. This time, President Warren let him go.

Before the Lizards came, what people called the White House these days had been the governor's residence, not far from the State Capitol in Little Rock, Arkansas. People kept talking about rebuilding on the site of Washington, D.C., but they were more willing to talk than they were to spend money. Some people also said the Lizards had known just what they were doing when they dropped an explosive-metal bomb on Washington. Sam had been known to say that a time or two himself.

He rather liked Little Rock, even the larger, more hectic city that had sprung up around and in the midst of the town he'd known during and right after the fighting. It was larger and more hectic than it had been, but still small and staid alongside Los Angeles. It was also much greener than Los Angeles, and full of trees. Both the Californian he was and the farm boy from the prairie he had been appreciated that.

Down the block, only a few embassies stood: that of the Lizards, biggest of all; those of Germany and the USSR, rival concrete cubes; smaller structures from Britain and Japan; those of Canada and Ireland and New Zealand and Germany's vassals: Switzerland, Finland, Sweden, Hungary, Italy, Romania, Bulgaria; and ones from the island nations of the

Caribbean – Cuba, the Dominican Republic, and Haiti. The Lizards had swallowed down the rest, with the exception of some the Germans had swallowed instead.

A man in a German uniform and a Lizard strolled down the street in earnest conversation. A colored fellow went past them the other way without even turning his head. Yeager chuckled to himself. Twenty years earlier, the local would either have tried to shoot both of them or run like hell. Sophistication had come to Little Rock, whether the Arkansans particularly wanted it or not.

Yeager stopped in a café for a hamburger. Endless years on the road had given him a connoisseur's appreciation of the differences between burgers. This was a good one, better than he was likely to have found in his ballplaying days: meaty, on a fresh, tasty bun, with equally fresh pickle and lettuce and tomato. He enjoyed every bite.

He also enjoyed the beer with which he washed down the burger. It was a local brew, rich and hoppy. With their deliveries disrupted by the Lizard invasion, the national breweries had lost some of their hold on the country. When local beers were good, they made Schlitz and Miller High Life and the rest taste like dishwater. When they were bad, of course, they bore a strong resemblance to horse piss. Bad local beers didn't last. Good ones seemed to be flourishing.

After leaving a dollar on the table, Sam left air-conditioning and went out into the muggy heat again. His face was thoughtful. As far as he was concerned, whoever had attacked the ships of the colonization fleet was a cold-blooded murderer. Whatever the Lizards did when they found out who it was, he wouldn't mind. He might have thought differently had there been any way to drive the Lizards out of the solar system and make sure they didn't come back. Since there wasn't . . .

'We've got to live with them,' he said, and then, more softly, 'I hope to God they nail the bastards.' As far as he was concerned, Lizards were people, too.

5

Mordechai Anielewicz rattled east across Poland on a train. The steam engine threw a black plume of coal smoke into the air; undoubtedly, it had been built before the Germans invaded, let alone the Lizards. The Race seemed horrified that such stinking survivals persisted. But trains moved people and goods more cheaply than Poland's inadequate road network, and so they kept on running.

Sharing the compartment with him were a farmer; a salesman who kept trying to sell his fellow passengers cheese graters, egg slicers, potato peelers, and other cheap metal goods; and a moderately pretty young woman who might have been either Polish or Jewish. Anielewicz kept trying to decide till she got out a couple of stops past Warsaw, but came to no conclusion.

He stayed aboard all the way to Pinsk. The border with the USSR lay just a few kilometers east of the city. The first thing Mordechai did when he got off the train was swat a mosquito. The Pripet Marshes surrounded Pinsk. He sometimes thought every mosquito in the world lived in the marshes. He might have been wrong, though; maybe only some of them lived there, with the rest coming to visit on holidays.

Swatting still, he made for the privies in the station. He'd eaten black bread and drunk tea all the way across Lizard-occupied Poland, and a man could do only so much of that without reaching the bursting point. The privies stank of stale piss. He didn't care. He left them much relieved.

Lizard soldiers prowled the streets of Pinsk. They were not happy Lizards. Twenty years of learning more about Lizards than he'd ever thought he would want to know had taught Anielewicz as much. They stalked along with furious delicacy, like cats that had been soaked with a hose.

He understood their language pretty well, and had long since mastered the art of listening without seeming to. 'If I don't come down with the purple itch or one of these horrible local fungi, it's not because I haven't been squelching through the mud the past four days,' one of them said.

'Truth,' another agreed with an emphatic cough. 'Impossible to do a proper job of patrolling that swamp. We'd need ten times the sensors and twenty times the males to have a chance of doing it right.'

'We have to try,' a third male said. 'If we didn't patrol the paths, who knows how much worse the smuggling would be?'

'Right now, I don't much care,' the first male said. 'I want to get back to the barracks and—' He lifted a claw-tipped hand to his face. His tongue shot out for a moment. The other males' mouths dropped open in laughter. They probably wouldn't have minded a taste of ginger, either.

A lot of the signs in Pinsk were in the Cyrillic alphabet Byelorussians used. Mordechai was less at home with it than he was with the Lizards' script. Some of the signs were in Yiddish. Pinsk had been in the Nazis' hands only a few months before the Lizards landed. The Jews here had had a hard time of it, but not so hard as the ones farther west, who'd lain under the German yoke for two and a half years.

ROZENZWEIG'S BAKERY. That sign was written in Yiddish, Byelorussian, and, as an afterthought, in Polish in letters half the size of those of the other two languages. Anielewicz went in. The good smell of baking bread and cakes and rolls and muffins almost made him fall over. Saliva gushed into his mouth. He reminded himself he hadn't been too hungry before he came inside. Remembering that wasn't easy.

A gray-haired man with a bushy mustache looked up from the bagels he was dusting with poppy seeds. 'You want something?' he asked in Yiddish.

'Yes,' Mordechai said. 'My name is Kaplan. You've got a special order for me in the back, don't you?'

The code phrase wasn't fancy, but it did the job. The baker eyed Anielewicz, then nodded. 'Yeah, it's here,' he said. 'You want to come look it over before you take it home?'

'I think I'd better, don't you?' Anielewicz said. He wondered what the Russians wanted, to have summoned him across Poland to handle it. If it wasn't important, he'd give the NKVD man or whoever his contact was a piece of his mind. He'd dealt with a good many Russians. He knew this one wouldn't care what he did or said. But it would make him feel better.

'Here,' Rozenzweig said. 'Talk. I don't want to know what you're talking about.' He turned and went back to his poppy seeds.

'Nu?' Mordechai asked the fellow sitting in the baker's back room: a nondescript, rather scrawny man not far from his own age, with a thin face and dark, intelligent eyes. *Another Jew,* Anielewicz thought. He'd dealt with a good many who worked for the Soviets. Every one, without exception, acted as a Soviet first and a Jew second if at all.

'Hello, Mordechai. Been a long time, hasn't it?' the man from the USSR asked in Yiddish that sounded as if it came from western Poland, not any part of the Soviet Union.

'Am I supposed to know you?' Anielewicz asked. He did his best to keep track of all the agents he met, but he'd met a lot of them. Every once in a while, he slipped up. He'd stopped worrying about it. He wasn't perfect, no matter how hard he tried to be.

The Soviet laughed and cocked his head to one side. He looked sly, like a man convinced he was smarter than everyone around him. And, where Anielewicz hadn't recognized him before, he did now.

'My God! David Nussboym!' he exclaimed. 'I might have known you'd turn up again.' His mouth hardened. 'Bad pennies usually do.'

'You shipped me off to the gulags to die, you and your collaborationist pals,' Nussboym said. 'I wouldn't be a *tukhus-lekher* for the Nazis, so you got rid of me.'

'You were going to sell us out to the Lizards,' Anielewicz said. 'They might have won the war if you had. Where would we be then?'

They stared at each other with a loathing apparently undimmed since the fighting ended. Nussboym said, 'The camps chew you up and spit you out dead. Russians, Jews, Lizards . . . it doesn't matter. Some people get by, though. The first denunciation I signed, I was sick for a week afterwards. The second left the taste of ashes in my mouth. But do you know what? After a while, you don't care. If you get the better rations; if you get the other bastard's job; if, after a while, you get out of the camp – you don't care any more.'

'I believe *you* don't,' Mordechai said, looking at him as he might have looked at a cockroach in his salad.

Nussboym looked back steadily, without showing he was insulted, with a small, superior smile, as if to say, *You haven't been where I have. You don't know what you're talking about.* And that was true. Anielewicz thanked God it was true. But he still thought that, even in the gulag, he would have found some way to fight back. Some people must have managed it.

He shrugged. It didn't really matter. 'So what do you want?' he asked harshly.

'I want you to know' – by which Nussboym meant his Russian bosses wanted Anielewicz to know –' the Germans were the ones who blew up the ships from the Lizards' colonization fleet.'

'You brought me all the way over here to tell me that?' Mordechai didn't laugh at him, but that took an effort. 'You

sneaked over the border to tell me that?' He was sure Nussboym hadn't crossed officially. Had Nussboym done so, they
wouldn't have met in Rozenzweig's bakery. 'Why would it
matter to me, even if it's true?'

'Oh, it's true.' David Nussboym sounded very sure. Of
course, his job was to sound sure. He would be nothing but
a recording, mouthing the words his bosses – NKVD men,
probably – had impressed on him.

'I have contacts with the Nazis, too,' Anielewicz said.

'Of course you do.' Now heat came into Nussboym's voice –
he was speaking for himself here, not for his bosses. 'Why do
you think I couldn't stomach working with you twenty years
ago?'

'So you work for Molotov, who got into bed with Hitler and
blew out the light – on Poland,' Mordechai said, and had the
dubious pleasure of watching Nussboym's sallow features
flush. He went on, 'The Nazis say Russia did it.'

'And what would you expect?' Nussboym returned. 'But we
have the evidence. I could give it to you—'

'Why would you?' Anielewicz asked. 'If you've got it, give it
to the Lizards.'

Nussboym coughed a couple of times. 'For some reason, the
Lizards don't always trust things they get straight from us.'

'Because you lie all the damned time, just like the Nazis?'
Anielewicz suggested. David Nussboym did not dignify that
with a reply; Mordechai hadn't really expected that he would.
The question he'd asked was a serious one, though, and
Nussboym hadn't answered it, either. That meant Anielewicz
had to do some thinking on his own. 'So you want the Lizards
to get this from us, do you?'

'They would be likelier to believe you than us, yes,' Nussboym said.

'Well, what if they do?' Anielewicz knew he was thinking out
loud; if his old rival didn't like it, too bad. 'That might embroil
them against the *Reich* – probably would, as a matter of fact.
You'd like that, wouldn't you?' Without waiting for an an-

swer, he went on, 'And if they did go at it, the Nazis would do their best to wipe Poland off the face of the Earth. I thought Molotov liked having a buffer between him and the swastika.'

'I have not spoken with him about that,' Nussboym said.

Did that mean he had spoken with Molotov about other things? How important a cog in the machine had he become? How important a cog did he want Anielewicz to think he'd become? How much of a difference was there between those last two?

Those were interesting questions. They were also beside the point. Anielewicz had no trouble seeing what the point was: 'You don't care what the *Reich* does to Poland, because you want to make the Lizards jump on the Nazis with both feet. If they do, the *Reich* won't be strong enough to worry you any more.'

He watched Nussboym closely. The skinny little man hadn't given away much when Anielewicz knew him before. He gave away nothing whatever now; he might have been carved from stone. But his very immobility was an answer of sorts.

Nodding, Mordechai said, 'I'm afraid you're going to have to do your own dirty work on this one.'

Nussboym raised an eyebrow. 'Do you mean to tell me you don't believe the Nazis did it?'

Anielewicz shook his head. 'As a matter of fact, I do believe it. Even with Hitler dead, they're crazier than your bosses are. What I don't believe is that you've got any evidence to prove they did it. If the Lizards haven't been able to come up with any, how are you supposed to?'

'The Lizards are very good with science and machines and instruments,' Nussboym answered. 'When it comes to people – no. We do that better.'

He was probably right. The Lizards had improved with people as time passed, but they weren't good. They'd probably never be good. They weren't people, after all. Even so . . . 'You'll have to do your own dirty work,' Anielewicz repeated.

142

Nussboym studied him in turn, then got up and left the bakery without another word.

There were times when Straha wondered whether the Tosevites who lived in the not-empire called the United States and who, for a reason he'd never grasped, styled themselves Americans had any more sense when it came to larger matters. Reporters were a prime example. These days, his telephone rang constantly.

'Straha here,' the ex-shiplord would answer in his own language. He had, in fact, learned a fair amount of English. He used the language of Home as a testing gauge. His working assumption was that no one ignorant of it would be able to tell him anything worth hearing.

Some Big Uglies, hearing the Race's hisses and pops, would hang up. That suited him fine. Some would try to go on in English. When they did, he would hang up. That also suited him fine.

But, even when reporters did know and use the language of the Race, they used it in a Tosevite fashion and for Tosevite purposes. 'I greet you, Shiplord,' one of them said after Straha had announced himself. 'I am Calvin Herter. I write for the *New York Times*. I would like to ask you a few questions, if I may.'

'Go ahead,' Straha said. Herter spoke his language fairly well – not so well as a real expert like Major Yeager, but well enough. 'Ask. I will answer as best I can.' It would pass the time.

He regretted saying that a moment later, for the Big Ugly asked the same question all the others had: 'Which not-empire do you think attacked the colonization fleet, and why?'

Having answered, *How should I know, when I am not a Tosevite?* any number of times already, Straha felt mischief stir in him. Had his character not had that streak, he wouldn't have tried to overthrow Atvar and he likely wouldn't have fled from the conquest fleet to the Tosevites. *And I would be better off today,* he thought, but not till after he had answered, 'Why, this one, of course – the United States.'

'Really?' Herter said. 'Why do you think that?'

'It stands to reason,' Straha answered. 'Your not-empire could hurt the Race more easily than either the *Reich* or the Soviet Union, because fewer folk would expect you to try it.'

He heard faint scratching sounds as the reporter wrote that down; recorders were less common here than among the Race. 'Really?' the Big Ugly repeated. 'Well, that is something, by the Emperor! That will give me a front-page headline every other newspaper in the not-empire will envy. Let me ask you some more questions about this. Why—?'

'Wait,' Straha said. He did not care to hear the reporter swearing by the Emperor. The Tosevite cared nothing about the Emperor, and was probably using the only oath in the language of the Race he knew – and the Emperor assuredly cared nothing about the Tosevite. But that was only a detail. Straha asked, 'You would print this in your newspaper?'

'Of course,' Herter answered. 'This will be the biggest story since the attack on the fleet.'

'But I have accused the government of this not-empire of perpetrating that attack,' Straha said, wondering if the Big Ugly could speak the language of the Race himself but had trouble understanding what he heard in it. Straha's English was sometimes like that.

But Herter did understand him. 'Oh, yes,' the reporter said brightly. 'That is what makes it such a big story. Now my next question is—'

'Wait,' Straha said again. 'The government of this not-empire would never allow you to print such a story.'

'Of course they will,' Herter said. 'This is not the *Reich*. This is not the Soviet Union. Here, we have freedom of the press.'

The phrase was in the language of the Race, but alien to it in spirit. Straha had heard it before, of course, but never in such a context as this: 'Your not-emperor would allow you to print a story that criticizes him? I find it hard to believe.'

'It is truth,' Herter said with an emphatic cough. 'We are a free not-empire. We are almost the only free not-empire left on the face of this planet. We have no censors telling us what goes in the newspapers and what does not.'

'None?' Straha had not really imagined the American passion for doing exactly as one pleased went so far as that.

'None,' the reporter answered. 'We did during the fighting, but we got rid of them again after that.'

'Why would your government let ordinary males and females criticize it?' Straha asked in honest bewilderment. 'What good does it do? What good do you imagine it does?' He could see none, not even turning both mental eye turrets in the direction of the problem.

But Calvin Herter could, and did: 'How better to make sure the government does what the males and females of the United States want it to do than by giving them the right to criticize freely?'

'Governments do not do what males and females want them to do.' Straha spoke as if quoting a law of nature. As far as he was concerned, he *was* quoting a law of nature. 'Governments do what governments want to do. How could it be otherwise, when they hold the power?'

'You have lived in America for a long time,' Herter said. 'How have you lived here so long without getting a better idea of how the government of the United States works?'

'You count snouts,' Straha said. 'Whichever side can persuade the most snouts to join it prevails. It does not have to be clever. It does not have to be wise. It only has to be popular.'

'There may be something to that,' Herter admitted. 'But with any other way to run a government, a policy does not have to be clever or wise or popular. There is the drawback the Race faces – and the Nazis and Communists, too.'

Underestimating a Big Ugly's wits rarely paid. The Tosevites were not stupid and, whatever else one said about them, were inspired argufiers. But Straha knew he was on solid ground in this dispute, and fired back: 'Often policies that are clever or wise are not popular. A snoutcounting government cannot use them, because not enough snouts will line up behind them. This is the drawback the United States faces.'

'No system is perfect,' Herter said.

'Our system is perfect – for us,' Straha said. 'I do not know that it would be perfect for Tosevites. But I do not know that it would not be, either. I am willing to believe – I am more than willing to believe – that Tosevites have yet to establish a social system perfect for themselves.' He let his mouth fall open at the neatness with which he had squelched Herter.

But, like so many other Big Uglies, Herter refused to stay squelched. 'If we are so imperfect, Shiplord, how is it that we, with our short history, fought the Race to a standstill even though you have a long history?'

Straha started to slap him down for his insolence: his first, automatic, response, as it would have been for any self-respecting male of the Race. Before he spoke, though, he realized what most other males of the Race would not have – the Big Ugly had a point. With a sigh, he answered, 'Scholars of the Race – and perhaps Tosevite scholars as well – will be studying that question for thousands of years to come. I do not believe it to be one with a simple answer.'

'You are probably right about that,' the reporter said. 'Now, can we return to the question I asked you before: Why do you believe the United States was the not-empire that exploded the ships from the colonization fleet?'

He was serious. Straha would not have believed it, and still did not want to believe it. But he had no choice but to believe it. That being so, he said, 'I do not really believe that. I find it highly unlikely. I wanted to place a biting pest on your tailstump, to watch you leap in the air when its proboscis pierced your skin. Do you understand what I am saying?'

'I think so,' Herter replied. 'In English, we call that a practical joke.' The two key words were in his own language.

'A practical joke,' Straha repeated. Thinking back on it,

he'd heard Sam Yeager use the phrase a couple of times. If anything, the Big Uglies seemed fonder of the thing than the Race was. He went on, 'Yes, I suppose that is what it was. I did not imagine you would publish it, so I said it to see what you would do.'

'Not funny, Shiplord. Not funny at all,' Calvin Herter said with another emphatic cough. 'You might have touched off a war between the United States and the Race. That goes too far for a practical joke.'

'I suppose so,' Straha said, at the same time wondering whether a war between the United States and the Race – one in which the Race wrecked the United States, of course – would be enough to allow him to return to the society of his own kind, assuming he survived it.

He had his doubts. As long as Atvar lived, nothing was likely to allow him to return to the society of his own kind. When the fleetlord got a grudge, he kept it.

Maybe Atvar would get killed in a war between the United States and the Race. As far as Straha was concerned, that would improve the Race's chances of winning such a war. Atvar would have been the ideal fleetlord for the conquest of the Tosev 3 the Race thought it would find. He was careful, methodical, and probably could have completed the job without losing a male. As things were . . .

As things were, Straha realized Herter had said something, but he had no idea what it was. 'Please repeat that,' he said. Speaking with another male of the Race, he would have been embarrassed. To a certain degree, he was embarrassed anyhow, but only to a certain degree.

'I asked whether, once the colonization fleet lands, you will be glad to have females with you once more,' the reporter said.

'In the sense that their arrival means we will be able to plant new generations of the Race on Tosev 3, yes,' Straha replied. 'In the sense that we will be wild for mating, as you Tosevites might be, of course not. Our nature is different.' *For which I am heartily glad,* he added to himself.

'You of the Race miss a lot of the spark in life, or so it seems to me,' Herter said.

'You Tosevites let your mating habits drive you wild, or so it seems to me,' Straha replied. 'I am content – more than content – to be as I am.'

'Me, too,' Herter said with an emphatic cough.

'I believe you,' Straha said. He wondered what sort of progress the Race's scientists had made since his defection toward unraveling the connection between the Big Uglies' sexual patterns and their society. Signals intercepts and conversations with other defectors and prisoners who had stayed in the USA did not tell him everything he wanted to know. He asked, 'Have you any further questions?'

'Shiplord, I have not,' the reporter answered. 'And if I did, how would I know you were telling the truth?'

Straha's mouth fell open. 'How would you know?' he echoed. 'You would not. That is part of the risk you run when you speak with me.'

To his surprise, Calvin Herter let out several yips of barking Big Ugly laughter. 'Shiplord, we will make a Tosevite of you yet,' he said. Straha hung up in some indignation. The reporter had no business insulting him that way.

Kassquit put on the artificial fingerclaws that made handling the Race's equipment so much easier for her. She turned on the computer terminal in her chamber, then turned off the overhead light. Sitting there in the darkness, her own body hidden from her eyes, she could pretend for a while that she was a female of the Race like any other female of the Race.

News bulletins told her the Race still did not know which Tosevite faction had dared raise its hand against the ships of the colonization fleet. 'Punish them all,' Kassquit whispered fiercely. 'They all deserve it. Of course they deserve it. They are Big Uglies.'

Her hands folded into fists in her anger at the natives of Tosev 3. As they did so, the artificial fingerclaws poked the soft, smooth flesh of her palms. She let out a long, misery-filled sigh. Even in the darkness, she could not escape what she was. Her flesh was the flesh of the natives of the world below.

'I cannot help that,' she said in the language of the Race, the only language she knew. 'I may be flesh of their flesh, but I am not spirit of their spirit. When they die, they will be gone. They will be gone forever. When I die, spirits of Emperors past will cherish me.'

She cast down her eyes in reverence for the Emperors who still watched over the Race, even though so many were tens of millennia dead. She also dared hope her spirit, when at last it was freed from the unfortunate form it bore, would resemble those of other females of the Race. Even if this flesh was not what it should be, surely no one and nothing could condemn her to be different forever.

She had sometimes thought of ending her life, to escape the prison of the body she was forced to wear. But she knew her existence helped the Race learn more about the perfidious Tosevites. If she ended it prematurely, she was all too likely to forfeit the good opinion of Emperors past. She dared not take the risk. If she were to be no more than a Big Ugly even after she was dead . . . how could she be expected to endure such a misfortune throughout eternity?

Of itself, her right hand strayed toward the joining of her legs. She noticed only when one of those fingerclaws scraped the skin of her inner thigh. She took the fingerclaws off that hand. The sole refuge she had from a difficult world was the sensation she could evoke from her Tosevite body.

But before she was well begun, the speaker beside her closed door emitted a hiss, the signal the Race used when someone wanted to enter. She jerked her hand away and flipped on the lights. 'Who is it?' she asked, removing the fingerclaws from her left hand as well.

'Ttomalss,' came the answer, as she had expected. He did do his best to treat her as if she were a proper part of the Race, for which she respected and admired him hardly less than she did the Emperor back on Home. When she was a hatchling, he had come and gone as he pleased. Now that she approached adulthood, though, he used her with all due courtesy: 'May I enter?'

'Of course,' she answered, and put one fingerclaw back on to touch the control that slid the door open. She folded herself into the posture of respect. 'I greet you, superior sir.' As he did not usually do, Ttomalss had someone with him. Kassquit remained in the posture of respect. 'And I greet you as well, superior female.'

'I greet you, Kassquit,' Felless said. 'I greet you indeed. It is good to see you again. You will be very valuable to my investigations.'

'I am glad to hear it, Senior Researcher,' Kassquit replied. 'Being useful to the Race is my goal and my purpose in life.'

Felless turned both eye turrets toward Ttomalss. 'Truly, she speaks the language as well as one could expect a Tosevite to do,' she said, 'and you have trained her well in the subordination due her superiors.'

Kassquit hid her anger. She did not like the way Felless talked about her as if she were not there, or as if she were too stupid to understand anything that was said about her. She glanced toward Ttomalss – he was not so far away from Felless that she had to embarrass herself by turning her whole head to do it – hoping he would reprove the researcher fresh from Home.

He said, 'I thank you, Senior Researcher. The effort involved has been considerable, but I agree that the result has been worthwhile.'

That was praise for Kassquit, if she chose to take it the right way. She was not inclined to take it the right way, not now. She did not want Ttomalss, who had raised her from earliest hatchlinghood, to speak of her as if she were only an experimental animal. He had always been her buffer, the one who eased the strain between her and other members of the Race.

Was that what he was doing now? Or did he really think of her as nothing more than a creature he had taught to imitate some of the ways of the Race? Did that not betray the bond between superiors and subordinates, the bond on account of which superiors deserved deference?

Oblivious to her annoyance, oblivious to her worries, Ttomalss pointed to the computer screen and said to Felless, 'As you see, she takes a keen interest in the events of the day.'

Kassquit coughed, trying to remind Ttomalss and Felless that she was there, that they were, in fact, standing in her chamber. Neither of them paid any attention to her. 'And what is her perspective on these events?' Felless asked Ttomalss.

She might have asked Kassquit. She did not. Ttomalss might have let Kassquit speak for herself. He did not. He answered for her: 'Why, the perspective of a female of the Race, of course.'

'Not the perspective of her own kind in any way?' Felless said. 'How interesting. What an excellent job you have done.'

'I thank you, Senior Researcher,' Ttomalss said. Kassquit recognized the tones of a male seeking favor.

At last, Felless deigned to notice her again. 'Since you have been studying the events of the day, what is your view on which band of Tosevites carried out this murderous attack against us?'

'My view, superior female, is that it matters very little, because all the Tosevite not-empires are bloodthirsty and murderous,' Kassquit replied. 'My view is that they should all be chastised, no matter which of them actually did it. That would discourage them from doing such a thing again.' She eyed Felless with something less than warmth. 'Only luck that your ship was not one of those targeted.' By her tone, she meant, *Only bad luck*.

Felless did not read that tone accurately. 'Only luck, yes,' she agreed. 'We are too vulnerable to these bloodthirsty maniacs, as you said; far too vulnerable.'

Thanks to his greater experience with her, Ttomalss did recognize the tone. After a series of splutters, he said, 'Indeed. It is most fortunate.'

Still feeling irritable, Kassquit eyed Felless and asked, 'Superior female, why did you seek my opinion of what the Tosevites have done, when I have never met a Big Ugly and so can have only limited knowledge of the differences, if any, among their various groups?'

Again, Felless was slower on the uptake than she might have been. She began, 'But you are a—'

'I am as much a female of the Race as I can possibly be,' Kassquit broke in. 'This is, I daresay, more than certain other individuals can claim.'

Now Felless could not ignore the insult. Neither could Ttomalss, who said, 'Kassquit . . .' in warning tones he had not used since she was a hatchling.

'What?' she flung back at him. Mortifyingly, her eyes began to fill with moisture, an emotional response built into her Tosevite body but alien to the Race. Sometimes the water would even spill down her face. By blinking rapidly – all she could do, since she had no nictitating membranes – she managed to keep that from happening now, though her nasal passages began to fill with mucus. 'If I cannot receive my due from this female, if I cannot receive my due from you, from whom shall I receive it? The fleetlord?'

She had not been guilty of such an outburst since she was a hatchling. Back then, her eruptions had been pure emotion. This one had logic behind it, too. Ttomalss and Felless both stared at her in astonishment. At last, Felless said, 'I think I may have been guilty of several false assumptions here. I apologize, Kassquit. You are more one of us and less a Tosevite than I had believed.'

'Ah,' Ttomalss said, finally understanding. 'Yes, Kassquit is indeed as much a female of the Race as she can be.'

'I wish you would have treated me as a female of the Race,' Kassquit said to both of them.

Felless quietly quivered, which meant she was angry at being criticized. Her anger bothered Kassquit not at all. Kassquit was angry, too, and felt she had every right to be. Felless had treated her as if she were somewhere between a half-wit and an animal. And Ttomalss had not done much better.

Had Ttomalss quivered in anger, too, Kassquit would have despaired. But the male who had raised her said, 'The point of this long exercise is, after all, to learn how much like one of us she can become. Since she has become so very much like us, we would be mistaken to treat her as if she were an uncultured Tosevite.'

'Truth,' Felless said, and then, with as much good grace as she could muster, 'I truly do apologize, Kassquit. You are indeed more nearly of the Race than I had imagined you could be, as I told you just now. In a way, this is good, for it says there is indeed a fine chance of accommodating Tosevites within the Empire. In another way, though, it makes matters more difficult for my research. You are not a good subject; you are too much like one of us to make a good subject.'

'I can only be what I am,' Kassquit said. 'I wish I could be like a female of the Race in all things. Since I cannot, I can only strive to be as much like a female of the Race as this body permits.'

Before, Felless' apologies had seemed grudging. Now the researcher said, 'Your words do you great credit. Surely the Emperor would be proud if he could listen to them with his own hearing diaphragms.'

'I thank you, superior female,' Kassquit said softly, and cast down her eyes. They were small and absurdly immobile, but they were what she had. Everything she had was at the service of the Emperor, at the service of the Empire.

'And I thank you, Kassquit, for what you have taught me today,' Felless said. One of her eye turrets turned toward Ttomalss and then toward the doorway. Ttomalss took the hint. The two of them left together, discussing Tosevite psychology.

As soon as they were gone, Kassquit darkened the chamber again. She sat in front of the computer screen, listening to the male there talking about preparations for landing some of the

153

ships of the colonization fleet. As long as she just listened to him and didn't think about herself or look at her soft, scaleless body, she could pretend she was fully a part of the Race . . . until her right hand wandered toward her private parts once more.

Smoke rose from the Tosevite city outside of which Nesseref intended to land her shuttlecraft. From what she'd seen, smoke often rose from Tosevite cities. Instead of nuclear energy and clean-burning hydrogen, the Big Uglies used the combustion of an astonishing variety of noxious substances to provide energy.

But, even for a Tosevite city, this one showed an uncommon amount of smoke. The Big Uglies were not merely burning their usual nasty fuels. They were burning a large stretch of their city, too, doing their best to burn it down around the males of the Race who occupied it. The more Nesseref saw of Tosev 3 and the Big Uglies, the gladder she was that she hadn't been part of the conquest fleet. They hadn't had an easy time of it, hadn't and still didn't.

'Shuttlecraft, this is Cairo Ground Control,' a male said. 'Your trajectory is on track for landing.'

'Acknowledged, Cairo Ground Control,' Nesseref said, and then, 'Tell me, will the site where I land be safe?'

She meant the question sardonically, which only proved she was new to Tosev 3. The male on the ground answered in all seriousness: 'It should be safe enough. We will have helicopter gunships patrolling at a radius to make small-arms or mortar attacks unlikely.'

'Thank you so much.' Nesseref meant that sardonically, too, but in an altogether different way. 'How have you males on the ground managed to stay alive since you got here?'

She meant that to be sympathetic. She thought it was sympathetic. But it was not sympathetic enough to suit the male on the ground, who replied, 'A lot of us have not,' and underlined with an emphatic cough how many hadn't.

Then she stopped worrying about fine shades of meaning, for black puffs of smoke began appearing out of nowhere in the air around her. A couple of clangs and bangs announced metal fragments ricocheting from or piercing the skin of the shuttlecraft. 'Ground Control, I am under attack!' she said urgently. She couldn't maneuver. All she could do was hope none of those bursting projectiles hit the shuttlecraft squarely.

The male with whom she'd been speaking cursed. 'The local Tosevites cannot build these weapons for themselves – they are too ignorant. But they are excellent smugglers, and the not-empires that can manufacture antiaircraft guns are more than happy to bring them in and make our lives more miserable than they were already.'

'I do not care about any of that,' Nesseref said furiously. 'All I want is not to get shot down. Make them stop firing at me!'

'We are trying to do that.' The male sounded perfectly calm. Part of that calm doubtless came because no one was shooting at him. And part was that he had done this before. Nesseref wondered how many times he had done it before, and if the Big Uglies had ever succeeded in shooting down a shuttlecraft. No sooner had that thought occurred to her than she wished it hadn't.

Regardless of whether the Big Uglies shot her down, she had to pay attention to what she was doing or she would end up killing herself. A fingerclaw stabbed a control. Her braking rockets lit, pressing her against her couch.

The Big Uglies had been tracking her descent by eye. When it slowed, they fired several rounds along the path she would have taken, then got her range again. She hissed something pungent. There she was, hanging in the sky like a fruit on a tree branch, all but shouting at the Tosevites to knock her down.

But the shellbursts stopped coming. She noticed new smoke rising from the edge of the city, smoke with flame at the base. She set the shuttlecraft down, as smoothly as if no one on Tosev 3 had ever heard of antiaircraft guns.

When I have time, she thought, *I will have a case of the fidgets. I do not have time right now.* She said that to herself over and over, till she eventually began to believe it.

As she descended from the shuttlecraft, a landcruiser pulled up alongside it. 'Get in,' a male called from the turret. 'We shall take you to the administration building. If you go in this, you'll make it there.'

'By the Emperor!' she said, and was almost too angry to lower her eye turrets. 'I thought the fighting was supposed to be over.' She scrambled down from the shuttlecraft and then up and into the landcruiser.

She was even more cramped inside the traveling fortress than she had been coming down from the *13th Emperor Makkakap*. Once she was settled as well as she could be, the landcruiser commander said, 'Everything was quiet – well, pretty quiet – till the colonization fleet got here. That addled the Big Uglies' eggs good and proper.'

'Why?' Nesseref asked. 'They must have known we were coming.'

'Oh, they did,' the landcruiser commander said. 'They knew, but they did not fret or plan much. They are not forethought-ful, not the way we are.'

'I guess not,' Nesseref said. After a moment, she brightened. 'Then we should not have much trouble figuring out which Big Uglies gave these Big Uglies the cannon they used to shoot at me.'

'No,' the male said regretfully. 'That is not right. The Tosevites are not forethoughtful, but they have their own kind of cleverness. Each not-empire will often give away guns it does not manufacture, to make it harder for us to blame outrages on any one group.'

Before Nesseref could answer, something clanged off the metal-and-ceramic hide of the landcruiser. 'What was that?' she asked nervously.

'Only a stone,' the male said. 'I ignore those. The Tosevites really pitch fits when we shoot them up for anything as small as a thrown stone. These Egyptian Big Uglies are very touchy that way.'

156

Nesseref asked, 'If this is what the Big Uglies give you, how did you stand the time between when you got here and when the colonization fleet finally came?'

'As I told you, we did not have too much to do after the fighting stopped, not until your fleet arrived.' The landcruiser commander paused to peer out through the periscopes mounted inside his cupola, then resumed: 'Besides, we would have been even more bored if Tosev 3 had been the sort of place we thought it was when we came here. Then the Big Uglies would not have been able to do anything but throw stones at us.'

'You enjoy fighting?' Nesseref said in some surprise.

'I am a soldier. I was chosen in a Soldiers' Time.' Sure enough, the voice of the male from the conquest fleet held pride. 'I have the honor of serving the Emperor by adding a new world to those he rules.'

'So you do.' As far as Nesseref was concerned, the landcruiser commander and his comrades were welcome to that honor. The Race had no standing army, only documentation on how to create one in time of need. Everything had gone as planned when the Rabotevs were conquered, and then again when the Hallessi became part of the Empire. On Tosev 3, not everything had gone as planned. On Tosev 3, as far as Nesseref could see, nothing had gone as planned. As if to underscore that, another rock crashed against the landcruiser's armored skin.

'It is a good thing we did not wait another few hundred years to start this conquest,' the landcruiser commander said, taking the conversation in a new direction, 'or the Big Uglies might have come to Home instead. We talk about that a lot here. It would have been very bad. It would mean all the time would become a Soldiers' Time.'

'That would be a change,' Nesseref said – to a male or female of the Race, sufficient condemnation in and of itself.

The landcruiser clanked to a halt. Over the intercom, the driver announced, 'Superior sir, superior female, we are here.'

'Good.' The commander opened the turret hatch, turning one eye turret toward Nesseref as he did. 'You should be fairly safe inside this compound. Once you are inside the building itself, you will be as safe as you can be in Cairo. I will await you and your passenger and return you to the shuttlecraft.'

'I thank you,' Nesseref said, and got out of the landcruiser. She hurried toward the building. If she had to be anywhere in Cairo, the safest place in the city struck her as a good choice. She was no soldier. She had no desire to make a Soldiers' Time – by its very nature, a temporary part of the Race's history – into a permanent condition. Idly, she wondered if the Big Uglies had permanent Soldiers' Times. Could even they be so foolishly wasteful of resources?

When she got inside, a male at a desk read her body paint and asked, 'What do you require, Shuttlecraft Pilot?'

'I seek Pshing, adjutant to Atvar, fleetlord of the conquest fleet,' she replied. 'I am ordered to bring him into the presence of Reffet, fleetlord of the colonization fleet.' Her opinion was that Pshing and Reffet could have conferred perfectly well by radio or video link. No one, however, had asked her opinion.

'I will inform him that you have arrived,' the male said, and spoke into a microphone in front of his snout. He turned an eye in Nesseref's direction. 'He tells me to tell you he will be here directly.'

Maybe *directly* meant something different for Pshing from what it meant to Nesseref. In her view, he took his time. She could not tell him so, not when a word from him whispered onto Atvar or Reffet's hearing diaphragm might blight her chances to advance. Such things were not supposed to happen, but they did. 'Let us go,' she said crisply when he did arrive, 'assuming, that is, that the shuttlecraft remains intact.'

She thought that might faze him, but it didn't. 'The odds favor us,' he said. 'Even with smuggled weapons, the local Big Uglies are not outstanding soldiers. Some of them are suicidally courageous, which can make them difficult to defend against, but raw ferocity has its limits.'

'I suppose so,' she said, and then vented a little more exasperation: 'Is this travel truly necessary, superior sir?'

'It is,' Pshing declared. 'The Tosevites have grown altogether too good at intercepting and decrypting our communications.' Nesseref sighed silently; they'd used the same excuse in Warsaw. Pshing went on, 'Details as to when and where ships from the colonization fleet are to land must for obvious reasons remain secure until the last possible moment.'

'Truth,' Nesseref said, however little she wanted to. 'Very well, then – we had best be off, to take advantage of the next launch window.'

The landcruiser was even more crowded with two passengers than with one. The gunner kept bumping into Nesseref, which did nothing to improve her temper. More stones thudded into the machine as it made its slow way through Cairo.

Nothing had happened to the shuttlecraft while Nesseref was gone. Praising Emperors past, she lifted on schedule and delivered Pshing to his meeting with Reffet.

When she opened her belt pouch in her own quarters aboard the *13th Emperor Makkakap* later that day, she found a small vial that hadn't been in there before. It was half full of finely ground brownish powder, and had a tiny note stuck to it. *A couple of tastes for when you get bored,* the note said.

Ginger, Nesseref thought. *It has to be more ginger.* She supposed the landcruiser driver had slipped the Tosevite spice in there. It hadn't got in there by itself, that was certain. It was, she knew, very much against regulations, even if males of the conquest fleet kept giving it to her. But she wasn't bored right now. She thought about throwing it away, then didn't. She hadn't thrown away the first vial, either. She might get bored one of these days. Who could say?

Rance Auerbach wondered whether he hated the Lizards worse for wrecking his life or for patching him up after they'd shot him as full of holes as a colander. People said both shooting the enemy and caring for him if you captured him were the right ways to go about making war. He wondered if any of those people had ever gone through close to twenty years of continuous pain. Better he should have bled out on the Colorado prairie southeast of Denver than put up with this.

But he hadn't bled out, which meant he still had the chance to pay the Lizards back for the unfavor they'd done by saving his life. 'And I will get even with them, if it's the last thing I ever do,' he muttered. Getting even with them as the last thing he ever did struck him as poetic justice. He would die happy if he could die knowing he'd hit them a good lick.

He sat down at the kitchen table, the closest thing to a desk his miserable little apartment boasted. His leg complained when he bent it to sit. It would complain again, a little louder, when he got up once more. He shifted on the chair a couple of times, and it half settled down.

He resumed the letter he'd begun the night before, writing, *And so I say again that I hope the Lizards never do figure out who blew up their ships. Let them fear all of us. Let them know we are all dangerous. And if they retaliate, kick 'em in the balls again.* He looked it over, nodded, and scrawled his signature. Then he put it in an envelope and stuck on an overseas airmail stamp.

'Let's hear it for airmail,' he said, and clapped his hands together a couple of times. Telephones and telegrams and telexes were too easy to monitor. The mail, though, the mail went through. Nobody would bother opening one envelope among hundreds, thousands, tens of thousands.

He started another letter, this one in German. He'd learned the language at West Point, then promptly forgotten it. Over the years, though, he'd brought it out of mothballs again, at least as far as reading and writing went. He knew a lot of people – classmates, men with whom he'd served when he could serve – and they knew people, too, people all over the world.

'Krauts better not hear me tryin' to talk their lingo, though,' he said with a raspy chuckle. German and a Texas twang hadn't gone together back at the Military Academy. They still didn't: even less so now.

But he understood how the grammar worked, and he knew what he wanted to say. He also knew his correspondent would agree with him when he said the same sorts of things he had to his English friend. Yeah, the Nazis were bastards, but they had the right idea about the Lizards.

'Kick 'em in the balls,' he said aloud. 'They don't even have balls to kick.'

The colonization fleet would be bringing lady Lizards. You couldn't very well have a colony – even the Lizards couldn't – without both sexes being there. Rance imagined a Lizard in a frilly bra and fishnet stockings held up by a garter belt. He laughed like a loon, so hard that he had trouble getting enough air into his poor, battered chest cavity. He knew the Lizards didn't really work that way; when the females weren't in season, the males didn't care. But it made a hell of a funny picture just the same.

He was addressing the envelope to his German associate when the telephone rang. It was back in the bedroom; getting to it took a while. Sometimes it would stop ringing just before he made it to the nightstand. He hated that. Even more, though, he hated making the long, painful trip – any trip for him was long and painful – to have a salesman try to get him to buy a new electric razor or a set of encyclopedias. He cussed those bastards up one side and down the other.

This time, the phone kept ringing long enough for him to answer it. 'Hello?'

'Rance?' A woman's voice. He raised an eyebrow. He didn't get that many calls from women. 'That you, Rance?'

'Who is this?' Whoever she was, she didn't come from Texas. Her voice held the flat, harsh tones of the Midwestern farm belt. And then, even though he hadn't heard it in more than fifteen years, he recognized it, or thought he did. 'Christ!' he said, and sweat sprang out on his forehead that had nothing to do with either heat or pain – not physical pain, anyhow. 'Penny?'

'It's not the Easter Bunny, Rance; I'll tell you that right

now,' she answered. Now that Auerbach heard more than four words from her, he wondered how he'd known who she was by her voice. It spoke of a lot of cigarettes, a lot of booze, and probably a lot of hard times. She asked, 'How are you doing, Rance?'

'Not too goddamn well,' he answered. The telephone trembled in his hand. If it hadn't been for Penny Summers, he might not have lived after the Lizards shot him up. They'd known each other before the Lizards' last big push toward Denver. The Race had scooped her up in Lamar, Colorado, before they wounded and captured him. Along with helping to keep him alive, she'd found ways to improve his morale no male nurse could have used. They'd stayed together for a while after the fighting ended, and then . . . 'How much trouble are you in, Penny?'

Her breath caught. 'How in God's name did you know I'm in trouble?'

He laughed again, pulling pain and mirth from his chest at the same time. 'If you weren't, darling, you sure as hell wouldn't be calling me.'

That should have struck her funny, too, but it didn't. 'Well, I'd be a liar if I said you was wrong.' Every word she spoke seemed chiseled from stone. Auerbach had grown very used to the lazy sounds of Texas English. Hearing those Kansas r's again made the hair prickle up at the back of his neck.

He knew he had to say something. 'Where are you calling from?' he asked. The question was innocuous enough that he didn't have to deal with the larger one of whether he hated her for helping to keep him alive.

'I'm in Fort Worth,' she answered.

'Thought so,' he said. 'The connection's too good for a long-distance call. What do you want me to do?'

'I don't know.' She sounded harried and worn. 'I don't know if anybody can do anything. But I didn't know who else to call.'

'That's too bad,' Rance said. If, after so much time, she

hadn't been able to find anybody on whom she could rely . . . 'You're as big a loser as I am,' he blurted. He wouldn't have said that to many people, no matter how down-and-out they might have seemed, not after he'd made the acquaintance of the Lizard machine gun. But the Lizards had blasted her father to red rags right before her eyes, and she didn't sound as if she'd gone uphill since.

'Maybe I am,' she said. 'Can I see you? I didn't want to just knock on your door, but—' She broke off, then resumed: 'Christ, I hate this.' She'd come a long way from the farm girl she'd been before the Lizards swept through western Kansas, and most of it down roads she wouldn't have dreamt of traveling then.

More than anything else, that bitterness decided Auerbach. 'Yeah, come on ahead,' he said: like called to like. 'You know where I'm staying?'

'You're in the phone book – if I found your number, I found your address, too,' Penny answered, which left him feeling foolish. 'Thanks, Rance. I'll be there in a little bit.' The line went dead.

Auerbach listened to the dial tone for a few seconds, then hung up the phone. 'Jesus Christ,' he said, with more reverence than he was accustomed to using. In similar tones, he went on, 'What the hell have I gone and done?'

He made his slow, creaky way out into the living room, where he stopped and looked around. The place wasn't in the worst shape in the world. It wasn't in the best, though, nor anywhere close. He shrugged. Penny didn't sound as if she was in the best shape, either. And if she didn't like the way he kept house, she could damn well leave.

Hobbling into the kitchen, he checked there, too. Bread on the counter, cold cuts in the refrigerator. He could make Penny sandwiches. If it meant he lived on oatmeal for a bit, till he had a hot day at the poker table or his next pension check came, then it did, that was all. And he had whiskey. He had plenty of whiskey. He didn't need to check to be sure of that.

He waited. 'Hurry up and wait,' he murmured, a phrase from his Army days. It still held truth. His heart thudded in his chest: more in the way of nerves than he'd known in years. He sat down. Maybe she wouldn't come. Maybe she'd get lost. Maybe she'd change her mind, or maybe she was playing some sort of practical joke.

Footsteps in the hall: sharp, quick, authoritative. The whole building shook slightly; it had been run up after the fighting stopped, and run up as quickly and cheaply as possible. He doubted they were her footsteps. She hadn't walked that way when he'd known her. But he hadn't known her for a long time. The footsteps stopped in front of his door. The knock that followed had the same abrupt, staccato quality to it.

Auerbach heaved himself up and opened the door. Sure enough, Penny Summers stood in the hall, impatiently tapping her foot on the worn linoleum and sucking on a cigarette. He stared at her in surprise he realized was completely absurd. Of course she wouldn't be the fresh-faced farm girl he'd more or less loved when he was young.

Her hair was cut short and dyed a brassy version of the blond it had been. Her skin stretched tight across her cheekbones and over her forehead. Powder didn't hide crow's-feet at the corners of her eyes and couldn't cover the harsh lines that ran like gullies from beside her nose to the corners of her mouth. The flesh under her chin sagged. Her pale eyes were faded and wary.

She took a last drag on the cigarette, threw it down, and ground it out under the sole of her shoe. Then she leaned forward and pecked Rance on the lips. Her mouth tasted of smoke. 'For God's sake, darling, get me a drink,' she said.

'Water?' Auerbach asked as he limped back to the kitchen. She wasn't young any more. She wasn't sweet any more. Neither was he, but that had nothing to do with anything. He knew what he was. She'd just ruined some of his memories.

'Just ice,' she said. The couch creaked as she sat down. He carried the glass out to her, with one of his own in his other hand. Her skirt was short and tight and had ridden up quite a ways. She still had good legs, long and smooth and muscular.

'Mud in your eye,' he said, and drank. She knocked back her whiskey at a gulp. He looked at her. 'What's going on? And what do you think I can do about it? I can't do much about anything.'

'You know people in the RAF.' It wasn't a question; she spoke with assurance. 'I got involved in a . . . business deal that didn't quite turn out the way it was supposed to. Some folks are mad at me.' She gave an emphatic cough. Maybe some of the folks she meant had scales, not hair.

'What am I supposed to do about it?' But that wasn't really what Auerbach wanted to ask. He wasn't shy about coming out with it. He wasn't shy about anything these days. 'Come on, Penny – why should I give a damn? You walked out on me a long time ago, remember?'

'Maybe I wasn't as smart as I should have been,' she said. Maybe she was buttering him up now, too, but he didn't say anything. He just waited. She went on, 'Once I did, though, I couldn't make it like it never happened. So – will you let a couple of your friends over in England know I'm trying to make things right? And will you let me stay here for a little while, till the heat in Detroit dies down?'

He hadn't known she'd been in Detroit. 'You know who you want me to write to?' he asked, and wasn't surprised when she nodded. She knew about him, whether he knew about her or not. 'Okay, I can write the letters,' he said, 'if you're not lying to me, and you really will fix this up.' He stuck his tongue in the palm of his hand, as if he were a Lizard tasting ginger.

'Good guess,' Penny said. 'All I need is a little time to straighten it out. I swear to God that's the truth.'

Once upon a time, she'd read the Bible a lot. Now . . . now he judged she'd swear whatever was convenient, same as most people. He shrugged, which hurt a little, then came to the point again: 'Only one bed in the bedroom.'

'That's all right,' she said. 'That's what I'm paying for, isn't it? – room and broad, I mean?' Her smile was a lot harder, a lot more knowing, than it had been in the old days. Auerbach laughed even so.

'I hate this,' Fotsev said. 'How are we supposed to find one male Big Ugly among all the ones who live here? For all we know, the miserable fanatic does not live here any more. If he has any sense, he does not.'

'If he had any sense, he would not be a miserable fanatic,' his friend Gorppet pointed out, a point with which Fotsev could hardly disagree. 'For that matter, if he had any sense, he would not be a Tosevite.'

Fotsev couldn't disagree with that, either, and didn't. His eye turrets swept the Basra street along which he and his small group were advancing – a narrow, stinking, muddy track between two rows of buildings, some whitewashed, more not, made from mud themselves. They showed only slits for windows, and had the look, though not really the strength, of fortresses.

'He is a crazy Big Ugly for preaching the way he does,' Fotsev said, 'and the rest of the Big Uglies are just as crazy for listening to him. And I can tell you somebody else who is crazy, too.'

'Who is that?' Gorppet asked.

Before Fotsev could answer, sudden movement from around a corner made him swing the muzzle of his personal weapon to cover it. A moment later, he relaxed. It was only one of the four-legged hairy creatures, part scavenger, part companion, that the Big Uglies kept as symbionts. It sat back on its haunches and yapped at him and his comrades.

'Miserable creature,' Gorppet said. 'I do not like dogs at all. Up in the SSSR, they used to train them to run under land-cruisers with explosives on their backs. Nasty to use animals that way. They do not know what they are doing.' He paused. 'But you were going to tell me who else is crazy. That is always worth hearing.'

'Truth,' one of their comrades said. 'Who else is crazy, Fotsev?'

'The shiplord of the colonization fleet,' Fotsev answered. 'With the Big Uglies on this part of the planet all stirred to a boil, why does he think he needs to bring any ships from the colonization fleet down here?'

'To keep the Big Uglies who know what they are doing from blowing up any more of them?' Gorppet suggested.

'Because the weather here is better than it is in most places on Tosev 3?' another male added.

Fotsev hissed in annoyance; those were both good answers. In his mind, though, they weren't good enough. He said, 'That madmale Khomeini is still stirring up the local Big Uglies. How much do you want to bet that they manage to wreck a colonization ship or two? They are so addled, a lot of them do not care whether they live or die.'

'It is that business of thinking they will get a happy afterlife if they die fighting us,' Gorppet said. 'We have given enough of them the chance to find out whether they are right or wrong lately, and that is truth.'

A male Tosevite came out of his house. Speaking the language of the Race with a rasping, guttural accent, he said, 'He is not here. Go away.'

'You do not tell us what to do,' Fotsev said. 'We tell you what to do.' The Big Uglies had had many years to figure that out. That they hadn't was, in Fotsev's view, a telling proof of their stupidity.

'He is not here,' the Big Ugly repeated. Swathed in his robes, he looked as much like a ragpile as an intelligent being.

'If a Big Ugly says something is not so, that makes it more likely to be so,' Gorppet said.

'You are right, of course,' Fotsev said. 'We had better search that house.'

The Big Ugly let out a howl of protest. Fotsev and the other males of the Race ignored it. Fotsev, as orders required, radioed back to the barracks that he and his comrades were entering a building. If they needed help, they would get it in a hurry. If they needed help, they would, very likely, get it too late no matter how fast it arrived. Fotsev chose not to dwell on that.

He pointed his personal weapon at the Tosevite. 'Open the door and go in ahead of us,' he ordered – if the local spoke his language, he was going to take advantage of it. 'If you have friends in there with guns, you had better tell them not to shoot, or they and we will surely shoot you.'

Against the Race, that would have been a perfect threat. Against a Big Ugly, it was a good one, but not, Fotsev knew, perfect. Too many Big Uglies all over Tosev 3 had proved themselves ready to die for what they reckoned important.

Without another word, the Tosevite turned and threw the door wide. Only after he had gone inside did he turn back and say, 'Here, do you see? There is no danger. And the male you seek is not here, as I told you before.'

Fotsev's mouth fell open in bitter laughter. No danger? He had been in danger every moment since coming down to the surface of Tosev 3 – and he had not been in the worst of the fighting. But he never expected to know another instant in which he was *not* looking now this way, now that, always anxious lest trouble see him before he saw it. The Emperor had called for a Soldiers' Time, and soldiers he had got. Fotsev did not think even the Emperor had the power to make soldiers back into ordinary males of the Race. He and his fellows had seen too much, done too much, had too much done to them, for that.

Such gloomy reflections did not keep him from doing his job. As he searched the house, he turned one eye turret back toward Gorppet and asked, 'Can you imagine living like this?'

'I would rather not,' his friend replied.

No computers. No televisor screens. Not even a radio receiver. No electricity of any sort; the walls held brackets for torches, and were stained black with soot above them. Fotsev saw only one book, printed in the sinuous squiggles of the alphabet used hereabouts. He knew what that book would be, too: the instruction manual for the local superstition. Most of the Big Uglies in this part of Tosev 3 who could read at all had that book and no others.

A couple of female Tosevites – even more thoroughly muffled in cloth wrappings than the males – squealed as males of the Race came into the kitchen. Fotsev looked at the pot bubbling over the fire. He could see the marks of hammering on it; it had been made by hand. The stew inside smelled good. Whatever had gone into it, though, hadn't been refrigerated beforehand, and Tosevite pests would have been free to walk over it and lay their eggs in it. *No wonder so many Big Uglies die sooner than they might,* he thought.

His scent receptors caught the tangy odor of ginger in the stew. It was just a cooking spice to the Big Uglies, not a drug. Fotsev pitied them for that, as for many other things. He was no fiend for ginger; he'd seen too many males endanger themselves and their comrades because they couldn't keep their tongues out of the ginger jar. The herb and duty simply did not mix. But, when he didn't have to go anywhere or do anything for a while . . .

He made himself ignore that temptingly delicious scent. A couple of other males seemed to be looking for excuses to get near the stew pot. One of the female Big Uglies hefted a large iron spoon in what was plainly a warning gesture; the Tosevites did not have so much food as to take lightly the idea of losing any.

Fotsev said, 'We are not here to steal. We are not here to stick out our tongues. We are here to see if that miserable Khomeini male is anywhere close by. Remember it, or else you will have something else to remember.'

His small group did as thorough a job as it could of ransacking the house. He did not think a male of the Race could have hidden from them, let alone one of the larger Tosevites. They did not discover the hairy Big Ugly who had stirred up so much hatred and unrest against the Race.

'Do you see?' said the Big Ugly who had asserted Khomeini was not there. 'I told the truth. And what did I get for it? You have torn my home to pieces.'

'You Tosevites have done plenty to us,' Fotsev replied. 'You cannot blame us if we want to keep you from doing more.'

'Cannot blame you?' The Tosevite yipped out the laughter of his kind. 'Of course we can blame you. We will blame you for a thousand years. We will blame you for ten thousand years.' He added an emphatic cough.

However emphatic he was, he spoke as if a thousand years were a very long time, ten thousand years an impossibly long time. Even if the years by which they reckoned were twice as long as those of the Race, Fotsev knew perfectly well that that was not so. 'Twenty thousand years from now,' he said, 'your descendants will be contented subjects of the Empire.'

The Big Ugly's small, deeply set eyes went as wide as they could. He said several things in his own tongue that did not sound like compliments. Then he returned to the language of the Race: 'You are as wrong as you were wrong when you thought the great Khomeini was here.'

'Our descendants will know.' Fotsev raised his voice: 'The Big Ugly male who preaches is not in this house. Let us go and see if we can find him elsewhere.' He doubted they would. But they did have some hope of keeping order in Basra, which was also important.

When he and his small group went out into the street, helicopters rumbled overhead. Alarm ran through him – what had the Big Uglies gone and done now? Then he heard and saw killercraft, some roaring low over the city, others high enough to scribe vapor trails in the upper atmosphere.

'What now?' Gorppet demanded. 'They have not needed killercraft in this part of Tosev 3 for a long time.'

Before Fotsev could answer, a new and different rumble filled his hearing diaphragms: a great endless roar of cloven air. He had not heard the like for many years. He looked into the sky. Sure enough: what he had thought he would see, he saw. At first, those specks were at the very edge of visibility, but they swelled rapidly. Before long, even if they never came too close to Basra, they swelled enough to let him gauge how truly huge they were.

'Ah,' Gorppet said.

'Yes.' Fotsev watched the globes descend toward bare ground south and west of the town. 'Whether in wisdom or not, the colonization fleet begins to land.'

6

David Goldfarb studied the radar screen with something between admiration and horror. He'd known how immense the Lizards' colonization fleet was, of course; he'd been seeing the echoes of those ships since they first began going into orbit around the Earth. But he'd grown used to them up in high orbit: they made a sort of background noise on his set. When they started dropping out of orbit, one detachment at a time, they actively impinged on his awareness once more.

'Will you *look* at the bloody things?' he exclaimed as yet another squadron, bound for Poland, passed over his station in Northern Ireland. 'How many Lizards have they got packed in each of those ships? Enough so they'll be stepping on each other's toes, I shouldn't wonder.'

'Aye, no doubt you're right, sir,' Sergeant Jack McDowell answered. 'And if they aren't stepping on their own toes, then they will step on the Nazis'.'

'That breaks my heart,' Goldfarb said. The sergeant chuckled; no, he didn't hold Goldfarb's being a Jew against him. If only the same held true for Goldfarb's superiors, he would have been a happier man. With Britain ever more closely aligned to the *Reich*, though, that wasn't in the cards. At least he hadn't been booted out of the RAF and into a concentration camp.

'They'll be low over German territory before they land, too,' he said with a certain sardonic satisfaction. 'Here's hoping Heinrich Himmler's hiding under the bed.'

McDowell nodded. He wasn't too far from Goldfarb's age: old enough to remember the Blitz, to remember the days when the Nazis were the worst enemies the British Empire had. To new recruits, the Greater German *Reich* might always have been the big, strong brother on the Continent. They had no sense of the past, or of what a nasty fellow the big, strong brother still was.

Of course, a fair number of the new recruits were as taken with the Lizards as they were with the Germans. Goldfarb let out a sigh. It hadn't been that way when he was a kid joining the RAF. He sighed again. For how many generations had people been complaining about the younger set? Enough for formidable antiquity even by Lizard standards, no doubt.

McDowell said, 'They're right where they ought to be, right where they said they'd be. The Germans haven't any excuse for throwing a rocket at them.'

'Except bloody-mindedness,' Goldfarb said. 'Never forget about sheer bloody-mindedness, especially when you're dealing with Germans.'

'They'll pay dear if they get gay this time,' McDowell said. The Lizards had made that very plain to the *Reich*, the USSR, and the USA: any attack on the ships of the colonization fleet as they landed would start up the fighting that had lain dormant for eighteen years. Goldfarb didn't think they were bluffing. His opinion counted for little. By all the signs, though, Himmler and Molotov and Warren agreed with him.

The Lizards hadn't bothered publicly warning either Britain or Japan to leave their colonization fleet alone. They didn't formally treat with either island nation as an equal, even if they had got their snouts bloodied when they invaded England.

Goldfarb followed the track of the ships from the colonization fleet till the curve of the Earth hid them from the prying eye of his radar. 'Doesn't look like the *Reich* will give this lot any trouble,' he said.

'Good, sir. That's good,' McDowell said. 'If the fighting starts up again, there won't be anything left of any of us when it's over.'

'Truth,' Goldfarb said in the Lizards' language. McDowell nodded; he understood those hisses and pops and coughs. For him, as for Goldfarb, learning them meant being able to do his job better. A lot of people half their age liked the Lizards' language for its own sake. *No accounting for taste,* Goldfarb thought.

After the alert caused by the descent of the detachment from the colonization fleet, the rest of Goldfarb's tour at the radar screen was uneventful. He preferred days like that; he'd had enough excitement when he was younger to last him a lifetime. He made his report to the flight lieutenant who replaced him at the radar, then escaped with a sigh of relief.

A cigarette in the pale sunlight outside took the edge off his tension. A pint of bitter, he knew, would do an even better job, or maybe Guinness from the Irish Republic. He was heading for his bicycle so he could let a specialist administer the proper dose – and perhaps even repeat it – when a shout made him whip his head around: 'Goldfarb!'

He stared in surprise. A good many years had gone by since he'd seen that handsome, ruddy face, but the only change in it he could see was that the handlebar mustache adorning the upper lip was streaked with gray. He stiffened to attention and saluted. 'Yes, sir!' he said loudly.

'Oh, in the bloody name of heaven, as you were,' Basil Roundbush said, returning the salute. 'I want to buy you a bloody pint, not put you on report.'

'Thank you, sir,' Goldfarb said, and extended his hand. Roundbush shook it; he still had a grip like a bear trap. Goldfarb eyed the four stripes on each sleeve of his gray-blue uniform. 'Thank you very much, Group Captain.'

Roundbush waved airily, as if the rank – the RAF's equivalent to colonel – meant nothing to him. Maybe it did mean nothing to him. He had the right accent; he'd gone to the right public school and the right university – Goldfarb couldn't recall if it was Oxford or Cambridge, but which hardly mattered. And, smiling his film-star smile, he said, 'You've done rather smashingly well yourself, Flight Lieutenant.' He didn't add, *For a Jew from the East End of London,* as he might have done. He didn't even look as if he thought it, which was rather remarkable. Instead, he went on, 'That's why I came over here to chat you up.'

Goldfarb's eyes widened again. 'You came to Belfast to . . . see me, sir?' he said slowly, wondering if he'd heard straight.

'I did indeed,' Roundbush answered, for all the world as if traveling to Northern Ireland to talk with a Jewish junior officer were the most normal thing in the world. 'Now – I've got a motorcar laid on, and you know this town, which I bloody well don't. Go fling your bicycle in the boot, and then tell me where we can get a pint.'

'Protestant pub or Catholic?' Goldfarb asked. 'It doesn't matter much to me, but . . .' He let his voice trail away. Maybe, after so long, Roundbush needed reminding about his faith.

He didn't. 'I know what you are,' he said. 'If you weren't, you'd not have caught that lovely lady of yours. I might have caught her myself, as a matter of fact.' He'd always had phenomenal luck with women. Goldfarb glanced at his left hand. He still wore no wedding band. Maybe that didn't signify, but maybe it did, too: could a tomcat change his stripes? He grinned at Goldfarb. 'I'm not fussy. Whichever you think is the best place.'

'There's the Crown Liquor Saloon on Great Victoria, sir, not far from the university, or Robinsons next door. Robinsons has the finest Guinness in town, I think.'

'Robinsons it is, then.' Roundbush spoke with decision befitting a senior officer. 'Guinness comes close to justifying the existence of Ireland, and I can't think of many other things that do. Come on, old man.'

Once ensconced in a snug with a pint of stout in front of

175

him, Goldfarb asked what he knew was the obvious question: 'And now, sir, what's all this in aid of?'

'Twisting the Lizards' nasty little tails – what else?' Roundbush answered, sucking foam out of that perfectly waxed mustache. 'One of the things we do on the sly, you know, is encourage them to stick their tongues in the ginger jar. A drugged Lizard is a long way from being a Lizard at his best.'

'No, I don't suppose he would be,' Goldfarb agreed, 'but – is it cricket?'

'Fine old tradition,' Basil Roundbush said. 'Goes back to the Opium Wars, you might say. It worked then, and it's working now. Oh, it's not working perfectly; we've had a spot of trouble with someone over in the States, but I do think that's being fixed. And we have hopes of getting some of our own back from Grand High Panjandrum Atvar and his scaly chums.'

Goldfarb didn't say anything at all to that. As far as he was concerned, Britain's survival was miracle enough. Dreams of resurrecting the old British Empire could only be just that: dreams. He did ask, 'How do I fit into this, sir?' If he sounded cautious, it was because he felt cautious.

'You've got connections in Poland, and you've got connections in Palestine, too,' Roundbush replied. 'We've had a couple of shipments go awry lately – this is apart from that business in the USA, mind you. Anything you can do to find out why would serve Queen and country, and might line your pockets quite nicely, too.' He made money-counting motions and then, as if suddenly noticing his glass was empty, signaled to the barmaid.

'Right away, dearie,' she said, and put something extra into her walk. Goldfarb shook his head in bemused amusement; whatever the group captain had had, he still retained it.

But that was beside the point. 'Is this RAF business, sir, or is it private business?' he asked. 'I've been happy enough here – more than happy enough. I'm not dead keen on turning my life upside down and inside out.'

'Of course you're not, old man,' Roundbush said soothingly. 'Of course you're not. That's why there'd be a little something special – or maybe more than a little something special – in it for you if you'd look into the matter for us. We do take care of our own; you needn't fret about that.'

The barmaid brought back fresh pints. Goldfarb paid her; Roundbush had bought the first round. Goldfarb always tipped generously – he couldn't afford a reputation for meanness. But despite scooping up his coins, the barmaid had eyes only for his companion.

'Cheers,' Roundbush said after she finally swayed away, and raised the new pint to his lips.

'Cheers,' Goldfarb echoed. He stared across the cramped little snug at the senior officer. 'Who exactly is "we," sir?'

'My colleagues,' Roundbush said: an answer that was not an answer. 'My notion was, a chap in your situation can use all the help' – he made that money-counting motion again – 'and all the friends he can find.'

'Isn't that interesting?' Goldfarb said. Oh, yes, Roundbush remembered he was a Jew, all right, and knew just how tenuous things were for Jews in Britain these days. 'And what would you want me to do?' he asked.

'Nose about a bit, see if you can find out how those shipments went wrong,' Roundbush answered. 'It's safe as houses.'

Goldfarb hadn't asked if it was safe as houses. Half a lifetime in the RAF convinced him that, if anyone told him it was safe as houses without his asking, it was most unlikely to be anything of the sort. If someone looked him up after some years to assure him it was safe as houses, it couldn't possibly be.

He took a pull at his Guinness. 'No, thank you, sir,' he said.

'Tut, tut,' Basil Roundbush said. 'That's the wrong answer. Believe you me, old man, whatever might happen to you if you say yes, something worse will happen to you if you say no. And you wouldn't want it to happen to your lovely family, too, now would you? That would be very sad.'

A nasty chill of alarm ran through Goldfarb. Roundbush and whatever friends he had were ideally placed to wreck his career if they wanted to badly enough. And if they wanted to play other sorts of games, how much help from the authorities could Goldfarb count on? The answer seemed only too plain. He gulped down the rest of his stout in a couple of swallows. 'I think I've changed my mind,' he said.

'Ah, capital.' Roundbush beamed. 'You won't regret it.'

'I regret it already,' Goldfarb said. The other RAF man laughed, just as if he'd been joking.

These days, Monique Dutourd was concentrating more on carved stones than on the Lizards' colonization fleet. She couldn't do anything about the fleet. If she pieced together enough interesting inscriptions, she could finally finish that paper on the cult of Isis hereabouts. She did look forward to reactions when it saw print. It was a more thorough synthesis than anyone had tried before, and might eventually lead to a promotion.

She was glad her field of specialization centered on the Mediterranean provinces in the early days of the Roman Empire rather than, for instance, the Germanic invasions. No matter what a French scholar had to say about the Germanic invasions, the modern Germanic invaders were only too likely to decide it was wrong. And the Germans were not in the habit of giving those with whom they disagreed a chance to revise their opinions.

Her mouth twisted in annoyance as she pulled out a photograph of an inscription from up near Arles. She'd taken the photograph herself, but it wasn't so good as it might have been. Had she waited a couple of hours longer, the sun would have filled the letters with shadow instead of washing them out. She bent low over the photo, doing her best to make sure she'd correctly inscribed the inscription.

The telephone rang. She jumped. *'Merde!'* she said; she hated interruptions of any sort. Muttering, she went to the phone. *'Allô?'* Whoever it was, she intended to get rid of him as fast as she could.

That proved harder than she'd hoped. *'Bonjour, Monique. Ici Dieter Kuhn,'* the SS man in her Roman history class said in his good if formal French. *'Comment ça va?'*

'Assez bien, merci,' she answered. *'Et vous?'* He'd taken her out for coffee several times, to dinner and a film once. Had he been a Frenchman, she likely would have slipped into using *tu* with him by now. But she was not ready – she wondered if she would ever be ready – to use the intimate pronoun with a German.

'Things go well enough for me, too, thanks,' Kuhn said. 'Would you care to drive down by the seaside with me for lunch?' He also used *vous*, not *tu*; he hadn't tried to force intimacy on her. She hadn't had to wrestle with him yet, as she almost surely would have after going out several times with one of her own countrymen. She wondered if he was normal, or if perhaps he squired her about to give the appearance of normality.

A lunch he bought – he always had plenty of cash – would be one she didn't have to pay for. She liked the idea of soaking the SS. Still . . . 'I am working,' she said, and cast a longing eye he couldn't see back toward her desk.

She sounded halfhearted even to herself. She wasn't a bit surprised when Dieter Kuhn laughed and said, 'You sound like you could use a break. Come on. I will be there in half an hour.'

'All right,' she said. Kuhn laughed again and hung up. So did she, shaking her head. Did he know she was afraid to say no? If he did, he hadn't used it to his advantage. That was another reason she wondered how normal he was.

He knocked on her front door exactly twenty-nine minutes after getting off the phone. His timing always lived up to every cliché about German efficiency. 'Does Chez Fonfon suit you?' he asked.

It was one of the better seafood bistros in Marseille. Monique only knew of it; she couldn't afford to eat there on her pay. 'It will do,' she said, and smiled a little at the regal acquiescence in her tone.

Kuhn held the door open for her to get into the passenger side of his battered green Volkswagen. She'd known he drove one of the buggy little cars since she'd thought him a Frenchman named Laforce. She hadn't thought anything of it; Volkswagens were the most common cars through the *Reich* and the territories it occupied.

The automobile rattled west toward the sea, past the basilica of St. Victor and Fort d'Entrecasteaux, which had helped guard the port back in the distant days when threats had to be visible to be dangerous. Kuhn drove with as much abandon as any Frenchman, and drove two wheels up onto the sidewalk when he parked near the restaurant. Seeing Monique's bemused expression, he chuckled and said, 'I follow the customs of the country where I am stationed.' He hopped out to open the door for her again.

At Chez Fonfon, she ordered bouillabaisse after a waiter fawned on them at hearing Kuhn's German accent. The fellow gave them what had to be the best table in the place, one overlooking the blue water of the Mediterranean.

'Et pour moi aussi,' Kuhn said. *'Et vin blanc.'*

'It does have mullet?' Monique asked, and the waiter's nod sent his forelock – alarmingly like Hitler's – bouncing up and down on his forehead. He hurried away. Monique turned her attention back to the SS man. 'The Romans would have approved. But for the tomatoes in the broth, people were eating bouillabaisse here – maybe on this very spot – in Roman days, too.'

'Some things change very slowly,' Kuhn said. 'Some things, however, change more quickly.' He looked to be on the point of saying more, but the waiter came bustling up with a carafe of white wine. Monique was not used to such speedy service. The SS man took it for granted. *Why not?* she thought. *He is one of the conquerors.*

Some wine took the edge off her bitterness. She did her best to relax and enjoy the view and the meal – which also came with marvelous promptness – and the company in which she found herself. But the food claimed most of her attention, as it should have. 'Very good,' she said, dabbing her lips with a napkin. 'Thank you.'

'It is my pleasure,' Kuhn answered. 'I do not suppose they would cook the mullet alive in a glass vessel here, to let us watch it change colors as it perished.'

She pointed an accusing finger at him. 'You have been studying too much.'

'I believe it is impossible to study too much,' he said, serious as usual. 'One never knows when a particular piece of information may be useful. Because of this, one should try to know everything.'

'I suppose this is a useful attitude in your profession,' Monique said. She did not really want to think about his profession. To keep from thinking about it, she emptied her wineglass. The waiter, who hovered around the table like a bee around a honey-filled flower, filled it again.

'It is a useful attitude in life,' Kuhn said. 'Do you not find this to be so?'

'It could be,' Monique answered. Had anyone but the SS man suggested it, she would have agreed without hesitation. She drank more white wine. As she drank, she discovered the wine had taken the edge off her caution, too, for she heard herself saying, 'One piece of information I would like to have is what you think you see in me.'

Kuhn could have evaded that. He could simply have refused to answer. The idea that she could force anything from him was absurd, and she knew as much. He sipped at his own wine and looked out at the Mediterranean for a few seconds before saying, 'You have a brother.'

Now she stared at him in frank astonishment. 'I may have a brother,' she said. 'I don't even know if I do or not. I haven't seen Pierre in more than twenty years, not since he was called to the front in 1940. We heard he was captured, and then we never heard again.' Excitement flowed through her. 'For a long time, I have thought he was dead. Is this not so?'

'No, it is not so,' Dieter Kuhn said. 'He is not only alive, he is living here in Marseille. I was hoping – I admit I was hoping – you would be able to lead me to him. But everything I have learned about you makes me believe you are telling the truth, and have no contact with him.' He sighed. *'C'est la vie.'*

'And what has my brother done to make you want to find him?' Monique inquired, before she could ask herself whether she really wanted to know.

'This town – it is not an orderly town,' the SS officer said, his voice stern with disapproval. 'Parts of this town might as well be thieves' markets, such as they have in the Arab towns of Africa.'

'It is Marseille,' Monique said. Where Kuhn was stern, she was amused. 'Marseille has always been like this, in France but not of it. The folk of Marseille have always traded where and in what they could get the best bargains.'

That had sometimes – often – included people. During and right after the fighting, Jews with money and connections had made it out of the *Reich* by the thousands from Marseille. Jews had a hard time of it nowadays, but other contraband still came in and went out. No one but the smugglers knew the details, but everybody had a notion of the broad outlines.

'You are familiar with the Porte d'Aix?' Kuhn asked.

'I don't think anyone is truly familiar with the Porte d'Aix, not with all of it,' Monique answered. 'It is a *souk*, a market-place of sorts like those in Algeria, as you said. Everyone goes into the edges now and then. I have done that. Why?'

'Because your brother, my dear Professor Dutourd, is the uncrowned king of Porte d'Aix,' Kuhn told her. 'It is my duty to attempt to arrange his abdication.'

'And why is that?' Monique asked. 'Is it not that whoever takes his place will be no different? If you ask the opinion of anyone who has studied history, he will tell you the same, I think.'

'It could be,' Kuhn said. 'But it could also be that whoever takes your brother's place will be more inclined to remember he is a human being and less inclined to be so friendly to the Lizards.'

Monique's first impulse was to drop everything she was doing and try to get hold of the brother she had not seen for so long, to warn him of his danger. Her second thought was that that was exactly what the SS man would want her to do. He would let her do the hunting, and then snatch Pierre once she'd guided him to his quarry. Doing nothing was not easy, but it was the best thing she could do if she wanted to go on having a brother, even one she did not know.

No. She could do one other thing, and she did it: 'Please be polite enough to take me back to my apartment. Please also be polite enough not to call on me again. And please have the courtesy no longer to attend the class I offer at the university.'

'The first, of course,' Kuhn said. 'I am not a barbarian.' Monique held her tongue, which was no doubt just as well. The SS man went on, 'As for the second, it shall also be as you wish, although I have enjoyed your company aside from any, ah, professional considerations. The last – no. Even if I learn nothing about your brother, I do learn about the Roman world, which interests me. I shall continue to attend – without, of course, making a nuisance of myself.'

Monique could hardly order him to stay away. Recognizing as much, she shrugged and got to her feet. Kuhn slapped banknotes on the table – he was not such a boor as to make her pay for her own lunch. As they went back out to his illegally parked Volkswagen, she thought she knew what was in his mind: as long as he stayed close to her, he might get a line on her brother. *You won't*, she thought fiercely, but at the same time she wondered how she would ever be able to keep from looking for Pierre now that she knew he dwelt in Marseille, too.

*   *   *

These days, the Communist Party hierarchy did not usually meet inside Peking, but out in the country. That lowered the risk of the little scaly devils wiping out the whole central committee at one stroke. The first time a meeting in a small town northwest of the city was called, Liu Han had eagerly looked forward to it, thinking it would take her back to the days of her youth and let Liu Mei see how she had lived then.

She'd ended up disappointed. Peasants hereabouts knew nothing of rice paddies like the ones she had tended near Hankow. They raised wheat and barley and millet, and ate noodles and porridge, not bowl after endless bowl of rice. The land was dry, not damp: a desert in summer, with yellow dust always in the breeze, and a frozen wasteland during the long winter.

Only one thing was the same among these peasants as among those with whom she'd grown up: their toil never ended.

Ducks and chickens and dogs and children made a racket in the narrow, dusty streets of Fengchen as Liu Han and Liu Mei came into the town in the foothills to talk with their comrades. 'Eee, my feet are weary,' Liu Han said. 'I feel I have walked ten thousand *li*.' She knew that would have taken her almost all the way across China, but wasn't the least bit embarrassed to exaggerate.

'And mine, Mother,' Liu Mei said dutifully. She looked around. 'I see no scaly devils here in Fengchen.'

'No, and I do not think you will,' Liu Han said. 'There are not enough little devils for them to garrison every town. They have the same trouble the Japanese had before them, and they rule the same way: they hold down the cities and they control the roads from one city to the next. All they do – all they can do – in the countryside is raid and steal.'

'Now that they have ships landing, though, there will be more of them.' Liu Mei spoke seriously, as she usually did. When she spoke of the little scaly devils, she spoke even more seriously than usual. She rarely smiled, but her frown was fierce and stormy.

A middle-aged man came out of one of the buildings on the main street: a tavern, by the pair of drunks who snored in front of it. The man was not drunk. Though dressed in a peasant's dark blue tunic and trousers, he carried himself with a soldier's erectness. 'Welcome,' he called. 'Welcome to you both.'

'Thank you, Nieh Ho-T'ing,' Liu Han said. Liu Mei nodded a greeting.

'It is good to have you here,' Nieh said. 'Mao has been asking after you. There are a couple of points on which he will be glad to have your views.' He hesitated, then went on, 'And I am glad to see you, too.'

'I am always glad to see you,' Liu Han said, more or less truthfully. They had been lovers for several years, fighting the little scaly devils side by side till Mao sent Nieh Ho-T'ing to the south to command resistance against the imperialism of the scaly devils there and Liu Han stayed behind to help radicalize the proletarian women of Peking. They'd both found other partners since.

Nieh smiled at Liu Mei. 'How lovely your daughter has become,' he said.

Liu Mei cast down her eyes in fitting modesty. Liu Han studied her. Her nose was too big, her face too long and narrow, her hair too wavy for her to conform to perfect Chinese standards of beauty: all tokens of her father. But Nieh was right – in her own way, she was lovely.

'So Mao is here?' Liu Han said, and Nieh Ho-T'ing nodded. 'Who else?'

'Lin Piao and Chu Te from the People's Liberation Army,' Nieh answered. 'Chou Enlai has not been able to get out of the south; the little devils are being very difficult down there.' He paused, grimaced, and added, 'And Hsia Shou-Tao is here with me.'

'Wherever you go, you have to bring your lapdog?' Liu Han asked, acid in her voice. Hsia Shou-Tao was a tireless and able revolutionary. He was also a tireless drinker and womanizer.

He'd once tried to rape Liu Han; she still sometimes wished she'd cut his throat when she had the chance.

Nieh Ho-T'ing pointed. 'We are staying at the inn yonder. They have a room waiting for the two of you.'

'Good,' Liu Han said. 'When will we meet?'

Nieh chuckled. 'You have not changed much, have you? Business first, everything else afterwards.' Liu Han did not answer; she stood there in the street, arms folded across her chest. Nieh shifted from foot to foot, then finally said, 'We will meet tomorrow morning, early. Mao is always up early; he never sleeps well.'

'Yes, I know,' Liu Han said. She turned to her daughter. 'Come on. Let's see what kind of room it is.'

It turned out to be about what she'd expected: well away from the main hall of the lodging house (what better did women deserve?), small, dark, but with enough blankets and with plenty of fuel for the *kang*, the low, thick, clay hearth on which they could lie to take greatest advantage of its warmth.

'It will be good to see Mao again,' Liu Mei said. 'It has been a few years.'

'He will be glad to see you, too,' Liu Han said. She wondered just how glad Mao would be to see her daughter. He had – and, she knew, deserved – a reputation for being attracted to young girls. He was especially fond of young, ignorant peasant girls, though: to them, as leader of China's hopes, he was the next thing to a god, or maybe not the next thing. Liu Mei had had the best education Liu Han was able to give her. She might admire and respect Mao, but she did not and would not worship him.

Liu Han had gone through a spell of worshiping Mao. She was glad she'd got over it. Some never did, not even after Mao cast them aside. Liu Han hadn't had the sort of education she'd got for her daughter, but her own hard core of common sense had never quite deserted her: or not for long, anyhow.

Next morning, she and Liu Mei came out to have breakfast.

Sitting in the main hall, chatting up a serving girl, was Hsia Shou-Tao. He scowled when Liu Han came in. He'd been subjected to stiff self-criticism any number of times, but his habits never changed.

By the way he looked at Liu Mei, he was imagining her body under her clothes. By the way he looked at Liu Han, he realized she knew what he was doing. His smile was half embarrassed, half afraid. Liu Han wished it were all afraid, but it would have to do. With it still on his face, Hsia said, 'Good morning, Comrade . . . er, Comrades.'

'Good morning,' Liu Han said before Liu Mei could reply – she did not want her daughter speaking to the lecher. 'Take me to the meeting place.'

She spoke like one who had the right to give orders. Hsia Shou-Tao obeyed as if she had that right, too. Since Liu Mei would not be at the meeting, he couldn't try to do anything with her – or to her – for a while. And he knew better than to bother Liu Han.

'Behold the palace of the proletariat,' he said sourly, pointing to a barn that had seen better days.

Inside, sitting on a mat on the dirt floor, were Mao Tse-tung, Chu Te, Nieh Ho-T'ing, and Lin Piao. After brief greetings, Mao came straight to the point: 'We have not received most of the weapons our comrades in the Soviet Union have promised us. Molotov tells me this is because the little scaly devils have intercepted several caravans lately.'

'That is very bad,' Hsia Shou-Tao said: for once, a remark of his with which Liu Han could not disagree.

'It is worse than very bad,' Mao said, running his hand through his hair. He was close to seventy; it had receded in front, leaving his forehead looking high and domed. As if to make up for that, he let his hair grow fuller in the sides and back than most Chinese men wore it. He went on, 'Molotov is lying to me. Most of those caravans were never sent.'

Liu Han exclaimed. That was news to her, and very bad news. By the horrified reactions of all her colleagues save Lin

Piao, it was news to them, too. Lin said, 'As Lenin asked, what is to be done?'

'We must have weapons,' Mao said, to which everyone nodded. Without weapons, the fight against the imperialist scaly devils would surely be lost. The Chinese revolutionary leader went on, 'The USSR seeks to curry favor with the little devils so they will not punish the Soviet Union for the attack on the ships of the colonization fleet. In my view, the USSR should have attacked these ships regardless of the cost, but Molotov is too much a reactionary to agree.'

'He betrays the international solidarity of the workers and peasants,' Hsia Shou-Tao thundered.

'So he does.' Mao's voice was dry. 'And all we can do about it is . . . remember.' He shook his head. 'No. That is all we can do to the USSR. But we must get weapons, whether Molotov supplies them to us or not.'

'That is the truth,' Chu Te said. He looked like an aging peasant, but he held the People's Liberation Army together no less than Mao did the Communist Party. If he said something military was so, then it was.

'Where else can we get weapons now?' Nieh asked. 'The Japanese?' He made a face to show what he thought of that. 'I do not want to give the eastern dwarfs a toehold in China again.'

'Nor I,' Mao said. 'They probably would not help us, though. They are not like the USSR or the USA or the *Reich*. They have no explosive-metal bombs. The scaly devils tolerate their independence, but do not admit they are equals. Dreadful things could happen to Japan very quickly, and the Japanese can do relatively little to resist.'

'In any case, if they helped anyone in China, they would help the Kuomintang,' Lin Piao said. 'Reactionaries love reactionaries.' Everyone nodded. Along with battling the scaly devils, the Chinese kept fighting among themselves. Liu Han thought Chiang Kai-shek would sooner have surrendered to the little devils than to Mao.

'We must have weapons,' Mao repeated. 'None of the three independent powers can truly want to see China altogether lost to the little scaly devils. The USSR will not help us for now. The *Reich* is not well placed, and is the most reactionary of the three; Hitler aided the Kuomintang during the 1930s. That leaves the United States.'

'America would sooner help the Kuomintang, too,' Hsia Shou-Tao said.

'Probably,' Mao said, 'but that does not mean America will not also help us. We had U.S. help in the fight against Japan. We have had some quiet help in the fight against the little devils, too. Now we need more.'

'How are we to get it? Japan and the islands Japan rules block us off from the USA.' Liu Han was proud she knew that. Back in her days in the village near Hankow, she hadn't even known the world was round.

'Not to put too fine a point on it, we must send an envoy to beg,' Mao said. 'Against the Lizards' imperialism, the U.S. capitalists will aid even revolutionaries – if we humble ourselves enough. In the cause of revolution, I have no pride.'

'A good example for us all,' Chu Te murmured.

Mao's gaze swung toward Liu Han. 'You, Comrade, not only are you a woman, and thus likely to appeal to bourgeois sentimentality, but you have an American connection none of the rest of us can match.'

For a moment, Liu Han did not understand what he was talking about. Then, all at once, she did. 'My daughter!' she exclaimed.

'Yes, Liu Mei and her American father, now conveniently and heroically dead,' Mao agreed, as if Bobby Fiore had had no more importance in Liu Han's life than his present convenience. 'If I can arrange the ways and means, I will send both of you to the United States with begging bowls. Do you remember any English?'

'Not more than one or two words,' Liu Han answered. The scaly devils had taken her into space. She'd survived that. If

Mao sent her to America, she would go. 'I will see how much I can learn before I leave.'

Johannes Drucker was glad to be back in space, not only because that meant he'd managed to free his wife from the specter of a Jewish grandmother lurking in her family tree but also because he – unlike a good many – enjoyed weightlessness and because he could better serve the Greater German *Reich* here than anywhere else – certainly better than in *Gestapo* detention.

An abrupt signal came into his ship: 'Spacecraft of the *Reich*! Spacecraft of the *Reich*! Acknowledge at once, space-craft of the *Reich*!' That was a Lizard talking, and he wasn't bothering to speak any human language.

'Acknowledging,' Drucker said. 'Go ahead, male of the Race.'

'I have information for you, and a warning,' the Lizard said. 'You will obey, or you will regret.' He gave an emphatic cough.

'Go on,' Drucker said. 'I cannot say what I will do until I hear what you have to tell me.'

'Information: the Race is punishing the *Reich* for the murder of the males and females aboard the destroyed ships of the colonization fleet,' the Lizard said. 'A warning: any attempt to interfere with the punishment will have the most severe con-sequences. Do you hear? Do you understand? Do you obey?'

'I hear. I understand,' Drucker answered. 'I cannot say whether I obey until I speak to my superiors. I shall do that now.'

'If your superiors are wise, they will obey. If they are not wise, we shall teach them wisdom.' The Lizard broke the connection.

After checking his position, Drucker radioed a German ship in the southern Indian Ocean and relayed what the Lizard had told him. 'I have not heard them sound so determined since we were fighting,' he finished. 'What are my orders?'

He was as near certain as made no difference what the

answer would be. The *Reich* could not keep its independence by knuckling under to the Lizards. He checked the radar screen for targets at which he could launch his missiles and aim his guns. He didn't expect to last long, but he would – what was the phrase the Americans used? Go down swinging, that was it.

And then, to his astonishment, the reply came: 'Take no action.'

'Repeat, please?' Drucker said, not sure he could believe his ears.

'Take no action,' came up again from the relay ship. 'We are told this punishment will be only symbolic, and will also be inflicted on Russia and America. If we were misinformed, you will proceed to avenge the *Vaterland* on the liars.'

'*Jawohl,*' Drucker said. Not sure the Lizards had monitored his conversation with the ship, he switched to the frequency they had used and back to their language: 'Spacecraft of the *Reich* calling the Race.'

'Go ahead.' The reply came back at once. 'Do you hear? Do you understand? Do you obey?'

'I hear. I understand,' Drucker said, as he had before. 'I will obey, unless the punishment you give is so severe, my superiors order me to fight. In that case, I will obey them, not you.'

'This does you credit as a warrior,' said the Lizard on the other end of the circuit. 'It will not keep you from dying if you are foolish enough to fight.'

'I serve the *Reich*,' Drucker answered. 'I serve the *Führer*.' The *Führer*, or at least Himmler's fair-haired boys in the SS, had treated him shabbily of late, and Käthe even worse. That didn't mean he was ready to give up on the Greater German *Reich*. Without the *Reich*, he thought, the Lizards would surely have overrun the whole world, not just around half of it.

'You would do better to serve the Emperor,' the Lizard said, adding another emphatic cough. Drucker had all he could do not to laugh out loud. The earnest alien sounded like nothing so much as a missionary trying to save a heathen savage's soul.

Lizards got offended when humans pointed such things out to them.

Drucker's radar showed several Lizard spacecraft dropping out of orbit. He estimated their courses, not bothering to feed the numbers into his computing machine. He didn't need precision, not when he'd been ordered to sit tight. But they were heading for the *Reich*.

He itched to change course and pursue them. He could knock down a couple, maybe more, before they wrecked him. The Lizards were technically proficient pilots, but they weren't inspired. He was, or could be.

'These are the punishment ships,' the Lizard told him. 'If you could see with your eyes and not with your sensors, you would see they have been painted to include the broad green bands that symbolize punishment.'

Drucker didn't answer. He kept nervously watching the radar screen. The Lizards were using a lot of force for a purely symbolic punishment. Had they been lying? Were they seizing this excuse to throw a sucker punch at each of the three main human powers still standing? If they were . . . How they would pay if they were! He would be one of the men who made them pay.

Then he got a signal from another German relay ship, one of the many that kept spacecraft in touch with the territorially limited *Reich*: 'They have destroyed an air base near the town of Flensburg. Many aircraft have been wrecked; there are casualities. They state they intend to take no further action.'

That sounded like more than a symbolic attack to Drucker. 'What are my orders?' he asked. 'Am I to retaliate?'

A long silence followed. Had the Lizards truly intended a strike on the *Reich*, he realized, one logical thing for them to do would have been to sink as many of the relay ships as they could. During the fighting, they hadn't paid so much attention to ships as they might have; later, men had discovered that seas on their home planet were small and unimportant compared to the oceans of Earth. But thinking the Lizards could not learn from experience was a deadly dangerous mistake.

He was just starting to worry in earnest when the relay ship did respond: 'No, no retaliation at this time, not unless the Lizards take some further action. The *Führer* has warned them in the strongest terms against thinking our forbearance will extend past this one occasion.'

'Good,' Drucker said. 'Even once is too often, if anyone cares what a pilot thinks.' He knew perfectly well that no one did. 'Have they also struck at the Russians and the Americans, as they said they would?' *Misery loves company,* he thought.

'Reports are coming in from the United States,' was the reply. 'They also hit an air base there. Radar indicates an attack was made on the USSR, but no comment from Radio Moscow.'

'Radio Moscow wouldn't tell anyone the sun had risen if they couldn't already see it for themselves,' Drucker said with a snort.

He sighed. He wasn't the least bit sorry the Lizards had had a good many ships from the colonization fleet blown to hell and gone. He wished they'd lost more. They kept landing more and more ships all over the territory they controlled. More and more Lizards, male and female, would be thawing out every day. The more of them there were, the harder getting rid of them would be. They'd got no better than a draw in the fighting, but they were liable to win the peace.

When he got over the United States, the American radioman with whom he spoke was full of righteous indignation. 'They had no business hitting us like that – none,' the fellow said. 'We didn't do anything to them. They didn't even claim we did. They hit us anyhow.'

'They did the same to the *Reich*,' Drucker said. 'They did the same to the Russians – I think. They got to do it because they are strong. The stronger always get to do what they like against the weaker.'

'That's not fair,' the American said.

'I am sure your Indians would be the first to agree with you,' Drucker said.

'So would your Jews – if you had any left,' the American retorted. Most Germans would have laughed at that. They were just as well pleased to be *Judenfrei* – free of Jews. Drucker would have laughed at it himself, only a handful of weeks before. He wasn't laughing now. Had he not figured out which strings to pull, and had he not been able to pull them, Käthe would have disappeared from his life forever. That changed the way he looked at things.

Drucker didn't say anything. The American radio operator kept jeering at him till he passed out of range. He had seldom been so glad to listen to a signal break up and dissolve in static.

The Lizards who controlled Africa did not give him so hard a time as the Americans had done. Part of that was because they were more polite than Americans had ever imagined being. The other part was that they didn't know how to get under his skin as well as a fellow human did.

American and German radio stations were full of reports of what the Lizards had done. All the German commentators said the same thing. Dr. Goebbels would never have permitted anything less. Some of the American broadcasters presented a generally similar line, but not all. Some even said the Lizards had the right to do what they'd done. In the *Reich*, anyone who dared utter such a disloyal sentiment in public – let alone on the radio – would have vanished into night and fog, very likely never to be seen again. Johannes Drucker approved. Americans, in his view, were disorderly to the point of anarchy, even to the point of insanity.

Radio Moscow played Tchaikovsky, Chopin, Rachmaninoff, Mussorgsky. The Russian news report, when it finally came on the air, bragged of the overfulfillment of the steel quota set forth in the latest Five-Year Plan and of the anticipated bountiful harvest. As far as the broadcaster was concerned, the Lizards might as well not have existed. Drucker snorted. The Russians put him in mind of so many ostriches, burying their heads in the sand.

He squeezed meat paste out of a tinfoil tube onto a slice of dark bread. After he ate, a few crumbs floated in the air. Eventually, the blower pushed them into one filter or another. Drucker drank fruit juice from a bladder of synthetic rubber that left a harsh, chemical taste. He wished the powers that be would let pilots take beer into space, though he understood why they didn't.

He sighed. 'The beer would taste lousy, too, if I had to drink it out of one of those miserable squeeze toys,' he muttered. But even bad beer looked good to him now.

He sighed again. Times were changing. He knew the Lizards didn't like that. Trouble was, he didn't like it, either. He'd lived most of his adult life at wary peace with the Lizards. Now that the colonization fleet was finally here, how could the peace survive?

Rance Auerbach peered west from his bedroom window toward the great pillar of smoke rising from Carswell Air and Space Force Base, over past the outskirts of Fort Worth. 'Son of a bitch,' he said. '*Son* of a bitch! The Lizards really went and did it, God damn them to hell and gone.'

Penny Summers put a hand on his arm. 'They said they were going to. Did you think they were bluffing? You ought to know better than that, Rance. When they say they're going to do something, they mean it.'

'Oh, I know that.' Auerbach shook his head, which sent pain shooting through his ruined shoulder. 'What really riles me is that we didn't fire a shot when they came down and shot up the field – just lay there with our legs in the air like a yellow dog and let 'em do it.' Talking hurt, too, but he didn't much care. He was too full of rage to care. If he didn't let it out, it would fester like an abscess at the base of a tooth. He sucked in another breath of air.

Before he could let it out again, the telephone rang. He limped over to the nightstand and picked it up. 'Hello?'

'Cut the broad loose, Auerbach,' the voice on the other end

of the line said. 'Cut her loose, or else your place will end up looking just like that airstrip out there.' The man who'd called hung up. Auerbach listened to the click, and then to the dial tone that followed it. Slowly, he hung up, too.

'Who was that?' Penny asked.

'Friend of yours, I reckon,' he answered.

For a moment, she simply accepted that. Then alarm washed over her face, leaving her looking older and harder than she had. 'I haven't got any friends, except maybe you,' she said bleakly. 'If anybody knows I'm here, I better get the hell out. What did they say they'd do if I didn't?' She sounded very sure they'd said something along those lines.

And, of course, she was right. Auerbach said, 'Burn the building down. You've gotten to know some really nice folks since you walked out on me the first time, haven't you, Penny?'

'You might say so,' she answered. 'Yeah, you just might say so. Okay, Rance. I don't want to put you on the spot, not if they know I'm here. This isn't turning out to be as easy to fix as I figured it would. I'll be out of here in an hour's time.' Her laugh came brittle. 'It's not like I've got a lot to pack.'

'You aren't going anywhere.' Auerbach opened the night-stand drawer, took out a .45, and stuck it in the waistband of his trousers. Then he pulled out another one and offered it to Penny. 'You know how to handle it?'

'I know how,' she said. 'I don't need it. I've got a .357 magnum in my handbag. But I still ought to leave. What can you do if they pour gasoline all over the downstairs and toss in a match?'

'Not much,' he admitted. 'You really made some people like you a hell of a lot, didn't you?' Without waiting for an answer, he went on, 'If you leave, where will you go?'

'Somewhere,' Penny said. 'Anywhere. Someplace where those bastards can't find me. I've got plenty of money – not enough to make 'em happy, but plenty. You've seen that.'

'Yeah, I've seen that,' Rance agreed, 'It doesn't do a dead person much good, though. How long can you last on the run?

You've got no place to run to, and you know it. You may as well stay here. You'll have somebody to cover your back.'

Penny stared at him, then looked away. 'God damn you, Rance Auerbach, you just made me want to cry, and I haven't come close to doing that in more years than you can shake a stick at. The crowd I've been running with isn't what you'd call chock full of gentlemen.'

'Gentleman, hell.' Auerbach felt himself flushing; he hadn't been so embarrassed since the day he'd found out where babies came from. 'All I am is a broken-down, busted-up cavalry captain who knows better than to let his troops get out of line.'

Penny Summers came to attention and saluted, which jerked startled laughter out of Rance. 'Call it whatever you want to call it, then. I don't care. But I don't want to get you into trouble on account of me.'

'You won't,' he answered. 'Worst thing your pals can do is kill me, and two weeks out of every month I'd reckon they were doing me a favor if they did the job. I haven't been afraid of anything since the night the Lizards shot me. Oh, I know how that sounds, but it's the Lord's truth.'

'I believe you,' Penny said. 'I nursed you back then, remember? I changed your bandages. I looked underneath. I know what they did to you. It's a miracle you aren't pushing up a lily somewhere in Colorado.'

Cautiously, he touched his shattered leg. 'If this here's a miracle, God's got a nasty sense of humor,' he said. He glanced toward her. 'You gave me the bedpan, too.'

'When you needed it.'

He laughed his ruined laugh. 'Every once in a while, you made like you were giving me the bedpan and then you did something else instead.'

'When you needed it,' Penny repeated in exactly the same tone of voice. Mischief sparked in her eyes. 'You think you need it now?' This time, she was the one who didn't wait for an answer. She set a hand on his chest and pushed. He didn't have much in the way of balance, not with one wrecked leg he didn't. In spite of flailing his arms, he went over on his back onto the bed.

Penny crouched above him. She undid his belt, she unzipped his fly, and she pulled down his chinos and his briefs. Then she took him in hand and bent her head low. 'Jesus!' he said hoarsely as her mouth came down on him, hot and wet. 'First time you did that, they set off an explosive-metal bomb outside of Denver just when I was shooting my load.'

'Sweetheart' – she looked up again for a moment – 'when I'm through with you, you're going to feel like they set off an explosive-metal bomb inside of you.' After that, she stopped talking for the next few minutes. And she turned out to be exactly right.

She went into the bathroom to wipe off her chin. Auerbach went in himself after she came out. When he emerged, he had a cigarette going. He took it out of his mouth and looked at it. 'Damn things are hell on your wind,' he said, 'but I don't have much wind anyhow. And I like 'em.'

'You had enough wind there,' Penny said. 'Let me have one of those, will you?' He tossed her the pack and a book of matches. After she lit her cigarette, she smoked it in quick, nervous puffs.

Auerbach sat down on the bed. His breath caught as his leg twinged when he shifted position, but he didn't feel too bad once he'd stopped moving. He laughed a little. Maybe afterglow was good for aches and pains. He wished he were able to experiment more often. Had he been younger, he could have.

But afterglow lasted only so long and meant only so much. After he stubbed out his cigarette in an ashtray made from the casing of a five-inch shell, he said, 'I didn't want to pry too much before, but now that they know you're here, I reckon I've earned the right to know: just who are *they*, anyway?'

By the way she nodded, Penny had been expecting the question. 'Yeah, you've got the right to know,' she agreed. 'Like I pretty much said, I was a go-between for some ginger smugglers. Ginger's not illegal here – I don't think it's illegal anywhere people still run their own affairs.'

'It's sure as hell illegal everywhere the Lizards run things, though,' Rance said.

'Oh, I know that,' Penny said. 'I didn't have any trouble. Lizards don't know everything there is to know about searching people, especially women. So I delivered the goods, and the Lizards paid me off, and . . .' She laughed out loud. 'And I decided to go into business for myself.'

'Did you?' Auerbach asked. 'That's not quite what you said when you showed up on my doorstep, you know. No wonder they aren't very happy with you.'

'No wonder at all,' Penny agreed. 'But I decided to take a chance. I didn't know if I'd ever get another one, you know what I mean? So I kept the money. Those people can do without it a hell of a lot better than I can. The only thing I wish is that they never got wise to me.'

'I believe that.' Auerbach's comment was completely matter-of-fact. Only after he'd spoken did he wonder how he'd come to take thieving and everything that went with it so much for granted. This wasn't the life he'd had in mind when he went off to West Point. He'd always known he might die for his country. The idea had never fazed him. But getting shot up and discarded as useless, left to live out the rest of his days as best he could – that had never crossed his mind, not then. 'God damn the Lizards,' he repeated, this time for a different reason.

'Amen,' Penny said, 'I wish there had been some way for me to give 'em poison to taste instead of ginger.'

'Yeah.' But thinking of the Lizards one way made Rance think of them another way. 'Christ! Those damn chameleon-faces aren't going to come after you along with the real people you stiffed, are they?'

'I don't know,' she answered. 'I don't think so, though. They've got enough trouble telling one person from another one, and they hadn't seen me all that often.' She lit another cigarette. Rance watched her cheeks hollow as she sucked in smoke. They'd hollowed the same way while she'd been . . . She forced his mind back onto the Lizards, saying, 'If they'd been after me, they'd have blown up this apartment house instead of the airfield outside of town.'

'Different batch of Lizards,' he said, before realizing she already knew that. He chuckled. 'Okay. A .45'll stop those bastards, too, believe you me it will – knock 'em ass over teakettle. Your gun'll do the job on a Lizard, probably better than it would on a person.'

'I can take care of myself,' Penny said. He just looked at her and didn't say anything. Under the rouge on her cheeks, she got redder still. If she'd been so sure she could take care of herself, she wouldn't have come to him for help. She stubbed out the cigarette, a sharp, savage gesture. 'Well, most of the time I can take care of myself, goddammit.'

'Sure, babe. Sure.' Auerbach didn't want to argue with her. He hadn't particularly wanted her here – she'd walked out on him, after all, and never looked back: never till she needed him again, anyhow. Now she'd walked back in without a backwards glance, too, and he'd discovered he was glad she had. In crassest terms, he couldn't remember the last time he'd got so much.

'We're all right, the two of us,' she said, as if she'd picked the thought out of his back pocket. 'We're both a couple of wrecks, and we deserve each other.'

'Yeah,' he said, one more time. But there was a difference, and he knew it even if she didn't. He'd *been* wrecked. If the Lizards hadn't done their best to kill him, he'd probably be a colonel by now, maybe even a brigadier general if he caught some breaks along the way. Penny, now, Penny had wrecked herself. Even after she'd left him, she could have settled down. He'd always figured she had. But no – and so she was here with him.

She said, 'The Lizards didn't do that much harm, not when you look at the whole country. Things'll be all right. And when you look at you and me, things'll be all right there, too, for as long as we want 'em to be.'

'If I had a drink, I'd drink to that,' Auerbach said. Penny ran out to the kitchen to fix him one. And if that didn't prove she had a point, he was damned if he knew what did.

'Comrade General Secretary,' Vyacheslav Molotov's secretary said, 'the Lizards' ambassador has arrived, along with his interpreter.'

'I quiver with delight,' Molotov said, his features expressionless as usual. His secretary gave him an odd look. *Good,* he thought. *I am not entirely predictable.* 'Send him – send them – in, Pyotr Maksimovich.'

In came Queek. In with him came the Pole who did his translating. After the usual exchange of politely insincere greetings, the Lizard said, 'We have struck at you, as we promised we would do. Remember, only our mercy and our uncertainty as to the degree of your guilt made the blow light. If we prove you were responsible for this outrage, we shall strike again, and heavily.'

'Since we were not responsible, you cannot possibly prove we were,' Molotov replied. He was, for once, telling the truth (unless Beria had lied to him). He delivered it exactly as he delivered lies he knew to be lies. Consistency was the key. He could have shouted and blustered and got the same results, so long as he shouted and blustered the same way every time.

'Your assertions have not always proved reliable,' Queek said: half a step short of calling Molotov a liar. The translator smiled as he turned the Lizard's words into Russian. Sure as sure, he had some axe to grind against the Soviet Union.

'Here is an assertion that is altogether reliable,' Molotov said: 'If you presume to violate our territory again, we shall move in our own interest. This may include combat with the Race. It may include rethinking our position on your imperialist aspirations in China. And it may include rethinking our relationship with the Greater German *Reich*.'

After the interpreter translated that, Queek spoke one word.

Again, the interpreter smiled as he turned it into Russian: 'Bluff.'

'You know better,' Molotov said, addressing the fellow directly. 'Remind your principal that the USSR and the *Reich* enjoyed a nonaggression pact for almost two years before coming to blows. We cooperated to some degree against the Race during the fighting. If we both see ourselves threatened, we can cooperate again.'

Not smiling any more, the Pole spoke in the Lizards' language. Queek listened intently, then said, 'It is precisely the instability of your species that makes you so dangerous.'

'We are not unstable,' Molotov said. 'We are progressive.'

'I cannot translate that,' the interpreter told him. 'The language of the Race has no such word, no such concept.'

'I believe it,' Molotov said, and then regretted wasting his time on a cut the interpreter would feel but the Lizard, even were it translated for him, would not. Reactionary that he was, he would take it for praise. Sighing, Molotov went on, 'I reiterate: we have tolerated one blow because we are a peace-loving nation and are, in the words of the old superstition, willing to turn our cheek. Once. We are willing once. If you also strike at the cheek we have turned, only the devil's grandfather knows where things will end.'

Whenever Russians brought the devil's kin into a conversation, they meant something had gone or would go dreadfully wrong somewhere. Molotov wondered how Queek's interpreter was getting that across in the language of the Lizards. The ambassador said, 'I have delivered my message. You have delivered yours, which I shall transmit to my superiors for their evaluation. Have we any further business?'

'I think not,' Molotov answered. 'We have threatened each other enough for a summer afternoon.' The interpreter gave him an odd look. He stared back, imperturbable as always. With a shrug that said the Pole couldn't believe what he'd heard, the fellow translated for Queek.

'Truth,' the ambassador said, one of the few words in his

language Molotov understood. He and the interpreter left together.

Molotov went into the chamber behind the office and changed clothes, then went into the other office onto which that chamber opened, the one no Lizard was allowed to enter. He spoke to the secretary there: 'Summon Lavrenti Pavlovich, Andrei Andreyevich, and Georgi Konstantinovich to meet me here in an hour's time.'

'Yes, Comrade General Secretary,' the man said.

What will they be thinking? Molotov wondered. *What will be going through Beria's mind? Through Gromyko's? Through Zhukov's?* Molotov had always trembled inside when Stalin summoned him to a meeting – often in the wee hours of the morning. Did his summons make his chief lieutenants shiver? He doubted it. He was as ruthless as Stalin had ever been, but less showy about it. And Stalin had enjoyed, and let people know he enjoyed, issuing death sentences. Molotov did it as routinely as Stalin ever had, but got no great pleasure from it. Maybe that made him less frightening than his great predecessor. So long as he held plots at bay, he didn't care.

Marshal Zhukov arrived first, fifty-eight minutes after Molotov told the secretary to call him. Gromyko was a minute behind him. This time, Beria was late: he strolled into the office ten minutes after Gromyko. He did not excuse himself, but simply sat down. Molotov did not think he was making a display of his power – just an uncultured lout from the Caucasus with no sense of time.

He did not make an issue of it. It would keep. Heading the NKVD did make Beria immensely powerful. But no chief of the secret police was ever loved. If Molotov decided to get rid of him, he would have the Party and the Red Army behind him, and a faction within the NKVD as well. So he did not worry about Beria . . . too much.

Of course, no one in the *Reich* had worried about Himmler too much, either. Molotov wished he hadn't had that thought.

Shoving it aside, he said, 'Now that we are all here' – as

much of a dig at Beria as he would take – 'let us discuss latest developments with the Lizards.' He summarized his conversation with Queek.

'Comrade General Secretary, I want you to know we could have inflicted severe losses on the Lizards when they attacked our air base,' Zhukov said. 'Only at your orders did we refrain from punishing the bandits.'

'It is as well you did,' Molotov said. He did not glance over to Zhukov. He did not need to see the man who looked like a peasant and fought the way *Wehrmacht* field marshals wished they could to worry about him. Like Beria, Zhukov was able. Unlike Beria, the marshal was also popular. But he had had many chances to stage a coup, and had taken none of them. Molotov trusted him as far as he trusted any man, which was not far. He went on, 'I do not know how harshly the Lizards would have retaliated had we struck at them, and I did not wish to discover this by expensive experiment.'

'They are sons of bitches, nothing but sons of bitches,' said Zhukov, who could affect a peasant's crudity to cloak his keen wits.

'They are powerful sons of bitches,' Gromyko said, another self-evident truth. 'Powerful sons of bitches have to be handled carefully.' He did glance over at Beria.

Beria either did not notice or affected not to. He said, 'The foreign commissar is right. And I can also tell you, Vyacheslav Mikhailovich, that the Lizards think we are powerful sons of bitches. Signals intercepts and reconnaissance satellite photos' – both provinces of the NKVD – 'show their colonists are not settling close to the southern borders of the USSR. You told them they did not have our leave to do so, and they are taking your word seriously.'

'That is good news,' Molotov said, and Zhukov and Gromyko both nodded. Molotov continued, 'That the colonists are continuing to land anywhere on the surface of the world is not good news, however.'

'From all I have learned, they will have a hard time making

the colonists into soldiers,' Zhukov said, 'a much harder time than we have in turning conscripts into fighting men. This works in our favor.'

'So it does, Georgi Konstantinovich, but only so far,' Molotov replied. 'They are landing many workers and many machines. Their industrial output will increase with more factories and more workers who do not seek to sabotage production. What soldiers they have will be better equipped.'

'They will also be able to exploit the resources of the territory they control more effectively than has been true up till now,' Gromyko added. In many ways, he thought very much like Molotov. Unlike Molotov, though, he seemed content with a subordinate role in affairs.

Zhukov said, 'If they train no more soldiers, they will run out sooner or later. How many weapons they make will not matter if they have no one who can fire them.'

'Interesting,' Molotov murmured. 'Perhaps very interesting.' Now he glanced over at Beria. 'Inquire among our prisoners as to how rapidly Lizards reproduce and how long they need to be trained to become proper parts of their society.'

'I will do that, Vyacheslav Mikhailovich,' the NKVD chief said. 'This is not information we needed before, and so we never tried to pull it out. Now that we see it might be useful, I expect we can get it.'

'Good,' Molotov said. 'Without the captives we took in the fighting, we would never have been able to move ahead in so many fields so fast. We have learned a great deal from them. And now that a new kind of knowledge becomes more valuable, as you say, we shall learn more.'

Beria nodded. 'I shall have the precise details for you very soon, even if it means testing a couple of Lizards to destruction, as the engineers say.' The electric lights overhead glinted from his spectacles, and perhaps from his eyes as well. He was no simple sadist, as were some of the men who worked for him, but he was not immune to the pleasures inherent in his job,

205

either. Molotov had heard stories about a couple of young girls who'd vanished without a trace. He'd never tried to find out if they were true. It didn't matter. If he ever decided to topple Beria, he'd trot out the stories whether they were true or not.

'Comrade General Secretary, were you serious when you told Queek we might consider realigning ourselves with the Greater German. *Reich* if pressure from the Lizards forced us in that direction?' Gromyko asked.

'I was not jocular,' Molotov replied. Gromyko gave him a reproachful look. Ignoring it, he elaborated: 'I shall act as circumstances force me to. If I judge the Lizards are a more dangerous threat than the Nazis, how in good conscience can I avoid seeking a rapprochement with Nuremberg?' The Germans had not rebuilt Berlin after the Lizards struck it with an atomic bomb, but left the city in ruins as a monument to the enemy's depravity – showing, in Molotov's view, a curious delicacy given their own habits.

Nodding at his words, Gromyko said, 'We have come through the first crisis since the arrival of the colonization fleet well enough – not perfectly, but well enough. May we likewise weather the storms ahead.'

'We shall not merely weather them. We shall prevail,' Molotov said. 'The dialectic demands it.' His colleagues solemnly nodded.

7

Just watching the way some of the newly defrosted colonists strolled around Basra made Fotsev's scales itch. 'By
the Emperor, they are asking to get killed,' he burst out. 'Some
of them will get what they are asking for, too.'

'Truth,' Gorppet said. 'I do not know whether they think the
Big Uglies are civilized, the way the Rabotevs and Hallessi are,
or whether they just figure they are tame, like meat animals.'

'Whatever they think, they are wrong,' Fotsev said. 'I am
just glad this *"Allahu akbar!"* business has died down for the
time being. If it had not, you would need to be addled to let
colonists into Basra at all.'

He watched and listened to a revived female dickering with a
Tosevite over an ornately decorated but useless brass ornament. She had not the faintest idea how to bargain, and paid
three times the going rate for such a trinket. Gorppet sighed
and said, 'Everything is going to get more expensive for all of
us.'

'So it is,' Fotsev agreed unhappily. 'They do not know
anything, do they?' One eye turret turned toward a male
who was wandering around photographing everything he
saw. Fotsev couldn't imagine why; Basra wasn't much, even
by the minimal standards of Tosev 3.

The male noticed him watching and called, 'Is it always so
chilly here?'

'Does not know anything,' Fotsev repeated in a low voice. Aloud, he answered, 'For Tosev 3, this is good weather. You will never see frozen water falling out of the sky here, for instance.'

'They told us about that,' the colonist said. 'I do not believe it.'

'Have you seen the videos?' Fotsev demanded.

'I do not care about videos,' the newcomer said. 'You can make a video look like anything. That does not mean it is true.' Off he went, camera in hand.

'Ought to send him up to the SSSR,' Gorppet muttered. 'He would learn something there – or else he would freeze to death. Either way, he would shut up.'

'That is cruel.' Fotsev thought about it. His mouth fell open in a nasty laugh. 'I do wonder how he would make out in that snow stuff up past his head, with the Big Uglies sliding along over it on boards. How would he like that? How much ginger do you suppose he would taste to keep himself from thinking about it?'

'Enough to make him mutiny, by the Emperor,' Gorppet exclaimed.

Fotsev eyed him warily. So did the other males in their small group. The last time he and Fotsev had spoken of mutiny, they'd been alone together. That was how males from the conquest fleet usually spoke of mutiny, when they spoke of it at all. Fotsev didn't think there was a male who was ignorant of the mutinies some troops had raised against their superiors. Talking much about them was something else. Like a lot of things on Tosev 3 – the death factories of the Deutsche sprang to mind – they were usually better ignored.

Gorppet looked defiantly at his comrades. 'They happened. We all know they happened.' But he lowered his voice before going on, 'Would not surprise me a bit if some of the officers deserved what they got, too.'

'Careful,' Fotsev said, and added an emphatic cough. 'If you go around saying things like that, people will say you think like a Tosevite, and that will not do you any good.'

'I do not think like a stinking Big Ugly,' Gorppet said. 'I am no snoutcounter. Nobody whose brains are not in his cloaca is a snoutcounter. But I will tell you this: when I have officers over me, I want them to know what they are doing. Is that too much to ask?'

'A lot of the ones who did not know what they were doing are dead now,' Fotsev said. 'The Big Uglies took care of them. We did not need mutineers.' The word felt odd coming off his tongue. Back on Home, no one had used it in tens of thousands of years, not unless he was creating a drama about the distant times before the Empire was unified.

Gorppet refused to spit it out and walk away from it. 'Truth – the ones who did not know what they were doing are dead now. But how many perfectly good males went to meet the spirits of Emperors past because of their bungling?'

Too many was the answer that hatched in Fotsev's mind. He didn't say it. He didn't want to think about it. It, too, was better left unexamined.

Before Gorppet could say anything more, a male from the colonization fleet came running toward the small group. In the years since coming to Tosev 3, Fotsev had fallen out of practice in reading civilians' body paint. He thought this fellow was a mid-senior cook, but wasn't quite sure.

Whatever the male was, he was excited. 'You soldiers!' he shouted. 'To the rescue! I need you!'

'For what?' Fotsev asked. Turning an eye turret in the direction from which the cook had come, he saw no Tosevites pounding after him with knives and pistols in their hands. By local standards, that meant things couldn't be too bad.

'For what?' the male from the colonization fleet cried. 'For what? Why, back around that corner yonder, one of these native creatures, these untamed native creatures everyone keeps warning us about, is carrying a gun twice the size of the one you have there.'

209

'Did he shoot you with it?' Gorppet asked. 'Does not look that way, on account of you are still here.'

'You do not understand!' the cook said. 'A wild native is walking these filthy streets with a gun. Go take it away from him.'

'Did he *try* to shoot you?' Fotsev asked.

'No, but he could have,' the newly revived colonist answered. 'What kind of world is this, anyhow?'

All the males in the small group began to laugh. 'This is Tosev 3, that's what,' Fotsev said. 'This is the kind of world where that Big Ugly probably will not try to shoot you unless you give him some sort of reason to want you dead. It's also the kind of world where, if we try to take his rifle away, everybody in this town will be shrieking *"Allahu akbar!"* and trying to kill us faster than you can flick your nictitating membrane across your eyeball.'

'You are crazy,' the other male said. His eye turrets swung to look over the males who accompanied Fotsev. 'You are all crazy. You have spent too much time with the horrible creatures that live here, and now you are as bad as they are.' Hissing in disgust, he stalked off, tailstump rigid with fury.

'Tell you what,' Gorppet said. 'If I had a choice, I would sooner act like a Big Ugly than like him.'

No one argued with him. The patrol made its way through Basra. Fotsev turned at the corner around which the excitable cook had come. Sure enough, there stood a Big Ugly with a rifle on his back. He was eating some of the fruits that grew on the local trees that looked like dusting tools. When he saw the soldiers of the Race, he bobbed his head up and down in a Tosevite gesture of greeting. Fotsev showed his empty right hand, palm out. That motion, unlike most, meant about the same thing to the Big Uglies as it did to the Race.

As Fotsev walked on, he did turn an eye turret back toward the Big Ugly to make sure he didn't have anything treacherous in mind. The Tosevite went on eating the small brown fruits –

they looked rather like turds, but tasted sweet – and spitting the seeds into the dust of the street.

'Oh, he is dangerous, all right,' Gorppet said, and laughed again.

After the males of the Race rounded another corner, a Big Ugly approached them. It was a male, Fotsev saw: it had hair on its jaw and cheeks, and it exposed its entire face to the view of outsiders, which violated local custom for females. A moment later, he realized it was a prosperous male. The Big Ugly's robes and headgear were fancier than those of most of his kind. That wasn't so reliable an indicator as body paint, but nothing on Tosev 3 seemed as reliable as its equivalent back on Home.

Then, to his surprise, the Big Ugly spoke in the language of the Race, and spoke well for one of its kind: 'You males, will you answer some questions of mine? I am an ignorant man, and I seek to learn.'

'Go ahead and ask,' Fotsev said, unused to such politeness from a Tosevite. The Big Ugly had given him more than the cook of his own species.

'I thank you,' the Tosevite said, polite still. 'Is it true that, in the ships the Race is now landing, there are both males and females, as Noah, peace be upon him, took male and female beasts aboard the Ark?'

Fotsev didn't know who Noah was, or anything about the Ark, a word the Big Ugly had of necessity put into his own language. Still, the question seemed straightforward enough. 'Yes, the colonization fleet carries both males and females. How could we colonize this world if it did not?'

He waited for the Big Ugly to pitch a fit. Instead, the fellow asked, 'And, of these new members of the Race we now see on the streets of Basra, some are males and some are females?'

'Yes,' Fotsev said. 'How else?'

'And your females are allowed to walk the streets naked, shamelessly showing themselves for your males to gaze upon and admire and desire?' the Big Ugly persisted.

Gorppet pulled Fotsev aside for a moment to whisper, 'What is this fool getting at?'

'How should I know? He is not making a fuss, and that is good enough for me,' Fotsev whispered back. To the Tosevite, he said, 'We do not wrap ourselves in cloths, the way you people do.'

'But you must, when male and female are together,' the Big Ugly said earnestly. 'Nakedness offends every custom.'

'Not our customs,' Fotsev said.

'But you will desire one another too much!' the Big Ugly cried in dismay.

Fotsev didn't laugh at him, though that wasn't easy. The Big Ugly was plainly intelligent, and as plainly ignorant, ever so ignorant. 'We do not mate because of what we see,' Fotsev said. 'We mate because of what we smell.'

'Nakedness is a crime against Allah,' the Tosevite said. 'He will punish you for your wickedness.'

'Let us get moving,' Fotsev said to his comrades. Arguing with a Big Ugly caused nothing but trouble. Leaving him to his own foolishness seemed a better idea.

But he wouldn't be left. He followed the males down the narrow, grimy, unpaved street, crying, 'You must clothe your females. Allah teaches it. Do you dare act contrary to the word of Allah?'

'This Allah of yours never talked to me,' Fotsev said, and laughed at the foolish Big Ugly. 'If he does, maybe I will listen to him. Until then, I am not going to worry about him. I will worry about things that are real instead.' He laughed again.

The Tosevite's little eyes got as big as they could. 'You say Allah is not real?' He turned and hurried away.

'You got rid of him,' Gorppet said. 'Well done!' To emphasize how well done, he folded himself into the posture of respect, as if Fotsev were at least an officer and perhaps a shiplord. Fotsev laughed once more, and so did his comrades. They got through the rest of their patrol with no trouble at all.

A few days later, fresh rioting against the Race broke out in

Basra. Three newly revived colonists got caught in the trouble and killed; a large number of Tosevites perished. Like his superiors, Fotsev hadn't the faintest idea what might have touched it off.

Mordechai Anielewicz was heading back toward his flat in Lodz when two Lizards came up to him. 'You are Anielewicz,' one of them said in Polish, looking from his face to a photograph and back again. Even with the photograph, he sounded unsure.

'I am Anielewicz,' Mordechai agreed, after briefly thinking about denying everything. It had worked for St. Peter, but he didn't know how well it would work for him. 'What do you want with me?'

'We are to bring you before the regional subadministrator,' the Lizard answered. He and his comrade both carried automatic weapons. They sounded nervous even so. They had reason to sound nervous. If Mordechai shouted, they'd last only moments in spite of the high-powered rifles. Jews with guns of their own were on the street and, no doubt, watching from windows, too.

But he did not shout. 'I'll come,' he said. 'Do you know why the regional subadministrator wants to talk to me?'

'No,' both males said together. Anielewicz believed them. The Lizards' bosses were in the habit of giving orders, not explanations.

'Well, I'll find out,' Anielewicz said. 'Let's go.' He started off for Bunim's headquarters near the square that housed the Bialut Market. The Lizards fell in on either side of him. He towered over them, but that didn't make him feel important. Size mattered little, power a great deal. He had it, but so did Bunim. One of the Lizards spoke into a portable radio set or telephone to let the regional subadministrator know they were on their way.

When he got there, Bunim addressed him in German: 'I have spoken to you of the threat against the colonists I received.'

213

'Regional Subadministrator, I remember,' Anielewicz replied. 'Many ships have landed in Poland now. Many colonists have landed in Poland now. I know of nothing bad that has happened to them, though not many have landed near Lodz.' In their shoes, he wouldn't have wanted to land near the border with the Greater German *Reich*, either.

'Nothing bad has happened – not yet,' Bunim said. 'But I am concerned. Is it the right word – concerned?' He didn't like to make mistakes. In that, he was a typical Lizard. Mistakes showed faulty planning, and the Lizards were much enamored of planning in general.

'Concerned is the right word, yes, Regional Subadministrator,' Anielewicz said, giving him what credit he could. 'You have come to speak this language well.' That was a lie, but not an outrageous one. Bunim did work hard. Having delivered the compliments, Mordechai got down to business: 'Why are you concerned? Have you received another threat?'

'No, no one has threatened,' Bunim told him. 'That is one reason I am concerned. When you Tosevites strut and bluster, we of the Race at least know where you stand. When you are quiet, that is the time for worry. That is the time when you are hatching plots in secret. And —' He fell silent.

Anielewicz exhaled in some exasperation. 'If no one had sent you the first message, you would not be worried now, even though everything was quiet. Since everything has been quiet since, why are you still worrying?'

Bunim's eye turrets flicked this way and that. He was an unhappy Lizard, no doubt about it. 'I have reason to be concerned,' he declared, and added an emphatic cough even though he was still speaking German.

'Well, if you do, you'd better show me why,' Mordechai said, his patience wearing thin. 'Otherwise, I'll just think you've been wasting my time.'

'Show you why? It shall be done,' Bunim said. Even in German, the phrase sounded odd, and seemed to imply Anielewicz was the regional subadministrator's superior.

Bunim took out one of the *skelkwank* disks the Lizards used for just about all their recording. He stuck it in a player. Out came the threat he had mentioned before to Anielewicz. Mordechai was not tremendously fluent in the language of the Race, but he followed it well enough to understand what he heard here.

'Well?' he said when the brief recording was done. 'I heard it. It was what you said it was, but so what?'

'You heard it, but you heard without full understanding,' Bunim said.

'You'd better explain, then,' Mordechai said. 'I must be missing something here, but I don't know what.'

'You heard the threat?' Bunim asked. Mordechai nodded. Bunim understood the human gesture. He went on, 'That threat, Anielewicz, was not spoken by a Tosevite. Without the tiniest fragment of doubt, it came from the mouth of a male of the Race.'

Anielewicz thought about that for a few seconds. Then, very softly, he said, *'Oy.'* Bunim was right. People didn't – couldn't – sound quite right speaking the Lizards' language. Sure as hell, that had been a Lizard. 'What do you suppose it means?' Anielewicz asked the regional subadministrator.

'One of two things.' Bunim held up a clawed middle finger. 'It could be some Tosevites holding a male of the Race prisoner. This is not good.' The Lizard held up his index finger. 'Or it could be a male of the Race plotting with Tosevites: a criminal, I mean to say. This also is not good.'

'You are right,' Mordechai said. 'Did any male go missing not long before you got this recording?'

'No, but this does not have to mean anything,' Bunim answered. 'We know both the *Reich* and the Soviet Union still have prisoners they took during the fighting. So does the USA. So do Britain and Nippon. Those not-empires are less likely to threaten Poland, though. If you were wondering, the recording was posted to me here from Pinsk. How it got to Pinsk, I do not know.' His eye turrets swung toward Anielewicz. 'You were in Pinsk not so long ago, *nicht wahr*?'

'Yes, it is so,' Anielewicz said, judging a lie there more dangerous than the truth. 'I was meeting an old friend' – which stretched the point about David Nussboym as far as it would go, and then another ten centimeters – 'I hadn't seen since the fighting stopped.' That last clause, at least, was true.

Bunim looked to be on the point of saying something, but closed his mouth instead. Maybe he'd expected Mordechai to lie about going to Pinsk. After a moment, he started again: 'You Jews could have captives, too. Do not think we do not know about this.'

'So could the Poles, more easily than we could,' Mordechai said. 'Or it could be a ginger smuggler angry at the administration here and wanting to embarrass you.'

'All these things may be true,' Bunim said. 'Only one of them *is* true, or perhaps truth lies in none of them, but in a place we have not yet found. But where is that place? I have males of the Race trying to learn. I have Poles trying to learn. And now I have Jews trying to learn, too.'

'Yes, we had better find out about that, hadn't we?' Mordechai said abstractedly. 'You are right, Regional Subadministrator. This could be trouble.'

'The colonization fleet has already had too much trouble,' Bunim said. 'We had better not have any more. If we have any more, Tosevites will also have trouble. They will have more trouble than they ever imagined.'

'I understand,' Anielewicz said. 'I tell you this, Regional Subadministrator: no humans like you any better than the Jews of Poland. If you will not find humans on your side among us, you will not find them anywhere.'

'Then it may be that we shall not find them anywhere,' Bunim said. 'I know you have had dealings with the *Reich* when you thought our eye turrets were turned the other way. I know you are not the only one to do this, too.'

Anielewicz felt a dull embarrassment, rather as if he'd been caught in bed with a woman other than Bertha. But his marriage to the Lizards was one of convenience, not of love.

216

And he'd been unfaithful not only with the Nazis but also with the Russians, as David Nussboym could attest. He shrugged. Like any adultery, his bouts of infidelity to the Race had seemed a good idea at the time.

He said, 'When the Race came to Earth, we Jews here in Poland were slaves to the *Reich*. Men are not meant to be slaves.'

'And we set you free,' Bunim said. 'And see the thanks we have had for it.'

Yes, he sounded like a woman betrayed. 'You set us free of the Germans,' Mordechai said.

'That is what I told you,' Bunim said.

But Anielewicz shook his head. 'No, it is not. You set us free of the Germans. You did not set us free. You aimed at becoming our masters yourselves. We do not care for that any more than we cared for having the Nazis enslave us.'

'And who would rule you if we left Poland?' Bunim inquired. Twenty years on Tosev 3 had taught him sarcasm.

He had also asked a question – *the* question – for which Anielewicz had no good answer, and indeed no answer of any sort. Instead of answering, he evaded: 'This is why we will help you now. For your safety, and for our own, we need to find out who is making threats against the arriving colonists.'

'So you do,' Bunim said. 'Any trouble that comes down on our heads – in the end, it comes down on your heads, too.'

Anielewicz sent him a stare of undisguised loathing. 'It's taken you all this time since you came to Earth, but you've finally figured out what being a Jew means, haven't you?'

'I do not know what you are talking about,' Bunim said, which might have been true or might not. The Lizard went on, 'I do know that my first duty is to preserve the Race, my next is to preserve the land on which the Race will dwell, and only after that do I concern myself with the welfare of Tosevites of any sort.'

From his perspective, that made perfectly good sense. Mordechai knew he himself put Jews ahead of Poles, Poles ahead –

far ahead – of Germans, and humans ahead of Lizards. But Bunim had resources he couldn't hope to match. If the Lizards decided the Jews deserved oppressing . . . if they decided that, how were they any different from the Nazis?

He shook his head. That wasn't fair to the Lizards. When they'd discovered Treblinka, they'd destroyed it in horror. Anielewicz did not think they would ever build an extermination camp of their own. A generation on Earth could not have corrupted the males of the conquest fleet that far, and the males and females of the colonization fleet would not be corrupt at all, not by Earthly standards.

Bunim said, 'Remember, our fates – is that the word? – our fates, yes, are tied together. If the Race fails on Tosev 3, your particular group of Tosevites is also likely to fail. The rest of the Tosevites, starting with the Poles, will make sure of this. Am I right or am I wrong?'

He was all too likely to be right. Anielewicz had no intention of admitting as much. In a stony voice, he replied, 'Jews got by for three thousand years before the Race came to Earth. If every male and female of the Race disappeared tomorrow, Jews would go right on getting by.'

Bunim's mouth fell open in Lizardly amusement. 'What are three thousand years?' he asked. 'Where will you be in three thousand more?'

'Dead,' Anielewicz answered, 'the same as you.'

'You, yes,' Bunim agreed. 'I, yes. The Tosevites? Possibly. The Race? No.' He spoke with absolute confidence.

'No, eh?' Anielewicz said. 'What about that male who threatened the colonists, then?' He had the somber satisfaction of seeing that he'd made Bunim loathe him as much as he loathed the Lizard.

Beside the *13th Emperor Makkakap*, the shuttlecraft seemed tiny. Beside the shuttlecraft, Nesseref seemed tiny. That surely made her seem infinitesimal alongside the enormous bulk of the starship now landed not far from the Tosevite town of Warsaw.

The logic was flawless. Nesseref, however, had other concerns besides logic. Turning to the male from the conquest fleet beside her, she asked, 'Why would anybody want to live in this miserable, cold place?'

'You think it is cold now, wait another season,' the male answered. 'Nobody from Home knows what cold is about. Winter here is like cold sleep without the drugs to make you unconscious.' He laughed. 'Tosev 3 has different drugs, believe you me it does. Have you found out about ginger yet, superior female?'

'Yes,' Nesseref said, which was not quite the truth and not quite a lie. She still had the two vials males had given her on earlier visits to Tosev 3. That in itself was against regulations, which grew more strident on the subject with each passing day. But she hadn't actually opened the vials and tasted the herb inside. As long as she didn't do that, she felt no enormous guilt.

'Good stuff, isn't it?' the male said enthusiastically. This time, Nesseref didn't answer at all. Every male from the conquest fleet who talked about ginger talked about it enthusiastically. That was one reason she hadn't tried it herself: she didn't trust anything that evoked such fervent responses. Being a shuttlecraft pilot had made her rely more on her own opinion than was usual among the Race.

Her own opinion at the moment was that things looked more confused than they should have. Newly awakened males and females from the colonization fleet wandered here and there, none of them with any clear notion of where they ought to be going or what they ought to be doing. The males from the conquest fleet who moved among them were easy to pick out by eye. They strode with purpose, to some destination familiar to them. They'd had years to get used to the vagaries of life on Tosev 3. A couple of hasty briefings couldn't possibly have the same effect.

Turning back to the male beside her, she asked, 'When you do not taste ginger, how do you stand Tosev 3? How do you keep from being bored to death?'

The male laughed again. 'Superior female, you can die a lot of ways on this planet, but being bored is not one of them. Of course, if you do get bored, one bunch of Big Uglies or another is liable to kill you, but I do not suppose that is what you were talking about.'

'No,' Nesseref said. Just how dangerous these natives could be hadn't really sunk in, despite her getting shot at on the way down to Cairo. Some Tosevites were laboring in the shadow of the *13th Emperor Makkakap*. 'They certainly do look funny, do they not? – wrapping themselves in cloths even when they work hard.'

'They stay warm that way,' the male from the conquest fleet said. 'But even the Tosevites who live where the weather is decent wear cloths, or most of them do. They use them for display – and for concealment, too, I think.'

'Why would they conceal with cloths?' Nesseref asked, puzzled. 'They are not hiding from predators, are they? No, of course not.' She answered her own question. 'They could not be.'

'No, no, no – concealment from one another.' The male from the conquest fleet gave a brief, highly colored account of Tosevite courtship and mating habits.

'That is revolting,' Nesseref said when he was through. 'I think you are making it up. I am new to this miserable world, so you figure I will believe anything.'

'By the spirits of Emperors past, I swear it is the truth,' the male said, and looked down at the ground. 'They are worse than animals, but they have a civilization. Nobody will ever figure them out.'

'Yes, we will, sooner or later.' The shuttlecraft pilot spoke with conviction. 'We just have not given it enough time yet. In a few hundred years, or maybe a few thousand years, our descendants will look back on this time and laugh at how foolish and upset we were. And the Big Uglies will be loyal subjects of the Emperor, just like everyone else.' She paused and peered over toward a couple of them. 'They will still be funny-looking, though.'

'That last is truth,' the male said. 'The rest . . . I tell you, superior female, you are still new-come from Home. You do not really know what things are like here. On Tosev 3, time is different, somehow. You can see things happen over years; they do not take centuries, the way they did with us. I am not sure there was a televisor on this planet when we got here. There are millions of them now.'

'I do not know what that proves,' Nesseref said. 'For all you know, they stole the idea from us. They seem to have stolen a lot of ideas from us.'

'Oh, they have,' the male from the conquest fleet said. 'They have, though it is not as if they have not got plenty of ideas of their own. But they do not just steal. They use what they steal, and they use it right away. Imagine the Race had never heard of televisors, but stole the idea for them from someone else. How long would we need before every other flat – every flat, some places – had a televisor in it?'

Even the form of the question felt strange to Nesseref. Imagining the history of the Race as different from the way it really was took a distinct and uncomfortable mental effort. She handled it as she would have handled a simulator session for the shuttlecraft: not real, but to be taken as real. The answer she got was obvious and disturbing at the same time: 'We would have needed thousands of years, because we would have to study the effects of televisors on a society that did not have them. We would have to be certain they were harmless before we began to use them.'

'Just so,' the male agreed. 'The Tosevites are not like that. They just start using things and then see what happens. Since we came, they have added televisors and computers and atomic energy and spacecraft and hydrogen engines and any number of different things – they tossed them into the pot to see how they flavor the stew. That is how they do things – and somehow they have not destroyed themselves.'

'Not yet,' Nesseref said. 'Slow and steady is better.'

221

'On Home, slow and steady is better,' the male said. 'Here – who knows?'

Nesseref didn't feel like arguing with him. 'Can you arrange transportation to the west for me?' she asked. 'I am supposed to visit a city called – Lodz, is it? – to examine the area for a possible shuttlecraft port site.'

'I can direct you to one who will make those arrangements for you,' the male replied. 'I can also tell you I think it is a bad idea: too close to the border with the Greater German *Reich*. Why do you think the ships from the colonization fleet have been landing in this part of Poland and not over there?'

'My superior has ordered me to examine the area, and so it shall be done,' Nesseref said. 'And I can also tell you that you seem to me to sound more like a Tosevite, or what I think a Tosevite would sound like from what I have heard, than a proper male of the Race.'

She thought that a crushing insult. The male from the conquest fleet only shrugged and answered, 'I am alive. That lets me talk however I like. And a lot of the males who used to sound so prim and proper are dead these days, so they do not sound like anything at all.'

Having got the last word, he also got his revenge on Nesseref, or so she assumed, for the transportation to which another male from the conquest fleet assigned her was a Tosevite railroad train propelled by an engine – a steam engine, she discovered by asking – that stained the sky with its plume of black exhaust smoke. She had one compartment of her railroad car to herself, but that did not keep Big Uglies from walking by, staring in at her, and using their own gluey-sounding languages to make remarks she could not understand.

Her compartment had seats made to accommodate backsides with tailstumps, which was something, but not much. Despite the seats, she had an uncomfortable trip. Railroads back on Home used magnetic levitation and had a smooth ride; here, iron wheels kept clattering along rails and over rail

222

junctions. Unpleasant, unfamiliar smells filled the car. When she opened a window to get some fresh air, she got soot from the engine's exhaust instead. Finally deciding that was worse, she closed the window again and watched the countryside through its none-too-clean glass.

Before long, she was thinking of going to sleep. The land between Warsaw and Lodz was flat and boring. Aside from being unusually green, it had nothing to commend itself to the eye. True, she was startled the first time she saw a Tosevite animal drawing a wagon, but then she saw several more in quick succession, which killed the novelty. She was also briefly interested at the first stop the train made in a small town, but she couldn't tell the Big Uglies who got on from the ones who got off. Also, every stop – and the train made a lot of them – meant she took even longer to get where she was going.

By the time she arrived, she was tempted to haul out a vial of ginger and have a taste, in the hope that the herb would make moments seem to move faster. But, unsure of what it would do to her common sense, she refrained. She wanted to be able to think clearly after she reached the town.

When, after what seemed like forever, she finally did leave the railroad car and go out into the train station, the officer who met her was energy personified. 'Of course we can find you what you need,' he said as he led her through the station, which seemed gloomy and cramped on the one fork of the tongue and ridiculously high-ceilinged on the other (only after she recalled it was built for Tosevites did the latter make sense). 'Wherever you want it, superior female, we will put it there. If you like, we will flatten out some ground special for you. We can do it. We can do anything.' He gave her not one but two emphatic coughs.

'I do not even know if this is a suitable place yet,' Nesseref said, a little taken aback at such vigor. 'Are the Big Uglies west of here not supposed to be dangerous?'

'Oh, we can take care of the Deutsche, too,' the officer said with another emphatic cough. 'If they give us trouble, we will give them a good kick in the snout.'

But, over the next little while, his enthusiasm and his boasts faded away. He started looking all around, as if afraid someone might be following him. 'Is something wrong?' Nesseref asked.

'No,' he said in a forlorn voice, but then added, 'Wait here, superior female,' and skittered around a corner. When he returned a moment later, he was strutting again, up on top of the world. 'Wrong?' he demanded. 'What could possibly be wrong? Everything is just as right as it could be, and this is the perfect – the *perfect*, I tell you – place for a shuttlecraft port, or my name isn't Emmitto.'

Before very long, Emmitto was subdued and worried again. Nesseref wondered what was wrong with him; such wild mood swings were most unusual in the Race. Only after he excused himself once more and once more returned full of exuberance did a warning light begin to glow on the instrument panel of her mind. She had everything she could do not to let her mouth fall open in sour laughter. *I should have tasted ginger, too,* she thought. *Then Emmitto would have had some company.*

Tosev blazed down out of a sky the wrong shade of blue, but with very respectable warmth all the same. Atvar smelled unfamiliar spicy odors far removed from the stinks of Cairo. 'I should come to Australia more often, regardless of where I make my capital,' he told his adjutant.

'Whatever pleases the Exalted Fleetlord,' Pshing replied. 'Since so many of the Race will be settling here, surely your duty might well be construed as requiring you to make frequent visits here.'

'It might indeed,' Atvar said, 'although I expect I can find my own excuses for doing what I want to do anyhow. Most males can, at any rate.'

He looked around with considerable satisfaction. Here as in few places on Tosev 3, the Race would have the land to itself.

The Big Uglies had made little use of the central part of the island continent. Now the Race would show them how foolish they had been to ignore it.

'Perhaps,' he said, 'just perhaps, mind you, the colonization fleet could establish its administrative center here, a center that would, in time, become the Race's chief administrative center, replacing Cairo. That would allow us to change capitals without confessing weakness to the Tosevites. If I spent my retirement here, I might yet come to think of Tosev 3 as a pleasant world.'

'A clever notion indeed, Exalted Fleetlord,' Pshing said. 'Shall I relay it to Fleetlord Reffet for his views?'

'Not yet,' Atvar answered. 'Let me study it for possible drawbacks first. We are males of the Race. I need not be hasty here, as I would when dealing with the Big Uglies. Returning to old habits feels good, after so long.' He paused, then let out an exasperated hiss. 'Or perhaps not so good. If I return to the habit of slowness, the Tosevites will make me regret it before long.'

'If we succeed in bringing this world into the Empire, I wonder if we shall ever be able to slow the Big Uglies down to a pace that the other races find tolerable,' Pshing said.

'I hope so, for the Tosevites' sake and ours,' Atvar said. 'I also hope we *can* bring this world fully into the Empire, for their sake and ours.'

Though he would not say as much to his adjutant, he feared the result if the Race failed to bring the independent not-empires into the Empire in a fairly short time. That the Big Uglies had succeeded in building a technological civilization in the relatively brief period since the Race's probe showed they had none warned of their prowess. What they had done since the colonization fleet made the warning even more urgent. Then, while astonishingly advanced, they had been behind the Race in every area. They'd hung on with an abundance of cunning and matériel. Now . . .

Some males brushed aside the Tosevites' progress by noting

how much they had borrowed – stolen, many said, and truthfully – from the Race. Atvar recognized the truth in that. But he also saw how the Tosevites did not blindly borrow, how they used machines and information taken from the Race to bring their own preexisting technology up to date, how they put their own slant on everything they stole.

His experts had run projections. He'd run secret projections of his own, too. They differed in detail, depending on just what assumptions went into them. The broad outlines, though, were startlingly, dismayingly, similar: before too long, the Big Uglies' technology would be more advanced than that of the Race.

Most of the projections said the Race would still enjoy a breathing space after that: the Big Uglies would need a while to realize what they'd achieved. Sooner or later, though, they would. They couldn't help it.

What would happen then? There too, the projections differed. *Nothing good for the Race,* though, was the theme that ran through them.

And I can't even destroy those not-empires, Atvar thought, *not without destroying the whole planet, which means destroying the colonization fleet.* One of the ideas haunting him was that such destruction might be worthwhile in spite of the cost: it might mean saving the Race as a whole.

Pshing pointed at something moving across the barren countryside, for which distraction Atvar was thoroughly glad. 'What are those things, Exalted Fleetlord?' his adjutant asked.

'Tosevite life of some sort, I suppose,' Atvar answered. 'If you have a monocular, you will be able to tell more.'

'I do, Exalted Fleetlord.' Pshing took the magnifier from a belt pouch, turned one eye turret toward the distant creatures, and raised the magnifying lenses. He let out a startled hiss. 'How peculiar! Are those Big Uglies? No, they cannot be. But still . . .' He gave Atvar the monocular. 'See for yourself, Exalted Fleetlord.'

'I will.' Atvar brought the little tube up to one of his own eyes. The creatures on the plain seemed to leap much closer. 'They *are* funny-looking.'

'They certainly are.' Pshing added an emphatic cough. 'I thought almost all Tosevite life forms except the Big Uglies themselves were quadrupeds, not bipeds.'

'I seem to recall reading that this island continent had an ecosystem long isolated from others on Tosev 3,' Atvar said. 'Maybe that accounts for these peculiar things. They look almost like a cross between the Big Uglies and ourselves, don't they? – though their tails are long.'

Just then, something must have startled the Tosevite creatures, which went bounding off at a very respectable turn of speed. 'Well!' Pshing said. 'I did not think they could move like that.'

'A lot of Tosevite creatures are deceptive, all the way up to the Big Uglies,' Atvar said. Suddenly, one of the animals crashed to the ground and lay kicking. The fleetlord could not see why until a Big Ugly emerged from concealment and ran over to the downed creature. 'Will you look at that!' Atvar exclaimed, and passed the monocular back to his adjutant.

'Yesss.' Pshing drew the word out into a hiss of his own. 'Not all Tosevites have moved forward from where the probe found them, have they?'

'By no means,' Atvar answered. The Big Ugly he'd been watching was naked, his dark brown hide filthy and daubed here and there with mud of various colors.

'He is bashing in the animal's head with a rock,' Pshing reported. 'I think his knife is metal, though. Looking at him, I do not think he could have made it for himself.'

'Perhaps he got it in trade from the more advanced Australians,' Atvar said, 'the ones whose principal cities we bombed so as to take possession of this continent.'

'It could be so,' Pshing agreed. 'That strikes me as more likely than his having made it for himself.'

'Speak to the folk hereabout – I want him captured and

227

brought before me,' Atvar said on sudden, almost Tosevite-like, impulse.

'It shall be done, Exalted Fleetlord.' Pshing got out his radio and spoke into it.

It was done, but only barely. When the Tosevite saw males and females of the Race approaching, he disappeared. That was how it seemed to Atvar, at any rate. One instant he was there in plain sight, running away; the next, he might have vanished off the face of Tosev 3.

His pursuers caught him nonetheless. Pshing, who was listening to their calls back and forth, said, 'One of them has an infrared detector, Exalted Fleetlord. Without it, I do not think they could have found him.'

The Big Ugly kept struggling for all he was worth. The males and females of the Race had to tie him before they could bring him in to Atvar. By then, the fleetlord wished he hadn't put them to so much trouble. To avoid disappointing them, he didn't show it, but praised them extravagantly.

Shouts poured from the Tosevite's throat, in whatever unintelligible language he spoke and then, to Atvar's surprise, in English, a speech he recognized even if he'd never learned to use it. Pshing had no trouble finding a male from the conquest fleet who understood it. The fellow said, 'Exalted Fleetlord, he says you mate with your own mother and also says you mate at an inappropriate orifice – the Big Uglies have more than we do, you know. He intends these as insults.'

'Ask him how he lives in this country,' Atvar said.

'It shall be done,' the male replied, and began speaking English. The dark-skinned Big Ugly kept yelling the same phrases he had used before. After a while, the male turned back to Atvar, saying, 'Exalted Fleetlord, I do not think he knows any more of this language than these few words.'

'How strange,' Atvar murmured. 'Why would anyone go to the trouble of learning insults in a language without learning any more in it? Having to try to understand more than one speech is bad enough as it is.' The language of the Race united three worlds, and had for time out of mind. Tosev 3 had even more languages than it had had empires and not-empires before the Race arrived.

'What shall we do with him, Exalted Fleetlord?' Pshing asked, pointing to the Tosevite. 'He is not going to tell us anything, I don't think.'

'He is also not going to harm us, for which spirits of Emperors past be praised,' Atvar said. 'He cannot harm us, being too ignorant – and how I wish that were true of every member of his species.' He turned to the male who spoke English. 'Take him well away from this starship. Give him a knife of ours, to make up for the one he no longer has, and let him go.'

'It shall be done, Exalted Fleetlord,' the male replied. 'May I give him some food, too? We have had some of these savages come around begging before; they mostly know how to pull the lid off a tin.'

'Yes, do that,' Atvar said. 'Otherwise, he might come back to rob rather than to beg. I want the Big Uglies to be dependent on us; I do not want them making worse nuisances of themselves than they have already.'

'Any Big Ugly is – or can be – a nuisance,' the male said. He and the ones who had brought the Tosevite to Atvar got him up on his feet in spite of his hoarse shouts and his efforts to bite and kick. As they led him away, he voided liquid waste.

'Disgusting,' said Pshing, who was fastidious even for a male of the Race.

'Big Uglies commonly are,' Atvar said. 'Some, though, are disgusting and dangerous. This one, fortunately, is not.'

'Even with the colonization fleet, will we be able to do all we want on Tosev 3?' Pshing asked. 'The natives will outnumber us to a far greater extent than anyone knew they would when we left Home.'

'I understand that, but we cannot expect more colonists for many years,' Atvar said. 'And, with the Big Uglies so thick on the ground most places, too large a colonization might exceed the carrying capacity of the land.'

229

'Local agricultural methods are not the most efficient,' Pshing said. 'And if a few, or more than a few, Big Uglies go hungry, there are many here among us who would not be overly disappointed.'

'I understand that,' the fleetlord said. 'If we ruled this whole world, what you are suggesting would be easy to achieve. But I fear the independent not-empires would not take kindly to the notion of our starving their fellow Tosevites. The independent not-empires do not take kindly to many notions of ours, except those they can steal.' He looked around again. The landscape definitely reminded him of Home. *Maybe I will retire here,* he thought. If he did, it couldn't come a day too soon.

Sam Yeager let out a sigh of relief. 'Well, honey,' he said, 'I could be wrong, but I think we've weathered another one.'

'Thank heaven,' Barbara said, carving another bite of lamb off her chop. 'I didn't know whether we would be able to manage it. We hadn't come so close to big trouble since the fighting stopped.'

'How much help did you give, Dad?' Jonathan Yeager asked. That his father worked with the Race impressed him. Anything that could impress an eighteen-year-old about his father was good, as far as Sam was concerned.

'Not that much,' he answered honestly. 'Mr. Lodge is a good ambassador. He let the Lizards know what we'd put up with and what we wouldn't. All I did was sort through the ways we might compromise.'

'Compromise.' It was in Jonathan's vocabulary, but he sounded about as keen on it as he was on lima beans.

'We need it,' Barbara said. 'If you were old enough to remember the fighting, you'd know how much we need it.'

'A fight would be worse this time, too,' Sam said. 'Nobody would wait very long before he started throwing atomic bombs around. And once that genie got out of the bottle, it'd be Katie bar the door.'

Barbara gave him a severe look. 'The *New Yorker* runs a

little feature called "Block That Metaphor." I think you just qualified, honey.'

'Did I?' Yeager mentally reviewed what he'd just said. With a sheepish grin, he admitted, 'Well, okay, I guess I did.'

Around a mouthful of lamb chop, Jonathan said, 'The Lizards should have stomped whoever did that to them into the mud.' He added an emphatic cough, to which his full mouth lent alarming authenticity.

'I won't say you're wrong,' Sam said slowly. 'The trick is being able to do that without setting the whole planet on fire.' People had talked that way after Pearl Harbor. It had been a metaphor then. It wasn't a metaphor any more. He went on, 'Whoever did it was pretty sly. He got in a good lick' – Barbara stirred but did not rise to that – 'and managed not to get hit back, or at least not very hard. Himmler or Molotov is laughing up his sleeve at Atvar.'

'They both say they didn't do it,' Barbara said.

'What are they going to say?' Jonathan Yeager waved his fork in the air to emphasize the point.

'Maybe they really didn't,' Barbara said. 'Maybe the Japanese did, or even the British.'

But Sam shook his head. 'No, hon, it couldn't have happened that way. The Japs and the English fly rockets, yeah, but they haven't got anything up in orbit, and it was an orbiting weapon that took out the Lizards' ships. The Japanese don't have nuclear weapons, either, though I know the British do.'

'One of the Big Three, then.' Barbara pursed her lips. 'Not us. The Russians or the Germans? The Lady or the Tiger?'

'I'd bet on the Russians,' Jonathan said suddenly.

'How come?' Sam asked. 'More people seem to think the Germans did it. More Lizards seem to think the Germans did it, too.'

'Because the Russians are better at keeping secrets,' his son answered. 'You hardly ever hear about anything that happens over there. When the Germans do something, they brag about it before they do it, they go on bragging while they're doing it, and then they brag that they've done it once they're through.'

Yeager laughed. 'You make 'em sound like a bunch of laying hens.' He paused and thought about it. 'You may have something. But you may not, too. The Germans can keep things quiet when they want to badly enough. Look at the way they sucker-punched the Russians the year before the Lizards came.'

'Look at the way they kept quiet about what they were doing to the Jews,' Barbara added. 'Nobody knew anything about that till the Lizards blew the whistle on them.'

'Nobody wanted to know anything about that,' Yeager said, at which Barbara nodded. He went on, 'Even so – you could be right, Jonathan. The president was going on about how close to the chest Molotov plays his cards.'

Jonathan looked down at the body paint on his own bare chest. At the moment, he was painted as a killercraft maintenance technician. He said, 'I wish you'd let me talk more with my friends about what you do. They'd think it was pretty hot.'

'No,' Sam said automatically. 'Not unless you want me to get into big trouble with my superiors. I deal with the Lizards because that's my job, not to let you impress your buddies.'

'I know,' Jonathan said, 'but still . . .' His voice trailed away. Yeager hid a smile. Jonathan and his friends spent a lot of time and effort acting as much like Lizards as they could, but rarely had anything to do with an actual male of the Race. Sam didn't paint his hide or shave his head or anything of the sort, but he knew as much about Lizards as any human being around. It probably didn't seem fair to Jonathan. A lot of things hadn't seemed fair to Sam at the same age: not least why people like Babe Ruth and Rogers Hornsby were in the big leagues while he himself had barely managed to hook on with a Class D team.

Because they were older than me and better than me. That seemed obvious now. It hadn't seemed obvious when he was eighteen and fresh off the farm. Life was like that, though at eighteen you didn't want to know it.

'It's got to be that way, son,' Sam said. 'As things are, I probably talk too much around here.'

'Huh!' Jonathan said. 'If you tell me "Good morning," you think you're talking too much. The only time you don't think you're talking too much is when you're telling me to do stuff I don't want to do.'

Spoken in a different tone of voice, that would have touched off a family brawl. Yeager knew a lot of people with kids his son's age who couldn't do anything with them and didn't want to do anything with them but hit them over the head with a brick. But Jonathan was laughing, showing Sam and Barbara he wasn't – altogether – serious. Shaved head and body paint aside, he was a pretty good kid. Whenever Sam got sick of looking at his son's bare scalp and painted torso, he reminded himself of that. Sometimes he had to remind himself several times.

After supper, Jonathan went back to his room to study; he'd started his freshman year at UCLA. Barbara washed dishes. Sam dried. Tomorrow night, they'd do it the other way round. 'We've got to buy a dishwasher,' Barbara said, as she did about once a week. 'They get better and cheaper every year.'

Sam answered as he did about once a week: 'We've already got two good dishwashers here: us. And we've got a spare in the back room. Where are you going to buy a dishwasher that can learn calculus and German?'

Before Barbara could make the next move in a sequence almost as formal as a chess opening, somebody rang the front doorbell. Sam was closer, so he went to open it. Standing on the porch was a pretty, freckle-faced, redheaded girl of Jonathan's age. She wore sandals, denim shorts, and a tiny, flesh-colored halter top; her body paint most improbably proclaimed her an expert sniper.

'Hello, Mr. Yeager.' She held up a book she carried under her arm. 'German test tomorrow.'

'Hi, Karen. Come on in.' Sam stood aside so she could.

'Jonathan's already hard at it, I think. Grab yourself a Coke from the icebox and you can give him a hand.'

'It shall be done, superior sir,' she said in the Lizards' language as she headed for the kitchen. She knew the way; she and Jonathan had gone to Peary High School together, and dated on and off their last year there. Sam followed. If he watched her as he followed – well, then, he did, that was all.

After Karen got the Coke, she chatted with Barbara for a minute or two before heading for Jonathan's room. There with his wife, Sam didn't eye her at all. Out of the side of her mouth, Barbara murmured, 'Oh, go ahead – enjoy yourself.'

'I don't know what you're talking about,' Sam said virtuously.

'No, eh? A likely story.' Barbara stuck out her tongue at him. 'Come on – let's finish the dishes.'

As he dried the last couple of pots and pans, Yeager listened for the sounds of Teutonic gutturals coming out of Jonathan's bedroom. He heard them, which meant he kept on drying. Studying with a girl with the door closed was against house rules. Remembering himself at Jonathan's age, he knew he might have tried to get away with things even with the door open.

'You have an evil mind, Sam,' Barbara said, but he noticed she was cocking her head in the direction of Jonathan's room every now and then, too.

'Takes one to know one,' he told her, and she stuck out her tongue at him again.

After the dishes were done and put away, he went into the study, turned on the radio, and tuned it to a band the Lizards used. The Race didn't reveal the details of its plans on public programs, any more than human governments did. But attitudes mattered, too; what they were telling their own people gave some clues about how they would respond to humans.

This was a sort of Lizard-in-the-street program. The interviewer asked, 'And what do you think of the Tosevites here in Mexico?'

'They are not so bad. They are not quite so big or so ugly as the males from the conquest fleet made me think they would be,' replied the Lizard he was interviewing, evidently a newly revived colonist. He went on, 'They seem friendly enough, too.'

'I am glad to hear it,' said the interviewer, who was as gooey with a microphone in his hand as any human ever born. 'And now—'

But the colonist interrupted: 'It still seems pretty strange, though: waking up and finding out the Race only owns half this planet, I mean. We ought to do something about that. It is not the way things were supposed to be in the plan, and the plan has to work.'

'Well, of course it does,' the interviewer said, 'and of course it will, even if it takes a while longer than we thought it would. Now I shall turn things over to Kekkefu in Australia, who will . . .'

Sam listened for a while longer, now and then jotting a note. He wondered if the notion that the plan from Home would work but needed more time, which was repeated several times, was intended to get the colonists used to the way things really were by easy stages, or if it reflected the Lizard brass' true beliefs. If the former, well and good. If the latter, there'd be more trouble ahead. He scribbled a new note.

Karen stuck her head in the door. 'Good night, Mr. Yeager.'

He looked up, then looked at his watch. How had it got so late? 'Oh. Good night, Karen. I hope you and Jonathan ace that test.'

Had she acted as if she didn't know what he was talking about, he would have figured she and Jonathan had been studying something other than German – biology, most likely. But she grinned and nodded and headed for the door, so he gave them the benefit of the doubt.

As the pilot opened the hatch to the shuttlecraft, Felless said, 'I never imagined my dealings with Tosevites would include dealings with those who have not yet submitted to the Race.'

'If you want to get along with the Deutsche, you will not even think about that *yet*, superior female,' said the pilot, who was a veteran of the conquest fleet. 'As far as they are concerned, they are the biggest and best around. They even call themselves the Master Race sometimes.'

Felless' mouth opened in a great chortle of mirth. 'The impudence!' she exclaimed. 'The arrogance!'

But, after she got down out of the shuttlecraft, the Deutsche seemed less impudent, even if she still got a strong impression of how arrogant they were. Their males, wrapped in gray cloth, steel helmets on their heads, automatic rifles in their hands, towered over her, so much so that she wondered if they were specially chosen for height. A couple of Deutsch landcruisers aimed their weapons at the shuttlecraft. They were recognizably the descendants of the machines the *Reich* had used during the fighting. They were also recognizably more formidable. Not being a soldier, she could not tell if they were a match for those the Race built. If they weren't, though, they couldn't have missed by much.

A male in civilian costume – white and black cloth, with a cloth headgear – came up and spoke in the language of the Race: 'You are Senior Researcher Felless?'

'I am,' she answered: her first words with a wild Big Ugly.

'I am Franz Eberlein, of the Foreign Ministry,' he said. 'You are to present your credentials to me before you may be permitted to enter Nuremberg.'

She had been briefed to expect such a demand. 'It shall be done,' she said, knowing it was for form's sake only. The sheet she gave him was written in both the language of the Race and in the odd, angular characters the Deutsche used to write their language. 'Is all in order?' Felless asked, also for form's sake.

Eberlein seemed to have been reading the document in her tongue, not in his own. *'Alles gut,'* he said, and then, in the language of the Race, 'Everything is good.' He nodded to the soldiers, who, without moving, contrived to look less menacing. Then he turned and waved to the edge of the great concrete slab on which the shuttlecraft had landed. A motor vehicle of Tosevite manufacture approached. 'Here is your transport to the embassy of the Race.'

It had, she was glad to see, a male of the Race steering. The Big Ugly from the Foreign Ministry opened the rear door when the vehicle stopped. As Felless went past him, he clicked his heels together and bent at the waist. That was, she had learned, a Tosevite equivalent to the posture of respect.

'Welcome to Nuremberg, Senior Researcher,' the driver said. 'I hope you will forgive me for a lack of conversation as we go. This vehicle has no automatic control, so I must pay attention to the road and to the Big Uglies using it. If I cause a crash, the Race is liable for damages.'

'Which Tosevites are liable for damages from the destruction of the ships from the colonization fleet?' Felless asked. The male did not answer, perhaps because he was minding the road, perhaps because the question, as yet, had no good answer.

Big Uglies stared at Felless and her driver as they went into the capital of the Greater German *Reich*. She stared, too, at what had to be the most bombastic architecture she'd ever seen. The Race, for the most part, built for reasons purely practical. It had not always been so, not quite, but even the very slow change the Empire knew had long since made other styles extinct.

Not here. When the Deutsche put up buildings, they seemed to want to boast about how splendid they were. The driver explained what some of the buildings were: 'That is the congress hall of the leading political faction here, the Nazis. It can hold fifty thousand. That sports palace holds four hundred thousand, though few are close enough to see well. This open area with the stands on either side is for ritualistic rallies. The Nazis have turned their ideology almost into a sort of emperor-worship. And now, as we go farther north, we come to the grand avenue, where our embassy and those of other Tosevite not-empires are located.'

Felless was not sure what made the avenue so grand. It was much wider than it needed to be, which sparked a thought. 'These Big Uglies seem to equate size and grandeur,' she said.

'Truth,' the driver agreed. Looking ahead, Felless saw a familiar, functional cube of a building in the middle of the absurdly ornate structures all around. The male pointed to it. 'There is our embassy. By the Tosevites' usages, it is reckoned part of the Empire. Our males guard it, not Big Uglies.'

'This is a surprisingly sophisticated concept,' Felless said.

'They insist on reciprocity, however,' the driver said in disparaging tones as he pulled to a halt in front of the building. 'The soldiers of the independent not-empires protect their embassies in Cairo.'

As far as Felless was concerned, that showed almost intolerable arrogance on the Big Uglies' part. She got out of the motorcar, which was heated to a level she found comfortable, and hurried inside the embassy. The males of the conquest fleet had dusted off a most archaic word there: the Race had had no need for embassies since the Empire unified Home.

Ambassador was a similarly obsolete term that turned out to be useful on Tosev 3. The Race's ambassador to the *Reich*, a male named Veffani, soon summoned Felless to his office. 'I greet you, Senior Researcher,' he said politely.

'I greet you.' Felless eyed him with no small curiosity. 'Tell me, superior sir, if you will – is that the body paint ambassadors wore in ancient days, or were you compelled to devise something new?'

Pride rang in Veffani's voice: 'It is authentic. Research provided an image of an ambassador from long, long ago, and my body paint matches his in every particular.'

'Excellent! I am glad to hear it,' Felless said. With some reluctance, she pulled her mind away from the distant past of Home and toward here and now on Tosev 3. 'My thanks for giving me this opportunity to sit in on your meeting with the not-emperor of the Deutsche tomorrow. The experience I gain should be valuable.'

'I hope that may be so, Senior Researcher,' Veffani said. 'The interview will be at his residence, and conducted through a Tosevite interpreter. The one Himmler uses is reasonably fluent in our language; you should have no difficulty following what both sides say.'

'Again, I thank you, superior sir,' Felless said. 'What should I look for in this – Hitler, was that the name?'

'No. Himmler. Hitler was his predecessor. Hitler was the most willful intelligent being I have ever met or, indeed, ever imagined. Himmler followed him after arcane political maneuverings no one of the Race fully understands. Before, he was in charge of the Deutsch secret police – and, in fact, he still is. He is less flamboyant, less strident, and also, I believe, less intelligent than Hitler. The one thing he is not is less stubborn. This, you will find, is a common factor among Tosevite leaders. The British Big Ugly named Churchill . . .' Veffani made distressed noises.

Felless shrugged. As far as she was concerned, one Big Ugly was very much like another. 'Where will you quarter me in the meanwhile?' she asked, a not so subtle hint.

Veffani, fortunately, recognized it for what it was. 'One of the secretaries will show you to a visitor's chamber,' he replied. 'You will, of course, want to settle in. The appointment with Himmler is at midmorning; I will see you then. As Tosevites go, the Deutsche are a punctual folk.'

'I shall not delay you,' Felless promised, and she didn't. The same driver took her and Veffani to the Deutsch not-emperor's residence so that they arrived just before the appointed time. A couple of tall Tosevites in long black mantlings and high-crowned caps that made them look even taller escorted the ambassador and the researcher into Himmler's presence. The room in which the Deutsch not-emperor received them was, by Tosevite standards, bare, being ornamented only by a Deutsch hooked-cross banner and by a portrait of a Tosevite whom

Felless recognized as Hitler by the peculiar little growth of hair under his snout.

Himmler had a growth of hair there, too, but one of a more common pattern for Big Ugly males. He looked at Veffani and Felless through corrective lenses, then spoke in his gargling language. As promised, the translator used the language of the Race well: 'He greets you in a polite and cordial way.'

'Return similar greetings on behalf of my associate and myself,' Veffani said.

'It shall be done,' the translator said.

Himmler listened. Big Uglies had more mobile features than the Race, but he seemed schooled at holding his face still. Veffani said, 'You know the SSSR and the United States both accuse the *Reich* of attacking the colonization fleet.'

'Of course they do,' Himmler said. He was an alien, but Felless thought she heard indifference in his voice. She could not imagine how he could be indifferent till he went on, 'What else would they say? If they say anything else, they endanger themselves. I deny it. I have always denied it. What the *Reich* does, it does not deny. It proclaims.'

Felless knew that held some truth. The ideology of the Deutsche seemed to involve continual boasting. *Master Race indeed*, she thought scornfully.

Unruffled, Veffani said, 'They have evidence for their claims.'

'The usual forgeries?' Yes, Himmler was indifferent, chillingly so. 'I have seen this so-called evidence. The U.S. and Soviet claims contradict each other. They cannot both be true. They can both be lies. They are. We have given you much better evidence concerning the Soviet Union.' By *better*, Felless took him to mean *more plausible*, not necessarily *true*.

Veffani took him the same way. The ambassador said, 'I have my own evidence that several Deutsch soldiers crossed the border into Poland the other day. They have no right to do this – Poland is still ours. I insist that they be punished.'

240

'They already have been,' Himmler said. 'Details of the punishment will be furnished to you.'

'I also require an apology to the Race,' Veffani said.

'We would not have punished them if we thought they were right,' the Deutsch not-emperor said. 'Since we have punished them, we must reckon them wrong. This makes any further apology unnecessary.'

He was logical. He was reasonable. Had he been a male of the Race, he might have been a schoolmaster. He also headed a not-empire that specialized in killing off certain groups of Big Uglies living within it for no logical, rational reason the Race had ever been able to find. Even as Veffani conceded that, under the circumstances Himmler had outlined, no apology would be necessary, Felless studied the Tosevite not-emperor. For his kind, he seemed utterly ordinary. Somehow, that made him more alarming, not less.

8

Having composed the document about which she'd been thinking for some time, Kassquit was polishing it when the speaker by the door hissed, announcing that someone outside wanted to come in. 'Who is it?' she asked, using her fingerclaw to make the document vanish from her computer screen.

'I: Ttomalss,' came the reply.

'Come in, superior sir,' she said. 'You are welcome.' That last was not altogether true, but she couldn't do anything about it. She intended to present the document to Ttomalss when she finished it, but she didn't want him seeing it till she did. And how could she work on it while he was here?

'I greet you, Kassquit,' he said as the door slid open to reveal his familiar face and form.

'I greet you, superior sir,' she replied. As she bent into the posture of respect, she realized how glad she was that he did not have Felless with him. No matter how the other researcher might have apologized, she still looked on Kassquit as half alien, half animal. When she was with Ttomalss, he seemed to look on Kassquit the same way. When he visited her by himself, though, he came closer to treating her as if she were a female of the Race in all fashions.

Whatever Ttomalss wanted now, he looked to be having some difficulty coming to the point. He said, 'I am glad you have grown out of hatchlinghood and into something approaching maturity.'

'I thank you, superior sir,' Kassquit said gravely. 'I am also glad of this as it makes me less of a burden for you and more readily able to care for myself.'

'You are gracious, Kassquit,' Ttomalss said.

'I know I was more difficult to raise than a proper hatchling would have been, superior sir, and I applaud your patience in caring for me as you have,' Kassquit said. 'I cannot help it if I was not so ready to begin life on my own as a hatchling of the Race would have been.'

Ttomalss shrugged. 'Now that the experience is behind me, I can truthfully say not all of it was negative. You must know that, while you were more dependent than a hatchling of the Race, you also acquired language more readily than such a hatchling would be likely to do. Once I could communicate with you, matters did improve considerably.'

'I am glad to hear this,' Kassquit said, one of the larger understatements of her young life. Usually, comparisons between the way she looked or behaved and the standards of the Race were to her disadvantage. Praise fell on her like rain on a desert that rarely saw it: a figure applicable to large stretches of Home.

'It is the truth,' Ttomalss said. 'And it is also the truth, as I mentioned before, that you are now mature, or nearly so.'

He was uncomfortable. Something was wrong. For the life of her, Kassquit couldn't tell what. Sometimes the direct approach worked well. She tried it now: 'What is troubling you, superior sir? If it is anything with which I can help, you know that is my privilege as well as my duty.'

It didn't work, not this time. It only made Ttomalss even twitchier than before. He strode back and forth across the chamber, his toeclaws clicking off metal, his tailstump twitching in agitation. At last, with what looked like a distinct effort of will, he stopped and cautiously turned one eye turret toward her. He said, 'Are you aware that this chamber can be illuminated with infrared light, light to which your eyes – and, to a lesser degree, mine as well – do not respond?'

Kassquit stared. She could not imagine a greater irrelevancy. Puzzled still, she said, 'I did not know such a thing could be done in this chamber, no. I did know it could be done, speaking more generally. Landcruisers, for example, can see targets by these infrared rays even in complete darkness.'

'Yes, that is so,' Ttomalss agreed. He started pacing again. His tailstump twitched harder than ever. 'That is precisely one of the purposes for which infrared rays are useful: seeing in what would otherwise be darkness, I mean.'

'Well, of course,' Kassquit said, still trying to understand why he was so agitated. Then she grew agitated herself, remembering the last time he and Felless had visited her together, and what she'd been doing when they visited her. 'You have been observing me in the dark,' she whispered.

Blood rushed to her cheeks and ears and scalp, as it did when she was mortified. He had seen her when she evoked pleasure by stroking her private parts. Of course she was mortified. What else could she be? By pleasuring herself thus, she proved beyond any hope of contradiction that she *was* a Big Ugly and not anything even close to a proper female of the Race.

She looked up at the ceiling in shame. 'I did not think you knew, superior sir,' she said, whispering still.

'I know,' Ttomalss said. 'I have known for some time. I am not angry, Kassquit.' He used an emphatic cough to stress that. 'I am not even disappointed in you. Please understand that. You are not only a product of your environment. You are also a product of your biology. If it were otherwise, you would now be a female of the Race, not . . . what you are.'

'Why do you tell me this?' Kassquit asked. 'Could you not have observed in silence and discretion?'

'I could have, yes,' Ttomalss said. 'I did, in fact. But now choices must be made: not this instant, you understand – we are not hasty, after all, as the wild Tosevites are – but consideration must nonetheless begin.'

'I suppose so,' Kassquit said reluctantly. 'What you say makes good logical sense.' What she felt when she touched herself, though, was about as far removed from good logical sense as anything could be. The Race, as far as she knew, was logical all the time. She wished she could be. Except when she was touching herself, she wished she could be. Then . . . She didn't know what she wished then, except that it could go on forever.

Ttomalss said, 'I must tell you, Kassquit, this is not easy for me. Matters pertaining to Tosevite reproduction behavior are most alien to the Race, and lie at the heart of the differences between us and the Big Uglies.'

He is embarrassed, too, Kassquit realized. Had he not felt it to be his duty to bring this up with her, he would without a doubt have been happier saying nothing. She admired him for doing his duty despite embarrassment.

She said, 'What are my possibilities, superior sir? The only ones I can see are continuing my present behavior and not continuing it . . . and not continuing it, at least occasionally, would be difficult for me.' Without some sort of release when the pressure of not quite belonging to the Race grew too great, what would she do? She had no idea. She did not want to have to find out.

'I understand,' Ttomalss said. 'That is, I understand as well as our differences in biology permit me to understand. Tosevite females have the potential to be sexually available to males at all seasons of the year. From this, it follows that there would be interest in and desire for activities pertaining to mating throughout the year as well. Your behavior seems to affirm this.'

'I suppose you may be correct, superior sir,' Kassquit said, 'although I have never thought of what I do as a mating behavior, only as something that gives me pleasure.'

'Mating behavior is designed to give pleasure, to ensure that organisms continue to pursue it,' Ttomalss said. Kassquit made an affirmative hand gesture; she had encountered that concept before. Ttomalss went on, 'There are, or could be, other possibilities available to you besides those you mention, though they might require considerable discussion before they could be implemented.'

'What other possibilities?' Kassquit demanded. 'If any other researchers have raised Big Uglies from hatchlinghood, I am not aware of it.'

'No, nothing of the sort,' Ttomalss said. 'It might have been better – I daresay it would have been better – for researchers other than myself to have undertaken such a project, but none chose to. Other than myself, none had the patience for it.'

'I understand, superior sir,' Kassquit said. 'You have spoken many times of the difficulties involved in rearing Tosevite hatchlings. This being so, what other alternatives are there for me?'

Ttomalss let out a hissing sigh. 'If the urge to mate grows uncontrollable, I suppose it could be arranged to bring a male up from the surface of Tosev 3 to attend to the matter. I do not urge this course, mind you; I merely mention it as a possibility.'

'A – wild Tosevite?' Kassquit used the negative hand gesture. 'I think not, superior sir. I want as little acquaintance with the Big Uglies as I may have; my destiny, for better or worse, is with the Race.'

'I agree, Kassquit,' Ttomalss said gravely. 'But, however much your spirit may belong to the Race, it is housed in a Tosevite body with Tosevite hormonal urges. The strength of these we are still in the process of ascertaining, but everything we have learned proves they are not to be despised.'

Kassquit bent into the posture of respect again. 'You are generous, superior sir, to show me so much consideration. But, first, I do not wish to meet any wild Tosevite males.' She used an emphatic cough. 'And, second, you understand that I am as ignorant of proper Tosevite mating behavior as the Race was before coming to this world. I suppose there is such a thing as proper Tosevite mating behavior; however beastly they may act, Big Uglies are not beasts.'

'This is all truth.' Ttomalss sounded surprised, and soon showed why: 'It is also truth that did not occur to me. If you wish to learn more of Tosevite mating behavior, you may consult our archives on the subject.' He gave her the code by which she could retrieve them from the data system.

'I thank you, superior sir,' Kassquit said. 'I did not realize these archives existed. One cannot search for what one does not know is there.'

'Again, truth,' Ttomalss said. 'Examine some of them, if you care to. It may help influence your decision. And now, having said what I came to say, I shall depart.' He did, with every sign of relief.

Kassquit went back to the computer. She intended to call up the document on which she had been working, the one in which she was requesting increased autonomy from Ttomalss. But here he had come to give her more autonomy of a different sort.

Curiosity overcame her. She supposed she had known it would. She used the access code Ttomalss had given her. The computer screen showed two wild, unshaven Tosevites coupling. Kassquit watched with fascination and horror mixed. The posture struck her as absurd, and what the male was doing as unlikely to cause pleasure. It looked, in fact, as if it ought to be acutely painful.

Evidently it was not, though. The female gave signs of the same pleasure Kassquit knew when stroking herself. The male's deeper groans seemed to be of the same kind, even if different in degree. After the recording finished, the computer menu asked if she wanted to view another. She gave an affirmative response.

Again, fascination and disgust warred. Some of the practices in which the Big Uglies indulged looked most unsanitary. Finally, Kassquit turned off the computer. She was very, very glad she had not asked Ttomalss to supply her with a wild Tosevite male.

* * *

Monique Dutourd stopped her bicycle in front of a public telephone kiosk on her way home from the university. Before she slid off the bicycle, though, she shook her head and started pedaling again, this time up a side street. A phone on her regular route was too likely to be tapped. After a few blocks, she came to another kiosk, this one in front of a little market.

'Better,' she said, and let down the kickstand. Before she approached the telephone, she looked all around, making certain the coast was clear. She even stuck her head into the market, to make sure *Sturmbannführer* Dieter Kuhn was not lurking there after outthinking her. The fellow inside washing squashes – rather a handsome young man, with a diabolical little chin beard – waved and blew her a kiss. She ignored him, as she ignored half a dozen casual invitations every day.

Rummaging in her purse, she found a twenty-five pfennig coin and put it in the telephone's coin slot. She was glad to hear a dial tone; she would not have wanted to place the call through an operator. She still wondered if she ought to be placing it at all. But surely the brother from whom she'd been so long separated got other calls. What was one more?

Everything, Monique thought. *Everything, or maybe nothing.*

She dialed the number. Finding it had taken a long time, and meant dealing with people of a sort she'd had nothing to do with since the tense days just after the fighting stopped. She hadn't trusted them then; she still did not. For all she knew, they'd taken her money and given her a number that would connect her with the city pound. And if they had, maybe that was just as well.

The telephone rang . . . and rang, and rang. Monique was about to hang up, get her quarter-mark back, and give up the whole thing as a bad job when someone answered: '*Allô?* Who's there?'

Monique had not expected a woman with a sexy voice on the other end of the line. Flustered, she blurted, 'Let me talk to Pierre.'

248

'And who the devil are you?' From sexy, the voice went to hard and suspicious in the blink of an eye.

'I'm his sister,' Monique said desperately.

'You're a lying bitch, is what you are,' the other woman snapped. 'He hasn't got a sister. So he's two-timing me again, is he? He'll be sorry.'

'I am not. He has. And he isn't,' Monique said. 'Tell him I remember that the name of the dog we had when he went off to war was Alexandre.'

She waited to discover whether the woman would hang up on her. Silence stretched. At last, the woman said, 'He has spoken of this dog to me. I do not think – I could be wrong, but I do not think – he would have spoken of it to any of his whores. You wait. I will see if he will speak to you.'

Wait Monique did. The operator frightened her out of a week's growth by demanding another twenty-five pfennigs. She paid. The operator got off the line again.

Another man came onto it. 'Tell me your name,' he said, his voice strange and familiar at the same time.

'Pierre? I am your sister Monique, Monique Dutourd,' she answered.

As she hadn't expected a woman to answer the phone, so the sigh now also took her by surprise. 'Well, I might have known you would catch up with me sooner or later,' he said. 'Life at the university finally got boring, eh?'

'You know about me?' That struck her as the most unfair thing she'd ever heard.

He laughed. 'My business is knowing things, little sister. The more things you know, the better, and the more you can do with them.'

'You sound just like the SS man who's looking for you,' Monique said, angry enough to try to blast him out of his complacency.

But he laughed. 'He can keep looking. Go on back home. Study your inscriptions. Forget all about it. I wish Kuhn had

249

kept his damned mouth shut, that's all.' If he knew the German's name, maybe he did know everything about her.

'Be careful, Pierre,' she said. 'Don't do anything foolish.'

'Don't you worry about me,' he said. 'I—Ah, the bastards are trying to tap the line. So long.' He hung up. The phone rang. The operator demanded yet another quarter of a mark. Monique paid again. She got back on her bicycle and headed home.

How had Pierre known what the Germans were doing? Dieter Kuhn had said he was too cozy with the Lizards to suit the *Reich*. Maybe they'd given him a gadget that would tell him such things. People had gained on the Lizards since the days when the conquest fleet came, but the aliens' electronics still outdid anything mere humans made.

Monique was struggling with an intractable inscription when the telephone in her flat rang. She guessed who it might be before she lifted the handset from its cradle. And sure enough, Dieter Kuhn spoke in precise, German-accented French: 'Good afternoon, Monique. A very interesting lecture, as always, and a very interesting telephone call as well. It did not help me so much as I might have liked, but it was interesting nonetheless.'

How much of her conversation with her brother had he heard? Had he heard any? Were his gadgets better than Pierre thought they were? Or was he running a bluff, hoping Monique would tell him more than he already knew?

Automatic distrust for Germans made her suspect the latter. She said, 'I told you I did not want you calling me any more.'

'My dear Professor Dutourd, I am not calling on a social occasion, I assure you,' Kuhn answered, still precise, still polite, but suddenly with iron in his voice that hadn't been there before. 'I am calling in regard to the security of the Greater German *Reich*.' French was not in the habit of capitalizing nouns, as German was. Monique heard, or imagined she heard, capital letters thudding into place just the same.

Picking her words with care, she said, 'I don't know anything more about the security of the Great German *Reich* than I did when you took me to Chez Fonfon, and I knew nothing then. You said as much yourself. The other thing I will tell you is that I do not desire to know anything more, either.'

'Ah, Monique,' he said, trying without much luck to sound playful, 'you know at least one thing more than you did then: a certain telephone number.' Before she could do any more than begin to wonder whether he really had it, he rattled it off.

'If you already knew that number, why did you need me?' she demanded. 'You could have done whatever you were going to do, and I would never have been the wiser.' Like so many in the lands the *Reich* occupied, she saw staying out of the eye of the authorities as the highest good.

'For one thing, I did not have that number until the day after you did,' Kuhn answered. 'For another, as I already told you, it is not so useful. It does not lead me directly to your brother. He has some *verdammte* Lizard machinery that relays from that telephone to wherever he happens to be. We know of this machinery, but we cannot match it.'

'What a pity,' Monique murmured, all but hugging herself with glee at having her guess confirmed. She felt extraordinarily clever, as if she'd proved what had killed Augustus' right-hand man Agrippa.

'Another ten years,' the SS officer said. 'Maybe less.' That brought her up short. Humanity had been at least fifty years – maybe twice that far – behind the Lizards when the conquest fleet arrived. Had the gap really narrowed so much so fast? In another generation, would the Lizards fall behind? There was an alarmingly modern thought for a Roman historian.

But then it was gone, replaced by one more urgent at the moment: 'Can't you just leave me alone?'

'I'm sorry,' Dieter Kuhn told her, and he actually did sound sorry. How good an actor was he? Pretty good, by everything she'd seen. He went on, 'When we deal with the Lizards here

251

inside the *Reich*, we want it to be on our terms, not theirs. Your brother makes that harder.'

'When you deal with anyone anywhere, you want it to be on your terms.' Only after the words were out of her mouth did Monique wonder whether Kuhn would take that as politically irresponsible. To her, they'd seemed a self-evident truth, as much a given as tomorrow's sunrise.

They seemed that way to him, too. With a chuckle, he said, *'Aber natürlich,'* and then went back to French: 'That is the way of the strong with the weak.'

'And who is strong and who is weak, between the *Reich* and the Lizards?' Monique asked: almost but not quite a rhetorical question.

'Oh, they are stronger, no doubt about it,' Dieter Kuhn answered at once, for which she reluctantly gave him credit. 'But we are – or we had better be – strong enough to make the rules on our own territory. Do you want the Lizards back again?'

'I am not a political person. It is not wise for anyone French to be a political person. And so I do not have to answer that question,' Monique said. 'And now, if you will excuse me, I would like to go back to my work.'

She started to hang up the phone. Before she could move it more than a few centimeters, Kuhn said, 'Wait.' His voice had the flat snap of command. Even as she obeyed, she wondered where he'd learned it. He couldn't be old enough to have fought against the Lizards when the conquest fleet landed.

'What do you *want* with me?' she cried. She wished he'd only been trying to seduce her; that, she could have dealt with, even if he'd succeeded. Here she felt like a mouse trying not to let a rhinoceros trample it. No, two rhinoceri: Kuhn had made it plain the Lizards were in this up to their eye turrets, too.

'Your help, for the sake of mankind,' Kuhn answered.

Some Frenchmen wore field-gray uniforms with tricolor patches on the left sleeves and coal-scuttle helmets with tricolor shields painted on them. They thought they were serving for the sake of mankind. As far as she was concerned, they were serving for the sake of the Nazis. 'Were you not listening when I said I cared nothing for politics?' she asked.

'I listened. I chose not to hear,' Kuhn said. 'Monique, it would be unfortunate if you failed to cooperate with us. It would be both professionally and personally unfortunate. I would regret that. You would regret it more.'

'I will not betray my brother, damn you,' Monique whispered. This time, she managed to hang up before the *Sturmbannführer* ordered her not to.

Afterwards, though, she stood by the phone, waiting for it to ring again, waiting for Dieter Kuhn to give her more orders in his calm, reasonable voice. *No,* she thought fiercely. *I will not. Not for anything. You can do whatever you want to me.*

She wondered how true that was. She'd never thought of herself as the stuff from which heroes were made. The Spartan boy had smiled when the fox under his cloak gnawed his belly. She was sure she would have screamed her head off. Who wouldn't have? Who couldn't have? A hero – and she wasn't.

The telephone did not ring. Eventually, she went back to her desk and tried to get more work done. She accomplished very little. Looking back on it, she found it startling she'd accomplished anything at all. She kept glancing over toward the phone, and toward the front door. One day soon, she would hear a ring, or a knock. She was sure of that. She could feel it in her bones. Then she would have to find out just how much of a hero hid inside her.

As Reuven Russie came into the house, he announced, 'Mother, I asked Jane Archibald if she'd have supper here with us tonight, and she said she would.'

'All right,' Rivka Russie answered. 'I'm making beef-and-barley soup. I'll put in some more barley and onions and carrots. There'll be plenty.' She didn't say anything about putting in more beef. Meat was harder to come by than produce. From what Reuven had learned from the Lizards, too much meat wasn't good for the human organism. Fat clogged the arteries, leading to heart attacks and strokes. *But it tastes so good*, he thought, wishing he'd skipped a lesson.

'Esther, chop the onion,' his mother called to his twin sisters. 'Judith, take care of the carrots.'

'Maybe you could throw them in the soup pot,' Reuven suggested. Before anyone could answer, he shook his head and went on, 'No, don't bother – I know they would spoil the taste of the soup.'

That got him a couple of almost inaudibly shrill squeals of rage, as he'd hoped it would. It also got him a dire threat: one of the twins – he couldn't tell which – said, 'Wait till you see what happens to your friend tonight. She'll be sorry she ever came around here.'

They'd done that before. They could be holy terrors when they chose – and even more terrifying when they chose to show how smart they were. But Reuven said, 'Good luck. It's Jane tonight. You weren't listening – and what else is new?'

As he'd hoped, his sisters shut up. Jane Archibald did intimidate them. For one thing, they had most of the height they'd have as adults, but almost none of the shapes they'd acquire. Jane was, most emphatically, a woman. And, for another, she was too good-natured to let them get her goat. They'd tried before, without any luck. Reuven hoped that didn't mean they'd try especially hard tonight.

His father came in a few minutes later. From the kitchen, his mother called, 'Moishe, you have a letter from your cousin in the RAF.'

'What's in it?' Moishe Russie asked.

'How should I know?' Rivka answered. 'It's in English. David speaks Yiddish well enough, he reads it, but I've never yet known him to try and write it.'

'I'll read it if you want, Father,' Reuven said. He saw the letter on the table by the sofa.

'Never mind,' his father said. He saw the sheet of paper, too.

'My English can always use practice. It's not perfect, but I can use it.'

'You'll get some more practice in a little while,' Reuven said. 'Jane is coming to supper, and then we're going to study.'

Moishe Russie raised an eyebrow. 'Is that what young people call it these days?' Reuven's ears got hot. His father went on, 'Should be interesting dinner-table conversation: Hebrew, English, and bits of the Lizards' language to fill in the cracks. Arabic, too, I shouldn't wonder. Jane has bits, doesn't she?'

'Hard to live here without learning some.' Reuven made a sour face. '*Allahu akbar*, for instance.' He pointed to the letter, which his father had picked up. 'What does your cousin have to say?'

'He's your cousin, too,' Moishe pointed out, 'only once further removed.' He read on; glum vertical lines filled his face. 'It's getting harder for his family to get by in Britain, even in Northern Ireland. Little by little, being next door to the *Reich* is turning the British into anti-Semites.'

'That's not good,' Reuven said, and his father nodded. He went on, 'He should take his family out while he still can and come here. If he can't come here, he should go to the USA. From everything you've always told me, too many people stayed in Poland too long.' He wished he remembered even less of Poland than was the case.

'*We* certainly stayed in Poland too long,' his father said, and tacked on an emphatic cough. 'If the Lizards hadn't come, we'd probably all be dead. If the Lizards hadn't come, all the Jews in Poland would probably be dead.'

'Hitler and Himmler have certainly done their best, haven't they?' Reuven said.

Moishe Russie shook his head. He couldn't be flippant about it. 'I can't imagine England going the same way, but they're starting down the path.' He lowered the letter for a moment, and in that moment looked older and tireder than Reuven ever remembered seeing him. Then he plainly made himself go back to reading. When he frowned a moment later, it was a different sort of frown, one of puzzlement rather than mourning.

'What is it, Father?' Reuven asked.

'He's wondering if I know anything about a couple of shipments of ginger that went awry,' his father answered. 'It seems an officer in a position to do him either a great deal of harm or a great deal of good is somehow involved in the ginger traffic, and wants to use him to use me to find out what happened to them and how to keep it from happening again.'

'And will you try to find out?' It was the obvious question, but still needed asking.

'Yes, I think so,' Moishe said. 'Ginger smuggling does the Lizards a lot of harm, I know that. And the Lizards have done us a lot of good. But David is family, and things are looking dark in Britain these days, so I'll find out what I can. If it does him some good . . . He broke into a Lizard prison to get me out, so how could I help doing everything I can for him?'

Reuven hadn't heard that story for a long time, and had forgotten most of it. Before he could ask any questions, though, someone knocked on the front door. Whatever the questions had been, they went clean out of his head. 'That will be Jane,' he said, and hurried to let her in.

She carried books and notebooks on her back in a khaki pack a British soldier might have used before the fighting stopped. Shrugging it off, she gave a sigh of relief. Then, in accented Hebrew, she said, 'Good evening, Dr. Russie.'

'Hello, Jane,' Reuven's father answered in English. 'I will practice in your language. I do not get to speak it so often.'

'All right by me,' Jane said. 'Better than all right by me, as a matter of fact.' Her smile was bemused. 'I still find it hard to believe I'm taking supper with the man my school is named for.'

Moishe Russie shrugged. 'I was in the right place at the right time – an English saying, isn't it? But you had better be careful – you will make Reuven jealous.'

'Thanks a lot, Father,' Reuven muttered under his breath. He'd worried that Judith and Esther might embarrass him. Well, his father had taken care of that for the evening.

His sisters came out and stared at Jane, as if wondering what they would look like when they grew up. They wouldn't look like her; they were both thin-faced and dark like Reuven, not pink and blond. If their figures came close to Jane's, though, they'd need to carry clubs to hold boys at bay.

'Supper's ready,' Rivka Russie called a few minutes later. She made sure Jane got a couple of marrow bones in her bowl. The Australian girl didn't waste them; she worked the marrow free with her knife and spooned it up. 'That's good,' she said. 'Takes me back, it does. My mum would make a soup not a whole lot different to this.' She frowned. 'I do wonder, I truly do, if the Lizards will let me go home after I finish here.'

'Why wouldn't they?' Esther asked – or maybe it was Judith.

'Because they want Australia all to themselves,' Jane answered. 'It never did have very many people in it. They killed a lot of them, and they aren't worrying very hard about whether the others are sick or well.'

'*Humanfrei*, not *Judenfrei*,' Reuven murmured in Yiddish. His father winced. His mother scowled at him. His sisters and Jane, perhaps fortunately, didn't get it.

After supper, Jane helped Rivka and Esther and Judith with the dishes. Moishe Russie lit a cigar. Reuven gave him a reproachful look. His father flushed, but didn't stub it out. Between puffs, he said, 'I got the tobacco habit before I knew – before anybody knew – how dangerous it was. Now people do know – but I still have the habit.'

With the ready intolerance of youth, Reuven remarked, 'Well, now that you do know, why don't you quit?'

'Ask a Lizard ginger-taster why he doesn't quit, too,' Moishe answered. 'He'll tell you the same thing I do: he can't.' Reuven raised an eyebrow. He was convinced anyone could do anything if only he applied enough willpower. He had never had to test this theory himself, which helped explain why he

257

remained convinced of it. His father said, 'Of course, one of the reasons we didn't know how dangerous tobacco was is that most people used to die of something else before it killed them.'

'It's a slow poison, certainly,' Reuven said. 'That doesn't mean it's not a poison. If the Lizards made us use it, we'd scream bloody murder – and we'd have a right to.'

'Scream bloody murder about what?' Jane asked, returning from the kitchen.

'Tobacco,' Reuven answered.

'Oh, of course,' she agreed – she didn't smoke, either. 'Nasty stuff.' Only then did she notice Moishe's cigar. A little defensively, she said, 'Well, it is.'

'Do you hear me quarreling with you?' Reuven's father asked. 'I know what it is. I keep smoking anyhow.'

'Speaking of nasty stuff . . .' Reuven pulled out his biochemistry text. 'Did you understand one word of today's lecture? He might as well have been speaking Hindustani for all the sense it made to me.'

'I got some of it, anyhow,' Jane said. 'Here, look . . .' From then on, most of the conversation was in the Lizards' language. That effectively excluded Reuven's mother, but she didn't let it bother her. She sat down in the front room and embroidered for a while and then, blowing a kiss to Reuven and nodding to Jane, headed for the bedroom.

Judith and Esther were less philosophical about being left in the dark. 'I think all those funny noises are just an excuse so they can talk mushy to each other,' one of them said to the other in Hebrew. They both giggled. Reuven hoped Jane hadn't understood. By the way she raised an eyebrow, she had.

Reuven took a deep breath, preparatory to reading his little sisters the riot act. Before he could, his father looked up from the newspaper he was reading. 'They aren't doing anything of the sort,' Moishe Russie told the twins. 'Kindly keep quiet and let them work, or you can go to bed right now.'

He rarely made such dire threats. When he did make them, he meant them. Esther and Judith got very quiet very fast.

They didn't stay quiet long, but they didn't bother Reuven and Jane any more, either. After a while, Moishe did send them to bed. Jane looked at her watch and said, 'I'd better get back to the dorm.'

'Do you want me to walk you back?' Reuven asked. 'I know things have quieted down some, but still—' He waited to see what she would say. Last time, she'd turned him down, and she'd got back without trouble.

She thought it over. 'All right,' she said at last. 'Thanks.'

The night was cool, heading toward chilly. Next to no one was on the streets, for which Reuven was heartily glad. Talking about being a protector was one thing, actually having to do the job something else again. When they got to the dorm – about a fifteen-minute walk from the Russie house – Reuven put his arms around Jane and again waited to see what would happen. She moved toward him instead of away. They kissed for a long time. Then, looking back over her shoulder, she went inside.

Reuven didn't remember a single step he took all the way home.

Glen Johnson walked into the bar at the Kitty Hawk officers' club and said, 'Scotch over ice, Julius.'

'Yes, suh, Lieutenant Colonel,' said the colored man behind the bar. He was about Johnson's age, or maybe a few years older, and walked with a limp. He built the drink with casual skill – not that there was anything fancy about scotch on the rocks – and slid it across the polished bar to Johnson. He plied a rag to get rid of the little wet trail the glass left, and contrived to make a couple of quarters disappear as if they'd never been there.

'Mud in your eye,' Johnson said, and sipped the drink. He reached into his pocket, pulled out an FDR half dollar, and set it on the bar by his glass. 'Go on, Julius – have one on me. Have a real one, not the phony drinks bartenders usually take. I'm wise to those tricks, I am.'

Julius looked at the big silver coin. He held out his white-jacketed arm to Johnson. 'You got to give it a twist.' Chuckling, the Marine pilot did. The barkeep let out a mock yelp for mercy, and Johnson released him. He scooped up the half dollar, then made himself a bourbon and water. 'Much obliged, suh.'

'You deserve it,' Johnson said. 'Why the hell not? Besides' – he looked around the otherwise empty bar – 'I don't much feel like drinking by my lonesome.'

'You got troubles, suh?' Julius raised the drink – by its color, not a very strong one – to his lips. The liquid in the glass went down hardly at all. No doubt he had practice at nursing a drink all night long. A bartender who drank too much of what he dispensed wouldn't last long in the business. One who asked sympathetic questions, on the other hand . . .

'Troubles?' Johnson said thoughtfully. 'You know a man without 'em? Christ on His cross, Julius, do you know a *Lizard* without 'em?'

'Don't know any man without troubles, no, suh,' the Negro said. 'Lizards? I found out more'n I ever wanted to about Lizards during the fighting, and that there's the God's truth.' He took another small sip from his bourbon and water, then stared down into the glass, as if wondering whether to go on.

Johnson started to ask him what was on his mind. A glance at Julius told him that, if he ever wanted to find out, he had better keep his mouth shut. He took a few salted peanuts from the bowl on the bar and munched on those instead. Maybe a bartender needed to talk to somebody every once in a while, too.

At last, still not looking up from the glass in front of him, Julius quietly asked, 'I ever tell you before, Lieutenant Colonel, that I was born and raised in Florida?'

'No, as a matter of fact, you never did,' Johnson said. If he'd let it go at that, he never would have found out anything more. But, as he put together Julius' color, his age, his limp, and now his place of birth . . . The pilot's eyes widened. 'You don't mean to tell me you were one of those—?' He stopped in some confusion. He didn't know how to say it, not in a way that wouldn't put the bartender's back up.

'One o' those colored boys that fought for the Lizards? Is that what you was gonna say, suh?' Julius asked.

'Well, yeah.' Johnson knocked back his drink. He laid more money on the bar. 'Give me another one of those, would you? Christ, how *did* you end up doing something like that? I mean, I know your unit mutinied against the scaly bastards, but how did you get sucked in in the first place?'

'I was hungry,' Julius answered simply. 'Everybody was hungry back then, you know – colored folks worse'n most, I reckon, an' the fighting killed all my livestock and knocked my farm all to hell. So when the Lizards came around an' promised they'd feed everybody who joined up good, I went.'

The pilot raised his glass. 'That wasn't the only thing they promised you, was it? The way I remember, they promised black men a chance to take it out on whites, too.' He grimaced. 'I hate to say it, but that wasn't the stupidest thing they ever did.'

Julius studied him. Here in North Carolina, things were still anything but easy for Negroes in spite of Martin Luther King and his preaching. Johnson saw him weighing how much he could say. After a long, long silence, the barman said, 'Well, I'd be lyin' if I told you there wasn't some who wanted that. Like you said, suh, the Lizards sort of knew what they was doin' there. But most o' the fellas who signed up did it on account of their bellies was rubbin' up against their backbones, same as me.'

He chuckled, looking back across a good many years. 'They had this one drill sergeant, Lieutenant Colonel, he scare the shell off a snappin' turtle. Lord, was that man mean! But he was a good sergeant, I reckon. He'd been in the Army in the First World War, so he knew what he was doin'. An' anybody who wasn't more scared o' him than whoever we was gonna fight was a natural-born damn fool.'

'I've known drill sergeants like that,' Johnson said. 'I have indeed. But was this fellow for the Lizards, or was he just in it for three squares a day like you?'

'I truly don't know, on account of nobody ever had the nerve to find out,' Julius answered. 'When the Lizards reckoned we was ready, they took some o' their soldiers out of the line they was holdin' against the U.S. Army and put us in. First time we went into action – Lord! You should have seen how fast we threw down them guns an' threw up our hands.'

'All of you?' Johnson asked.

The bartender hesitated again. Johnson didn't suppose he could blame him. He wouldn't have wanted to admit anything that brought his race discredit, either. 'Hell, it don't matter none now,' Julius said, more than half to himself. He looked over at Johnson. 'No, not all of us, God damn it. Like I said, some o' those boys flat hated white folks, hated 'em worse'n they hated the Lizards. What they said was, the Lizards was honest – to them, everybody was a nigger. And they fought. They fought like sons of bitches. Don't reckon there's one of 'em came out of that battle alive. So what do you think of that, Lieutenant Colonel?'

Johnson shrugged. 'It was a long time ago, and they're all dead, like you say, so it doesn't make a hell of a lot of difference what I think. Was that when you got wounded?'

'Noticed I ain't so spry, did you?' Julius said. 'Yeah, I was tryin' to surrender and this damnfool kid – he couldn't have been seventeen, even – shot me on account of he reckoned I was foolin'. Hurt like *hell*.'

'Oh, yes,' Johnson said. 'It's not a picnic out there, is it? And the crazy thing is, the politicians who send the soldiers out have fought in wars themselves, or a lot of them have. But they go ahead and give the orders that send out the kids every single time.'

'Sort of different with the Lizards,' Julius observed. 'We didn't have no choice when they went and hit us, and I don't reckon their Emperor ever did any fighting hisself. From what folks say, the Lizards hadn't done no fighting for a hell of a long time before they decided to come on over here and take away what's ours.'

'That's what I've heard, too,' Johnson agreed. 'It's what the Lizards say themselves, as a matter of fact. I don't swear it's true, mind you, but I don't think they'd lie about something like that, something where it's not to their advantage to lie, if you know what I mean.'

'Yes, suh, I do.' The bartender nodded. 'From what I seen of 'em, they don't lie as much as people any which way. Oh, they will – don't get me wrong, they will – but they're a little more honest than just plain people, I reckon. Don't suppose that did 'em a whole lot o' good when they come up against the likes of us.'

'We're a sinful lot, all right,' Johnson said, and Julius nodded. The pilot went on, 'Good thing we are, too. We tricked the Lizards as often as we beat 'em fair and square – more often than we beat 'em fair and square, I shouldn't wonder.' He pointed to the black man. 'That's what your unit did, or most of them, anyway.'

'Yeah, most of 'em.' Julius took another small sip from the drink Johnson had bought him. 'Some o' those boys, they didn't care how the Lizards treated them, long as they treated white folks the same way.'

Johnson thought it was a good time to finish his own drink. Negroes still didn't get treated like white men in the United States. He said the most he could say: 'It's better than it used to be.' He didn't know that from his own experience before the war; up till then, he'd seen only a handful of Negroes. He waited to see how the bartender would respond.

Julius chose his words with care; Johnson got the idea that Julius always chose his words with care. 'Yeah, it's better than it used to be,' the bartender said at last. 'But it ain't as good as it ought to be, you don't mind my sayin' so. Doctor King say that, too, an' he's *right*.'

'Nothing here is as good as it ought to be,' Glen Johnson

said at once. 'That's what the USA is about – making things better, I mean. The Lizards think what they've got is perfect. We know better. We aren't at the top, but we're trying to get there.'

The bartender ran his rag over the already-gleaming surface of the bar. 'I think you're right, Lieutenant Colonel, suh, but you got to remember, some of us is closer to the top than the rest.'

Since he didn't have a good comeback to that one, Johnson asked for another drink instead. He looked around at the empty stools and the empty chairs around the tables. 'Slow tonight,' he remarked. 'Real slow tonight, as a matter of fact.'

'Yes, suh,' Julius said, giving him another glass of scotch. 'You're about all that's keepin' me in business. Otherwise I'd just pack up and go home and see if there was anything good on the TV.'

'Yeah,' Johnson said. He got partway through his third drink before realizing a colored man who'd had some pointed things to say – and with justice – about the inequalities of life in the United States owned a television set. Ten years earlier, that would have been unlikely. Twenty years earlier, it would have been unimaginable, even if the Lizards hadn't come.

Johnson was about to finish the scotch and head on over to the barracks when Captain Gus Wilhelm came in, spotted him, waved, and sat down beside him. 'Looks like you're ahead of me,' he remarked. 'Have to do something about that. Martini might help.' He set coins on the bar. Julius made them disappear.

'I said things were slow tonight,' Johnson told his fellow pilot. 'Now they just went and got slower.'

'Heh,' Wilhelm said, and then, remembering protocol, 'Heh – sir.' He was in his mid-thirties, and had just got into the Army when the fighting stopped. He raised his glass in salute. 'Confusion to the Lizards.'

'I'll drink to that,' Johnson said, and did. 'That's what this whole planet is – confusion to the Lizards, I mean.'

'Good thing, too,' Wilhelm said. 'If they understood us a little better, they would have kicked the crap out of us, and where would we be then? "It shall be done, superior sir" ' – he used the Lizards' language for the phrase – 'that's where. No way in hell we'd be out in space yet.'

'I won't argue with that,' said Johnson, who wasn't inclined to argue with much of anything. He lifted his own glass on high. 'Confusion to the Lizards, yeah – and a big thank-you to 'em, too, for making us want to get ourselves off the ground.' Solemnly, both men drank.

'Sir,' Flight Lieutenant David Goldfarb said, 'I've just had a letter back from my cousin in Palestine.'

'Ah, that's first-rate, Goldfarb,' Basil Roundbush answered. 'There. Do you see? I knew you could do it.' He waved to the Robinsons barmaid. 'Another round here, darling.' She smiled and nodded and swayed away to draw two more pints of Guinness. The group captain watched her with the innocent pleasure of a tot in a toy shop.

'Yes, sir.' Goldfarb suppressed a sigh. He hadn't wanted to get involved in this whole highly unofficial business. Not for the first time in his military career, no one had cared whether he wanted to get involved. 'It appears – my cousin had to be careful with the questions he asked, so he's not perfectly sure – it appears, I say, that things got disarranged in Marseille.'

'Disarranged, eh? That's not bad.' Roundbush tugged at his mustache. 'And Marseille? Why am I not surprised? Was it the bloody Frenchmen or the Nazis who made free with what doesn't belong to them?'

Goldfarb would have said *the Frenchmen or the bloody Nazis*. In 1940, Basil Roundbush would have, too. Not now. He would no doubt have said he'd changed with the times. Goldfarb hadn't. He was glad he hadn't.

He said, 'Moishe doesn't know that, I'm afraid. Which means the Lizards he was talking to don't know, either.'

'Well, if they don't know, they can't get too upset with us for

265

'not knowing,' Roundbush said. The barmaid returned and set their pints of stout in front of them. 'Ah, thank you, sweetheart.' He beamed up at her, then turned his attention back to Goldfarb. 'You've been a good deal of help, old man. You will not find us ungrateful.'

'Thank you, sir,' Goldfarb said, which was not at all what he was thinking. *You won't find us so ungrateful as to murder your wife, or maybe your children. You won't find us so ungrateful as to trump up a charge to drum you out of the RAF and keep you from finding honest work anywhere else.* Roundbush's friends were generous men, all right. By the standards of today's Britain, they were extraordinarily generous. *Which says more about today's Britain than it does about generosity.*

'Marseille.' Roundbush spoke the name as if it were an off-color word in a language he didn't speak well. 'All sorts of things can go wrong there, no doubt about it. I wonder which one has. I shouldn't have thought Pierre would play such a shabby trick, but one never can tell.'

'Pierre, sir?' Goldfarb asked. An instant later, he wished he'd kept his mouth shut. The less he knew about his former colleague's business, the less risk he ran of being drawn into that business.

'Pierre moves things hither and yon,' Roundbush explained. That much, Goldfarb had gathered for himself. The senior RAF officer went on, 'He has a finger in every pie in Marseille – and that's a good many fingers. If he's taken up thievery, we may have to whisper in the ears of some chums we have there.'

Some German chums we have there. Goldfarb had no trouble figuring out what he meant. He took a long pull at his Guinness to disguise what he was thinking. What had the world come to, if a couple of Jews were helping Englishmen turn Germans loose on Frenchmen?

No. What had come to the world? The Lizards had, and things would, could, never be the same.

'It's a rum old world,' he said, a sentiment fueled both by his thoughts of a moment before and by the Guinness he'd drunk.

266

'Too right it is, old man,' Basil Roundbush agreed. Why he should agree, with his good looks, his rank, and his upper-crust accent, was beyond Goldfarb. He went on, 'What we have to make sure of is that it's even more of a rum old world for the Lizards than it is for us.'

'Right,' Goldfarb said tightly. He shouldn't have gone through the latest pint so fast, for he burst out, 'And if we have to get into bed with the Nazi bastards who murdered all my kin they could catch, we just turn out the bloody lights and do it, because we have to pay the Lizards back first.'

Well, that's torn it, he thought. Whatever Roundbush and his friends decided to do, he hoped they'd do it to him and not to his family. If anything happened to his wife or his children, he didn't know what he'd do. On second thought, that wasn't true. He knew exactly what he'd do. He'd go hunting. He didn't know how many he'd get, but it would be as many as he could.

To his surprise, Group Captain Roundbush nodded in evident sympathy. 'I can see how you would feel that way,' he said. 'Can't say that I blame you, even, not sitting where you sit. But can you see there are others who might push the Lizards up to the front of the queue and leave the Jerries behind them?'

'Oh, yes, I can see that. I haven't even got trouble with it,' Goldfarb answered. If he could speak his mind to Roundbush without the world's ending, he damn well would: 'But what I can't see is the people who push the Lizards up to the front of the queue and then cozy up to the Jerries because they don't like the Lizards, either. And there are too damned many of that lot.' He looked defiantly at Roundbush. If the other RAF officer wanted to make something of it, he was ready.

But Roundbush again kept his tone mild. 'We haven't got the empire any more,' he said, as if to a schoolchild. 'We aren't strong enough to pretend the *Reich* isn't there, right across the Channel from us.'

'I know that, too.' The other thing Goldfarb knew was that he was floundering; he hadn't expected these smooth answers.

He fell back on an argument with which no one – no one decent – could disagree, or so he was convinced: 'Too bloody many people too high up like the Nazis too bloody well.'

'You'll never make a practical man,' Basil Roundbush said. 'But that's all right, too; you've already done the practical men who drive the Lizards crazy a good turn, and we shan't forget. I've already said that, and I mean it.'

'One of the most practical things you and your practical friends could do would be to help my family and me emigrate to Canada or the United States,' Goldfarb said, his voice bitter. 'My kin and my wife's have been lucky to get out of places where the trouble was bad before it got as bad as it could. It's looking more and more like things will just keep getting worse here.'

'I hope not,' Roundbush said. 'I do hope not.' He even sounded as if he meant it. 'But if that's what you want, old boy, I daresay it could be arranged.'

He didn't even blink. Goldfarb thought he might have deserved some token surprise, something like, *Wouldn't you sooner stay, in view of your service to the country?* But no. If he wanted to go, Roundbush would wave bye-bye.

Or maybe he wouldn't even do that. He said, 'One thing you must bear in mind, though, wherever you turn up, is that people may still ask you to do things for them from time to time. You've helped once. Easier to unscramble an egg than to stop helping now.'

Goldfarb looked him straight in the eye. 'I took the King's shilling, sir. I never took yours.'

Roundbush rummaged in his pockets till he found a silver coin. He set it in front of David Goldfarb. 'Now you have.'

And Goldfarb did not have the nerve to send the shilling flying across the pub. 'Damn you,' he said quietly. He was trapped, and he knew it.

'Don't fret about it,' Roundbush advised him. 'We shall do our best not to make our requests' – he didn't even say *demands* – 'too onerous.' Oh, the trap had velvet jaws. That did not mean it bit any the less.

Tossing back the last of his Guinness, Goldfarb got to his feet. 'I'd better head on home, sir. My wife will be wondering what's become of me.' Naomi knew he was going to have this meeting with Roundbush, but Roundbush didn't need to know she knew. Roundbush already knew altogether too much about Goldfarb's affairs.

He didn't argue now, saying, 'Give her my best. You are a lucky dog; if you must stay with one woman, you couldn't have picked a finer one. One of these days before too long, I may have another small bit of business on which you can lend a hand. Until then—' He gave Goldfarb an affable nod.

Goldfarb stalked out of Robinsons and retrieved his bicycle from the rack in front of the pub. He couldn't even be properly angry at Roundbush; getting angry at him was like beating the air with your fists. It accomplished nothing.

He pedaled away from the pub at a slow, deliberate pace. With several pints of Guinness in him, it was the best pace he could manage. He didn't particularly notice the pack of punks on bicycles till they'd surrounded him. 'All right, buddy, which is it? Protestant or Catholic?' one of them snarled.

If he guessed wrong, they'd stomp him for the pleasure of putting down heresy. If he guessed right, they might stomp him even so, just for the hell of it. If he laughed in their faces – what would they do then? He tried it.

They looked astonished. That made him laugh harder than ever. 'Sorry, boys,' he said when he got some of his breath back. 'You can't have me. The goddamn Nazis have first claim.'

'Bloody hebe,' one of the punks muttered. They all looked disgusted. He realized he wasn't out of the woods yet. They might decide to stomp him for spoiling their fun. But they didn't. They rode off. Some of them threw curses over their shoulders as they went, but he'd heard worse in London.

When he got home, he spoke of that first with Naomi. She laughed. 'It is better here than in England,' she said. 'In

England, you would have got into trouble anyhow. Here, they let you go.'

'I wasn't what they were after, that's all,' he answered. 'That doesn't mean they weren't after somebody. And besides, I've got more important people after me.' He told his wife of what had passed with Basil Roundbush.

'They will help us emigrate if we must?' Naomi asked. 'This could be very important.' Her family had got out of Germany just before the *Kristallnacht*. She knew everything she needed to know about leaving and not looking back.

'They'll help me if I keep helping them,' Goldfarb said. 'If I keep helping them, the Nazis are going to give it to some poor Frenchman in the neck.'

Naomi spoke with ruthless practicality. 'If he is a ginger smuggler, he is not a poor Frenchman. He is much more likely to be a rich Frenchman. No one who trades with the Lizards stays poor long.'

'Truth,' Goldfarb said in the language of the Race. He returned to English: 'But I still don't want to be the one who put the *Gestapo* on his tail.'

'I don't want a lot of things that have happened to have happened,' his wife answered. 'That does not mean I can do anything about them.'

Goldfarb considered. 'I'll tell you what,' he said at last. 'I'll stay home and tend to things here, and you go on out into the world. You're obviously better suited to it than I am.' Naomi laughed, just as if he'd been joking.

Ttomalss did not care to leave space, to come to the surface of Tosev 3. He especially did not care to visit the independent Tosevite not-empires. Having been kidnapped in China, he did not want to risk falling into the hands of hostile Big Uglies again.

But, when Felless asked him to assist her down in the Greater German *Reich*, he did not see how he could refuse. And the *Reich*, he noted after checking a map, was a long way from China.

270

He watched with more than a little interest as the shuttle-craft descended to the landing field outside Nuremberg, the capital of the *Reich*. He had landed but seldom since taking Kassquit up from China. The former capital of the *Reich*, he remembered, had been vaporized. Were Tosevites sensible beings, that would have taught the Deutsche respect for the Race. But very little taught the Big Uglies respect for anything, and the Deutsche, by all evidence, were among the more stubborn Big Uglies.

After disembarking from the shuttlecraft, he endured the formalities with the Tosevite male from the Deutsch Foreign Ministry on the broad expanse of concrete. The conversation, fortunately, was in the language of the Race. Ttomalss under-stood and still spoke some Chinese, but he very much doubted whether this Eberlein creature did. The language in which the official addressed the armed Big Uglies on the landing field sounded nothing like Chinese, at any rate.

Getting into a motorized vehicle of Tosevite manufacture also made Ttomalss nervous, although he was glad to see a male of the Race driving. 'Have no great fear, superior sir,' the driver said. 'For Big Uglies, the firm of Daimler-Benz is quite capable, and builds relatively reliable machines.'

'How long have they been building them?' Ttomalss asked.

'Longer than almost any other Tosevite firm engaged in such work,' the driver answered: 'about seventy-five of the years of Tosev 3. Twice as many of ours,' he added helpfully.

'If it is all the same to you,' Ttomalss said with dignity, 'I shall go right on being nervous.'

Having seen a great deal – more than he ever wanted – of the architecture of China, Ttomalss was struck by how different Nuremberg looked. That held true not only for the outsized Nazi ceremonial buildings the driver pointed out to him but also for the smaller structures that held businesses or Deutsch sexual groupings – families, the Big Uglies called them. What struck him was how unhomogenized a world Tosev 3 was. Home, after a hundred thousand years of Empire, had no real regional differences left. One city was much like another. That wasn't so here.

'Ah, there it is,' he said with no small relief when he saw the familiar-looking cube of the Race's embassy to the *Reich*. 'A touch of Home on Tosev 3.'

'Only when you're indoors, superior sir, only when you're indoors,' the driver said. 'And we're coming into the cold season of the year, too. You'll want to muffle yourself up good and snug when you stick your snout outdoors, that you will.'

'I will not want to muffle myself,' Ttomalss said. 'I may do it, but I will not want to.'

'Better than freezing your scales off,' the driver told him, and with that Ttomalss could not disagree. The motorcar, which had run well enough – if more noisily than a vehicle manufactured back on Home – pulled to a halt in front of the embassy.

Veffani, the Race's ambassador to the Deutsche, greeted Ttomalss just inside the entrance. Even the hallway that led back to the main chambers of the embassy was heated exactly to the temperature the Race found most comfortable. Ttomalss hissed with pleasure. 'We shall try to make your stay here as pleasant as we can, Senior Researcher,' Veffani said. 'Felless impressed me strongly with how important she thinks your contribution can be.'

'Of course, I will do everything in my power to serve the Race,' Ttomalss replied. 'I am not quite certain about what sort of aid Felless seeks from me. Whatever it is, I shall do my best to give it.'

'Spoken like the sensible male you have proved yourself to be,' the ambassador said. 'And, even though this is a city of Big Uglies, there are certain worthwhile aspects to life here. You must try the *bratwürste*, for instance.'

'Why must I?' Ttomalss asked suspiciously, and then, 'What are they?'

'Little sausages,' Veffani answered, which seemed harmless enough. 'They are quite flavorful, so much so that we send them to other embassies all over Tosev 3, and even to the fleetlord's table in Cairo.'

'If the fleetlord enjoys them, I am sure I will, too,' Ttomalss said.

Veffani grew more enthusiastic still: 'When commerce between Tosev 3 and Home begins, plans are to freeze some in liquid nitrogen for transport to the table of the Emperor himself.'

'They must truly be very fine, then,' Ttomalss said. *Either that or, because you like them, you think every other male and female will, too.* He didn't say that. Instead, he remained polite to his superior: 'I shall make a point of trying them.' He paused. 'And here is Felless. I greet you, superior female.' He folded himself into the posture of respect, as he had for the ambassador.

Unlike Veffani, Felless returned the gesture. 'I greet you, superior sir,' she said, 'for while my formal rank may be somewhat higher, I want to draw once more on your superior expertise. Every meeting with these Tosevites, every analysis of what they do, brings only fresh confusion.'

'If you think I do not suffer from these same symptoms, I fear you run the risk of disappointment,' Ttomalss said. 'Each day's work with the Big Uglies only illuminates the width and breadth of our ignorance.'

'I see that,' Felless said. 'I have arranged with Ambassador Veffani to quarter you in the chamber next to mine, that we may confer as conveniently as possible.' Her laugh was rueful. 'Or, on the other fork of the tongue, I may simply scream in frustration. If I do, I hope it will not disturb your rest.'

'If you think I have not screamed on account of the Big Uglies – in frustration and in terror – you are mistaken, superior female,' Ttomalss said. 'I shall find any screams of yours easy to forgive.'

His chamber proved more spacious and more comfortably appointed than the one aboard the ship from the conquest fleet: easier to find room in a building than in a starship, even an enormous starship. He telephoned Kassquit to make sure his Tosevite fosterling was all right and to let her know he was thinking about her even if his work called him away. He had discovered early on that she needed far more reassurance than a male or female of the Race would have.

Felless gave him a little while to settle in, then asked for admittance. When she entered the chamber, she was carrying a tray full of little sausages. 'Try some of these while we work,' she said. 'They are very tasty.'

'*Bratwürste?*' Ttomalss asked.

'Why, yes,' Felless said. 'How did you know?'

Ttomalss laughed. 'The ambassador already praised them.' He picked one up and popped it into his mouth. 'Well, I will say he was not wrong. They *are* quite good.' He ate several, then turned an eye turret toward Felless. 'And now, superior female, what troubles you about the Deutsche?'

'Everything!' Felless said with an emphatic cough. 'They administer this not-empire on the basis of a whole series of false concepts. They assume they are superior to all other Tosevites, on the basis of no credible evidence whatever—'

'This is common among groups of Tosevites,' Ttomalss broke in. 'The Chinese believe the same thing of themselves.'

'But the Deutsche go further, as you must know,' Felless said. 'They maintain that certain other groups – some perhaps genetically differentiated, others simply following a relatively unpopular superstition – are so inferior as to deserve extermination, and they mete it out to these groups in immense numbers.'

'We have been pondering that since our arrival on Tosev 3,' Ttomalss said. 'It has, if anything, worked to our advantage. One group they persecute, the Jews, has given us a good deal of aid.'

'So I am told,' Felless said. 'That, it strikes me, is as it should be. What is not as it should be is the continued survival and scientific progressivism of the Greater German *Reich*. How can beings so dedicated to utterly irrational premises at the same time fly spacecraft and control missiles tipped with nuclear weapons?'

'I congratulate you,' Ttomalss said. 'You have pierced with your fingerclaw a central perplexity of Tosev 3. Part of the answer, I think, is that they have so recently emerged from complete savagery that a good deal remains just under the scales, so to speak: far more than among us.'

'They drive me mad,' Felless said with another emphatic cough. 'One moment, they will be as logical, as rational, and as intelligent in conversation as any member of the Race. The next moment, they will confidently assert the truth of a premise that is, to any eye but their own, at best ludicrous, at worst preposterous. And they will proceed to reason from that premise with the same rigor they use on other, more rational, ones. It is madness, and they cannot see it. And they continue to thrive even though it is madness, and aim to infect all of Tosev 3 with these mad doctrines. How is one to deal with what strikes the unbiased observer as a pathological condition?'

'Superior female, you do not strike me as an unbiased observer toward the Deutsche,' Ttomalss said with amusement.

'Very well, then. I shall revise that: with what strikes the non-Deutsch observer as a pathological condition,' Felless answered tartly. 'There. Does that satisfy you? Will you now answer the question? How does one deal with Big Uglies whose ideology is nothing but a systematized delusion?'

'All Big Uglies sophisticated enough to have ideologies have them laced with delusions,' Ttomalss replied. 'The Deutsche believe themselves to be biologically superior, as you have mentioned here. The Tosevites of the SSSR believe the workers will rule and then no one will rule, for perfect goodness and equity will come to all Big Uglies.'

'Looking for goodness and equity among the Big Uglies is indeed a systematized delusion,' Felless said.

'Truth,' Ttomalss said with a laugh. 'And the Big Uglies of

the United States believe that counting the snouts of the ignorant and clever together will somehow automatically create wise policy. Much as I have pondered this, I have never grasped its philosophical underpinnings, if there are any.'

'Madness. Utter madness,' Felless said with yet another emphatic cough. 'As one researcher to another, I tell you I am near despair. There have been times when I have been tempted to withdraw to my spacecraft, and other times when I have been even more tempted to indulge in the Tosevite herb that has gained such popularity among the conquest fleet.'

'Ginger? I do not think that would be wise, superior female,' Ttomalss said. 'Whatever the pleasures of the herb, it is without a doubt destructive of sound intellect and sensible habits. I have seen no exceptions to this rule.'

'Then it might make me better able to understand Big Uglies, don't you think?' Felless said. 'That in itself could make the herb valuable.' Ttomalss must have shown his alarm, for the female added, 'I was but joking.'

'Superior female, I should hope so,' Ttomalss said primly.

9

'Where will it be today, superior sir?' Straha's Tosevite driver asked him after closing the door to the motorcar. The ex-shiplord had learned to rely on the machine even though it broke down more often than the Race would have tolerated. Los Angeles was not a city wherein it was convenient for even a Big Ugly without a motorcar to travel, let alone a male of the Race.

He gave the driver the address. Like his own residence, it was in the district called the Valley – a place-name that, unlike a lot of the ones the Tosevites used, made perfect sense to him. This part of the city was warmer in summer than the rest, and so endeared itself to the Race. It was also colder in winter, but winter anywhere in Los Angeles was chilly enough to be unpleasant.

Even hereabouts, the air tasted wet and green to Straha on warm days and cold alike. That had amused Sam Yeager, who probably would have failed to be comfortable on the coolest, dampest days Home had to offer. The mere idea that Straha would consider the comfort of a Big Ugly was a telling measure of how far he had fallen since defecting from the conquest fleet.

'May I ask you something, superior sir?' the driver asked.

'Ask,' Straha said resignedly. The Big Uglies never stopped trying to learn this, that, and the other thing from him. He didn't suppose he could blame them – were he still with the conquest fleet, he would have done the same with any prominent Tosevite defector – but it grew wearisome at times.

'You usually refuse invitations from other males of the Race to functions such as the one tonight,' the driver said. 'Why did you choose to accept this one?'

The Tosevite spoke Straha's language about as well as a Big Ugly could. In terms of grammar and pronunciation, he probably spoke it as well as Yeager, who was Straha's touchstone in such matters. But he did not think like a male of the Race, as Yeager was able to do.

Straha tried to explain: 'Why did I accept? First of all, because I usually decline: I have learned from you Tosevites that being too predictable does not pay. And, second, the males who sent me this invitation are old acquaintances. I have known them since not long after my arrival in the United States, when I was being concealed and interrogated at the place called Hot Springs.' That was another sensible, descriptive place-name, of the sort common back on Home.

'I understand now,' the driver said. 'You are visiting old friends.'

'In a manner of speaking, yes,' Straha said. But he had recently found an English word that came closer to what he was doing tonight: *slumming*. During his days as shiplord, he would never have associated with ordinary males like these two, and they would never have presumed to ask him to associate with them. Association at Hot Springs was surely one of the reasons they did so presume now, but the pervasive and corrosive American doctrine of equality was as surely another.

He did not hold to the doctrine of equality. What was civilization itself, if not a graduated structure of inequalities? But many prisoners who had elected to stay among the American Tosevites had become infected by their foolish politics. That made sense to Straha. They had been low, so naturally they wanted to consider themselves on the same plane as those who had been above them.

'Here we are, superior sir,' the driver said as the motorcar squeaked to a stop just past a rather garish yellow house with a low hedge out in front of it. Decorative plants were used back on Home, too, but not in such profusion. The driver nodded to Straha. 'I shall stay out here and keep an eye on things.' He was not just a driver, of course. He carried a considerable assortment of lethal hardware, and knew how to use all of it.

'If you must smoke cigarettes while you wait for me, have the courtesy to step out of the motorcar before you do so,' Straha said. He and the Big Ugly had had previous disagreements on that subject.

Now, though, the driver yipped out Tosevite laughter. 'It shall be done, Shiplord,' he said. 'And do enjoy the ginger I am sure a lot of the males there will be tasting.' He laughed again. Straha headed for the house, feeling oddly punctured.

One of the two males who shared the house folded himself into the posture of respect in the doorway. 'I greet you, Shiplord,' he said. 'You honor our home by your presence.'

'I greet you, Ristin,' Straha replied. Ristin wore red-white-and-blue body paint of no pattern authorized by the Race. Sam Yeager had devised it in Hot Springs to designate prisoners of the United States. It still scandalized Straha, even after so many years. To Ristin, though, it symbolized his abandonment of the Race and entrance into the world of the Tosevites.

'I trust all is well with you, Shiplord?' Ristin asked with perhaps a tenth of the deference an infantrymale should have given an officer of Straha's rank.

'As well as it can be, yes,' Straha said.

'Come in, then, and use our house as your own,' Ristin told him. 'We have food. We have alcohol, in several flavors. We have ginger, for those who care for it.' He and the male with whom he shared the house had never got the habit. Straha did not know whether to feel scorn or pity or envy at that.

'I thank you,' Straha said, and went inside. As in many houses built by Tosevites, he felt a little too small. The ceiling was too high, as were the counters in the kitchen. Even the light switches – aside from being a strange shape – were set higher in the wall than he would have had to reach back on Home.

Music blared out of a playing machine in the front room. It was not the music of the Race, but some Tosevite tune. When Straha turned an eye turret toward the player, he discovered it was also of Tosevite manufacture. Instead of using a *skelkwank* light to release the information digitally stored on a small disk, the player had a stylus that rode the grooves of a large platter – and, with every playing, degraded them a little, so the platter eventually became unusable. That was like the Big Uglies, Straha thought – they had no consideration for the long term.

Straha had no use for most Tosevite music, though the Big Ugly called Bach sometimes created patterns he found interesting. This was not Bach. It was, in his view, hardly music at all, even by Tosevite standards. It was full of crashes and horns – not the horns with which the Big Uglies made music, but the ones they used as warning devices on motorcars – and other absurdities.

Through the cacophonous din, a singer howled in English:

'When the fleetlord say, "We'll rule this world from space,"
We – *hiss, hiss,* – right in the fleetlord's face.
The fleetlord thinks the Earth is for the Race.
We – *hiss, hiss,* – right in the fleetlord's face.'

The hisses did not come from a Big Ugly's throat. They sounded more as if they were made by pouring water onto red-hot metal. That would have fit in well with the other strange noises coming out of the playing machine.

Several males stood in front of the player. Their mouths hung wide open. They thought the recording was the funniest thing they'd ever heard. Straha considered. It was barbaric, it was crude, it was rude – and it was aimed at Atvar. That made up Straha's mind for him: he decided the recording was pretty funny, too.

'I greet you, Shiplord.' That was Ullhass, the male with whom Ristin shared his home. Like his comrade, he wore U.S. prisoner-of-war body paint. Maybe he found that funny, in the same sort of way the Tosevite song was funny. That was as close as Straha had ever come to understanding why these two males preferred U.S. body paint to that of the Race.

'I greet you, Ullhass.' Straha took pride in keeping his own ornate body paint touched up, even though he would never again command the *206th Emperor Yower* or any other ship of the Race. He had made sure of that.

'Help yourself to anything that suits you, Shiplord,' Ullhass said, much as Ristin had at the entrance. 'Plenty to eat, plenty to drink, plenty to taste. Plenty of gossip, too. I am glad you decided to join us. We are pleased to see you. You do not come among your own kind often enough.'

'I am here.' Straha let it go at that. These former captives who had happily settled into Tosevite society and who had one another for company were hardly more his own kind than were the Big Uglies. Because they had been captured, the Race readily forgave them. Many of them had traveled back and forth between the United States and areas of Tosev 3 the Race ruled.

Straha had not. He would not. He could not. The Race had made it very plain that he was liable to arrest if he ever left the USA. The leaders of the local not-empire had also made it very plain they did not want him to leave. Just as he knew too much about the Race, so he also knew too much about them.

He went into the kitchen, took some ham and some potato chips – as long as he was here, he would enjoy himself – and poured some clear spirits. The Big Uglies flavored a lot of their alcohol with things most males of the Race found highly unpleasant – burnt wood and tree berries were a couple of their favorites – but they also distilled it without flavorings. That Straha could drink without qualms, and he did.

A ginger jar sat on the high counter. Anyone who wanted a taste could have one, or more than one. *Later,* Straha told himself. Had he told himself *no*, he would have known he was lying. *Later* was easier to deal with.

Skittering in, a male almost bumped into Straha. 'Sorry, friend,' he said as he spooned some ginger out into the palm of his hand. Then one of his eye turrets swung toward Straha, taking in his complex swirls of paint. The other male gave him respect. 'Uh, sorry, Shiplord.'

'It is all right,' Straha said, and the other male tasted the ginger he'd taken. Seeing his pleasure made Straha abruptly decide *later* had become *now*. After a good-sized taste of his own, even exile seemed more palatable than it had. But, through the exaltation, he knew it would not last.

'Did I hear true, Shiplord?' the other male asked. 'Did you tell one of those Big Uglies you thought this not-empire had shot up the colonization fleet?' Without waiting for an answer, he opened his mouth to laugh. 'That is even funnier than Spike Jones.' Seeing Straha's incomprehension, he added, 'The Tosevite with the silly song.'

'Oh,' Straha said, and then, wary as usual, asked, 'How did you hear of that? I know it never appeared in a newspaper.'

'That Big Ugly male who interviewed you – Herter, is that the name? – spoke with me a little later,' the other male replied. 'He talked about the way you yanked his tailstump. He thought it was funny, too, once he realized you did not mean it.'

'What I did not realize was that he was ready to print it,' Straha said. 'The Big Uglies in this not-empire carry freedom to the point of license.'

Several other males had heard the story of Straha's misadventure with the reporter, too. That let him have a more entertaining time at the gathering than he'd expected. Even males who used English as readily as their own original speech would laugh at the follies of Tosevites.

But, when Straha related the tale to his driver on the way back to his own home, the Big Ugly was anything but amused. 'Do not ever tell that story again, Shiplord,' he said with an emphatic cough. 'The *Reich* and the USSR can gain too much benefit if you do.' He remained polite, even deferential, but he was giving an order just the same.

To this I have been reduced: to taking orders from Big Uglies. Straha sighed. He had been reduced to worse circumstances than that, but few more humiliating. He sighed again, a long, mournful hiss. 'It shall be done.'

The *Liberty Explorer* had been a long time crossing the Pacific from Shanghai to San Pedro, with stops in Japanese-held Manila and in Honolulu. Even though the paperwork for her daughter and her was in good order, Liu Han had stayed in her cabin aboard the U.S. freighter all through the stop in Manila, and had made sure Liu Mei did the same. Liu Han still felt lucky to have survived the Japanese attack on her village north of Hankow. She did not want to give the eastern dwarfs a chance to finish the job, not when she had to put out a bowl for alms – and arms – in the USA.

Liu Mei had wanted at least to go out on deck and see more of Manila than she could from the cabin's porthole. When Liu Han vetoed that, her daughter had protested, 'The Japanese are not going to bomb this ship.'

'Not openly – they cannot afford to anger the USA,' Liu Han had answered. 'But they do not want the progressive forces in China gaining strength in the United States. If they know we are aboard – and they have spies, and so does the Kuomintang – they may try to make us or the ship suffer a misfortune. Best take no chances.'

Neither the *Liberty Explorer* nor its handful of passengers had suffered any undue misfortune on the long passage across the ocean. Liu Han had taken advantage of the slow voyage to study English as best she could, and to work with Liu Mei on it. She would never be fluent. She hoped she would be able to make herself understood, and to understand some of what people said to her.

Now, standing at the bow of the old freighter, she looked

ahead and spoke in Chinese to her daughter: 'There it is. Now we will have to convince the Americans to give arms and money to us as well as to the Kuomintang.'

'We could have done this in Hawaii,' Liu Mei said.

Liu Han shook her head. 'No. It is not part of the mainland, so what happens there does not always reach the rest of the country. And Honolulu is not the port it was before the little scaly devils dropped one of their big, horrid bombs on it. We had to finish this journey, to come to the province – no, the state – of California.'

She did not mention her biggest fear: that the Americans would have forgotten she was coming. All that was supposed to be arranged. Liu Han knew how often things that were supposed to be arranged went wrong in China, and the Chinese, it went without saying, were the best people in the world. Relying on these round-eyed foreign devils to do as they should tested her nerves.

San Pedro looked to be about as busy a port as Shanghai, though all the boats and ships, as far as she could tell, had engines. She saw no sail-powered junks hauling freight from one harbor to another, as she would have in Chinese waters. As the *Liberty Explorer* drew closer to land, she did spot a few tiny sailboats, too tiny for any use she could find.

She went up to a sailor and pointed at one. 'That boat, what for?' she asked, learning and practicing her English at the same time.

'Ma'am, that's a pleasure boat,' the American foreign devil answered. 'Whoever's in it is just sailing to have a good time, maybe do a little fishing, too.'

'Boat for good time?' Liu Han wasn't sure she'd understood, but the sailor nodded, so she had. 'Eee!' she said. 'Fellow sail boat, he very rich.' In her mind, she pictured the unknown man ruthlessly exploiting foreign devils so he could gain the wealth he needed to buy his own boat.

But the sailor shook his head. 'Don't have to be all that rich, ma'am. My brother makes parts for clocks here in L.A, and

284

he's got himself a little sailboat. He likes it. I spend enough time on the water as is, so I don't go out with him all that often, but he has a fine old time.'

Liu Han didn't follow all of that, but she got most of it. Either boats here were much cheaper than she'd imagined, or American proletarians made far more money than she'd thought possible.

A tugboat came out to help nudge the *Liberty Explorer* up against a pier. Liu Han looked at the men working on the pier. They had no basic similarity, one to another, as Chinese did. Some of the white men she saw had yellow hair, some had black, and one, astonishingly, had hair the color of a newly minted copper coin. Along with the whites, there were also black men and brown men who did look a little like Chinese, save that they were stockier and hairier.

Liu Mei stared at the various workers. 'So many different kinds, all together,' she murmured. She'd seen a few Russians, but not many others who were something besides Chinese. 'How can they live together and make a nation?'

'It is a good question,' Liu Han said. 'I do not know the answer.' Looking at the Americans, she kept trying to spot ones who looked like Bobby Fiore. In a way, that was foolishness, and she knew it. But, in another way, it made sense. Liu Mei's father was the only American she'd ever known. What could be more natural than looking for others like him?

Liu Mei pointed. 'And look! There is a man holding up a sign in Chinese. That must be for you, Mother.' She beamed with pride. 'See. It says, "The American people welcome Liu Han." Oh!'

Before she could finish reading the sign, her mother did it for her. 'It also says, "The American people welcome Liu Mei." And the last line reads, "Two heroes in the fight for freedom."'

'I am not a hero,' Liu Mei said with becoming modesty. 'I am only your comrade, your fellow traveler.'

'You are young yet,' Liu Han said. 'With the world as it is, you will have your chances to become a hero.' She prayed to the gods and spirits in whom, as a good Communist, she was not supposed to believe to protect her daughter. Bobby Fiore had been a hero, giving his life in the revolutionary struggle against the imperialism of the little scaly devils. Liu Han hoped with all her heart that her daughter would never be called upon to make the same sacrifice.

Lines fore and aft moored the *Liberty Explorer* fast to the pier. The gangplank thudded down. 'Come on, Mother,' Liu Mei said when Liu Han didn't move right away. 'We have to get the arms for the People's Liberation Army.'

'You are right, of course,' Liu Han said. 'Just let me make sure these stupid turtles don't lose our baggage or run off with it.' Actually, she did not think the sailors would. They struck her as being unusually honest. Maybe they were just unusually well paid. She had heard that Americans were, but hadn't taken it seriously till that one sailor spoke of his brother the factory worker owning a sailboat.

When she was satisfied the few belongings she and Liu Mei had brought from China would accompany them off the freighter, she went down the gangplank, her daughter following. The man holding the Chinese sign came up to them. 'You are Miss Liu Han?' he asked, speaking Mandarin with an accent that said he was more at home in Cantonese.

'I am Comrade Liu Han, yes,' Liu Han answered in English. 'This is my daughter, Comrade Liu Mei. Who are you?' She was wary of traps. She would be wary of traps as long as she lived.

The Chinese man grinned, set down the sign, and clapped his hands together. 'Nobody told me you spoke English,' he said in that language, using it rapidly and slangily. 'My name's Frankie Wong. I'm supposed to be your helper – your driver, your translator, whatever you need. You follow me?'

'I understand most, yes,' Liu Han said, and took more than a little pleasure in disconcerting him. Still in English, she went on, 'You with Kuomintang?'

'I'm not *with* anybody,' Frankie Wong said. He dropped back into Chinese: 'Why would I want to be with any faction over there? My grandfather was a peasant when he came here to help build the railroads. All the round-eyes hated him and called him filthy names. But he was a laborer, and I am a lawyer. If he'd stayed in China, he would have stayed a peasant all his life, and I would be a peasant, too.'

'That does not have to be true,' Liu Mei said. 'Look at my mother. She was born a peasant, and now she is on the Central Committee.'

Frankie Wong looked from mother to daughter and back again. 'I think maybe Mao did a better job of picking people to come to the United States for him than anyone over here thought he did,' he said slowly. A sailor with a dolly brought a crate down the gangplank and rolled it toward the Chinese women. Wong eyed it. 'Is that your stuff?' At Liu Han's nod, he spoke to the sailor in rapid-fire English, now faster than she could keep up with. He turned back to her. 'Okay. It'll follow us to the hotel. Come on; I'll take you to my car.'

That a lawyer would own an automobile did not surprise Liu Han. Lawyers were important people in China; she had no reason to believe they wouldn't be important people here. But a lot of the people who drove automobiles here were plainly not important. Liu Han could judge that by the way they dressed, and by the battered, rusty cars some of them had. She could also judge it by how many automobiles were on the streets: hundreds, thousands, tens of thousands, enough to clog them the way people on foot and on bicycles clogged the streets of Peking.

Liu Mei noticed that, and noticed something else as well. 'Look how wide all the streets are, Mother,' she said. 'They hold the automobiles so well, I think they were made to hold them.'

'You are right,' Frankie Wong said. 'You are right, and you are clever. A hundred years ago, Los Angeles was only a village. These streets were made with cars in mind.'

Liu Han thought about that as he drove them past the buildings and houses of the city, which also seemed to her to be set very far apart from one another. A large city growing from a village in only a hundred years? All of China's great cities had been great for many centuries. She laughed a little. Los Angeles struck her the same way Earth as a whole struck the little scaly devils: it had grown too great too fast to seem quite natural.

In front of the hotel, a crowd of people had gathered. Some waved U.S. flags. Some waved red flags. Some waved Kuomintang flags, too, with their twelve-pointed stars. 'Don't worry about that,' Frankie Wong said. 'It just means they know you're from China.'

Warily, Liu Han let herself be reassured. 'When will we see officials who can help us?' she asked. 'Will they come to this' – she read the letters slowly and carefully – 'Biltmore Hotel, or will we have to travel to them?'

Now Wong looked at her with frank respect. 'From what I heard, you didn't have any English before you got ready to come to the USA.'

'A little. A very little, from a long time ago,' Liu Han answered with a glance over toward Liu Mei. 'But I could not read it then. Learning this alphabet is easier than learning Chinese characters, I think. It would be easier still if the letters sounded the same way all the time.' Her daughter, who had studied with her, nodded agreement to that.

Frankie Wong laughed. 'A lot of people who grow up speaking English would agree with you there. I'm one of them, as a matter of fact. But let's get you settled in here first before we worry about reforming English. How does that sound?'

'It will have to do,' Liu Han said. Wong laughed again, though she didn't think she'd been joking.

Sam Yeager knotted his khaki tie, then checked the result in the mirror on the sliding door to the bedroom closet. 'You look very handsome, dear,' Barbara said.

288

'Take more than a uniform to do that for me,' Yeager answered. His wife snorted. He eyed her. 'You now, babe, you look good.'

Barbara examined herself. Her azure dress played up her eyes. She tapped a curl back into place. 'If you like middle-aged women, I may possibly do,' she said. 'Possibly.'

He slid an arm around her waist and brushed her lips with his, not hard enough to disturb her lipstick. 'I don't know about middle-aged women in general, but I can think of one in particular I like.' His hand closed on her hipbone. 'And I like what you do, too. I just wish I could do it more often. But I'm middle-aged, too.'

'Middle-aged going on seventeen, by the way you're pawing me,' Barbara said as she twisted away. But she had a smile on her face and a smile in her voice. 'Now – is our son ready?'

'He'd better be,' Sam said. Both as a ballplayer and as a soldier, his life had run by the clock. That was second nature to him. It wasn't yet second nature to Jonathan, which produced friction every now and then, or sometimes more often than every now and then. Sam raised his voice: 'You ready to go, Jonathan?'

'Just about,' Jonathan answered, something less than a smile in his voice. 'Do I really have to come to this thing, Dad?'

'Yes, you do.' Yeager held on to his temper with both hands. 'We've been over this before, you know. This is officially an informal reception, which means family and all. What would you do if we weren't here – call Karen and see if she could come over?' He made it seem as if being alone in the house with her didn't sound like fun.

'Well, yeah, I might do that.' Jonathan made it seem as if his father were the one who'd put that thought in his mind, as if he never would have had it without Sam's help. They were both lying through their teeth, and they both knew it.

'You'll have to find another time, that's all,' Sam said. 'But cheer up. I hear this emissary has a daughter about your age. Maybe she'll be cute.'

289

'Fat chance,' Jonathan said.

Sam shook his head. He hadn't been so cynical at that age. He was sure he hadn't. And if anybody had offered him a chance to meet a girl who might be cute, he'd have been off like a shot. He was sure of that, too. After another glance at his watch, he said, 'Come on, let's have a look at you. We've got to get going, you know.'

'I'm coming, I'm coming.' When Jonathan came into the bedroom, he did pass muster. He couldn't do anything about his shaved head, but that was far from unique among kids his age. His suit wasn't of flashy cut or color, and, if his tie bore a pattern that looked like body paint, it wasn't gaudy body paint.

'Let me grab my handbag, and we can go.' Barbara put the strap on her shoulder. 'This should be fun.'

Jonathan muttered something, his *voce* just *sotto* enough to keep him out of trouble. Sam had his doubts, too, but kept them to himself. He'd been to enough official functions over the years to know that a few were interesting, most weren't much of anything one way or the other, and a few made him wish he'd stayed far, far away. He even understood how he'd got ordered to attend this one: he was an expert on Lizards, this Liu Han came from a country oppressed by Lizards, and so . . . To the brass' minds, no doubt it all seemed perfectly logical.

Barbara found one more inducement for her son as the three of them headed out to the Buick: 'The food will probably be good.'

'Yeah?' Jonathan weighed that. He'd been to a few of these affairs himself. After a moment, he nodded. 'Okay, that's pretty hot.' To show how hot it was, he gave an emphatic cough.

'Some Lizards will be there, I expect – some of the ones living here, I mean,' Sam said, unlocking the driver's-side door. 'If you want to talk to them in their language, that's fine. It'll be good practice for you.' That proved an even better incentive than food. However much the Lizards fascinated Jonathan and his set, he didn't find all that many chances to meet them.

Sam got on the Harbor Freeway at Rosecrans. The freeway had pushed that far south only a couple of years earlier; it made getting to downtown L.A. a snap – except when an accident addled things, as one did this evening. Yeager muttered and fumed till they were past it, then stepped on the gas as hard as he could.

'Good thing we left a little early,' Barbara remarked.

'Have to build in some extra time,' he answered, passing a car that wasn't going fast enough to suit him. He laughed. 'The Lizards think we're out of our minds for driving without seat belts. But they'd never sell, never in a million years. The only thing people care about is going fast.' As if to prove his point, he zoomed past a gasoline-burning machine that couldn't get out of its own way.

He left the freeway at Sixth and went east a few blocks to Olive, on which the Biltmore stood, across from Pershing Square. He parked in a lot north of the hotel. U.S. flags, the red banners of the People's Liberation Army, and national flags of China – Kuomintang flags, in other words – all flew outside the twelve-story, E-shaped building. Pointing to those last, Barbara said, 'She probably wishes they weren't there.'

'You're right. She probably does,' said Sam, who'd spent the couple of days he'd known about the reception boning up on China. He nodded toward the hotel as they came up to the entrance. 'Pretty fancy place, eh, Jonathan?' He didn't say *hot*; that wasn't his slang, any more than *swell* was his son's.

'It's all right, I guess,' Jonathan answered, determined to be unimpressed.

Inside, Sam was asked to show identification. He did so without hesitation. He might have been a Lizard stooge, a Kuomintang supporter, or even a Japanese agent, none of whom had any reason to love the People's Liberation Army. He might even have worked for the NKVD; Molotov wouldn't

291

want the Chinese Communists shopping anywhere but at his store. When he'd satisfied the guards that he was none of those things, they checked off his name and those of his wife and son and let them go into the reception hall.

Jonathan made a beeline for the buffet. As soon as he'd filled his plate, he stood around looking to see if any other fogies had brought along people – with luck, good-looking female people – his own age. Sam and Barbara looked at each other with identical amused expressions. At Jonathan's age, Sam would have behaved the same way. At Jonathan's age, though, barn dances were about the biggest social events Sam had ever seen. Even the small towns of Class D ball had seemed sophisticated to him. He shook his head. The world was a different place, a faster place, these days.

He looked around, too, not for pretty girls but to see what kind of crowd it was. When he spotted Straha, an eyebrow shot up. The shiplord raised a hand in greeting. Sam nodded back. If the chief Lizard defector was here, that put a seal of approval on the event, all right.

And there was the guest of honor, a Chinese woman who would have had to stand on her toes to make five feet. Her daughter was several inches taller – and if Jonathan hadn't noticed her, he wasn't paying attention, because she was a very pretty girl. Yeager got a drink, then drifted toward them to do his ceremonial duty.

Listening to Liu Han and Liu Mei, he realized they had only a little English. A Chinese man in a suit snappier than any civvies Sam owned was translating for them. Having done a good deal of translating himself, Yeager recognized its limits. The only Chinese he understood was chop suey. Still . . . *Where there's a will, there's a lawyer,* he thought.

When he came up to the two women, he nodded to them – he'd seen they didn't shake hands as if they were used to doing it – and spoke in the language of the Race: 'I greet you, females from a distant land.'

They both exclaimed in Chinese, then both started talking at the same time in the Lizards' language. After a moment, Liu Mei fell silent and let her mother go ahead: 'I greet you, Tosevite soldier, American soldier.' She was less fluent than Sam, but he had no trouble understanding her.

He gave her his name and his rank, and explained that his specialty was dealing with the Race. While he spoke, he noticed the Chinese man – he wore a button giving his name as Frank Wong – looking more and more unhappy. Liu Han noticed, too; Sam saw at once she had no flies on her. She spoke to Wong in Chinese. He relaxed and went off to get a drink.

Liu Han let out a sly chuckle. 'I persuaded him that he was working too hard. Now he has a chance to recover.'

'Clever.' Yeager used an emphatic cough. He and Liu Han traded sly grins. He asked, 'And what do you think of Americans, now that you are meeting us for the first time?'

'This is not my first meeting with Americans. Liu Mei's father is an American,' Liu Han said. 'He was a captive, as was I. We were part of the Race's experiments on Tosevite mating habits. You know of these things?'

'I know of them, yes.' For a moment, Sam wondered why she was so openly admitting something so shameful. Then he gave himself a mental kick in the pants. She wanted to paint the Lizards black, so she could gain as much sympathy for her cause as she could.

She went on, 'He was a good man. He was far and away the best man I met in these experiments. When I knew I would have a baby' – that came out as, *When I knew I would lay an egg,* but Sam understood—' he came down to China with me. He used to play your not-empire's game, and he made money in China throwing and catching a ball as a show.'

'Baseball?' Sam said in English, and Liu Han nodded. Liu Mei turned away; Yeager wondered how often she'd heard this story. Laughing a little, he told Liu Han, 'Before I was a soldier, I used to play baseball myself.'

'Truth?' she said, and he nodded. She cocked her head to

one side. 'Maybe you knew him.' He started to say it wasn't likely, considering how many people played baseball in the United States. Before he could, she went on, 'His name was Bobby Fiore.' She pronounced it very clearly.

'Jesus Christ!' He knocked back his scotch-and-soda at a gulp. 'Bobby Fiore?' Liu Han's head went up and down. Yeager stared. 'Bobby Fiore? We played on the same team. We shared a room when we traveled. We were on the train together when the Race came down and shot it up. I got out before their helicopters landed. I never found out what happened to him.'

He stared over at Liu Mei. Now that he knew, he could see the Italian second baseman in her, in her chin, in her nose, in her hair. On her, though, it all looked good. Across twenty years, he could hear his old roomie laughing at the friendly insult.

Liu Han said, 'He is dead. He died in Shanghai, fighting the Race. I was not there. But I have heard the died very bravely.'

'Bobby Fiore. My God.' Sam wished his glass weren't empty. He wanted another slug of scotch, but he didn't want to go away. 'May I introduce my son' – he pointed toward Jonathan, and then waved for him to come over – 'to your daughter, who is also the daughter of my old friend?'

'You may.' Liu Han looked in Jonathan's direction. She must have fixed on his shaved head, for she asked, 'Is he one of those who try to act like the Race?'

'He is.' Sam saw no point in beating around the bush or lying. 'There are those who go further with it than he does.' That was also true, thank heaven.

'We have young males and young females like that in China, too,' Liu Han said. 'I used to hate the very idea. I do not hate it so much now. The Race is here. We have to learn to live with its males and now its females. This is one way to do so.'

'I think you have good sense,' Yeager answered as Jonathan and Liu Mei exchanged polite greetings in the language of the Race. *Ain't that something?* he thought. Barbara, could she have seen into his mind, would have disapproved of the grammar. He shrugged and went off to get that fresh drink after all. *Ain't that something?* he thought again.

Vyacheslav Molotov examined the report from the Soviet consul in Los Angeles. He shoved the telexed sheet across his desk at Andrei Gromyko. 'Have you seen this?' he asked the foreign commissar.

'I have, Vyacheslav Mikhailovich,' Gromyko answered. 'Mao shows more imagination than we believed he had.'

'Mao shows himself a nationalist first and a Marxist-Leninist second,' Molotov said. 'This is, of course, one of the sins for which he so noisily condemned Stalin.'

'He could afford to be noisy in condemning Stalin,' Gromyko said. 'He lives well beyond the frontier.'

Both men warily looked around. Stalin had been dead for most of a decade, but his spirit lingered in the Kremlin. Molotov had to remind himself his predecessor could not harm him. Even after reminding himself, he said, 'Living beyond the frontier did not always make a difference, Andrei Andreyevich. Remember what happened to Trotsky.'

'An ice axe in the brain?' Gromyko considered. 'I can think of ways I would sooner leave the world, yes.' He glanced at Molotov. 'Are you suggesting that Mao should worry about such a thing? If you are, you would do better to whisper it in Lavrenti Pavlovich's ear than in mine.'

'No.' Not without some regret, Molotov shook his head. 'Trotsky was an annoyance, a loose end. Mao leads a formidable force in the fight against the Lizards' imperialism. I can think of no one else in the Chinese party who could take his place.'

'And we did provoke him, too,' Gromyko said musingly.

'What has that to do with anything?' Molotov asked in genuine curiosity. 'He is useful to us, so we have to put up with him for the time being. But we do not want him getting too friendly with the Americans. Having their influence on the

Siberian frontier would be even more of a nuisance than having the Lizards there, because the Americans are less likely to keep whatever agreements they make.'

Gromyko paused to light a cigarette: a Russian one, a little tobacco in a tube like a holder. After taking a puff, he said, 'If we want to bring Mao back into the fold, we will have to start moving weapons into China again.'

'I think we can do that,' Molotov said. 'The fuss the Lizards put up over the attack on the colonization fleet has died down. Whoever did that planned with great wisdom. My only qualm is that I do not care to believe either Himmler or Warren is so wise. But yes, I think we can safely resume shipments.'

'Very well,' Gromyko said. 'I think you are right. If we are caught, the usual denials will serve in a case like that.'

Molotov looked at him with something as close to affection as he gave anyone but his wife. If Gromyko's cynicism did not match his own, it came close. A man without cynicism had no business running a great country, as far as the General Secretary was concerned. That was one reason Earl Warren made him nervous.

Gromyko said, 'I have also learned, Vyacheslav Mikhailovich, that there is some derangement in the networks of officials and other criminals who smuggle ginger into the Lizards' territory. The Germans, the British, and the Americans are all in full cry. I hope their internal struggles do not disrupt the trade.'

'Indeed,' Molotov said indifferently. 'I have heard something of this from Beria. He will be watching it, too.'

Gromyko did not flinch, for which Molotov admired him. Molotov had not actually heard anything from the NKVD chief. But keeping his followers eyeing each other was one way to keep them from eyeing the top spot in the hierarchy.

'I hope,' Gromyko said slowly, 'that whatever ginger-smuggling channels the NKVD has set up will not be deranged by this fuss among the capitalists. We have made considerable profit from ginger.'

'And what could be more important to good Marxist-Leninists than profit?' Molotov returned. His wintry sense of humor was a good match for Gromyko's. He went on, 'Now that you know the line we are to take in regard to Mao, can I rely on Lavrenti Pavlovich and you to implement it?'

'One never knows how far one may rely on Beria,' Gromyko answered, which Molotov found most unfortunate, but which was also true. 'On me, and on the Foreign Commissariat, you may of course rely.'

Beria, had he been there, would have claimed he was loyal and the Foreign Commissariat riddled with spies for the Nazis and the Americans and the Lizards. Beria was loyal to himself and the Soviet Union, in that order. He had been loyal to Stalin, a countryman of his, or as near as made no difference. Molotov eyed Gromyko. Was Gromyko loyal to him in particular? In a struggle against Beria, yes, he judged. Otherwise? Maybe, maybe not. But Gromyko was not the sort to head a *coup d'état*. That would do. It would have to do.

'See to it, then,' Molotov said. Gromyko nodded and left. Molotov's dismissals were brusque, but they weren't brutal, as Stalin's had been.

Molotov's secretary stuck his head into the office. 'Comrade General Secretary, your next appointment is here.'

'Send him in, Pyotr Maksimovich,' Molotov said. The secretary bobbed his head in a gesture of respect that went back to the days of the Tsars, then went out and murmured to the man in the waiting room.

The fellow came in a moment later. He was thin and middle-aged, with an intelligent face that clearly showed he was a Jew. He carried a topcoat and a fur hat against the nasty weather outside. Here in the Kremlin, sweat beaded his face. Also going back to the days of the Tsars, and to long before the days of the Tsars, was the Russian habit of heating buildings very warm to fight the winter cold. Molotov waved the man to the chair Gromyko had just vacated.

'Thank you, Comrade General Secretary,' the fellow said.

His Polish accent put Molotov in mind of that of the Lizard ambassador's interpreter.

'You are welcome, David Aronovich,' Molotov replied. 'And what is the latest news from Poland?'

'Colonization by the Lizards is proceeding more rapidly than either the Poles or the Jews expected,' David Nussboym answered. 'This suits the Jews better than the Poles. The Jews know they could not rule on their own. Many Poles still harbor nationalist fantasies.'

'Polish delusions, for the time being, are the Lizards' problem and not mine,' Molotov said. 'The Lizards are welcome to the Poles, too. If we cannot embroil the Lizards against the *Reich*, next best is to use them as a buffer against the Nazis and, as you say, as an object for the Poles' nationalist desires. Russians have filled that role in the past; I am content to leave it to the Race now.'

'That strikes me as wise, Comrade General Secretary,' Nussboym said.

Molotov gave him a hooded stare. He had not asked for any such endorsement. Nussboym plainly had not grown to manhood in the USSR, else he would not have been so quick to speak his mind. Even years in the gulag, evidently, had not taught him that lesson. Then Molotov gave a mental shrug. If Nussboym proved a nuisance, he could go back to the gulag. He wasn't so important that Beria would lift a finger to protect him.

'And I have another piece of information you need to know,' Nussboym said, doing his best to make himself out to be more important than he was.

'Tell me the information,' Molotov said icily. 'Then I will tell you whether I need to know it. Do you understand?'

'Yes,' Nussboym said, flinching: he understood some things, anyhow. 'The information is, I have located the hiding place the Jews use for the atomic bomb they stole from the Nazis in Lodz.'

'Have you?' Molotov rubbed his chin. 'I do not know yet

whether that is information I need to know, but it is certainly interesting.' He eyed Nussboym. 'You would sell out your coreligionists and former countrymen to tell me this?'

'Why not?' the Polish Jew now serving in the NKVD replied. 'They sold me out. Why should I not repay them? I owe the Party more loyalty than I owe them, anyhow.'

He said that, and said it with evident sincerity, even though the first thing the Party had done when it got its hands on him was throw him in a gulag for some years. Molotov believed him. For one thing, he was far from the only man to come out of the gulag and serve the Soviet Union well. Every time Molotov flew in a Tupolev passenger plane, he remembered how Stalin had plucked the designer out of the camps and set him to work at his proper job when the Germans invaded. General Rokossovsky was another such case. Either of them was worth a hundred of the likes of David Nussboym.

But that did not make Nussboym worthless. Molotov considered how best to use him. Subtlety seemed wasted here. 'Very well, then,' Molotov said. 'Where is this bomb hidden away? Somewhere not far from Lodz, I am sure.'

'Yes.' Nussboym nodded. 'In or near the town of Glowno, to the northeast.'

'In or near?' Molotov raised an eyebrow. 'Can you not be more precise than that, David Aronovich? Those first bombs were huge things, weighing tonnes apiece. You cannot hide them under the mattress.'

'Up till now, the Jews have kept this one hidden for close to twenty years,' Nussboym retorted, which held enough truth to keep Molotov from getting angry at the sardonic relish the NKVD man took in saying it.

'Did you also find out whether the bomb could still function?' Molotov asked. 'Scientists tell me these weapons must have periodic maintenance if they are to go off.'

'Comrade General Secretary, that I do not know,' Nussboym said. 'The Jews have done their best to keep the bomb working, but I do not know how good their best is. From everything I have been able to learn, neither they nor the Poles nor the Lizards know whether the bomb would work.'

'And no one, I suppose, is anxious to find out,' Molotov said. Nussboym nodded. Molotov studied him. 'And you have told Comrade Beria the same.'

'He will hear the same from me, yes,' Nussboym said.

Molotov studied him again. Would he report here before he went to Dzerzhinsky Square? Maybe. Molotov dared hope so, but dared not be sure.

What to do about the bomb? Let the Lizards know it was there? He shook his head. They were clever enough to sit tight. Let the nationalist Poles know it was there? That was a happy thought. The Poles were headstrong, foolish, and frustrated. They could almost be relied upon to do something everyone else around them would regret.

Mordechai Anielewicz chuckled as he rode his bicycle toward Glowno. His legs were behaving very well, almost as if he'd never breathed in too much nerve gas. That wasn't why he chuckled, though. The name of the town never failed to remind him of *gowno*, the Polish word for shit.

No Lizard starships had landed close enough to Glowno to go up if the Jews ever had to set off their atomic bomb – if it could be set off, which Anielewicz did not know. He was a little sorry the Race hadn't offered him such a hostage to fortune. Samson never would have made it into the Bible if he hadn't had the Philistines' temple to pull down.

'Now politicians can kill millions with their jawbones of asses, not just a thousand,' Anielewicz murmured. He grunted. That held true for him, too – if the bomb still worked.

Every now and then, he wished he'd been able to figure out a way to smuggle the bomb into the *Reich* and set it off there. It would have been fitting vengeance for everything the Nazis had done to the Jews. But it might have set the world afire – and the bomb wasn't easy to smuggle, anyhow. He ordered it moved every so often to keep the Lizards from getting their hands on it, and that wasn't easy, either, not when the damn thing weighed closed to ten tonnes.

Cars and lorries zoomed past him as he pedaled along at the edge of the highway. A lot more of the lorries, these days, were Lizard models with Lizards driving them: males and females from the colonization fleet, no doubt. He wondered how they liked the weather. It was a bright, sunny day, with the temperature only a little below freezing – otherwise, Anielewicz would have taken a car himself instead of bicycling. For a Polish winter, it was good weather indeed. Once he'd gone far enough to warm himself up, Mordechai actively enjoyed it.

But the Lizards didn't like the cold, not even a little. They didn't have cold weather on their home planet, and they didn't know how to deal with it. That thought had hardly crossed Anielewicz's mind when he came upon a Lizard lorry in the ditch by the side of the road. The driver kept turning his eye turrets from the truck to the road and back again, as if he hadn't the faintest notion of how he'd come to grief.

Mordechai applied the brake – with care, for the road was icy in places – and stopped alongside the lorry, which was canted at an odd angle in the mud. 'What happened?' he asked in the language of the Race.

'I will tell you what happened,' the Lizard said angrily. 'I will be glad to tell you what happened. A Big Ugly in a stinking motorcar cut in front of me. I do not think the stupid creature had the faintest notion I was there.' He had to be a newly revived colonist; he had no idea that one human being might find his comments about another offensive. 'I hit the brake to keep from colliding with the worthless Tosevite, and the next thing I knew, I was here.'

'You must have hit a patch of ice and skidded,' Mordechai said. 'That can happen to anybody. You have to be careful at this season of the year.'

'Ice?' the Lizard echoed, as if it had never heard the word in its own speech before. It was, no doubt, used far less often in

301

the Lizards' language than in Polish or Yiddish. 'Why is ice permitted on the surface of a road?' The poor creature sounded bewildered, as if Anielewicz had started talking about a rain of frogs.

'Ice,' Mordechai repeated patiently. The sooner the Lizard learned the facts of life about weather here, the less likely it was to kill itself – and perhaps several people with it. 'The temperature on this part of Tosev 3 is often below freezing, as it is now. Rain will freeze. So will dew. And ice, as you have discovered, is very slippery. Your tires cannot hold their grip on it.'

'Why isn't it scraped off the road as soon as it forms?' the Lizard demanded. 'Your practices here strike me as most unsafe. The Race has held this part of the planet for some time, and should have done a better job of preparing it for colonization.'

Anielewicz didn't laugh out loud, though holding back wasn't easy. But he didn't want to make the poor, ignorant, indignant Lizard any more indignant than it already was. Patiently, he said, 'Sometimes there are only patches of ice, as today. Sometimes all the roads are icy, and there is no equipment for all the scraping it would take to keep them clear. Sometimes, when . . .' He hesitated. He didn't know how to say *snow* in the Lizards' language. Circumlocution, then: 'When powdery frozen water falls from the sky, it covers the roads higher than a male. In this season of the year, that could happen at any time.'

'When I was awakened, I was warned of this kind of frozen water,' the Lizard said. 'I still find it hard to believe any planet could have such an absurd form of precipitation.'

'You will find out how absurd it is,' Mordechai said. 'And now, I must be on my way.' Off he went, slowly building up speed.

The Lizard looked as if it wanted to order him to stop and help. But, as usual, he had a rifle on his back. Maybe the briefing the Lizard had got included the idea that it wasn't a good idea to give orders to Tosevites who might open fire instead of obeying. For the colonists' sake, Mordechai hoped it included that thought. If it didn't, they'd learn some expensive lessons in a hurry.

When he got into Glowno, he was alarmed to discover a Lizard prowling the streets. He didn't dare approach the shed where the bomb was kept till he found out why the alien was going around. Glowno wasn't much more than a wide spot on the highway between Lodz and Warsaw. Lizards came through the place, but they rarely stopped.

He went up to the Lizard and asked his question straight out: 'What are you doing here?'

'Freezing,' the Lizard answered, which wasn't what he'd expected but was perfectly reasonable. As an afterthought, the Lizard went on, 'And looking for a place to put a shuttlecraft port.'

'Ah,' Anielewicz said. 'I heard you were in Lodz, my home city, not long ago. You did not find any place that suited you there?'

'Would I be here if I had?' the Lizard retorted, again catching him off guard.

He tried to rally: 'You are the female Nesseref, not so? That is the name of the shuttlecraft pilot I heard.'

'Yes, I am Nesseref,' she answered. 'Who are you, to know who I am?'

He found himself in a trap of his own making. If he admitted who he was and his status, she would wonder why such a prominent personage had come to such an unprominent town as Glowno. After a moment's thought, he said, 'I am Mordechai Anielewicz,' and let it go at that. If she realized who he was, she did; if not, not. To keep her from having much time to think, he went on, 'To me, you look much as a male of the Race would. How can a Tosevite tell a female from a male?'

Nesseref's mouth fell open. She found the question funny. 'We have the same trouble with you Big Uglies, you know. You all look the same to us, and you do not even use body

303

paint to help us tell you apart. Some of the males from the conquest fleet can tell your males and females apart, but I cannot, not yet.'

'But you have not answered my question,' Anielewicz said.

'It is easy enough, for anyone with eyes in his head,' the Lizard said with another laugh. 'My stance is somewhat wider than a male's; I am the one who lays the eggs, and so need wider hips. My tailstump is a little longer, my snout is a little more pointed than a male's would be. Do you understand now?'

'I do, yes. I thank you.' Armed with his new knowledge, Mordechai tried to pick out the things she said made her distinct from males of the Race. For the life of him, he couldn't. She looked like a Lizard, and that was that. He laughed. 'Now I understand why the Race has trouble with us.'

'But our differences are so obvious!' Nesseref exclaimed. 'They are not subtle, like the differences between male and female Tosevites.'

'Obvious differences are the differences one is used to,' Anielewicz said. 'Subtle differences are the differences someone else is used to.'

Nesseref thought about that. After a moment, she laughed again. 'Truth!' she said, and added an emphatic cough. She turned both eye turrets toward Mordechai. 'You are different from most Big Uglies I have met. You do not bluster and swagger, as so many of your kind seem to do.'

'I thank you,' Anielewicz said again. It would have been a compliment of a different sort from a female of his own species. In an odd way, he valued it more from the Lizard, who was disinterested – or, at least, uninterested. And he returned it: 'Nor do you seem like most males of the Race I know. You are not so certain you know everything there is to know.'

'And I thank you,' Nesseref returned. 'Perhaps we shall be friends.'

'Perhaps we shall,' Mordechai said in some surprise. Having a Lizard as a friend had not occurred to him till that moment. He had always dealt with Lizards because he had to, not because he wanted to. The Lizards he'd known had always made it clear they were dealing with him for the same reason. 'Are all females like you?'

'By the Emperor, no,' Nesseref said. 'Are all Tosevite males – I presume you are a male – like you?'

'No,' Anielewicz said. 'All right. We are a couple of individuals who happen to get on well. That will do, I think.'

'Yes, I also think so,' Nesseref said. 'From much of what I had heard and seen on this planet, I wondered if having a Tosevite friend was even possible. We of the Race have friendships with Rabotevs and Hallessi, but they are more like us in temperament – not in appearance, necessarily, but in temperament – than you Big Uglies.'

'I have heard that from other members of the Race,' Anielewicz said. 'I notice you have not brought any of these peoples to Tosev 3.'

'No: both these expeditions were fitted out from Home,' Nesseref answered. 'Once this world is brought fully into the Empire, though, Hallessi and Rabotevs will come here, as they have gone to each other's worlds and to Home as well.'

'You will find many Tosevites who do not think this world will ever be fully brought into the Empire,' Anielewicz said. 'As a matter of fact, I am one of them. I hope this does not offend you.'

'Offend me? No. Why should it?' Nesseref said. 'But that is not to say I believe you are right. By all appearances, you Tosevites are an impatient species. The Race is a great many things. Impatient it is not. Time is on our side. In a few thousand years, you Tosevites will be contented subjects of the Emperor.'

Bunim, the regional subadministrator in Lodz, had said much the same thing. Such confidence was unnerving. Were the Lizards right? The only thing Mordechai knew was that he wouldn't live long enough to find out. Seeking to shake the female's calm confidence a bit, he said, 'I do wish you the best of luck finding a spot for your shuttlecraft port.'

'I thank you,' Nesseref replied. 'You are well-spoken indeed, for a Tosevite.'

'And I thank you,' Mordechai said. 'And now, if you will excuse me, I have to check on the security of my explosive-metal bomb.'

Nesseref's mouth fell open. 'You are a funny Big Ugly, Mordechai Anielewicz,' she said, 'but you cannot fool me so easily as that.' Anielewicz shrugged. Just as well – better than just as well – she hadn't believed him.

As much as Johannes Drucker relished going into space, he also treasured leave time with his family. He treasured it more than ever these days; he'd come too close to losing Käthe. He didn't know what he would have done without her. He didn't know what his children would have done, either. Heinrich was fifteen now, Claudia twelve, and Adolf ten: old enough to get through better than they would have a few years before, perhaps, but losing a mother could never be easy. And losing a mother for the reason the *Gestapo* had put forward . . .

'Go on, Father,' Heinrich said from the back seat of the Volkswagen. 'The light is green. That means you can.' He would be eligible to learn to drive next year. The thought made Drucker cringe, or at least want to go back behind the steering controls of a Panther or some other panzer the next time he needed to hit the road.

He put the car into gear. It was a 1960 model, and burned hydrogen rather than gasoline. The engine was a lot quieter than those of the older buggy VWs that helped clog the streets of Greifswald. Christmas candles and lamps burned in the windows of shops and taverns and houses. They did only so much to relieve the grayness the town shared with so many others near the Baltic.

'Maybe it's the weather,' Drucker muttered under his breath. In wintertime this far north, the sun rose late and set early and never climbed very far above the southern horizon. Mists from the sea often obscured it even during the brief hours when it condescended to appear at all. Most days from November to February, streetlights shone around the clock. But they could not make up for the sun, any more than a distant cousin could make up for a missing mother.

Drucker wished that particular figure of speech had not occurred to him. He wished he'd had no cause to think of it. He glanced over to Käthe, who sat in the front seat beside him, with the children crowded into the back. She smiled. For once, evidently, she hadn't guessed what he was thinking.

'When we go into the shops, you will not come with me,' she said, as much at home with giving orders as Major General Dornberger. 'I want your present to be a surprise.'

'All right,' he agreed, so mildly that she gave him a suspicious stare. He returned it as blandly as he had turned aside the *Gestapo* interrogation earlier in the year. 'After all, I want to get you a surprise or two myself.'

'Hans—' She shook her head. Light brown curls flew. 'Hans, I am here. That is your doing. What greater present could you give me?'

'Greater? I don't know.' Drucker shrugged, and then, steering the Volkswagen as precisely as if it were the upper stage of an A-45, took for his own a parking space into which it barely fit. That done, he gave his wife his attention once more. 'I can go on giving you things if I want to, I think. And I do want to.'

Käthe leaned across the gearshift and kissed him on the cheek. In the back seat, Claudia giggled. She was at the age where public displays of affection amused, horrified, and fascinated her all at the same time. Drucker supposed he ought to count his blessings. All too soon, she'd likely put on public displays of affection that would horrify him without amusing him in the slightest.

'Heinrich, for whom will you shop?' Käthe asked.

Drucker's older son said, 'Why, for you and Father, of course. And for—' He broke off, two words too late, and turned red.

'For Ilse,' Claudia said; she was becoming an accomplished

tease. 'When are you going to give her your Hitler Youth pin, Heinrich?' Her voice was sweet and sticky as treacle.

Heinrich turned redder still. 'That's none of your business, you little snoop. You're not the *Gestapo*.'

'Nobody should be the *Gestapo*,' Adolf said fiercely. 'The *Gestapo* doesn't do anything but cause trouble for people.'

Privately, Drucker agreed with that. Privately, he'd said much worse than that. But Adolf was only ten. He couldn't be relied upon to keep private what absolutely had to be kept private. Drucker said, 'The *Gestapo* does do more than that. They hunt down traitors to the *Reich* and rebels and spies for the Lizards and the Bolsheviks and the Americans.'

'They tried to hunt down Mother,' Adolf said. 'They can—' The phrase he used would have made a *Feldwebel* with thirty years' experience as a non-com blush.

'Keep a civil tongue in your head, young man,' Drucker told him, hoping he sounded severe. He'd never said anything like that about the *Gestapo*, even if he agreed with the sentiment expressed. 'You must always keep a civil tongue in your head, for your family may not be the only people listening to you. What would happen to you, do you suppose, if the *Gestapo* had planted a microphone in our auto?'

Adolf looked appalled. Drucker had hoped he would. Drucker also hoped – devoutly – that the *Gestapo* hadn't planted a microphone in the VW. Such a thing was far from impossible. The snoops might have planted one to see if they could catch Käthe admitting her grandmother was a Jew. Or they might have planted it in the hope of hearing some other seditious statement.

Adults–adults with a gram of sense, anyhow – watched what they said as automatically as they breathed. Children had to learn they couldn't shout out the first thing that came into their heads. If they didn't learn fast, they didn't last long.

'Just remember,' Drucker told his son – told all three of his children, actually, 'no matter what you think, no matter how good your reasons for thinking it may be, what you say is a different business. Nobody can hear what you think. You never can tell who might hear what you say.' He paused a moment to let the lesson sink in, then went on, 'Now let's not say any more about it. Let's go shopping and see what sorts of nice things the stores have in them.'

He remembered the war years and the ones right after the fighting. In those days, the stores had had next to nothing in them. They'd tried to trick out the nothing with tinsel and candles, but hadn't had much luck. Now, though, the lean times were over. The German people could enjoy themselves again.

Käthe went off in one direction, with Claudia and Adolf in tow. Heinrich made his own way down the street. Maybe he was shopping for Ilse. Had Drucker been his son's age, he would have gone shopping for her; he was sure of that.

As things were, he went shopping for his wife. He found an excellent buy on Limoges porcelain at a shop not far from the town council hall. The shop stocked a wide variety of goods imported from France, all at very reasonable prices. He remarked on that as he made his purchase. 'Yes, sir,' the clerk said, nodding. 'In Paris itself, you could not buy these things so cheap.'

'I believe it,' Drucker said. Why that might be so never entered his mind. He took it for granted that Germany was entitled to first claim on whatever France produced. Germany, after all, was the beating heart of the *Reich*.

'Would you like me to do that up in gift-wrapping, sir?' the clerk asked.

'Yes, please.' Drucker hated wrapping presents himself. 'Thank you very much. And put it in a plain bag afterwards, if you'd be so kind.' He left the shop well pleased with himself. The plate, which reproduced an eighteenth-century painting of a shaded grotto, would look splendid on the mantel, or perhaps mounted on the wall.

He didn't bother heading back toward the Volkswagen, not yet. He knew he shopped more efficiently than Käthe and the children. Instead, he window-shopped as he wandered through the streets of Greifswald. He paused thoughtfully in front of a shop that stocked goods imported not from France but from Italy. A slow smile stole across his face. He went inside and made a purchase. He had that one gift-wrapped, too. The clerk, a pretty young woman, was most obliging. By the way she smiled, she might have been obliging if he'd been interested in something other than the shop's stock in trade. But he had no great interest in anyone but Käthe, and so did not experiment.

When he went back to the car, he found the rest of the family there ahead of him, and had to endure their teasing all the way home. 'You'll get coal for Christmas, every one of you,' he growled in mock anger, 'brown coal that won't even burn without stinking and smoking.'

On Christmas morning, before sunup, he took his family outside. They looked toward the east, not toward Bethlehem but toward Peenemünde, about thirty kilometers away. To his disappointment, the fog lay too thick to let them see the latest A-45 ascend to the heavens, but the roar of the rocket reverberated inside their bones.

'Maybe you'll ride it one of these days, Heinrich, Adolf,' he said.

His sons' faces glowed with pride. Claudia said, 'And what about me?' The best he could do to answer her was change the subject.

They went inside and opened presents, which provided plenty of distraction. Käthe exclaimed in delight at the plate from Limoges. She'd got Drucker a fancy meerschaum, and some Turkish tobacco to smoke in it. He puffed away in delight. Heinrich got a fancy one-liter beer stein. He proceeded to fill and then empty it, after which he got sleepy and red in the face.

'Maybe we should have bought the half-liter stein after all,' Drucker said. Käthe laughed. Heinrich looked offended and woozy at the same time.

Adolf got a battery-powered Leopard panzer with a control on the end of a long wire. He blitzkrieged through the living room and around the Christmas tree, till he wrapped the wire around the tree and couldn't undo things by reversing. Claudia squealed ecstatically when she opened her present, a blond plastic doll with a spectacular wardrobe and even more spectacular figure. That one hadn't been cheap, since it was imported from the USA, but it made her so happy, Drucker judged it well worth the cost.

'All my friends will be jealous,' Claudia chortled,' especially Eva. She's wanted one for weeks – practically forever.'

'Maybe she got one, too,' Drucker said. A little of Claudia's joy evaporated; she hadn't thought of that. But then, because it was Christmas, she brightened and made the best of it.

After a Christmas supper of fat roast goose, all her resentment went away, and, for the evening, all of Drucker's too. Heinrich went out to take Ilse to a party. Adolf kept destroying the *Reich*'s enemies till bedtime, while Claudia played with the American doll.

Heinrich had a key. After the younger children went to sleep, there was nothing to keep Käthe and Drucker from climbing the stairs to their own bedroom. With the air of a magician pulling a rabbit out of a hat, Drucker took the second gift-wrapped package from under a spare pillow in the closet and handed it to her. She let out a small shriek of happy surprise. 'Why didn't you give this to me with everything else?' she asked.

'You'll see,' he answered, and closed the bedroom door as she opened the package. She let out another small shriek: it held a pair of frilly garters and other bits of lace and near-transparency. He grinned. 'Gift-wrapping for you.'

She looked at him sidelong. 'And then, I suppose, you'll expect to unwrap me.'

Before very long, he did just that. Some little while after she was unwrapped, they lay side by side, naked and happy. He toyed idly with her nipple. 'Merry Christmas,' he said.

311

'I hope it was,' she told him, her voice arch.

'Jawohl!' he answered, as he might have to his commanding general. He wished he could have raised a different sort of salute, but that took longer in middle age.

She lay quiet for so long, he wondered if she'd fallen asleep. Then she said 'Hans?' in tones altogether different from the ones she had been using. He made a wordless noise to show he was listening. She leaned over and whispered in his ear: 'My father's mother . . . I think she really was a Jew.'

He didn't say anything right away. Whatever he said, he knew, would touch, would shape, the rest of their lives together. Silence, on the other hand, would only alarm her. He whispered back: 'As long as the *Gestapo* doesn't think so, who cares?' She hugged him, then burst into tears, and then, very quickly, did go to sleep. After a couple of hours, so did he.

10

'**I** do not understand,' Felless said. She had said that many, many times since coming to the Greater German *Reich*. Most of the time, as now, she did not mean she could not understand the translator who was rendering some official's words into the language of the Race. For a Big Ugly, this translator spoke the language well enough. What he said, though, and what the official said, made no sense to her.

'I will repeat myself,' the security official said. He seemed patient enough, willing enough, to make himself clear. Because he had lost most of the hair on top of his head, he looked a little less alien to her than did a lot of Tosevites. Below a wide forehead, his face was narrow, with a pointed chin. He spoke in the guttural Deutsch language. The translator turned his words into those Felless could follow: 'The Jews deserve extermination because they are an inferior race.'

'Yes, you have said that before, *Gruppenführer* Eichmann,' Felless said. 'But saying something and demonstrating it is true are not the same. Is it not so that the Jews have given the Tosevite not-empire known as the United States many able scientists? Is it not true that the Jews under the rule of the Race are thriving in Poland and Palestine and . . . and elsewhere?' She had learned some Tosevite geography, but not much.

'These things are true, Senior Researcher, yes,' Eichmann said calmly. 'In fact, they prove my point.'

Felless' jaw muscles tensed. She wanted to bite him. The urge was atavistic, and she knew it. But maybe pain would make him come out with something she recognized as sense. '*How* does it prove your point?' she demanded. 'Does it not seem to prove exactly the opposite?'

'By no means,' Eichmann said. 'For the purpose and highest destiny of any race is to form a—' The interpreter hesitated. He said, 'The term *"volkisch"* has no exact translation in the language of the Race. What the *Gruppenführer* means is that it is the destiny of each kind of Tosevite to form a not-empire made up of that particular kind and no other.'

A thousand questions occurred to Felless, starting with, *Why?* She suspected – indeed, she was certain – that one would not take her anywhere she wanted to go. She tried a different one instead: 'How are the Jews in any way different from this?'

'They are incapable of forming a not-empire of their own,' Eichmann answered, still sounding unimpassioned, matter-of-fact. 'Instead, they dwell within not-empires other, better races have created, as disease viruses dwell within a body. And, again like viruses, they poison and destroy the bodies in which they dwell.'

'Let us assume much of what you say is true,' Felless said. 'Has this conclusion you draw from the data been proved experimentally? Has anyone given these Jews land on which to set up a not-empire? Have they tried and failed? What sort of experimental control could you devise?'

'They have not tried and failed,' Eichmann replied. 'They have not tried at all, which demonstrates they are incapable.'

'Perhaps it only demonstrates they have not had an opportunity,' Felless said.

Eichmann shook his head back and forth, a Big Ugly gesture of negation. 'There has been no independent Jewish not-empire for two thousand years.'

Felless laughed in his face. 'First, this is an inadequate sample. Two thousand years – even two thousand of your long years – is no great time in terms of the history of a race or group, regardless of your opinion. Second, you are arguing in a circle. You say the Jews cannot form a not-empire because for this period of time they have had no opportunity because they cannot form a not-empire. You may have one fork of the tongue or the other on that argument; you may not have both.'

Gruppenführer Eichmann stirred behind his desk. The translator murmured to Felless: 'The *Gruppenführer* is not used to such disrespect, even from a male of the Race.'

That made Felless laugh again. 'For one thing. I am not a male of the Race. I am a female of the Race, as should be obvious to you. For another, when elementary logic is classed as disrespect, I am not sure rational discussion between the *Gruppenführer* and me is possible.' *I am not sure the* Gruppenführer *is even an intelligent creature. But his kind controls explosive-metal weapons. One day soon, they may begin to try to build a starship. What do we do then?*

'I have here a choice,' Eichmann said. 'I can follow what you say, a female of an alien species who has no personal experience of Tosev 3 and its races and kinds. Or I can follow the words and teachings of Hitler in his famous book *My Struggle*. Hitler spent his whole life pondering these problems. I trust his solutions far more than I trust yours. If this makes me seem illogical in your eyes, I am willing to pay such a price.'

He was as impervious as landcruiser armor. From his perspective, what he said made a certain amount of sense – but only a certain amount, for his conclusions, as far as Felless could see, remained those of a lunatic. His notions – and, presumably, this Hitler's notions – of the importance of an individual not-empire for every minutely different variety of Tosevite also struck her as absurd. Her own bias, she admitted to herself, was for the unity and simplicity of the Empire.

She tried again: 'If every Tosevite faction should have its own not-empire, how do you justify the rule of the *Reich* over the Français and the Belgians and the Danes and other such different groups of – of Tosevites?' Big Uglies, she recalled just in time, sometimes took offense at being called Big Uglies to their big, ugly faces.

'That, Senior Researcher, is very simple,' Eichmann answered. 'We have defeated them on the battlefield. This proves our superiority over them and demonstrates our right to rule them.'

'Is it not that they have also defeated you on the battlefield from time to time?' Felless asked. 'Are these events not random fluctuations of strength rather than tests of competitive virtue in the evolutionary sense?'

'By no means,' the Deutsch male answered through the interpreter. 'Truth, at one time the Français defeated us. But that was a hundred fifty years ago, and since that time they have mongrelized themselves, thus weakening their race to the point where we were easily able to defeat them not once but three times – though in the middle conflict we were robbed of our victory by a stab in the back.'

Felless did laugh again. She couldn't help it. 'The absurdity of imagining that evolution proceeds in such a fashion, or can have profound results in so few generations, is almost beyond description.'

'What is beyond description is the arrogance of the Race in imagining it can come to our planet and presume to understand us in so short a time,' Eichmann said.

Understand the Tosevites? Especially the Deutsch Tosevites? Fellness did not think she would ever do that. She said, 'Even the Tosevite authorities in the other not-empires, and also those in areas ruled by the Race, disagree with the interpretation offered by the *Reich*.'

'And what would you expect?' Eichmann's shoulders moved up and down in a Tosevite gesture of indifference similar to the one the Race used. 'When Jews dominate these other not-empires – and also the areas of the planet that you administer – they will naturally try to conceal scientific fact that places them in a bad light.'

'Jews do not dominate the areas of this planet that the Race rules,' Felless said, and added an emphatic cough. 'The Race dominates those areas.'

'So you think now,' the Deutsch security official said. 'One day before too long, you will say something else – if you ever notice the puppet strings attached to your wrists and ankles. But perhaps you will not even realize you wear shackles.'

That did it. The idea of Big Uglies of any sort manipulating the Race without the Race's knowledge was too absurd to contemplate. Felless rose from her chair – which, being made for Big Uglies, was none too comfortable anyhow – and said, 'I see no point to further discussion along these lines. I must say, I find it strange that Tosevites who accept the Race's superior knowledge in so many areas refuse to believe our knowledge superior in others.'

To her disappointment, Eichmann did not rise to the bait. 'I agree: this is pointless,' he said. 'I acceded to your request for an interview as a courtesy, nothing more. I have long been aware of the Race's profound ignorance in matters having to do with the relations among groups of Tosevites and the menace of the Jews. Good day.'

'Good day.' Tailstump quivering with rage, Felless stalked out of Eichmann's office, out of the bleak stone pile known as the Kaiserburg, and into the Tosevite-made vehicle waiting for her without even noticing the frozen water on the ground or the temperatures conducive to keeping water frozen. 'Take me back to the embassy this instant,' she snarled to the driver. 'This instant, do you hear me?'

'It shall be done, superior female,' the driver said. Wisely, he said not another word till he had delivered the researcher to the one Homelike place in all Nuremberg.

She went up to her quarters in the same high dudgeon in which she had departed from Eichmann's workplace. Once there, she entered into the data system the conversation she'd had with the Big Ugly while it was still fresh – revoltingly fresh – in her memory. Even the acid commentary she entered along with the interview failed to relieve her temper.

I should have bitten him, she thought. *By the Emperor, I really should have bitten him.* Then she stopped and shuddered. *By associating with Big Uglies, I am becoming as uncivilized as they are.*

She went next door and asked for admittance to Ttomalss' chamber. Instead of admittance, she got a recorded message saying he was doing field research of his own and would be back in the midafternoon.

Felless muttered and hissed discontentedly. She'd asked Ttomalss to assist her. She had not asked him to undertake autonomous research. Being around the Big Uglies, with their passion for individualism, had corrupted him, too.

Back to her own quarters she went. She remained anything but happy. Associating with Tosevites could not possibly leave anyone happy, or so she was convinced. But the depth of her own rage and frustration and despair appalled her. Ever since her premature revival, she had had nothing but bad news about Tosev 3 and its inhabitants.

Maybe she could find better news. Maybe the better news would come, in a way, from Tosev 3. The way she felt now, any change would be an improvement. Ttomalss would not approve, but, at the moment, she didn't care what Ttomalss thought. Ttomalss had gone off to do something on his own. Felless laughed. She wondered if, when he returned – it wouldn't be too long – he would know what she'd done. She laughed again. She doubted it. He knew plenty about Big Uglies, but that seemed to be all he knew.

She went over to her desk and opened one of the drawers. In it, after not so long on Tosev 3, she'd already stowed four or five vials of the herb called ginger. This male or that one, all of them longtimers on this dreadful, chilly world, had given the herb to her, saying it would improve the way the place looked. Up till now, she hadn't experimented; the stuff *was* against regulations. After the meeting with the Deutsch male called Eichmann, she didn't care. All she cared about was relief.

She poured some ginger into the palm of her hand. The odor

hit her scent receptors: spicy, alien, alluring. Her tongue shot out, almost of itself. In moments, the ginger was gone. In only moments more, the herb reached Felless' brain.

'Why did somebody not *tell* me?' she murmured through the ecstasy suffusing her. She had never imagined it could be so good. She was smarter, quicker, more powerful than she'd ever imagined being. The only sensation that compared to it was mating, which she suddenly recalled much more vividly than she had since the last time she came into her season.

Mirth and joy filled her. So did the desire for another taste. She poured more ginger onto her palm. Would Ttomalss notice? She'd find out soon.

Ttomalss did not like the Deutsche. He knew no one among the males of the Race who did like the Deutsche. Many of the males who had fought against them respected their military abilities. Some of the males who worked for the embassy also respected their ability to acquire and develop new technology. But no one liked them.

'They are arrogant,' Veffani, the Race's ambassador, had told him, 'as arrogant as if they had done something to justify such arrogance, as the Race had unquestionably done. They are murderous, and are not only unapologetic but proud of it.'

Understanding how and why that was so would have been useful for the Race. To try to gain some of that understanding, Ttomalss had spoken with a certain Rudolf Höss, an officer in charge of one of the industrial murder facilities the Deutsche operated. His question had been the most basic one possible: 'How can you stand to do what you do? Does it not oppress you?'

'Why should it?' Höss had answered with a yawn. 'It is my assignment. My duty is to obey the orders of my superiors and to carry out my assignment to the best of my ability.'

Had a male of the Race said that, it would have been laudable. But no male of the Race would have dreamt of getting an assignment like Höss'. Rather desperately, Ttomalss had asked, 'But did you not think of rejecting this assignment when it was given to you?'

'Why should I have done that?' Höss had seemed genuinely puzzled. 'My training suits me for the work. Besides, if I did not do it, someone else would have to, and I can do it better than most.'

'But the nature of the task—' Ttomalss began to wonder if his translator was doing a proper job. Could the Big Ugly across the desk from him be so oblivious to the kind of thing he did?

Evidently, Höss could. He said, 'It is an assignment, like any other.'

No matter how Ttomalss tried, he could not penetrate below that insistence on duty to the true feelings Höss had about his work. maybe he had no true feelings about it. Ttomalss would not have believed that possible, but it seemed to be so.

He had returned to the embassy with a mixture of relief at coming back to Homelike surroundings and frustration at failing to accomplish his object. The mixture of feelings made him hiss in annoyance when someone asked for admittance to his chamber. 'Who is it?' he demanded irritably.

'I: Felless,' was the reply from outside the chamber.

The female's voice sounded odd, but Ttomalss did not dwell on that. The unfortunate fact was that he could not refuse her entry, not when she had summoned him here to assist in her research. 'Come in, superior female,' he said, and thumbed the control that opened the airtight door. Given the proficiency of the Deutsche with poisonous gases, that struck Ttomalss as a more than reasonable precaution.

'I greet you,' Felless said, skittering toward him.

'I greet you, superior female,' Ttomalss said resignedly. He swung his eye turrets toward Felless with a certain amount of curiosity. She did sound strange, and she moved strangely, too, almost as if she were going faster than she had any business doing.

'Do you know, Senior Researcher, that the Tosevites are

very likely the most aggravating species evolved anywhere in the entire galaxy?' Felless said.

'Truth,' Ttomalss said with an emphatic cough. It didn't matter if Felless' voice wasn't quite right, not when she said things like that. 'As a matter of fact, the Big Uglies are . . .'

He took a deep breath, preparatory to cataloguing the Tosevites' many iniquities. As the air went into his lung, it went past his scent receptors. The odor they caught was familiar but altogether unexpected. He stared at Felless. The long scales between his eye turrets stood up to form a sort of a crest, as they had not done since he came to Tosev 3.

Felless stared at him, too. The erection of his crest was only one response his body made on smelling that odor. Almost without conscious thought, he pushed his chair back and came around his desk toward Felless. With each stride, he grew more nearly upright, till at last he walked almost like a Big Ugly. The female bent into a position somewhat similar to the posture of respect, one which left her posterior high and swung her tailstump out of the way.

Ttomalss hurried to place himself behind her. His reproductive organ jutted from his cloaca. He thrust it into hers. A moment later, he let out a whistling hiss as pleasure shot through his body.

When he released her, he said, 'I did not know you were coming into your season, superior female.'

'Neither did I,' Felless said. 'My body usually gives me some warning. This time, I had none. I tasted ginger a little while ago, and—'

She got no further than that. The pheromones pouring from her still filled the air and still intoxicated Ttomalss. The visual cues he gave excited Felless once more, and she reassumed the mating posture. Ttomalss coupled with her again, just as he had observed male Big Uglies repeatedly joining with females.

After the second mating, he was as worn as she. He had trouble thinking straight. He could still smell the pheromones. He wanted to couple again, even if he was not sure his body would respond to his desire. Hoarsely, he said, 'Maybe you had better go. The embassy will be a chaotic place for a while, if this is truly our females' season on Tosev 3.'

'But it should not be.' Felless sounded as dazed as Ttomalss felt. 'I did not think I was coming into season, as I said. I do not think I am due to come into season for some time. But I did. By the Emperor, I did.' She cast down her eyes, as she should have. Then, of itself, her head began to lower. Her hindquarters began to rise.

Ttomalss started to move behind her once more. Had he not already coupled twice in mere moments, he would have joined with her yet again. Instead, in a strangled voice, he said, 'Get out.'

Felless, still half in the mating posture, scuttled for the door. She poked the recessed button beside it with a fingerclaw. The door slid open. She scurried out – and almost ran into Veffani, who had a hand raised to activate the intercom and ask for admittance.

'Your pardon, superior sir,' Felless gasped.

'No apology necessary, Senior Researcher,' the ambassador to the *Reich* replied. As Ttomalss had done, he took a breath so he could say something more. As Ttomalss had done, he stopped with the words unspoken. The long scales at the top of his head lifted up, as Ttomalss' were still doing. He stood more nearly erect.

Felless began to assume the full mating posture once more. But to Ttomalss, Veffani's visual cues were not a signal for mating. To him, millions of years of evolution made them scream, *Rival!* He stalked toward Veffani, fingerclaws spread, mouth open in what was anything but a laugh.

It was not rational. It was anything but rational. Some small part of his mind knew that perfectly well. It watched in horror as the larger, dominant, part commanded him to hunt down and slaughter the male who was his superior.

Veffani was locked in the grip of fury, too, now that he saw Ttomalss' visual cues along with smelling Felless' pheromones.

With what must have taken great effort, he said, 'This is madness. We have to stop.'

'Truth.' The remaining part of Ttomalss' mind that could still think clearly seized on the excuse not to tear and snap at Veffani. Then the telephone hissed for his attention. That was a stimulus against which evolution had developed few defenses. He turned away to answer it. Veffani did not spring upon him.

The call turned out to be inconsequential. When Ttomalss disconnected, he saw that Veffani was just disconnecting from Felless. The ambassador had taken advantage of his distraction to mate.

'Superior female, please leave before we are all completely addled,' Ttomalss said. Felless straightened from the mating posture and scurried off up the hallway.

Her pheromones lingered in the air, but not at a level to send Ttomalss and Veffani wild. 'Now that the season is here, it is sweet,' Veffani said. 'Soon it will be over, and we can go back to being ourselves.'

'Truth,' Ttomalss said. 'And that will be sweet, too. I am glad to have mated, but I did not miss it while going so long without.'

'Well, of course not,' Veffani said. 'Are we Tosevites, to be thinking of mating every moment of the day and night?' He paused, then waggled his tongue in self-deprecation. 'At the moment, we might as well be Big Uglies. I still feel the urge – and the urge to quarrel with you as well.'

'And I with you, superior sir.' Ttomalss' wits, distracted by the mating urge, remained less sharp than they should have been. When something new occurred to him, he cursed himself for not having seen it sooner. 'How the Tosevites will laugh at us now that we are interested in such matters once more.'

'As I said, soon it will be over,' Veffani replied. 'And of one thing you may be sure: Tosevites have short memories. Very soon, they will forget their mockery and accept our behavior as normal for us, just as their behavior, however revolting we find it, is normal for them.'

'In one way, superior sir, that is a most perceptive observation on your part,' Ttomalss said, and explained to the ambassador to the *Reich* how Kassquit, even though raised as nearly as possible as a female of the Race, still sought physical relief at regular intervals. The researcher went on, 'In a different way, though, I fear you may be too optimistic, for when have the Big Uglies ever proved accepting either of us or of other factions of their own kind?'

'Well, that is also a truth.' Veffani let out an annoyed hiss. 'I cannot think straight, not with these pheromones still in the air. And every male in the place will have scent receptors tingling, looking for the female in her season.'

'And soon the rest of the females will be in heat, too – and so the mating season will go,' Ttomalss said. 'And then it will be over for another year. We shall have a new crop of hatchlings to begin to civilize, which will afford the Big Uglies further chances for mirth, not that their own hatchlings are anything save risible.' He checked himself. 'No, that is not strictly true. Their hatchlings are risible while they are raising them. When one of us attempts the task, it is, I assure you, no laughing matter.'

'That I believe. You have my admiration for your efforts along those lines,' Veffani said. 'I should not have cared to try to emulate them. What I should care for is—' He broke off and made another self-mocking tongue waggle. 'What I should care for is another mating. Being in the season makes us strange, does it not?'

Before Ttomalss could answer, a male came hurrying down the hall. The scales of his crest were raised; he had the determined stride of one who knew exactly what he wanted, though not exactly where it was. A moment later, another similarly intent male followed him. Ttomalss laughed. 'It has begun.'

With his mouth open, he caught more of Felless' pheromones. His crest stood higher, too.

* * *

Nesseref was fed up with Tosev 3: not with the Big Uglies – who, while their reproductive habits were revolting, had proved to have some interesting and even personable individuals among them – but with her own kind. She gave Bunim, the regional subadministrator headquartered in Lodz, a sour stare. 'In my opinion, superior sir, you cannot have it both ways. You wanted the shuttlecraft port in this area, but now you keep raising objections to every site I propose.'

'That, Shuttlecraft Pilot, is because you continue to propose objectionable sites,' Bunim replied. 'Things in this region are more complicated than you seem to understand.'

'Enlighten me, then,' Nesseref said, with more sarcasm than she should have aimed at a superior. At the moment, she would cheerfully have aimed a weapon at Bunim. *Obstructionist,* she thought.

Through the window of his office, she could see little clumps of frozen water twisting and swirling in the icy breeze. The stuff was interesting, perhaps even attractive in a bizarre way – when seen through a window. Nesseref had acquired more experience of snow than she'd ever wanted, trying to find a landing site that would satisfy her and Bunim both.

Despite the cold, despite the snow, Tosevites still met to buy and sell in the market square on which Bunim's office faced. They put on more layers of muffling and went about their business. In a way, such determination was admirable. In another way, it made her reckon the Big Uglies addled.

Bunim said, 'The situation is complicated in this way: the Race rules Poland, but not in the way we rule Rabotev 2 or even the way we rule most other parts of Tosev 3. The two groups of Tosevites here – the Poles and the Jews – are both heavily armed and could, should they rise up against us, cause us a great deal of difficulty. The Jews are even said to possess an explosive-metal device, though I do not know for certain if this is true.'

'I met a Tosevite who said he was checking the security for such a bomb,' Nesseref said.

'All Tosevites lie,' Bunim said dismissively. 'But the point is, the only reason the locals tolerate us is that they loathe the not-empires to either side of them, the Greater German *Reich* and the SSSR, more than they loathe us. We do not want them to loathe us more than they loathe these not-empires, or they might succeed in expelling us. Thus we have to step carefully. We cannot simply move in and take whatever we want. This includes taking land we want, provided the Big Uglies now owning it do not care to give it up. Now do you begin to see?'

'I do, superior sir.' What Nesseref thought she saw was a confession of weakness, but saying so would not do. What she did say was, 'You are telling me you are treating these Big Uglies as if, in property rights and such, they were males and females of the Race.'

'Essentially, yes,' Bunim said.

Nesseref's opinion of that policy was not high. Bunim, however, would not care what her opinion was, and his superiors would support his opinion. Nesseref said what she could: 'I do wish this policy had been communicated to me some time ago rather than now. Doing so would have prevented a great deal of friction between us.' *I could have done my job properly and gone away,* she thought savagely. *This is not a garden spot. From what I have seen of Tosev 3, it has no garden spots.*

'I suppose I assumed you understood what the situation was here,' Bunim said. 'We of the conquest fleet take matters Tosevite so much for granted by now, we are liable to forget that you colonists are less familiar with them.'

'It would be better if you did not.' Nesseref got up. 'And now, superior sir, if you will excuse me . . .' She turned and departed without looking back at Bunim, so she never found out whether he excused her or not.

Outside, the wind snapped at her as if it had teeth, blowing snow into her face and into the front of the building where Bunim had his office. She drew her own mufflings more tightly around her. Her eye turrets turned toward the guards around the building. She pitied them. They had to endure this brutal weather for far longer stretches than she.

They'd also had to endure Bunim for a far longer stretch than she had. She pitied them for that, too. Now she turned an eye turret back toward his office. He infuriated her. He knew things, didn't bother to tell them to her, and then blamed her when her work had problems.

'Unconscionable,' she muttered. But his superiors would back him. She was very sure of that. They'd served with him since the conquest fleet arrived. She was only a newcomer, and a newcomer of lower rank at that. 'Unfair.' That was a low mumble, too. It was also the way the world – any world – worked.

She hated it, hated Bunim, hated everything about Tosev 3 except, strangely, a Tosevite or two. Rummaging in her belt pouch, she pulled out one of the vials of ginger males had given her. Maybe that would make her feel better. *Nice if something could,* she thought.

The breeze threatened to blow the ginger out of the palm of her hand. It was so cold that she wondered if her tongue would freeze to her skin when she shot it out. The taste of the herb was like nothing she'd ever known, sharp and sweet at the same time. And its effect was everything the males of the conquest fleet had said it would be, everything and then some. The truth of that amazed her as much as the sensation itself; she knew perfectly well how much males were in the habit of exaggerating.

Bliss filled her. The sensation reminded her of how she felt during mating season. She hadn't thought much about that since her last season ended. Like the rest of the Race, she kept the mating season and what went on then in a separate compartment of her mind from the rest of her life. Ginger seemed to make the walls around that compartment crumble.

She shivered in the breeze, a shiver that had very little to do with the wretched Tosevite weather. To be interested in mating when she was not in season frightened her; some severe hormonal disorders had symptoms like that. But, at the same time, she enjoyed – she couldn't help enjoying – the delicious feeling of longing that stole over her.

She took another taste, bending her head low over the ginger still in the palm of her hand. Bending her head low was also the beginning of the mating posture. She did her best not to think about that. With the herb coursing through her, not thinking was easy.

Nesseref swung her eye turrets back toward the building in which Bunim had his headquarters, to make sure the sentries hadn't noticed her tasting ginger. Despite the number of males from the conquest fleet who used the stuff, it remained against regulations. The penalties imposed for using it struck her as absurdly harsh. She did not want to get caught.

Whether she wanted to or not, though, she was about to get caught, for both sentries were approaching her. She started to move away, hoping for the chance to sidle round a corner and disappear. But they were advancing on her with quick and determined strides.

Then she saw that their erectile scales had risen, and that they were moving with a more nearly upright gait than the Race usually used. 'By the Emperor,' she whispered, 'I was not just thinking about mating after all.' The breeze blew her words away – the same breeze that had blown her pheromones to the two males standing outside Bunim's building.

One of them gestured, motioning for her to stick her head down farther and her hindquarters in the air. It was a gesture only used, only seen, during the mating season. She obeyed it without thinking. That seemed easier than ever.

Sometimes, in the wildness of the season, males fought over females. Sometimes they simply took turns. That was what happened here. The male who had not gestured tugged at Nesseref's wrappings, then at his own, so they could join. 'Miserable, clumsy things,' he grumbled.

He thrust his reproductive organ into hers. The pleasure that gave, when added to the pleasure of the ginger, was almost more than Nesseref could bear. When the male finished, the other one took his place. She enjoyed his attentions as much as those of his predecessor.

Dimly, she noticed a crowd of Tosevites gathering around her and the two males she had aroused. The Big Uglies stared and pointed and said things in their incomprehensible language. Some of them made strange barking, yapping sounds. Nesseref had heard that was how they laughed. She didn't care. She didn't care about anything except the ginger and what the males were doing.

They'd switched again. A moment later, the one who'd gone first finished his new coupling. The other one took his place once more.

By the time he finished, the ginger was beginning the ebb from Nesseref's system. She raised her head and lowered her rump, turning her eye turrets back toward the males. 'Enough,' she said. Suddenly, what she'd just been doing disgusted her. She felt as low as she'd been filled with delight a moment before.

'No such thing as enough,' one of the guards said, and gave an emphatic cough. But he'd mated with her twice, so both the words and the cough sounded halfhearted.

'Funny a female should come into season in winter,' the male remarked. 'Probably has something to do with the long Tosevite years.'

Sunk in depression as she was – something about which ginger-tasters had not warned her – Nesseref did not answer. *But I wasn't coming into season,* she thought. *I wasn't. I would know if I were. I always know a few days before I do. Every female knows beforehand.*

She hadn't been close to coming into season till she tasted ginger. As soon as she'd tasted it, thoughts of mating started going through her head. That was very strange. She wondered if it would happen every time she tasted. Maybe she would find out, because she wanted to taste again. From these depths, the heights to which she'd ascended on the herb seemed all the more desirable.

329

Desirable . . . 'Do you males go into season when you taste ginger?' she asked the guards, figuring one or both of them was likely to use the herb.

'No,' one answered. 'That's foolish. How can a male go into season without a female in heat to send him there?' The other sentry gestured to show he agreed.

I don't know, Nesseref thought. *How can a female go into season when it's not her time?* She didn't know that, either, not for certain, but she'd just done it. Now she noticed the gaping, laughing Tosevites. *By the Emperor, how am I any different from them?* One more question for which she had no answer.

'I greet you, Exalted Fleetlord,' Kirel said. 'I trust your stay in Australia proved enjoyable and restorative?'

'Oh, indeed, Shiplord, indeed,' Atvar said. 'And I trust there are new crises and disasters awaiting me here.' His mouth opened in a wry laugh. 'There always are.'

'No crises or disasters,' Kirel said, and Atvar felt a strange mixture of disappointment and relief. The shiplord of the bannership went on, 'There is one thing, however, which has come up in the last few days that does appear worthy of your attention.'

'There always is,' Atvar said with a sigh. 'Very well, Shiplord: enlighten me. You were on the point of doing so anyhow, I have no doubt.'

'As a matter of fact, I was,' Kirel agreed. 'It appears that, here and there across Tosev 3, a certain number of females from the colonization fleet have come into season. Matings have taken place, and one male near Basra was badly bitten in a fight over a female.'

'That *is* curious,' the fleetlord said. 'A certain number of females, you tell me? They should all enter their season at about the same time, not piecemeal. Did Reffet use some peculiar selection criteria for them? Are some from the worlds of the Rabotevs and Hallessi rather than Home?'

'I do not believe that to be the case,' Kirel replied. 'Nevertheless, there does appear to be a common factor in these incidents.'

His tone warned that good news did not lie ahead. Atvar fixed him with a baleful stare. 'I suppose you are going to tell me what this common factor is, too. Before you do, tell me whether I really want to know.'

'I do not know whether you do or not, Exalted Fleetlord,' Kirel said, 'but I will tell you that you need to know.'

'Very well,' Atvar said, with the air of a male who expected the enemy to do his worst.

Kirel proceeded to do just that: 'It appears that all the females who suddenly came into season had tasted ginger shortly before they did so. This is not certain, due to natural reluctance to admit to ginger-tasting, but it appears likely to be true.'

'I think I will go back to Australia now,' Atvar said. 'No, on second thought, I believe I will go into cold sleep and have my miserable, frozen carcass shipped back to Home. When I am revived there, everything that has happened to me here will seem to be only a dream remembered from hibernation. Yes, I like the sound of that very much.'

'Exalted Fleetlord, you led us into battle against the Big Uglies,' Kirel said loyally. 'You gained as satisfactory a peace as you could after conditions turned out to be different from those we anticipated. Do you now despair over an herb we have been fighting since not long after our landing on Tosev 3?'

'I am tempted to,' Atvar replied. 'Are you not? Fight as we would, we could not keep a great many males from becoming regular ginger users. Do you think we shall have any better luck with the females from the colonization fleet?'

'Who can say, with any certainty?' Kirel replied. 'We may yet find a way to overcome the craving the herb causes.'

'I hope you are right,' Atvar said. 'But I wish I truly believed it.' He studied Kirel. The shiplord of the *127th Emperor Hetto* truly did not seem too upset at the news he had given Atvar.

331

Perhaps he did not understand its implications. Atvar did. Tosev 3 had given him practice in recognizing catastrophes while they were still hatching. He proceeded to spell this one out: 'You say it is truth that females who taste ginger go into their season?'

'Some females, yes: this is truth,' Kirel said. 'I do not know if it is truth for all females.'

'Spirits of Emperors past grant that it not be,' Atvar said, and cast his eyes down to the floor of his office in Shepheard's Hotel. 'Females going into season will mean males going into season, sure as night follows day.'

'That is also truth, Exalted Fleetlord,' Kirel admitted. 'I have no doubt it will prove a nuisance, but—'

'A nuisance,' Atvar exclaimed. 'A nuisance? Is that all you see?' Kirel was sound, conservative, reliable. He had as much imagination now as he'd had in his eggshell, when he'd had nothing to imagine. Atvar said, 'Females will not taste ginger at only one season of the year, any more than males do.'

'No doubt you are right once more, Exalted Fleetlord.' No, Kirel really did not grasp the size of the disaster looming ahead.

Atvar made it unmistakably clear: 'Shiplord, if we have females accessible to mating at any season of the year and males accessible to mating at any season of the year, *how are we any different from Big Uglies?*'

'That is a . . . fascinating question, Exalted Fleetlord,' Kirel said slowly. 'I must confess, I have no good answer for it at the moment.'

'I was hoping you might, because I have none, either,' Atvar said. 'The accursed Tosevites have evolved to cope with their bizarre biology. If our biology on this world becomes bizarre, how are we to cope? Evolution has not prepared us to be in season the year around. Can you imagine anything more wearing? How are we to get done that which will assuredly need doing if our minds are constantly filled with thoughts of mating?'

Kirel's eye turrets were rigid and still with horror as he stared at the fleetlord. 'No analysis up to this time has suggested such a chain of events,' he said. 'That does not necessarily mean they are improbable, however. Indeed, they strike me as all too probable.' He folded himself into the posture of respect. 'How did you come to postulate them?'

'When dealing with matters on this planet, my standard method is to take the worst thing I can imagine, multiply it by ten, and then begin to suspect I have something a quarter of the way to the true level of misfortune,' Atvar said.

Kirel laughed. Atvar wished he had been joking. Kirel asked, 'What is now to be done?'

'I do not know,' Atvar answered. His laugh, unlike Kirel's, was bitter. 'We have been studying the Tosevites' sexuality since we arrived here. Who would have imagined our research might have practical applications to our own situation?'

'We must do everything we can to keep ginger out of the hands and off the tongues of females,' Kirel said. 'That will not eliminate the problem, but it will help reduce it.'

'Draft the appropriate orders for my approval,' Atvar said. 'As you say, that will not remove the problem, but it will make it smaller. And, like an army that has taken a heavy blow, we need to buy time and regroup.'

'Truth. It shall be done, Exalted Fleetlord.' Kirel hesitated, then went on, 'If I may offer a suggestion?'

'Please do,' Atvar said. 'The more suggestions we have now, the better.'

'Very well, then.' Kirel looked away from Atvar with both eye turrets for a moment. He was embarrassed at what he was about to say, then. Nevertheless, he said it: 'In matters pertaining to year-round sexuality, we are the ignorant ones, the Big Uglies the experts. You could do worse than consult with them in regard to this problem. We shall not be able to keep it secret. In fact, if some of the reports reaching Cairo are true, it is no longer secret. Some very public matings have occurred.'

'Have they?' Atvar shrugged. Such things happened all the

time during mating season. Still, Kirel's point was well taken. Atvar said, 'A good notion. I shall summon Moishe Russie. Not only is he a Big Ugly, but also a physician, or what passes for such among his kind. He will undoubtedly be able to tell us much that we do not yet know or suspect about what lies ahead for us.'

He wasted no time, but telephoned Russie at his practice in Jerusalem. Being the most powerful individual on the planet had its advantages: Russie did not refuse to speak to him. Atvar couched his orders in polite terms; he had seen over the years how touchy and stubborn Russie could be. But they were orders, and of that the fleetlord left no doubt.

Next morning, Russie presented himself at Shepheard's Hotel. 'I greet you, Exalted Fleetlord,' he said when Pshing escorted him into Atvar's presence. 'How may I assist you?' He spoke the language of the Race well if pedantically.

Atvar remembered there had been a time when Russie was unwilling to assist the Race in anything. He had, to some degree, mellowed. If he could help the Race without hurting his own kind, he would. The situation was not ideal from the fleetlord's point of view, but it was acceptable. On Tosev 3, that ranked as something of a triumph.

'I shall explain,' Atvar said, and he did.

Russie listened intently. Atvar had studied Tosevite expressions – far more varied and less subtle than those of the Race – but saw nothing on the Big Ugly's face save polite interest. When the fleetlord finished, Russie said, 'I have already heard something of this. There was an incident in Jerusalem the other day that shocked both Jews and Muslims, but no one knew its likely cause till now.'

An incident that shocked the Muslims was the last thing the fleetlord wanted; that Tosevite faction was already far too restive. He said, 'How are we to prevent further such incidents?'

'As you surely know, it is our strong custom to mate privately,' Russie said. 'A ban on public mating by the Race would help keep order in areas of the planet you rule.'

'Our custom is the opposite,' Atvar said. 'We are in the habit of mating wherever we chance to be when the urge strikes us. Still, for the sake of good order among the Tosevites, a ban such as you suggest might be worthwhile.' It would be a palliative, as would tighter controls on ginger-smuggling, but Tosev 3 had taught him palliatives were not always to be despised.

'If your females, or some of them, are to be in season all the time, you will also need rules about with whom they can mate, and perhaps about what happens when a male mates with a female against her will,' Russie said.

'If a female is in season, mating is not against her will,' Atvar answered.

Russie shrugged. 'You know better than I.'

'Not necessarily,' Atvar said. 'This is unfamiliar territory for the Race, as unfamiliar as Tosev 3 was before our probe landed here – and as unfamiliar as Tosev 3 was after the probe landed here, too.'

'Why exactly, then, have you summoned me?' the Tosevite asked.

Atvar turned both eye turrets toward him. 'For your suggestions,' the fleetlord replied. 'You have already given some. I hope you will give more. The Race will have to cope, as we have had to cope with so much on your world.'

'If you had thought of it as our world from the beginning, you would not have these problems now.' Moishe Russie's face twisted into a peculiar grimace. 'And I, very likely, would be dead. I will do what I can for you, Exalted Fleetlord.'

'I thank you.' Atvar sounded more sincere than he had expected. With luck, Russie would not notice.

Monique Dutourd kept noticing Lizards on the streets of Marseille as she bicycled to work. She hadn't seen so many since the Race ruled the south of France back in the days when she was a girl. Normally, she would not have taken much notice of them. After learning how her brother made his living – after learning Pierre was alive to make a living – she paid more attention to them. She couldn't help wondering whether they were here to smuggle things into and out of the city.

Semester break had come and gone. Now she was teaching about the later Roman Empire, all the way through the sixth-century era of Justinian. Sure as the devil – in more ways than one, she supposed – Dieter Kuhn was enrolled in the class, still under the name of Laforce.

She wished he weren't. She wished he weren't for a couple of reasons, in fact. For one thing, of course, he still wanted to use her to do something dreadful to Pierre. And, for another, she had to teach about the Germanic invasions of the Roman Empire in this part of the course. She knew by his examinations that he took meticulous notes. Having meticulous notes on a Frenchwoman's opinions about the Germanic invasions of the Empire in *Gestapo* hands might not have been the last thing she wanted, but it came close.

On she pedaled, threading her way through the traffic with nearly automatic ease. She was glad trousers were more acceptable on women than they had been when she was a girl. They helped preserve modesty on a bicycle and, in winter, they also kept her legs warm – not that Marseille winter was all that cold.

Just south of Rue Grignan, traffic came to a halt. Even on a bicycle, Monique could barely squeeze forward. She tilted her left wrist to look at her watch. When she saw the time, she muttered a curse. She was liable to be late to her lecture, which meant she was liable to be in trouble with the university authorities.

Up ahead, someone in a motorcar blew his horn, and then someone else and someone else again. But, curiously, she heard none of the ripe oaths she would have expected motorists and bicyclists caught in a traffic jam to loose. Instead, what floated back to her ears was laughter, laughter and rude suggestions: 'Turn a hose on them!' 'In the name of God, find them a hotel room!' 'Yes, for heaven's sake – one with a bidet!' That brought more coarse laughter.

'What *is* going on up there?' Monique exclaimed, picking her way between a fat man on a bicycle too small for him and a German soldier in a field-gray Volkswagen utility vehicle. The soldier blew her a kiss. The fat man winked at her. She ignored them both. Standing on tiptoe while straddling the bicycle, she tried to see what was going on up ahead. People couldn't have been so shameless as to prove their affection for each other in the middle of a crosswalk . . . could they?

A man who should have shaved the day before yesterday looked back over his shoulder and said, 'There's a couple of Lizards up ahead there, fucking their brains out.'

'No,' Monique said, not so much contradiction as simple disbelief.

But, as she edged up even with the man with the stubbled cheeks and chin, she discovered he was telling the truth. There in the middle of the road, a couple of Lizards were going at it for all they were worth. She'd never seen, never imagined seeing, such a thing. In an abstract way, she admired the male's stamina and enthusiasm, though she wouldn't have wanted to stand so long with her head down by her toes, as the female was doing.

Aesthetic considerations here were very much by the way. What mattered to her was that the Lizards, by blocking traffic, were going to make her late. 'Yes, turn a fire hose on them!' she shouted.

After what seemed like forever but was about five minutes, she got past them. They were still mating as enthusiastically as ever. Half a block down, she spied a policeman. 'Why don't you arrest them?' she shouted, still furious at the delay.

With a shrug, the *flic* replied, 'My dear *mademoiselle*, I do not know whether it is against the law for Lizards to fornicate in public. So far as I am aware, no statute covers such an eventuality.' He shrugged again and took a bite from a sandwich he carried in place of his billy club, which swung on his belt.

'Arrest them for blocking traffic if you can't arrest them for screwing,' Monique snapped. The policeman only shrugged again. Monique had no time to argue with him. She pedaled furiously – in every sense of the word – toward the south.

When she strode into the lecture hall, sweat stained her blouse. But she was on time, with about fifteen seconds to spare. She began to talk about the Gothic incursions into the Roman Empire in the middle of the third century, incursions that had cost the Emperor Decius his life, as dispassionately – or so she hoped – as if no such people as the Germans had troubled the world in the seventeen hundred years since Decius' unfortunate and untimely demise.

At least I don't publish anything touching on this period, she thought. A lecture could be thought of as written on the wind. A scholarly article left a record as permanent as the inscriptions she pursued. The *Gestapo* could, if it so chose, do all sorts of unpleasant things with that.

The *Gestapo*, in the person of *Sturmbannführer* Dieter Kuhn, came up to her after the lecture and said, 'Another stimulating discussion of the issues. You have my compliments, for whatever you think they may be worth.'

'Thank you,' Monique said, and turned away to answer a genuine student's question about where the Goths had landed along the coast of Asia Minor. It was the last real question she had. When she finished dealing with it, Dieter Kuhn still stood waiting. Her temper flared. 'Damn you. What do you want?'

'If it is all right with you, we will ride back to your flat together,' Kuhn said.

'And if it is not all right with me?' Monique set her hands on her hips.

Kuhn shrugged, not quite as a Frenchman would have done. 'Then we will ride back to your flat together anyhow.' He had never been anything but polite to her, but he made it very plain he did not intend to take no for an answer.

'Why?' she asked, playing for time.

She did not really expect an answer, but the SS officer gave her one: 'Because something strange is happening in your brother's dealings with the Lizards. It could be that, before too long, he will see us as friends, or at least as professional colleagues, rather than as foes.'

It did not sound like a lie. But then, if it was, it wouldn't. Still, Monique started to dismiss it . . . till she remembered the morning traffic snarl. 'Does it have to do with Lizards screwing?' she asked.

His eyes, brown as hers, widened slightly. 'You are very clever,' he said, as if wondering whether she was too clever for her own good. 'How did you figure that out? The situation has made itself plain only in the past few weeks. There has been no talk of it in the newspapers or on the wireless. We have made certain of that.'

'I wish I could take more credit for intelligence, but I saw a pair of them, ah, enjoying themselves as I rode down to the university this morning,' Monique answered.

'Ah,' Kuhn said. 'I see. And now, shall we go?'

Monique considered. The only other choice she saw was screaming and hoping enough Frenchmen came running to give the SS man a good beating. But that would be dangerous not only for her but also for anyone who came to her aid. She sighed. 'Very well,' she said, though it wasn't.

Kuhn had, as usual, come prepared. The bicycle he rode was almost as old and disreputable as hers. She rode every day. So far as she knew, he didn't. He had no trouble staying with her even so. She got the feeling he was, if anything, holding back. She sped up till she might have been racing. Kuhn stuck like a burr. He glanced over to her and nodded, plainly enjoying himself. Damn him, he wasn't even breathing hard.

As she let him into her flat, she wished, not for the first time, that she only had to worry about him tearing off his trousers. She suspected she wouldn't be able to stop him if he tried – and a Frenchwoman who dared lodge a complaint against the all-powerful SS would be lucky if she just got ignored. But Kuhn wasn't interested in her body – or not interested enough to do anything along those lines. To him, she was a tool, a key, not an object of desire.

'Call your brother,' he said now. He must have seen the mulish resistance on her face, for he went on, 'You may tell him I am forcing you to do it. You may, if you like, tell him I wish to speak with him, for I do.'

'Why don't you just call him yourself, then, and leave me out of it?' Monique demanded. More than anything else, she wanted not to be stuck between the brother she didn't know and the SS she knew too well.

'He is more likely to pay attention to his sister than to someone who has been hunting him for some time,' Dieter Kuhn answered.

'He hasn't paid any attention to me for more than twenty years,' Monique said. Kuhn looked at her. The look said, *Get on with it.* Hating herself, she picked up the telephone and dialed the number she'd worked so hard to learn.

'Allô?' It was the woman with the sexy voice. Pierre's wife? His mistress? Only his secretary? Did smugglers have secretaries? Monique didn't know.

'Hello,' she said back. 'This is Pierre's sister. There is an SS man in my flat who needs to speak with him.'

That got her a few seconds of silence, and then Pierre's voice, as full of suspicion as the woman's had been the first time Monique spoke to her: 'Hello, little sister. What nonsense is this about an SS man? Is it the fellow who wanted to be your boyfriend?'

'Yes.' Monique's face heated. She thrust the handset at Kuhn. 'Here.'

'Thank you.' He took it with complete aplomb. '*Bonjour*, Dutourd. I just thought you ought to know that ginger is a genuine aphrodisiac for female Lizards. They didn't like the trade before. Now they have an even bigger reason to hate it. If they come after you – when they come after you – we won't lift a finger to stop them, not unless we get some cooperation on your end.'

340

He played the game well. Monique already knew that. Now she saw it again. She wondered how much difference it would make to her brother. Not much, she hoped. If Pierre didn't play this game well, he wouldn't have been able to stay in business so long himself.

He said something. Monique could hear his voice coming out of the telephone, but not the words. Dieter Kuhn obviously heard the words. 'I think you are being an optimist,' he replied. 'I think, in fact, you are being a fool. As I said, if you do not cooperate with us, we shall not cooperate with you. *Au revoir*.' He hung up, then turned to Monique. 'Your brother is stubborn. He will live to regret it – for how long, I cannot say.'

Monique burst into tears. Through them, she pointed to the door. 'Get out.' Rather to her surprise, Kuhn left. She cried for a long time even so.

Straha turned one eye up from the documents and photographs Major Sam Yeager had given him toward the Tosevite himself. 'You are confirming what my sources in lands ruled by the Race have already reported to me,' he said. 'I find it highly amusing. Would you not agree?'

'I just might, Shiplord,' Yeager answered. 'For the past twenty years, the Race has been calling us sexually wild, and now your males and females are mating whenever they get the chance. Yes, that is pretty funny, all right.'

'Atvar will be shedding his skin in patches,' Straha said with a certain morbid relish. 'Females coming into heat outside the proper mating season will be something new and unexpected. The Race is not at its best dealing with the new and unexpected.' He added an emphatic cough. 'And Atvar is not good at dealing with the new and unexpected even for a male of the Race.'

Yeager said, 'If you already knew this, Shiplord, I am sorry I had you come down to my house to look at these things.'

'Do not concern yourself,' Straha answered. 'I know that one of the things I am is a Tosevite tool. I chose the role myself,

341

if you will recall.' He laughed a small laugh. 'How strange that the herb which gives males so much pleasure turns out to give females and males even more.'

'Shiplord, that is one of the things I wanted to ask you,' Yeager said. 'There are a couple of females of the Race in Los Angeles now. If we were to arrange to give them some ginger while you were around . . . if you want us to do that, we can take care of it for you. You have done a lot for us over the years.'

Straha thought about it, then made the negative hand gesture. 'You mean this generously, I have no doubt. I believe a Big Ugly who had gone without a female for as long as I have would be inclined to accept. But a male of the Race, you must understand, has no desire until his scent receptors catch the odor of a female in her season.'

'No, I do understand that,' Yeager answered. 'If we gave one of these females ginger, you would smell that odor. I wondered if you wanted to, is all.'

'Again, I say thank you, but no,' Straha said. 'I am content to remain as I am. If I could join fully in the colonies now forming, it might be something else, but I know it will never be permitted.'

Exile. Once more, the word beat at him. It was what he was. He would never be anything else. He could never be anything else. If Atvar died tomorrow, his replacement would be Kirel, who might as well have hatched from the same egg. And Reffet, the fleetlord of the colonization fleet, was too new-come to Tosev 3 to understand what had driven Straha to do as he did.

Suppose he had succeeded in overthrowing Atvar, after the Big Uglies set off their first explosive-metal bomb. Suppose he had gone on to conquer the whole chilly, miserable planet. What would he do now? – for surely some females would taste ginger under his regime. He longed for a taste himself right now, as he sat here talking with Yeager.

He truly did not know what he would do. He did know

Atvar was welcome to the problem. Whatever Atvar did would probably be a half measure, too little and too late. That was Atvar's way. Straha said as much.

'It is not easy to figure out what he might do,' Yeager said, echoing Straha's thought. 'A lot of ginger goes into the parts of Tosev 3 the Race occupies, and a lot gets grown there, too. I do not see how the Race will be able to stop females from tasting it. And when they do . . .'

'Indeed, Sam Yeager,' Straha said. 'Preventing that will be difficult. And I have heard that females continue to give off the pheromones for some time after first being stimulated to do so by the herb.'

'I had not heard that. I had better write it down.' Yeager did. The chimes at his front door pealed. He got to his feet. 'Excuse me.' He hurried out to see who was there; he had no intercom to check from back here in his study.

After the door opened, Straha heard Yeager speaking English: 'Oh, hello, Karen. Come on in. Jonathan's back in his bedroom. Chemistry tonight, isn't it?'

'That's right, Mr. Yeager. He's got to help me on this one – he's better at it than I am.' This voice was higher and thinner than Yeager's: it came, Straha judged, from a female Big Ugly. And, sure enough, the Tosevite who walked past the doorway wore her coppery hair long and possessed – and, indeed, displayed – prominent mammary glands. She also displayed a lot of skin, which was painted in a good imitation of the pattern a mine-clearance underofficer wore.

Straha did not know what to make of young Big Uglies imitating the Race like that. The first time he'd seen it, a couple of years before, he'd been offended. Now he was more nearly resigned, and hoped it meant assimilation in action. Even Sam Yeager's offspring decorated himself so.

'Oh,' the young Tosevite said, seeing him. She assumed the posture of respect about as well as a Big Ugly could and shifted from English to the language of the Race: 'I greet you, superior sir.'

'I greet you, Mine-Clearance Underofficer,' Straha replied with wry amusement. 'My proper title is Shiplord.'

'Ship—?' The female's small eyes went as wide as they could. Still in the posture of respect, she said, 'I meant no offense.'

'I do not reckon myself insulted.' Straha watched her staring at his ornate body paint, and wondered if she would be sporting something like it soon. 'You speak and understand my language well,' he said. 'Now go and study your chemistry. It may prove useful to you later in life.'

From behind the young female, Sam Yeager spoke again in English: 'Yeah, run along, Karen. I'm talking shop here, I'm afraid.' On she went, that bright hair shining. Yeager came back into the study. 'I hope she did not disturb you too much, Shiplord.'

'By her presence? No,' Straha replied. 'I spoke truth when I said she spoke well. But I hope you will not be insulted when I say I would sooner have a more experienced underofficer in charge of securing a mined area.'

'As a matter of fact, I agree with you.' Yeager shook his head, a gesture of bemusement Straha understood. 'But I sometimes think a lot of young males and females would sooner belong to the Race than to their own kind.' He laughed a loud Tosevite laugh. 'Even the ones who imitate the Race most closely, though, forget how different your mating habits are from ours. Imitating those would not be easy for them.'

'As things seem to have turned out, your young females and males would say they are imitating our females and males under the influence of ginger,' Straha observed. 'That would let them do anything they like in matters pertaining to mating.'

'They already come too close to doing anything they like,' Yeager answered. 'It was not like this when I was an adolescent. And my father could have said the same thing before me, and his father before him.'

'There in a sentence you have the difference between your species and mine,' Straha replied. 'With us, everything is

344

always the same from one generation to the next.' He paused. 'Though I do wonder whether that will hold as true on Tosev 3 as it has on the other worlds we rule. Everything we do here seems built on sand.'

'If you cannot change on this world, you are going to have problems, sure enough,' Sam Yeager said.

'Changing our mating habits will not be easy,' Straha said. 'But I can also see that keeping from changing our mating habits will not be easy, either. I crave ginger right now. Surely females will crave it as much as males. If at each taste it stimulates them to give off the pheromones that indicate they are in season . . . life on this planet will grow even more complicated for us than it is already.'

'You had better get used to the idea, then,' Yeager said. 'How do you suppose it will change your society?'

'I do not know. In the absence of data, I would sooner not try to guess,' Straha replied. 'My kind is not so given to reckless speculation as is yours.' He pointed to the Tosevite. 'I will tell you this, however: life for you independent Big Uglies has also grown more complicated than it used to be.'

'How do you mean?' Yeager asked, and then checked himself. 'Oh. Of course. The attack against the colonization fleet.'

'Yes, the attack against the colonization fleet,' Straha agreed. 'You Big Uglies learn quickly, but you also forget quickly. The Race is different. If, two hundred years from now, the Race learns which not-empire is guilty of that attack, we will punish that not-empire. And we will be searching for the truth through all those two hundred years.'

'I understand,' Yeager said, but Straha wondered if he really did. He was, after all, a Tosevite himself, even if he had unusual insight into the way the Race thought.

'Is there anything else?' Straha asked him. Yeager shook his head again, this time in negation. Typical Tosevite inefficiency, Straha thought, to have one gesture do duty for two separate meanings. The exile shiplord got to his feet. 'Then I shall depart. I now have much to think about, and so, I would imagine, have you.'

'Truth,' said Yeager. He walked with Straha to the front door, and stood watching till the male had got into the Tosevite vehicle in which he was conveyed from one point to another in this city – which was not small even by the standards of the Race.

'Take me back to my home,' he told the Big Ugly who was his driver and guard.

'It shall be done, Shiplord.' The fellow started the vehicle's motor. As he did so, he remarked, 'That was an attractive female who went into Major Yeager's house.' He appended an emphatic cough.

'If you say so,' Straha answered. 'I am glad you found something to amuse you while I was talking with the major. On me, I assure you, the attractiveness, if any, of the female was wasted. I did note, however, that she made a most improbable mine-clearance underofficer.'

His driver laughed. 'I believe it!' He glanced back at Straha, a habit the shiplord wished he would forget while the motorcar was moving. 'How do you judge if a female of the Race is attractive?'

'By scent more than by sight,' Straha answered absently. He wondered if he should have told Yeager he wanted to mate with a female after all. If he was lucky, his eggs would join in the new society the Race was building here, even if he could not. He shrugged. Mating simply was not the urgent matter with him that it was for Tosevites. He missed it not at all. Getting home to his ginger struck him as much more urgent. 'Do not dawdle,' he told the driver, and the motorcar went faster.

11

Rance Auerbach's laugh, a harsh rasp, sounded almost as much like a death rattle as like honest mirth. 'You think it's true?' he asked Penny Summers. 'You reckon ginger really does make those scaly bastards come into heat like it was springtime?'

'Too many people saying it for it to be a lie,' Penny answered. 'I think it's funny as hell, too, matter of fact. Sort of pays them back for all the nasty things they've thought about us, you know what I mean?' She lit a Raleigh.

'Give me one of those, will you?' Auerbach said. After he got it going and helped take one more step in wrecking his already damaged lungs, he went on, 'Yeah, turnabout's fair play, all right.'

That made him look out the bedroom window of his Fort Worth apartment, just to see if he noticed anything out of the ordinary. He didn't. The people whose money Penny had walked off with had promised some turnabout, too. They hadn't delivered. He was beginning to hope that meant they wouldn't.

Penny said, 'Ought to get some more ginger and smuggle it down into Mexico. Lots of females there, I hear.'

'Think you can?' If Rance didn't sound dubious, it wasn't from lack of effort. 'There's some people who aren't real fond of you, remember?'

347

'It doesn't take a whole lot of work to get ginger,' Penny said with a curl to her lip. 'Hell, I can buy some down at the grocery store. But I'd want to lime-cure it, make it so the Lizards get all hot and bothered for it, before I took it down. The really tricky part is selling in someone else's territory. You're not careful about that, someday somebody'll find you floating in an irrigation ditch.'

'Why take the chance, then?' Auerbach asked. Ever since the Lizards filled him full of holes, he'd been a lot less enthusiastic about taking chances than back in his Army days.

But Penny's eyes glittered. 'To get a really big stake, why else? I've got a good start on one, after I went and stiffed the boys back in Detroit. But I want more. I want enough so I can just go somewhere, get away from everything, and not have to worry about where my next dime is coming from for the rest of my days.'

'Like where?' Rance said, dubious again. 'The Big Rock Candy Mountain?'

Penny shook her head. 'No, I really mean it. How's Tahiti sound? About as far away from Kansas as you can get, this side of Oz, anyway.'

Rance grunted thoughtfully. The outfit calling itself Free France still ran Tahiti and the neighboring islands. Neither the USA nor Japan had bothered gobbling them up, partly because that would have set the two at loggerheads, partly because the Free French made themselves very useful: they did business with everybody, people and Lizards alike, and didn't ask questions of anybody.

'How would you like that?' Penny asked. 'You could lay on the beach all day, suck up rum like it was going out of style, and smile at the native girls when they go by without their shirts on. And if you do anything more than smile at 'em, I'll kick you right in the nuts.'

'You're a sweetheart,' Auerbach said, and Penny laughed. Before he could say anything else, somebody knocked on the door. 'Who the hell's that?' he muttered, and made his slow way toward it. 'It's not like I get a whole lot of company.'

When he opened the door, he found two men standing in the hallway. One of them, a broad-shouldered, meaty fellow, put a big hand in the center of his chest and pushed, hard. With one bad leg under him, he went over backwards as if he'd been shot. As he fell, the muscular guy's skinny pal said, 'Don't fuck with us, gimpy, and you'll keep breathing. We've got some business to finish up with your lady friend. I bet you even know what we're talking about, don't you?'

Both bruisers started past him, certain Penny was there and also certain he was no danger to them. They'd likely been casing the joint, so their first certainty was accurate. Their second certainty, however, had some flaws. Rance had got used to wearing that .45 in the waistband of his trousers, and the reflexes he'd honed in the Army still worked. Even though both his leg and his shoulder bellowed at him when he hit, he had the heavy pistol in his hand less than a heartbeat later.

He fired without a word of warning. The .45 bucked in his grip. A hole appeared in the back of the heavy man's jacket. Gore and guts blew out a much bigger hole in the front of his belly – the sort of hole, Auerbach knew from experience, you could throw a dog through.

The bruiser let out a hoarse scream and crumpled. His friend whirled, hand darting for a trouser pocket. He had commend-ably quick reflexes, but not quick enough to let him outdraw a gun already aimed at him. Auerbach's first bullet caught him in the chest. He looked very surprised as he stood there swaying. Auerbach shot him again, this time in the face, and the back of his head exploded. He fell on top of the other thug, who was still writhing and shrieking. Auerbach smelled blood and shit and smokeless powder.

Penny came around the corner from the bedroom, pistol in her hand. She didn't scream or puke or faint. She aimed the pistol at the head of the heavyset ruffian, the one Auerbach had shot from behind, plainly intending to finish him off.

'Don't,' Rance told her. 'Put your piece away. Go back into the bedroom and call the cops. If half a dozen people haven't done it already, I'm a Chinaman. These two bastards broke in here intending to rob us or whatever the hell, and I plugged 'em. We don't have to say a word about ginger.'

'Okay, Rance.' She nodded. The broad-shouldered goon had stopped moaning, anyhow; with a wound like that, he wouldn't last long. 'Keep an eye on 'em anyhow, just in case.'

'I will.' With his usual slow, painful movements, Auerbach levered himself up into a chair. He took a look at the carnage, then shook his head. 'What do you want to bet the goddamn landlord tries to stick me with the bill for cleaning this up?'

Penny didn't answer; she'd already gone back into the bedroom to use the telephone. One of Rance's neighbors stuck her head into his apartment through the open doorway. She saw him before noticing anything else, and started to talk: 'Howdy, Rance. Lucille said there was gunshots somewheres, but I told her it wasn't nothin' but firecra—' That was when she noticed the two blood-drenched corpses at the back of the living room. She turned white. 'Oh, sweet, suffering Jesus!' she blurted, and got the hell out of there.

Auerbach laughed, but he sounded shaky even to himself. He felt shaky, too, as he had after combat against the Lizards. *Reaction setting in,* he thought. He *was* shaky; the .45 trembled in his hand. Deciding neither of the thugs was going to give him any more trouble, he put the safety back on.

From the bedroom, Penny called, 'Cops are on the way. You were right— I wasn't the first one who got through to them.' A minute or so later, Rance heard sirens coming closer. The police cars stopped in front of the apartment building.

Four cops in blue uniforms came running up the stairs, all of them carrying pistols. The first policeman into the apartment looked, whistled, and said over his shoulder, 'We ain't gonna need the ambulance, Eddie, just the coroner's meat wagon.' He turned to Auerbach. 'All right, buddy, what the hell happened here?'

Rance told him what had happened, though he made it sound as if he thought the dead men in his living room were a

350

couple of ordinary robbers, not hired muscle for the ginger smugglers. Another policeman – Eddie? – stepped around the bodies and went to talk with Penny in the bedroom. After a while, he and the cop who'd been talking with Auerbach (his name was Charlie McMillan) put their heads together.

McMillan said, 'You and your lady friend tell the same story. I don't reckon we've got any reason to charge you with anything, not when those boys came busting into your place.'

One of the other Fort Worth policemen had stooped beside the bodies. He said, 'They're both packing, Charlie.'

'Okay.' McMillan eyed Rance in a speculative way. 'Mighty fine shooting for somebody who'd just got knocked on his ass. Where'd you learn to handle a weapon like that?'

'West Point,' Auerbach answered, which made the policeman's eyes widen. 'I was in the Army till the Lizards shot me up a few months before the fighting stopped. I can't get around very fast any more – hell, I can't hardly get around at all any more – but I still know what to do with a .45 in my hand.'

'He sure as hell does,' the cop by the body said. 'These boys are history. I don't make either one of them. You recognize 'em, Charlie?'

McMillan sauntered over and looked at the corpses. As he lit a cigarette, he shook his head. 'Sure don't. They've got to be from out of town. I'd know any strongarm boys of our own who were trying to pull jobs like this.' He turned back toward Auerbach. 'They picked the wrong guy to start on, that's for sure.'

'That's a fact,' the other cop agreed. 'You're not going to charge these folks?'

'Charge 'em? Hell, no.' McMillan shook his head almost hard enough to make his hat fall off.' 'Ought to be a bounty on sons of bitches like these. All I'm going to do is take Mr. Auerbach's formal statement, and his lady friend's, and then wait for the coroner to come take his pictures and haul the bodies away.'

'Okay. Sounds good to me,' the cop by the corpses said. It sounded good to Auerbach, too. *Off the hook,* he thought.

McMillan took out a notebook and a pen. Before he started taking the statement, he remarked, 'Maybe their prints'll tell us who they are. Little Rock may know, even if we don't.' He stubbed out his cigarette, then said, 'All right, Mr. Auerbach, tell it to me again, only slow and easy this time, so I can get it down on paper.'

Auerbach was less than halfway through his statement when a rangy fellow the policemen all called Doc ambled into his apartment. He had a physician's black bag in one hand and a camera with a flash in the other. After looking at the bodies, he sadly shook his head and said, 'That rug's never gonna be the same.'

As if his words were some kind of signal, Rance's landlord came in on his heels. He took one look and said, 'You get the cleaning bill, Auerbach.'

'I knew you'd tell me that, Jasper,' Auerbach answered. 'Have a heart. If they'd shot me, you'd have to pay it yourself.'

'They damn well didn't, so you can damn well fork over,' the landlord said. The cops rolled their eyes. Auerbach let out a racking sigh. This was a fight he knew he was going to lose.

A couple of husky coroner's assistants carried the bodies downstairs one at a time on stretchers. The coroner left with them. Jasper was already gone; he'd said what he came to say. Charlie McMillan finished getting statements. Then he and his pals took off, too, leaving Auerbach alone in the apartment with the blood-soaked carpeting.

After putting a couple of ice cubes in a glass, Rance poured whiskey over them. While Penny was building her own drink, he took a long pull at his and said, 'You know what? Tahiti sounds pretty goddamn good.'

'Amen,' Penny said, and finished her whiskey at a gulp.

Kassquit wished Ttomalss would return from the surface of Tosev 3. He had never been gone for so long before. None of the other males on the orbiting starship truly treated her like a member of the Race. Up till now, Ttomalss had served as a buffer between her and them. Now, whenever she let herself out of her compartment, she had to deal with them herself. As a result, she left the compartment as seldom as she could.

Even worse than the long-familiar researchers were the males and females from the colonization fleet. As far as they were concerned, she was nothing but a Big Ugly – a barbarian at best, a talking animal at worst. She'd pined for Home; everything she'd read and viewed made her pine for Home. But the males and females new-come from the world at the center of the Empire were far more callous toward her than those more familiar with Tosev 3 and its natives. That hurt.

It hurt so much, she would have spent all her time in her compartment if she could. Unfortunately for her, the Race had long ago determined it was more efficient to gather males and females in one place to eat than to distribute food to each compartment in which someone dwelt or worked.

She'd taken to eating her meals at odd times, times shifted away from those during which males and females normally crowded the galley. That minimized friction with those who did not care for her. Try as she would, though, she could not eliminate it altogether.

One day, she was heading back from the galley when she almost collided with a male named Tessrek, who skittered around a corner straight into her path. She barely managed to stop in time. Had she failed, the collision would of course have been her fault. 'I beg your pardon, superior sir,' she said from the posture of respect.

'Watch where you plant your large, homely, flat feet,' Tessrek snapped. He had never cared for her. Ttomalss had told her Tessrek hadn't cared for the previous Tosevite infant he'd tried to rear, either.

'It shall be done, superior sir,' Kassquit replied now. All she wanted to do was end the conversation and return to the lonely peace of her compartment.

But Tessrek was in no mood to let her off so easily. ' "It shall be done, superior sir," ' he echoed, imitating her intonation as best he could with his different mouthparts. 'Down on Tosev 3, they have animals that can be trained to talk. How do I know you are not just another such animal?'

'By whether what I say makes sense,' Kassquit answered, refusing to let Tessrek see he had made her angry. 'I can imagine no other way to do it, superior sir.' Sometimes a soft reply made him give up his attempts to disconcert or simply to hurt her.

It didn't work this time. 'You are only a Big Ugly,' Tessrek said. 'No one cares about your imaginings. No one cares about your kind's imaginings.'

A female from one of the ships of the colonization fleet walked past as Kassquit was doing her best to come up with another polite answer instead of telling Tessrek to flush himself down the waste-disposal opening in his compartment. 'My imaginings, such as they are, are not typical of those of Big Uglies, superior sir,' she said. 'They are much closer to those of the Race, because . . .'

Her voice trailed away as she realized, a little slower than she should have, that Tessrek was no longer paying her any attention. Both his eye turrets were fixed on the female who had just gone by. The scales on top of his head rose into a crest, something Kassquit had never seen before on any male. He stood up straight – unnaturally straight for a male of the Race, almost as straight as Kassquit herself. With a peculiar wordless hiss, he hurried after the female.

Her eye turrets swiveled so she could look back at him. She hissed, too, a lower, softer sound than his, and bent into a posture similar but not identical to the posture of respect, a posture that left her head low and her rump high. Tessrek moved into place behind her. Kassquit got a brief glimpse of an organ that, like the male's erectile scales, she had never seen before. It reminded her a little of the sort of organ male Tosevites possessed. And Tessrek used it rather as she had seen male Tosevites use theirs in the recordings that fascinated and disgusted her at the same time.

No sooner had Tessrek made yet another sound that was not a word than another male came hurrying along the corridor. He also had eyes only for the female. With every step he took, he strode more nearly upright. Like Tessrek, he had a row of scales standing upright on his head.

'Back,' Tessrek snarled at him, and stressed the word with an emphatic cough. But the other male paid him no attention. Tessrek let out a shriek and sprang at him before he could reach the female, who still stood waiting with her head near the floor.

They thrashed and twisted, biting and clawing at each other. Kassquit had to spring back to keep from being dragged into the fight. 'Help!' she cried. 'These two males have gone mad!'

Her shout brought a couple more males out to see what was going on. But both of them immediately displayed the same excitement as Tessrek and his opponent had shown. One, in fact, promptly joined in the brawl. The other nimbly dodged around it and began to couple with the compliant female.

Kassquit stared in astonished horror. She had never dreamt males of the Race could behave thus. Ttomalss had never talked much about what males and females were like during the breeding season. Kassquit had got the idea even thinking about it made him – and all the other males she'd known – nervous. Now, all at once, she understood why.

Males kept running along the corridor. They either piled into the fight or tried to mate with the female. A new fight soon hatched because of that. Kassquit backed away. None of the males showed the slightest interest in her. Unlike the females of their own kind, she did not smell exciting to them. She couldn't imagine what she would have done if she had.

After backing along the corridor to another one that intersected it, she made her way back to her own compartment by a roundabout route. Once there, she made sure the door would not open without her authorization. Then she sat down –

rather uncomfortably, in a chair too small and made for a backside with a tailstump – and put her face in her hands. That was not a gesture the Race used, but it seemed appropriate. Her mind whirled. For as long as she could remember, Ttomalss and other males had mocked the Tosevites' mating habits. Had the Big Uglies been able to see what she had just witnessed, Kassquit was sure they would have been able to do some mocking of their own.

She wondered why the female had gone into heat, and why no others seemed to have done so with her. As Kassquit had understood things, all females back on Home had their season at about the same time and, once it was done, it was done for another year. That didn't seem to be what had happened here.

She heard shouts in the corridor outside her compartment. Someone slammed into the door, hard. That wasn't a knock; it was a male – she assumed it was a male – getting hurled into the metal panel. To her vast relief, the door held. The shouts went down the corridor.

'By the Emperor!' Kassquit burst out. 'Are they all addled?' As far as she could tell, they were. She turned on the computer to find out what the Race made of the madness sweeping through it.

But the continuous news broadcast she listened to for a while said nothing about females suddenly entering their season or about males clawing and biting one another in their frenzied eagerness to couple. Instead, the newscaster spent most of his time condemning the ginger habit and everything associated with it. 'Were it not for ginger,' he declared, 'the Race would be far more tranquil and secure than it is today.'

Kassquit laughed out loud, as a Tosevite would have. That embarrassed her, but not so much as it might have done; at the moment, she was embarrassed for the Race. 'Only proves how much you know,' she said, and used an emphatic cough.

She went through the other media channels, trying to find one that would admit the Race was faced with females coming into season at what seemed to be an unexpected time. She could not.

Everywhere she checked, though, commentators were inveighing against the insidious Tosevite herb called ginger.

She was about ready to pitch something through the screen when the computer announced she had an incoming telephone call from Ttomalss. 'Will you accept?' the electronic voice inquired.

'Yes,' Kassquit said, and had to remind herself not to add on another emphatic cough, which would have confused the machinery. Ttomalss' image appeared on the screen in front of her. 'Superior sir, I am so glad to see you!' she burst out, and did append that second emphatic cough after all.

'I am always glad to see you, Kassquit,' Ttomalss said, solemn as usual. *He is steady,* Kassquit thought. *He is reliable.* He went on, 'And why are you so particularly glad to see me now?'

'Because madness is going through the ship right now,' she answered, and explained what sort of madness she meant.

'Oh,' Ttomalss said when she'd finished. After that, he said nothing for a little while. *He is embarrassed by my speaking frankly,* Kassquit thought. But Ttomalss was embarrassed for other reasons than that, as he showed when he spoke again: 'I must tell you, this problem of females' apparently ultimately coming into season has also occurred here in Nuremberg and elsewhere on the surface of Tosev 3. I myself have succumbed to the mating urge.'

'You have?' Logically, Kassquit knew she had no right, no reason, to feel betrayed. She did nonetheless. 'Superior sir, how could you?'

'No. The question is, how could I not? The answer is, there was no way I could not, not after the female's pheromones reached my scent receptors,' Ttomalss replied. 'I must also tell you that it appears as if ingesting ginger triggers females to release the pheromones indicating they are in season. This is not yet confirmed, but appears likely.'

'I see,' Kassquit said, and she did. When the commentators condemned ginger, they'd known what they were doing after all. She found the next question right away: 'How much confusion will that cause in the Race?'

'I do not know,' Ttomalss answered. 'I do not know if anyone knows. I do not even know if proper projections can be drawn, or whether data on ginger use are too inaccurate to permit such extrapolation. In my own instance, I believe it was the first time Senior Researcher Felless had ever tasted—'

'Felless?' Kassquit broke in, her narrow eyes wide with horror. 'You mated with *Felless*?' Ttomalss' mating with any other female of the Race she could have tolerated. That one? The one who treated her like a specimen and, by her example, made Ttomalss go halfway toward doing the same? 'Oh, I hate you!' Kassquit cried, and ended the connection. Water poured from her eyes and ran altogether unheeded down her face.

Fotsev was jumpy as he patrolled the narrow, stinking streets of Basra. Every other male in his group was jumpy, too. He could see that by the way his comrades moved. And it was a different sort of jumpiness from the one they'd had before the ships of the colonization fleet started coming. That had been a simple, rational concern about fanatical Tosevites starting to screech *'Allahu akbar!'* and opening up on them with automatic weapons.

Yes, this was different. It was anything but rational, as Fotsev – rationally – knew. He didn't want to put what it was into words. If he did, he knew he would only think about it more.

His friend Gorppet wasn't so shy. He let his tongue loll out into the open, which made the scent receptors on it more sensitive. 'Put me in cold sleep and ship me Home if I do not smell a ripe female around here somewhere,' he said.

All the males in the patrol sighed at the same time. All of them, for a couple of paces, walked more nearly erect, as if beginning to assume their half of the mating posture. 'Whoever she is, wherever she is, she is nowhere near,' Fotsev said, as if reminding himself, calming himself.

'Truth,' Gorppet said, 'but I still want her.'

'I wish you had not said that,' Fotsev told him. 'Now I am going to be thinking about her instead of about what I am supposed to be doing on patrol, and that is liable to get me killed.'

A stocky veteran named Shaspwikk said, 'Does not seem right, smelling a female but not being able to get at one.'

'Truth.' The whole patrol spoke as one male. Fotsev added, 'Back on Home, the streets are crazy during the season. So are the corridors of any good-sized building, come to that. And the smell of females gets so thick, you can poke an eating tong into it. And then it is over, and everything gets back to normal again.'

'Shaspwikk said it,' Gorppet agreed. 'The way it is on Home, that is the way it ought to be. You smell a female, you go and mate, and that is that. What will it be like if we keep smelling females all the time but there are none in heat close by? We will get as addled as the Tosevites are.'

'It is a wonder we can smell anything here except the stinks the Big Uglies make,' Shaspwikk said.

'Smelling out females – that is different somehow,' Fotsev said. 'I would know those pheromones through all the stinks the Big Uglies make all over Tosev 3.'

'Truth,' Gorppet said. 'Of course, if we could not smell those pheromones no matter what, we would get no eggs, and after a while there would be no more Race.'

'But when I do smell them, I want to mate, by the Emperor,' Shaspwikk said.

'Good thing there is no female close by right now,' Fotsev said. 'We would fight each other to get at her, and nobody would care what the Big Uglies are doing.'

Gorppet turned one eye turret toward him. 'I would not mind fighting now, even if I cannot get my cloaca next to a female's. Smelling the pheromones is plenty to put me on the edge of brawling.' A couple of other males made the hand gesture of agreement.

'I feel the same way,' Fotsev said, 'but may the spirits of Emperors past turn their backs on me if I let the Tosevites know. They would laugh themselves silly, the miserable creatures, and then start plotting even more mischief than they get into already.'

He swung his own eye turrets from one male in the small group to another, defying his comrades to argue with him. None of them did. None of them would meet his glance, either. They might not be happy about agreeing with him, but they couldn't argue.

'And another thing,' he said. 'You want to be careful about sticking your own tongues too far into the ginger jar these days. Smelling females in heat makes us twitchy enough all by itself. Pile the herb on top of that and you have trouble waiting to happen.'

'Pile the herb on top of anything that puts too much strain on a male and you have trouble waiting to happen,' Gorppet said. His eye turrets turned every which way, to make sure no one outside the patrol, whether Big Ugly or male of the Race, could overhear. In a low voice, he went on, 'That is what happened when things went bad up in the SSSR, or so they say.'

Fotsev wished he wouldn't have mentioned mutiny, even obliquely. 'Put ginger and females' pheromones together and the trouble they had up in the SSSR is liable to look like hatchlings' games,' he said.

Again, no one disagreed with him. The problem was, whenever trouble came, he wanted to taste ginger so he wouldn't have to think about it any more. But that kind of not thinking was what could start troubles with females involved. He saw as much, and saw it clearly. He didn't see what to do about it.

And then, abruptly, he stopped worrying about it. Along with the usual stenches of Basra, the breeze wafted to his scent receptors the tantalizing odor of a female in season. This was no distant, diffuse scent. It came from somewhere close by –

only a few alleys over, if he was any judge. He let out a soft hiss. His head came up. So did the erectile scales on top of it. His mouth opened, not in a laugh but to let more air stream past his tongue and the scent receptors on it.

He wasn't the only male to catch the scent, either. His comrades' crests were rising, too. All of them tasted the breeze, ready to follow where it led them. Now they looked warily at one another, each fearing a sudden attack to keep him from getting what he craved.

Gorppet pointed. 'That way,' he said, his voice rough.

'We all go together,' Fotsev said. 'And we all be careful of what we do. Fighting with teeth and claws is one thing. Fighting with rifles and grenades, though, is a different business.'

Back on Home, they wouldn't have had to worry about it. Back on Home, weapons were few and far between. No one needed them there, and no one except police and a few criminals could get hold of anything more lethal than knives. Fotsev wished Tosev 3 were like that. But it wasn't. A male without weapons here was by the nature of things a male in danger. With females in heat around, however, a male with weapons was also likely to be a male in danger . . . from his own kind, similarly armed.

Its members still eyeing one another, the patrol picked its way through the maze of narrow, crowded lanes toward the females. Before long, they did not need their scent receptors alone to guide them. Shouts from a crowd of Big Uglies ahead told them they had to be getting close. 'You speak some of this language,' Fotsev said to Gorppet. 'What are they yelling?'

'For someone to pour water over them,' Gorppet answered. 'That's what they do when their domestic animals – you know, the yapping ones – couple in the street. So somebody's mating up there.'

'Truth.' The rage and jealousy surging through Fotsev shocked him. He wanted that female, wherever she was, and he wanted her this instant. Of itself, his posture grew more upright. He noticed his fellow males were not leaning so far forward as they usually did.

He and the rest of the patrol came round the last corner just as the male finished with the female. The fellow, whose body paint proclaimed him an accountant, was from the colonization fleet. Instead of challenging the newcomers, he turned and skittered off, forcing his way through the crowd of laughing, jeering Tosevites. He must have fully sated himself, then.

The female remained in the mating posture. Her head near the ground, she spoke in a small, bewildered voice: 'But I was not coming into heat. By the Emperor, I was not.' She cast down her eyes, not that they could look much farther down than they were already.

'You are in heat now,' Fotsev said. 'We can smell it.' The female did not disagree. She remained in place, waiting for him and his comrades. The odor coming from her inflamed him. He clung to coherent thought as best he could. 'We shall take turns,' he declared. 'And those who are not mating shall stay alert, to make sure these Tosevites here cause no trouble.'

He knew about the new regulations about coupling where Big Uglies could watch, but knowing and remembering were two different things. One after another, he and the other males of the patrol coupled with the female, who remained compliant but perplexed. But, by the time each of them had mated once, the female said, 'Enough,' and straightened up. With her pheromones still stimulating him, Fotsev would have liked to couple again. She showed no interest in further mating, though. 'I feel so strange,' she muttered. 'Just a little while ago, I was happy as I could be, as happy as I have ever been. Now . . . Now I just want to sink into the ground.'

'Sounds like she has been tasting ginger,' Shaspwikk observed.

'It does,' Fotsev agreed. 'That would account for her coming into heat all at once, too.'

'I have not tasted ginger, and you need not talk about me as if I were not here,' the female said sharply. 'That other male,

362

wherever he went, the accountant, tried raising his scales at me a while ago. He said he smelled pheromones. Well, he did not smell mine. I got something to drink from one of these ridiculous creatures here. He asked for a sip. I gave him the cup. When he gave it back to me and I drank, my season came upon me without warning. But you know about that.'

'Yes, we know about that.' Now that he had mated once, Fotsev's mind was working again, after a fashion. 'Where is this cup?'

'Right there.' The female pointed.

Fotsev picked it up from the ground. He inhaled sharply, drawing air over his scent receptors. 'I thought so,' he said. 'The drink in here has ginger in it.'

Thinking along with him, Gorppet exclaimed, 'That other male must have slipped it in there. He wanted to mate because he could smell pheromones off in the distance, the same as we did, but this female was not in season, so he got her heated whether she wanted to be or not. What a sneaky fellow!' His emphatic cough said he half admired the vanished accountant.

'He did that to me? He deliberately did that to me?' The female did not sound admiring. She sounded furious, outraged. 'He used this herb to make me do something I had no intention of doing, something I could not have done had he not given me the herb to bring me into my season. I do not even know his name, but curse him and all his ancestors from the first egg they hatched out of.'

'Back on Home, this could not have happened,' Fotsev said slowly. 'Back on Home, females all come into their season at about the same time, and there are plenty to go around for the males. It is not like that here on Tosev 3.'

'I do not like the way it is here on Tosev 3,' the female said with an emphatic cough of her own. 'He used me without my consent. He coupled with me against what would have been my will. That is not right.'

'I agree – that is not right,' Fotsev said. 'I think that male committed a crime. I think he committed a new crime, a crime

363

that would have been impossible back on Home. This is a crime that could only happen on Tosev 3.'

'What do we do about it?' Gorppet asked. 'If female pheromones keep lingering in the air, more males will think to use ginger to get what they want from females who would not otherwise be ready to give it to them.'

'Truth.' Fotsev took his radio off his belt. 'For now, we can only report it – report it and hope our superiors have better ideas than we do.' Even as he began to speak, he could see that neither Gorppet nor the female who'd been fed ginger thought the authorities would. He didn't think so, either, but did his best not to show it.

Shpaaka looked out at his human students at the Russie Medical College. Along with the rest of the class, Reuven Russie stared at the male Lizard. He poised his pen to record whatever wisdom Shpaaka saw fit to dispense this morning.

Instead of beginning his lecture in the usual way, though, Shpaaka said, 'I think I must call on you Tosevites for assistance today.'

A low buzz of surprise went through the chamber. Shpaaka did nothing to check it. That was surprising, too. The male usually took sardonic pleasure in inveighing against Tosevite rudeness and lack of self-control when what he reckoned to be those things manifested themselves in his lecture hall. Reuven raised a hand and waited to be recognized. Jane Archibald came straight out and asked a question: 'What is the difficulty, superior sir?'

Shpaaka did not discipline her. He did not even reprove her for the breach of decorum. 'The difficulty, I daresay, is one with which you are already familiar,' he replied. 'You are intelligent; you have good sources of information. Surely it will not come as any great surprise when I say that the Tosevite herb known as ginger has a pharmacological effect on females of the Race both unexpected and disconcerting.'

It was no surprise to Reuven, not when Atvar had summoned his father to Cairo to confer with him about the problem. Looking around the hall, he saw that his classmates didn't look astonished, either. Stories of Lizards seen coupling in the streets of Jerusalem had been making the rounds at the medical college for the past few days. Some students had doubted them. Reuven knew better.

Now Jane showed proper etiquette: 'Superior sir, permission to ask another question?'

'Granted,' Shpaaka said. 'The search for understanding proceeds through questions. It can proceed no other way.'

'How do you believe we Tosevites can help you, superior sir?' Jane asked. Reuven knew what she thought of the Race, and of what the Race had done to Australia. None of that showed in her speech as she went on, 'We know little or nothing about the reproductive behavior of the Race. We have had no chance to learn about it until now, when females have come to Tosev 3. In what way, then, can we possibly assist you?'

'This is a good question, a cogent question,' Shpaaka said. 'But I must tell you, the reproductive behavior the Race has begun exhibiting here on Tosev 3 is not similar to that which we display on Home.' He sighed, an amazingly humanlike sound. 'Very little the Race does on Tosev 3 appears to be similar to what we do back on Home.' An emphatic cough stressed that.

After a moment during which he seemed to gather himself, he went on, 'Back on Home, virtually all females come into their season within a short time. Virtually all males are stimulated by the pheromones they release and have the opportunity to mate with at least one of them. That is normality.'

It was normality for most life on Earth, too. Reuven understood that perfectly well. He also understood it was not normality for humans. Glancing over at Jane Archibald, he was glad things worked the way they did, even if he hadn't had the chance to put all the theory into practice.

Maybe Jane felt his eye on her. She looked his way and impudently stuck out her tongue. He laughed and looked toward Shpaaka again.

The Lizard physician had needed another pause to marshal his thoughts. After that second – embarrassed? – hesitation, he said, 'Here on Tosev 3, it appears that ginger causes females almost immediately to enter their season, and to emit the pheromones showing males they have done so. But only a relatively small number of females taste ginger. More males are apt to scent the pheromones than have an in-season female readily accessible to them. This causes tension and frustration of a sort we are not used to.

'Furthermore, females – and males – do not taste ginger only during one short season of the year, but continuously. This means pheromones showing females to be in season are, or will be, released into the air throughout the year. Sexual tension of the sort I previously mentioned will likewise be continuous.

'Now, this runs contrary to all our long-established instinctual patterns. It is, however, the paradigm of normality for you Big Uglies. Your insights on how we are to cope with it will be greatly appreciated.'

Atvar had made the identical appeal to Reuven's father. Reuven wondered if, all over the world, Lizards were asking such questions of humans they thought they could trust. He pitied them and laughed at them at the same time. They'd been smugly superior for a long time. Now, abruptly, things weren't so simple for them.

With sudden indignation, Shpaaka added, 'We have even had a couple of incidents where a male, smelling a distant female's pheromones, has surreptitiously given an adjacent female ginger so he could mate with her. This is a depth of iniquity to which I doubt even you Tosevites have ever plunged.'

The lecture hall erupted in loud Tosevite laughter. Reuven joined in. He couldn't help himself. Even after twenty years on Earth, after twenty years of intensive research on human beings, the Lizards remained painfully naive. They were likely to be right, too: they would need human help in dealing with problems of sexuality. Reuven doubted they could do it on their own.

Shpaaka looked out at his students. 'Perhaps I was mistaken,' he said, his voice dry. 'Do you find it amusing that your kind may be more iniquitous than I had previously imagined?'

'Yes, superior sir,' they chorused, which touched off another round of raucous laughter.

Shpaaka laughed, too, in the silent manner of his kind. 'Very well, perhaps it is amusing,' he said. 'But tell me, how do we prevent more such unfortunate incidents in the future?'

That was a serious question, seriously meant. After a little thought, Reuven raised his hand. When Shpaaka recognized him, he said, 'Superior sir, I do not know if you will be able to prevent them altogether. We cannot; we have never been able to. We do work to keep them to a minimum.'

'You Tosevites are, in many circumstances, more readily satisfied than we would be,' Shpaaka returned. Reuven glowered; the Lizard had asked for advice, but then what had he done with it? Mocked it, nothing else. Shpaaka seemed to realize his discontent, saying, 'In matters pertaining to desire, perfect success may be more difficult to obtain than elsewhere.'

'Permission to speak, superior sir?' an Argentine student named Pedro Magallanes asked. When he got it, he said, 'Do the other races in your Empire ever have, ah, problems of this sort?'

'Only in rare instances, due to one hormonal imbalance or another,' Shpaaka replied. 'The same holds true for the Race. Until becoming acquainted with you Tosevites, we thought it must necessarily hold true for any intelligent species. Now we discover it does not even necessarily hold true for ourselves. I would appreciate the irony more were it less painful.'

That he noticed it at all spoke well for him. The human rulers of the Greater German *Reich* and the Soviet Union could not recognize irony if it cocked its leg and pissed on their ankles; of that Reuven was certain.

'You Tosevites have had long practice controlling continuous reproductive urges,' Shpaaka went on. 'Since we are newcomers to the business, we shall probably end up borrowing from you: yes, I know, another irony.'

Shpaaka's students whispered and murmured to one another. The Lizard affected not to notice, an indulgence he seldom granted them. Bahadur Singh, a turbaned Sikh, spoke to Reuven in English: 'This will drive the Lizards to distraction – assuredly, to distraction – for some time to come.' His eyes glowed. 'Maybe my country can use the distraction to make itself free.'

'It could be so.' Reuven didn't really think it likely. The Lizards, distracted or not, would do whatever they had to do to hold on to India. But Bahadur Singh had hope. Reuven had no hope that Palestine could ever shake off the Lizards' yoke. Even if it could, it would be torn between Arabs and Jews. The aliens' rule was about as good as anyone here could hope for, having at least the advantage of disinterest.

Most of the time, Reuven took that for granted. Now, when he looked at it, he found it depressing. Couldn't people get along well enough so they didn't need to have disinterested aliens keeping them from quarreling with one another?

His quiet laugh was rueful. His father would have known better even than to bother shaping the question in his own mind. If Poland hadn't taught that the only possible answer was, *Of course not, you fool,* what would? The squabbles in Palestine even under Lizard rule should have driven the point home with a sledgehammer.

Before he let it depress him too much, a student from the Soviet Union named Anna Suslova asked, 'Permission to speak, superior sir?' Reuven sometimes wondered how she'd got into the medical college, and whether someone capable had taken the entrance exams for her. She often seemed out of her depth here. The question she put to Shpaaka showed how her mind worked: 'Superior sir, why not punish ginger users so severely, fear of punishment keeps females from using the drug?'

'We have been trying to do this with our males since we came to Tosev 3,' Shpaaka replied. 'We have not succeeded. By all indications, ginger causes pleasure even more acute in females. How likely is it that we will eliminate its use among them through intimidation?'

Maybe he'd thought that sardonic rejoinder would quash Anna Suslova. If so, he had misjudged her. With a toss of her head, she replied, 'It could be that you have not yet made the punishment severe enough to intimidate properly.'

'Yes, it could be,' Shpaaka admitted. 'But it could also be that we are not so fond of spilling one another's blood as Tosevites often seem to be.'

Anna Suslova tossed her head again. 'In an emergency, superior sir, one does what is immediately necessary and worries about its consequences later. Had the Soviet Union not followed this principle, is it not likely my not-empire would be under the rule of the Race today?'

'Yes, I suppose that is likely,' Shpaaka said. 'My opinion is, many of the Tosevites of your not-empire would be happier were that so.'

Where he hadn't before, he got through to the Russian girl with that. She glared at him, furious and not even trying to hide it. For a Lizard, he was good at recognizing human facial expressions, but he didn't call her on this one. Reuven Russie scratched his head. If he'd justified the Race's rule in Palestine on the grounds of utility for the human population, how could he avoid extending the principle over the whole planet?

He contributed little to the discussion for the rest of the period.

Liu Han looked out from the window of her suite in the Biltmore Hotel at the wide street and the automobiles that packed it to the point where hardly any of them could move.

With no small reluctance, she turned to her daughter and said, 'I am beginning to believe that the Americans' constant boasting about their prosperity is not boasting, but is a simple statement of fact.'

'They eat well,' Liu Mei said. Then she corrected herself: 'They have plenty to eat, and they eat whenever they like. I see that, even if I do not care for much of their food. They have many more motorcars and televisors and radios than we do. They have more *room* than we do. This is a large city, not so large as Peking but still large, but it does not feel crowded. All these things do make for prosperity, yes. Who could disagree?'

'I myself disagreed,' Liu Han said. 'This hotel is a hotel for rich people. Anyone can see that. The Americans do not bother pretending otherwise. Any country will treat rich people, important people, well, no matter how it treats its workers and peasants. You cannot judge how prosperous the United States is by the way the American ruling classes treat us.'

'I understand that, Mother.' Liu Mei's voice showed amusement, even if her face did not. 'It is good, though, that the Americans treat us as important people. They cannot be treating us as rich people, for we are not.'

'No, we are not rich people,' Liu Han agreed. 'We should have trouble paying for a day's stay in this hotel, let alone a stay of weeks like the one they are giving us. But we have been enough other places and seen enough other things for me to be sure they are not simply showing us their best, as we have sometimes done for foreign visitors over the years.'

She thought of televisors and radios and motorcars, as Liu Mei had. She thought of machines to wash dishes, which she'd seen in some of the homes she'd visited, and machines to wash clothes, which she'd seen in almost all of the homes. Those machines were like proletarians who could not be oppressed and so would never need to rise up in revolution against their capitalist overlords.

And she thought of something simpler, something far more fundamental. In every house she visited, she made sure she asked to use the toilet. And every house boasted one, some-times more than one, not just a squatting-style toilet like those some rich men in China had, but a veritable porcelain throne. And every house boasted not just the cold running water that made the toilet flush but also hot, hers to command at the turn of a tap. If that was not prosperity, what was?

Liu Mei said, 'And all the books they have! So many more people have libraries of their own here than back home. That major's house, for instance, had more bookshelves than I was able to count.'

'Yes, I remember,' Liu Han said, more than a little dis-contentedly. When she and Liu Mei went to visit Major Yeager, she'd thought the books that packed his house another attempt at deception – *a Potemkin village,* the Russians called it: something meant to be seen but not used. But when she plucked a book off a shelf at random, Yeager had talked animatedly about it in both English and the language of the Race. Liu Han sighed. 'His wife is a scholar. Maybe that helps account for it.'

'He knew my father,' Liu Mei said in tones of wonder. 'I never thought I would meet anyone who knew my father. I have cousins in this country. I never thought I would have cousins anywhere.'

Absurdly, Liu Han felt a stab of jealousy. So far as she could tell, she had no relatives except Liu Mei alive anywhere in China. Between them, the little scaly devils and the Japanese had ground her ancestral village to powder; of her family, only she had got out from between the millstones.

'Major Yeager knew your father better than I ever did,' Liu Han said slowly. a strange thing to say, she knew, when Bobby Fiore had sown the seed that grew into Liu Mei deep inside her womb. Strange – but true. 'He knew him longer than I did, and they spoke the same language, so they could understand each other. Your father and I spoke in broken bits of Chinese and the little scaly devils' language and English. He never learned to speak Chinese very well.'

And with our bodies, she thought, though she did not say that aloud. *Our bodies understood, even when we did not.* That, by the spirit of the compassionate Buddha, was knowledge of Bobby Fiore Major Yeager did not have.

Liu Mei said, 'Is it tonight we are going back to Major Yeager's house?'

'Yes, tonight,' Liu Han answered. 'Why do you ask?'

'Because it is good to go to a place where people understand the little devils' language,' her daughter answered. 'It is not as good as if Major Yeager and his wife and his son spoke Chinese, but we both know more of the little devils' language than we do English, and all three of them are fluent in it.'

'I will not tell you are wrong,' Liu Han said. Even so, she glanced over toward Liu Mei. 'And you will have a chance to talk with that son – Jonathan, his name is. Do not be too free with him. The Americans have less restraint in their dealings between young people than we do.'

'Do you know what he reminded me of?' Liu Mei said. 'The young people in Peking who imitate the scaly devils, that's what. Except he knows more about them than the young people in Peking do.'

'There was that one we saw,' Liu Han began. But then she shrugged. 'You are probably right. You have to remember, though, that his father and mother deal with the scaly devils every day. If he has learned much of them, he has learned it because of what his parents do.' Liu Mei nodded, accepting that. Liu Han let out a silent sigh of relief. She did not want her daughter to have any excuse for developing an infatuation for any American youth.

By the time evening came, she was ready and more than ready to go down to Major Yeager's home, if only to relax. She had spent the day conferring with several American members of Congress. Frankie Wong helped by interpreting, but she tried to speak as much English as she could, because she did not fully trust him to translate accurately. That made it a grueling session, one in which she felt as if her brains were

372

being rolled out onto something flat and hard like dough being made into noodles.

And the congressmen were less sympathetic than she'd hoped they would be. 'Let me say I do not see why we should be helping international Communism,' declared one, a man with a long nose and jowls that showed even more dark stubble than Bobby Fiore had had.

Frankie Wong gave her an expectant look, but she answered that one herself, in English: 'You help us, you help people go free from Lizards.' The long-nosed American abruptly stopped asking questions.

Another congressman said, 'Why shouldn't we just send you lots of ginger, to keep the Lizards too drugged up and too horny' – Wong did have to translate that for her – 'to be able to fight back?'

'Power come from barrel of a gun. War and politics never separate,' Liu Han replied. 'So say Mao. He say true, I think.'

She got through the hearing. She thought she held her own. But letting an American drive her and Liu Mei down the wide but still crowded highways of Los Angeles was still a relief. She'd spent more time in motorcars here in the American city than in all her life in China. Fair enough: these foreign devils did reckon her an important personage. But so many people in the city had automobiles, had them and took them for granted. Even the way the city was built took them for granted. She'd seen that from the start. *Prosperity,* she thought again.

Only the richest Chinese would have been able to afford the home in which the Yeagers lived. Only those who collaborated with the little scaly devils would have been able to get the electrically powered machines that were so common in this country. 'We greet you,' Barbara Yeager said in the little devils' language when Liu Han and Liu Mei rang the doorbell (even it ran on electricity). Her husband and son nodded behind her. She went on, 'Supper will be ready soon.'

Supper was an extravagantly large slab of beef served with a baked potato. Potatoes, Liu Han had found, were harmless;

they took the place of rice and noodles in a lot of American cooking. The beefsteak was another declaration of U.S. affluence. Liu Han had never eaten so much meat in China as she did at almost every supper in the United States.

After supper, Major Yeager surprised her by helping his wife clean up. No Chinese man would have done such a thing, despite the Communists' preaching of equality between the sexes. When the job was done, he went into the front room and pulled a paperbound book off a shelf. 'I had to do some shopping around before I found this,' he said in English, sounding pleased with himself, 'but I did.'

He handed it to Liu Han. She read English haltingly. '*Nineteen Thirty-eight Spalding Official Base Ball Guide*.' She looked over at him. 'Why you show me this?'

'Open it at the page where I put a card in,' he answered. She did, and looked down at small pictures of men in caps of the sort Americans still sometimes wore. After a moment, one of the faces leapt out at her. She pointed. 'That is Bobby Fiore.'

Major Yeager nodded. Yes, he was pleased with himself. 'Truth,' he said in the scaly devils' tongue before returning to English: 'He is wearing a baseball uniform there. I wanted your daughter to have the chance to see what her father looked like.'

Liu Mei had gone off to talk with Jonathan Yeager. When she came into the room after Liu Han called, her mother looked closely to see if she was rumpled. Liu Han would not have bet American youths behaved much differently from their Chinese counterparts if they got the chance. But everything here seemed as it should.

Liu Han pointed to the photograph. 'Your father,' she said, first in English and then in Chinese. Liu Mei's eyes got very wide as she stared and stared at the picture. When at last she looked up, they were wet with tears. Liu Han understood that. She and her daughter were good Marxist-Leninists, but the ancient Chinese tradition of respect for one's ancestors lived in both of them.

'Thank you,' Liu Mei said to Major Yeager. She'd spoken in

English, but added an emphatic cough. That let her shift to the little devils' language: 'This means very much to me.'

'I am glad to do it,' Yeager replied in the same language. 'He was your father, and he was my friend.' He turned to Liu Han. 'Keep the book, if you want to. It will help you remember, even when you go home.'

'I thank you,' Liu Han said softly. She still believed – she had to believe – the American system was flawed, regardless of the prosperity it produced. But some of the foreign devils could be men as good as any Chinese. She'd seen that with Bobby Fiore, and now she saw it again with this other man who had been his friend.

Flight Lieutenant David Goldfarb studied the radar screen. 'Another American launch,' he remarked. 'The Yanks have been busy the past couple of weeks, haven't they?'

'Aye, sir,' Sergeant Jack McKinnon answered. He chuckled. 'Likely they've got a lot o' ginger to fly up to all those poor Lizards who've had to do without their womenfolks for so long.' He laughed at his own wit.

So did Goldfarb, but he had a harder time of it. He wished the Lizards had never discovered that ginger made their females randy. Such a discovery could only mean they'd want more of the stuff. Oh, their leaders would do their best to keep them from getting more, but those same leaders had been doing their best for a long time. They'd had little luck yet.

He didn't think they'd have much luck in future, either. He sighed – not too loud, so the sergeant wouldn't notice. That meant Group Captain Roundbush would keep moving the stuff by the bushel basket, which meant Roundbush was liable to ask him for more help one day before too long.

And he would have to give it. The way things were in Britain these days, he would have to do whatever Roundbush told him to do. The group captain had said he would help Goldfarb emigrate. With each passing day, that looked like a better idea . . . if Roundbush had told the truth.

Putting the group captain out of his mind – for a little while – Goldfarb studied the radar screen. 'Looks like they're going hammer and tongs at that space station of theirs,' he remarked. 'They'll really have something when they finally get it done.'

'Oh, that they will, sir – summat grand.' But McKinnon, in spite of what he said, did not sound as if he agreed with Goldfarb. A moment later, he explained why: 'And once they've got it, what will they do with it? What good will it do them? We can get our toes out into space, aye, but it really belongs to the Lizards.'

'For now it does, yes,' Goldfarb admitted. 'And it doesn't look like it'll ever belong to Britain, does it?' Saying that pained him. Back before the Lizards came, Britain had been at the forefront of science and technology. British radar had kept the Nazis from invading in 1940. British jet engines had been well in advance of everybody else's, including the Germans'. When space travel came, what was more natural than to assume it would come from the British Empire?

But the British Empire was only a memory now. And the British Isles lacked the resources for a space program of their own. What resources they had, they'd put into land- and submarine-based rockets with which they could make any invader – Lizards, Nazis, even Americans – pay a dreadful price.

And so Britain remained independent. But the continent-bestriding powers – the USA, the USSR, the Greater German *Reich* – also strode beyond the planets, strode on the moon, on Mars, and even on the asteroids. As a boy, Goldfarb had dreamt of being the first man on the moon, of walking beside a Martian canal.

A Nazi had been the first man on the moon. There were no Martian canals. So the Lizards said, and they turned out to be right. They still couldn't understand why men wanted to set foot on such a useless, worthless world.

Goldfarb understood it. But, even for the Yanks who'd gone

to Mars and then come home again, it must have seemed like a consolation prize. Whatever people did in space, the Lizards had done it thousands of years before.

'If we could build a ship that would pay a call on Home, that would be something,' Goldfarb said dreamily.

'It'd be summat the Lizards didn't fancy, and go ahead and try telling me I'm wrong, sir,' McKinnon said. 'That'd be the last thing they wanted: us coming to pay them a call, I mean.'

'So it would. They wouldn't know what kind of call we aimed to pay them,' Goldfarb answered. He thought about it for a moment. 'And I'm damned if I know what kind of call we ought to pay them, either. It would be nice if we could give them as much to think about as they've given us, wouldn't it?'

McKinnon's expression of naked longing reminded Goldfarb that the Scot's relatively recent ancestors had been in the habit of painting themselves blue and swinging claymores as tall as they were. 'Aye, wouldn't it be sweet to drop a nice, fat atomic bomb down the Emperor's chimney? The Lizards could scarce blame us, not after all they've done here.'

'Somehow, I don't think that would stop them from blaming us.' Goldfarb's voice was dry. 'What I'd like to do, though, is send ships to other planets in the Empire and see if we could free the Rabotevs and Hallessi. They can't like the Lizards lording it over them, can they?'

But even as he said that, he wondered. The Lizards had ruled those other two worlds for a long time. Maybe the aliens on them really did take the Empire for granted. People didn't work that way, but the Lizards didn't work like people, so why should their subjects? And people hadn't ruled other people for anywhere near that many thousand years. Maybe obedience, even acquiescence, had become ingrained into the natives of Halless 1 and Rabotev 2.

'Might be worth finding out,' McKinnon said. 'Pity they aren't closer. Likely wouldn't do, sending leaflets through space to 'em.'

'Workers of the worlds, unite!' Goldfarb said, grinning. 'You have nothing to lose but your chains.'

The joke should have gone over better than it did. McKinnon's smile, now, looked distinctly strained. His lips moved – silently, but Goldfarb had no trouble understanding the word they shaped. *Bolshie.*

It could have been worse. McKinnon could have said it out loud. That might have wrecked Goldfarb's career for good, assuming his being a Jew hadn't already done the job. Being labeled a Bolshevik Jew in a country tilting toward the Greater German *Reich* wasn't just asking for trouble. It was begging for trouble on bended knee.

'Never mind,' Goldfarb said wearily. 'Never bloody mind. That'll teach me to try to be bloody funny, won't it?'

McKinnon stared at him as if he'd never seen him before. Goldfarb was not in the habit of making his speech so peppery. He was not in the habit of banging his head against a stone wall, either. He wondered why not. Metaphorically, he did it every day. Why not be literal about it, too?

He looked at his watch. The luminous dots by the numbers and the hands told him the time in the darkened room. 'Shift's almost over,' he remarked in something close to his normal tone of voice. 'Thank heaven.'

Jack McKinnon did not argue with him. Maybe that meant the veteran sergeant would be relieved to go outside and get some fresh air, or something as close to it as Belfast's sooty atmosphere yielded. But maybe, and more likely, it meant McKinnon would be glad to escape from being cooped up in the same room with a damned crazy Jew.

At last, after what certainly seemed like forever, McKinnon and Goldfarb's reliefs showed up. The Scotsman hurried away without words, without even his usual, *See you tomorrow.* He would see Goldfarb tomorrow, whether he liked it or not. *Not*, at the moment, seemed ahead on points.

Shaking his head, Goldfarb got onto his bicycle and pedaled for home as fast as he could. Since everyone else in Belfast had got off at about the same time, that was not very fast. He hated traffic jams. Too many people in motorcars pretended they could not see the plebeians on bicycles. He had to swerve sharply a couple of times to keep from getting hit.

When he did get back to his flat in the married officers' quarters, he was something a good deal less than his best. Normally patient with his children, he barked at them till they retreated in dismay. He barked at Naomi, too, something he scarcely ever did. She used a privilege denied the children and barked back. That brought him up short.

'Here,' she said with brisk practicality. 'Drink this.' *This* was a couple of jiggers of neat whiskey poured into a glass. 'Maybe it will make you decent company again. If it doesn't, it will put you to sleep.'

'Maybe it will make me beat you,' he said, full of mock ferocity. Had there been the slightest likelihood he would actually do that, the words would never have passed his lips. But, while he might talk too much when he'd had a drop or two too many, he'd never yet turned mean.

'If you're going to beat me, why don't you wait till after supper?' Naomi suggested. 'That way, I won't be tempted to pour a pot of boiling potato soup in your lap.' She cocked her head to one side. 'Well, not very tempted, anyhow.'

'No, eh?' he said, and knocked back the whiskey. 'In that case, I'd better behave myself.'

He behaved himself to the extent of keeping quiet through the soup and through the roast chicken that followed. Then he plopped himself down in front of the televisor to watch the Cologne-Manchester football match. Most of the time, he had no use for the hooligans who came to the stadium to make trouble and to stomp anyone who showed signs of supporting the wrong team. He listened with benign approval as they cursed and booed and hissed the Germans.

'You'd better win,' a leather-lunged heckler bawled, 'or it's the gas chamber for the lot of you!'

Cologne did not win. Neither did they lose. The match

ended in a 1–1 tie. Goldfarb scowled as he turned off the set. He wanted, he craved certainties, and the match, like life, offered nothing but ambiguity.

Although the Manchester coach spent several minutes explaining why the tie was really as good as a victory, he didn't sound as if he believed it himself. Goldfarb was glad when he disappeared and the blandly handsome face of a BBC newsreader filled the screen.

'Another round of public fornication among the Lizards was observed in London today,' he remarked after touching on larger disasters. 'Fortunately, in this day and age, there are few horses left to startle, and mere human beings have grown increasingly blasé in the face of the Race's continued randiness. In fashion news—'

Goldfarb snorted. He tremendously admired traditional British restraint, not least because he had so little of it in his own makeup. He'd once thought the Lizards similarly restrained, but ginger and the arrival of females had changed his mind there. With what ginger had done to his own life, he wished the Lizards had never heard of it.

'Finally this evening,' the newsreader went on, 'M.P. Sir Oswald Mosley of the British Union of Fascists introduced a bill in Parliament proposing to restrict the legal privileges of certain citizens of the United Kingdom. Despite the fact that the bill appears to have no chance of passage, Sir Oswald said it continued an important statement of principle, and—'

With a curse, Goldfarb got up and turned off the televisor. He stood by it, shaking. Was that fury or fear? Both at once, he judged. It had started here. At last, it had started here.

12

Glen Johnson studied *Peregrine's* radar screen. More than anything else up here, including his bare eyes, it told him what he needed to know. Everything was, or seemed to be, as it should have been. He didn't know exactly what all the targets he saw were, but he hadn't known that for some time: all three spacegoing human powers and the Lizards kept right on changing the orbits on their weapons installations.

He sighed. Everyone should have cut that crap out after whoever it was struck at the colonizing fleet. Down on Earth, somebody was laughing himself silly because he'd hit the Lizards a good lick and got away with it.

But that stunt could not work twice. The Lizards had made it very plain they wouldn't let it work twice. Looking at things out of their eye turrets, Johnson couldn't blame them. If anyone struck at them now, everyone would regret it. That made all the maneuvering out here seem pointless at best, provocative at worst. It went on even so.

'Stupid,' he muttered under his breath, and stupid it undoubtedly was. That didn't mean it would stop. Who'd said, *Nobody ever went broke underestimating the stupidity of the American people?* He couldn't recall, but it was true, and not only of Americans.

His low, fast orbit meant he kept passing things traveling in higher, slower paths around the Earth. Several *Falcon*-class

381

ships were in orbit at any given time, to make sure they kept a close eye on everything that was going on. When Johnson spotted the large target on his radar, he thought for a moment that it was a ship from the colonization fleet. But the orbit was wrong for that. Moreover, by its transponder signal, it didn't belong to the Lizards at all. As a matter of fact, it was as American as the *Peregrine*.

He whistled softly and thumbed on his radio. '*Peregrine* to Space Station. *Peregrine* to Space Station. Over.'

The signal came back a moment later: 'Go ahead, *Peregrine*. Over.'

'That thing is really going up there, isn't it?' Johnson had to remember to add, 'Over.'

He got laughter back. 'Sure is, *Peregrine*. Any day now, we're opening up our own supermarket.'

'Damned if I don't believe you,' he said. 'My last flight up, you weren't anything special at all on my radar. This time, first thing I thought was that you belonged to the colonization fleet.'

That won him more laughter. 'Pretty funny, *Peregrine*. We've got a lot we're going to be doing up here, that's all, so the place has to get bigger.'

'Roger that,' Johnson answered. 'But what do the Lizards think about you? They don't like anybody coming up here but them.'

'Oh, they don't worry about us,' the radio operator on the space station said. 'We're a great, big, fat target, and we're too damn heavy to do much in the way of maneuvering. If real trouble starts, you can call us the *Sitting Duck*.'

'Okay,' Johnson said. He didn't ask what sort of weapons the space station carried. That was none of his business, and even less the business of whoever might be monitoring this frequency. 'Over and out.'

Sitting Duck, *eh?* he thought, and shook his head. *More likely the* Sitting Porcupine. If that radioman hadn't been sandbagging, he was a monkey's uncle. The USA wouldn't put anything so big and prominent into space without giving it some way to take care of itself. Even the Lizards weren't that naive. They'd thought they would be facing knights in shining armor (or rusty armor – he remembered some of the pictures from their probe), but they'd come loaded for bear.

What impressed him most about the space station wasn't its likely armament but, as he'd told the radio operator, how fast it was growing. An awful lot of launches had to be ferrying men and supplies up there. As far as he was concerned, that sort of spaceflight was bus driver's work, but there was a lot of bus driver's work going on to make the station expand so quickly.

He scratched his chin, wondering if he'd be able to finagle a ride up there himself, to see with his own eyes what was going on. After a moment, he nodded. That shouldn't be hard to arrange.

A Lizard radar station called from the ground to inform him his orbit was satisfactory. 'I thank you,' he answered in the language of the Race. The Lizard on the radio had sounded sniffy, as Lizards had a way of doing. If his orbit hadn't been satisfactory, the Lizard would have been screaming his head off.

Johnson suddenly laughed. 'That's what it is!' he exclaimed, speaking aloud to enjoy the joke more. 'There's thousands of tons of powdered ginger up there, and they're going to drop it on the Lizards' heads. Wouldn't that produce some satisfied customers?'

He knew he was anthropomorphizing. When the Lizards didn't have it, they didn't miss it the way people would. But when they were interested, they were a lot more interested than anybody above the age of nineteen could hope to understand.

'Hello, American spacecraft. Over.' The call was in crisp, gutturally flavored English. 'Who are you?'

'*Peregrine* here, Johnson speaking,' Johnson answered. 'Who are you, German spacecraft?' The German equivalents of his ship had orbits with about the same period as his own, but, because Peenemünde was a lot farther north than Kitty Hawk, they swung farther north and south than he did, and met only intermittently.

'Drucker here, in *Käthe*,' the flier from the *Reich* answered. 'And I wish I were in Käthe right now, and not up here. Do I say this right *auf Englisch*?'

'If you mean what I think you mean, yeah, that's how you say it,' Johnson replied with a chuckle. 'Wife or girlfriend, Drucker? I forget.'

'Wife,' Drucker answered. 'I am a lucky man, I know, to be still in love with the woman I married. Have you a wife, Johnson?'

'Divorced,' Johnson said shortly. 'Spent too much time away from her, I guess. She got fed up with it.' She'd run away with a traveling salesman, was what Stella had done, but Johnson didn't advertise that. Unless somebody asked him about her, he didn't think of her twice a month. He wasn't a man inclined to dwell on his mistakes.

'I am sorry that to hear,' Drucker said. 'Here is to peace between us and confusion to the Lizards.'

'Yeah, I'll drink to that any old day, and twice on Sunday,' Johnson said. 'Every day I'm not up here, I mean.'

'They think all I have here is water and ersatz coffee and a horrible powder that turns water into something that is supposed to taste like orange juice,' Drucker said. 'They are wrong.' He sounded happy they were wrong.

'Somebody's listening to you,' Johnson warned.

'They will not shoot me for saying I do not like the tang of their orange drink,' the German answered. 'They need a better reason than that.'

For once, Johnson wished the radio speaker in the *Peregrine* weren't so tinny. He thought Drucker's voice had an edge to it, but couldn't be sure. He was probably imagining things. Spacemen were part of the Nazi elite. The *Gestapo* wouldn't go after them. It would pick some poor, beat-up foreigners who couldn't even complain.

After a pause that stretched, Drucker went on, 'You and I and even the Bolsheviks in their flying tin cans – if we were not here, the Lizards would be able to do whatever they chose.'

'That's so,' Johnson agreed. 'Doesn't mean we get along with each other, though.'

'Well enough not to use the rockets and bombs we have all built,' Drucker said. 'That is well enough, when you think of how the world is.'

His signal was starting to break up as his flight path carried him south of the *Peregrine*. Glen Johnson found himself nodding. 'I'm not going to tell you you're wrong, pal. Safe landing to you.'

'Safe . . .' A burst of static drowned out the last of the German's words.

The rest of Johnson's tour was uneventful. He approved of that. Events in space meant things going wrong – either in *Peregrine*, which was liable to kill him, or outside the ship, which was liable to mean the whole world and most of the spacecraft in orbit around it would go up in smoke.

He got down to Kitty Hawk in one piece. After the usual interrogation – almost as if he were a captured prisoner and not an officer in the U.S. Marine Corps – the bright young captain who'd grilled him asked, 'And do you have any questions of your own, sir?'

It was, for the most part, a ritualistic question. Past the latest sports scores, what would a returning pilot want to know about what had happened during the mission he'd just completed? He knew better than anybody.

But, this time, Johnson said, 'Yeah, as a matter of fact, I do.' The captain's eyes widened; Johnson had taken him by surprise. But he recovered quickly, using a gracious gesture to urge the *Peregrine*'s pilot to go ahead. And Johnson did: 'What are they throwing into that space station to make it grow so fast?'

'Sorry, sir, but I really don't know a thing about that,' the captain replied. 'Not my area of responsibility.'

'Okay,' Johnson said with a smile and a shrug. He got to his feet. So did the young captain, who gave him a precise salute. He did an about-face and left the interrogation room. As soon as he got outside, he scratched his head. Unless everything he'd learned about human nature over a lot of tables with poker chips on them was wrong, that bright young captain had been lying through his shiny white teeth.

Johnson scratched his head again. He could think of only one reason why the captain would lie: whatever was going on aboard the space station was secret. It had to be a pretty juicy secret, too, because the captain didn't want him to know it was there at all. Had the fellow just said, *Sorry, sir – classified*, Johnson would have shrugged and gone about his business. Now, though, his bump of curiosity itched. What were they hiding, up there a few hundred miles?

Something the Lizards wouldn't like. He didn't need an Ivy League degree to figure that one out. He couldn't see the Race breaking out in a sweat about whatever it was, though, not when they had starships from two different fleets practically blanketing the Earth.

'Security,' Johnson muttered, making it into a dirty word. And at that, he had it good. He wouldn't have traded places with the Nazi in the upper stage of that A-45, not for all the tea in China he wouldn't. And Russia was no better place to live than Germany, not if half of what people said was true.

Let's hear it for the last free country in the world, he thought as he headed toward the bar to buy himself a drink to celebrate being alive. Even England was slipping these days. Johnson sadly shook his head. Who would have thought, back in the days when the limeys battled Germany single-handed, they would have ended up sliding toward the *Reich* an inch at a time?

He shrugged again. Who would have thought . . . a whole lot of things over the past twenty years? If the United States had to get secret to stay free, he didn't see anything in the whole wide world wrong with that.

He was on his second whiskey before the irony there struck him. By the time he'd started his third one, he'd forgotten all about it.

Atvar was glad to return to Australia. It was late summer in this hemisphere now, and the weather was fine by any standards, those of Home included. Even in Cairo, though, the weather had been better than bearable. What pleased him more was how far the colony had come since his last visit.

'Then, all we had were the starships,' he said to Pshing. 'Now look! A whole thriving city! Streets, vehicles, shops, a power plant, a pipeline to the desalination center – a proper city for the Race.'

'Truth, Exalted Fleetlord,' his adjutant replied. 'Before very much longer, it will be like any city back on Home.'

'Indeed it will,' Atvar said with an emphatic cough. 'This is going according to plan. When we proceed according to plan, we can move at least as fast as the Big Uglies. And here in the center of Australia, we shall have no Big Uglies interfering with our designs, except for the occasional savage like the one I saw the last time I was here. But this is and shall forevermore be *our* place on Tosev 3.'

'As you say, Exalted Fleetlord,' Pshing answered. 'My only concern is that we are, in certain areas, still vulnerable to sabotage from the Tosevites. The desalination plant and pipeline spring to mind.'

'I am assured the security plans are good,' Atvar said. 'They had better be good; we have had enough painful lessons from the Big Uglies on how to construct them and where our vulnerabilities lie.'

He did not want to think about security plans and sabotage, not now. He wanted to walk along the sidewalks of the growing city, to watch males and females peacefully going about their business and getting on with their lives. Before too many generations, if all went well, they would rule the whole planet, not just a little more than half. And the Empire could get on with the job of civilizing another world.

If all went well . . .

Very faintly, he could smell the pheromones that meant a female somewhere upwind was ripe for mating. He tried to ignore the odor. He couldn't quite. For one thing, it made him a little more irritable than he would have been otherwise. Even here, in the heart of the Race's haven on Tosev 3, the Tosevite herb had come. He sighed. The troubles this world brought seemed inescapable.

All over the town, alarms began hissing. Amplified voices shouted: 'Missile attack! Incoming missile attack! Take cover against missile attack!'

'No!' Atvar screeched. All around him, the colonists stared foolishly. Every moment counted, but they did not seem to realize it. They had not been trained for this. Atvar did not know which way to start himself. The missiles could be coming from any direction. If they'd been launched from one of the accursed submersible ships the Big Uglies had developed, they would be here all too soon.

Antimissile sites ringed the city, as they ringed the whole area of settlement here in Australia. But they were not infallible. They had not been infallible against even the crude missiles the Big Uglies had had during the fighting. And Tosevite technology was better now than it had been then.

Atvar turned his eye turrets toward Pshing. 'If we perish here, Kirel will take vengeance the likes of which this world has never seen.'

'Of course, Exalted Fleetlord.' Pshing sounded so calm, Atvar envied him. The fleetlord did not want to fall here. He wanted to bring the assimilation of this world into the Empire as far forward as he could. How much the universe cared about what he wanted was liable to be another question.

Alarms kept hissing. Atvar looked around for someplace to shelter against the nuclear missile he assumed would momentarily burst overhead. He saw nowhere to hide. Turning to

Pshing, he said, 'I am sorry you had to come here with me as part of your duties.' If he was about to die, he didn't want to die with the apology unspoken.

Before Pshing could answer, antimissiles roared off their launch platforms. They would do what they could, but Atvar knew some of their targets were all too likely to elude them.

Explosions to the north, to the northwest, and overhead smote his hearing diaphragms. Debris fell out of the sky, crashing down around and in the city the Race was building. A great chunk dug a hole in the ground not far from Atvar. The leg and tailstump of a male or female stuck out from under it. That leg still twitched feebly, but no one could have lived after so much metal fell on him.

Still, despite the bursts overhead, no new temporary sun blazed into life above the city. 'Exalted Fleetlord, we may live!' Pshing cried.

'We may indeed,' Atvar said. 'The antimissiles are performing excellently.' They were performing better than he'd imagined they could, let alone hoped. Those continuing explosions above him had to be Tosevite missiles intercepted and blasted out of the sky. Had they been anything else, one of those missiles would have ensured that he never heard anything again.

He opened his mouth to laugh exultantly. As he inhaled, all the strange, alien scents of the Australian desert went past his scent receptors and into his lung. Among them was a spicy scent he did not remember from his previous visit. He had never smelled anything like it before. It was, he thought, the most delicious odor he'd ever known, with the possible exception of a female's pheromones. It reminded him of those pheromones, as a matter of fact.

'What is that splendid smell?' he asked aloud.

No sooner asked than answered. The response formed in his head even as Pshing spoke the words: 'Exalted Fleetlord, I do not know for certain, but I think that must be ginger.'

'Yes. Truth,' Atvar said. He could *see* the truth, all but

hanging there in front of his eyes. It was as obvious as Venteff's Theorem on the relationship between the squares of the sides of a right triangle and the square of the hypotenuse. Everything suddenly seemed obvious to him. He had never felt so brilliant, never since the day when he'd used the egg tooth at the end of his snout to break through the shell that separated him from the wider world.

'I never tasted ginger before,' Pshing said.

'Neither did I.' Regret filled Atvar. If he'd been using the Tosevite herb during the fighting, the Big Uglies surely would have had to yield to the Race. He felt certain and swift and strong, very strong.

Other males and females must have felt the same way, for they rushed upon the chunk of metal that had crushed one of their comrades and hauled it away. Some of them exclaimed in horror and disgust, for they were colonists, not males from the conquest fleet, and the crushed remains they uncovered were outside their experience. But they had acted swiftly and decisively, without the Race's usual long pauses for thought.

'They did well,' Pshing said. For the moment, the action was what counted, not what resulted from it.

'Truth,' Atvar said again. He wondered which Tosevite not-empire had launched this attack against the Race in its citadel on Tosev 3. Whoever it was certainly had some strange notions of what an attack was. But for the handful of males and females hit by falling pieces of rocket, the rest of the members of the Race on whom the Big Uglies had chosen to shower so much ginger were, if anything, enjoying themselves more than they had before.

He paused and looked about, now here, now there, his eye turrets moving independently of each other. The smell of ginger was not the only marvelous odor coming to his scent receptors now. Along with it, he smelled female pheromones.

Yes, of course, he thought. *I remember. Ginger brings them into their season.* The Big Uglies had spent all the years since his arrival on Tosev 3 raising his ire; never once had the erectile scales atop his head risen with it. They were for only one sort of display, the sort he made now.

Pshing was also displaying his crest. So were other males, too, as far as the eye turret could reach. And females were lowering their heads and raising their hindquarters into the mating posture. They might have been uninterested mere moments before, but the ginger floating through the air in a fine, delicious cloud did to them what the coming of the season would have done back on Home.

Atvar advanced on the nearest female he saw. With every step he took, his own posture grew more nearly upright. But he was not the only male approaching her. Fury filled him, lest the other male get there before him. 'Go back!' he shouted. 'I am the fleetlord!' He showed his claws in a threatening gesture.

The other male also displayed his claws. 'I do not care who you are!' he shouted back, a shocking lack of decorum at any time but the season. Then, it was every male for himself. 'I am going to mate with this female.'

'No!' Atvar hurled himself at the male from the colonization fleet. He was older, but he also knew how to fight, not only as a commander but also as an individual. Before long, the other male fled, hissing and wailing in dismay.

The female over whom they'd fought turned an eye turret back toward Atvar. 'Hurry!' she said. 'This is uncomfortable.'

He did his best to oblige. It wasn't uncomfortable while it went on: very much the reverse. As soon as he'd finished, the female skittered away. But he, like the other males in the city, kept right on smelling the pheromones from other females that announced they were still receptive.

It was, in fact, very much the way a day during the season would have gone back on Home. In other words, not a cursed thing got done. Males sought females and brawled among themselves. Females stopped and waited where they stood for males. Sometimes a single mating was enough to satisfy them. Sometimes, perhaps depending on how much ginger they'd inhaled and tasted, they wanted more.

Only slowly did the difference between here and Home sink into Atvar's mind: what with ginger and pheromones, he was far more distracted than he should have been. Back on Home, everyone expected the season. It was part of the rhythm of the year, not a disruption.

Here in Australia, the reverse was true. This city had just hatched from its egg. Much of it, in fact, still remained inside the shell. Males and females had plenty to do without worrying about the distraction of mating as if they were so many Big Uglies. Some of that work would get done wrong now. Some of it would not get done at all. Out across the city, more males and females were liable to be hurt by the sudden onset of the season than from debris falling out of the sky.

Clever, Atvar thought after a while. The Big Uglies who had done this were liable to be more clever than he was at the moment. His wits working far less clearly than they should have, he wondered whether inciting the Race to mate could be construed as an act of war. Was it not closer to what the Tosevites called, for no obvious reason, a practical joke?

And yet, if they chose to do it again, would they not disrupt life here once more? If, after disrupting life, they followed with an attack that did include nuclear weapons or poisonous gas, what then? *We would be in trouble then,* Atvar thought.

He'd never imagined he might wish he had not had the joy of mating.

Felless craved ginger. She fought against the craving with a grim intensity the likes of which she'd never imagined. It wasn't so much that she worried about the immediate effects of the ginger itself. But what it would do to her, what it would do to the males around her . . .

Whenever she tasted, she went into her season. She'd done that often enough to be convinced it was the ginger. She didn't want to do it again. It turned her into an animal, one whose desires were even more alien to her than those of the Tosevites she was supposed to be studying. She knew all that. She understood it down to the core.

She still craved ginger.

Every so often, on the streets of Nuremberg or in the corridors of the Race's embassy to the *Reich*, she would pass males and females coupling. New regulations had done little to stop it. Every so often, a male filled with lust by some other female's pheromones would advance upon her with raised head scales and erect posture.

When she had no ginger in her, when she wasn't chemically stimulated to go along with such nonsense, she enjoyed telling those males what she thought of them. Most of them looked astonished. One had been so drunk on pheromones, she'd had to bite him to get him to leave her alone.

And one, a clever fellow, had offered her ginger. 'Have a taste,' he'd said, those upright scales on his head quivering. 'You'll feel like mating then.'

'I do not want to feel like mating!' she'd shouted in a transport of fury that still astonished her. 'If my season had come on its own, that would have been one thing. Drugging myself for the sake of your mating urge is something else again.'

'Spoilsport,' he'd hissed, and gone off in a huff. He was Ambassador Veffani's first secretary, an important male in the embassy. Felless had to hope he wouldn't hold a grudge against her once female pheromones weren't addling his scent receptors.

The trouble was, males remained in a state of low-grade lust for days at a time. One female or another in the embassy would taste ginger and set them off. Every so often, Felless proved unable to resist temptation herself. One of the males who coupled with her during a slip was the first secretary. Maybe that made him stop resenting her for her earlier refusal.

Even the Big Uglies noticed the disruption that had come over the Race. One of them, a male with a Deutsch chemical firm, complained to her about it: 'Before, we could make arrangements and rely on them. Now, nothing your males

393

and females say can be trusted from one day to the next. This is not good.'

'Were it not for the herb that comes from this planet, were it not for the Tosevites who supply us this herb, we would not have such difficulties,' she answered, not wanting all the blame to rest on her back.

She failed to impress the Big Ugly. 'We Tosevites have also drugs,' he answered. 'They do not turn all of us unreliable. When we catch Tosevites who use drugs, we treat them as criminals. We punish them. Sometimes we punish them severely.'

What a Deutsch male meant by severe punishment was either death or something that would make the victim long for it. Felless did not care to imagine herself on the receiving end of such punishment. She said, 'We also punish those who use ginger.'

'You do not punish them enough, or they would not dare use it,' the Tosevite told her.

He sounded logical. He also sounded sure of himself. The Deutsche had a way of doing both those things at once. Sometimes, that made them very effective. Others, it just meant they went more spectacularly wrong than they would have otherwise. 'Your ways are too harsh for us,' Felless said.

'Then you will suffer because of this,' the Big Ugly said, 'and those of us who do business with you, unfortunately, will also suffer.' He got up and bowed stiffly from the waist, the Tosevite equivalent of the posture of respect. Then he turned and marched out of Felless' office.

Troubled, she went to see the ambassador to the Deutsche. 'Superior sir,' she said, 'we are becoming the laughingstock of the Tosevites. Something must be done to minimize the effect ginger has on us.'

'In principle, Senior Researcher, I agree,' Veffani answered. 'After the ginger bombs above our new city in Australia, I could scarcely disagree. Wherever we have both males and females, the Big Uglies have it within their power to incapacitate us. This is a danger we did not face even during the fighting.'

394

'What are we to do?' Felless asked.

'I do not know,' the ambassador said. 'This is still under discussion by leading officials of both the conquest fleet and the colonization fleet. One part of the emerging solution – or emerging effort to find a solution – is the imposition of harsher penalties on those guilty of tasting ginger.'

'That solution would appeal to the Big Uglies,' Felless said, and explained the conversation she'd just had with the Deutsch male. 'Shall we imitate their barbarism?'

'We may have no choice,' Veffani replied. 'If we do not imitate their barbarism, we seem to be heading in the direction of imitating their reproductive habits, as you must realize.' Felless realized it all too well; he had coupled with her that first time she'd tasted ginger, when she still did not know what it would do to her. The ambassador went on, 'Which would you prefer?'

'Neither, superior sir,' Felless answered at once. 'I would prefer for things to return to the way they have always been.'

'A sentiment worthy of the Race,' Veffani said. 'Tell me, then, how to make this particular situation unhatch and return to its egg.'

'I cannot,' Felless said softly. 'I wish I could. And, speaking of eggs . . .'

She could feel a pair growing inside her, though they would not be ready to lay for some time yet. She had thought a successful mating – whichever one it had been – would shut down her desire and her production of pheromones. That was the sensible way things had worked back on Home.

As the males of the conquest fleet said over and over again, nothing on Tosev 3 worked the way it did back on Home. Ginger short-circuited the end of her cycle. Even though she was gravid, she still released pheromones and wanted to mate every time she tasted. The matings, she knew, were no more than meaningless sensation, like the meaningless sensation suffusing so much of Tosevite sexuality. That did not mean she did not hunger for them.

395

Ginger also produced nothing but meaningless sensation. That did not mean she did not hunger for it, either.

Veffani said, 'If you should have any ginger, Senior Researcher, I strongly suggest you divest yourself of it. Penalties for possession and intoxication *are* going to increase. They are going to increase more for females than for males, too.'

'That is unjust!' Felless exclaimed.

'Perhaps in one sense, it is. In another sense, however, it most assuredly is not,' Veffani replied. 'Consider: a male under the influence of the herb is likely to disrupt only his own life. If he is an experienced user, and not too greedy, he does not even do that to any great extent. But a female disrupts not only her own life but also the lives of all the males who scent her pheromones. Does that not make a greater penalty for females appropriate?'

'Perhaps,' Felless said grudgingly. 'But there should also be a penalty, and a severe one, for males who give females ginger in order to induce them to mate when they would not do so otherwise.'

'Such penalties are also being drafted,' the ambassador said. 'We have had cases of this sort of behavior reported. Males with pheromones filling their scent receptors are less rational than we would like. Even now, I find a certain difficulty in concentrating. Somewhere in this building, a female is in her season, and the pheromones drift in through my open door. I can understand how thoughts of mating, even by trickery, might come to mind.'

'The Tosevites have a term for this disgusting trickery, which is not unknown among them,' Felless said. 'They call it *seduction*.'

'Tosevite languages have borrowed many words from our tongue,' Veffani said. 'How unfortunate that we should have to take such a sordid term from theirs. We never needed it before.'

'Truth,' Felless said. 'And I wish we did not need it now.' She let out a worried hiss. 'Eventually, smugglers are bound to carry ginger Home. What will it do there, by the Emperor?'

'Nothing good,' the ambassador answered. 'I can say no more than that; I have, as yet, no data from which to program the computer to evaluate possible scenarios. But this herb can bring nothing but trouble and disruption to Home. I need no computer to see the truth in that. It brings nothing but trouble and disruption here.'

'With that, superior sir, I cannot possibly disagree,' Felless said. 'And now, with your permission, I shall withdraw from your presence.' She did not say she was withdrawing so she could dispose of the ginger in her quarters; after what Veffani had told her, she did not want to admit she had any of the Tosevite herb. If he drew his conclusions from the way she acted, that was one thing. If he had actual evidence of her possessing ginger, that could be something else again.

Her mouth dropped open. He'd mated with her. She'd gone into her season, as ginger made females do. If that didn't give him some sort of hint that she used the herb, what would?

It was on his mind, for, after using the affirmative hand gesture, he added, 'Do bear in mind what I have said, Senior Researcher.'

'It shall be done,' Felless said, and departed. She sneaked back up to the chamber the embassy staff had assigned her, and managed to get inside without having Ttomalss notice her. As males went, he wasn't a bad fellow. He hadn't given her ginger in the hope of inciting her to mate, as Veffani's first secretary had done. So far as she knew, he did not even use the herb. He'd warned her against it before anyone knew the effect it had on females. But even so . . .

Even so, he'd mated with her. Under most circumstances, that bond was far more casual in the Race than among the Tosevites. Under many circumstances, it was no bond at all. During the season, who could say with certainty with whom one had mated? But ginger changed that, as ginger changed everything Felless knew. She knew only too well, in the cases of Ttomalss and Veffani.

She also knew only too well that she did still have ginger

hidden in her office. She opened a drawer, lifted up the folders full of printouts, and took out the vial. Pouring the herb down the sink, letting water wash away the herb, was surely the most expedient course.

Her craving rose up to smite her. She could not throw the ginger away, no matter how hard she tried. She thrust the vial back into the drawer and slammed it shut. Then she stood and quivered for some little while. The temptation was not to take out the vial again and get rid of the ginger. The temptation was to take out the vial again and taste till the ginger was gone.

And then it would do what it did with her mind, bringing exaltation and then crushing depression. And it would do what it did with her body, making her randier than any Big Ugly. And she still craved it. 'What am I going to do?' she whispered in desperation and despair. 'What *can* I do?'

A male sidled toward Nesseref as she walked through Lodz. The shuttlecraft pilot watched him with a wariness she'd had to acquire in a hurry. Sure enough, his posture was a little more upright than it might have been. Sure enough, the scales along the midline of his skull kept starting to twitch upright. Sure enough, all that meant the pheromones of an upwind female had addled whatever wits he owned.

'I greet you, superior female,' he said, his voice as ingratiating as he could make it. At least he recognized she was of higher rank; she'd met males too far gone in lust to know or to care.

'I greet you,' she answered resignedly. Maybe she was wrong. Maybe he wouldn't do what she thought he would.

But he did. He reached into his belt pouch and pulled out a small glass vial. 'How would you like a taste of this?' he asked.

'No!' she said, and used an emphatic cough. That wasn't empathic enough to make him understand and pay attention to her. He poured some into the palm of his hand, then invitingly held that hand in front of her snout. All she had to do was flick out her tongue and taste the herb.

She pushed him away. He let out a startled squawk, and then a low cry of dismay as the ginger was lost forever. 'Curse you, that is not friendly!' he exclaimed.

'It is not friendly to try to make me want to mate when I do not feel like mating, either,' Nesseref said angrily. The male advanced – now, if she was any judge, to hurt her because she'd made him lose some of his precious herb. Used to making quick decisions, she made one here: she lashed out and kicked him as hard as she could. 'Go away!' she shouted.

Maybe he hadn't expected her to fight back. Maybe he hadn't expected her to start fighting before she did. Whatever he'd expected, she'd given him something else. He hissed in surprise and pain and did scuttle away.

'Well, well,' said someone – a Tosevite – behind her. 'That was interesting. Did it mean what I thought it meant?'

Nesseref whirled. The Big Ugly's voice was familiar, though she still had scant skill at telling Tosevites apart by appearance. 'You are Anielewicz, the male I met in Glowno?' she asked. If she was right, splendid. If she was wrong, she would not be embarrassed.

But, as she had been with the male of her own kind, she was right. The Big Ugly's head bobbed up and down in his kind's gesture of agreement. 'Yes, I am Anielewicz,' he said. 'And you are Nesseref. And I have answered your question, and you have not answered mine.'

Was that irony in his voice? With a male of the Race, she would have been certain. Reading Tosevites was harder. Cautiously – but with less caution than she used with the male of her kind – Nesseref said, 'How can I answer your question when I do not know what you thought it meant?'

'Did he give you ginger there, or try to, so you would mate with him?' Anielewicz asked.

'Yes, that is what he did.' Spelling it out infuriated Nesseref all over again. 'I have tasted ginger, and I have mated while the herb excited me. That male had no business trying to make it excite me.'

'We think alike there,' Anielewicz said. 'Sometimes a male Tosevite will give a female alcohol, to make her want to mate or to make her too drunk to stop him from mating with her. We also think this is wrong. Among us, in fact, it is reckoned a crime.'

'It should be,' Nesseref said. 'Among us, it is not, though there is talk of making it one. Among us, no one would have or could have done such a thing without this cursed herb, so we did not even consider such possibilities.' She paused thoughtfully. 'You Big Uglies have had to do more planning about problems pertaining to reproduction than we have.'

'It has been necessary for us,' Mordechai Anielewicz answered. 'Now, with ginger, it may become necessary for you, too.'

'Us, imitating Tosevites?' Nesseref started to laugh, but stopped. 'I suppose it could happen. You may have already found solutions for which we would need to spend a long time searching.'

'Truth,' the Big Ugly said. 'And now, Shuttlecraft Pilot, may I ask you one question more?'

'You may ask,' Nesseref told him. 'I do not promise to answer.'

'You would be a fool if you did promise,' Anielewicz replied. He had good sense for a Big Ugly. *No,* Nesseref thought. *He has good sense. He would have good sense as a male of the Race.* He asked his question: 'Did you not crave the ginger when the male offered it to you?'

'Some,' Nesseref said. 'But, as best I can, I do the things I ought to do, not the things I crave doing.'

To her surprise, Anielewicz burst into the barking laughter of his kind. 'You had better be careful, or you will end up a Jew.'

'I do not understand the differences between one group of Tosevites and another,' Nesseref said. 'I know there are differences, but I do not see why you put such weight on them.'

'That . . . is not simple,' the Big Ugly said. 'Not all the

differences are weighed rationally. I think you of the Race, taken as a whole, are more rational than we Tosevites. We think with our feelings as much as with our brains.'

'I have heard that this is so,' Nesseref replied. 'I have seen that it is so, in my small experience of Big Uglies. I find it interesting that a Tosevite should also believe it is so.'

Anielewicz grimaced in such a way that the outer corners of his mouth turned up. Nesseref could not remember whether that meant he was happy or sad. Happy, evidently, for he said, 'One friend should not lie to another.'

'Truth,' Nesseref said, and then decided to tease him: 'Were you lying to me when you told me you were going to check on that explosive-metal bomb in Glowno? I thought you were, but was I wrong?'

The Big Ugly stood very still. He had a rifle slung on his back, a weapon of Tosevite manufacture. Nesseref had paid it no mind till that moment. She wouldn't have then, save that he started to reach for it before arresting the motion. 'I made a mistake when I ever mentioned that,' he said slowly. 'And you, of course, went and told others of the Race.'

She had told Bunim, who hadn't believed her. She started to say as much, but checked herself. If Anielewicz had been telling the truth then and did not want her or anyone of the Race to know it was truth, she would be in danger if she gave the impression she was the only one who did believe it – with her disposed of, no one would credit it. So all she said was, 'Yes, I did that.'

'And now the Race knows where the weapon is,' Anielewicz said with a sigh. He began to reach for the rifle again. Nesseref braced herself to leap for him as she'd attacked the male of her own kind. But he checked himself once more. After shaking his head, he continued, 'No blame attaches to you. You could not have known how much this would inconvenience me and my fellow Jews.'

'I do not understand why it does inconvenience you,' Nesseref said. 'The Race rules here. No group of Tosevites does. No group of Tosevites can. What need has a small faction like yours for an explosive-metal bomb?'

'You are new to Tosev 3, sure enough,' Mordechai Anielewicz answered patiently. 'I must remember: this means you are new to the way groups deal with one another, for the Race has no groups, not as we Tosevites do.'

'And a good thing, too,' Nesseref said, with an emphatic cough. 'We do not spend our time squabbling among ourselves. In our unity is our strength.'

Anielewicz's mouth went up at the corners. 'That holds some truth, but only some. With us Tosevites, disunity is our strength. Had we not had so many groups competing against one another, we could never have come far enough fast enough to have resisted when the Race landed on our planet.'

Nesseref wished the Big Uglies had not come far enough fast enough to be able to resist the Race. At the moment, though, that was a side issue. She returned to the main point: 'I still do not understand why a small group of Tosevites would need such a thing as an explosive-metal bomb.'

'Because even a large group will think twice about harming a small group that can, if pressed, do a great deal of harm in return,' Mordechai Anielewicz replied. 'Even the Race will think twice about harming a small group of Tosevites that can do it a great deal of harm in return. Do you understand now, my friend?'

'Yes, now I understand – at least in theory,' Nesseref said. 'But I do not understand why so many Tosevite groups remain small and separate instead of joining together with others.'

'Old hatreds,' Anielewicz said. Nesseref had to laugh at that. Anielewicz laughed, too, in the yipping Tosevite way. He continued, 'Nothing here seems old to the Race. I understand that. But it does not matter. Anything that seems old to us may as well be old in truth.'

In one way, that was an absurdity, a logical contradiction. On the other fork of the tongue, though, it made a twisted kind of sense. Many things on Tosev 3, Nesseref was discovering, made that kind of sense if they made any.

Anielewicz had trouble telling females of the Race from males, but he'd gained some skill in reading the reactions males and females had in common. He said, 'I think you begin to understand the problem.'

'All I understand is that this world is a much more complicated place than Home,' Nesseref said. 'This little place called Poland, for instance. It has Poles in it, which makes sense, and you Jews, which does not.'

'If you think I will argue with that, you are mistaken,' the Tosevite said.

Ignoring the interruption, Nesseref went on, 'In one direction are the Deutsche, who hate both Poles and Jews. In the other direction are the Russkis, who also hate both Poles and Jews. Does this make them allies? No! They hate each other, too. Where is the sense in this?'

'Nowhere I can find,' Anielewicz replied; Nesseref got the idea she'd amused him, though she couldn't understand why. He went on, 'Oh, by the way, you missed one thing.'

'And that is?' She was not sure she wanted to know.

Anielewicz told her nonetheless: 'Poles and Jews hate each other, too.'

'Why am I not surprised?' Nesseref asked.

'I do not know. Why are you not surprised?' The Tosevite laughed his kind's laugh once more. Then he asked, 'Did you ever find a site you thought would make a good shuttlecraft port?'

'None yet that satisfied me and Bunim both,' Nesseref replied. 'And anything near Glowno is also near the explosive-metal bomb you may have.' She chose those words with great care; she did not want him to reach for the rifle again.

'Tell me where you do decide to put the shuttlecraft port, and I will move the bomb close to it,' Anielewicz said, just as if he seriously meant to help.

'Thank you so much,' Nesseref said. 'Maybe it is the nature

of your reproductive patterns that makes you Big Uglies so full of deceit.'

'Maybe it is,' Anielewicz said. 'And maybe the Race will learn such deceit now, too.' And off he went, having got the last word.

Today, of course, Mordechai Anielewicz's legs decided to act up on him. He had to keep stopping to rest as he bicycled up to Glowno. Had he not breathed in that nerve gas all those years before, he would have been able to make the trip with ease. Of course, had he not breathed in that nerve gas, the Nazis might have touched off the atomic bomb with which he was presently concerned. In that case, he wouldn't be breathing at all at the moment.

He had radio and telephone codes warning the Jews who kept an eye on the bomb of an emergency. He hadn't used them. He hoped he wasn't making a mistake by not using them. He'd feared those warnings might be intercepted. If he brought the alert himself, it couldn't very well be. He didn't think Lizard commandos would rush the shed where the bomb lay hidden before he could get up to it. He wasn't sure they would rush it at all. But he'd run his mouth when he shouldn't have, and now he was paying the price in worry. And he wanted to be on the spot if the alarm came – that was the other reason he hadn't used his codes.

He dug his fingers into the backs of his calves, trying to loosen up the muscles there. The rest of him could be philosophical about breathing in nerve gas. His legs hurt. As if in sympathy, his shoulders started aching, too. Trying to rub one's own back was among the most unsatisfactory procedures ever devised.

Pain or no pain, he got rolling again. Ludmila Jäger lived with more discomfort every day than he felt when his aches and pains were at their worst. But, again, that was philosophy. It might spur him on, but didn't make his body feel any better.

Grunting, he leaned forward and put his back into the work.

No matter what he did, he couldn't recapture the ease of motion he'd known the last time he went up to Glowno. By the time he got to the small Polish town, he was about ready to fall off his bicycle.

Before he went to the shed where the bomb hid, he walked into a tavern to wash the dust of the road from his throat. 'A mug of beer,' he said to the Pole behind the bar, and set down a coin.

'Here you go, pal.' The fellow slid the mug to him without a second glance. He looked no more Jewish than the half dozen or so men already in the place. As usual, he had his Mauser on his back. Compared to them, he was underdressed. A couple of them wore crisscrossed bandoleers, giving themselves a fine piratical aspect. One had an old Polish helmet on his head, another a German model with the swastika-bearing shield on one side painted over.

'Yeah, we'll take it,' the tough in the Polish helmet said, knocking back some plum brandy. 'We'll take it, and we'll get it the hell out of here.'

One of his pals sighed. It might have been the sigh of a lover pining for his beloved. 'And when we've got it, *we'll* be the big shots,' he crooned.

Mordechai sipped his beer, wondering what sort of robbery the roughnecks were plotting. Finding out seemed a bad idea. They had a lot more fire-power than he did. He wondered how much cash the local bank held. Then he wondered if Glowno boasted a local bank.

'We'll be big, all right,' another ruffian said. 'And about time, too. The kikes will all burn in hell, but they act like cocks o' the walk here. Been going on too damn long, anybody wants to know.'

'Won't last forever,' said the first tough, the one with the helmet. 'As soon as they lose it and we get it, everybody's going to have to listen to us.'

After that, Anielewicz didn't think they were going to knock over a bank any more. He knew how Nesseref had found out the explosive-metal bomb was here: he'd talked too damn much. He had no idea how these Poles had found out, but how they'd found out didn't matter. That they'd found out did.

He finished the beer and slipped out of the tavern. The ruffians paid him no attention. They had no idea they'd said anything he might understand – or care about if he did. He looked like a Pole. If he knew what they were talking about, they'd figure he'd be cheering them on.

A lot of Poles would have cheered. The Lizards in Poland did lean toward the Jews. That was partly because the Jews had leaned toward them and against the Nazis in 1942. It was also because there were a lot more Poles than Jews; the Lizards got more benefit from supporting small faction against large than they would have the other way round.

Furthermore, Jews did not dream of an independent Poland strong enough to defy all its neighbors. Poles did. Anielewicz thought the dream a delusion even if the Poles got their hands on an explosive-metal bomb. They didn't, for which he could hardly blame them – except that they wanted *his* bomb.

His legs groaned when he got back on the bicycle. He didn't think the Polish nationalists could touch off the bomb even if they got it, but he didn't want to find out. He wasn't sure the Jews could touch it off, either. He didn't want to find that out any more than the other. Pulling down the Philistines' temple while he was in it had made Samson famous, but he never got to hear about it.

The shed in which the bomb was stored lay at, or rather just beyond, the northern edge of Glowno. Before the war, it had been attached to a livery stable. Livery stables, these days, were in no greater demand in Glowno than anywhere else. That part of town had taken damage in the fighting between the Nazis and the Poles, too, and then again in the fighting between the Nazis and the Lizards. Rubble and scrubby second growth surrounded the shed. There were only a couple of houses in the area, both owned by Jews. The Poles were just as glad the Jews had chosen an area where they didn't draw attention to themselves.

Anielewicz swung off his bicycle as soon as the poplars and birches and bushy plants of whose names he wasn't sure screened him from most of the town. 'Good thing you did that,' somebody remarked, 'or you'd have been mighty sorry you were ever born.'

That warning might have been in Yiddish, but Anielewicz had all he could do to keep from laughing out loud: it came straight from a U.S. Western film he'd watched the week before dubbed into Polish. He fought down the temptation to respond in kind. Instead, he said, 'How many guards can we get in a hurry, Joshua? We're about to be attacked.'

'*Oy!*' the unseen Jew said. 'There's Mottel and there's me, and we can get Pinkhas, I guess. Benjamin and Yitzkhak would be around, but their cousin got hit by a bus in Warsaw, so they're there.'

'Get everybody here, fast but quiet,' Mordechai ordered. 'Who's on the switch?' If that switch was tripped, the bomb would go up – if it could go up. Somebody always had to be ready to use it.

'You are, now,' Joshua answered. 'You know the bomb better than anybody, and—' He broke off. He'd undoubtedly been about to say something like, *and you'd have the nerve to do it*. Anielewicz didn't know if he would or not. One more thing he wasn't anxious to discover by experiment. After a moment, Joshua asked, 'How much time have we got?'

'I don't know, not exactly,' Anielewicz answered. 'I saw six Poles drinking in a tavern. I don't know how long it'll be before they do what they came to do. I don't know if they have any friends along, either.'

'It would be nice if you did know a few things,' Joshua remarked.

Ignoring that, Anielewicz picked his way up the twisting path to the shed. The wooden building looked weathered and sad. The two locks on the door seemed to have seen better days. Anielewicz opened them in the right order. Had he

407

unlocked the top one first, something unpleasant would have happened to him.

He went inside. It was dark and dusty in there; a cobweb caught in his hair. But the interior was very different from the exterior. Inside the rain- and sun-faded timbers the shed showed the world was reinforced concrete thick enough to challenge medium artillery. It had firing slits for a German-made machine gun; the MG-42 was at least as good a weapon as any the Lizards manufactured.

Also keeping Anielewicz company was the big crate that housed the bomb. He wondered what those half-dozen Poles would do with it if they got it. Did they think they could put it in their back pocket and walk off with it? That would need to be a big, sturdy pocket, considering the size and weight of the thing.

He supposed he should have been glad the Lizards weren't attacking. They would have known what they were doing, and would have come in overwhelming force. All the Poles knew was that the Jews had something they wanted. Back in the old days, that was all the Poles had needed to know. Things were different now, even if the nationalists hadn't figured that out.

'A good gun battle will teach them,' Mordechai muttered under his breath. But that wasn't the answer, either. With or without a gun battle, the bomb would have to leave Glowno now. That was obvious. One small hitch, though: how could it leave? Everyone would be watching the shed from now on.

Joshua came in, not through the door but up out of a tunnel that ran from somewhere in the middle of the rank second growth. 'People are posted,' he said. 'We'll give them more than what they want.'

'Good,' Anielewicz said. Sudden decision crystallized in him. 'You stay here. You can handle the detonator if you have to. I'm going to try to make sure you don't have to.'

Before Joshua could protest, Anielewicz opened the door – it was very heavy, but well balanced and mounted on strong hinges, so it swung easily – and stepped outside again. He stooped and picked up a rather rusty large nail or small spike from the dirt by the shed. Smiling a little, he went down the track and waited.

After about half an hour, his patience was rewarded. Here came the Polish nationalists, all of them with weapons at the ready. Mordechai stepped out into the open where they could see him. He held up the nail or spike so the head and a little of the shank protruded from his fist. 'Hello, boys,' he said in friendly tones. 'If I drop this, the bomb goes off. That means you want to be careful where you point those guns, doesn't it?'

One of the Poles crossed himself. Another one said, 'Christ, it's that bastard from the tavern. Damn him, he doesn't look like a Jew!'

'Life is full of surprises,' Anielewicz said, still bland. 'The last surprise you'll ever get, though, is how high you'll blow. If we Jews don't keep the bomb, nobody gets it, and that's a promise.'

If another band was heading for the shed from a different direction, none of this playacting would matter. But, by the way the Poles talked furiously among themselves, Anielewicz didn't think that was so.

A tough shook a fist in his direction. 'You damned Jews won't keep this thing forever!'

'Maybe not,' Mordechai answered. He thought it all too likely, in fact. They'd have to move the bomb and hide it again, which wouldn't be easy – it wasn't the simplest thing either to move or to conceal. But if they didn't, they'd face more raids, a stronger one from the Polish nationalists or one from the Lizards or the Nazis or even the Russians. He went on, 'But we've got it now, and you won't be the ones who get it away from us.'

A Pole raised a submachine gun and started to point it at him. Two of the fellow's pals slapped the weapon down again. They believed the nail was a dead-man switch. Slowly, sullenly, they withdrew. One of them shook his fist at Mordechai. Anielewicz made as if to wave with the hand holding the nail. That got all the Poles moving faster.

He allowed himself a sigh of relief. This raid had fizzled. He owed Nesseref a big thank-you for getting him worried about Glowno. He wondered if he'd ever be able to explain that to her. He doubted it. *Too bad*, he thought.

Vyacheslav Molotov looked at his leading advisors. 'Comrades, the Lizards have shown us a weakness we did not previously know they possessed. The question before us is, how can we most effectively exploit it?'

'It is not a military weakness, not in the strict sense of the words,' Georgi Zhukov observed. 'I wish it were, but it is not.'

'Why do you say that, Georgi Konstantinovich?' Molotov asked.

'Because the Lizards' military personnel are all males,' the Soviet marshal answered. 'A ginger bomb at a front would not send them into a mating frenzy, as there would be no females close by to incite.'

Lavrenti Beria smiled. 'Against the Lizards, ginger is *not* a military weapon – I agree with Georgi Konstantinovich. Rather, it is a weapon of terror, a weapon of subversion. I look forward to using it.'

Of course you do, Molotov thought. *Is that the smile you wear when you do dreadful things to a young girl?* He forced his mind back to the meeting. *And of course you agree with Zhukov. If ginger is a weapon of subversion, it is a weapon for the NKVD, not the Red Army. Zhukov was careless, to renounce it so fast.*

He turned to the foreign commissar. 'Has anyone learned who fired the missiles at the Lizards' Australian colony, Andrei Andreyevich?'

Gromyko sipped from a glass of sweet tea before shaking his head. 'No, Comrade General Secretary, not with certainty – or, if the Lizards know, they are holding the information tight against their chests.'

'Lavrenti Pavlovich?' Molotov asked. Beria had channels Gromyko lacked.

But the chief of the NKVD shook his bald head. 'Too many candidates. We did not do it; I know that. But the Nazis might have. The Americans might. And this is a more difficult problem than the massacre of the ships from the colonization fleet in orbit, because the British or the Japanese might also have done it.'

'In a way, I am glad we did not do it,' Molotov said. His colleagues nodded. All of them, even Beria, were at bottom prudes. Beria, Molotov suspected, got some of his vicious pleasure because of the strength of the rules he was breaking.

As Hitler had before him, Himmler made loud noises about the high moral tone of the Greater German *Reich*. Would that keep him from doing whatever he could to advance his interests? Molotov didn't believe it for a minute. The Americans and British were decadent capitalists, so they would have few moral scruples. And the Japanese Empire had never shown scruples of any sort. Sure enough, the field was wide open.

Zhukov said, 'For myself, I am sorry we did not think of it.' A leer spread over his broad peasant face. 'I would have paid money to watch all the Lizards screwing their heads off. Serves them right for laughing at us for so long.'

Gromyko took another sip from his glass of tea. 'It does disrupt them, as Lavrenti Pavlovich has said. But I wish whoever had this idea would have saved it till a critical moment instead of using it to make a nuisance of himself and no more.'

'Spoken like a good pragmatist,' Molotov said: high praise from him. He turned to Beria and Zhukov. 'Would the wreckage from the missiles have given the Lizards some clues as to who did this?'

'Comrade General Secretary, anyone who would launch his own missiles at the Lizards is such a fool, he would deserve to get caught,' Beria said.

'I agree,' Zhukov said, not sounding happy about agreeing with Beria on anything. 'But my colleagues in the Red Navy tell me it would not be so easy to fire a mongrel missile from a

411

submarine. If anything went wrong, the missile might explode in its launch tube, which would destroy the ship.'

'Boat,' Gromyko said. 'Submarines are called boats.'

'Submarines are toys for the devil's grandson,' Zhukov retorted. He muttered something else. Molotov's hearing wasn't what it had been; he didn't catch all of it. He did catch *boats* and *damned civilians* and a couple of new references to Satan's near relations.

Gromyko might have heard all of Zhukov's bad-tempered tirade, or he might have heard none of it. If he had heard, his face didn't know about it. He said, 'On the basis of geography, the Japanese are likeliest to be guilty.'

'Submarines are sneaky devils,' Zhukov said, apparently determined to disagree with the foreign commissar because Gromyko had presumed to correct him. 'The new ones, the ones with atomic motors, hardly need to surface at all. And even a diesel *boat*' – he gave Gromyko another sour look – 'with a breathing tube could be a long, long way from Australia before it had to fuel.'

However spiteful that was, it was also true. 'No evidence, then,' Molotov said. No one disagreed with him. He wished someone would have.

'Ginger bombs are not something over which the Lizards will start a war, as they would over atomic weapons.' Gromyko coughed. 'No one goes to war because he is made too happy.'

Beria chuckled at that. Zhukov remained grumpy. Molotov asked, 'Were the Lizards made so happy, they could not carry on? If happiness of that sort incapacitates them, they may well fight to prevent it.'

'I believe that to be so, Comrade General Secretary,' Beria said. 'Signals intercepts indicate that they feared nuclear missiles following on the heels of the ones loaded with ginger.'

Zhukov nodded. If he was annoyed enough at Gromyko to take Beria's side, Molotov would have to do something about that. Before he could speak, Zhukov added, 'Intercepts also indicate that the Lizards' fleetlord was in Australia during the ginger attack. That must have made them even jumpier than they would have been anyhow.'

'Are you certain?' Beria leaned forward. 'I have received no such reports.'

Zhukov looked smug. 'Sometimes military intelligence can do what ordinary spies cannot. This is why we have the GRU as well as the NKVD.'

Beria scribbled something on a notepad, then angrily tore off the sheet, ripped it to shreds, and threw it away. Molotov sat motionless. Inside, though, he was grinning from ear to ear. He hadn't even needed to turn Zhukov and Beria against each other; they'd taken care of it for themselves. *And a good thing, too,* he thought. Anything he could do to keep the Red Army and the NKVD at odds with each other, he would. And if he didn't have to . . . so much the better.

Gromyko coughed. 'In another matter, I have heard that there was an attempt to hijack the nuclear bomb the Jews are said to have in Poland. I am given to understand that it failed.'

'Too bad,' Molotov said insincerely.

'Not necessarily,' Zhukov said. 'Some of those Poles might want to use the bomb against us, not the Lizards.'

'That is an unpleasant thought,' Molotov said in the same tone of voice he'd used before. 'Even so, the greater the instability within Poland, the greater the advantages for us.' Everyone nodded at that. Molotov added, 'This merely proves the nationalists' incompetence. Knowing them to be ineffective is valuable for us. Were they better at what they do, they would be more dangerous.'

'Were they better at what they do, they would be Nazis,' Gromyko said.

Molotov nodded. 'Many of them would like to be Nazis. Many of them, in 1939, were even more reactionary than the Nazis. Spending a couple of years under German rule would have been a useful corrective for that. But they have been under Lizard control for a generation now: time enough to

413

forget such lessons. They will cause the Lizards trouble one day before too long, and that means they will also cause trouble for the Germans and us.'

'Then why,' Beria asked, 'did you authorize our operative to tell the nationalists where the Jews were hiding their bomb?'

Before answering, Molotov weighed the startled expression on Zhukov's face and the stony one on Gromyko's. Gromyko looked that stony only when concealing what he really thought. Here he was probably concealing horror. Molotov did not look toward Beria. Maybe the NKVD chief would prove smug, maybe he would manage to hold in what he was thinking. But, just as Molotov stirred up dissension among his advisors, so Beria was trying to rouse dissension against the General Secretary. Yes, Lavrenti Pavlovich wanted to follow Himmler to the top.

'Why?' Molotov said, letting none of that show in his face or his voice. 'Because I expected the reactionaries to fail and be discredited: a bomb like this early German model weighs a good many tonnes, and is not easy to move. And even if the nationalists did succeed in stealing it, they are likelier to use it against the Lizards or the Jews or the Nazis than against us. A small risk, I thought – and I was right.'

Zhukov relaxed. Gromyko went right on showing the world nothing. And Beria – Beria fumed. Like so many from down in the Caucasus, he had trouble holding on to his temper. Stalin had been the same way. Stalin, though, had been even more frightening. Molotov used Zhukov and Gromyko to check Beria. No one had been able to check Stalin, not in anything that really mattered.

Perhaps realizing he was checked now, Beria changed the subject: 'Comrade General Secretary, I am pleased to report that we have successfully delivered a sizable shipment of arms to the Chinese People's Liberation Army.'

'That is good news,' Molotov agreed. 'I am given to understand, however, that Mao's emissary to the United States still attracts a good deal of favorable notice in the American press, and that it is likely President Warren will try to get weapons through to the People's Liberation Army.'

'If you want her assassinated, I will see what I can do,' Beria said. 'Blaming it on the Lizards should not be too difficult.'

'Assassinations have dangerous and unpredictable consequences,' Gromyko said. 'They are a strategy of last resort, not one of first instance. The risks here outweigh the benefits.'

'How so?' Beria said defiantly.

'America can never have the influence in China we do,' the foreign commissar replied. 'Never, with geography as it is and politics as they are now. U.S. access to the mainland of Asia is too limited. The Japanese Empire and the Pacific Ocean prevent it from being anything else – especially when Japan has her own ambitions in China, which she does. We, on the other hand, can penetrate the Chinese frontier at any point of our choosing along thousands of kilometers. Let the Americans do the Lizards in China a little harm. It is all they can do.'

'A reasonable answer, I think, Lavrenti Pavlovich,' Molotov said. 'Your comments? Counterarguments?'

'Never mind.' Beria turned his head to glare at Gromyko. The chandeliers overhead made the lenses of his spectacles look like opaque golden ellipses to Molotov. *Yes, a barn owl*, Molotov thought. *That's what he reminds me of.* Gromyko looked back at Beria, imperturbable as always.

Molotov dismissed the meeting a few minutes later. He had a better sense now of what the Soviet Union should and should not try to do. He'd also kept his subordinates divided. As he lit a cigarette, he wondered which was more important.

13

'No, I'm sorry, Karen,' Major Sam Yeager said into the telephone, 'but I can tell you right now that Jonathan isn't going to be around tomorrow night. There's a reception scheduled downtown, and he's got to be there with Barbara and me.'

'Oh,' Karen said in a dull voice, and then, 'Is it another reception for these Chinese women? I'd thought they'd have gone home by now.'

'Not for a while yet,' Yeager answered, which, he realized too late, was probably more than he should have said.

'The one my age—' Karen began. After a moment, she sighed and said, 'I'd better go. I've got studying to do. Goodbye, Mr. Yeager.'

'Goodbye,' Sam said, but he was talking into a dead telephone. With a sigh of his own, he hung up. Sitting on the bed beside him, Barbara gave him a quizzical look. He shook his head. 'Karen's jealous of Liu Mei, that's what it is.'

'Oh, dear.' Barbara raised an eyebrow. 'Does she have reason to be jealous, do you think?'

'Why are you asking me? The one you need to ask is Jonathan.' Yeager held up a hasty hand. 'I know, I know – he'll say, "None of your business." I probably would have said the same thing when I was his age – but when I was nineteen, I was out on the road playing ball, making my own living.'

'Not so easy to do that nowadays,' Barbara said.

'No, especially if you can't hit a curveball,' Sam said, a little sadly. Jonathan wasn't a terrible sandlot player, but he'd never make a pro, not in a million years.

Barbara said, 'Maybe he is sweet on Liu Mei. You used to have to drag him to these receptions. Now he goes without any fuss, and the two of them do spend a lot of time together.'

'I know. Wouldn't that be something, though?' Yeager shook his head in slow wonder. 'Bobby Fiore's kid . . .'

'Who is half Chinese,' Barbara said with brisk feminine practicality. 'Who was raised in China – except when she was raised by the Lizards – who doesn't speak much English, and who's going back to China some time in the not too indefinite future.'

'You know all that,' Sam said. 'I know all that. Jonathan knows all that, too. Question is, does he care?'

He got another chance to find out the next evening, when he and Barbara and Jonathan piled into the Buick to go up to the reception at City Hall. The building dominated the Los Angeles skyline, being the only one permitted to exceed the twelve-story limit enforced from fear of earthquakes.

People still turned out to meet and be seen with Liu Han and Liu Mei: the local Chinese community, politicians, military men, and the kind of people Sam had come to think of as prominent gawkers. He'd been astonished to meet John Wayne at one of these bashes. Barbara's only comment was, 'Why couldn't it have been Cary Grant?'

Here and now, Sam got a drink, made a run at the buffet, and dutifully circulated through the crowd. If he ended up in a knot of men in uniform, that was no great surprise. The officers' wives formed a similar knot a few feet away.

After a while, Liu Han gave a little speech about how much China in general and the People's Liberation Army in particular needed American help. Her English was better than it had been when she got to the USA the summer before. When

417

she sat down, the mayor of Los Angeles got up and made a much longer speech covering the same points.

Actually, Sam only thought it covered the same points, for he soon stopped listening. Turning to the colonel next to him, he murmured, 'Sir, isn't there something against this in the Geneva Convention?'

The colonel snorted. 'We're not prisoners of war,' he said, and then paused. 'It does seem that way, though, doesn't it?'

'Yes, sir,' Yeager answered. 'And to think: I could be at the dentist's office now.'

That won him another snort from the colonel, a big, bluff fellow with pilot's wings and the rocket that showed he'd flown in space. 'You're a dangerous man – though not half as dangerous as the windbag up there.'

'He'll shut up sooner or later,' Sam said. 'He has to . . . doesn't he?'

Eventually, the mayor did descend from the podium. He got a heartfelt round of applause, and looked delighted. Sam shook his head. The damn fool couldn't tell the audience was cheering not because of anything he'd said but because he'd finally stopped saying it.

'That calls for a drink, Major,' the colonel said. 'I never thought we ought to get hazardous-duty pay for these affairs, but I may just change my mind.' He stuck out a hand. 'Name's Eli Hollins.'

Yeager shook it. 'Pleased to meet you, sir.' He gave his own name.

'Oh, the alien-liaison fellow.' Hollins nodded. 'I've heard of you. Read some of your reports, too. Solid stuff in there; I used pieces of it when I was talking with the Lizards up in orbit.' He cocked his head to one side. 'You get right inside 'em, seems like. How do you do that?'

A grin stretched across Yeager's face. He was no more immune to praise than anybody else. 'Thank you very much, sir,' he said. 'How? I don't know. You try to see things from a

418

Lizard's point of view, that's all. You see what makes him tick, and then reason from that the way he would.'

'You make it sound easy,' Hollins said. 'Any ten-year-old kid can fly a fighter plane – with about thirty years of practice.' He and Yeager finally made it through the crowd to the bar; after the mayor at last fell silent, a lot of people had decided they needed refreshing. Hollins ordered scotch for himself, then raised an eyebrow at Sam. 'What'll it be?'

'Let me have a Lucky Lager,' Yeager told the barkeep. Hollins covered both drinks. 'Thanks again, sir,' Sam said. 'Next round's mine.'

'That's a deal,' the flier said equably. He raised his glass. 'Confusion to the Lizards – may we cause plenty of it.'

'I'll drink to that,' Sam said, and did. 'And we do cause 'em plenty. We have, ever since they got here. They figured they'd be knocking over savages, but we were already geared up for a hell of a big war. They're still trying to figure that out. They'll be trying to figure it out ten thousand years from now. That's how they work: slow, patient, thorough.' He took another swig from his Lucky. 'I'm going on like His Honor.'

'Yeah, but there's a difference: you make sense, and he didn't.' Eli Hollins studied Yeager. 'The Lizards'll still be figuring us out ten thousand years from now – if we don't lick 'em first. Am I right or am I wrong?'

'Sir, you're right,' Sam answered. 'No question about it: you're right. Sooner or later, we'll have the edge on them. We come up with new things faster than they do, and they know it. Question is, do they give us the chance to use what we've got when we do start sliding past them?'

'Once we're ahead of them, they won't stop us.' Hollins had a fighter pilot's arrogance, all right. He was fifteen years younger than Yeager, too. That also probably had something to do with it.

Yeager said, 'If they think we can go after Home, sir, they're liable to try to wreck Earth, destroy us as a species. I know they've talked about it. They've seen how dangerous we are now, and they aren't stupid. They may have a better idea of where we'll be a hundred years from now than we do.'

'That's . . . interesting,' Hollins said. 'Cold-blooded little bastards, aren't they?'

'They don't want to do it,' Sam said. 'I think they're more squeamish about mass murder than we are. The Nazis' death camps almost made them turn up their toes. That's one of the reasons they'll go on hunting whoever blew up the ships from the colonization fleet till they catch 'em. I wouldn't want to be in Himmler or Molotov's shoes when that happens, either.'

'Makes sense to me.' Colonel Hollins finished his drink. 'But steer on back to what you were saying before, why don't you? If the Lizards are squeamish about mass murder, how come they're thinking about wiping out Earth?'

'I asked Straha about that once.' Sam looked around, but didn't see the shiplord here. 'What he said was, "If you have a leg with a cancer in it, sometimes you have to cut it off to save the body." ' Yeager paused for effect, then added, 'Can I get you that other drink now?'

'Don't mind if I do – don't mind if you do,' Hollins said, and Sam bought him another scotch. His own beer had some mileage left.

Sipping it, he looked around the City Hall reception room again. Barbara was talking with the mayor's wife. Maybe that didn't rate hazard pay; Sam hoped the lady was less dull than her husband. And Jonathan was having an animated conversation with Liu Mei. It was animated on his side, anyhow; her face never changed expression much.

Yeager turned back to Hollins; nobody in his family looked eager to flee, as sometimes happened. He polished off his beer, then said, 'I've been poking around a little, trying to see what I can find out. If I can whisper something into a Lizard's hearing diaphragm, maybe the Race will come down on the Russians or the Germans, and that'll be the end of it. Nobody will have to look over his shoulder any more, and nobody will ever try such a dumb stunt again.'

Hollins' voice was dry: 'Tell you what, Major – you tend to your knitting and let the Lizards tend to theirs.'

'Well, yeah, sure,' Sam said. 'Even Molotov's a human being. Even Himmler's a human being . . . I suppose. But I can think of a hell of a lot of Lizards I'd sooner have living next door to me than either one of them.'

'Damned if I'll argue with you there,' Hollins said with a chuckle, 'but there's a hell of a lot of *people* I'd sooner have living next door to me than those guys, too. Like all the rest of the human race, for instance.'

'That's true,' Sam admitted. 'Other thing is, though, the Lizards are sort of distracted right now. They're trying to decide what to do about ginger and what it does to their females. That'll keep them busy for a while, unless I miss my guess. I've been trying to lend a hand, you might say.'

'I don't know about a hand,' Colonel Hollins said. 'I'd give 'em a finger any old day, though.' Sam laughed. Hollins went on, 'Yeah, if sex won't distract you, I don't know what will. Here's hoping they stay distracted for a long time, too.'

'They may,' Yeager said. 'This isn't like anything they've run into before. The ginger bomb somebody threw at Australia showed how big a problem it could be. And just being horny from one day to the next is confusing the heck out of them.'

'Good,' Hollins said. 'We already drank to that once, remember? Let 'em stay confused. The more confused they are, the less time they have to go poking their snouts into our affairs. And that's what it's all about, Major.' He spoke with great certainty. Yeager got the idea he usually did.

'Yes, sir,' Sam said. It wasn't as if Hollins were wrong. If he came down a little hard for human beings, well, why not? He was one. So was Sam. He still wanted justice done on the human beings who had committed the perfectly human crime of murder by blowing up the ships of the colonization fleet.

Rance Auerbach looked toward the border between the United States and Lizard-held Mexico. 'I hear they've got dogs trained to sniff for ginger these days,' he said as Penny Summers eased the old Ford she'd bought one step closer to the checkpoint.

'Yeah, they've been doing that for a little while now,' Penny said. 'Just don't be a worrywart, okay? Whatever they've got, it doesn't keep the stuff out – and it won't keep this stuff out. Relax. Enjoy the ride.'

'You don't ask for much, do you?' Auerbach said. Penny laughed, but he hadn't been joking. She had more in the way of balls than he did. He wasn't ashamed to admit it. He'd been pretty much content to vegetate for years till she bounced back into his life. He didn't know what to call what he was doing now, but it wasn't vegetating. He was sure of that.

They crawled over the toll bridge from Rio Grande City south into Ciudad Camargo. The Mexican cops and customs men were working for the Lizards these days, but that didn't mean they liked *yanquis* any better than they had before. 'Purpose for coming here?' one of them demanded, pencil poised over a form.

'We're tourists,' Auerbach answered. Penny nodded.

'Ha!' the customs man said. 'Everyone who smuggles ginger, he says he's a tourist.' If he thought he could rattle the Americans, he was barking up the wrong tree. Penny had played these games before, and Rance didn't much care what happened to him. He leaned back in his seat and relaxed, as Penny had suggested.

Then the customs man whistled shrilly. Up came one of his pals, leading a female German shepherd on a leash. The dog sniffed all around the automobile. Auerbach's breath came short – but then, it always did. Penny hid whatever jitters she had by lighting a cigarette.

When the dog didn't start barking its head off, its handler led it away. The customs man waved the Ford forward. As soon as they were out of earshot, Penny turned to Auerbach and said, 'See? Piece of cake. If I'm not smarter than a damn Mexican dog—'

'Takes one bitch to outfox another,' Rance said. Penny hit him in the arm, a gesture half friendly, half angry. After a couple of seconds, she decided it was funny and laughed.

Ciudad Camargo was a pleasant little town nestled in a green valley. Lots of cattle and a few sheep grazed in that green valley. The town itself smelled powerfully of manure. The road paralleled the Rio Grande till it got past San Miguel, then went inland. Away from the river, the countryside stopped being pleasant and green and turned into a sun-blasted desert.

'No wonder the Lizards like it here,' Rance said, sweat pouring off him. 'Christ, it's worse than Fort Worth, and I didn't reckon anything could be.'

'It's hot, all right,' Penny agreed. 'But we're going looking for Lizards, after all. Aren't a whole lot of 'em in Greenland.'

'Just don't let the car boil over,' Auerbach said. 'I haven't seen any other traffic on this miserable road. If we get stuck here, buzzards are liable to pick our bones.' He looked up into the bake oven of the sky. Sure as hell, several broad-winged black shapes floated on the currents of hot air rising from the ground. They didn't have to work very hard to stay airborne, not in this weather.

'Don't worry about it,' Penny said, which was like asking him not to worry about the endless gnawing pain in his leg. She could ask, but that didn't mean she'd get what she asked for.

Smoking one cigarette after another, she drove south with assurance. Every so often, the Ford would go past a farm where a family tried to scratch out a living without enough land, water, or livestock. Back in the States, hardly anyone plowed with mules any more. Here, even having a mule looked to be a mark of some prosperity. Children stared at the battered old Ford as it went by. It was almost as alien to them as one of the Lizard's starships would have been.

A drunkenly leaning sign marked the border between the states of Tamaulipas and Nuevo Léon. The road ran into a bigger, better one running southwest from Reynosa. Penny turned onto that one. It went through a little town called

General Bravo, and then, on the eastern bank of a trickle called the San Juan River, an even littler one implausibly called China.

On the western bank of the San Juan sat a Lizard town, tiny and neat and clean, the buildings sharp-edged and perfectly white, the streets all paved, everything in perfect order. The Lizards went about whatever business they had. A couple of them might have turned an eye turret toward the American car. Most paid no attention to it whatever.

'That's new,' Penny said as she drove out of the Lizard town. 'They are settling down to stay, aren't they?'

'Yeah,' Rance said harshly. 'They'd be doing that on the other side of the Rio Grande, too, if we hadn't fought 'em to a standstill.' Peering back over his shoulder hurt, but he did it anyhow. 'Wonder if they've brought any crops from their planet that'll grow around these parts. Too early to tell; they haven't even been here a year yet.'

Penny looked over toward him – safe enough, with so little traffic on the road. 'You think of all kinds of funny things, don't you? I was just wondering how many Lizards in that place taste ginger.'

'That's sensible thing to wonder,' Auerbach said. 'I'm full of moonshine, that's all. You could have stopped and found out.'

He wasn't serious. Luckily for him, Penny knew it. 'Didn't want to take the chance,' she answered. 'Up ahead, I'll be dealing with Lizards I know. That's a lot safer – you bet it is.'

'Okay,' Auerbach said. 'I'm just along for the company.' He slid closer to Penny, reached under her pleated cotton skirt, and ran his hand up the inside of her thigh all the way to her panties.

She laughed. 'If a gal did that to a guy, he'd drive right off the damn road. We'll have plenty of time for games later, all right?' She sounded almost like a mother trying to keep a rambunctious little boy in line.

The Lizard air base and antiaircraft missile station sat in the desert about halfway between China and Monterrey. Unlike the new colonists' center, it had been there a long time; planes from it had undoubtedly flown against the United States during the fighting. The buildings were still neat and clean, but they'd lost something of that razor-edged look newer ones had. The comparison was easy to make, because some buildings close by *were* new.

'Colonists here, too.' Now Penny didn't sound so happy. 'I hope the Lizards I knew are still around. If they aren't, that complicates things.' She shrugged. 'Only one way to find out.'

She pulled the Ford to a stop next to one of the shanties of the little human hamlet that had grown up to serve the Lizards and the people who labored for them. When she got out, Auerbach did, too. The fellow behind the battered bar of what turned out to be a tavern looked up and addressed Penny not in Spanish or English but in the Lizards' language: 'I greet you, superior female. I have not seen you for too long.'

'I greet you, Estéban,' Penny answered in the same language. Auerbach followed it haltingly. She went on, 'I need to see Kahanass. Is he still here?' When the Mexican nodded, she broke into a grin. 'Can you get someone to tell him I am here?'

'It shall be done,' Estéban said, one phrase in the Lizards' language almost everyone understood. He shouted in Spanish. When a teenage kid stuck his head in the door, he sent him off. Then, to Rance's relief, he turned out to speak some English: 'You want beers?'

'Oh, Christ, yes!' Rance exclaimed. He sucked down a blood-temperature Dos Equis as if it were the nectar of the gods.

Before too long, the teenager came back, a Lizard in tow. 'I greet you, Kahanass,' Penny said. 'I have things you may want to see, if you have things you can give me.'

Kahanass wore the body paint of a radar operator. 'Truth?' he asked, another Lizard word with broad currency among humans. 'I did not expect you to come back here with things for me to see, but I will look at them. If I like them, I may have things to give you.' He swung an eye turret toward Auerbach. 'Who is this Tosevite? Have I seen him before? I do not think so. Can I trust him?'

'You can trust him,' Penny said. 'He and I have mated. He has killed my enemies.'

'It is good,' Kahanass said. 'Bring me these things, then, so I may look at them. If I like them . . .' His voice trailed away. People who bought and sold ginger spoke in circumlocutions. If someone was listening, if someone was recording, that made proving what they were up to harder.

'It shall be done.' Penny went out and opened the Ford's trunk, returning with a couple of suitcases.

Kahanass recoiled from them. 'Phew! What is that horrible stink?'

'Lighter fluid,' she answered in English. The Lizard evidently understood, for he didn't ask her to explain. She went on, 'It keeps the animals from smelling whatever else is inside. None of it got on whatever else is inside.' She opened a suitcase. 'You can tell that for yourself, if you like.'

Kahanass took a taste. He hissed with pleasure. 'Yes!' He used an emphatic cough. 'Yes, I shall have things. I shall indeed. You wait here. Estéban has a scale. He will weigh out these things and weigh out the pay.'

'It shall be done,' Penny said as the Lizard hurried out of the tavern. She turned to Auerbach. 'You see, sweetheart? No trouble at all.'

'Yeah.' Rance nodded. For the first time, Tahiti started to look real to him. He thought about island girls not overly burdened with clothing. A man could get used to that, even if he didn't do anything but watch. And if he did . . . well, if he was careful, odds were he could get away with it.

Estéban took a scale out from under the bar and set it on the counter. It looked like the balances Rance had used in chemistry classes at West Point. Penny nodded at it. 'We're gonna be a while, weighing all I got on those litty bitty scales.'

'That's okay,' Rance said expansively. 'We haven't got

anywhere more important we're supposed to be.' With money or gold or whatever the Lizards paid in straight ahead, all they had to do was get back across the border and into the USA again. And that was the easy part; as a general rule, folks didn't smuggle things into the United States from Mexico, but rather the other way around.

Penny looked out the window. 'Here he comes back again,' she said. 'Boy, he didn't waste any time there, did he? He wants some for himself, and he'll sell the rest.'

'Sounds good to me,' Auerbach agreed.

In came Kahanass. 'I will pay gold at the usual rate,' he said. 'Is it good?'

'Superior sir, it is very good,' Penny said.

That was when things went to hell. A couple of Lizards with rifles burst into the tavern behind Kahanass. 'You are prisoners!' they shouted, first in their own language and then in English. Three more burst in from a back entrance behind the bar. They also yelled, 'You are prisoners! Do not move, or you are dead prisoners!'

Kahanass cried out in horror. Rance's hand started to slide toward the waistband of his trousers. It didn't get more than an inch or two before it froze. Unlike the bruisers in his apartment, the Lizards didn't take him for granted. If he pulled out a pistol, they'd plug him.

He wondered what had gone wrong. Had the Lizards been watching Kahanass? Or had some of Penny's former friends tipped them off that she might be going into business for herself? He glanced over to her. Her face was set and tense. Like him, she'd looked for a chance to fight and hadn't seen any. He shrugged, which hurt. 'Well, babe, so much for Tahiti,' he said, which hurt even worse.

When her telephone rang these days, Monique Dutourd flinched. Calls were all too likely to be from people with whom she didn't want to talk. But she had to answer anyhow, on the chance things would be different this time. *'Allô?'*

'Hello, Monique,' came the quiet, steady voice on the other end of the line. She sighed. As if she didn't know that voice better than she wanted to, it continued, '*Ici* Dieter Kuhn. I have an interesting story to tell you.'

'I don't want to hear it,' she snapped. 'I don't want to hear from you at all. Don't you understand that?'

'It is relevant,' the SS man said. 'You would be well advised to listen to me.'

'Go ahead, then,' Monique said tightly. Kuhn could have done much worse than he had. She kept reminding herself of that. No doubt he wanted her to remind herself of that. If she terrorized herself, she did his work for him. She understood as much, but couldn't help the fear.

'*Merci,*' Kuhn said. 'I want to tell you about the inventiveness of a certain Lizard.' Monique blinked; that wasn't what she'd expected. The German officer went on, 'It seems a certain female recently agreed to taste ginger and come into season so males could mate with her – provided they first transferred funds from their credit balances to hers.'

It needed a moment to sink in. When it did, Monique blurted, '*Merde alors!* The Lizards have invented prostitution!'

'Exactly,' Kuhn said. 'And what one has thought to do, others will think of before long. This will make the problem they face from ginger even worse than it is already. It will make the pressure on your brother even worse than it is already. He remains uncooperative, you know.'

'There's nothing I can do about it,' Monique answered. 'If you don't know that, you should. He doesn't care whether I live or die.' In a way, saying that wounded her. In a different way, her words were like a paid-up life-insurance policy. If Pierre didn't care what happened to her, and if the SS knew he didn't care, they wouldn't have any incentive to start carving chunks off her.

'Unfortunately, I believe you have reason,' Dieter Kuhn said. 'Otherwise, we might have made the experiment by now.'

She did not, she would not, let him know he had frightened

her. 'If that is all you have to say, you wasted your time calling,' she told him, and hung up.

But going back to work after a call like that was almost impossible. The Latin inscriptions might have been composed in Annamese, for all the sense they made to Monique. And whatever she had been on the point of saying about them had gone clean out of her head. She cursed Kuhn both in standard French and with the rich *galéjades* of the Marseille dialect.

Having done that, she spent a while cursing her brother. If he'd chosen a more reputable profession than smuggler, she wouldn't be in trouble now. With a sigh, she shook her head. That probably wasn't so. She might not be in this particular trouble right now. She would probably be in some other trouble. Trouble, her whole life argued, was part of the human condition – and an all too prominent part, at that.

She went back to the inscriptions. They still didn't mean much. The Lizards thought humans very strange because the past of less than two thousand years before was different enough to be of interest. Almost all their history was modern history: history of well-known beings who thought much like them.

The knock on her door came two nights later. She was brushing her teeth, getting ready for bed. At that sharp, peremptory sound, she had to grab desperately to keep from dropping the glass. The Nazis did not let late-night knocks appear in books or films or televisor or radio plays. Such silence fooled no one Monique knew. The knock came again, louder than before.

Monique thanked heaven that she hadn't yet changed into her night-clothes. Still in the day's attire, she kept a shred of dignity she would have lost. Even so, she went to the door as slowly as she could. Had she not been sure the SS men outside would kick it in, she would not have gone at all.

She opened it. Of course none of the neighbors had come out to see what the racket was; they would be glad it wasn't *their* racket. To her surprise, there in the hallway stood neither

Dieter Kuhn nor his friends in field-gray uniforms and black jackboots but a dumpy, middle-aged Frenchman in baggy trousers and a beret that sat on his head like a cowflop.

'Took you long enough,' he grumbled in accents identical to her own.

Despite that, she needed a moment before she realized who he was, who he had to be. 'Pierre!' she whispered, and grabbed him by the arm and pulled him inside. 'What are you doing here? Are you out of your mind? The *Boches* will be watching this place. They may have microphones in here, and—'

'I can find out about that.' Her brother took from a pocket a small instrument of obvious Lizard manufacture. He used a pencil point to poke a recessed button. After a moment, a light at the end glowed amber. 'Unless the Germans have come up with something new, they aren't listening,' he said. 'For the love of God, Monique, how about some wine?'

'I'll get it,' she said numbly. She poured a glass for herself, too. When she brought the wine back from the kitchen, she stared at the brother she hadn't seen in two-thirds of a lifetime. He was shorter than she remembered, only a few centimeters taller than she. Of course, she'd been shorter the last time she saw him.

He was looking her over, too, with a smile she thought she remembered. 'You look like me,' he said, his voice almost accusing, 'but on you it looks good.' He glanced around the flat. 'So many books! And have you read them all?'

'Almost all,' she answered. A lot of people who saw the crowded bookshelves asked the same question. But then she gathered herself and asked a question of her own: 'What are you doing here? When we talked on the telephone, you wanted nothing to do with me.'

'Times change,' he answered, resolutely imperturbable. He had, no doubt, seen a lot of changes. With a shrug, he went on, 'You must know what ginger does to female Lizards, *n'est-ce pas?*'

'Yes, I know that,' Monique said. 'If you will recall' – she could not resist letting her voice take on a sardonic edge – 'I was here when the SS man warned you the Lizards in authority would be more upset about your trade than you thought.'

'So you were.' No, Pierre was not easy to unsettle. In that, though Monique did not think of it so, he was very much like her. He went on, 'Kuhn is not stupid. If the Nazis were stupid, they would be much less dangerous than they are. If they were stupid, we would have beaten them in 1940. Instead, we were stupid, France was stupid, and see what it got us.' Almost as an aside, he added, 'The trouble with the Nazis is not that they are stupid. The trouble with the Nazis is that they are crazy.'

'And what,' Monique inquired, 'if you would be so kind as to inform me, is the trouble with the Lizards?'

'The trouble with the Lizards, my dear little sister?' Pierre Dutourd finished his wine and set the glass on the table in front of him. 'I should think that would be obvious. The trouble with the Lizards is that they are here.'

Startled, Monique laughed. 'So they are. But would we be better off if they were not? The Nazis – the crazy Nazis – could have conquered the whole world by now, and then where would we be?'

'Trying to get along, one way or another,' Pierre answered. 'That is all I ever wanted to do. I did not intend to become a smuggler. Who grows up saying, "I, I shall become a smuggler when I am a man"? I was working in a café in Avignon when it became clear the male Lizards were mad for ginger. I helped them get it and' – a classic Gallic shrug – 'one thing led to another.'

'What do you want from me?' Monique asked. 'You still have not told me that.'

'If I go home . . . if I go to any of the places I might call home, I believe I will end up slightly dead,' her brother answered with what was, under the circumstances, commendable aplomb. 'As you will have gathered, the Lizards are less than happy with me and others in my trade right now. If they get their tongues on what I sell, then they are happy, but that is a different matter.'

'Do you want help from the Germans, then?' Monique asked. 'I don't know how much I can do. I don't know if I can do anything.'

'Even though you are so fond of this Kuhn?' Pierre said. He sounded serious, damn him.

Monique was serious, too, and seriously furious. 'If you weren't my brother, I'd throw you out of here on your arse,' she snapped. 'I ought to do it anyway. Of all the things you could have said—'

'It could be that I do not have reason here,' Pierre said. 'If I am mistaken, I can only apologize.'

Before Monique could answer, someone else knocked on her door. This knock was soft and casual. It could have come from a friend, even a lover. Monique didn't think it did. By the way he stiffened, neither did Pierre. His hand darted into a trouser pocket and stayed there. Monique said, 'For what may be the first time in the history of the *Reich*, I hope that is the SS out there.'

'Yes, that is a curiosity, isn't it?' her brother agreed. 'Well, you had better find out, hadn't you?'

She went to the door and opened it. Sure as sure, there stood Dieter Kuhn, bold as the devil. Behind him were three uniformed SS men, all carrying submachine guns. 'May I come in?' he asked mildly. 'I know who your company is. I assure you, I shall not be jealous.'

Too much was happening too fast. Monique stood aside. The SS men tramped into her flat and closed the door behind them. One spoke in German to Kuhn: 'Now we do not have to look as if we captured you, Herr *Sturmbannführer*.' Monique's spoken German was rusty but functional.

'*Ja,*' Kuhn agreed. 'But if I came here in uniform, Professor Dutourd's reputation among her neighbors would suffer.' He shifted back to French as he turned toward Pierre Dutourd: 'We meet at last. Your scaly friends are less friendly now than they used to be. Did I not predict this?'

'Sometimes anyone can be right,' Pierre replied. 'But yes,

there are leading Lizards who want me out of the business I have been in.'

'We do not want you out of business,' Kuhn said. 'We want you to go right on doing what you have been doing. Is this not agreeable to you?'

'Doing it under your auspices,' Pierre said glumly.

'But of course.' The SS man was cordial, genial.

'It must be that you don't understand,' Monique's brother said. 'I had grown used to being free. I am one of the few people in the *Reich* who was.'

'You were one of the few people who was,' Kuhn returned, genial still. 'But there is a difference between what you call unfreedom and what the *Reich* can call unfreedom. If you care to experience that, I assure you I can arrange it.' He nodded to his tough-looking henchmen. Monique's heart leapt into her throat.

But Pierre sighed. 'One does what one can do. One does only what one can do. Without you and without the Lizards, I cannot go on. Since the Lizards seem in a bit of a temper for the time being, I must place myself in your hands.' He sounded anything but overjoyed.

With the airtight door to his quarters shut, Ttomalss felt safe and secure. The Race had included such doors to the embassy in Nuremberg because the Deutsche were so proficient at manufacturing poisonous gases. But, when closed, the doors also kept out the females' pheromones that had cast the Race into so much confusion.

Ttomalss wished he could stay in there and never come out. He had psychological training; he understood the concept of wanting to return to the egg. Most of the time, such desires were pathological. Here, though, he had solid practical reasons for viewing the outside world as a source of peril.

Had he so desired, he could have gone to the computer to find out how many of the workers at the embassy were females. The computer, unfortunately, could not tell him how many of those females tasted ginger. More did so every day, though; he was sure of that. And when they tasted, and for a while after they tasted, they went into their season.

And the pheromones they released stayed in the air, and excited any male who smelled them. Ttomalss, having almost fought the Race's ambassador to the *Reich*, did not care to brawl again. Nor did he care for the half addled feeling even a thin dose of pheromones gave him. His eye turrets kept swinging this way and that, searching for ripe females who, frustratingly, were not there. And he had trouble thinking straight; the desire for mating kept clouding his mind, distracting him, teasing him.

His mouth fell open in a bitter laugh. Veffani had said the mating season would be sweet, back there at the start when Ttomalss and the ambassador both coupled with Felless for the first time. Veffani was a clever, cultured male, but seldom had any member of the Race made a greater blunder on Tosev 3.

At the computer, Ttomalss struggled once more with the problem the Deutsche posed the Race: not so much in the sense of physically endangering it, although this not-empire was dangerous, but in ideological terms. He could not grasp how and why intelligent, capable individuals would subscribe to what appeared to him to be such obvious nonsense. The Race had been grappling with that since the arrival of the conquest fleet, and grappling in vain.

He examined Felless' notes on her talk with Eichmann and his own interview with the Big Ugly called Höss. They were consistent with other data the Race had compiled on the *Reich*. The Deutsche, all evidence to the contrary notwithstanding, remained convinced they were genetically superior to other Tosevites; that the Deutsch word *Herrenvolk* translated as *Master Race* hatched endless sardonic mirth among Ttomalss and his fellows.

That the Deutsche put their theory into practice by attempting to exterminate those they judged genetically inferior had puzzled and horrified the Race ever since it came to Tosev 3. The government of the *Reich* had not changed its policy in all that time, either. The only reason its exterminations had slowed was the increasing scarcity within its borders of members of the proscribed groups.

Ttomalss dictated a note for the computer to record: 'Recent interviews confirm that one reason the Deutsche have been able to succeed with their policy of extermination is the equally relentless policy of euphemism they use in connection with it. Big Uglies tend to focus on words as opposed to actions to a greater degree than is common among the Race. If they conceive themselves to be "carrying out a final solution" rather than "killing fellow Tosevites of all ages and sexes," they do so without worrying about the truth behind the screen of words. A male or female of the Race, if faced with such a prospect, would be likelier to go mad.'

But the Tosevites are mad to begin with, he thought. Nevertheless, he left the note unrevised. No one – certainly no one among the Race – could argue against the madness of the Deutsch not-empire. Unfortunately, no one could argue against the success of the Deutsch not-empire during the time just before and after the arrival of the Race, either.

What did that combination of success and madness mean? The most obvious answer was, a quick end to success. Pundits among the Race had been predicting that for the Greater German *Reich* ever since its noxious nature became obvious. So far, they'd been wrong. Anyone who chose anything obvious pertaining to Tosev 3 seemed doomed to disappointment.

He had just thought of something new to add to the note when the door hissed for attention. Whatever the thought was, it fled for good. He cursed in mild annoyance, then turned on the exterior microphone to ask, 'Who is it?'

'I: Felless,' came the reply from the corridor.

Ttomalss felt like jumping out the window. Unfortunately, he would have bounced off it instead; it was made from an armored glass substitute. 'Superior female, have you tasted ginger during the past day?'

'I have not,' Felless said. 'I swear by the Emperor.'

'Very well.' Ttomalss cast down his eyes in automatic respect undimmed by living so long on Tosev 3. 'You may enter.' He hit the control that opened the door. 'If you are lying, we shall both regret it.'

As soon as Felless had come into the room, Ttomalss closed the door behind her. Not much air from the corridor could have come in with her, but he still got a whiff of pheromones. For a bad moment, he thought they were hers, and that she had lied to him. Then he realized he did not smell them strongly enough to send him into the full frenzy of the season, only enough to make him jumpy and edgy and acutely aware she was a female, where in normal times he would have ignored the sex difference.

'I greet you, superior female,' he said, as dispassionately as he could.

'I greet you,' Felless returned. Then she pointed. 'The scales of your crest are trying to rise. I am *not* in my season now.'

With an effort of will, Ttomalss was able to make the offending scales lie flat. He did his best to quell the turmoil he could not help feeling. 'No doubt it is someone else's pheromones I smell, then, superior female,' he said. 'And how may I help you today?'

Part of what he meant was, *Could you have sent me a message and not disturbed me by coming in person?* The pheromones had not – quite – addled him enough to make him say that out loud.

If Felless understood the subtext of the question, she gave no sign of it, which was probably just as well. She said, 'I want to discuss with you the ideology of the Deutsch Big Uglies as it relates to their policy of massacring other groups of Tosevites of whom, for whatever obscure reasons, they fail to approve.'

'Ah,' Ttomalss said. 'As it happens, I was just recording a few notes on that very topic.' She'd made him forget what he was going to say next, too, but he was not so pheromone-addled as to tell her that, either.

'I should be grateful for your insights,' Felless said, sounding more like a working member of the Race and less like a female in heat than she had for some time. Maybe she really was fighting the urge to taste ginger.

'Insights?' Ttomalss shrugged. 'I am far from sure I have any of significance. I do not pretend to be an expert on the Deutsche, only a student of Tosevites in general who is attempting with limited success to apply that general knowledge to a particular situation more unusual than most.'

'You do yourself too little credit,' Felless said. 'I have heard males speak of Tosevites with unusual insight into the Race. I think your experience in rearing Big Ugly hatchlings makes you the converse to these.'

'It could be so. I had hoped it would be so,' Ttomalss answered. 'But I must confess, I am still puzzled by Kassquit's reaction on learning you and I had mated.' He'd spent a good deal of the time since that unfortunate telephone conversation trying to repair the bond he had formerly established with the Tosevite fosterling. He remained unsure how far he had succeeded.

Felless said, 'Mating, as I have been forcibly reminded of late, is not a rational behavior among us. Things relating to it must be even less subject to rational control among the Big Uglies.'

'Now that, superior female, is an insight worth having,' Ttomalss said enthusiastically. 'It shows why you were chosen for your present position.' It was, in fact, the first thing he'd noted that showed why Felless was chosen for her present position, but that was one more thing he did not mention.

'You flatter me,' Felless said. As a matter of fact, Ttomalss *did* flatter her, but she offered the sentence as a conversational commonplace, and so he did not have to rise to it.

He had just finished recording Felless' remark when the computer announced he had a telephone call. He started to

437

instruct it to record a message, but Felless motioned for him to accept it. With a shrug, he did. The computer screen showed a familiar face. Kassquit said, 'I greet you, superior sir.'

'I greet you, Kassquit,' Ttomalss said, and waited for the sky to fall: she would be seeing not only his image but also Felless'.

To make matters worse, Felless added, 'And I greet you, Kassquit.'

'I greet you, superior female,' Kassquit said in tones indicating she would sooner have greeted the female researcher as pilot of a killercraft equipped with tactical explosive-metal missiles.

'What do you want, Kassquit?' Ttomalss asked, hoping he could keep the conversation short and peaceful.

'It was nothing of great importance, superior sir,' the Tosevite he'd raised from a hatchling replied. 'I see that you are busy with more important matters, and so will call back another time.'

Had he taught her to flay him with guilt in that fashion? If he hadn't, where had she learned it? She reached for the switch that would break the connection. 'Wait!' Ttomalss said. 'Tell me what you want.' Only later, much later, would he wonder if she had moved more slowly than she might have, to make him beg her to stay on the line.

'It shall be done, superior sir,' she said now, and even her obedience wounded. 'I was wondering if you, in the capital of the Deutsch not-empire, could hope to have any influence over the smuggling of the illegal herb ginger through the territory of the Greater German *Reich*.'

'I do not know,' Ttomalss said. 'The Deutsche, like other Tosevites, have a habit of ignoring such requests. They would doubtless want something from us in exchange for acting otherwise, and might well want something we do not care to yield to them.'

'Still, the notion might be worth considering,' Felless said. Ttomalss had studied Kassquit for a long time. He knew her expressions as well as anyone of a different species could.

This was, he thought, the first approval Felless had won from her.

Lieutenant Colonel Johannes Drucker looked from his fitness report to Major General Walter Dornberger's face. 'Sir, if you can explain to me why my marks have slipped from "excellent" to "adequate" in the past year, I would appreciate it.'

That that was all he said, that he didn't scream at Dornberger about highway robbery struck him as restraint above and beyond the call of duty. He was, he knew perfectly well, one of the best and most experienced pilots at Peenemünde. A fitness report like this said he'd stay a lieutenant colonel till age ninety-two, no matter how good he was.

Dornberger didn't answer at once, pausing instead to light a cigar. When the base commandant leaned back in his chair, it squeaked. Unlike some – unlike many – in high authority in the *Reich*, he hadn't used his position to aggrandize himself. That chair, his desk, and the chair in front of it in which Drucker sat were all ordinary service issue. The only ornaments on the walls were photographs of Hitler and Himmler and of the A-10, the A-45's great-grandfather, ascending to the heavens on a pillar of fire, soon to come down on the Lizards' heads.

After a couple of puffs and a sharp cough, Major General Dornberger said, 'You should know, Lieutenant Colonel, that I was strongly urged to rate you as "inadequate" straight down the line and drum you out of the *Wehrmacht*.'

'Sir?' Drucker coughed, too, without the excuse of tobacco smoke in his lungs. 'For the love of God, why, sir?'

'Yes, for the love of God,' Dornberger said, as if in a story by Edgar Allan Poe. 'If you think along those lines for a moment, a possible explanation will come to you.'

A moment was all Drucker needed. 'Käthe,' he said grimly, and Dornberger nodded. Drucker threw his hands in the air. 'But she was cleared of those ridiculous charges!' They weren't so ridiculous, as he knew better than he would have liked. He chose a different avenue of attack: 'And it was thanks to your good offices that she was cleared, too.'

'So it was,' the commandant at Peenemünde said. 'And I called in a lot of markers to do the job. I had enough pull left to keep from throwing you out in the street, but not enough to let you keep rising as you should. I'm sorry, old man, but if you haven't learned by now that life isn't always fair, you're a luckier fellow than most your age.'

One of the things Drucker had on his record – the one he bore in his head and heart, fortunately not the one that went down on paper – was joining with the rest of his panzer crew in murdering a couple of SS men in a forest near the Polish-German border to let their colonel and commander go free. As long as that old crime remained undiscovered, he was ahead of the game. That made the present injustice easier to tolerate, though not much.

With a sigh, he said, 'I suppose you're right, sir, but it still seems dreadfully unfair. I'm not that old, and I had hoped to advance in the service of the *Reich*.' That was true. Considering what the *Reich* had done to him and tried to do to his family, though, he wondered why it should be true.

If it weren't for the Reich*, we would all be the Lizards' slaves today*. That was also likely to be true. *So what?* Drucker wondered. He'd always set the personal and immediate ahead of the broad and general. Maybe, because he'd done that, he didn't deserve to make brigadier, or even colonel. But that would have been a real reason, not the put-up job Dornberger was forcing on him.

'I can give you a consolation prize, if you like,' the base commandant said. Drucker raised a skeptical eyebrow. Dornberger said, 'You will fly more this way than you would have had you gone on to promotion.'

Rather to his own surprise, Drucker nodded. 'That's true, sir. Only a consolation prize, though.'

'Yes, I understand as much,' Dornberger said. 'But there are people in Nuremberg who are not at all fond of you. That you have come away with a consolation prize is in a way a victory. It is for you now as it was for the *Reich* and the Soviet Union and the United States at the end of the fighting: we kept what we had, but had to yield what we were not directly holding.'

'And we have been plotting ever since to see what sort of changes to that arrangement we can make,' Drucker said. 'Very well, sir, I will accept this for now – but if you think I will stop trying to change it, you are mistaken.'

'I understand. I wish you all good fortune,' Major General Dornberger said. 'You may even succeed, though I confess it would surprise me.'

'Yes, sir. May I please have the report back?' Drucker said. Dornberger pushed it across the desk to him. Drucker took a pen from his breast pocket and filled out the space on the form reserved for the evaluated officer's comments with a summary of the reasons he thought the report inadequate. Nine times out of ten, ninety-nine out of a hundred, that section of the form stayed blank even on the worst fitness reports. It was universally regarded as being the space where an officer could give his superiors more rope with which to hang him. Having already been hanged, Drucker did not see that he had anything left to lose.

When he finished, he passed the report back to Major General Dornberger. The base commandant read Drucker's impassioned protest, then scrawled one sentence below it. He held up the sheet so the A-45 pilot could see: *I endorse the accuracy of the above. W.R.D.*

That took nerve, especially in view of the pressure to which he'd partially yielded when he wrote the fitness report. 'Thank you, sir,' Drucker said. 'Of course, most likely the report will go straight into my dossier with no one ever reading it again.'

'Yes, and that may be just as well, too,' Dornberger said. 'But now you are on the record, and so am I.' He glanced toward a framed photograph of his wife and children on his desk, then added, 'I wish I could have gone further for you, Drucker.'

He said no more, but Drucker understood what he meant. If he hadn't yielded to at least some of the pressure, he might never have seen his family again. Even major generals could prove little more than pawns in the game of power within the *Reich*. Drucker sighed again. 'It shouldn't be this way, sir.'

'Maybe it shouldn't, but it is. Sometimes we do what we can, not what we want.' Dornberger took out another cigar. 'Dismissed.'

'*Heil* Himmler!' Drucker said as he rose. The words tasted like ashes in his mouth. He saluted and left the commandant's office.

Outside the office, outside the administration building, Peenemünde bustled on as it had for the past twenty years and more. A breeze blew in from the Baltic, full of the odors of mud and slowly spoiling seaweed. Somewhere along the barbed-wire perimeter of the base, a guard dog yelped excitedly. It was, Drucker knew, more likely to have seen a stray cat than a spy.

Everything at Peenemünde was camouflaged as well as German ingenuity could devise, not so much against spies on the ground as against satellite reconnaissance. Many of the buildings weren't buildings at all, but dummies of cloth and boards. Some of those even had heaters burning inside, to make them appear as they should to infrared detectors. And all the real buildings were elaborately disguised to seem like nothing but pieces of landscape overhead.

In a way, all that ingenuity was wasted. If the Lizards – or, for that matter, the Bolsheviks or the Americans – ever decided to attack Peenemünde, they weren't likely to be clinical about it. An explosive-metal bomb would wreck camouflaged and uncamouflaged alike . . . although some of the reinforced-concrete installations underground would stand up to anything but a hit right on top of them.

Drucker shook his head. Everything here was as it had been. Only he'd changed. No, even he hadn't changed. It was only that the *Reich* had just told him his adult lifetime of service to his country didn't amount to a pile of potatoes. That hurt. He'd never dreamt how much it would hurt.

Officers of junior grade and enlisted men still stiffened to attention and saluted as he went past. They didn't notice any changes: as far as they were concerned, a lieutenant colonel remained a figure of godlike authority. His mouth twisted. Eventually, he would be saluting some of them, for his place in the firmament was fixed now, while they might keep on rising.

Drizzle started falling, which perfectly suited his mood. He strode on through the base. A couple of A-45s stood at their gantries, in different stages of preparation for launch. Drucker nodded toward them. They were, in a way, the only friends he had left at Peenemünde. Major General Dornberger's fitness report, as the commandant pointed out, did leave him clear to keep going into space. That was something: less than he would have liked, but something.

He gave the immense rockets another nod. In an odd way, they looked less futuristic than the old A-10s – vengeance weapons, Hitler had called them. A-10s had had the sharp noses and graceful curves everyone in the pre-Lizard days had thought necessary for rocket ships. The A-45s were simple cylinders, the upper stages as blunt-nosed as Bavarians. Blunt noses had more area with which to absorb the heat of atmospheric friction; cylinders were easier and cheaper to manufacture than the fancier chunks of sheet metal that had flown in the early days.

Drucker sighed. Here as elsewhere, reality proved less romantic than dreamers had thought it would be. He shook his head. Maybe things would have been better had the Lizards never come. With the Russians beaten and rolled back across the Urals, the *Reich* would have had all the *Lebensraum* it needed to show what it could do in Europe. Maybe he and Käthe and the children, instead of living near here, would be growing wheat or maize on the boundless plains of the Ukraine today.

A moment later, the daydream turned to nightmare. The SS

could have plucked her off the plains of the Ukraine as readily as from Greifswald. As a simple farmer, he wouldn't have had friends in high places. They'd have shot her or thrown her in a gas chamber. He'd kept that from happening in the real world. If he was upset at the fitness report's wrecking his chances for further promotion, how would he have felt with Käthe liquidated?

That thought spawned another one, a blacker one. Liquidating Käthe for having a Jewish grandmother struck Drucker as outrageously unjust, but that was because he knew her and loved her. What about other people with one Jewish grandparent? Was liquidating them just? What about people with two Jewish grandparents? What about people with three? With four? What about people who were out-and-out Jews?

Where did you draw the line?

The *Reich* drew it at one Jewish grandparent. That left Käthe in danger and her children safe. Drucker hadn't been able to see the sense in it. Would there have been more sense in drawing it at two Jewish grandparents? That would have left Käthe safe, but . . . Was there any sense in liquidating *anybody* because he was Jewish or partly Jewish?

The *Reich* thought so. Up till the trouble over Käthe, Drucker hadn't thought much about it one way or the other. Now . . . Now he remembered that Colonel Heinrich Jäger, for whom his elder son was named, for whom he'd helped murder a couple of SS *Schweinhunde*, had never had anything good to say about such massacres.

He'd helped Jäger disappear into Poland with that pretty Russian pilot, and never heard of or from him since. Now, solemnly, he turned to the east – the southeast, actually – and saluted. 'Colonel,' he said, 'I think you may have been smarter than I was.'

Fotsev strode into the administrative offices of his barracks complex. A clerk looked up from his computer screen. 'Name and pay number?' the male asked. 'Purpose for coming here?'

'Purpose for coming here is to report before commencing three days' leave, superior sir.' Fotsev put what was uppermost in his mind first. That done, he gave the clerk his name and the number that separated him from every other Fotsev ever hatched.

After entering the name and pay number into the computer, the male gave the affirmative hand gesture. 'Your leave is confirmed: three days,' he said. 'Will you be going into the new town?'

'Of course, superior sir,' Fotsev answered. 'I have been away from Home, and from the way life was on Home, for a very long time now. I look forward to being reminded of it. From what other males have said, the new town is the best antidote possible for the mud and the stinks and the mad Tosevites of Basra.'

'I have heard the same,' the clerk said. 'My leave time has not yet come, but it is approaching. When it arrives, I too shall go to the new town.' He pointed out the door. 'The shuttle bus leaves from there. It should arrive very soon.'

'I thank you.' Fotsev knew where the shuttle bus left. He knew when, too. With barracks cleverness, he had timed the beginning of his leave to spend as little time as he could manage waiting for transportation.

As usual, the bus rolled up on time. Had it been late, he would have suspected Tosevite terrorism. Being late through inefficiency was a failing of the Big Uglies, not the Race. Fotsev and a small knot of similarly canny males waited for the fellows returning from leave to descend, then filed aboard.

With a rumble, the bus – of Tosevite manufacture, and so noisy and smelly and none too comfortable – rolled off down the new highway leading southwest. Big Ugly farmers grubbing in their fields would sometimes look up as it passed. Before long, though, it left the region river water irrigated and entered more barren country that put Fotsev in mind of Home. The plants that did grow here were different from the ones he'd

445

known before going into cold sleep, but not all that different, not from the window of a bus.

He twisted, trying to find as comfortable a position as he could. After a while, he wrestled a window open, and sighed with pleasure as the mild breeze blew across his scales. This was the weather the Race was made for. With the Big Uglies and their noxious city and their even more noxious habits and superstitions fading behind him, he was ready to enjoy himself until he had to return to unpleasant, mundane duty.

'Look!' Another male pointed. 'You can see the ships of the colonization fleet ahead in the distance. There is a sight to make a male feel good.'

'Truth!' Several troopers spoke at the same time. A volley of emphatic coughs rang through the bus.

'They were smart,' Fotsev said. 'They gave the ships and the new town a good safety zone, so the local Tosevites will have a hard time sneaking up on them and doing anything frightful.' The converse of that was, all three independent Tosevite not-empires doubtless had explosive-metal-tipped missiles aimed at the ships and the town. But Fotsev chose not to dwell on the converse. He was on leave.

He thought about tasting ginger, but decided to wait till he got to the new town. Since finding out what the herb did to females, officers had acted like males with the purple itch. The driver was too likely to be watching for that sort of thing.

'No pheromones in my scent receptors,' another trooper remarked. 'Such a relief to feel normal again, not to have mating in the back of my mind all the time. I can think straight again.'

Not one of the other males argued with him. Several voiced loud agreement. Fotsev didn't, but he didn't think the fellow was wrong, either.

The ships from the colonization fleet dwarfed the buildings of the new town, even the taller ones, so those buildings didn't come into view till the males on the bus had seen the ships for some little while. When Fotsev spied the buildings, he let out a

446

hiss of pleasure. 'By the Emperor,' he said softly, 'it really is a piece of Home dropped down onto Tosev 3.'

With a squeal of brakes, the bus stopped in the middle of the new town. The driver said, 'You males have yourselves a good time.'

'How can we help it?' Fotsev said as he descended from the bus and rapturously stared this way and that. With every motion of his eye turrets, he catalogued new marvels. Paved streets. Better yet – clean paved streets. Buildings like the practical, functional cubes he'd known from hatchlinghood till the day when, in a Soldiers' Time, he was made a soldier. Males and females of the Race strolling those streets and going into and out of those buildings. No guards, or at least no obtrusive ones. Perhaps best of all, no Big Uglies.

He sighed with delight. As he inhaled afterwards, he caught the pheromones of a distant female. She'd surely been tasting ginger. He sighed again, on a different note: half stimulation, half resignation. He shouldn't have been surprised the chief vice for the Race on Tosev 3 had reached the new city, but somehow he was.

After a moment, he laughed at himself, a laugh full of mockery. He'd brought ginger here himself, to help make the leave more pleasant. If he'd done it, other males had done it. If other males had done it, some of the new colonists would have got ginger by now. And half those colonists, more or less, were females.

Instead of tasting as soon as he found a quiet place, as he'd intended, he strolled along the streets, looking into shop windows. Restaurants and places to drink alcohol were open and doing well. So were the establishments of males and females who sold services: physicians, brokers, and the like.

Few manufactured goods were yet on sale. After a moment, Fotsev corrected himself about that. Few goods manufactured by the Race were yet on sale. Factories hadn't had a chance to start producing. He did see Tosevite goods for sale, imported

447

from one or another of the not-empires whose technical standards were higher than those prevailing around Basra.

He made a discontented noise. He wouldn't have wanted to watch a Tosevite televisor, even if the Big Uglies had borrowed, or rather stolen, the technology from the Race. On the other fork of the tongue, if it was a choice between a Tosevite televisor and none, as it would be for a while . . . He made another discontented noise. If the Big Uglies could manufacture televisors more cheaply than the Race, what would the males and females who would have made them do? That was not a problem the colonization fleet would have worried about before leaving Home. As far as anyone knew then, the Big Uglies had no manufacturing capacity.

If only it were so, Fotsev thought. He'd had too many painful lessons about what the Tosevites could do. And he hadn't had a particularly hard time of it, not as the fighting went. Other males told stories much worse than any he had.

Still, thinking about what he'd seen over the years since the conquest fleet arrived was enough to tempt him to reach for one of the vials of ginger he carried in his belt pouch. With a distinct effort of will, he checked himself. He'd have time later. He wouldn't have tasted back on Home, and he was trying his best to pretend he was there now.

What would he have done? He would have gone and drunk some distilled potation. He could do that here, easily enough. He strolled into one of the places that sold such potations.

As per custom immemorial, it was dark and quiet inside. What light there was suited his eyes better than the somewhat harsher glare of the star Tosev. Several males from the new city sat on chairs and stools, talking about work and friends, as they would have back on Home.

Fotsev walked up to the server. The bottles behind the male were all of Tosevite manufacture. Fotsev supposed he shouldn't have been disappointed. As with realizing ginger had reached the new town, he was. He gave the server his account card. 'Let me have a glass from that one there,' he said, pointing to the drink he wanted. 'I have had it before, and it is not bad.'

The server billed his card, then gave him the drink. The price he had to pay for it disappointed him, too. He could have got the like from a Big Ugly in Basra for half as much in barter. He'd heard the local Tosevites' superstition forbade them from drinking alcohol, but had seen little proof of it.

But some of the things he was paying for here were a room that suited his kind and getting away from the Big Uglies. He raised his glass in salute. 'To the Emperor!' he exclaimed, and drank.

'To the Emperor,' the server echoed, and cast down his eyes, as he should have done. Then, after reading Fotsev's body paint, he said, 'I would have thought you soldiers would forget the Emperor after so many years on this miserable planet.'

'That could never happen,' Fotsev said with an emphatic cough. 'If I do not remember him, spirits of Emperors past will forget me when I die.'

'How can you males of the conquest fleet remember anything?' the server asked. 'Everything on this world seems topsy-turvy; nothing is the same from one moment to the next.'

'Truth there,' Fotsev agreed.

A female sitting at the table not far away turned an eye turret toward him. 'How could you of the conquest fleet not give us a properly conquered planet?' she demanded. 'Too many of these wild Big Ugly creatures are still running their own affairs, and even the ones that are supposed to be conquered are not safe. That is what everyone keeps shouting at us, anyhow.'

'Those creatures turned out not to be what we thought they were,' Fotsev answered. 'They were much more advanced than we expected, and are still more advanced today.'

'When the conquest fleet came, they were less advanced than we are,' the server said. 'Is that truth, or is it not?'

'It is,' Fotsev began, 'but—'

'Then you should have defeated them,' the server broke in, as if the continued independence of some Tosevites were Fotsev's fault and his alone. 'That you failed speaks only of your own incompetence.'

'Truth,' the female said, and a couple of her companions made the affirmative hand gesture. 'We came here to a world that was not ready for us, and whose fault is that? Yours!'

Fotsev finished his alcohol, slid off his seat, and left the establishment without another word. He had already seen that the colonists had a hard time fitting in when they came to Basra. But he'd never imagined the reverse might be true, that he might have a hard time fitting in when he came to the new town.

Tosev 3 had changed him. Tosev 3 had changed every male in the conquest fleet. The males and females of the colonization fleet remained unchanged. They might have been on Home yesterday. And he did not fit with them. What did that say? Nothing he wanted to hear. He took out the ginger after all, and had a big taste. With the herb coursing through him, he didn't have to listen, whatever it was.

14

'**S**orry, Lieutenant Colonel.' The first lieutenant with whom Glen Johnson was speaking couldn't have been much more than half his age, but the fellow's voice held brisk assurance. 'No can do. Personally, I'd say yes, but I have my orders, and they leave me no discretion.'

'Pretty funny orders,' Johnson said. 'All I want to do is pilot one cargo flight up to the space station and have a look around. I'm cleared for the controls – I'd better be; they're a lot simpler than *Peregrine*'s. So what's the trouble about putting me into the rotation during a stretch when I'm not patrolling? It's not like I charge overtime.'

'Of course not, sir.' The lieutenant smiled to show what a good, patient, understanding fellow he was. 'But you must know rotations are made up some time in advance, and are not casually revised.'

'What I know is, I'm getting the runaround,' Johnson said. The immovable young lieutenant looked hurt. Johnson didn't care. He went on, 'What I don't know is why.'

He didn't find out, either. The lieutenant sat there, prim and proper as a nineteenth-century Midwestern schoolmarm. Johnson muttered something about his ancestry, just loud enough to let him hear. He turned red, but otherwise did not change expression. Johnson muttered again, louder this time, and stalked out of the air-conditioned office.

Even early in spring, even so close to the coast, humidity made his shirt cling to him like a hooker who'd just spotted a C-note. Something bit him on the wrist: one of the nasty little gnats the locals called no-see-ums. He slapped and cursed. He sure hadn't seen this one.

'When the going gets tough,' he muttered, 'the tough get . . . plastered.' He wasn't so sure about getting plastered, but damned if he couldn't use a drink. Getting one seemed a far better idea than going off to his sterile little cubicle in the bachelor officers' quarters and brooding.

In the bar, he spotted Gus Wilhelm. After snagging a scotch on the rocks, he sat down next to his friend. 'What are you doing here?' Wilhelm said.

'I might ask you the same question, especially since you were here first,' Johnson answered.

'Sun's got to be over the yardarm somewhere,' Wilhelm said. 'And besides, it's air-conditioned in here.' He eyed Johnson. 'Looks like you could use the cool even more than me. If that's not steam coming out of your ears, I've never seen any.'

'Bastards,' Johnson muttered, and gulped down half his drink.

'Well, yeah, a lot of people are,' Wilhelm said reasonably. He let very little faze him. 'Which bastards are you talking about in particular?'

'The ones who don't want to let me go up there and have a look at our space station,' Johnson answered. He could feel the scotch; he didn't usually drink before noon. 'I'm a taxpayer, dammit. Christ, I'm even a taxpayer with a security clearance. So why won't they let me fly a load up there?'

'Ah,' Gus Wilhelm said, and nodded wisely. 'I tried that not so long ago. They wouldn't let me go, either.'

'Why the hell not?' Johnson demanded.

Wilhelm shrugged. 'They wouldn't say. C'mon, sir – if they started telling people why, what kind of service would this be?'

Before Johnson could respond to that, another officer came into the bar: a large, good-looking, easygoing fellow who wore his brown hair as long as regulations allowed, and then maybe half an inch longer. He was one of the pilots who regularly took loads up to the space station. Johnson waved to him, half friendly, half peremptory. 'Over here!' he called.

Captain Alan Stahl peered his way, then grinned and nodded. 'Let me grab myself a beer, sir,' he said, his accent balanced between Midwest and South: he was from St. Louis. After corralling the Budweiser, he ambled over to the table where Johnson and Wilhelm were sitting. 'What can I do for you gents?'

'Leave me out of it,' Wilhelm said. 'I'm just here to drag the bodies away.'

Stahl gave him a quizzical look. 'How much of a start have you got on me?'

Instead of answering that, Johnson asked a question of his own: 'What are you bus drivers hauling up to the space station, anyhow, that makes it so precious ordinary working stiffs like me can't get a peek come hell or high water?'

Stahl's open, friendly face closed like a slamming door. 'Now, sir, you know I'm not supposed to talk about that,' he said. 'I don't ask you how you run your business. Isn't polite to ask me how I run mine, especially when you've got to know I can't answer.'

'*Why* the devil can't you?' Johnson snarled. He didn't like being balked. Nobody who had the temperament to climb into the cockpit of a fighter plane took well to frustration. But Alan Stahl didn't give him anything else; he just sipped his Bud and kept his mouth shut.

Gus Wilhelm put a hand on Johnson's arm. 'You may as well give it up. You aren't going to get anywhere.'

'Well, what the hell are people hiding up there?' Johnson said.

'Sir, if more people know, the Lizards are likelier to know, too,' Stahl said. 'And now I'm talking too much, so if you'll excuse me—' He gulped down his beer, nodded – he was always polite – and hurried out of the bar.

453

'Well, you spooked him,' Wilhelm remarked.

'I already said once, I'm a taxpayer with a security clearance,' Johnson said. 'What am I going to do, step into a telephone booth and call the fleet-lord? Radio whatever the hell I find out down to a Lizard ground station next time I ride *Peregrine*? Not too damn likely, I don't think.'

'Oh, a lot of security's nothing but nonsense – I know that as well as the next guy,' Wilhelm answered. 'But you might say some little thing to somebody, and he might say something to somebody, and on down the chain, and somewhere down there whatever you said might bounce off a Lizard's hearing diaphragm. And you're sure as hell a taxpayer, but maybe your security clearance isn't high enough for whatever's going on upstairs.'

'A bus driver like Stahl knows, and I don't?' That wasn't fair to the other pilot, but Johnson was in no mood to be fair.

'Give it up,' Wilhelm said again. 'That's the best advice I've got for you. Give it up. If you don't, you're going to end up in more trouble than you can shake a stick at. If Stahl reports you, you may be there already.'

'Screw him,' Johnson muttered, but he did his best to calm down; he knew it was good advice, too. He thought about buying himself another drink, then decided not to. If he got smashed now, or even high, he would end up in trouble. He could feel it, the way fellows with old wounds or broken bones could feel bad weather before it happened.

When Johnson got to his feet without another word and without waving to the bartender, Gus Wilhelm let out a not quite silent sigh of relief. Wilhelm misunderstood. Johnson hadn't given up – far from it. But, plainly, he couldn't do any more here and now. His friend knew no more than he did, and wasn't curious. The bird who did know something had flown the coop.

Deciding he ought to do something useful with his time, Johnson went over to the big hangar where *Peregrine* was being fixed up between flights. He shot the breeze with the technicians, examined the latest pieces of modified equipment they were installing, and shot the breeze some more. Some of the modifications were undoubted improvements; others looked to be change for change's sake.

'All right,' he said, 'it's a digital clock, not one with hands. Is it more accurate?'

'Not so you'd notice,' the fellow who'd installed it answered cheerfully. 'But the numbers are supposed to be easier to read.' Johnson wasn't convinced, but didn't see how the new clock would do any lasting harm, either. He held his peace.

After lunch, he did go back to his cubicle. He was rereading *The War of the Worlds* and reflecting, not for the first time, that Wells' Martians would have been a hell of a lot easier to lick than the Lizards when somebody knocked on his door. He stuck a three-by-five card in the book to keep his place and got up off the bed to see who it was.

His visitor had three stars on his shoulder straps. Johnson stiffened to attention; the Kitty Hawk base commandant was only a major general. He hadn't known any higher-ranking officer was on the base. He couldn't imagine why a lieutenant general wanted to see him.

The officer in question, a bulldog-faced fellow whose name tag read LeMAY, didn't keep him in suspense for long. He stabbed out a stubby forefinger and tapped Johnson in the chest, forcing him back a pace. 'You have been asking questions,' he growled in a voice raspy from too many years of too many cigarettes.

'Sir! Yes, sir!' Johnson replied, as if back in Parris Island boot camp. Gus Wilhelm had warned he might get into trouble. Gus hadn't dreamt how much trouble he might get into, or how fast. Neither had Johnson.

'You have been asking questions about things that are none of your business,' Lieutenant General Curtis LeMay said. 'People whose business they are told you they were none of yours, but you kept on asking questions.' That forefinger probed again. Johnson gave back another pace. One more and he'd be backed up against the bed. LeMay strode after him. 'That's not smart, Lieutenant Colonel. Do you understand me?'

'Sir! Yes, sir!' Johnson had to work to keep from shouting it out, as he would have to a drill instructor. Rather desperately, he said, 'Permission to ask a question, sir?'

'No.' The lieutenant general turned even redder than he had been. 'You've already asked too goddamn many questions, Johnson. That's what I came here for: to tell you to button your lip and keep it buttoned. And you will do it, or you will regret it. Have you got that?'

For a moment, Johnson thought LeMay was going to haul off and belt him. If the lieutenant general tried that, he resolved, the lieutenant general would get a hell of a surprise. But LeMay mastered himself and waited for an answer. Johnson gave him the one he wanted: 'Sir! Yes, sir!'

Still breathing hard, LeMay rumbled, 'You'd damn well better.' He turned and stomped out of the BOQ.

'Jesus.' Glen Johnson's legs didn't want to hold him up. Facing his furious superior was harder than going into battle had ever been. It was as if one of his own wingmen had started shooting at him along with the Lizards. 'What the hell have I stumbled over?' he muttered as he sank down onto the bed.

Whatever it was, Gus Wilhelm had been dead right: it was a lot more secret than his security clearance could handle. The United States trusted him to fly a spacecraft armed with explosive-metal missiles. What didn't his own government trust him to know? If he tried to find out, he was history. Curtis LeMay had made that more than perfectly clear. *Crazy,* he thought. *Absolutely goddamn crazy.*

'Where to, Shiplord?' Straha's Tosevite driver asked him as he got into the motorcar.

'Major Yeager's, as you no doubt know already,' the ex-shiplord replied. 'I have had the appointment for several days.' The driver said nothing, but started the motorcar's engine. He put the machine in gear and rolled away from Straha's house in the Valley.

Yeager lived in Gardena, a toponym presumably derived from the English word *garden*. The place did not look like a garden to Straha, though Yeager had told him fruit trees grew there before houses went up. It looked like most other sections of Los Angeles and the surrounding suburbs. As for the toponym *Los Angeles* . . . Straha did not believe in angels, even in Spanish, and never would. When he imagined winged Big Uglies, he imagined them flying through the air and voiding on the heads of the Race down below. Tosevites would find that sort of thing very funny. That he might find it funny himself only meant he'd been associating with Tosevites too long.

'Wait for me,' he told the driver as the motorcar pulled to a stop in front of Major Yeager's home. He knew it was an unnecessary order as soon as he gave it, but, though he commanded no one any more, he still liked to see things clawed down tight.

'It shall be done,' the driver said, and took out a paperbound book. The cover showed an intelligent being unlike any with which Straha was familiar. Seeing Straha's eye turrets turn toward it, the driver remarked, 'Science fiction.' In the language of the Race, it would have been a contradiction in terms. But Straha remembered that Yeager was also addicted to the stuff, and claimed it had helped give him his unmatched insight into the way the Race thought. Straha reckoned that one more proof of how strange the Big Uglies were.

'I greet you, Shiplord,' Yeager said as Straha came to the door. 'The two emissaries from the Chinese People's Liberation Army will be coming in an hour or so. I hope you do not mind.'

'Would it matter if I did?' Straha asked before remembering his manners: 'I greet you, Major Yeager.'

Not directly answering the exile's bitter question, Yeager said, 'I hoped you might be able to tell them useful things

457

about how the Race conducts itself, things they could take back to their homeland with them. They will be returning soon.'

'It is possible,' Straha said. 'I do not claim it is likely, but it is possible. And what shall we discuss before these other Big Uglies arrive?'

'Come into the study,' Yeager said obliquely. 'Make yourself comfortable. Can I get you alcohol? Can I get you ginger?'

'Alcohol, please – rum.' Straha used an English word. 'Ginger later, perhaps. I have been trying to cut back on my tasting lately.' He hadn't succeeded, but he had been trying.

'Rum. It shall be done.' Yeager attended to it. He had some himself, with cubes of ice in it. Straha did not care for drinks so cold. After they had both sipped, the Tosevite asked, 'And have you heard anything new about who might have attacked the ships of the colonization fleet?'

'I have not,' Straha answered, 'and, I admit, this perplexes me. You Big Uglies are not usually so astute in such matters. The incentive here, of course, is larger than it would be in other cases.'

'Yes, I would say so,' Yeager agreed. 'Whoever did it, the Race will punish – and whoever did it deserves to be punished, too. I wonder if your contacts with males – maybe even with females now, for all I know – in the occupied parts of Tosev 3 had brought you any new information.'

'As far as who the culprit may be, no,' Straha said. 'I have learned that one of the ships destroyed carried most of the specialists in imperial administration. Whether the guilty party knew this in advance or not, I cannot say. My sources cannot say, either. I would be inclined to doubt it, but am without strong evidence for my doubt.'

'I think you are right. The attack came too soon for Tosevites to have known such details about the colonization fleet – I believe,' Major Yeager said. 'But it is an interesting datum, and not one I had met before. I thank you, Shiplord.'

'You are welcome.' Straha drank more rum. Another minor treachery to his kind. After so many larger acts of treason, one more was hardly noticeable.

Yeager did not scorn him as a traitor, not where it showed. He did not think Yeager scorned him at any deeper level. The Big Ugly was too interested in the Race in general to do anything of that sort: one more part of his character that made him so unusual.

Before too long, the Chinese Tosevites came. Yeager introduced them as Liu Han and Liu Mei. They spoke the language of the Race fairly well, with an accent different from the American's. Straha noted that Yeager's son, who had paid little attention to his own arrival despite fascination with the Race, joined the group and made polite conversation for a time after the new Big Uglies arrived.

From their voices, both of them were female. Did Jonathan Yeager find one of them sexually attractive? If so, which? After a while, Straha remembered that Liu Mei was Liu Han's daughter. Since Jonathan was younger than Sam Yeager, that made him more likely to be interested in Liu Mei – or so Straha thought. The subtleties of Tosevite behavior patterns were lost on him, and he knew it.

Presently, Sam Yeager spoke in English: 'Enough chitchat – time to talk turkey.' Straha didn't follow the idiom, but Jonathan evidently did, for he left. Liu Mei stayed. Maybe that meant she didn't find him attractive. Maybe it meant she put duty above desire, which Straha found admirable. Or maybe it just meant the exiled shiplord didn't fully grasp the situation.

Liu Han said, 'Shiplord, how do we best use ginger against the Race?'

'Give it to females, obviously,' Straha answered. 'The more females in season, the more addled males become.'

'I understand this,' the Chinese female said – was that impatience in her voice? 'How to give ginger to females over and over to keep males addled all the time?'

'Ah,' Straha said. Liu Han did see the obvious, then; the ex-shiplord hadn't been sure. He went on, 'Introducing it into food or drink would do the job, I think. They might not even know they were tasting . . . No, they would, because they would come into their season.'

'Truth,' Liu Han said. 'This endangers those who prepare food for the Race; they would naturally be suspect.'

'Ah,' Straha said again. 'Yes, that is so.' He hadn't thought the Big Uglies would care; they hadn't seemed to worry much about spending lives during the fighting.

'If we could get enough females and males excited at the same time, it might be worth the risk,' Liu Mei said: maybe the Tosevites, or some of them, retained their ruthlessness after all.

Jonathan Yeager came back into the study. Did the younger female's voice draw him, as pheromones would have drawn a male of the Race? 'That could get a lot of people hurt,' he observed. He might be interested in Liu Mei, but was not addled by her; Straha heard reproof in his voice.

'It is war,' Liu Mei said simply. 'Here, the fighting is over. You Americans have won your freedom. In China, the struggle against the imperialism of the Race goes on. The People's Liberation Army shall free my not-empire, too.'

'And make it as free as the SSSR?' Straha inquired with sarcasm he thoroughly enjoyed. 'That is the model the People's Liberation Army uses, is it not?'

Sam Yeager whistled softly. Straha had learned Big Uglies sometimes did that when they thought someone had made a good point. But Liu Han said, 'We would be freer under our own kind at their worst than the Race at their best, for we did not choose to have the Race come here and try to set itself over us.'

Straha leaned forward. 'Now there is a topic on which we could have considerable debate,' he said, anticipating that debate. 'If you believe that—'

Several loud pops resounded outside, followed by a fierce, ripping roar. Straha was slower to recognise the noise than he should have been; as shiplord, he'd had no experience with close combat. Before he could react, Sam Yeager spoke in English: 'That's gunfire. Everybody down!'

Straha dove for the floor. Yeager did not follow his own order. He grabbed a pistol from a desk drawer in the study and hurried out toward the front of the house. 'Be careful, Sam,' his wife called from the next room.

More gunfire sounded from the direction of the street. A window – or maybe more than one – shattered. Yeager's pistol resounded, the noise shockingly loud indoors. Liu Han came as close to taking the shots calmly as anyone could – closer than Straha was doing, for that matter. Liu Mei never seemed to get excited about anything. And Jonathan Yeager, though he had no weapon, hurried to his father's aid.

'It's over,' Sam Yeager called from the front room. 'I think it's over, anyhow. Barbara, call the cops, not that half the neighborhood hasn't already. Jesus, I can't afford new window glass, but we sure as hell need it.'

Barbara Yeager came in and picked up the telephone. Straha went out into the front room to see what had happened. His driver was coming toward the house, an automatic weapon in his hand. 'Is the shiplord all right?' he shouted.

'I am well,' Straha answered.

'He's fine,' Yeager said at the same time. 'What the devil happened out there?'

'I was sitting in the car, reading my book,' the driver answered. 'The guy who drives for the Chinese women was in the car behind me, doing whatever he was doing. A car came by. A couple of guys leaned out the window and started blazing away. Lousy technique. I think I may have nailed one of them. Thanks for the backup, Yeager.'

'Any time,' Sam Yeager said. 'You okay?'

'Right as rain,' Straha's driver answered. 'The Chinese guy, though, he took one right in the ear, poor bastard. Never knew what hit him, anyway.'

Through the howls that Tosevite constabulary vehicles used

to warn others out of their way, Yeager said, 'Whom were they after? The shiplord? The Chinese women? Could have been either one.'

Someone trying to kill me? Straha thought. He hadn't imagined Atvar could sink so low. Assassination was a Tosevite ploy, not one the Race used. *No,* he thought. *Not one the Race had used.* Maybe Atvar was able to learn some unpleasant things from the Tosevites after all.

'Either one's possible,' his driver said. 'And how about you, Major? Got any people who aren't fond of you?'

'I didn't think so,' Yeager said slowly. 'It'd be a real kick in the teeth finding out I was wrong. The shiplord and the Red Chinese are a lot more important targets than I'll ever be, though.'

'Yeah, you're right,' Straha's driver agreed, adding, 'No offense.'

While Sam Yeager yipped Tosevite laughter, Straha stared out at the dead Big Ugly in the motorcar behind his own. *That could have been me,* he thought, with a chill worse than any Tosevite winter. *By the Emperor whom I betrayed, that could have been me.*

Back at the Biltmore Hotel after endless questioning by American policemen and others from the FBI (which Liu Han thought of as the American NKVD), her daughter asked, 'Were those bullets meant for us or for the scaly devil?'

'I am not sure. How can I be sure?' Liu Han answered. 'But I think they were meant for the little devil. Can you guess why?' She sent Liu Mei an appraising glance.

Her daughter considered that with her usual seriousness. 'If the NKVD had sent assassins after us, they would not have made such a poor attack.'

'Exactly so,' Liu Han answered, pleased. 'The Russians do not attempt assassinations. They assassinate.'

'But' – Liu Mei sounded abashed at disagreeing, as a good daughter should, but disagreed nonetheless – 'what about the

Kuomintang or the Japanese? They might have sent killers after us, too, and theirs would not be so good as the ones Beria could hire.'

'I had not thought of them for a while,' Liu Han admitted in a small voice. 'Next to the Russians, everything else seemed such a small worry, I forgot about it. But that was a mistake, and you are right to remind me of it.' She grimaced. 'No one will remind Frankie Wong of it, not now.'

'No,' Liu Mei said. 'He helped us.'

'Yes, he did,' Liu Han said. 'He did not do it out of the goodness of his heart – I am certain of that. But he did help us, even if he was helping himself and maybe others at the same time. But his wife is a widow tonight, and his children are orphans. And now they have reason to hate us, too. A bad business, oh, a very bad business.'

'The Americans were brave when the shooting started,' Liu Mei said. 'They knew just what to do.'

'Major Yeager is a soldier,' Liu Han replied, a little tartly. 'His job is to know what to do when shooting starts.' She glanced over at her daughter out of the corner of her eye. 'Or were you thinking of his son?'

Liu Mei did not look flustered. Liu Mei's face had trouble holding any expression. But she sounded troubled as she answered, 'The father had a gun. The son had none, but went forward anyhow.'

'He went to aid his father,' Liu Han said. 'That is what a son should do. It is what a daughter should do for a mother, too.'

'Yes, Mother,' Liu Mei said dutifully. Less dutifully, she went on, 'Will we be able to go outside this hotel again, now that assassins are loose?'

'I do not know the answer to that,' Liu Han said. 'In part, it will be up to the Americans. I do not know if they will want to take the chance.'

'Why should they worry?' Liu Mei's voice was expressive, even if her face was not. She sounded bitter now. 'China cannot harm the United States. The People's Liberation Army cannot conquer America – the People's Liberation Army cannot even conquer China. We are not the little scaly devils, or even the Russian or German foreign devils. The Americans will not be very worried about letting us go into danger.'

She was probably right. That did not make her words any more pleasant for Liu Han to hear. 'Mao would think well of you,' Liu Han said at last. 'You see things in terms of power.'

'How else?' Liu Mei sounded surprised. Liu Han was surprised to hear that in her daughter's voice, but realized she shouldn't have been. She herself had been involved in the revolutionary struggle since before she'd managed to liberate Liu Mei from the scaly devils. That meant Liu Mei had been involved in the revolutionary struggle for as long as she could remember. No wonder she thought in those terms.

'I hope the assassins were after the little scaly devil,' Liu Han said, tacitly yielding the earlier point to her daughter. 'I also hope the Americans can catch them and get answers out of them. That should not be too hard; this country does not have so many people among whom they could disappear.'

'No, but they were in a motorcar – the American who serves the little devil said so,' Liu Mei countered. 'With a motorcar, they could go a long way from Major Yeager's house, to a place where no one was looking for them.'

'You are right again.' Now Liu Han eyed her daughter with respectful curiosity. Liu Mei was getting the hang of the way the USA worked faster than her mother did. Maybe that was just because she was younger. Maybe it was because she was smarter, too. Liu Han didn't like to admit the possibility even to herself, but she was too much a realist to be blind to it.

And Liu Mei, no matter how clever she was, still had certain blind spots of her own. In musing tones, she repeated, 'The Americans were very brave when the shooting started.'

Liu Han didn't know whether to laugh or to go over to her and shake her. 'When you say "the Americans," you are talking about the younger one, the one called Jonathan, aren't you?'

Liu Mei flushed. Her skin was slightly fairer than it would have been were she of pure Chinese blood, which let Liu Han more easily see the flush rise and spread. Her daughter lifted her head, which also made her stick out her chin. 'What if I am?' she asked defiantly. She was bigger and heavier-boned than Liu Han; if they quarreled, she might do some shaking of her own.

'He is an American, a foreign devil.' Liu Han pointed out the obvious.

'He is the son of my father's friend,' Liu Mei answered. Liu Han hadn't realized how much that meant to her daughter till Liu Mei started learning about Bobby Fiore. Liu Han had known the American, known his virtues and his flaws – and he'd had plenty of each. He hadn't – he couldn't have – seemed quite real to Liu Mei, not till chance let her meet his friend. Jonathan Yeager drew especially favorable notice in her eyes because he was associated with Bobby Fiore.

Picking her words with care, Liu Han said, 'He is one who likes the scaly devils a great deal, you know.' If her daughter was infatuated with Major Yeager's son, she did not want to push too hard. That would only make Liu Mei cling to him and cling to everything he represented harder than she would have otherwise. Liu Han remembered the paradox from her own girlhood.

'So what?' Liu Mei tossed her head. Her hair bounced, as Liu Han's would not have; Bobby Fiore had had wavy hair. Liu Mei went on, 'Is it not so that having more people who better understood the little scaly devils would be useful for the People's Liberation Army?'

'Yes, that is always so,' Liu Han admitted. She pointed a finger at her daughter. 'What? Are you thinking of showing him your body to lure him back to China to help us against the scaly devils? Not even a maker of bad films would think such a plan could work.' *And so much for being careful of what I say,* she thought.

Liu Mei blushed again. 'I would not do such a thing!' she

465

exclaimed. 'I would never do such a thing!' Liu Han believed her, though some young girls would have lied in such a situation. She remembered the scandal surrounding one in her home village . . . But the village was gone, and the girl who'd had a bulging belly very likely dead. Liu Mei went on, in more thoughtful tones, 'But he is a nice young man, even if he is a foreign devil.'

And Liu Han could not even disagree with that, not when she'd thought the same thing herself. She did say, 'Remember, he may have a foreign devil for a sweetheart.'

'I know that,' her daughter answered. 'In fact, he does, or he did. He has spoken of her to me. She had hair the color of a new copper coin, he says. I have seen a few people like that here. They look even stranger to me than black people and blonds.'

'There is a fable,' Liu Han said. 'When the gods first made the world, they did not bake the first men they made long enough, so they came out pale. Those are the usual foreign devils. They left the second batch of men in too long, and that is how blacks came to be. The third time, they baked them perfectly, and made Chinese. It is only a fable, because there are no gods, but we look the way people are supposed to look.'

'I understand,' Liu Mei said. 'But I have got used to pale skins, because I see them around me all the time these days. Red hair, though, still seems strange.'

'And to me, too,' Liu Han agreed, remembering the red-headed man she'd seen the day the *Liberty Explorer* came into the harbor at San Pedro.

Before she could say anything more, someone knocked on the door to the suite the two Chinese women shared. Liu Han went to open it without hesitation; the U.S. government had posted armed guards in the hallway, and so she did not fear another attempt at murder.

Indeed, the fellow standing in the hallway could not have looked less like an assassin. He was pudgy and wore dark-rimmed spectacles. To her surprise, he spoke fairly good

Mandarin, even though he was a white man: 'Comrade Liu Han, I am Calvin Gordon, aide to the Undersecretary of State for the Occupied Territories. I am pleased to be able to tell you that the first shipments of arms for the People's Liberation Army left San Francisco and San Pedro harbors, bound for China. I hope they will reach your country safely, and that your comrades use them well and wisely against the little scaly devils.'

'I thank you very much,' Liu Han said. 'I did not expect anyone to tell me, especially in person.' She glanced toward the telephone that sat on a table by one end of the overstuffed sofa in the suite. Americans seemed to think talking on it was as good as actually being with a person.

But Calvin Gordon said, 'President Warren ordered me to fly out from Little Rock and let you know. He wants you to understand that China is important to the United States, and we will do everything we can to help free your country.'

'That is good,' Liu Han said. 'That is very good. But, of course, we do not know if these arms will actually reach the People's Liberation Army.'

'No, we do not know that,' Gordon agreed. 'The world is an uncertain place. If the weapons get past the Japanese and the little devils and the Kuomintang, the People's Liberation Army will use them. And if they do not get past the Japanese and the little devils and the Kuomintang, we will send some more, and we will keep sending them until the People's Liberation Army has them. Does that satisfy you?'

'How could I ask for anything better?' Liu Han said. 'I thank you, and I thank President Warren, and I thank the United States. Now that you have done this, I have done what I came here to do.'

She exchanged polite pleasantries with Gordon for a few minutes. Then he gave her what was almost a bow and left. As she turned in triumph to Liu Mei, she realized she had told the American diplomat the exact truth. Nothing held her daughter and her in the United States any more. She could go home.

467

*   *   *

Existence crawled past for Kassquit. She had never had nor wanted a great deal of contact with males of the Race other than Ttomalss. She would undoubtedly have spent much of her time in her chamber while he was in Nuremberg even without the confusion females and ginger brought to her ship. With it, she felt even more alone than she had before.

Penalties for tasting ginger – especially for females – kept getting harsher. Males and females kept on tasting, though. Kassquit hadn't found herself in the middle of any more mating brawls since that first one, but she knew she could at any time. That made her even less interested in coming out of her chamber than she would have been otherwise.

But, as always, she had to come out to eat. Although she avoided the busiest times at the refectory, she still did need to deal with occasional males and females of the Race. Sometimes they would be eating when she came in. More often, she would encounter them in the corridors on her way to and from eating.

She met Tessrek more often than she wanted. For one thing, the researcher's compartment was close to her own. For another, he had enjoyed baiting her for as long as she could remember, and perhaps for longer than that.

'What is that sour smell?' he said one day as she was returning to her compartment. 'It must be the reek of a Big Ugly.'

Of themselves, Kassquit's lips drew back, displaying her teeth in an expression that was anything but a smile. 'Not the smell you want, is it, superior sir?' she said, sardonic and polite at the same time. 'You would sooner sniff a female of your own kind drugged into her season, would you not? Then you can behave like an animal without shame, truth?'

Tessrek recoiled. He was not used to counterattacks from Kassquit. 'You are only a Tosevite,' he snapped. 'How dare you presume to question a male of the Race on what he does?'

'I am an intelligent being,' Kassquit returned. 'When I see a

468

male of the Race acting like an animal, I am intelligent enough to recognize it, which is more than can be said for the male in question.'

'Your tongue is abominable, not only in its shape but also in the uses to which you put it,' Tessrek said.

Kassquit stuck out the organ in question. She thought it abominable, too, but she would not admit that to Tessrek. Nor would she tell him that she had thought of having it surgically split to make her more like a proper member of the Race. What she did say was, 'The things my tongue describes are abominable. The things you do are abominable, worse than any for which the Race has mocked the Tosevites.'

And Tessrek recoiled again. When not in his season, he, like any other male or female of the Race, found reproductive behavior of any sort repugnant. Being reminded of his own had to flay him. 'What a little monster Ttomalss raised up among us!' he said angrily.

'I have only told the truth,' Kassquit said. 'You are the one who tells lies about me. You have got away with it up till now, but I will not tolerate it any more. Do you understand me, Tessrek?' It was, as best she could remember, the first time she had used his name instead of an honorific.

He noticed, too, and took offense. 'Do you presume to use me as an equal?' he demanded.

'I beg your pardon,' Kassquit said sweetly. Tessrek started to relax. Kassquit sank the dart with double enjoyment because of that: 'No doubt I gave you too much credit.'

For a moment, she thought Tessrek would physically assail her. He displayed his sharp teeth in a threat gesture more fearsome than hers, and also spread his fingerclaws. Kassquit made herself stand her ground. *If he attacks,* she told herself, *I will kick him as hard as I can.*

Tessrek took a step toward her. Feeling as curious as she was frightened, she took a step toward him, as if answering his challenge. And he, with a hiss both furious and frustrated, turned and skittered down the corridor in retreat that rapidly turned into rout. Still hissing, he rounded a corridor and disappeared.

'By the Emperor,' Kassquit said softly. Never in her life had she faced down a male of the Race. Never in her life had she tried to do that. As soon as she stopped assuming she was inferior, she stopped being inferior. Astonished, she murmured, 'I can match myself against them. I truly can.'

For the first time, she had an insight into how ginger made males and females of the Race feel. The power surging through her was sweet. It was not the satisfaction or release she got from touching herself, but in a certain way it was even more enjoyable. *I overcame him,* she thought. *I never overcame anyone before.* A moment later, another thought struck her: *I wonder why I never tried to overcome anyone before.*

She saw Tessrek again later that day. The male left her alone, as he had not done since Ttomalss went down to the surface of Tosev 3. Nor did he seek to quarrel with her again after that.

When Ttomalss next telephoned her, a day later, she gave him a quick summary of her triumph. 'I congratulate you, Kassquit,' he said. 'You have routed a bully. May you have many further such successes, though I know Tessrek was your most difficult and annoying tormentor. With him defeated, you should have less trouble from now on.'

'I thank you, superior sir,' Kassquit said. 'May you prove correct.' Then, having pressed Tessrek, she decided to press Ttomalss as well: 'Have you had any luck in getting the Deutsche to revise their policy concerning ginger-smuggling?'

'I have not,' Ttomalss said. 'I do not know if I have any hope of success there. Smuggling ginger is in the interest of the Deutsche because of the disruption it causes the Race.'

'Perhaps you should recruit Senior Researcher Felless to this cause,' Kassquit said, only a little acid in her voice. 'It would surely be in her interest to see that ginger-smuggling was curtailed.'

470

'Er, yes – a clever notion,' Ttomalss said. Kassquit did not smile, because she'd lost that response in hatchlinghood: Ttomalss had not been able to smile back at her when she began smiling then. Had she been able to, though, she would have smiled now. She'd embarrassed him by reminding him he'd coupled with Felless. *He deserves to be embarrassed,* she thought. *He will pay for that as long as I can make him do it.*

Logically, her anger at Ttomalss made no sense. Felless had not even known what ginger would do to her when she tasted. Once he smelled her pheromones, Ttomalss could hardly have helped mating with her. But logic had very little to do with it. Kassquit still felt betrayed, and was still taking her vengeance.

Ttomalss said, 'Perhaps another male, one more experienced in the ways of Tosev 3 than Felless, would be a more suitable partner in this endeavor.'

'Perhaps,' Kassquit said, making it plain she truly believed no such thing. 'But was not Felless specially chosen for her expertise in aliens? Surely she would have more insight into the Deutsche than most males from the conquest fleet.'

'I do not believe it is possible to have insight into the Deutsche and to stay sane,' Ttomalss said. 'A member of the Race may do one or the other, but not both.'

'They are Tosevites,' Kassquit said with a sniff, altogether forgetting her own blood. 'Of course they are addled. What could you give them that would make them keep ginger to themselves?'

'Something else that would be disadvantageous to the Race,' Ttomalss answered. 'I can conceive of the Deutsche making no other demand. They may be mad, but they are not such fools as to throw away something that hurts us without getting something else in return.'

'A pity,' Kassquit remarked. 'Perhaps you can arrange to give them something that seems to be to their advantage but is not.'

'And what happens when they discover this?' Ttomalss asked. 'They begin smuggling ginger again, no longer having any disincentive to restrain them.'

'Oh,' Kassquit said in a small voice. 'I had not thought of that. It is truth, superior sir.' Regardless of whether she'd prevailed over Tessrek, she wasn't going to be right all the time.

'Have general conditions on the ship grown more stable since last we talked?' Ttomalss asked. 'I hope so. Being in Nuremberg is a trial, but, despite appearances, I do not expect to stay here forever.'

'Somewhat, but only somewhat,' Kassquit answered. 'As I told you, I fear I was rude to Tessrek not long ago.' She did not fear that; she took an almost feral joy in it. The language of the Race, though, lent itself more readily to polite phrases.

Ttomalss said, 'Tessrek is the only male I know whose central nervous system connects directly to his cloaca.' He waited for Kassquit to use the hand gesture that showed she thought he was right, then went on, 'I hope you were thoroughly rude to the obnoxious obscurantist.'

'I believe so, yes.' Kassquit took a new pleasure in recounting in greater detail the exchange between the researcher and her, and yet another in watching Ttomalss laugh.

After he'd closed his mouth again, Ttomalss said, 'Good for you. He has been insolent for too long. High time he truly learned he can no longer sharpen his claws on your hide with impunity.'

'I do thank you for your support, superior sir,' Kassquit said. 'Lately, I have not had so much of that support as I might have liked. I am glad to see it return.'

'You need less support than you did at one time,' the male who had fostered her from hatchlinghood replied. 'Your adolescence is nearly completed. Soon you will be an adult, as independent as any other.'

'Yes, superior sir,' Kassquit said dutifully, but she could not help adding, 'An adult *what*? For I am not a Tosevite, not in any sense except my biology, but I cannot fully be a female of the Race, for that same biology prevents me from doing so.'

She did not think Ttomalss would have an answer for her; he

never had before when she'd asked similar questions. But now he did: 'An adult citizen of the Empire, Kassquit. Rabotevs and Hallessi are not members of the Race, either, but they reverence the Emperor, and spirits of Emperors past watch over them when they die. The same will be true for you in all respects.'

She tasted the words. 'An adult citizen of the Empire,' she repeated. 'I would be the first Tosevite citizen of the Empire, would I not?'

'You would indeed,' Ttomalss agreed. 'By your actions – even by your standing up to a male who unjustly abused you – you have proved you deserve the designation. Eventually, all Tosevites will be citizens of the Empire. You will be remembered as the one who showed the way, as one who made a bridge between Tosevites on the one fork of the tongue and the Empire on the other.'

Kassquit's tongue, as Tessrek had reminded her, had no fork. For the first time since she'd realized how different she was from everyone around her, she didn't care. 'It is good, superior sir,' she said to Ttomalss. She meant every word of it. For the first time since she'd realized how different she was, she knew her place again.

The telephone in David Goldfarb's flat rang. Naomi, who was closer, went and answered it: 'Hullo?' She paused, listening, then turned to her husband. 'It's for you, David.'

He got off the sofa. 'Who is it?'

'I don't know,' Naomi answered, a hand cupped over the mouthpiece. 'Not a familiar voice . . . I don't think.' She sounded a little doubtful.

With a shrug, he took the telephone. 'Goldfarb here.'

'And I'm glad of it, old man,' the fellow on the other end of the line replied. 'How are you and your lovely wife this evening?'

'Fine, thank you, Group Captain Roundbush,' Goldfarb answered tightly. He'd recognized that upper-crust accent at once, though Naomi would have heard it only a few times over the years. 'What can I do for you, sir?' He knew, with a grim and mournful certainty, that Basil Roundbush had not rung him up to pass a few pleasant minutes.

'Funny you should ask that,' Roundbush said, though Goldfarb didn't think it was funny at all. 'There is a spot of work you could do for me, if you happen to feel like it.'

He made it sound as if he were truly asking a favour rather than giving a thinly veiled order. Maybe that amused him. It didn't amuse David Goldfarb. 'What have you got in mind, sir?' he asked. 'Canvassing for Mosley's bill, perhaps? A bit late for that, I'm afraid; it seems dead for this session of Parliament.' Naomi's eyes got round.

'Why, so it does, and, if you want my opinion, a good thing, too,' Roundbush said. 'Tell me the truth, Goldfarb: have I ever denigrated you on account of your faith? Ever in all the years we've known each other?'

'You've *used* me on account of my faith,' Goldfarb said. 'Isn't that enough?'

'Oh, but my dear fellow, that's business. It's not personal.' Roundbush sounded hurt that Goldfarb couldn't make the distinction.

'It's not just business when I'm so vulnerable to it.' Goldfarb wondered if he should have said that, but it couldn't be anything Roundbush didn't know. 'You still haven't told me what you want from me tonight.'

'Quite,' Roundbush said, which wasn't an answer. 'Perhaps we could meet tomorrow afternoon at that pub with the excellent Guinness – what was the name of the place again? – and discuss it there.'

'Robinsons,' Goldfarb said automatically.

'Right. See you at Robinsons, then, at half past five to-morrow.' The line went dead.

'What was that in aid of?' Naomi asked after David hung up, too.

'I don't precisely know,' he answered. 'Whatever it was, it

was something the distinguished group captain' – he laced the words with as much sarcasm as he could – 'didn't care to discuss over the telephone wires. Which means, all too likely, it's something that won't stand the light of day.'

'Something to do with ginger,' Naomi said.

'I can't think of any other business Roundbush is involved in that he doesn't care to discuss over the telephone,' David said. 'Of course, I don't know all the business he's involved in, either.'

'Can't you stay away, then?' she asked.

He shook his head. 'I wish I could, but you know it's impossible as well as I do. I have to see what he wants – and see if I can talk him out of it.'

He got his chance the next evening, pulling up in front of Robinsons on his bicycle at exactly the appointed time in spite of a cold, nasty drizzle. When he went inside, he bought himself a whiskey – it didn't seem a night for stout – and sat as close to the fire as he could get. He'd beaten Roundbush to the pub, which left him glowing with virtue – and hoping his superior wouldn't show up.

But in Group Captain Roundbush came, dapper as ever, and sat down at the table with Goldfarb. 'That's not the worst idea anyone ever had,' he said, pointing to the whiskey, and ordered one for himself. When it came, he raised the glass high. 'Here's to you, old man.'

'You don't need to butter me up, sir,' Goldfarb said. 'Whatever it is you've got in mind, I'm probably stuck with it.'

'Now that's a fine attitude!' Basil Roundbush said. 'I'm about to offer the man an expense-paid holiday on the French Riviera – sounds all the better, doesn't it, with the drips and trickles outside? – and he says he's stuck with it. Plenty of chaps'd be happy to pay to go there, believe you me they would.'

'The German-occupied French Riviera?' Goldfarb's shudder had nothing to do with the weather. 'Yes, sir, that's a splendid place to send a Jew. Why not pick one of your other chaps instead?'

475

'You'll have a British passport,' Roundbush said patiently. 'Or, if you'd rather, you can have an American one. Might even be better: plenty of gentiles in the States who look the way you do, so to speak. And you're the right man for this job. You speak the Lizards' language and you can get along in German with your Yiddish.'

'There is the small matter of French,' Goldfarb remarked.

'Small matter is right.' Roundbush remained imperturbable. 'Anyone you need to talk to will speak German or the Lizards' language or both. As I may have mentioned once or twice, we have a spot of trouble down there. Seems as if the Germans have got their claws into a chap who was a freelance operator who did a deal of business for us. Anything you can do to set things right will be greatly appreciated, on that you may rest assured.'

'What do you imagine I can do there that one of your other chaps couldn't do a thousand times better?' Goldfarb asked.

'But, my dear fellow, you *are* one of our chaps,' Roundbush said. 'You have a more personal interest in the success of your undertaking than anyone else we could send. Do you deny it?'

'I bloody well can't deny it, not with you beggars soaring over my family and me like vultures over a dying sheep,' Goldfarb snarled. 'You have the whip hand, and you're not ashamed to use it.'

'You take things so personally,' Roundbush said. Unspoken but hanging in the air between them was, *Just another excitable Jew.*

'All right: I have an interest,' Goldfarb said. 'What I haven't got is any knowledge of your operation. How am I supposed to set it to rights if I can't tell what's right and what's wrong?' That was a legitimate question. A not so legitimate thought tagged along behind it. *If Roundbush gives me enough dirt about his pals, maybe I can bury them in it.*

'I can tell you some of what you need to know,' Roundbush said. 'I can also give you the names of people down there to ask. They'll be able to tell you far more.' He signaled to a barmaid: 'Two more whiskies, dear.' As soon as she'd gone off to fetch them, he turned back to Goldfarb. 'So you'll take it on, then?'

'What choice have I got?' David asked bitterly.

'A man always has choices,' Group Captain Roundbush replied. 'Some may be better than others, but they're always there.' *Thanks so much,* Goldfarb thought. *Yes, I could stick a gun in my mouth and blow out my brains. That's the sort you mean.* Roundbush was going cheerfully along his own line of thought: 'For instance, would you sooner carry a British passport or an American one?'

'With this accent?' Goldfarb shook his head. 'No choice there. If I ever run into anyone who can tell the difference – and I might – I'd be made out a liar in less time than it takes to tell.'

'Not necessarily. You could be a recent immigrant,' Roundbush said.

'I wish I *were* a recent immigrant,' Goldfarb said. 'Then you couldn't be twisting my arm like this.'

'Not personally,' the senior RAF man agreed. 'As I told you when we had our last discussion about your possibly leaving the country, though, I do have colleagues in the same line of work on the other side of the Atlantic. They might need your services from time to time. And, because they don't know at first hand what a sterling fellow you are, they might be rather more importunate than I am in requiring your assistance.'

Goldfarb had no trouble figuring out what that meant. 'They're a pack of American gangsters, and they'll shoot me if I talk back.'

Basil Roundbush didn't admit that. On the other hand, he didn't deny it, either. Instead, he turned the subject, saying, 'Jolly good to have you on board again. I expect you'll do splendidly.'

'*I* expect I'll make a bloody hash of it – or I would make a bloody hash of it if I dared, if something dreadful wouldn't happen to my family,' Goldfarb said. He knocked back his

477

new whiskey, which the barmaid had brought while he and Roundbush were talking. She'd damn near plopped herself down in Roundbush's lap afterwards, too. After coughing a couple of times, David asked, 'Tell me something, sir: did you and your chums blow the ships from the colonization fleet out of the sky?'

He had, for once, succeeded in startling the normally imperturbable Roundbush. 'Oh, good heavens, no!' the group captain exclaimed. 'We can do a great many interesting things – far be it from me to deny that – but we have no satellites and no direct control over any explosive metal even here on Earth.'

Did he say *no direct control* because he wanted to imply indirect control? Very likely, Goldfarb judged. He wondered if the implication held any truth. He hoped not. 'Do you know who did attack the colonization fleet?' *If you do – especially if it's the* Reich, *I can pass that on to the Lizards*. Doing Heinrich Himmler a bad turn was reason enough and to spare for going down to Marseille.

But Roundbush disappointed him by shaking his head. 'Haven't the foggiest idea, I'm afraid. Whoever did manage that one isn't letting on. He'd be a fool to let on, but that hasn't always stopped people in the past.'

'True enough,' David said. The trouble was, too much of what Roundbush said made too much sense to dismiss him out of hand as just a bloke who'd gone bad. From the standpoint of mankind at large – as opposed to the standpoint of one particular British Jew – he might not even have gone bad at all. Something else occurred to Goldfarb: 'Did you have anything to do with the ginger bombs that went off over Australia and made the Lizards have an orgy?'

'I haven't got the faintest notion of what you're talking about, old man,' Roundbush said, and laid a finger by the side of his nose. That was a denial far less ringing than the one he'd used in connection with the colonization fleet. Goldfarb noticed as much, as he was no doubt intended to. With a chuckle,

Roundbush went on, 'Only goes to show there really may be such a thing as killing them with kindness.'

'Yes, sir.' The whiskey mounted to Goldfarb's head, making him add, 'That's not how the *Reich* kills its Jews.'

'I fought the *Reich*,' Roundbush said. 'I have no love for it now. But it's there. I can't very well pretend it's not – and neither can you.'

'No, sir,' David Goldfarb agreed mournfully. 'But *Gottenyu*, how I wish I could.'

'Another letter from your cousin in England?' Reuven Russie said to his father. 'That's more often than you usually hear from him.'

'He has more *tsuris* than usual, too,' Dr. Moishe Rusie answered. 'Some of his friends – this is what he calls them, anyhow – are going to send him to Marseille, to help them in their ginger-trafficking.'

'Send a Jew to the Greater German *Reich*?' Reuven exclaimed. 'If those are Cousin David's friends, God forbid he should ever get enemies.'

'*Omayn,*' his father said. 'But when all the other choices are worse . . .' Moishe Russie shook his head. 'I know. It hardly seems possible. But he wants me to find out what I can from the Lizards about ginger-smuggling through Marseille, so he doesn't go in completely blind.'

'How much of that can you do?' Reuven asked.

'There are males who will tell me some,' his father said. 'I've spent a lot of time getting to know them. For something like that, they will give me answers, I think. And what I cannot learn from them, I may be able to find out from the Lizards' computers.'

'Yes, that's true,' Reuven agreed. 'You can find out almost anything from them if you know where to look and which questions to ask.'

His father laughed, which irked him till Moishe remarked, 'If you know where to look and which questions to ask, you can find out almost anything almost anywhere – you don't need computers to do it.'

Reuven's twin sisters came out of the kitchen to announce supper would be ready in a few minutes. Fixing Judith and Esther with a mild and speculative eye, he remarked, 'You're right, Father. They already know everything already.'

'What is he talking about now?' Esther asked, at the same time as Judith was saying, 'He doesn't know what he's talking about.'

'If you'd listened carefully, he was paying you a compliment,' their father said.

They both sniffed. One of them said, 'I'd sooner get a compliment where I don't have to listen carefully.'

'I'll give you one,' Reuven said. 'You're the most—' His father coughed before he could say anything more. That probably kept him out of trouble. Even so, he didn't appreciate it. His sisters rarely gave him such a golden opportunity, and here he couldn't even take advantage of it.

A moment later, his mother quelled the budding argument for the time being, calling, 'Supper!' The ploy might not have been so subtle as Solomon's, but it did the job. Next to boiled-beef-and-barley soup with carrots and onions and celery, squabbling with his sisters suddenly seemed less important.

His father approved, too, saying, 'This is fine, Rivka. It takes me back to the days before the fighting all started, when we were living in Warsaw and things . . . weren't so bad.'

'Why would you want to remember Warsaw?' Reuven asked with a shudder. His own memories of the place, such as they were, began only after the Nazis had taken it. They were filled with cold and fear and hunger, endless gnawing hunger. He couldn't imagine how a pleasant bowl of soup took anyone back there in memory.

But his mother's smile also looked into the past. She said, 'Don't forget, your father and I fell in love in Warsaw.'

'And if we hadn't,' Moishe Russie added, 'you wouldn't be here now.' He glanced over to the twins. 'And neither would you.'

'Oh, yes, we would,' Esther said. Judith added, 'Somehow or other, we would have found a way.' Reuven was about to blast the twins for logical inconsistency when he saw they were both holding in giggles. He went back to his soup, which evidently disappointed them.

'What did Cousin David say?' Rivka Russie asked. 'I heard you talking about his letter out in the front room, but I couldn't make out everything you were saying.' Moishe explained. Rivka frowned. 'That's very bad,' she said, shaking her head. 'That such trouble should happen in England . . . Who would have dreamt such trouble could happen in England?'

Moishe Russie sighed. 'When you and I were small, dear, who would have dreamt such trouble could happen in Germany? In Poland, yes. We always knew that. In Russia, yes. We always knew that, too. But Germany? David's wife is from Germany. She and her family were lucky – they got out in time. But when she was small, Germany was a good place to be a Jew.'

'America, now,' Reuven said. 'America, and here, and maybe South Africa and Argentina. But if you want to live under human beings and not the Race, America is about the only place left where you can breathe free.'

'Mosley's bill failed, thank heaven,' his father said. 'It's not against the law to be a Jew in England, the way it is in the *Reich*. It's only that you'd better not, or people will make you wish you weren't.'

'Poland was like that,' Reuven's mother said. 'I don't think England is as bad as Poland was, but it could be one of these days.'

Reuven watched his sisters stir. He waited for one of them to ask why gentiles persecuted Jews. He'd asked that himself, till finally deciding it wasn't worth asking. That it was so mattered. Why it was so . . . Ask a thousand different anti-Semites and you'd get a thousand different answers. Which of them was true? Was any of them true? *Why* questions too often lost you in a maze of mirrors, each reflecting back on another till you weren't sure where you stood, or if you stood anywhere.

And, sure enough, one of the twins did ask a *why* question, though not the one Reuven expected: 'Why does it matter if anyone – especially anyone Jewish – lives under people or under the Race? It doesn't look like Jews will ever live under other Jews, and the Lizards do a better job of keeping people from bothering us than just about any human beings do – you said so yourself.'

'That is an important question,' Moishe Russie said gravely. Reuven found himself nodding. It was a more important question than he'd thought his sisters had in them. His father went on, 'Who the rulers are matters because they set the tone for the people who live under them. The Nazis didn't *make* the Germans anti-Semites, but they *let* them be anti-Semites and *helped* them be anti-Semites. Do you see what I mean?'

Both twins nodded. Judith, who hadn't asked the question, said, 'The Lizards would never do anything like that.'

'*Never* is a long time,' Reuven said before his father could speak. 'Jews are useful to them right now. One of the reasons we're useful to them is that so many people treat us so badly – we haven't got many other places to turn. But that could change, or the Lizards could decide they need to make the Arabs happy instead of us. If either one of those things happens, where are we? In trouble, that's where.'

He waited for Esther and Judith to argue with him, not so much because of what he'd said as because he'd been the one who said it. But they both nodded solemnly. Either he'd made more sense than usual, or they were starting to grow up.

His father quoted the Psalm: 'Put not your trust in princes.'

'Or even fleetlords,' Reuven added.

'If we don't trust princes, if we don't trust fleetlords, whom do we trust?' Esther asked.

'God,' Moishe Russie said. 'That's what the Psalm is talking about.'

'Nobody,' Reuven said. He'd been raised in the Holy Land, in the cradle of Judaism, but was far less observant than either of his parents. Maybe it was because he'd been persecuted less. Maybe it was because he had a better secular education, though his father had had a good one by the standards of his time. Maybe he just had a hard time believing in anything he couldn't see.

'Reuven,' his mother said reprovingly.

And maybe he had reasons for doubt his parents hadn't had when they were young. 'What's the use of believing in a God who lets His chosen people go through what the *Reich* has put them through?'

'I'm sure men thought the same in the time of Philistines, and in the time of the Greeks, and in the time of the Romans, and in the Middle Ages, and in the time of the pogroms, too,' his father said. 'Jews have gone on anyhow.'

'They didn't have any other answers in the old days,' Reuven said defiantly. 'We have science and technology now. God was a guess that did well enough when there wasn't any competition. Today, there is.'

He waited for his parents to pitch a fit. His mother looked as if she were on the point of it. His father raised an eyebrow. 'The Nazis have science and technology, too,' Dr. Moishe Russie observed. 'Science and technology tell them how to build the extermination camps they like so well. But what tells them they shouldn't like those camps and shouldn't want to build them?'

Reuven said, 'Wait a minute. You're confusing things.'

'Am I?' his father asked. 'I don't think so. Science and technology talk about *what* and *how*. We know more about *what* and *how* than they did in the days of the Bible. I have to admit that – I could hardly deny it. But science and technology don't say anything about *why*.'

'You can't really answer questions about *why*,' Reuven protested: the same thought he'd had not long before. 'There's no evidence.'

'Maybe you're right,' Moishe Russie said. 'In a strictly scientific sense, I suppose you are. But if someone asks a question like "Why not slaughter all the Jews we can reach?" – what kind of answer do science and technology have to give him?'

'That Jews don't deserve to be slaughtered because we aren't really any different from anybody else,' Reuven said.

It wasn't the strongest reply, and he knew it. In case he hadn't known it, his father drove the point home: 'We're different enough to tell apart, and that's all the Germans care about. And we aren't the only ones. They know they can do it, and they don't know why they shouldn't. How and why should they know that?'

Reuven glared at him. 'You're waiting for me to say God should tell them. You were talking about the Middle Ages. In the Middle Ages, God told the *goyim* to go out and slaughter all the Jews they could catch. That's what they thought, anyhow. How do you go about proving they were wrong?'

His father grimaced. 'We're not going to get anywhere. I should have known we wouldn't get anywhere. If you won't believe, there's nothing I can do to make you believe. I'm not a *goy*, to convert you by force.'

'And a good thing, too,' Reuven said.

His twin sisters looked at each other. He didn't believe in telepathy. The Lizards thought the idea was laughable. But if they weren't passing a message back and forth without using words, he didn't know what they were doing. They both spoke at the same time: 'Maybe you should convert Jane instead, Father.'

Moishe Russie raised an eyebrow. 'How about that, Reuven?' he asked.

Glaring at Esther and Judith failed to help. They laughed at Reuven, their eyes wide and shining. He couldn't strangle them, not with his parents watching. In a choked voice, he said, 'I don't think that would be a good idea.' It wasn't quite true, but he wouldn't admit as much. He went on, 'Maybe I'll bother you two when you have boyfriends.' It didn't do a bit of good. The twins just laughed.

15

Living in Texas since the fighting stopped, Rance Auerbach had heard a lot of horror stories about Mexican jails. The one in which the Lizards kept him didn't live up to any of them, much to his surprise. It was, in fact, not a great deal less comfortable than his apartment, if a lot more cramped. The Lizards even let him have cigarettes.

Every so often, they'd take him out and question him. He sang like a canary. Why not? The only person he could implicate was Penny, and he couldn't get her in any deeper than she was already, not when they'd caught her with lime-cured ginger in her fists.

One day – he'd lost track of time, lost track and stopped worrying about it – a pair of Lizard guards with automatic rifles opened the door to his cell and spoke in the language of the Race: 'You will come with us at once.'

'It shall be done,' Auerbach said, and slowly rose from his cot. The Lizards backed away so he couldn't grab their weapons. That was standard procedure, but he still found it pretty funny. However much he might have wanted to, he couldn't have leapt at them to save his life.

They took him to the interrogation chamber, as he'd expected. Like the rest of the jail, it was well-lighted and clean. Unlike the rest, it boasted a chair built for human beings. Unlike people, the Lizards didn't seem to go in for the third degree. That did nothing but relieve Rance; had they felt like working him over, what could he have done about it?

Today, he noticed, the interrogation chamber held two human-made chairs. That gave him hope of seeing Penny, which the Lizards hadn't let him do since capturing the two of them. She wasn't there now, though. Only the guards and his chief interrogator, a male named Hesskett, were. With Rance's bad leg and shoulder, assuming the posture of respect was painful for him. He did it anyway, then nodded to Hesskett human-style and said, 'I greet you, superior sir.' Politeness didn't hurt, not in the jam he was in.

'I greet you, Prisoner Auerbach.' Hesskett knew enough to keep reminding him he was in a jam. Having done so, the Lizard pointed to a chair. 'You have leave to sit.'

'I thank you,' Auerbach said. Once, he'd sat without leave. The next time, he hadn't had a chair. Standing through a grilling came closer to torture than his captors perhaps realized. He'd minded his manners ever since.

As he sank into the chair now, two more guards escorted Penny into the chamber. She looked tired – and, without any makeup, older than she had – but damn good. He grinned at her. She blew him a kiss before going through the greeting ritual with Hesskett.

Once she was in the other chair – too far away to let Auerbach touch her, dammit – Hesskett started speaking pretty fluent English: 'You are both found guilty of trafficking in ginger with the Race.'

'You can't do that! We haven't had a trial,' Auerbach exclaimed.

'You were caught with much of the herb in your possession,' the Lizard said. 'We can find you guilty without a trial. We have. You are.'

Rance didn't think a lawyer, whether human or Lizard, would have done him much good, but he'd have liked a chance to find out. Penny asked the question uppermost in his mind, too: 'What are you going to do with us?'

'With a crime this bad, we can do what we want,' Hesskett said. 'We can leave you in jail for many years, many long Tosevite years. We can leave you in jail till you die. No one would miss you. No one of the Race would miss either one of you at all.'

That wasn't true. A lot of customers, from Kahanass on down, would miss Penny quite a bit. Saying so didn't strike Rance as likely to help his cause. But he didn't think Hesskett had brought them here so he could gloat before locking them up and losing the key. The Lizard wasn't talking that way, anyhow. Auerbach asked, 'What do we have to do to keep you from throwing us in jail for life?'

Hesskett's posture was already forward-sloping. Now he leaned even farther toward the two humans. 'You are guilty of smuggling ginger,' he said. 'You know other Big Uglies involved in this criminal traffic.'

'That's right,' Penny agreed at once. She really did. Aside from her, the only ones Rance knew at the moment were the plug-uglies he'd plugged back in Fort Worth.

'Do you know the ginger smuggler and thief called Pierre Dutourd?' Hesskett said the name several times, pronouncing it as carefully as he could.

'Yeah, I do. The big-time dealer in the south of France, isn't he?' Penny said. Auerbach nodded so Hesskett wouldn't get the idea – the accurate idea – that he didn't know Pierre the Turd or whatever the hell his name was from a hole in the ground.

'It is good,' the Lizard interrogator said. 'We have tried to end his business with the Race, but we have not succeeded. We believe the Deutsche are protecting him from us. We need his trade stopped. If you help us stop it, we will reward you greatly. We will not put you in jail for long Tosevite years. If you refuse, we will do to you what we have the right to do to you. Do you understand? Is it agreed?'

'How are we going to do anything to this fellow in France?' Auerbach asked. 'We're here, not there.'

'We will fly you to Marseille, his city,' Hesskett answered. 'We will give you documents that will satisfy the *Reich*. You will deal with our operatives already in Marseille and with this Pierre Dutourd. Is it agreed?'

'I've got one problem – I don't speak French for beans,' Penny said. 'Apart from that, I'll do whatever you say. I don't like jail.'

'That is the idea,' Hesskett said smugly.

'I've got a little French and a little German,' Rance said. 'They're rusty as hell, but they might still work some. I'll be able to read some, anyway, even if I can't do much talking.'

'You Tosevites would be better off with one language for all of you instead of languages in patches like fungus diseases on your planet,' Hesskett said. 'But that is not to be changed today. Do you both agree to aid the Race in putting out of business the smuggler Pierre Dutourd?'

Penny nodded at once. Auerbach didn't. Going into Nazi-occupied France after a smuggler the *Reich* was propping up wouldn't be a walk in the park. He wanted some reassurance he'd come out again. Of course, if he went into jail, he had Hesskett's reassurance he wouldn't come out again. That made up his mind for him. With a rasping sigh, he said, 'I'll take a shot at it.'

Things moved very quickly after that. Hesskett put Rance and Penny in a Lizard airplane from the air base near Monterrey to Mexico City. When they got out of the plane a little more than an hour later (it seemed much longer to Auerbach; his seat was cramped and not made for the shape of his rear end), more Lizards who fought ginger-smuggling took charge of them. Only moments after their photographs were taken, they got handed copies of U.S. passports that Auerbach couldn't have told from the real McCoy to save himself from the firing squad. Stamps showed visas issued by the *Reich*'s consulate in Mexico City. Auerbach knew they had to be as phony as the passports, but didn't ask questions.

The next morning, after a Lizard-paid shopping spree to get

them more than the clothes they'd had on when they were captured, they boarded the small human-adapted section of an airplane bound from Mexico City to Marseille. 'Well, now,' Penny said, glancing over to Rance beside her, 'you can't tell me this worked out so bad. We got caught, and what did we get? A trip to the Riviera, that's what. Could be a heck of a lot worse, if anybody wants to know.'

'Yeah, it could,' Auerbach agreed. 'And if we don't do whatever we're supposed to do about this Dutourd guy, it'll get worse, too. The damn Lizards'll lock us up and forget about us.'

Penny leaned over and gave him a big, wet kiss. It felt good – hell, it felt great – but he wondered what had brought it on. She breathed in his ear. Then, very low to defeat possible (no, probable) listening devices, she whispered, 'Don't be dumb, sweetheart. If we can't make the damn Lizards happy, we start singing songs for the Nazis.'

Rance didn't say anything. He just shook his head, as automatically as if at a bad smell. In spite of occasional correspondence he'd had, the Nazis had been the number-one enemy before the Lizards came, the enemy the USA was really gearing up to fight. Oh, the Japs were nasty, but Hitler's boys had been trouble with a capital T. As far as he was concerned, they still were.

The flight was far and away the longest one he'd ever taken. Sitting cooped up in an airplane hour after hour turned out to be a crashing bore. He necked a little with Penny, but they couldn't do anything more than neck a little, not with Lizards strolling through every so often. The Lizards didn't act quite so high and mighty as they had before the colonization fleet brought their females. He wondered how many of them had found a female who'd tasted ginger.

After what seemed like forever, water gave way to land below the airplane. Then came more water: the improbably blue Mediterranean Sea. And then the plane rolled to a stop more smoothly than a human aircraft was likely to have done, at the airport northwest of Marseille.

When Rance and Penny got off the plane and went into the terminal to get their baggage and clear customs, spicy smells filled the air: laurel, oleander, others Auerbach couldn't name so readily. The sky tried to outdo the sea for blueness, but didn't quite succeed.

Some of the customs officials were Frenchmen, others Germans. They all spoke English. They also all seemed interested in why Americans should have come to Marseille aboard a Lizard airplane. They went through the suitcases with microscopic attention to detail and even had them X-rayed. Finding nothing made the Germans more suspicious than contraband would have; the French didn't seem to give two whoops in hell.

'Purpose of this visit?' demanded a customs man in a uniform that would have made a field marshal jealous.

'Honeymoon,' Auerbach answered, slipping his good arm around Penny's waist. She snuggled against him. They'd concocted the story on the airplane. Penny had shifted one of her rings to the third finger of her left hand. It didn't fit very well there, but only a supremely alert man would have noticed that.

This Aryan superman – actually, a blond dumpling who wore his fancy uniform about as badly as he could – wasn't that alert. He did remain dubious. 'Honeymoon in Mexico and Marseille?' he said. 'Strange even for Americans.'

Auerbach shrugged, which hurt his bad shoulder. Penny knew when to keep her mouth shut. The customs official muttered something guttural. Then he stamped both their passports with unnecessary vehemence. He didn't know what they were up to, but he wouldn't believe they weren't up to something.

Outside the terminal, a cab driver with a cigarette hanging from the corner of his mouth stuffed their bags into the trunk at the front of his battered Volkswagen. He spoke in bad, French-accented German: *'Wo willen gehen Sie?'*

'Hôtel Beauveau, s'il vous plaît,' Auerbach answered and went on in slow French: 'It is near the old port, *n'es-ce pas?'* If

he'd impressed the cabby, the fellow didn't let on. He slammed down the trunk lid – what would have been the hood on any self-respecting car – got in, and started to drive.

Getting to know her brother turned out to be less of a pleasure than Monique Dutourd had imagined it would. Pierre might not have planned to be a smuggler when he was young, but he'd lived in the role so long that it fit him tighter than his underwear. And all his acquaintances came out of the smugglers' den of Porte d'Aix, too. Having met Lucie, his lady friend with the sexy voice, Monique came away convinced her voice was the best thing she had going for her.

Pierre spent much of his time cursing the Nazis in general and *Sturmbannführer* Dieter Kuhn in particular. 'They are cutting my profit margin in half, it could be even more than in half,' he groused.

He seemed to have forgotten that the Lizards would have cut his life in half. Monique had more general reasons to loathe the Germans – what they'd done to France, for instance. Pierre didn't care about that. He dealt with people all over the world, but remained invincibly provincial at heart: if something didn't affect him in the most direct way, it had no reality for him.

Between Pierre and *Sturmbannführer* Kuhn, Monique's work suffered. The paper on the epigraphy relating to the cult of Isis in Gallia Narbonensis remained unfinished. The SS man started asking her out again. 'Dammit, you have my brother in your hip pocket,' she flared. 'Aren't you satisfied?'

'That is business,' Kuhn replied. 'This is, or would be, or could be, pleasure.'

'For you, perhaps,' Monique said. 'Not for me.' But not even the direct insult was enough to keep him from asking her to lunch or dinner every few days. She kept saying no. He kept asking. He kept being polite about it, which gave her no more excuse to lose her temper – not that losing her temper at an SS officer was the smartest thing she might have done under any circumstances.

491

Once more, she grew to hate the telephone. She had to answer it, and too often it was the German. Whenever it rang, she winced. And it kept ringing. One night, just as she was starting to make some fitful progress on the inscriptions, it derailed her train of thought with its insistent jangle. She called it a name unlikely to appear in any standard French dictionary. When that didn't make it shut up, she marched over to it, picked up the handset, and snarled, '*Allô?*'

'Hello, is this Professor Dutourd?' The words were in German, but it wasn't Dieter Kuhn. For that matter, it wasn't standard German, either; it differed at least as much from what she'd learned in school as the Marseille dialect differed from Parisian French.

'Yes,' Monique answered. 'Who's calling, please?' Her first guess was, another SS man from some backwards province.

But the fellow on the other end of the line said, 'I'm a friend of some friends of your brother's. I'm looking to do him a good turn, if I can.'

She almost hung up on him then and there. Instead, she snapped, 'Why are you calling me? Why aren't you bothering the SS?' Then she added insult to injury: 'But don't worry. They probably hear you now, because they listen on this line whenever they choose.'

She'd expected that would make the caller hang up on her, but he didn't. He muttered something that wasn't German at all, whether standard or dialect: 'Oh, bloody hell.'

Monique read English, but had had far fewer occasions to speak it than she'd had with German. Still, she recognized it when she heard it. And hearing it made her revise her notion of who Pierre's 'friends' were: probably not Nazi gangsters after all. *Not this batch, anyhow,* she thought. 'What do you want?' she asked, sticking to German.

He answered in that throaty, guttural dialect: 'I already told you. I want to give him as much help as I can. I don't know how much that will be, or just how I'll be able to do it.' He laughed without much humor. 'I don't know all kinds of things I wish I knew.'

'Who are you?' she asked. 'How do you know Pierre?'

'I don't know him at all – my friends do,' the stranger answered. 'Who am I?' That bitter laugh again. 'My name is David Goldfarb.'

'Goldfarb,' Monique echoed. It could have been a German name, but he didn't pronounce it as a German would have. And he'd cursed in English when provoked. Maybe his dialect wasn't really, or wasn't quite, German at all. 'You're a Jew!' she blurted.

An instant too late, she realized she shouldn't have said that. Goldfarb muttered something pungent in English, then returned to what had to be Yiddish: 'If anybody is listening to your phone . . .' He sighed. 'I'm a British citizen. I have a legal right to be here.' Another sigh. 'I hope the Jerries remember that.'

By the way he said it, *Jerries* had the same flavor as *Boches*. Monique found herself liking him, and also found herself wondering if he was setting her up to like him. If he really was a Jew, he was risking his neck to come here. If he was a liar, he was – no, not a smooth one, for there was nothing smooth about him, but a good one. 'What do you want with my brother?' Monique asked.

'What do you think?' he answered. He did believe someone was tapping her line, then: he was saying no more than he had to.

She came to a sudden decision. 'You know where I teach?' Without waiting for him to say yes or no, she hurried on: 'Be there at noon tomorrow with a bicycle.'

He said something in the Lizards' language. That, unlike French, German, or English, was not a tongue of classical scholarship. A generation of films had taught her the phrase he used, though: 'It shall be done.' The line went dead.

When she finished her lecture the next day, she wondered if Dieter Kuhn would try to take her out to lunch. He didn't.

Maybe that meant the Nazis hadn't been listening after all. Maybe it meant they had, and were seeing what kind of trouble she'd get into if they let her. She left her lecture hall, curious about the same thing.

That fellow standing in the hall had to be David Goldfarb. He looked like a Jew – not like a Nazi propaganda poster, but like a Jew. He was eight or ten years older than she, with wavy brown hair going gray, rather sallow skin, and a prominent nose. *Not bad-looking*. The thought left her vaguely surprised, and more sympathetic than she'd expected. 'How does it feel to be here?' she asked.

She'd spoken French. He grimaced. 'English or German, please,' he said in English. 'I haven't got a word of French. Fine chap to send here, eh?' He grinned ruefully. When Monique repeated herself – in German, in which she was more fluent than English – the grin slipped. He returned to his rasping dialect: 'Coming here is bad for me. Not coming here would have been bad for me and my family. What can you do?'

'What can you do?' Monique repeated. She'd been asking herself the same thing ever since *Sturmbannführer* Kuhn let her know Pierre was alive. Too often, the answer was, *Not much.* 'You do have a bicycle?' she asked. He nodded, and then had to brush a lock of hair off his forehead. She said, 'Good. Come along with me, then, and we'll go to a café, and you can tell me what this is all about.'

'It shall be done,' he said again, in the language of the Race.

She led him to Tire-Bouchon, on Rue Julien, in a turn-of-the-century building not far from her route home. A couple of soldiers in *Wehrmacht* field-gray were eating there, but they paid her no undue attention. To her relief, they paid Goldfarb no undue attention, either.

She ordered a garlicky beef stew. The waiter turned out to speak German. That wouldn't have surprised her even if the *Wehrmacht* men hadn't been in the place. After some back-and-forth, Goldfarb chose chicken in wine. He turned back to

Monique as the waiter left. 'This is on me. One thing I will say about my friends' – he gave the word an ironic twist – 'is that they've got plenty of money.'

'*Merci,*' Monique said, and then, 'So . . . What exactly do your friends want from my brother?'

'They don't want anything *from* him,' the Jew from England answered. 'They want him to go back into business for himself, buying some of the ginger he sells the Lizards from them and keeping them full of money. They don't want him to be a German cat's-paw.'

'I am sure he would like that very much,' Monique said. 'The only trouble is, the Lizards will kill him if he stays in business for himself. They, or their leaders, do not want to put up with ginger now, not with what it does to their females and how it upsets their males. The Nazis can keep him in business and protect him. Can your friends do the same?'

She expected him to blanch at the blunt question. French opinions of England had not been high in the fighting or after it, and many Frenchmen laughed to see Britain fight so hard to retain her independence and then be shorn of the empire that made such independence genuine. But Goldfarb said, 'I'm not sure. I think we'd have a better chance to get the Lizards to call off their dogs. I have a cousin with good connections – he's even one of the fleetlord's advisors every now and then.'

Monique's wave of disbelief almost caught the waiter who was bringing them their lunches. After he'd set the food on the table and left again, she said, 'You cannot expect me to think you are telling the truth.'

'Think whatever you want,' David Goldfarb told her. 'My cousin's name is Moishe Russie. Your brother ought to know it.' He cut off a bite of chicken. A smile lit up his lean, melancholy face. 'This is very, very good.'

Monique resolved to remember the name; if Goldfarb was a liar, he'd been well prepared. The way he attacked his plate amused her. Tire-Buchon served hearty bourgeois fare, but surely nothing to cause such ecstasy. Then she recalled he came from England, poor fellow, and so no doubt had lower standards than hers.

After a bit, he looked astonished to have no more chicken left. 'Is it possible for me to meet your brother?' he asked. 'I'm staying at Le Petit Nice.' He butchered the name, but she understood it.

She also understood he was not a professional agent or anything of the sort. Someone more skilled would have been more careful about telling her where he was staying. His English associates must have chosen him for whom he knew, not for what he knew. But his very lack of skill at intrigue, oddly, made him more convincing. If he wasn't what he said he was, he had to be something close to it.

'It could be that you might see my brother,' Monique said, picking her way through the German conditionals. 'I do not yet know, of course, whether he would want to see you.'

'If he wants to get back into business for himself, I'm the best hope he has,' David Goldfarb said.

'I'll tell him you said so,' Monique answered. 'He will know better than I how far to trust you.'

Goldfarb paid for lunch with crisp new *Reichsmarks*. He stayed even more thoroughly a gentleman than Dieter Kuhn had, and seemed to have to remember to wave as he rode off on his bicycle. Unlike the SS man, he wore a wedding band, but experience had taught Monique how little the lack of one had to do with anything.

Once she'd got back to her block of flats, she sighed as she lugged her bicycle upstairs. Maybe, just maybe, she could get some work done. But when she opened the apartment door, she let out a gasp. Dieter Kuhn was sitting on the sofa.

'*Bonjour*, Monique,' he said with a pleasant smile. 'Now, what did the damned kike have to tell you?'

David Goldfarb was astonished to discover how much he liked Marseille. He liked the weather, he loved the food, and the people – even the Germans – were nicer to him than he'd expected. What the Germans would have done to him had he been one of theirs rather than one of the Queen's was a question on which he preferred not to dwell.

He hadn't lived in such luxury as at Le Petit Nice before. It wasn't even his money. That made him spend it less recklessly, not more, as it might have with a lot of men. He didn't need to be extravagant to have a good time, and so he wasn't.

Three days after he'd had lunch with Monique Dutourd – who was, without a doubt, the most interesting professor he'd ever met – the telephone in his room rang as he was trying not to cut his throat while shaving. 'Hello?' he said, getting shaving soap on the handset as he held it to his mouth.

A man spoke in the language of the Race: 'I greet you. Meet me tomorrow at midday behind the old synagogue. Do you understand? Is it agreed?'

'It shall be done,' Goldfarb said, and only then, 'Dutourd?' He got no answer; the line was dead.

Maybe it was a trap. In fact, the odds were depressingly good it was a trap. That had nothing to do with anything. David had to stick his head into it. If he went home without doing whatever he could to get the ginger dealer out from under the Germans' muscular thumbs, his family would regret it. Group Captain Roundbush hadn't said so in so many words, but he hadn't needed to, either.

With a camera slung around his neck, dark glasses on his nose, and a preposterous hat shielding his head from the Mediterranean sun, Goldfarb hoped he looked like a man on holiday. He walked along the hilly streets of Marseille, peering down at a city map to make sure he didn't get lost.

When he found the synagogue on Rue Breteuil, he grimaced. Rank weeds grew in front of the building. The boards nailed across the door had been in place long enough to grow grainy and pale, except for the streaks of rust trailing down from the nailheads. More boards kept men without better homes from climbing through the windows. Vandals – or, for all David knew, Nazi officials – had painted swastikas and anti-Semitic slogans on the bricks of the front wall.

Passersby gave Goldfarb curious looks as he kicked his way through the weeds toward the back of the synagogue. He ignored them. Not least because he proceeded as if he had every right to be doing as he did, the passersby stopped paying attention to him almost at once. In the Greater German *Reich*, no one questioned a man who acted as if he had the right to do what he was doing. Basil Roundbush had told him it would be so, and it was.

Other buildings huddled close on either side of the synagogue. In their shadows, the weeds did not flourish quite so much. Behind the closed and desecrated shrine, though, they grew even more vigorously than in front, growing almost as tall as a man. Anything or anyone might be lurking there. Goldfarb wished for a pistol. Softly, he called, 'Dutourd?' For good measure, he tacked on an interrogative cough.

The weeds stirred. 'I am here,' a man answered in the language of the Race. He did have a pistol, and pointed it at Goldfarb. Under his beret, his sad-eyed face was nervous. 'Did anyone follow you here? Anyone at all? Germans? Males of the Race? Were you careful?'

'I think so,' Goldfarb answered. 'I am not a spy. I am a soldier, and not so used to sneaking here and there.'

'Then you may well die before your time,' Pierre Dutourd remarked. He took from his belt a gadget probably of Lizard manufacture. After glancing at it, he relaxed a little. 'I do not detect any electronics planted in or aimed at this place. That means – I hope that means – no one is listening to us. Very well, then – say your say.' Even speaking the Lizards' language, Dutourd sounded like a Frenchman.

'Good,' Goldfarb said, though he wasn't sure how good it was. 'My friends back in Britain want to see if they can return you to doing business for yourself. They do not think you should have to subordinate yourself to the *Reich*.' The Race's language was made for distinguishing subtle gradations of status. The relationship Goldfarb described was one of menial to master.

Dutourd caught the shade of meaning and grimaced at it. 'They do not treat me quite so badly as that,' he said, then paused and shook his head. 'They say they will not treat me so badly as that. Whether it proves true remains to be seen.'

'Anyone who trusts the Germans—' Goldfarb began.

'Trust them? Do I look like such a fool as that?' Pierre Dutourd sounded offended. 'But I did and do trust the Race to kill me if I did not have the *Reich* protecting me. And so . . .' He shrugged. Still aiming the pistol in David's general direction, he pointed with his free hand. 'What can your English friends do to keep me going without the Germans and without getting myself killed?'

Goldfarb would have asked exactly that question had he worn Dutourd's shoes. It was a question for which he had no good answer. He did his best to disguise that, saying, 'They will do whatever proves necessary to keep you afloat.'

Dutourd's lip curled. 'As the Royal Navy did at Oran, when your ships opened fire on and sank so many of the ships of France? Why should I trust Englishmen? With the Germans and with the Race, one is always sure of what one gets. With the English, who can say? I sometimes think you do not know that yourselves.'

'We can give you money,' Goldfarb said. 'We also have good connections with the Lizards. They can help take the pressure off you.'

'A likely story,' Dutourd said, unconvinced. 'Next you will tell me of a tunnel from London to Marseille, so the Germans will not be able to tell what ginger you bring me. If these are the best stories you can tell, better you should go back to England.'

'These are not just stories,' Goldfarb said. *Miserable frog,* he thought. *He's lived under the Nazis so long, he's used to it.* Aloud, he went on, 'My cousin in Jerusalem is Moishe Russie, of whom you may have heard. Did Monique tell you that?'

'Yes, she told me. And my cousin is Marie Antoinette, of whom you may have heard,' Dutourd answered. 'More lies. Nothing else.'

Goldfarb pulled out his wallet and displayed a picture he carried in it. 'Here is a photograph of Cousin Moishe and me. I should very much like to see a photograph of you and Cousin Marie.'

Pierre Dutourd bared his teeth in something close to a smile. 'I must say that I have not got one with me. If you are a liar, you are a thoroughgoing liar. I know of this Moishe Russie, as who with a hearing diaphragm' – using the Lizards' language could produce some odd images – 'does not? I am surprised to find his cousin, if you are his cousin, working with the ginger smugglers, I must also say.'

'Why?' Goldfarb asked. 'If you think I love the Race, you are mistaken. My empire might have beaten Hitler. Thanks to the Race, that did not happen. And Britain is not a friendly home for Jews any more.'

'It could be,' Dutourd said, 'that you are telling the truth after all. Whether this matters in the slightest, however, remains to be seen.'

'How can I do more to convince you?' Goldfarb asked, though he had already come closer to convincing the Frenchman than he'd thought he would.

'By showing me that—' The ginger smuggler abruptly broke off, for the device on his belt let out a warning hiss. With surprising speed and silence, he disappeared back into the weeds.

That left David Goldfarb out in the open by himself as he listened to someone crunching through the plants by the side of the synagogue as he had done. He wished for a pistol more than ever. His hand darted into his pocket. It closed on the best single protection he did have: his British passport. Against certain kinds of danger, it was sovereign. Against others, though . . .

'Jesus!' a woman said in American English, 'why in hell

would anybody want to set up a meeting in this goddamn place?'

A man laughed hoarsely. 'You just covered the waterfront there, Penny,' he said, pausing for breath every few words. 'But I don't reckon the Jews'd reckon you got 'em wet once.'

'Am I supposed to care?' the woman – Penny – asked. 'The tracer gadget says that Frenchman's in there, so we've got to keep going.'

'You'll get yourself killed if you charge ahead like that,' the man remarked. His accent, while still from the other side of the Atlantic, was different from Penny's. 'Let me get out in front of you.'

He came out from around the corner with a soldier's caution – and with a pistol in his hand. None of that would have kept Dutourd from spotting him, as David Goldfarb knew very well. Before any fireworks started, Goldfarb said, 'Good day, there. Lovely weather, we're having, eh?'

'You must be the limey. We've heard something about you.' The man leaned on a stick, but the gun in his other hand remained very steady. 'Don't tell me you don't have that Frenchman around here somewhere.'

The woman, a brassy blond, came into sight behind him. She also carried a pistol. Goldfarb didn't think either of their weapons would do them much good if Pierre Dutourd opened up: he'd be able to get off at least a couple of shots before they realized just where he was.

For the moment, Dutourd stayed hidden. Goldfarb asked, 'What do you want with him? And who are you, anyway?'

'Name's Rance Auerbach – U.S. Army, retired,' the man answered. 'This here's Penny Summers. We'll talk about what we want when we see Dutourd. And just whose side are you on, buddy? Come on, speak up.' He gestured with the pistol, a large, heavy weapon.

Goldfarb gave his name. 'As for whose side I'm on, *my own* is the answer that springs to mind.'

'You can tell whose side he's on, Rance,' Penny said. 'He's

got to be hooked up with those British smugglers – probably that Roundbush fellow, the guy you wrote a letter to for me. Only thing they ever wanted was to keep more ginger going through to the Lizards.'

'You know Group Captain Roundbush?' Goldfarb asked in surprise.

'Yeah,' the American named Rance answered. 'We used to do some business together, a long time ago. I haven't been in that business for a while – I haven't been in much in the way of any business for a while – but we've sorta stayed in touch. I suppose he reckoned he could get some use out of me sooner or later.'

That sounded very much like Basil Roundbush, damned if it didn't. 'And what's wrong with getting more ginger through to the Lizards?' David asked. He could think of several things offhand, but, much against his will, felt compelled to take the side of those from whom he was also compelled to take orders. He wondered if Dutourd spoke English. The Frenchman had given no sign of it, but that didn't necessarily signify.

'Not a damn thing as far as we're concerned – not personally, anyhow,' Auerbach said. 'But we've got to do what those little scaly bastards tell us to do. And so . . .' He took a step forward.

Knowing the Lizards would oppose anything that had to do with ginger, Goldfarb got ready to throw himself to one side, with luck escaping the fire-fight bound to break out in a moment. Before anyone could start shooting, the back door to the synagogue burst open. Germans in SS uniforms with submachine guns stormed out and covered Goldfarb and the two Americans. Others aimed into the undergrowth. The officer who emerged behind them spoke in the language of the Race: 'Come forth, Dutourd. If you do not, we will have to kill you.' Sullenly, Pierre Dutourd stood up and raised his hands high. The SS *Sturmbannführer* nodded. 'Very good. In the name of the Greater German *Reich*, you are all under arrest.'

* * *

Pshing came into Atvar's private office. 'Excuse me for interrupting, Exalted Fleetlord, but the Tosevite Moishe Russie is attempting to reach you by telephone. Shall I put him off?'

'No, I will speak to him,' Atvar answered. 'The situation in India remains too muddled to offer any easy or quick solution. I am willing to put aside consideration of it for the time being.' He was, in fact, eager to put aside consideration of it for the time being, but Pshing did not have to know that. 'Transfer the call to my terminal,' he told his adjutant.

'It shall be done,' Pshing said, and went out to do it.

Moishe Russie's image appeared on the screen in front of Atvar. 'I greet you, Exalted Fleetlord,' the Tosevite said. 'I thank you for agreeing to hear of my troubles.'

'I greet you,' Atvar said. 'Do note that I have agreed to nothing of the sort. If you prove wearisome, I shall return to the work in which I was previously engaged. Keeping that warning in mind at all times, you may proceed.'

'For your generosity, I thank you,' Russie said. Was that irony? Would the Big Ugly be so presumptuous while seeking a favor? Atvar could not be sure, even after long acquaintance with him. With a sigh that might have come from the throat of a male of the Race, Russie went on, 'I have just learned that a relative of mine, a certain David Goldfarb, is a prisoner in the Greater German *Reich*. If you can use your good offices to help obtain his release, I shall be forever in your debt.'

'You are already in my debt,' Atvar pointed out, in case the Tosevite had forgotten. 'And how did this relative of yours become a prisoner inside the *Reich*?'

While asking the question, he checked the computer. As he'd thought, Russie had no relatives living inside the *Reich*: only in Palestine and Poland, both of which the Race held, and in Britain, which retained a tenuous independence from both the Race and the *Reich*. Meanwhile, he turned his other eye turret toward the part of the screen on which Russie was saying, 'The Germans arrested him in the company of two Americans

503

named Auerbach and Summers. You will please recall, Exalted Fleetlord, that my cousin is also a Jew.'

'Then he was unwise to enter the *Reich*,' Atvar said. Yet Moishe Russie's shot struck home. The Race remained appalled at the savage campaign the Deutsche waged against the Jews. And any opportunity to irritate this particular lot of Big Uglies was sweet to Atvar.

Furthermore, the names of the other two Big Uglies Russie had mentioned were somehow familiar. Not wanting to say them aloud, the fleetlord keyed them into the computer. Sure enough, a report about those two had come to his notice not long before. Officials over on the lesser continental mass had recruited them to help suppress the trade in smuggled ginger coming out of the *Reich*.

'Your relative was cooperating with these Tosevites, then?' Atvar asked. That would give him another reason for demanding this Goldfarb's release and infuriating whatever Deutsch officials had to arrange it.

'He was caught with them, so how could he have been doing anything different?' Russie asked reasonably. 'But they are not Jews, and so do not face the immediate danger in which he finds himself.'

'I understand,' Atvar said. 'Very well: I will see what can be done. And what can be done, Dr. Russie, shall be done.'

'I thank you, Exalted Fleetlord,' Moishe Russie said. 'These Tosevites, for your information, were seized in the city of Marseille.'

'Yes, yes,' Atvar said impatiently. Russie didn't know he already knew that: it was, at any rate, the city in which Summers and Auerbach (he gathered the female was more important, or at least more deeply involved in the ginger trade, than the male) had been sent. 'I shall investigate, and I shall do what I think best in this regard.'

Russie thanked him again, then broke the connection. Atvar looked at the square on the screen, now blank, where the Big Ugly's image had appeared. He hissed in slow, almost reluctant approval. A male of the Race could not have begged for a favor any more effectively than Russie had done. And Russie had known Atvar would be likely to give him what he wanted for the sake of irking the Deutsche.

After replaying his conversation with Moishe Russie to remind himself of the name of the doctor's relatives, Atvar telephoned the Deutsch Foreign Ministry in Nuremberg. The image of the Big Ugly on the screen was less sharp than Moishe Russie's had been; Tosevite video equipment did not measure up to that which the Race manufactured.

Despite the poor quality of the image, Atvar thought he saw surprise on the Big Ugly's mobile features when the fellow got a good look at his body paint. 'Are you familiar with the matter of David Goldfarb?' the fleetlord demanded, as if to a subordinate he knew to be none too bright.

Rather to his surprise, the Tosevite answered, 'I am. In what way does this case interest the Race?'

'I want this Tosevite released – and,' Atvar added, 'the other two Tosevites, the Americans, seized with him.'

'Three other Tosevites were seized with him,' the Deutsch male replied. 'One of them was Pierre Dutourd, the notorious ginger smuggler. Do you want him released, too? He and the other three were, I repeat, all seized together.'

Moishe Russie hadn't said anything about that. Atvar suddenly wondered whether this Goldfarb had been helping Auerbach and Summers or whether he'd been on the smuggler's side. Still, the Tosevite's question had an obvious answer: 'Yes, give us this Pierre Dutourd, too. Ginger-smuggling is a wicked business; we will punish him.'

'Ginger-smuggling is not a crime under the laws of the *Reich*,' the Deutsch functionary observed.

'If it is not a crime, why is this Dutourd' – Atvar pronounced the Big Ugly's name as best he could – 'in a Deutsch prison?'

'Why?' The official's face twisted into the expression that showed amusement. 'He is in our prison because we say he ought to be there. We need no more reason than that. The

Reich does not propose to let anyone who might be dangerous to it run around loose causing trouble.'

That made a certain amount of sense to Atvar: more sense than the bizarre and self-destructive policies of the snoutcounting Americans, at any rate. The fleetlord let out an angry hiss, anger directed at himself. If a Deutsch policy made sense to him, something had to be wrong with the policy or with him or with both.

He said, 'I assure you, the Race will punish this smuggler as he deserves. You need have no doubts on that score.'

'You of the Race hardly know what punishment is,' the Big Ugly replied. 'We will keep this male for ourselves. We do know these things. We know them in detail.' Though he spoke the language of the Race, gloating anticipation that seemed unique to the Tosevites filled his voice.

Atvar suppressed a shudder. The Big Uglies, and especially the Deutsch Big Uglies, exulted in the ferocity of the punishments they meted out. The fleetlord forced himself not to dwell on that, but to concentrate on the business at hand. This male had refused to release Dutourd, but had not said a word about the other prisoners. 'Very well, then – you may keep this smuggler,' Atvar said. 'But turn over to us the two American Tosevites, and also the British Jew, Goldfarb. They did not come to your territory with the intent of harming you.'

He hoped that wasn't true of Auerbach and Summers, but could not be sure, and it made a good bargaining point. He hated having to try to get a Tosevite's leave to obtain his desires. He hated even more the idea of having to admit that a Tosevite not-empire had territory to which it was entitled. And he hoped mentioning that Goldfarb was a Jew wouldn't get Moishe Russie's relative liquidated out of hand. He thought as well of Russie as he did of any Tosevite.

'If you want the Americans, Exalted Fleetlord, you are welcome to them,' the Deutsch official said. 'We have no use for them, and giving them to you will help embarrass the United States. As for the Jew . . . You know that we aim to keep the *Reich* free of his kind.'

'Yes, I know that,' Atvar said, and did his best not to let his disgust with the policy the Deutsche pursued show. 'If you removed him from your not-empire by sending him here to me, you would be keeping your not-empire as free of Jews as if you killed him.'

'He could still cause trouble for the *Reich* if we let him live,' the Big Ugly replied. 'And the British would care very little about what happened to him: they are slowly coming round to our way of thinking.' But he did not reject the fleetlord's request out of hand, as he might have – as Tosevites often seemed to take a perverse pleasure in doing.

Noting that, Atvar said, 'If you kill him, the Race will care, whether the British Big Uglies do or not. Do you understand me?'

The Deutsch Big Ugly used his short, blunt, forkless tongue to lick his lips. That was a sign of cautious consideration among the Big Uglies, or so researchers had assured Atvar. After a pause, the official said, 'You are taking an improperly high-handed attitude, Exalted Fleetlord.' Atvar said nothing. The Big Ugly licked his lips again. He made a fist and slammed it down onto the top of the desk behind which he sat. In any species, that would have been a sign of anger. 'Very well,' he snapped. 'Since you love Jews so well, you may have this one, too.'

Time had proved it was useless to point out that the Race did not particularly love Jews, that their Tosevite neighbors treated them so badly as to make the Race seem a better alternative. Since the Deutsche seemed unable to figure that out for themselves, Atvar had no interest in enlightening them. The fleetlord contented himself with saying, 'I thank you. My subordinates will arrange to retrieve this Tosevite.'

'If he should ever enter the *Reich* again, he will be sorry he was ever hatched,' the Deutsch male said, which had to translate a Tosevite idiom all too literally into the language of the Race. 'Farewell.' The Big Ugly's image disappeared.

No male or female of the Race would have been so rude to Atvar. Big Uglies, though, had already proved they could be far ruder than this. The fleetlord telephoned Moishe Russie. 'It is accomplished,' he said when the connection was made. 'Your relative will in due course be returned to you.'

'I thank you, Exalted Fleetlord.' Russie added an emphatic cough.

'You are welcome.' Atvar said. Maybe Russie did not know this Big Ugly named Goldfarb had been involved in the ginger-smuggling trade – or more likely, maybe he did not know Atvar would know. But know the fleetlord did. And he also knew he would do everything he could to learn as much about the trade as Goldfarb could or would tell him.

'He should be here any minute now,' Dr. Moishe Russie said, peering out though one of the narrow windows that gave a view of the street.

'Father, you've been saying that for the past hour,' Reuven Russie pointed out with such patient as he could muster.

'The Nazis are punctual,' his father said. 'The Lizards are also punctual. So I ought to know when he will be here.'

'We know it, too,' Reuven said, even less patiently than before. 'You don't have to keep reminding us every five minutes.'

'No, eh?' Moishe Russie said. 'and why not?' His eyes twinkled.

Reuven smiled, too, but it took effort. He knew his father was joking, but the jokes had turned into what Jane Archibald would have called kidding on the square. His father was too worried about his distant cousin to be anything but serious behind those twinkling eyes.

Silent as a thought, a hydrogen-powered motorcar glided to a stop in front of the house. A door opened. A man in utterly ordinary clothes got out and walked up the short path to the door. He knocked.

Moishe Russie let him in. 'Welcome to Jerusalem, Cousin,'

he said, folding David Goldfarb into an embrace. 'It's been too long.' He spoke Yiddish, not the Hebrew the Jews of Palestine used most of the time.

'Thanks, Moishe,' Goldfarb answered in the same language. 'One thing I'll tell you – it's good to be here. It's good to be anywhere but a Nazi gaol.' His Yiddish was fluent enough, but had an odd accent. After a moment, Reuven realized the flavoring came from the English that was his relative's first language. David Goldfarb turned toward him and stuck out a hand. 'Hello. You're a man now. That hardly seems possible.'

'Time does go on.' Reuven spoke English, not Yiddish. It seemed every bit as natural to him, if not more so. He hadn't used Yiddish much since coming to Palestine. While he had no trouble understanding it, forming anything but childish sentences didn't come easy.

'Too bloody right it does,' Goldfarb said, also in English. He was a few years younger than Reuven's father. Unlike Moishe Russie, he still kept most of his hair, but it had more gray in it than the senior Russie's. He must have seen that for himself, for he went on, 'And it's a miracle I'm not white as snow on top after the past couple of weeks. Thank God you could help, Moishe.'

Reuven's father shrugged. 'I did not have to go into a gaol after you,' he said, sticking to Yiddish. 'You did that for me. All I did was ask the Lizards to help get you out, and they did it.'

'They must think a lot of you,' Goldfarb answered; now he returned to his odd-sounding Yiddish. *If Jane spoke Yiddish, she'd speak it like that,* Reuven thought. His cousin added, 'They'd better think a lot of you now, after everything they put you through back then.'

Moishe Russie shrugged again. 'That was a long time ago.'

'Too right it was,' Goldfarb muttered in English; he didn't seem to notice going back and forth between languages. Still in English, he continued, 'We'd all be better off if the buggers had never come in the first place.'

'You might be,' Moishe Russie said. 'England might be. But me? My family?' He shook his head. 'No. If the Race had not come, we would all be dead. I am sure of it. You saw Lodz. You never saw Warsaw. And Warsaw would only have got worse as the war went on.'

'Warsaw was bad, very bad,' Reuven agreed; he had no happy recollections of the city in which he'd been born. 'But what the Nazis did with their killing factories is worse. If they'd stayed in Poland, I think Father is right: we would all have gone through them. Next to Hitler, Haman was nothing much.'

Goldfarb frowned. Plainly, he wanted to argue. As plainly, he had trouble seeing how he could. Before he found anything to say, the twins came out of the kitchen. The scowl disappeared from his face. Grinning, he turned to Moishe. 'All right, they're as cute as their photos. I didn't think they could be.'

Reuven suppressed the strong urge to retch. The twins stretched like cats, being charming on purpose. As with cats, it struck Reuven as an act. 'They're miserable nuisances a lot of the time,' he said – in Yiddish, of which Esther and Judith had only a smattering: his father and mother often spoke it when they didn't want the twins to know what was going on.

'Well, I have children of my own, and every one of them thinks the others are nuisances,' Goldfarb said, also in Yiddish. He eyed Judith and Esther, then switched to slow, clear English: 'Which one of you is which?'

'I'm Esther,' Judith said.

'I'm Judith,' Esther echoed.

Reuven coughed. So did his father. David Goldfarb raised an eyebrow. He'd had practice with children, all right; his expression was identical to the one Moishe Russie used when he caught Reuven or Judith or Esther stretching the truth.

'Oh, all right,' Esther said. 'Maybe it is the other way around.'

'You couldn't prove it by me,' Goldfarb said. 'But your father and your brother have their suspicions.'

'We came out here to say that supper was ready,' Judith said. 'Who says that doesn't really matter, does it?'

'Not if it's true,' Reuven said. Both his sisters sniffed indignantly at the possibility that he could doubt them. Having failed to doubt them a few times when he should have been wary, he bore up under their disapproval.

Supper was a couple of roasted chickens, with chickpeas and carrots and a white wine that made Goldfarb nod in what seemed surprised approval. 'I don't usually drink wine, except during *Pesach*,' he said. 'This is good.'

'It's not bad, anyhow,' Moishe Russie said. 'When I drink anything these days, it's mostly wine. I haven't got the head for whiskey or vodka any more, and the beer you can get here is a lot nastier than what they made in Poland – in England, too, for that matter.'

'If you get used to drinking wine, you won't want to drink beer, anyhow,' Reuven said. 'Beer's thin, sour stuff by comparison.'

'That only goes to show you've been drinking bad beer,' David Goldfarb answered. 'From what your father said, I don't suppose it's any wonder.'

Rivka Russie brought matters back to the more immediate by softly saying, 'It's good to see you here and safe, David.'

'*Omayn,*' Moishe Russie added.

Their cousin – Reuven's cousin once further removed – emptied his wineglass with a convulsive gulp less closely related to how much he enjoyed the vintage than to its anesthetic properties. 'It's bloody good to be here, believe me,' he said, and inclined his head to Reuven's father. 'Thanks again for pulling the wires to help get me out. You did more than the British consul in Marseille. You couldn't very well have done less, let me tell you, because he didn't do anything.'

'It was my pleasure, you believe me,' Moishe Russie said, waving away the thanks. Reuven had seen many times that his father had a hard time accepting praise.

'What was it like, there in the Nazis' prison?' one of the twins asked.

'It was the worst place in the world,' David Goldfarb said. Esther and Judith both gasped. Goldfarb looked at his glass, as if regretting it was empty. Moishe Russie saw that glance and proceeded to remedy the situation. After drinking, Goldfarb went on, 'The cell was only a cell, with a cot and a bucket. Not much different to a British cell, I shouldn't wonder. They fed me – I got a little hungry, but not very. They asked me questions. They didn't knock my teeth out or hit me very often or very hard. It was still the worst place in the world.'

'Why?' Esther asked, while Judith said, 'I don't understand.'

'I'll tell you why,' Goldfarb said. 'Because even though they didn't do any of those things, they could have. I knew it, and they knew it, and they knew I knew it. Knowing it did almost as good a job of breaking me as real torture would have done.'

He'd spoken English; word by word, the twins couldn't have had any trouble following what he said. But they didn't understand it. Reuven could see as much. He did, or thought he did, though he was just as well pleased not to have had the experience that would have made understanding certain.

His mother asked, 'What were you doing there in the first place?'

'Trying to help some of my British . . . friends,' Goldfarb said. 'They did some of their dealings through a Frenchman who had been operating on his own, but they started losing money – or not making so much money, I'm not sure which – when the Germans got their hooks into him. So they sent me down to the south of France to see if I couldn't persuade him to go back to being an independent operator. Why not?' His mouth twisted; he emptied the wineglass again. 'I was just an expendable Jew.'

'Ginger is as bad for the Lizards as cocaine or heroin is for us,' Reuven's father observed, 'maybe worse. I wish you'd never got caught up in that.'

'So do I,' Goldfarb said. '*Vey iz mir*, so do I. But having dreadful things happen to my family would have been even worse, and so off I went.'

Moishe Russie reached for more wine himself when he heard that, something he rarely did. Nodding heavily, he said, 'When I was having trouble with the Lizards in Warsaw, I had help getting Rivka and Reuven to a place where the Race couldn't get their hands on them, so I understand how you feel.'

'We were in a cellar!' Reuven exclaimed, astonished at how the memory came back. 'It was dark all the time, because we didn't have many lamps or candles.'

'That's right,' his father said. Reuven shook his head in astonishment; he hadn't so much as thought of that hideaway for many years. His father looked across the table at Goldfarb. 'And the Lizards were trying to put Dutourd out of business while you were trying to set him up again – and the Nazis caught their people, too.'

'If you stick your head in the lion's mouth, you know there's a chance he'll bite down,' Goldfarb said with a shrug. 'I gather you got the Americans out of their cells, too?'

'Yes, I managed that,' Moishe Russie said. 'Getting them was easier than getting you, in fact. The Germans worry more about offending the Race than they do about offending England.'

'I can understand that, worse luck for me,' David Goldfarb said. 'The only one who got left behind was Dutourd. He would have dealt with me, I think. I hope he doesn't get into too much trouble for that.' He paused. 'The Lizards started asking me questions the minute I got on their plane in Marseille. And do you know what? I answered every one of them. If my "friends" back home don't like it, too bloody bad.'

'Good for you,' Reuven said.

His father nodded and remarked, 'My guess is that the Frenchman won't. He's useful to the Nazis – he's not just another damned Jew.'

Goldfarb inclined his head. 'As one damned Jew to another – to a whole family full of others – I thank you.' He poured

513

more wine into his glass, then raised it high. *'L'chaim!'* he said loudly.

'To life!' Reuven echoed, and was proud to have answered a beat ahead of his father and mother and sister. He drank his wine; it went down sweet and smooth as honey.

Felless felt like a hypocrite as she accompanied Ambassador Veffani into the *Reichs* Ministry of Justice in Nuremberg. She also felt even smaller than she usually did while entering a building the Big Uglies had built to suit themselves. The Ministry of Justice, like a lot of public buildings of the *Reich*, was deliberately designed to minimize the importance of the individual, whether that individual was a Tosevite or belonged to the Race.

'They know not the Emperor, so they have to build like this,' Veffani said when Felless remarked on the style. 'They hope false splendor will make their not-emperor and his minions seem as impressive to their subjects as generations of tradition have made the Emperor seem to us.'

'That is . . . a very perceptive remark, superior sir,' Felless said. 'I have seen similar speculations, but seldom so pithily expressed.' For a moment, interest made her forget her craving for ginger – but only for a moment. The craving never left for long – and now she and Veffani were visiting the Deutsch minister of justice to plead for harsher treatment of a captured ginger smuggler. If that was not irony, the stuff had never hatched from its shell.

Deutsch soldiers in steel helmets stiffened as Veffani and Felless reached the top of the broad stone stairway leading to the entrance. They clicked their booted heels together, a courtesy rather like assuming the posture of respect. One of them proved to speak the language of the Race: 'I greet you, Ambassador, and your colleague. How may I serve you?'

'We have an appointment with Justice Minister Dietrich,' Veffani answered, observing protocol. 'Please escort us to him.'

'It shall be done.' The Deutsch guard's about-turn had none of the smooth elegance a member of the Race would have given it, but possessed a stiff impressiveness of its own. Over his shoulder, the Big Ugly added, 'Follow me.'

Follow him Veffani and Felless did, down corridors that dwarfed Big Uglies, let alone the two of them. Deutsch functionaries, some in the business clothes the Tosevites favored, more in the uniform wrappings the Deutsche used to show status in place of body paint (and, Felless realized, to overawe Tosevites not similarly wrapped), bustled here and there. As with the Race, they seemed to feel that the busier they looked, the more important they actually were.

Minister Dietrich had a doorway even larger and higher than any of the others. A Tosevite miscreant hauled before him would surely feel he had committed some crime for which he could never atone. Felless felt the Big Ugly architect had committed a breach of taste for which he could never atone. A great deal of Deutsch monumental architecture inspired the same feeling in her.

The guard escorting Felless and Veffani spoke back and forth with Dietrich's secretary in the Deutsch language. Felless had picked up a few words of it, but could not follow a conversation. 'It is all formality, of no great consequence,' Veffani whispered to her.

She made the hand gesture of agreement. The secretary spoke the language of the Race about as well as a Tosevite could: 'Come with me, Ambassador, Senior Researcher. Minister Dietrich will be pleased to hear whatever you may have to say, although, of course, he cannot promise to fulfill all your desires.'

'I understand,' Veffani said. 'As always, I look forward to seeing him.'

Veffani is a hypocrite, too, Felless thought. The ambassador's hypocrisy, luckily for him, had nothing to do with the herb. He merely had to pretend the Big Uglies with whom he dealt not only were but deserved to be his equals. Felless still found that concept outrageous. She had come to Tosev 3 assuming the world would be altogether conquered, subservient to the will of the Race. That hadn't happened, but she remained convinced it should have.

After more formal pleasantries, the secretary – who would also serve as translator – escorted the male and female of the Race into the presence of Justice Minister Dietrich. His gray hair and flabby face showed him to be an elderly male. 'I greet you, Veffani,' he said in the language of the Race. His accent was far thicker than that of his secretary.

'I greet you, Sepp,' Veffani replied. Sepp, he had given Felless to understand, was a nickname for Josef. The Big Uglies, already possessed of too many names from the standpoint of the Race, added to the confusion by using informal versions of them whenever they felt like it. *One more piece of Tosevite inefficiency,* Felless thought. Veffani went on, 'I present to you Senior Researcher Felless, who is also concerned with the problem ginger poses for the Race.'

'I greet you, Senior Researcher,' Dietrich said.

'I greet you, Justice Minister,' Felless answered; using his title let her avoid calling him *superior sir,* an honorific she did not care to give to any Tosevite.

Dietrich spoke in the Deutsch language. The secretary translated: 'And are you intimately concerned with the problem of ginger, Senior Researcher?' He put undue stress on the word *intimately*. Both he and his superior let out the yips the Big Uglies used for laughter.

Failing to see any joke, Felless answered, 'Yes, I am,' which seemed to amuse the Tosevites all over again.

'Shall we begin?' Veffani asked, and Sepp Dietrich, seeming to recall his manners, waved him and Felless to chairs. They were built for Tosevites, and so not comfortable to the male and female of the Race, but refusing would have been most impolite.

'So,' Minister Dietrich said, 'we come again to the matter of this Dutourd, do we? The Foreign Ministry has already told the fleetlord that he shall not be surrendered.'

'So it has,' Veffani said. To Felless, his tone indicated strong disapproval. Whether Dietrich and his secretary understood that, she could not tell. The ambassador resumed, 'That you seek to use him for your own purposes and against the interests of the Race is, however, not acceptable to us.'

'How can you say such a thing?' Dietrich asked. 'We have him in prison. We are keeping him in prison for the time being. If he can do anything against you while in prison, he is a formidable character indeed, not so?'

'You are not keeping him in prison because of what he has done against the Race,' Veffani said. 'You are keeping him in prison because he wanted to go on doing it on his own, and not for you.'

'He is in prison,' Dietrich said, not bothering to deny the assertion. 'You cannot ask for more, since dealing in ginger is not a crime under the laws of the *Reich*.'

'Superior sir, may I speak?' Felless asked. When Veffani used the affirmative hand gesture, she turned both her eye turrets toward Sepp Dietrich. 'Justice Minister, if under your laws it is not a crime to deal in ginger, we can and will revise our laws to make it no crime to deal in narcotics that appeal to Tosevites, and to make it legal and indeed encouraged to smuggle those narcotics into the independent Tosevite not-empires.'

As one of the ornaments on the wrapping around his torso, Dietrich wore a small silvery pin showing a Big Ugly's skull with a couple of crossed bones behind it. His own features froze into an expression no more lively than that skull's. 'If you wish to play that game, we can play it,' he said through his interpreter. 'No drug you can bring into the *Reich* will do as much to us as ginger does to you.'

'Truth.' Felless admitted what she could scarcely deny. 'But you are already doing all you can to us with ginger.' She knew the truth in that to a degree Dietrich did not realize. 'If you keep trying to do all you can to us with ginger, why should we do anything less to you?'

517

She waited until the interpreter put that into the language of the Deutsche. Sepp Dietrich's jaw worked as he chewed on it both literally and metaphorically. He said, 'This is not far from a threat of war.'

Veffani's eye turrets slewed rapidly toward Felless. The ambassador was undoubtedly wondering what sort of trouble she'd got herself into. So was she, but she went ahead regardless: 'Why is it a threat of war when we do it to you, but nothing of the sort when you do it to us?'

Dietrich grunted. 'Perhaps you should be talking with the foreign minister and not with me.'

'Perhaps you should not evade your responsibilities,' Felless shot back. 'This male Tosevite is in a Deutsch prison. An official from the Foreign Ministry has already refused to turn him over to the Race, as Ambassador Veffani said. That leaves him in your hands.'

'It also constitutes an act unfriendly to the Race,' Veffani put in. 'From the actions of the *Reich*, someone might conclude that peace between your not-empire and the Empire does not matter to you. I think that would be an unfortunate and dangerous conclusion for anyone to reach. Do you not agree?'

Watching the Big Ugly squirm gave Felless pleasure approaching that of a taste of ginger. After coughing and wiping metabolic cooling water away from his forehead (a sign of distress among Tosevites, the experts agreed), Dietrich said, 'I am not unfriendly to anyone. The *Reich* is not unfriendly to anyone except Jews and other racial inferiors, and Dutourd, whatever else you may say of him, is not a Jew.'

'He is an enemy of the Race,' Veffani said. 'Keeping him in prison for a long time would be an act of courtesy to the Race.'

'I shall take what you say under advisement,' Sepp Dietrich replied. 'The matter may have to be decided at a level higher than mine, though.'

'Who is higher than you, Justice Minister Dietrich?' Felless demanded. 'If you cannot decide here, who can?'

'Why, *Reichs* Chancellor Himmler, of course.' Dietrich

seemed surprised she needed to ask. She was surprised the head of the Deutsch not-empire would concern himself about the fate of a ginger smuggler. Dietrich proceeded to explain why: 'The *Reichs* Chancellor yielded to the Race when he let you destroy an air base after the attack on your colonization fleet, though the *Reich*, he has insisted, was not guilty of that attack. To yield to you again might be taken as a sign of weakness, and we Deutsche are not weak. We are strong, and we grow stronger day by day.'

That was true. It was also, to the Race's way of thinking, extremely unfortunate. From the point of view of the *Reich*, Dietrich's words did make a certain amount of sense. Felless reluctantly admitted as much to herself.

But Veffani said, 'Protecting criminals is not a sign of strength. It is a sign of criminality.'

'I did not agree to receive you to listen to insults,' Sepp Dietrich said. 'Now I must bid you good day. And I remind you that this Dutourd has committed no crimes in the view of the *Reich*.'

'And I remind you that the *Reich* can also redefine crimes to suit itself,' Veffani answered as he rose from his chair. Felless imitated the ambassador, who added, 'I shall report the substance of your remarks to the fleetlord.'

Dietrich made a sort of noise the interpreter did not translate. Felless followed Veffani out of the justice minister's office. When she started to say something, he made the negative hand gesture. *I am a fool,* she thought. *If the Deutsche are recording anywhere, they are recording here.*

Only after the two members of the Race had left the Ministry of Justice could she say what had in mind: 'Congratulations. You showed them we are not to be trifled with.'

'And to you, Senior Researcher,' Veffani said, 'for your able assistance.'

16

Vyacheslav Molotov woke with a head pounding like a mechanical hammer in the biggest steel mill in Magnitogorsk. *By the devil's grandmother,* he thought blurrily, *I haven't had a hangover like that since I was a student before the Revolution.*

Only gradually, as full awareness seeped back into him, did he realize how long ago the Revolution had been. For some reason, he remembered that before remembering he'd had nothing stronger than fizzy mineral water the night before. That alarmed him.

He sat up in bed, which forcibly brought his attention to its not being his bed, not being the one in which he'd fallen asleep. It was a cheap cot on which a newly conscripted recruit would have had trouble getting any rest. He looked around. He was not in his bedroom, either. Somehow, that didn't hit him too hard. By then, it was scarcely a surprise.

He tried to figure out where he was and how he'd got there. *Where* quickly became obvious. If this wasn't a cell, he'd never seen one. As cells went, it was fairly luxurious; most would have had straw on the floor rather than a cot of any sort, no matter how unsatisfactory. Watery sunlight dodged past the bars over the narrow windows.

Who would put me in a cell? Molotov's mind was still slower than it should have been (*someone's drugged me,* he realized, which should have been obvious from the start), but only two candidates presented themselves. Beria or Zhukov? Zhukov or Beria? *The lady or the tiger?* The drug – chloroform? – had to be what let that fragment of foolishness float up into the light of day.

'Guard!' he called, his voice hoarse, his throat raspy and sore. 'Guard!' How many counterrevolutionaries had called out to their gaolers during the great days? How few had got even the slightest particle of what they wanted? How little Molotov had expected to find himself in the position in which he'd put so many others, both during the Revolution and throughout the endless rounds of purges that followed.

He wondered why he wasn't simply dead. Had he been staging a coup, he would not have let his opponents survive. Lenin had thought the same way, and disposed of Tsar Nicholas and his family. With wry amusement, Molotov remembered how shocked the Lizards had been to learn that bit of Soviet history.

To his surprise, a guard did come peer into the cell through the little barred window set into the door. 'Awake, are you?' he grunted, his accent White Russian.

'No, I always shout for guards in my sleep,' Molotov snapped.

He might have known the fellow would prove imperturbable. 'Good thing you're with it again. You have some papers to sign. Or maybe you could have done that in your sleep, too.'

'I am not going to sign anything,' Molotov declared. He wondered if he meant it. He'd dished out a lot of pain, but he'd never had to try to take much. People who weren't on the business end of torture talked about withstanding it. People who were knew how rare an ability that was. Most men, once the anguish started, would do anything to make it stop. He dared a question: 'Where am I?'

Beria or Zhukov? Zhukov or Beria? Zhukov, he judged, would not have left him alive if he ever decided to strike for the top. But he didn't think Beria would have, either. Beria, though, might be inclined to gloat, and . . .

He didn't get much chance to think about it. The guard answered, 'You're right where you belong, that's where.' He laughed at his own cleverness, rocking back on his heels to do it. Then he shoved his face up close to the window again. 'And you'll do what you're told, or you'll never do anything else again.' He went on his way, whistling a song that had been popular a few years before.

Molotov's stomach growled. It was ravenous, no matter how his head felt. He wondered how long he'd been drugged asleep. One more thing they wouldn't tell him, of course. He looked at the window. Was the stripe of sunlight it admitted higher or lower than before? That would eventually tell him whether this was morning or afternoon. But even if he knew, what could he do with the knowledge? Nothing he could see.

Knowing in whose prison he sat . . . That could be all-important. And he didn't need long to figure it out, either, once the cell took on a little more immediate reality for him. Here and there, previous occupants had scrawled or scratched their opinions on the walls. Quite a few were uncomplimentary toward the NKVD. None said a word about the Red Army.

'Beria,' Molotov said softly. So. The Mingrelian wanted to go where the Georgian had blazed the trail, did he? With cold political horse sense behind his judgment, Molotov didn't think Beria could get away with it for long. The Soviet Union had had one ruler from the Caucasus, and that was plenty for a long time. But horse sense, unfortunately, said nothing about Molotov's personal chances for escape.

And here came the guard again. He shoved papers between the bars of the window set into the door. A cheap pen followed the papers. 'Sign here. Don't take all day about it, either, not if you know what's good for you.'

'I will remember your face and learn your name,' Molotov said. The guard walked off again, laughing.

Molotov read the papers. According to them, he had resigned as General Secretary because of failing health. They maintained he looked forward to retirement in some place with a warm climate – perhaps the Caucasus, so Beria could make sure he didn't get into mischief, perhaps the hell in which, as a good Marxist-Leninist, he wasn't supposed to believe.

If he signed those papers, how long would Beria let him live? He had the idea he was still breathing for no other reason than to put his name on the requisite lines. But if he didn't, what would Lavrenti Pavlovich do to him? Did he want to find out? Did he have the nerve to find out?

Whatever it was, it couldn't be worse than killing him. So he told himself, at any rate. A few minutes later, the guard opened the door. He was big and beefy. So were his three pals. When he checked the papers, he scowled. 'You forget how to write?' he demanded, his voice scratchy from too many cigarettes.

'No,' Molotov said. It was the last coherent sound he made for the next several minutes. The goons set on him with a gusto that showed they enjoyed their work. They also showed a certain amount of skill, inflicting a maximum of pain with a minimum of actual damage. The one who wrapped Molotov's fingers around a pencil in a particular way and then squeezed his hand had especially nasty talents along those lines. Molotov howled like a dog baying at the moon.

After a bit, the guard shoved the papers in front of his face again. 'Remember your name yet, old man?' *Yes* leapt into Molotov's throat. But then he thought, *If I yield, I am likely to die*. He made himself shake his head. The guard sighed, as if at a bad run of cards. The beating went on.

Feigning unconsciousness came easy for Molotov, though lying still when one of the bastards kicked him in the ribs was anything but. Grumbling, the guards stamped out of the cell. But they would be back. Molotov knew too well they would be back. Maybe the next round of torment would break him. Maybe they wouldn't bother with another round. Maybe they would just kill him and get it over with.

He gathered his strength, such as it was. He'd sent a lot of men to executions without wondering what went through their minds while they awaited death. What went through his mind was surprisingly banal: he didn't want things to end this way. But no one, now, cared what he wanted.

Sooner than he'd expected, the door opened again. He braced himself, not that that would do any good. Only one NKVD man this time, with a silenced pistol in his hand. *It is the end,* Molotov thought. Then the fellow spoke: 'Comrade General Secretary?' His Russian had a rhythmic Polish accent.

And, suddenly, hope lived in Molotov's narrow, heaving chest. 'Nussboym,' he said, pleased and proud he'd remembered the name. He spoke with desperate urgency: 'Get me out of here and you can name your own price.'

David Nussboym nodded. 'Come along, then,' he said. 'Keep your head down – make yourself hard to recognize. If anyone does figure out who you are, look abused.'

'It will not be hard.' Molotov heaved himself to his feet. Nussboym aimed the pistol at him. He shambled out of the cell, looking down at the cheap linoleum of the floor as he'd been ordered.

A few men passed them in the halls, but a guard leading a prisoner excited no special comment. Molotov was nearing the doorway and realizing Nussboym would have to shoot the guards there when something outside emitted a rumbling roar and the door came crashing in. One of the guards cursed and grabbed for his pistol. A burst of machine-gun fire cut him down.

An immensely amplified voice bellowed: 'Surrender in there! Resistance is hopeless! The Red Army has this prison surrounded! Come out with your hands up!'

Molotov wasted no time whatever in obeying. Only later did he wonder if the tank machine-gunner might have shot him down for rushing forward so quickly. David Nussboym threw down his pistol and followed a heartbeat later.

A Red Army infantry lieutenant with a clipboard stood behind the tank. The fellow looked too young to shave, let alone serve the Soviet Union. 'Give me your name, old-timer, and make it snappy,' he barked.

'Vyacheslav Mikhailovich Molotov,' Molotov said in tones like a Murmansk winter. 'Now give me yours.'

The lieutenant visibly started to call him a liar, but then took another look. He stiffened, as if suddenly afflicted with rigor mortis. Then he bawled for a superior. In something under fifteen minutes, Molotov was whisked into the presence of Marshal Zhukov back at the Kremlin. 'Well, well,' Zhukov said. 'So Beria didn't do you in, eh?'

'No, Georgi Konstantinovich,' Molotov answered. 'I remain at the helm, as you see, and not badly the worse for wear. And tell me, where is Lavrenti Pavlovich now?'

'Deceased,' Zhukov answered. 'Your office carpet will need changing; it has stains on it.' The Red Army officer didn't say anything for a while. Molotov didn't care for the way Zhukov was studying him. If he had an unfortunate accident about now, who would stop Zhukov from seizing the reins of the Soviet Union? *No one at all,* Molotov thought bleakly. Zhukov lit a cigarette, inhaled, coughed a couple of times, and said, 'Well, well, good to have you back.'

Molotov breathed again, and didn't even notice how his ribs twinged. He'd known the habit of subordination was deeply ingrained in Zhukov, but he hadn't known how deeply. Maybe Zhukov himself hadn't known, either, not till the test came. 'Good to be back,' Molotov said, no more emotionally than he said anything else. He raised an eyebrow. 'And how did you become involved in the drama?'

'Beria announced your indisposition over Radio Moscow this morning,' Zhukov answered. 'He also announced mine. Mine would have been fatal, except that my bodyguards shot faster and straighter than his assassins. I suspect he had a puppet waiting to take over the Army, but the rank and file are fond of me, even if some officers and *apparatchiks* aren't. And, while the NKVD is strong, the Red Army is stronger. I have made very sure of this. We suppress the *Chekists* everywhere.'

'Good,' Molotov said. Beria had aimed to kill Zhukov at once, but had been willing to keep Molotov himself alive for a while. That spoke volumes about whom the NKVD chief had thought more dangerous. The way things had turned out proved he'd had a point. Molotov chose not to dwell on it. He said, 'The NKVD man who came out with me – his name is Nussboym – deserves reward, not punishment. He got me out of my cell. Without him, Beria's men might have liquidated me even with Red Army troops filling Dzerzhinsky Square.'

'So they might have,' Zhukov said – wistfully? Molotov chose not to dwell on that, either. Zhukov went on, 'I leave it to you to tend to that, then, Comrade General Secretary. Meanwhile, we have retaken the Radio Moscow transmitter and announced that all is well, but you might want to think about broadcasting a message yourself, to show that you are well and in control.'

'Yes, I will do that,' Molotov agreed at once. Chloroform? Beatings? He shrugged them off. That he hadn't eaten since before Beria's thugs seized him? He shrugged that off, too. 'Take me to a broadcast studio.' Only after he was on his way did he realize he hadn't asked about his wife. He shrugged once more. That could wait, too.

As she set a boiled brisket of beef on the table, Bertha Anielewicz said, 'I wonder what really happened in Moscow the other day.'

'So do I,' Mordechai Anielewicz answered, picking up the serving fork and carving knife. While he cut portions for his wife, his children, and himself, he went on, 'I ran into Ludmila this morning. She doesn't know any more than we do, but she was almost dancing in the street to hear that Beria's dead.'

'She ought to know,' Bertha said.

'That's what I thought,' Mordechai agreed. 'She said the only thing she was really sorry about was that Molotov didn't go with him.'

'Can't have everything,' his wife said. 'The way things are, sometimes you can't have anything.'

'And isn't that the truth?' After a moment's gloom, Anielewicz brightened. 'David Nussboym ended up in the NKVD, remember. He ought to be sinking like a stone about now. *Nu*, can you tell that that breaks my heart?'

'Oh, of course,' Bertha answered. 'Twenty years ago, he would have sunk you like a stone, too, if we hadn't beaten him to the punch.'

Their children listened with wide eyes. Anielewicz wasn't in the habit of hashing over things that had happened before they were born. He didn't do it now, either, contenting himself with a nod. 'We'll have to see what goes on in Russia,' he said in an effort to pull matters back toward the present. 'They say Molotov is on top again, but they say all sorts of things that turn out not to be true.'

Before Bertha could answer, the telephone rang. She got up and went into the parlor to answer it. After a moment, she called, 'It's for you, Mordechai.'

'I'm coming. At least it waited till I was almost finished with supper.' Anielewicz equated telephone calls with trouble. A lot of years had burned that equation into his mind. He took the handset from his wife, who returned to the table. 'Hello?'

'Anielewicz? This is Yitzkhak, up in Glowno. We're going to take the sheep to market tomorrow. Do you want a last look at them before they go?'

'No, you can send them without me,' Anielewicz said, to confuse anyone one who might be listening despite the German- and Lizard-made gadgets he'd had installed on his phone line to defeat would-be snoops. He operated on the assumption that, whatever the *Reich* and the Race could manufacture, they could also find a way to defeat. If he'd admitted wanting to go up to Glowno, Yitzkhak would have known something was badly wrong. To make things sound as normal as they could, he went on, 'How's your cousin doing?'

'Pretty well, thanks,' Yitzkhak answered. 'She's up on

crutches now, and the cast will come off her leg in another month. Then it's just a matter of getting the strength back into the muscles. It'll take time, but she'll do it.'

'Of course she will,' Mordechai said. 'That's good news.' He'd seen enough wounded men during the fighting to know it might not be so easy as Yitzkhak was saying, but only time would tell. After stepping in front of a bus, the other Jew's cousin was lucky to have got off with only a broken leg.

After a little inconsequential talk, Yitzkhak got off the line. Anielewicz went back to the supper table. When he sat down, his wife raised a questioning eyebrow.

'That miserable flock of sheep,' he said; he couldn't be quite sure who was listening to what he said inside his flat, either. 'Yitzkhak wanted to know if I needed to check them before he got rid of them. I told him to go ahead; I'm sick of the foolish things.'

His children stared; they knew he owned no sheep and had no interest in owning any. He held up a hand to keep them from asking questions. They understood the signal, and refrained. Bertha knew what he was talking about. 'Well, we have some leftovers here,' she remarked, by which Mordechai knew he'd be taking them with him for lunch when he went up to Glowno.

Sure enough, his wife had a sack waiting for him when he headed off early the next morning. He took it with a word of thanks, kissed her, and climbed aboard his bicycle. He could have ridden the bus and arrived faster and fresher, but he and his colleagues had been talking over their plans ever since the Polish nationalists tried to abscond with the explosive-metal bomb. The Jews hadn't intended to sneak it out of Glowno in the dead of night. Anielewicz grinned – very much the opposite.

And he always liked to measure himself by exercise. His legs began to ache dully before he'd got very far outside of Lodz, but he settled into a kilometer-eating rhythm and the pain got no worse. After a while, it even receded. That marked the day as a good one. He hoped it would prove an omen.

He was not the only Jew on the road with a rifle or a submachine gun on his back. That would have been true any day, but was more true today than most. And motorcars and even lorries full of armed Jews rolled past him. Some of the men in those cars and lorries, recognizing him as one of their own, waved when they went by. Every now and then, he would take a hand off the handlebars and wave back.

By the time he got to Glowno, Jewish fighters filled the town. Signs in the windows of shops owned by Jews welcomed the militia to town and invited the fighters to come in and spend money on food or drink or soap or clothes or any of two dozen other different things.

The Poles on the streets of Glowno eyed the armed Jews with expressions ranging from resignation to alarm. A generation earlier, such a gathering of Jews would have been impossible, and would have been broken up with bloodshed if attempted. Now . . . Now, here in Glowno, the Jews would have won any fighting that started.

A crackle of rifle fire began outside of town. Anielewicz cocked his head to make sure just where it was coming from, then relaxed. The fighters had a marksmanship contest planned, and that was what he heard. A few minutes later, on the other side of Glowno, a machine gun came to deadly, raucous life. Mordechai knew the fellow handling it. He'd fought against the Germans in a machine-gun company in 1939, and had specialized in the weapons ever since. Thanks to the Lizards, the Jews had plenty of machine guns of German, Polish, and Soviet manufacture (along with a few oddities such as Austro-Hungarian Schwarzloses left over from the First World War), but not all the fighters knew how to keep them in top working order.

Loud blasts announced grenades tearing up a meadow. The man giving lessons in how to throw them was a rarity in football-mad Poland: he'd spent his childhood in the United States, and had played a lot of baseball there. Anielewicz knew next to nothing about baseball, but did understand it involved plenty of throwing.

His own role at the gathering was more theoretical. He closeted himself with leaders of Jewish militias from all around Lizard-occupied Poland and gave them the best advice he could on how to get along with the Race. 'Never let the Lizards forget how badly the Poles outnumber us,' he said. 'The more reason they think we have to be loyal to them, the likelier they are to give us all the toys we want and to back us if we do have trouble with the *goyim*.'

His listeners nodded sagely. A lot of them had used the same tactics over the years. Like Anielewicz, a lot of them had also intrigued with the *Reich* or the Soviet Union to keep the Lizards from gaining too dominant a position. The trick in playing that game was so simple, Mordechai didn't bother mentioning it: *don't get caught*.

He was drinking a stein of beer in the tavern where he'd overheard the Polish nationalists plotting to hijack the bomb when Yitzkhak found him. Yitzkhak looked like a clerk: he was short and slight and had a pinched-up face that didn't approve of anything. Like Mordechai, he was from Warsaw. He'd fought like a madman against the Nazis, and later against the Lizards.

When he spoke, he sounded faintly accusing: 'On the telephone, you said you weren't coming up.'

'I changed my mind – is this against the law?' Anielewicz returned. Even here, they were careful of what they said and how they said it.

'Well, you can't see your sheep,' Yitzkhak said petulantly. 'The mob here, they all got sold, and I don't know where the devil they've gone now. I don't much care, either, if you want to know the truth.'

The bomb had gone, then. Mordechai let out a sigh of relief and ordered another mug of beer. The hubbub the Jewish fighters had raised in and around Glowno had let Yitzkhak and his friends get the weapon out of town with no one the wiser. Anielewicz had counted on that – and had counted on the fighters to bail Yitzkhak and his friends out of trouble if they got into any.

Aloud, he said, 'Well, let me buy you a shot for all the trouble you've gone through on account of those damn sheep.'

'A shot doesn't begin to do it,' Yitzkhak said, sour still, but that didn't mean he refused the vodka. Anielewicz bought himself another beer, too. All things considered, he was of the opinion he'd earned it.

After he'd drunk it, he went out to see if anyone had stolen his bicycle. Unlike the bomb, it was still there. As he started to climb aboard it for the ride back to Lodz, he saw a couple of Lizards coming along the street. Judging what they were thinking wasn't easy, but to him they looked horrified at seeing so many humans swaggering around with guns.

That – and the steins of beer he'd drunk – made him smile. If they weren't used to the idea that people weren't their slaves by now, too bad. With more than a little bravado, he waved to them, calling, 'I greet you, males of the Race.'

'I greet you,' one of the Lizards said . . . cautiously. His eye turrets swung this way and that. 'What is the purpose of this, ah, gathering?'

Camouflage, Mordechai thought. Aloud, he said, 'To make sure we Jews can strongly oppose anyone who tries to trouble us: Germans, Russians, Poles – or anyone else.' By that last, he could only have meant the Race.

'They *are* barbarians,' one of the Lizards said to the other. Anielewicz didn't think he was supposed to hear, but he did.

'Barbarians, truth,' the other Lizard agreed, 'but if these are the Jews, they are the barbarians who are useful to us.'

'Ah,' the first Lizard said. *Ah,* Mordechai thought. Hearing that from the Lizard was no great surprise. He knew the Race found the Jews useful. Jews found the Lizards useful, too. *And so the world goes round.* He waved to the males again, then started pedaling south and west, back toward Lodz. His legs hardly pained him at all, and, once he'd got out of town, he could go quite fast. *And so the wheels go round.* He bent his back to the work.

* * *

531

Nesseref felt like hissing at her Tosevite workmen in the tones of an alarm signal. 'Why have you not poured the concrete, as we discussed the other day?' she demanded indignantly.

The Big Ugly foremale peered down at her from his preposterous height. He did not speak the language of the Race with any great grammatical precision, but he made himself understood: 'Rain too hard,' he said, and added an emphatic cough. 'Ground all muddily. Pour now, not set good. Pour now, not hardly set at all.' He placed hands on his hips. The shuttlecraft pilot had never seen the gesture before, but it had to be one of defiance.

And the Big Ugly – Casimir, his name was – had a point, or she supposed he did. She'd never seen it rain so hard back on Home as it had rained here near Glowno these past couple of days. Males from the conquest fleet, the ones who didn't keep trying to ply her with ginger, told her such things weren't rare on this part of Tosev 3, and were even more common elsewhere.

'Very well, Casimir,' she said, yielding ground. 'How long do you think it will be before we can pour the concrete for the shuttlecraft field?'

'Don't know.' Where the Big Ugly's hands-on-hips gesture had been alien, his shrug could almost have come from a male of the Race. 'Ground dry in four, five, six days – if no more rain before then.' He shrugged again. 'Don't know nothing about rain then now. Nobody don't know nothing about rain then now.'

That wasn't strictly true – the Race's meteorologists were better at forecasting Tosev 3's weather than they had been when the conquest fleet arrived. Then, from the reports Nesseref had read, they'd wanted nothing more than to crawl back into their eggshells and hide. Their models had not been built for this world's extremes of climate. They had improved, but remained a long way from perfect.

Casimir said, 'Taste some ginger, Shuttlecraft Pilot. You feel better then.' He used another emphatic cough.

'No,' Nesseref said with an emphatic cough of her own. 'Do not suggest that to me again, or this crew will have a new foremale the next instant.'

She glared at the Big Ugly. He was taller and bulkier, but she was fiercer. He turned away, mumbling, 'It shall be done, superior female.' The pat phrase, unlike most of his speech, he brought out correctly.

'It had better be done,' Nesseref snapped.

She still craved ginger, craved the way it made her feel, even craved the way it brought her into her season. The more she craved, the more strongly she resisted the craving. She was, and was determined to remain, her own person, bending her will to those of others only when she had to and to a Tosevite herb not at all, not if she could help it. No matter how good it made her feel, ginger turned her into an animal. Worse, it turned the males around her into animals, too.

When she strode off, her feet squelched in the offending mud. She hissed again, wishing someone more familiar than she with conditions on this planet had got the job of laying out the shuttlecraft port.

'At least I found some land we could use,' she muttered. It was up to Bunim or his superiors to compensate the Big Uglies who had formerly owned the land. By all the signs, the Tosevites were holding the Race for ransom, or thought they were. But the Race had more resources than these peasants thought, and paying them what they thought they deserved was a tolerable expense.

The idea of having to pay them still offended Nesseref. This wasn't one of the independent not-empires whose existence had once astonished her; the Race really had conquered this stretch of Tosev 3. But the local administrators seemed to be doing their best to deny they'd accomplished any such thing. No matter how often Bunim explained it, it still seemed wrong.

Nesseref glanced north and west toward Glowno, then south and east in the direction of Jezow, the other nearby Tosevite town. On the map, in fact, Jezow was closer to the site she'd chosen than was Glowno. Her eye turrets kept twisting back toward the latter town, though. The Big Ugly called Anielewicz had said he had an explosive-metal bomb there. She still didn't know whether he'd been telling the truth. She hoped she – and the shuttlecraft port that would eventually come into being here despite the delays the ghastly weather caused – would never have to find out.

She swung her eye turrets in the direction of the Big Uglies who labored for her. Anielewicz had joked – she hoped he'd joked – about moving the bomb he might or might not have so that it could destroy her shuttlecraft port. Were any of these Tosevites his spies? She could hardly come out and ask them.

Almost all the workers, she knew, were of the larger sub-group called Poles, not the smaller subgroup called Jews. By what Nesseref had learned from both Bunim and Anielewicz, the two subgroups disliked and distrusted each other. That made it less likely the Poles were spying for Anielewicz.

Whatever reassurance that thought brought her did not last long. That the Poles weren't spying for Anielewicz didn't mean they weren't spying for someone. She wished she could have had males and females of the Race laboring here, but, even after the arrival of the colonization fleet, there weren't enough to go around. There wasn't enough heavy equipment to go around, either, not with so much of it in use building housing for the colonists.

She glared up at the gray, gloomy sky. She'd decided to use Tosevite labor because, with it, she could have had the shuttle-craft port finished before her turn came for the heavy equip-ment the Race had hereabouts. But the weather wasn't cooperating. She'd been through an interminable winter here. She'd talked with veterans from the conquest fleet. Tosev 3's weather was not in the habit of cooperating with anyone.

As if to prove the point, a drop of rain fell on her snout, and then another and another. This wasn't going to be the sort of cloudburst that had halted the concrete pouring, but it wasn't weather in which her laborers could do much, either. They seemed anything but unhappy about that. Some pulled cloth caps down lower over their eyes. Others stood in whatever shelter they could find and inhaled the smoke from the burning leaves of some Tosevite plant. That struck Nesseref as a nasty habit, but they enjoyed it.

After a while, Casimir came over to her and said, 'Not can working in weather like these.'

'I know,' Nesseref said resignedly.

'You dismissing we?' the foremale asked. 'With pay? Weather not ours fault.'

'Yes, with pay,' Nesseref said, more resignedly still. She would have done the same for workers of the Race, and her instructions were to treat the Big Uglies like workers of the Race, or at least like Rabotevs and Hallessi. She doubted these Tosevites deserved to be treated in such a fashion, but was willing – less willing than she had been, but still willing – to believe the males who'd come with the conquest fleet knew more about the situation than she did.

Now Casimir took off his cap and bent from the waist in her direction. 'You is good to working for, superior female.'

'I thank you,' Nesseref said. To be perfectly polite, she should have given the foremale a compliment in return, praising him for the hard work he and the other Big Uglies had done. She could not bring herself to say the words. From everything she'd seen, the Polish males worked no harder than they had to.

They did not seem to miss the reciprocal compliment. After Casimir had shouted to them in their own language, they let out the cries that meant they were happy. Some of them bowed to Nesseref, as the foremale had done. Some waved: a friendly gesture she had seen them use among themselves. And some simply headed off toward Jezow without a backwards glance. A lot of those, she knew from experience, would overindulge in alcohol during their free time and return to work in the morning a good deal the worse for wear.

A raindrop hit her in the eye. Her nictitating membrane

flashed across the eyeball, flicking away the moisture. She wondered how long the rain would go on. Too long, without a doubt. She sighed. She couldn't do anything about that. She couldn't do anything about far too many things on Tosev 3.

She pulled a telephone from her belt pouch and punched in Bunim's code. The regional subadministrator took longer to answer than she thought he should have. Nor was his voice particularly gleeful as he asked, 'Well, Shuttlecraft Pilot, what has gone wrong now? I assume something has, or you would not be calling me.'

'Truth, superior sir – something has,' Nesseref said. 'Because of this rain, the concrete pouring cannot commence as scheduled.'

She was glad the portable telephone had no vision link; though the Race's features were less mobile than those of the Big Uglies, she did not think Bunim would look happy. But all he said, after a sigh of his own, was, 'Very few things on Tosev 3 move in exact accord with prearranged schedules. This is naturally distressing to our kind, but it is a truth of its own here. Better the schedule should become somewhat addled than those trying to fulfill it.'

'I thank you, superior sir,' Nesseref said in some surprise. 'That is generous of you.' It was more generous than she'd expected him to be.

'Anyone who tries to hurry things on Tosev 3 is doomed to disappointment, just as anyone with the purple itch is doomed to scratching,' Bunim replied. 'I am given to understand the problem is worse elsewhere on Tosev 3 than here.'

'Emperor preserve me from those regions, then,' the shuttle-craft pilot said.

'Indeed,' Bunim said. 'But you must also remember that the Big Uglies, when moving to their own purposes rather than to ours, are capable of bursts of speed we could not hope to match. Thus their acquisition of industrial technology in a mere handful of years. Thus also their extremely rapid growth in technical ability both while fighting the conquest fleet and since the fighting stopped.'

'I do remember this,' Nesseref said. 'I do not understand it, but I remember it. My opinion, for whatever it may be worth to you, is that they have more technical ability than they know what to do with. If they had more social stability, they might not advance so fast, but they would be better off.'

'I agree with you,' Bunim said. 'They were already working on explosive-metal weapons when the conquest fleet arrived. By now, the Deutsche and the Americans, say, might already have fought a nuclear war. Had we come in the aftermath of such a fight, we would only have had to pick up the pieces.' He sighed. 'It would have been much easier.'

'For the conquest fleet, certainly,' Nesseref said. 'The colonization fleet would have had a harder time dealing with a wrecked planet, though.'

'Truth.' Bunim sighed again. 'That is one reason we did not use many explosive-metal bombs. Even so, however, there are times when I think it would have been worth it.' He broke the connection, leaving Nesseref standing alone in the chilly rain.

The science officer at the Race's embassy in Nuremberg was a male named Slomikk. Ttomalss had had occasional questions for him since coming down to the surface of Tosev 3, and had generally been pleased with his replies. He seemed to have more insight into the way the Tosevites thought than was common among the Race.

Today, though, Ttomalss came to him with a query of a different sort: 'How much danger am I in from the abnormal amount of background radiation in this part of Deutschland?'

Slomikk swung both eye turrets toward the researcher into Tosevite psychology. 'How did you learn of this increase in radiation?' he inquired. 'You are correct – it does exist – but we do not go out of our way to advertise it.'

'I can see that you would not,' Ttomalss said with considerable warmth. 'I stumbled upon it by accident; I was investigating the effects of local climate on agriculture, and the next map to leap onto the screen was one of radiation distribution as related to wind patterns.'

'I . . . see,' Slomikk said slowly. 'Well, that is one link I shall have to remove from the computer system.'

'Is that all you have to say about it?' Ttomalss demanded, more indignantly than before. 'Can you do nothing more than conceal the evidence from those who are compelled to serve here?'

'What else would you recommend, Senior Researcher?' the science officer said. 'I cannot make the radiation disappear, and the Deutsche insist on placing their center here. Their former center, Berlin, was during an early stage of the fighting a great deal more radioactive than this.'

'I am aware of that, of course,' Ttomalss said, 'as I am aware that we also bombed the Deutsch city of München, south of here. But both those events took place during the fighting; the radioactivity from them should have subsided by now, should it not?'

'Indeed it should have, were that the only radioactivity we were discussing,' Slomikk said. 'But the Deutsche, back in the days when they were first experimenting with explosive metals, built a pile with inadequate moderators, or perhaps with no moderators at all. As you would expect, it melted down, and its radioactivity has not declined to any great degree in the years since. It is still too strong for anyone, even condemned criminals, to go in and clean it out, and it is the source of the increased radioactivity you noticed in this area.'

'A pile without moderators?' Ttomalss shuddered at the mere idea. 'Big Uglies are mad. What prompted them to do such a thing?'

'As best I can gather – you will understand, the Deutsche are not forthcoming about this – the answers are, desperate haste and complete inexperience,' Slomikk replied. 'From our point of view, it is unfortunate that they acquired technical proficiency so fast.'

'Yes.' Ttomalss used the affirmative hand gesture. 'Better by far for us had they succeeded in rendering a good stretch of their not-empire completely uninhabitable rather than . . .' He returned to the question that had brought him to Slomikk in the first place: 'How dangerous is this environment, anyhow?'

'Risk of malignancy is certainly higher than it would be had the Deutsche not acted with such flagrant stupidity,' Slomikk said. 'That does not mean it is extremely high. Among the Deutsche of Nuremberg, the incidence of neoplasms is about thirty percent higher than it is in areas with lower radiation levels. Closer to the site of the meltdown, that increases considerably.'

'How do you know this?' Ttomalss answered his own question: 'You have access to Deutsch records, then?'

'Some of them,' Slomikk said. 'Frustratingly, only some. Many of their records remain handwritten or produced on machines that are not electronic. We have to examine them physically, which is not easy for us to do without revealing ourselves. And working through Tosevite intermediaries to gain access to what these records contain is not everything it might be, either, for there is always the question of whom a Big Ugly truly works for.'

'So there is,' Ttomalss agreed. 'Tosevites have played us false so many times in the past, we have every reason to be alert to treachery now.'

Slomikk was the sort of methodical male who, once he got started on an explanation, kept right on no matter what the male to whom he was explaining said: 'And not all the Deutsch security systems for the data they do have in electronic format are easy to penetrate. Big Uglies worry about espionage far more than the Race has done since the formative days of our species.'

'With all the competing sovereignties among the Big Uglies, they have needed such fears,' Ttomalss observed. 'This is an area where unity has not given us strength.'

'They have even entrapped us a few times,' Slomikk said,

'defending data with all their strength, making us exert great effort and ingenuity to win them. Then, when we had done so, we eventually discovered the data were thoroughly falsified.' He let out an irate hiss.

'I have had firsthand experience of Tosevite treachery,' Ttomalss said. 'I can well believe these Big Uglies could be as devious as you say. Do you suppose they could have penetrated any of our data networks without our knowing it?'

'That is not my area of expertise, but I would doubt it very much,' Slomikk said. 'You would be better advised seeking such answers from the head of Security here. But I, for my part, am certain the Deutsche are too ignorant to attempt, let alone succeed at, electronic espionage of their own.'

'I hope you are right,' Ttomalss said, 'but one of the things I have seen again and again is that the Tosevites encourage us to underestimate them, which enables them to prepare for and carry out outrageous deeds under our snouts. They have given us so many large, unpleasant surprises that successful espionage here would be only a small, unpleasant surprise.'

'Surprises from espionage are not always small.' Slomikk paused thoughtfully. 'Perhaps it would be wise if one of us did mention this matter to the head of Security here. I will take care of it, if you like.'

The science officer's voice was casual – too casual. *I will take the credit if you turn out to be right* was what he meant. Ttomalss should have got angry. He knew that. He couldn't make himself do it. The embassy to the *Reich* was not his permanent station. He didn't much care what the males and females here thought of him, and their opinions would have no large effect on his career.

'Go ahead,' he said, as if it were a small matter. To him, it was. If it wasn't to Slomikk, fine.

'I thank you.' Slomikk scribbled a note to himself.

'You are wise not to note this problem electronically,' Ttomalss observed. Slomikk did his best to look wise. What he did look like was a male who had reached for a pen without the least concern for security, with only the thought that it would be the quickest way to set down the idea and make sure he did not forget it.

'If you are right,' he said, 'it will be good that we find out about it.'

'Truth,' Ttomalss said. If he was right, the embassy's security officer would end up wishing he'd never been hatched. Thinking about hatchlings put Ttomalss on a new line of thought: 'Is increased background radiation more likely to affect eggs and hatchlings than adults? We have several gravid females here in the embassy, you know.'

'Obviously, there is more concern where cell growth is rapid,' Slomikk said. 'We have few data to suggest how urgent that concern should be. We, unlike the Big Uglies, have been sensible enough to minimize exposure of the vulnerable to radiation.' He hesitated. 'Or we have until now, at any rate. I may have to discuss with Veffani the wisdom of moving gravid females out of this area until such time as they have laid their eggs.'

One more notion you did not think of, but for which you are willing to take the credit, Ttomalss thought. Again, he had trouble being as angry as he might have. The only gravid female he knew well was Felless. He wondered whether he or Veffani had fertilized the eggs she bore.

Had he been a Tosevite, the question would have been of enormous importance to him. All his own research and most of the Tosevite literature he'd studied convinced him of the truth of that. Back on Home, the question of paternity would scarcely have arisen. During her season, Felless would have mated with any number of males. Here on Tosev 3, Ttomalss found himself in the middle: more than curious, less than concerned.

'You seem to have a knack for posing stimulating questions, Senior Researcher,' Slomikk said. 'You are to be congratulated.'

'I thank you,' Ttomalss said, in what he feared were abstracted tones. He'd asked himself an interesting question, and one for which he had as yet no good answer. Ginger seemed certain to make more females here on Tosev 3 become gravid after mating with a smaller number of males, or perhaps with only one, than happened back on Home. There were more circumstances in which that could make important who the father was: if he'd given the female ginger to induce her to mate with him, for instance, or if she'd taken credit from his account in exchange for tasting ginger and becoming sexually receptive.

Ttomalss sighed. 'This world is doing its best to change us, no matter how much we are in the habit of resisting change.'

'I agree. You are not the first to raise this notion, of course,' Slomikk said. 'Even creating embassies and reviving the title of ambassador was new and strange, for the Race has needed neither embassies nor ambassadors these past tens of thousands of years.'

'Forcing us to revive the old is one thing,' Ttomalss said. 'It is, in itself, not a small thing. But we have had to respond to so much that is new both from the Tosevites and among ourselves, that the revivals pale to insignificance by comparison.'

'Again, I agree. I wish I could disagree. Too much change is not good for a male, or for a female, either,' the science officer said. 'Change swift enough to be perceptible in the course of an individual's lifetime is too much. This is one of the reasons the Race so seldom goes conquering: to spare the large majority of individuals from ever experiencing the stress of drastic change. It is not the only reason, but it is not the least of reasons. Indeed, we have endured such stress here on Tosev 3 better than I thought we could.'

'Now there is an interesting observation,' Ttomalss said. 'The Big Uglies have been in the throes of drastic change for generations. Do you suppose that is one of the reasons they are so strange?'

'I do not know, but it strikes me as something worth investigating,' Slomikk said. 'You would, I suppose, have to compare their present behavior with the way they acted before change was a daily occurrence in their lives.'

'So I would,' Ttomalss said. 'As best I can tell, they have always behaved badly. Whether they have behaved badly in different ways of late . . . may be worth learning.'

Thanks to his Army security clearance and his connections with Lizard expatriates and exiles, Sam Yeager had access to as much sensitive computer data as any but a handful of men. Some of those data were on the USA's computers, others on those that belonged to the Race. The only place where the separate streams flowed together was inside his head. That suited him fine.

Every time he had to switch from a computer built by the Race to one made in the USA, he was reminded of the gap in both technology and engineering that still existed. *Apples and oranges,* he thought. *The Lizards have had a lot more practice at this than we have.*

He shrugged. Back before the Lizards came, he'd never imagined one computer would fit on his desk, let alone two. Back before the Lizards came, he'd scarcely imagined computing machines at all. If he had, he'd imagined them the size of a building and half mechanical, half electronic. That was about as far as science-fiction writers had seen by 1942.

Putting on artificial fingerclaws to deal with the keyboard of the Lizard machine, he grinned. He could see a lot further now. Had he really been a Lizard, he could have done most of his work on their machine by talking to it rather than typing. Its voice-recognition system, though, wasn't set up to deal with a human's accent. Voice commands sometimes went spectacularly wrong, so he avoided them. The computer didn't care who typed into it.

Because he was an expert on the Race, he was one of the few humans in the independent countries allowed even limited access to the Lizards' vast data network; in his case, the connection was wired through the Race's consulate in downtown Los Angeles. He admired that network tremendously, but sometimes – often – felt going through it for information made looking for a needle in a haystack seem simple by comparison.

That was especially true because he had access to more of the data network than the Lizards at the consulate or back in Cairo thought he did. Some of his friends among the former prisoners who'd decided to stay in the United States after the fighting ended were clever with computers. They'd forked – their idiom – the programs the consulate had given him to let him range more widely than Lizard officialdom thought it was permitting. They reckoned that a good joke on their own kind. Yeager reckoned it highly useful.

The Lizards had never stopped discussing the attack on the colonization fleet. The topic filled several fora – the best translation Sam could make. He wasn't supposed to be able to read what was said in those fora, but he could. That topic interested him, too. If he could pin the crime on the Greater German *Reich* or the Soviet Union, the Lizards would punish the guilty party – preferably with a two-by-four – and life could finally get back to normal.

A name – Vesstil – caught his notice. 'I knew a Vesstil once upon a time,' he muttered, and noted down the number that accompanied the Lizard's name. Then he had to take off the fingerclaw so he could use the American-made computer that took up twice as much desk space as its Lizardly counterpart. It didn't run as well, either, despite using technology borrowed – or, more accurately, stolen – from the Race. But one of the things that computer stored was a list of all the Lizard prisoners the United States had captured.

Sure enough, there was Vesstil's name. And, sure enough, the number attached to it matched that of the Lizard now holding forth about the attack on the colonization fleet. This was the shuttlecraft pilot who'd flown Straha down to the USA when the shiplord decided to defect. Yeager remembered that he had repatriated himself not long after the fighting ended.

It is unlike the Big Uglies to keep secrets so well, Vesstil had written. *Even with their safety hanging in the balance, it is unlike them. This argues something unusual even for Tosevites went on in relation to this attack.*

Another Lizard had answered, *Interesting speculation, but useless to us,* and the discussion had drifted on to other things.

'I'm not sure it is useless,' Sam muttered, deliberately using English to get himself out of the chattering among the Lizards in which he'd been immersed. In fact, he'd been collecting examples of unusual actions by the Germans and Russians in the hope that one of them would lead to more clues he could use to pin down the guilty party. It hadn't happened yet, and didn't look as if it would happen any time soon, but that didn't mean he'd abandoned hope.

Yeager also collected examples of strange American behavior: those were easier for him to come by and let him hone his analytical skills, though they had nothing to do with the colonization fleet. He wondered why one of the spacemen who flew out of Kitty Hawk had got a black mark by his name for getting too curious about the growing U.S. space station.

He suspected he could have found out with a couple of phone calls, but playing detective through the American computer network gave him more practice at manipulating such creations, so he went at it that way. Back in the bush leagues, he'd always asked for curves from the batting-practice pitchers because he'd had more trouble hitting them than fastballs.

He grumbled as he waited for the human-made computer to spit out the information he needed. It was slower than the one the Lizards made, and the U.S. computer network, a creation of the past five years, far smaller and more fragmented than the one the Lizards took for granted.

As things turned out, he had to make the phone calls anyhow, because the network let him down. He really did have U.S. security clearances – unlike the ones the Lizards had flanged up for him for a lark – but they didn't seem to be high enough to take him where he needed to go. They should have been, or so he thought, but they weren't.

He wondered what that meant. Whatever it was, it couldn't have anything to do with the attack on the colonization fleet. The space station hadn't been involved in that; the Lizards had detected a signal from a submarine that promptly submerged, and then somebody's nasty chunk of hardware had gone into action. Somebody's. Whose? He had no more proof than the Lizards did.

Then he stopped worrying about it for a while, because Barbara came home with the trunk of the car full of groceries, and he had to help haul them into the house. She put away the food that went into the refrigerator, he what went into the pantries. About halfway through the job, Barbara looked over to him and said, 'This is all for Jonathan, you know. There wasn't enough room in the car for a week's worth of groceries for him and us both. As soon as we're done here, I'll have to go back to the store for some food for us.'

'You expect me to laugh and think that's a joke,' Sam said. 'Trouble is, I've seen the way the kid eats. I believe you, or close enough, anyhow.' He put a couple of cans of tomatoes on a shelf, then said, 'Karen seems happier when she comes around here these days.'

'Of course she does,' his wife answered at once. 'Liu Mei is five thousand miles away now. I hope she and her mother have made it back to China all right, but I wouldn't be surprised if Karen hoped their ship sank. Hand me that sack of oranges, would you? They're nice and ripe.'

They were just finishing when the telephone rang. Barbara answered it, then called out for Sam. He took the handpiece from her and spoke: 'Yeager.'

'Good morning, Major.' The crisp voice on the other end of the line belonged to Colonel Edwin Webster, Sam's immediate superior. 'You are to report in tomorrow at 0800: no working out of the house. We have a visiting fireman who wants to see you. He's asked for you by name, and he's not somebody who'll take no for an answer. Have you got that?'

'Yes, sir: report in at 0800,' Yeager said in martyred tones. He much preferred working from his home, which, thanks to his personal library and his computer connection, he got to do most of the time. 'Who is this fellow, anyway?' he asked, but Webster had hung up on hearing him acknowledge the order.

Barbara was properly sympathetic. Jonathan, when he got home from classes, wasn't. 'I have to go in at eight o'clock three mornings a week this term,' he said.

'That's because you're young – and if you don't watch the way you talk, you won't get much older,' Sam told him. With the heartlessness of youth, Jonathan laughed.

Fortified by two cups of coffee, Yeager drove downtown the next morning. He poured himself another cup as soon as he'd reported to Colonel Webster, who looked disgustingly wide awake himself. Sam repeated the question he'd asked the day before. Webster didn't answer it this time, either.

Before long, though, Sam found out. Colonel Webster's adjutant, a harried-looking captain named Markowitz, came into his cubicle and said, 'Sir, if you'll come with me . . . ?' Yeager put down his pen and forgot about the meaningless piece of busywork he was doing. He got up and followed Captain Markowitz.

In the office to which the adjutant led him sat a three-star general smoking a cigarette with sharp, savage puffs. The general waited till Markowitz had gone and closed the door behind him, then stubbed out the butt and impaled Yeager with a glare that held him in place as a specimen pin held a preserved butterfly to a collecting board. 'You have been poking your nose into places where it has no business going, Major,' he rasped. 'That will cease, or your military career will, forthwith. Have you got that?'

'Sir?' Sam said in astonishment. He'd expected a visiting fireman who wanted to know something special about the Lizards, not one who aimed to carve chunks off him and roast them over the fire. And he didn't even know what he was supposed to have done.

Lieutenant General Curtis LeMay didn't keep him in suspense for long: 'You have been snooping about the space station. Whatever may be going on there, it is none of your goddamn business. You are not authorized to have that information. If you try to get it from us again, you will regret it for the rest of your days. Do you understand what I am saying to you, Major Yeager?'

'Sir, I understand what you're saying,' Yeager answered carefully, 'but I don't understand why you're saying it.'

'*Why* is not your business, Major,' LeMay said. 'I've come a long way to give you that order, and I expect to have it obeyed. Is there any danger I am laboring under a misapprehension?' His tone warned that there had better not be. He lit another cigarette and started smoking it down to a nub.

'No, sir,' Sam said, the only thing he could say under the circumstances. If LeMay didn't want him taking a look at the space station, he wouldn't . . . or he wouldn't get caught again, anyhow. Why Lieutenant General LeMay was so vehement about the matter, he couldn't guess – but LeMay wasn't in the mood to answer questions.

'You had better not,' the general growled, and seemed to notice Yeager still standing at attention in front of him. 'Dismissed. Get the hell out of here.' Yeager saluted, then frankly fled.

Straha had the best computer equipment money could buy. It wasn't his money, either, but that of the Tosevites with whom he had chosen to make his home. The equipment, though, was regulation issue for the Race. How the Americans had got it for him, he found it wiser not to ask. But get it they had. They had also managed, in some highly unofficial fashion, to connect it to the Race's network by way of the consulate in downtown Los Angeles. That gave Straha one more window on the way of life he had deliberately abandoned.

It was, necessarily, a one-way window. He could observe, but did not interact. If he did interact – if he sent messages for placement on the network – he might reveal and forfeit his highly unofficial connection. In the American phrase, he stayed on the outside looking in.

And so, when he turned on the computer and discovered he had a message waiting, his first reaction was alarm. If the Race discovered his connection on its own, he was liable to lose that window.

But the message, he discovered, was not from any male of the Race, or even from some new and snoopy female. It was from Major Sam Yeager, who had connections of his own. It asked nothing more dangerous than whether Yeager could come and visit the exiled shiplord at his home one day before too long.

'Of course you may visit,' Straha said on the telephone, still not eager to send a message and make the system notice him. 'I do not understand why you did not simply call, as I am doing now.'

'I like the message system the Race uses,' replied the Tosevite, whose access to that system was somewhat – but only somewhat – more official than Straha's. It did not seem a good enough reason to the ex-shiplord, but Straha chose not to pursue the point. He proposed a time at which Yeager might come, the Big Ugly agreed, and they both hung up.

Yeager was punctual, as Straha had expected him to be. 'I do not see your driver here,' the Tosevite remarked after he had exchanged greetings with Straha.

'No, he is not here; I gave him the morning off, knowing I would not be going anywhere because you would be coming here,' Straha answered. 'I can quickly summon him by radio link, if that is what you require.'

'No,' Yeager said, and used an emphatic cough. 'Perhaps we could go out into the back yard and talk there.'

'It is warmer inside,' Straha said unhappily. Yeager stood quiet, not saying anything more. Straha's eye turrets swung sharply toward him. 'You think my house may be—' He broke off even before Yeager began to raise a warning hand. 'Yes, let us go out into the back yard.'

By local standards, it was not much of a yard, being dirt and rocks and sand and a few cacti rather than the green grass and gaudy flowers customary in the United States. But in essence if not in detail, it put Straha in mind of Home. Yeager said, 'Shiplord, what do you know and what can you find out about the American space station?'

'Rather less than you can, I suspect,' Straha answered. 'I have access only to what the Race knows about it. Your own people, the builders, will surely have whatever detailed knowledge you may require.'

Yeager shook his head. 'I have been ordered not to inquire into it, and American computers are closed against me – indeed, are warned against me.'

Straha needed no elaborate calculation to understand what that was liable to mean. 'You have in some way triggered a security alert?' he asked.

'Oh, you might say so,' the Big Ugly answered in English. Before Straha could grow too confused, he shifted back to the language of the Race: 'That is an idiom of agreement.'

'Is it? I thank you; I had not encountered it before,' Straha said. 'But you are a military officer, and one who, because of your dealings with the Race, is privy to many secrets. Why would questions about your space station be closed to you?'

'That is also my question,' Yeager said. 'I have not found an answer for it. I have been discouraged from seeking an answer for it.'

'Something most highly secret must be going on in connection with the space station, then,' Straha said. All at once, he wondered whether his wisecrack to the Tosevite reporter who'd questioned him held truth after all. But no. 'It cannot be connected to the attack on the colonization fleet.'

'My thoughts also ran in that direction,' Yeager said. 'I agree; there can be no possible connection. And that there can be no possible connection gives me great relief. But I cannot imagine what else would be so secret as to keep me from inquiring about the station: indeed, would lead to my being discouraged from making any further inquiries along those lines.'

Straha knew he was no expert in reading the tones in which Tosevites spoke, but he would have placed a fair-sized bet that Yeager had been strongly discouraged from making such inquiries. The exiled shiplord asked, 'Are you disobeying orders in asking these questions of me?'

'No, or not precisely,' Yeager replied. 'I have been ordered not to seek more information from American sources. I do not think it occurred to anyone above me that I might seek information from other sources.'

'Ah,' Straha said. 'You are what we call in the language of the Race a beam-deflector – you twist your orders to your own purposes.'

'I'm obeying the letter, we would say in English,' Yeager said. 'As for the spirit . . .' He shrugged.

'We would have a good deal to say to an officer who played so fast and loose with his orders,' Straha observed. 'I know you Big Uglies are looser than we, but in your military, I had always believed, less so than in other areas.'

'That is truth,' Yeager admitted. 'I am at – or perhaps over – the limit of my discretion. But this is something that is kept secret when it should not be. I want to know why it is. Sometimes things are made secret for no reason at all, other times to conceal bad mistakes. My not-empire needs to know of that last, should it be true.'

Straha studied Yeager. He spoke the Race's language well. He could think like a male of the Race. But he was, at bottom, alien, as was the society that had hatched him.

A large bird with a blue back and wings and a gray belly landed near one of the cacti. It turned its head toward Straha and Yeager. 'Jeep!' it screeched. 'Jeep! Jeep!' It hopped a couple of paces, then pecked at something in the dirt.

'Scrub jay,' Yeager remarked in English.

'Is that what you call it?' Straha said in the same language. Birds were alien to him, too. Back on Home, flying creatures – of which there were fewer than on Tosev 3 – had membranous wings, something like Tosevite bats. But their bodies were scaly like the Race's, not hairy like the Big Uglies'. No beasts back on Home had hair or feathers; they needed less insulation than Tosevite creatures.

Another bird, a smaller one with a glistening green back and purple-red throat and crown, buzzed into the yard and hovered above the scrub jay, letting out a series of small, squeaky, indignant chirps. Its wings beat so fast, they were only a blur. Straha could hear the buzz they made. The jay paid no attention to the smaller bird, but went on looking for seeds and crawling things.

'Hummingbirds don't like jays,' Yeager said, again in English. 'I suppose jays will eat their eggs and babies if they get a chance. Jays will eat just about anything if they get a chance.'

The hummingbird finished cursing the jay and darted away. One instant it was there, the next it was gone, or so it seemed to Straha. The scrub jay pecked for a little longer, then flew off at a much more sedate pace.

'You Big Uglies are hummingbirds, now here, now there, moving faster than the eye turret can follow,' Straha said. 'We of the Race are more like the jay. We are steady. We are sure. If you know where we are at one moment, you may predict where we will be for some time to come.'

Yeager's mouth corners twisted upward in the expression Tosevites used to show amusement. Still speaking English, he said, 'And you of the Race will eat just about any planet if you get a chance. We didn't give you as much of a chance as you thought you'd have.'

'That I can scarcely deny,' Straha said. He swung his eye turrets away from the jay, which had perched in a tree in a neighbor's yard and was screeching again. Giving Yeager his full attention, he went on, 'You realize my investigations, if I make them, will have to be indirect? You also realize I may alert not only your not-empire to wrongdoing, but also the Race? I ask you these things before proceeding as you requested. If you like, I will forget the request you have made.' He could not think of another Tosevite to whom he would have made that offer.

'No, go ahead,' Yeager said. 'I cannot imagine anything at the space station that would endanger your ships more than other, more secret, installations we already have in space.'

'Indeed,' Straha said. 'Since you put it in those terms, neither can I. It would be easier if I could safely have a more active presence on our computer network, but I will do what I can by scanning and searching out messages pertaining to this subject, and by using surrogates to plant questions that may lead to interesting and informative answers.'

'I thank you,' Yeager said. 'More than that I cannot ask. Very likely, you understand, all of this will prove to be of no consequence.'

'Of course,' Straha replied. 'But then, most of my life since defecting to the United States has proved to be of no consequence, so this is not of any great concern to me.' He could not think of another Tosevite – for that matter, he could not think of a male of the Race – to whom he would have exposed his bitterness thus. He longed for a taste of ginger.

Yeager said, 'Shiplord, that is not true. Your presence here has meant a great deal to my not-empire and to all Tosevites. Thanks in no small part to you and to what we learned from you, we were able to make and for the most part to keep our armistice with the Race.' He held up a hand. 'I know this may only make you think of yourself as a tremendous traitor, but that is not so. You have helped save everyone on Tosev 3: males of the conquest fleet, males and females of the colonization fleet, and Big Uglies.' He used the Race's nickname for his kind without self-consciousness.

'I wish I could believe everything you tell me,' Straha said slowly. 'I also try to tell it to myself, but I do not believe it from my own mouth, either.'

'Well, you should,' Yeager said, like one male encouraging another to go forward in combat. 'You should, for it is truth.'

Straha had never imagined he could be so preposterously grateful to a Big Ugly. He wondered if Yeager understood his own kind as well as he understood the Race. 'You are a friend,' he said, and sounded surprised after the words came out: the idea of a Tosevite friend seemed very strange to him. But that he had one was also truth. 'You are a friend,' he repeated, 'and I will help you as one friend helps another.'

17

Kassquit pondered the computer screen in front of her. She often kept one eye turret turned toward discussions about objects in orbit around Tosev 3 (so she thought of it, though she, of course, had no eye turrets and usually had to turn her whole head to see something). This was, after all, the environment in which she'd spent her whole life. It was the environment in which she would likely spend the rest of her life. Tracking what went on here mattered to her.

After the disaster that befell the colonization fleet, Kassquit paid more attention than she had to discussions about Tosevite space objects. Before that attack, she'd wanted nothing to do with the species of which she was biologically a part. She still didn't, not really, but she'd had to realize the wild Tosevites were dangerous to her. Their missiles could have vaporized her ship as easily as one from the colonization fleet. Only chance had put her on the opposite side of the planet from the ships that were destroyed. Chance, to a member of the Race (or even to a Tosevite trained to act like a member of the Race), did not seem protection enough.

Little by little and then more and more, the messages of a male named Regeya drew her notice. They stood out for a couple of reasons: Regeya seemed quite well informed about the doings of the not-empire called the United States, and he wrote oddly. Most males and females sounded very much alike, but he spiced his messages with peculiar turns of phrase and hardly seemed to notice he was doing it.

Those qualities finally prompted her to send him a private message. *Who are you?* she wrote. *What is your rank? How have you become so knowledgeable about these Big Uglies?* She did not ask him why he wrote strangely. She was strange herself, in ways more intimate than writing quirks. But, in writing, her strangeness didn't show. That was another reason she cherished computer discussions: males and females who couldn't see her assumed she was normal.

Regeya took his time about answering. Just when Kassquit began to wonder if he would answer at all – he would have been within his rights, though on the abrupt side, to ignore her – he did send a reply: *I am a senior tube technician. The American Big Uglies taught me, and were so interesting, I got hooked on them.* She admired the phrase for a moment before reading his last sentence: *Other than that, I am an ordinary male. What about you?*

'What about me?' Kassquit asked rhetorically. She wrote, *I am a junior researcher in Tosevite psychology, which comes close to addling me.* That was all true, and proved truth could be the best deception. She added, *You have an interesting way of writing,* and sent the message.

Wondering just what a senior tube technician did and what his body paint looked like, she checked a data store. The answer came back in moments: there was no such classification as senior tube technician. As usual, her face showed little expression, but she found that puzzling. She checked the computer to see how many Regeyas had come to Tosev 3 with the conquest fleet: the male showed too much knowledge of American Tosevites to belong to the colonization fleet, or so it seemed to her.

In short order, the answer came back. Unless the computer was mistaken, only one male bearing that name had belonged to the conquest fleet, and he had been killed in the early days of the invasion. Kassquit checked the records for the colonization fleet. They showed two Regeyas. One had been a bureaucrat aboard a ship destroyed in the attack on the fleet. The other, a graphic designer, was newly revived. Kassquit checked past messages in the discussion section. Regeya, whoever he was, had sent messages while the graphic designer remained in cold sleep.

'That is very strange,' Kassquit said, a considerable understatement. She wondered what to do next.

While she was wondering, a message from Regeya – *from the mysterious Regeya,* she thought – reached her. *Tosevites are strange creatures, but not so bad once you get to know them,* he wrote, and then, *I write with my fingerclaws, the same as everybody else.*

Kassquit would have forgiven him a good deal for his kind words about Big Uglies. He, of course, whoever he was, could have no way of knowing she'd been hatched (no, born: a thoroughly disgusting process) one herself. And she liked his strange slant on the world. But he was not who and what he pretended to be. Such deceptions, she had gathered, were common among the Tosevites, but rarely practiced by members of the Race.

What does a senior tube technician do? she wrote, hoping that in answering the would betray himself.

But his reply was altogether matter-of-fact: *I tell intermediate and junior tube technicians what to do. What would you expect?*

She stared at the screen. Her mouth fell open. That was laughter in the style of the Race. In the privacy of her chamber, she also laughed aloud, as Big Uglies did. Whoever this Regeya was, he had both wit and nerve.

But who was he? Why was he using a name not his own? She could find no good reason. Nothing in the discussions in which he took part could gain him any profit, only, at most, a little information. Unable to solve the problem herself, she mentioned it to Ttomalss the next time they spoke.

'I can think of two possibilities,' the senior researcher said. 'One is that he is indeed a male of the Race using a false name for deceptive purposes of his own. The other is that he is a Tosevite who has partially penetrated our computer system.'

'A Tosevite!' Kassquit exclaimed. That had not occurred to her – nor would it have. 'Could a Big Ugly seem like a male of the Race in discussion groups and electronic messages?'

'Why not?' Ttomalss asked. 'You certainly seem like a female of the Race whenever your physiognomy is not visible.'

'But that is different,' Kassquit said. 'This Regeya, by your hypothesis, would be a wild Big Ugly, not one civilized from birth, as I have been.' She heard the pride in her voice.

'We have been studying the Tosevites since our arrival here,' Ttomalss said. 'Indeed, thanks to our probe, we studied them before we arrived here – although, as events proved, not well enough. And they have been studying us, too. Some of them, I suppose, will have learned a good deal about us by now.'

'Learned enough to imitate us that well?' Kassquit had trouble believing it. She'd not only taken this Regeya for a male of the Race, she'd taken him for a clever one. He had an unusual way of looking at the world, one that made her see things in a new light. But perhaps that sprang not from cleverness but from an alienness he couldn't fully conceal. She said as much to Ttomalss.

'It could be so,' he answered. 'I will not say that it is, but it could be. I fear you will have to conduct that investigation for yourself. I am too occupied with matters here to lend you much assistance. Felless will soon be laying her pair of eggs – she stubbornly refuses to leave Deutschland, despite possible health hazards – and will not be able to do as much work as usual for a little while before she finally does. That means I will have to do some of hers as well as my own.'

'Very well, superior sir,' Kassquit said coolly. To her, Felless remained an unscratchable itch deep under the scales she did not have. 'I shall attempt to draw out this Regeya, whoever and whatever he may be, and to see exactly what information he is seeking. Armed with that knowledge, I may be able to convince the authorities to take me seriously.'

'I approve of this course,' Ttomalss said, and broke the connection. Kassquit wasn't sure she approved of it. Being a Tosevite, *would* she be able to convince the authorities to take her seriously no matter what she did? She was not looking forward to the experiment, but saw no alternative.

Meanwhile, she had the chance to converse with Regeya and monitor his messages to learn what interested him. He knew where he wanted to sink his claws, that was plain: he aimed to learn all he could about whatever the Race knew of the American space station. That puzzled Kassquit. If he was a Big Ugly himself, why wouldn't he know such things?

Her first assumption had been that, if he was a Tosevite, he was an American – how else would he know so much about the United States? Then she began to wonder. She supposed the Big Uglies spied on one another as well as on the Race. Was Regeya from the *Reich* or the SSSR, seeking what the Race knew about a rival?

She couldn't ask him that, not in so many words. She did ask, *How and why do you know so much about these particular Big Uglies?*

In due course, Regeya answered, *I have followed their doings since they freed me after the fighting stopped. The Race and the Big Uglies will be sharing this planet for a long time. Sooner or later, Tosevites will travel to other worlds of the Empire, as Rabotevs and Hallessi will come here. We and the Big Uglies had better get to know each other, do you not think?* After the interrogative character, he used the Race's conventional symbol for an emphatic cough.

Kassquit studied that. No matter who – or what sort of being – had written it, it made good sense. *Truth,* she replied.

Some in the discussion group reported that the Americans were again increasing the number of shipments up to their station. *No one can tell what they are shipping, though,* the male who sent the message said. *Whatever it is, it stays crated until inside the station. This is inefficient even by Tosevite standards.*

What are the Big Uglies hiding? Regeya asked on noting that message.

If they were not hiding it, we would know, the male who had sent the earlier message replied. Kassquit laughed to see that. The message continued, *Whatever it is, we know enough always to keep an eye turret on that station.*

A good thing, too, Regeya replied.

Kassquit made a small, exasperated sound. Would an American Big Ugly have said such a thing? Would any Big Ugly have said such a thing? Didn't the Big Uglies know enough to show solidarity against the Race, as the Race showed solidarity against them? She knew the Big Uglies did not show solidarity among themselves, but still . . .

Finally, curiosity got the better of her. *Are you a Tosevite?* she sent to Regeya.

If he was, she thought that had a decent chance of scaring him out of the Race's computer network. But she did not have to wait long for his reply. *Of course I am,* he answered. *Just as much as you are.*

She stared at that. Her heart fluttered. Did Regeya, could Regeya, know who and what she was? He would have to have excellent connections indeed to gain even a hint of that. And Kassquit, unlike Regeya, was a fairly common name. Or was he just making a joke? She had gathered he was fond of joking.

What do I tell him? she wondered. *By the Emperor* – dutifully, she cast down her eyes – *what do I tell him?*

What if I am? she wrote back.

We would both be surprised, Regeya replied, again very quickly. He had to be waiting at the computer for her messages. *What is your telephone code?* he asked. *Perhaps we need to discuss this in person.* Kassquit was appalled. Even if she left the vision blank, Regeya would be able to hear that she did not fully belong to the Race.

I would rather leave things as they are, she wrote. She knew that was rude, but better to be rude than to betray herself.

As you wish, Regeya answered promptly. *We may be more alike than you think.* Kassquit made the negative hand gesture.

Whether Regeya belonged to the Race or to the Tosevites, she would not be much like him. She was sure of that.

Getting back into space felt good to Glen Johnson. After his run-in with Lieutenant General Curtis LeMay, he'd wondered if his superiors would let him ride *Peregrine* again. But nobody else at the Kitty Hawk launch site had said boo to him about LeMay's appalling visit to the BOQ. It was as if the general had delivered his tongue-lashing and then cleared out without mentioning it to anybody, which was possible but not in accord with the usual habits of general officers. Johnson had feared his career would be blighted for good.

His orbit was lower and therefore faster than that of the American space station. Whenever he passed below it, he paid close attention to the radio chatter coming from it. The traffic told him the station was getting yet another new load of surprises, which didn't surprise him. So many bus drivers were going up there, the Greyhound lines probably had to shut down half their routes.

He couldn't tell what the supplies were. That didn't surprise him, either. If he heard exactly what was going on up there, the Lizards and the Germans and the Russians would, too. He didn't want that. But he did want to know what was going on.

One thing he could tell, both by radar and by spotting scope: whatever those supplies were, the crew aboard the space station wasn't letting them go to waste. Sometimes he thought it looked bigger than it had on his previous pass each time he caught up with it. It was as big as one of the Lizards' starships these days, and showed no signs of slowing its growth.

'What the *hell* are they doing up there?' he asked a universe that did not answer. Construction in vacuum and weightlessness wasn't easy, but the station kept shifts going around the clock.

He couldn't ignore everything else in space, much as he would have liked to. During his tour, Peenemünde launched a couple of A-45s and brought the manned upper stages back to

Earth quite a bit faster than was their usual practice. Anything out of the ordinary was suspicious, as far as Johnson was concerned – and as far as his superiors were concerned, too, even if they didn't seem suspicious about what was going on at the American space station.

He tried pumping the Nazi spacemen about what their bosses were up to. That was doctrine. The Germans didn't tell him doodly-squat, which was doubtless part of their doctrine. They tried pumping him about the U.S. space station, too.

'Dammit, Drucker, I don't know what's going on up there,' he told one of his German opposite numbers when the fellow got not just nosy but pushy to boot. 'And if I did, I wouldn't tell you anyway.'

Drucker laughed. 'And you so angry with me got when I told you the same thing. I do not know what we are here with these test launches doing.'

Listening to the Germans, Johnson had discovered, was a matter of staying patient till they got around to the verb. He laughed, too, but sourly. 'Yeah, but the difference between us is that I know I'm telling the truth, but I've got the nasty feeling you're lying to me.'

'I speak truth,' Drucker declared, with a burst of static warning that they were drifting out of radio range of each other. 'It is you Americans who are liars.' More static gave him the last word in the argument.

'Screw him,' Johnson muttered, and then, 'On second thought, no thanks. I didn't come up here to be Mata Hari.' Spying with his eyes and ears and instruments was one thing. Using his fair white body . . . Again, his laugh was less than wholehearted. Nobody, Nazi pilot or good old American waitress or secretary or schoolteacher, had shown much interest in his fair white body lately.

He brought the *Peregrine* down to a good landing – about as smooth as he'd ever managed – at Kitty Hawk and then went through debriefing. He remarked that the Germans were curious about what was going on up at the space station.

The major taking notes just nodded and waited for him to say something else. If the fellow knew anything, he wasn't talking.

After a while, Johnson ran dry about the Germans and Russians and Lizards in space. The first debriefer left. His replacement came in and started grilling the spaceman about the changes the mechanics and technicians had made in *Peregrine* since his last flight. He had answers and opinions, some of them strong ones, about those modifications.

When they finally let him go, he thought about heading for the bar for a bit of high-proof tension relief. Instead, he went back to the BOQ. He was shaking his head as he did it – *Christ, don't I even have the energy to go buy myself a drink?* – but the direction in which he kept walking argued that he didn't.

He took a shower, then went back to his room and flopped down on the bed. Instead of falling asleep, which he'd thought he would do, he lay there for a bit, then pulled a Hornblower novel out of the GI nightstand by the bed and started to read. Things had been simple back in Hornblower's day, with only people to worry about.

The telephone on the nightstand rang, making him jump. He didn't like jumping, especially not when he was just back in full gravity. He picked up the phone and said, 'Johnson.'

'Lieutenant Colonel, I'm Major Sam Yeager, calling from Los Angeles,' the voice on the other end of the line said. He sounded as if he was calling from the other end of the country; there weren't so many hisses and pops on the line as there would have been before the Lizards came, but enough to notice remained.

'What can I do for you, Major?' Johnson asked. Yeager's name seemed vaguely familiar. After a moment, he placed it: a hotshot expert on the Lizards.

He expected Yeager to ask him about dealing with the Race in space. Instead, the fellow came straight out of left field: 'Lieutenant Colonel, if you don't mind my asking, did you by any chance get your ass chewed by General LeMay not so long ago?'

'How the hell did you know that?' Johnson sat up so suddenly, he knocked the Hornblower novel onto the floor.

Across three thousand miles, Major Yeager chuckled. 'Because I'm in the same boat – and I think it's the *Titanic*. General LeMay gets ants in his pants when people start asking about the space station, doesn't he?'

'He sure does. He—' Johnson shut up with a snap. He suddenly realized he had only Yeager's assurance that he was who and what he said he was. For all he knew, Yeager – or somebody claiming to be Yeager – might be one of LeMay's spies, trying to catch him in an indiscretion and sink him like a battleship. In a tight voice, he said, 'I don't think I'd better talk about that.'

'I'm not after your scalp, Lieutenant Colonel,' Yeager said. Johnson went right on saying nothing. With a sigh, Yeager went on, 'I don't like this any better than you do. Whatever's going on up there smells fishy to me. The Lizards have it on their minds, too, and I don't like that for beans. We could end up in big trouble on account of this.'

That matched perfectly with what Glen Johnson thought: so perfectly that it made him suspicious. He picked his words with care: 'Major, I don't know you. I'm not going to talk about this business with somebody who's only a voice.'

After a pause, Yeager answered, 'Well, I don't suppose I can blame you. The general is convincing, isn't he?'

'I don't know what you're talking about,' Johnson said, which might as well have meant, *Hell, yes!*

Another pause. Then Yeager said, 'Okay, sir, you don't trust me, and you don't have any reason to trust me. But I'm going to lay it on the line. The way it looks to me now, whatever the hell we're doing up there, it's something real big. It's something so big, whoever's in charge – which may be General LeMay and may be whoever *his* boss is – doesn't want anybody, and I mean anybody, finding out about it. How does that sound to you?'

Yeager might have been echoing Johnson's thoughts. But Johnson was damned if he'd admit it. He'd trusted Stella, and that hadn't got him anything but pain and lawyers' bills. If he trusted Yeager, he was liable to get his tit in a worse wringer yet. So all he said was, 'This is your nickel, Major. I'm still listening.' If by some chance this wasn't Yeager, or if it was and he was trying to get Johnson in Dutch, maybe he'd end up hanging himself instead.

'You think I'm setting you up, don't you?' Yeager asked, which couldn't have been a better echo of what was going on in Glen Johnson's mind.

'It did occur to me, yeah,' Johnson said dryly.

'I wonder why.' Yeager could be dry, too. That made Johnson more inclined to believe him, not less. Maybe he'd known it would. He went on, 'Listen. This isn't how you keep a secret. The way you do that is to pretend you don't have one, not to make a big hairy thing out of yourself and go around yelling, "I've got a secret and I won't tell you what it is, so you'd better not ask – or else!" Come on, Lieutenant Colonel. You're a big boy. Am I right or am I wrong?'

Johnson laughed. He didn't want to – he knew he was handing Yeager an edge – but he couldn't help himself. 'I tell you what,' he said. 'That's how I'd play it, anyway.'

'Me, too,' Yeager said. 'Some of the big shots don't understand anything but killing a mosquito with a tank, though. All that does is get a secret noticed. You noticed it—'

'Yeah,' Johnson broke in. Again, he couldn't help himself. If they'd let him go up to the space station, they could have shown him around, kept him from seeing anything he wasn't supposed to see, and sent him home. Yeager was right. They hadn't played it smart, not even a little.

'I noticed, too,' Yeager said. 'I'm not the only one, either. The Lizards have noticed something funny's going on up there. There's this one female of the Race named Kassquit – at least I think she's a female of the Race; that's a little strange – who's real curious about things that have to do with the space station. And we don't want the Lizards curious that way, not after what happened to the colonization fleet we don't.'

'Amen,' Johnson said. 'The next time anything goes wrong, they're going to shoot first and ask questions later.' He listened to himself with no small surprise. Somehow or other, Major Yeager had convinced him while he wasn't looking.

'That's what I think, too,' Yeager said. 'If you ask me, that's what anybody with an ounce of sense would think. But that's probably too much to ask of some people with a lot of stars on their shoulders.'

'Yeah,' Johnson said again. He'd spent a lot of time fishing for bluegill when he was a kid. He knew what setting a hook was like. Yeager had set a hook in him, all right. 'Next question is, what can we do about it? Can we do anything about it?'

'I don't know,' Yeager answered. 'Part of that depends on just what they really are doing at the space station. I haven't been able to find out, and I've got better and stranger connections than you might think. I got in big trouble the first time, but I didn't know I would, so I went in straight up and didn't bother sliding, if you follow me. I'm not playing it like that any more.'

Johnson pondered. Yeager was still taking chances, or he wouldn't have got on the phone. But there were a lot of different ways to be sneaky. A slow grin spread over Johnson's face. 'Maybe, Major, just maybe, I can get a closeup look at that critter after all.'

Fotsev hated Basra. His reasons for hating Basra were easy to understand. The place stank. It was full of Big Uglies, and not only Big Uglies, but Big Uglies fanatically devoted to their superstition who might at any moment rise in rebellion against the Race. Patrols in Basra were never routine; any cloth-shrouded Tosevite might be an assassin, and some, expecting a happy afterlife from their preposterous outsized Big Ugly beyond the sky if they sacrificed themselves to his cause on Tosev 3, were willing, even eager, to slay themselves if only they could take males of the Race with them.

So Fotsev hated Basra. As far as he was concerned, the only decent thing about it was the weather. Compared to that of Buenos Aires, where he'd been stationed before, it seemed a delightful reminder of Home.

He let out a small, discontented hiss as he and his squad tramped through Basra's central market square. 'What is itching your tailstump?' Gorppet asked him. The male's mouth fell open in amusement. 'This place, I should not wonder. More filth and disease right here – I mean this miserable square, not the whole city: spirits of Emperors past, I don't want to think about the whole city – than on all of Home put together.'

'You need leave again,' another male told Fotsev. 'Go on out to one of the new towns and you will see how things ought to be.'

And that made Fotsev realize why he was so discontented. 'I went out to the first one a while ago,' he said. 'Once was enough. I have not been back. I do not want to go back. I hated the new town just about as much as I hate this place.'

'You are mad, as addled as any Tosevite ever hatched,' said the other male, a fellow named Betvoss. Only astonishment could have prompted him to come out with such a thing, for Fotsev outranked him.

A couple of males on the patrol hissed in alarm. A couple more gestured to show they agreed with Betvoss. Fotsev could have taken offense, but he didn't. When he spoke, he sounded more weary than anything else: 'Home is an egg I have hatched out of. I am something different now. It may not be something better – I do not think it is something better. But I do not fit inside that shell any more. The males and females who live in the new towns know little of Tosev 3, and do not wish to learn. They still dwell inside the old shell. I have learned too much of Tosev 3, which I suppose is why I do not.'

Betvoss twisted his eye turrets in a way that suggested he did not understand and that there was nothing for him to understand. Fotsev had expected as much. Betvoss said, 'If you hate the new town and you also hate Basra, what is left for you?'

'Nothing, probably,' Fotsev answered. 'I think that will be the fate of many of us from the conquest fleet: caught betwixt and between, belonging nowhere.'

'Not me,' Betvoss said. 'I like the new towns. They remind me of how things were and how they will be again.'

'I think Fotsev speaks truth,' Gorppet said, which astonished Fotsev; the dour veteran seldom took his part. Gorppet had seen much worse action during the fighting than Fotsev had, and Fotsev often thought the other male resented him for coming through so easily. But now Gorppet went on, 'I went into the new town a couple of times, maybe three. I do not bother going any more, either.'

'I enjoy it,' Betvoss said. 'I would sooner be there than here. I would sooner be anywhere than here.'

'They do not understand the males of the Soldiers' Time in the new town,' Fotsev said. 'They did not go through what we went through, and they cannot see why we did not deliver Tosev 3 to them as we would have if all the Big Uglies truly had ridden animals and swung swords, as the probe made us think they would.'

Betvoss seized the first part of that. 'You say the colonists do not understand us? What of the Tosevites?' His wave encompassed the Big Ugly males in their wrappings of brown or white and the females in black with only their eyes showing and sometimes even those veiled away behind cloth.

Fotsev shrugged. 'I do not expect Big Uglies to understand – they are Big Uglies. But the folk of the new town are my own kind – or they look like me, at any rate. I expected more than I got, and I was disappointed.'

'And I as well,' Gorppet agreed. 'Only we who have been through it can understand what we endured. Some of the Tosevites who fought against us come closer than the males and females of the Race who did not.' He sighed. 'When the males of the conquest fleet die, no one will understand.' After a couple of strides, he swung an eye turret toward Betvoss. 'Some males do not understand now.'

'Truth,' Betvoss said. 'And you are one of them.'

'Enough,' Fotsev said with a slow, tired, emphatic cough. 'Are we Big Uglies, to brawl among ourselves?'

By the Emperor, I need a taste of ginger, he thought. However much he might need one, though, he was not so sure where he might come by it. The herb was in shorter supply than he could ever remember. Those above him had always fumed and grumbled about ginger, and every so often made examples of males caught tasting or dealing in it. But there had always been plenty – till females from the colonization fleet showed what the herb did to them. Now the authorities were serious about keeping it off everyone's tongue.

One of Fotsev's eye turrets slid toward Gorppet. If anyone could still get ginger, he was the male. And if he understood why Fotsev stayed away from the new towns, maybe he would be more willing to share some of what he had, if he had any.

The breeze shifted, changing the notes in the symphony of stinks that played over Fotsev's scent receptors. One odor cut through the usual array of Tosevite stenches, though: the pheromones of a female in her season. *Somebody is getting ginger,* Fotsev thought. He wasn't the only male to note that scent, of course. His whole squad suddenly seemed more alert. A couple of troopers began to take on the erect posture associated with mating. Betvoss started away from his comrades, toward that wonderful scent.

'Back!' Fotsev said sharply, relishing the chance to rebuke the male who'd thought he was addled. 'She is a long way off. We just have to go on about our business and pretend she is not there.'

'I smell her. I want to mate with her,' Betvoss whined. Fotsev wanted to mate with her, too, wherever she was, but not to the point where he forgot himself and forgot his duty. Even as he kept eyeing the market square, the urge remained, an itch inside his head – and inside his cloaca – he couldn't scratch. It made him irritable; he was ever so ready to leap down Betvoss' throat if the other male got more unruly than he had already proved.

But Betvoss, though he stayed sulky, obeyed: obedience was nearly as ingrained in the Race as was desire when presented with the proper stimuli.

Small male Tosevites came running up to the patrol, jabbering in their own language. Gorppet gestured with his rifle. He did not want them to get too close. Fotsev didn't blame him. The Race had learned from painful experience that stopping suicide attackers wasn't easy.

So far, the fanatical Tosevites had not begun using hatchlings as suicide warriors. That did not mean they would not do such a thing, though. In all truth, Gorppet was right to be cautious.

Caution came hard, though, when the small Big Uglies (a notion that made Fotsev laugh, but that was true: he overtopped almost all of them) came up in spite of Gorppet's warning. They'd learned a few words from the language of the Race. 'Food!' they shouted. 'Want food!' Others shouted, 'Want money!'

'No money,' Gorppet said, gesturing with the rifle again. The Race's credit would have been useless to these ragamuffins, and handing out the metal disks the Tosevites used as their medium of exchange went against orders.

Food was something else. Fotsev had never seen hunger till he came to Tosev 3. He'd thought hunger was the feeling he knew just before it was time for a meal. Maybe that was hunger, of a sort. But it was not the kind of hunger that came from having no food at all, from having to do without meals. Fotsev knew such conditions had existed back on Home in ancient history, before the Empire unified his planet. But those days were more than a hundred thousand years in the past, a very long time ago even by the standards of the Race. Seeing that kind of hunger had jolted him, and he was far from the only male it had jolted.

So now he took little cubes of pressed meat and concentrated nutrients and tossed a handful of them to the Big Ugly hatchlings. So did three or four other males from the squad. The Tosevites squalled in delight and squabbled with one another over the food. They had no trouble eating the Race's rations, as Fotsev and his fellows had no trouble except occasional disgust with Tosevite foods. And some Tosevite food products were even more delectable to the Race than to Big Uglies . . . and so Fotsev's mind, almost inevitably, came back to ginger.

The one problem with feeding some Tosevite beggars was that their success drew more, sure as carrion drew scavengers. After a while, Fotsev and his fellows ran low on ration cubes and started saying, 'Enough! All gone!' The hatchlings cursed them in the language of the Race and, Fotsev was sure, even more hotly in their own tongue.

Gorppet said something in that language that made them stop cursing and bark out the laughter of their kind. After that, the patrol had less trouble getting rid of them. When Fotsev asked Gorppet what he'd said, the other veteran replied, 'I wished that predators would find the eggs of all their descendants.' It seemed a fine strong curse to Fotsev till he remembered the Big Uglies did not lay eggs. Then he understood why the hatchlings laughed. But anything that avoided trouble suited him fine.

After what seemed forever, the patrol returned to barracks. Fotsev made his report, not that he had anything much to report. And then, for a little while, his time was his own. As he'd been sure he would, he hunted up Gorppet. 'Come for a walk with me,' he said. Rumor had it that the barracks held listening devices. Fotsev neither knew whether rumor was true nor cared to learn.

Out in the open, he hadn't even broached the subject before Gorppet said, 'You look like a male who could use a taste – maybe even a couple of tastes.'

'Truth,' Fotsev said, with an emphatic cough. After a couple of tastes, Tosev 3 improved – and would stay improved till the

571

ginger left his system. He asked, 'How did you come by the herb? I am empty.'

'Your friend' – a common euphemism for a ginger dealer – 'must be one of the males who got his from a Big Ugly west of here who's out of business – for the time being, anyhow,' Gorppet answered. 'I have lots of friends. That is why I never go dry.'

'I never thought I would,' Fotsev said ruefully, or as ruefully as he could with the herb exulting through him, 'but I did.'

'The males with the fancy body paint want to get their teeth into this, all right,' Gorppet said. 'They do not want females coming into season any old time.' He laughed; he'd had a couple of tastes, too. 'You smelled how well it works while we were out on patrol. They can slow the trade down, but they can't stop it.'

'I think you are right,' Fotsev said. 'Hard to try to do other things, normal things, while on the edge of my own season. I understand why our superiors are fighting ginger so hard – but I still want one more taste.'

'It shall be done,' Gorppet said, and it was. He had another taste himself. They spent the rest of their free time enjoyably cutting Betvoss into little strips.

The Americans had a phrase: a slow boat to China. Liu Han and Liu Mei heard that phrase any number of times on their journey west across the Pacific, so often that they got good and sick of it. It was, if anything, an understatement for their homeward voyage aboard the *Liberty Princess*, a ship whose self-contradictory name never failed to amuse Liu Han.

Everything went fine from Los Angeles to Hawaii, but Hawaii, of course, still belonged to the United States. Past Hawaii, from the island of Midway (which the Japanese had seized, almost unnoticed, during the time of fighting against the little scaly devils) on, every stop the *Liberty Princess* made before Shanghai was in the Empire of Japan.

And the Japanese were suspicious. Now Liu Han wished her

visit to the United States had drawn less public notice. Whenever Japanese inspectors came aboard the ship, they naturally tried to prove she and Liu Mei were, in fact, just who they were, despite papers purporting to prove them to be other people altogether.

They never quite managed. Liu Han thanked the gods and spirits in whom she was not supposed to believe for the English Liu Mei and she had picked up getting ready to visit the USA and improved while there. They used it as much as they could, baffling the Japanese who did not speak it and holding their own with the ones who did. Even in the Philippines, where many puppets of the eastern dwarfs were fluent in English, Liu Han and Liu Mei kept steadfastly insisting they were people other than their true selves, and got by with it. Without absolute proof – which they could not get – the Japanese did not care to embroil themselves with the United States.

After the last Japanese official gave up in frustration, after the *Liberty Princess* was finally cleared to sail for Shanghai with the two Chinese women aboard, Liu Han turned to her daughter and said, 'Do you see? This is what the power of a strong country is worth. The United States protects its people and protects its ships. One day, China will be able to do the same.'

Liu Mei did not try to hide her bitterness. 'Before we become a strong country, Mother, we have to become a country of any sort. As far as the little scaly imperialist devils are concerned, we are nothing but part of their Empire.'

'That is why we have traveled so far,' Liu Han answered. 'We did everything we could in the United States, I think. Weapons are coming. I do not know just when they will reach us: the Japanese and the Kuomintang and the little devils will all make that as hard as they can. But the weapons will come sooner or later. The People's Liberation Army will take advantage of them sooner or later. And, sooner or later, the scaly devils will pay for their aggression and oppression. How long that takes doesn't matter. Sooner or later, it will happen. The dialectic demands it.'

Except for mentioning the dialectic, she might have been a little scaly devil talking. One of the things that made them so dangerous was their habit of thinking in the long term. Mao had coined a good term to describe them: he called them incrementalists. They never retreated, and kept moving forward half an inch here, a quarter of an inch there. If they needed a hundred years or a thousand years to reach their goals, they didn't care. Sooner or later, they would get there – or so they thought.

But then Liu Mei said, 'If the little scaly devils had come here sooner, they could have easily conquered us. We also have to worry about whether we can afford to wait.'

'We have the dialectic on our side. They did not,' Liu Han said. But her daughter's words worried her. The dialectic said nothing about when victory would come. She could only hope it would come in her lifetime. Most of the time, she didn't worry about not knowing. Every once in a while, as today, it ate at her.

The *Liberty Princess* sailed up the Yangtze to Shanghai. The city had more Western-style buildings than any other in China, having been the center of the round-eyed devils' imperialist ambitions before the coming of first the eastern dwarfs from Japan and then the little scaly devils. Liu Han had known that, of course, but it had meant little to her because she'd seen few Western-style buildings before coming to the United States. Now she'd spent months in a city of nothing but Western-style buildings. She studied the ones in Shanghai with new eyes.

The city meant something different to Liu Mei. 'So this is where my father died,' she said in musing tones. 'That did not mean so much to me before I learned about him from the American who knows so much about the little devils.'

'Nieh Ho-T'ing always said he died very bravely,' Liu Han said, which was true. 'He helped men of the People's Liberation Army escape after they struck the little devils a stinging blow.' She looked at Shanghai with new eyes herself. Memories of Bobby Fiore came flooding into her mind – and a little

574

jealousy at how interested Liu Mei had been in the American half of her family.

Again, her daughter might have picked the thought from her mind. 'In everything that matters, I am Chinese,' Liu Mei said. 'You were the one who raised me. We are going home.' Liu Han smiled and nodded. Liu Mei wasn't as right as she thought, thanks to the little scaly devil named Ttomalss. Liu Han's daughter did not smile, because the little devil had not – could not – smile at her while trying to raise her after stealing her as a newborn from Liu Han. Liu Mei knew that had happened to her, but remembered none of it. It had marked her just the same.

'Now we have only to get off this ship, get onto the train, and go home to Peking,' Liu Han said. 'And, I think, before we do that, we have to stop somewhere and get something to eat. It will be good to eat proper food again.'

'Truth,' Liu Mei said, and used an emphatic cough. 'The Americans eat some very strange things indeed. Fried potatoes are not bad once you get used to them, but cheese – how do they eat cheese?'

'I don't know.' Liu Han shuddered. 'What else is it but rotten milk? They should throw it away or feed it to pigs.'

Shortly thereafter, she conceived the identical opinion of the Chinese customs officials who manned the Shanghai customs office for the little scaly devils. She had hoped – she had, in fact, been assured – officials who sympathized with the Party and the People's Liberation Army would ease her passage back into China. Hopes and assurances or not, it didn't happen. The customs men who dealt with her daughter and her might have been working for the Kuomintang, or they might have completely prostituted themselves to the little devils. Liu Han never was sure of that. She was sure they thought her false papers were false papers, no matter how artfully they'd been forged.

'Stupid women!' one of the customs men shouted. 'We know who you are! You are Reds! Do not deny it. You cannot deceive us.'

575

Liu Mei said nothing. Her face stayed expressionless, as it usually did, but her eyes blazed. She got angry at being called a Red, even though she was one. When Liu Han had time, she would laugh about that. She didn't have time now.

'We are the people our papers say we are,' she said, over and over and over again.

'You are liars!' the boss customs man said. 'I will haul you up in front of the little scaly devils. Let us see you tell your lies to them. They will know your papers are as false as a dragon's wings on a duck.'

The threat worried Liu Han to some degree: the little scaly devils might be able to tell the papers were false where human beings could not. Underestimating their technical skill was always dangerous. But they were disastrously bad at interrogation; next to them, the Americans were paragons. And so, with a sneer, Liu Han said, 'Yes, take us to the little scaly devils. I can tell them the truth and hope they will listen.' She could tell them a pack of lies and hope they believed her.

But her willingness to go before them rocked the customs man, as she'd thought it would. To most Chinese, the little devils remained objects of superstitious dread. Surely no one with anything to hide would want to talk to them. The customs man took a somewhat more conciliatory tone: 'If you are not the people we think you are, how is it that you come off the American ship?'

'We got aboard in Manila,' Liu Han said for about the tenth time. The false papers said the same thing; a good many Chinese merchants lived in the Philippines. 'Maybe, while you have been badgering us, the people you want, whoever they are, have gotten away. They are probably halfway to Harbin by now.'

'Harbin!' the customs man shouted. 'Stupid woman! Foolish woman! Ignorant woman! The Reds are not strong in Harbin.'

'I do not know anything about that,' answered Liu Han, who knew quite a bit about it. 'I have been telling you for a long, long time now, I do not know anything about that. And neither does my niece here, either.'

'You do not know anything about anything,' the customs man said. 'Go on, get out of here, and your stupid turtle of a niece, too.'

'He is the stupid turtle,' Liu Mei said once they were well out of the boss customs man's hearing.

Liu Han shook her head. 'No, he did his job well – he was right to be suspicious of us, and I had to work hard to make him let us go. If he were stupid, I would have had an easier time. That was not the trouble. The trouble was that he serves the imperialist little devils – or maybe our enemies in the Kuomintang – with too much zeal.'

'Something should happen to him, then,' Liu Mei said.

'And maybe something will,' Liu Han said. 'The Party here in Shanghai must know about him. And if they do not, we can pass the word from Peking. Yes, maybe something will happen to the running dog.'

The Shanghai train station stood not far from the docks: a large gray stone pile of a building, again in the Western style. Because it was not far, Liu Han and Liu Mei walked. To go with their assumption of the role of Chinese from the Philippines, they now had less baggage than they'd taken aboard the *Liberty Princess* in Los Angeles. Liu Han was glad not to have to exploit the labor of a rickshaw puller or a pedicab driver. Such work might be necessary, but it was degrading. Now that she had seen the United States, she felt that more strongly than ever.

Lines in front of the ticket sellers were not neat and orderly, as they would have been back in the USA. They were hardly lines at all. People jostled and shouted and cursed one another, all shoving forward to wave money in the faces of the clerks. Liu Han felt swamped, smothered in humanity. Shanghai was no more crowded than Peking, but her most recent standard of comparison was Los Angeles, a town far more spread out than either Chinese city. Liu Mei at her back, she elbowed her way forward.

After much bad blood, she managed to buy two second-class

577

tickets north to Peking. The platform on which she and her daughter had to wait was as crowded as the cramped space in front of the ticket sellers. She'd expected that. The train came into the station three hours late. She'd expected that, too.

But, after she and Liu Mei fought their way to seats on the hard benches of a second-class car, she relaxed. In spite of all inconveniences, they were going home.

Johannes Drucker muttered something unpleasant under his breath as he floated weightless in *Käthe*, the upper stage of his A-45. The radio wasn't set to transmit, so nobody down on the ground could hear him. That was doubtless just as well.

He checked himself. He hoped nobody down on the ground could hear him. He remained politically suspect, and knew it. He wouldn't have put it past the SS to sneak a secret microphone and transmitter into *Käthe*, in the hope he would say something damning when he thought no one was listening. If he had any opinions about Heinrich Himmler and sheep, he'd be smart to pull the wool over them.

'*Baah!*' he said, softly and derisively. Let the boys in the black coats figure out what that meant, if they were listening. He had more important things to worry about. Had he been wearing a hat, he would have tipped it in the direction of General Dornberger. The commandant at Peenemünde had been able to keep him in space. As far as he was concerned, this was the most fun he could have with his clothes on.

A radar ping almost bright enough to make him blink appeared on his screen. '*Du lieber Gott,*' he said, not caring at all whether anyone was listening to him. 'I think the Americans are building New York City up here.' The station was noticeably bigger than it had been on his last trip up into orbit, and it had been enormous even then. Its German equivalent could not compete.

He turned his radio receiver to the bands the Americans favored. They got careless with their signals traffic every so often. Not often enough. They were up to *Wehrmacht* standards – or perhaps a little beyond – when they talked with one another. His best hope was catching them in the middle of an accident, so he could hear what they said when they weren't thinking so much of whether he was listening.

Thinking that way made him feel a little guilty. Wishing an accident on anybody in space probably meant wishing death on him, too. Very few minor accidents happened out beyond the atmosphere – everything worked fine, or else you were dead. Drucker didn't want anybody wishing that kind of misfortune on him.

He listened to the chatter that went on around the space station. The workers expanding it complained more than their German counterparts would have done. 'I'm so damn tired, I'd be grateful to be dead,' one of them said.

That proved too much even for the other Americans. 'Oh, shut up, Jerry,' one of them said, a sentiment with which Drucker heartily agreed.

After a little while, Drucker decided not to wait and see if something would happen, but to try to make something happen instead. 'You certainly are getting large there,' he radioed to the American space station. 'When do you intend to attack the colonization fleet again?'

That *again* made him particularly proud. If it didn't make any listening Lizard sit up and take notice, he didn't know what would. He must have struck a nerve inside the station, too, for the answer came back in a tearing hurry: 'Go peddle your papers, you Nazi bastard! If you guys didn't blow up the Lizards, Molotov's boys sure as hell did, on account of it wasn't us.'

'Ha!' Drucker said. 'You Americans the crazy ones are, making this great huge . . . thing up here.' He'd done his duty by his country. Anybody who didn't think the SS was crazy, though, didn't know the current *Führer*'s precious pets.

And the American radio operator kept jeering at him: 'You're just jealous 'cause you don't have a big one yourself.'

Only belatedly did Drucker realize the American might not

be talking about space stations. 'I have never on that score any complaints had,' he said smugly.

'Another Nazi superman, eh?' the radio operator said. 'Listen up, pal – what do you think your wife is doing while you're up here?'

'The laundry,' Drucker said. 'Now your mother, I cannot for her answer.'

He smiled, listening to the American curse him. Before long, the curses faded as he went out of range and the bulge of the Earth hid the space station. He nodded to himself. He had given at least as good as he got. But then his satisfaction dribbled away. He hadn't learned anything, which was what he'd hoped for. Like everybody else, the *Wehrmacht* paid for what you did, not for how good you looked when you didn't do much.

Or had he learned something after all, something he would sooner not have known? When the *Reich* began fighting Poland, when the *Reich* began fighting the Bolsheviks, it had termed both campaigns counterattacks. Drucker couldn't prove those statements were lies, but he knew few foreigners believed them. Could Himmler be lying here, too?

If Germany had launched the missiles of an orbiting weapon against the Race, she was wise to lie about it. Even bestriding Europe like a colossus, the Greater German *Reich* was the smallest independent human power, its population fearsomely concentrated. The Lizards could take a terrible revenge.

He reported his conversation with the American to a German radio relay ship in the Indian Ocean. 'That is good, Lieutenant Colonel,' the radioman told him. 'The Lizards do not pay enough attention to the United States. Perhaps we can persuade them to do so. For some reason, they always suspect us and accuse us instead.' His voice took on a faint whining tone. 'I do not understand why.'

'I can't imagine,' Drucker said, and then hoped the fellow down there on the ship didn't notice how dry he sounded. But his own hope for promotion had slammed into a stone wall not for anything he'd done, but because of suspicions about his

580

wife's ancestry. And a lot worse than that would have happened to Käthe had the SS been able to nail their suspicions down tight.

The Lizards had to know such things. Was it any wonder they suspected the *Reich* on account of them?

'See if you can learn more still on your next pass under the space station,' the radio operator told Drucker.

'I'll try,' he answered, and broke the connection. The signal for the attack on the colonization fleet, he remembered, had come from the Indian Ocean. It was supposed to have come from a U-boat, but was everyone dead certain of that?

Centimeter by centimeter, he made himself relax. The USA had a relay ship down there in the waters between Africa and Australia, and so did the USSR. Anyone could have done it.

As his orbit carried him over Australia, he chuckled to himself. Undoubtedly a U-boat had lobbed ginger bombs at the Lizards' cities going up in the desert there. Nobody knew whose U-boat had done it. Drucker chuckled again, thinking of the orgy the Lizards must have had. 'Killing them with kindness,' he said, and then came right out and laughed, because *kindness* didn't begin to describe it.

Up over the long stretch of the Pacific Ocean he flew, passing not far from the island the self-styled Free French still ruled. That notion made him laugh, too, in a different way. If petty criminals and gambling lords wanted to call their little bailiwick a country, he couldn't stop them, but that didn't mean he had to take them seriously.

Eventually, he caught up with the space station again. When he called to report his presence in the neighborhood (not that the station wouldn't know unless its radar was out), the same radio operator as before answered him: 'Your mouth is so big, pal, I figured you'd have sucked all the air out of your cabin by now.'

'You talk about big,' Drucker said, laughing once more. 'When do you take that big boat of yours onto the sea instead of leaving it in orbit docked?'

581

'Wouldn't you like to know?' the American answered.

Drucker started to make another gibe, but then he really listened to what the radioman had said. 'What was that?' he asked, wanting to make sure he'd heard what he thought he had.

But the American didn't repeat himself. Instead, he replied, 'I said, you don't know what you're doing.'

He hadn't said that. Drucker's English wasn't perfect, but he was sure the American hadn't said that or anything like it. What did that mean? Drucker could think of only one thing: the American had slipped and was trying to cover it up. 'You will never get that ugly beast moving,' he jeered, trying to rattle the radioman into another mistake.

To his sorrow, it didn't work. 'We're doing five miles a second now,' the American said. 'Eight kilometers a second for you, buddy. That's fast enough, don't you figure?'

'Whatever you say,' Drucker answered. 'You are the one who likes to brag.'

This time, he got no answer. He hadn't gone out of range of the space station. It still glowed like a Christmas-tree ornament on his radar screen. That had to mean the American was clamming up on purpose. And *that* had to mean the fellow had put his foot in it, and knew he had, too.

No more questions, Drucker thought. Let the radioman think he hadn't noticed a thing out of the ordinary. The American would be hoping he hadn't, anyhow. Drucker sped on in delicious, thoughtful silence.

He started to radio what he'd learned – no, what he'd heard, because he wasn't sure what he'd learned – down to the next German relay ship over which he crossed. He stopped with his index finger already on the TRANSMIT button. Someone, no doubt, would be monitoring his traffic with the relay ship. With a little luck, nobody'd noticed his unusual exchange with the space station. He decided to hang onto it and what it might mean till he got down.

Earth unrolled below, going now into darkness, now into light. Blue ocean, white and grays wirls of cloud, land in shades of green and brown – it was all very beautiful. Drucker wondered whether Lizard pilots with this view felt the same. From what they said, Home held more land and less water. If they thought the Sahara and the Australian outback were comfortable, their opinion of both forests and oceans was liable to be a lot lower than his.

When he was up here, he usually wanted to stay in orbit as long as he could. He liked spaceflight. And, when he was up here, he didn't have to worry about things going wrong down below. They couldn't do anything to him up here no matter what went wrong down below.

A moment after that comforting thought, he had one less comforting: they could, if they wanted to badly enough. Another pilot in the upper stage of an A-45 could come after him and shoot him down, just as if he were in a fighter plane.

He patted the control panel. He'd do his best to make anybody who tried that very unhappy. He thought he could manage it, too. Radar made sneaking up to shoot somebody in the back much harder.

And if anyone did come gunning for him . . . He patted the control panel again. With her two explosive-metal-tipped missiles, *Käthe* carried a lot of death. If anyone came after him and didn't get him, he would be in a position to exact the greatest revenge in the history of the world.

Well, maybe he would be in position. Part of that would depend on how close he was to Nuremberg and Peenemünde, and whether he could get to either one as he came out of orbit.

'Still, the *Führer* wouldn't want to find out the hard way,' Drucker murmured, 'not if he's smart, he wouldn't.'

The transmitter was off. He almost wished it weren't. The *Reich* trusted him to fly with atomic weapons. He wouldn't have minded putting a flea in the ear of some Party bigwigs: a man who flew with atomic weapons was probably not a good man to annoy. Anyone with any brains should have been able to figure that out for himself. Drucker wasn't so sure how many Party bigwigs had any brains.

Once upon a time, he'd read somewhere, the Americans had flown a rattlesnake flag with the legend DON'T TREAD ON ME. Drucker slowly nodded. He had two fangs of his own. If people pushed him too hard, he might use them.

Flight Lieutenant David Goldfarb felt as if he were moving back through time. He'd flown from Jerusalem to London in one of the Lizards' jets, a machine as modern as next year. Then he'd taken the train from London to Liverpool, a technology less than a century and a half old – on Earth, anyhow. And then he'd traveled from Liverpool to Belfast on a ferry, and the waves of the Irish Sea had made him as miserably sick as any passenger in any boat since the dawn of time.

Back on solid ground, he'd recovered fast. Seeing Naomi and his children again hadn't hurt, either. Nor had returning to work. He even seemed to have won some small amount of respect for going into Germany and coming out in one piece.

None of that, though, made him feel as if he'd put the dreadful time behind him. He knew what would. *Only a matter of waiting,* he thought, and didn't expect he'd have to wait long.

And he was right. When he came off duty after his second day back at the radar installation, a familiar voice called, 'Welcome home, old chap!' There came Group Captain Roundbush, a broad smile on his handsome face, his right hand extended.

Instead of clasping it, Goldfarb came to attention and saluted. 'Sir,' he said.

'Oh, my dear fellow,' Roundbush said. 'You're not going to take it that way, I hope?'

'Sir—' Goldfarb looked around before going on. No, no one else was close enough to hear what he had to say to Basil Roundbush. He took a deep breath. 'Fuck you, sir.'

Roundbush blinked, but didn't quite lose his smile. 'I can understand why you might feel that way, old man, but really,

584

you mustn't.' He sounded as cheerful, as ingratiating, as ever. 'Here, I've got a motorcar laid on. Come along with me to Robinsons. We'll put down some Guinness, and then the world will seem a happier place.' He turned to go, confident Goldfarb would follow.

Goldfarb didn't. After a couple of steps, Group Captain Roundbush noticed. He turned back, puzzlement on his features. Goldfarb said, 'Sir, from now on I'm not having one bloody thing to do with you that isn't strictly required by duty. So no, I'm bloody well not going to Robinsons with you, or anywhere else, either.'

Now Roundbush looked grave. 'I'm afraid you don't know what you're saying.'

'I'm afraid I do – so sod off,' Goldfarb answered. 'Excuse me. Sod off – sir.' His right hand slipped to the holster of his pistol. 'The way I feel right now, for half a crown I'd blow your fucking head off.'

He didn't think he could put Roundbush in fear. The medals on the group captain's chest said he didn't frighten easily, if at all. But bravery and goodness didn't necessarily go hand in hand. If the Nazis didn't prove that, the Russians did. Still, Goldfarb wanted him to know he meant what he was saying.

Roundbush did know it. His eyes narrowed, which left him a little less handsome and a lot more dangerous-looking. 'You do want to have a care about what you're saying, you know,' he remarked.

'Why?' Goldfarb didn't bother hiding his bitterness. 'What kind of trouble can my big mouth get me into that's worse than what my big nose has already done?'

'I'd say you were doing your best to find out,' Group Captain Roundbush answered. 'I know you've been through a lot, but—'

'You don't bloody know the tenth part of it,' David broke in.

'Perhaps I don't, Roundbush said. 'If you like, I shall be happy to admit I don't. But what I do know' – he fixed

Goldfarb with a cool and menacing stare – 'is that you will find yourself in more trouble than you ever dreamt of if you don't button your lip this very minute.'

'I've already *been* in more trouble than I ever dreamt of,' David Goldfarb said. 'I've been in more trouble than you and your pals could buy me in a thousand years. And so, sir, with all due respect, as far as I'm concerned, you can bend over and kiss my bleeding arse.'

'You will regret this foolish outburst,' Roundbush said. That, David thought, was very likely to be true. But he would have regretted going along with Roundbush and the ginger smugglers even more. The senior RAF officer went on, 'And I am afraid your military career has just taken a large shell to the engine.'

'Go peddle your papers.' Goldfarb enjoyed defiance. It tingled through his veins, heady as good whiskey. He doubted the RAF could give him an assignment a great deal worse than the one he already had. He didn't say that, though, as he was certain his former colleague and current oppressor would move heaven and earth to prove him wrong.

Roundbush said, 'Do bear in mind that your family may suffer on account of your pigheadedness.'

'You've talked about my family too much,' Goldfarb answered. 'Now I'm going to say something about them: If any harm – any harm at all, mind you – comes to them, something will happen to you, too. Have you got that?'

'Your spirit does you credit,' Basil Roundbush said. 'You would be better off if your good sense did, too.' He nodded to Goldfarb, then turned and walked away, shaking his head as if washing his hands of the other RAF officer.

Goldfarb watched him go. As if after combat, reaction began to set in. Goldfarb's knees wobbled. His hands shook. He was panting as if he'd run a long way. He began to think he'd been a fool after all.

If he ran after Roundbush and begged forgiveness, he was sure he would get it. Why not? He remained useful to the group captain and his ginger-smuggling pals. They were, and prided themselves on being, businessmen. Personal animosity? They'd wave it aside.

He stayed where he was. He didn't want Roundbush and his associates to forgive him. He wanted them to leave him alone. Maybe, if he wasn't useful to them, they'd do just that. Maybe they wouldn't, too. Again, his hand glided toward his holster. If Group Captain Roundbush thought he'd been kidding when he made his warning, the much-decorated officer was badly mistaken.

The motorcar in which Roundbush would have taken him to the pub rolled away. Goldfarb sighed and headed for his bicycle. It was the sort of transportation he was more used to, anyhow.

When he got back to the quarters he shared with his family, his first words were, 'Pour me a whiskey, darling, would you please?'

'Of course,' Naomi said, and did. The request was unusual from him, but not unheard of. The way he knocked back the smoky amber liquid, though, made her raise an eyebrow. 'You had a bad day?'

'I had about the worst day a man could have, as a matter of fact.' He held out the glass to her. 'Fill me up again. I'm going to get drunk and beat you, the way my father said the Poles would do to their wives.'

His wife got him another drink. When he sipped it instead of gulping it down, she nodded in approval and relief; maybe, even after all these years of marriage, she'd taken him literally when she shouldn't have. She let him get about halfway down the glass before she said, 'Don't you think you should tell me about it? The children are all out doing one thing or another. You don't have to be shy.'

'Good,' he answered. 'I told Basil Roundbush to go fly a kite in a thunderstorm, is what I did.' As best he could, bowdlerizing only slightly, he recounted the conversation he'd had with the group captain. When he was finished, he sighed and said, 'I should have played along, shouldn't I?'

Naomi took the glass out of his hand and set it on the counter by the icebox. Then she wrapped her arms around him and squeezed the breath out of him. 'I'm proud of you,' she said.

'You are?' He reached for his drink again. 'Why? I'm not particularly proud of myself, and you're liable to suffer for what I did.'

'I don't think so,' Naomi said. 'They will not get you to help them like that – and I think Roundbush knows you were not joking.'

'I'll tell you what I think.' Goldfarb spoke more positively than usual: the whiskey talking through him, no doubt. 'I think we ought to emigrate as fast as we can . . . if they'll let us out.'

'The United States?' Naomi asked. 'I would not mind going to the United States at all.' By her voice, that was an understatement.

But Goldfarb shook his head. 'Canada, I think. Fewer formalities getting into Canada.' Seeing how disappointed his wife looked, he added, 'We could go to the States later, you know.'

'I suppose so.' Naomi brightened. 'That wouldn't be bad. And you're right – Canada wouldn't be bad, either. If you think it's easier to go to Canada than to the USA, that's what we ought to do. If my family had waited till they could get into the United States in 1938, we'd still be waiting.'

'Except you wouldn't be waiting,' Goldfarb said, 'not when you were trying to get out of Germany. You'd be . . .' He let his voice trail off. He was very glad when Naomi took the point and nodded. He went on, 'Sometimes, the idea is to be able to get out when you have to; you can worry about where you end up later.'

'All right,' she said. 'See the Canadian consul tomorrow. If you want to see the American consul, too, that's all right.'

'Fair enough.' David finished the second whiskey. It was a hefty tot; he could feel it. 'If I went out now, they could nick me for drunken cycling.' Naomi laughed, but he remembered how many times over the years he'd pedaled back to his bed somewhat, or more than somewhat, the worse for wear.

He was sober when he cycled over to the Canadian consulate after his next tour in front of the radar. When he explained what he wanted, a clerk there said, 'I'm sorry, sir, but we can't accept serving officers.'

'If you accept me, I won't be a serving officer,' David answered. 'If you accept me, I'll resign my commission like *that*.' He snapped his fingers. 'Will you give me the forms on that basis?' The clerk nodded and handed him a set. He filled them out on the spot and gave them back. They seemed straightforward enough.

The clerk glanced at them. He looked up at Goldfarb. 'Your government would be idiotic to let you go.'

'Perhaps you didn't notice I'm a Jew,' Goldfarb said. Then, seeing the surprise on the clerk's face, he realized the fellow *hadn't* noticed. Such indifference was rare in the United Kingdom of 1963. He hoped it was common in Canada.

He rode to the American consulate a few blocks away. The clerk there was female and pretty. The forms, however, were much longer and uglier than the ones the Canadians used. Goldfarb slogged through them, too, and turned them in.

'Thank you, Flight Lieutenant,' the clerk said. She, too, looked over the papers. 'The USA can pick and choose whom we let in, you know, but by these I'd say – unofficially, of course – you have a fair chance. Better than fair, in fact.'

He grinned all the way back to his flat. The Canadians wanted him. So did the Americans. He wasn't used to that, not in Britain these days he wasn't. 'I ought to be,' he said, careless of the looks he might get for talking to himself. 'By God, I bloody well ought to be.'

18

'I remain of the opinion that you are making too much of this,' Ttomalss said.

Kassquit glared at him out of his computer screen. 'My investigation shows otherwise, superior sir,' she replied, deferential but unyielding, 'and I remain of the opinion that you make too little of it. It is a serious matter.'

'It may be,' Ttomalss said. 'You have no real proof.'

'Superior sir, are you being deliberately blind?' Kassquit asked. 'There is no such title as senior tube specialist. This Regeya, whoever he may be, does not write like any member of the Race whose words are familiar to me. I think – as you yourself suggested – he really must be a Big Ugly.'

Hearing that come from one Tosevite's mouth to describe another amused Ttomalss. He didn't let that show, not wanting to offend Kassquit. He did say, 'I have done a little investigating of my own.' And he had – a very little. 'It would not be easy for a Tosevite to gain access to our network from the outside, so to speak.'

'You have always told me how the wild Big Uglies succeed in doing what seems most difficult to us,' Kassquit said. 'If we can gain access to their computers – and I assume we can and do – they may be able to do the same to us.'

Ttomalss knew the Race did just that; his conversation with the embassy's science officer would have told him as much had

590

he been naive enough to believe otherwise. But he did not fancy having his own words thrown back in his snout. 'We can do things to them that they cannot do to us in return.'

'Can you be sure computer spying is one of those things?' Kassquit asked. 'If I were a Big Ugly' – she paused in momentary confusion, for in biological terms she *was* a Big Ugly – 'I would try my best to reach the Race's computers.'

'Well, so would I,' Ttomalss agreed, 'but I have since spoken with Slomikk, the science officer here' – his research, a casual conversation – 'and he does not think the Tosevites have this ability regardless of what they may desire.'

'No one will listen to me!' Kassquit said angrily. 'I have tried and tried to persuade males and females involved in computer security to investigate this Regeya, and they ignore me, because to them I am nothing but a Big Ugly myself. I had hoped they would take me seriously, but now I discover that even you do not take me seriously. Farewell, then.' She broke the connection.

'Foolishness,' Ttomalss muttered. Kassquit was surely seeing things that were not there. Big Uglies seemed far more susceptible to wild imaginings than did males and females of the Race.

And yet, as the senior researcher had to admit, his Tosevite ward did make a sort of circumstantial case. He could not imagine what sort of body paint a senior tube technician would wear. Checking a data store, he found Kassquit was right: no such classification existed. And Regeya was an unusual name. But not all males and females used their true names under all circumstances. When aiming criticism at a superior, for instance, anonymity came in handy.

With a sigh, Ttomalss began sifting through computer records in search of the elusive Regeya, whoever he might be. Because the fellow had that unusual name, his messages were easy to track, even without knowing his pay number. And, Ttomalss discovered, Kassquit was right: Regeya did

591

have an unusual turn of phrase. But did that make him a Big Ugly, or just a male with a mind of his own?

The more Ttomalss read of Regeya's messages, the more he doubted the fellow whose phosphors he followed was a Tosevite. He did not believe any Big Ugly could have such insight into the way the Race thought and felt. No, Regeya might be eccentric, but Ttomalss felt nearly certain he was a male of the Race.

Being in Nuremberg and concerned with the Deutsche, Ttomalss had paid no attention to the American space station and to whatever the Big Uglies from the lesser continental mass were doing to it. Whatever it was, it struck him as suspicious. He did not seem to be the only one who thought it was, either. By all the signs, this Regeya did, too.

Because of that more than because of Regeya, whoever the individual behind the messages under the name might be, Ttomalss did send a message of his own to Security, asking what was known about the American space station.

Nothing that can be released to unauthorized personnel. The answer, sharp and stinging, came back almost at once.

It infuriated Ttomalss, who, unlike Kassquit, wasn't used to being ignored. He did what he almost certainly would not have done otherwise: he wrote back, saying, *Are you aware that a possible Tosevite under an assumed identity as a male of the Race is also seeking information about this space station?*

Again, the response was very prompt. *A Tosevite? Impossible.*

To his bemusement, Ttomalss found himself using with Security all the arguments Kassquit had used with him. And Security was little more impressed with them than he had been. *Tell me the individual named Regeya is demonstrably a male of the Race, and I will be convinced there is no need for concern here,* he wrote.

This time, he waited a long time for an answer. He waited, and waited, and waited, and no answer came. At last, when he'd almost given up, he did get one last message. *Your continued interest in the security of the Race is appreciated,* it said: only that, and nothing more.

He stared at the screen. 'Well, what does that mean?' he asked. 'Did I make them think of something that had not occurred to them before, or are they just trying to get rid of me?' The words displayed gave him no answer.

He did not get long to wonder, for he had just turned away to try to do some other work when Felless telephoned. He guessed that meant she'd been tasting ginger; otherwise, she would have come to his office. 'Those idiots!' she exclaimed. 'Those treacherous, lying, double-dealing idiots!'

'What have the Deutsche done now?' Ttomalss asked. He did not think the Race could have infuriated her so.

He turned out to be right. 'They have released from imprisonment the ginger smuggler Dutourd,' she blazed. That incensed reply almost made him laugh, considering how fond of the Tosevite herb she was. She went on, 'They promised he would stay imprisoned for a long time. They promised, and they lied.'

'This is unfortunate, but hardly unique in our experience on Tosev 3,' Ttomalss said. 'Big Uglies, I sometimes think, lie for the sport of it.'

'So I gather,' Felless answered. 'Rather more than the sport of it is involved here, however. The Deutsch minister of justice, a male named Dietrich, all but said – I thought he did say – to Ambassador Veffani that this Dutourd would remain imprisoned for a long time to come. I was there. I heard him.'

'Ah,' Ttomalss said. 'That does put things in a different light.'

'I should say so!' Felless said. 'The ambassador is furious. He has already begun composing a memorandum of protest to the justice minister and another one to the ruler of this not-empire: to Himmler, whatever his title may be.'

'*Reichs* Chancellor,' Ttomalss supplied.

'*Reichs* Chancellor, General Secretary, President – what difference does it make?' Felless said impatiently. 'All these titles are only fancy names pasted over emptiness. But this one has the nerve to defy the Race. I cannot believe his duplicity will stand.'

'Is making Himmler and, ah, Dietrich change their minds worth a possible nuclear exchange with the *Reich*?' Ttomalss asked. 'That is the question the fleetlord will have to answer for himself before proceeding.'

'If we do not persuade the Big Uglies that they must keep their word, they will promise us peace one day and then begin a nuclear exchange themselves the next,' Felless said.

'This is likely to be truth,' Ttomalss agreed. 'It is also my point: we should not let their lies take us by surprise.'

'They yielded on all other matters pertaining to this incident,' Felless said. 'They released the American Tosevites who were acting as our agents. Despite protests, they even released a Tosevite in some way related to a Big Ugly who advises the fleetlord of the conquest fleet. And then they defy us about this smuggler – defy us after saying they would not.'

'As I said, they are known to be devious. Competing against one another has made them so,' Ttomalss said. He wondered whether the Big Uglies really were devious enough to impersonate a male of the Race on the computer network. As he'd told Kassquit, it was possible, but he still had trouble believing it.

Felless said, 'I will be laying my eggs soon. I would like to think my hatchlings will become adults on a world where the Race is able to hold the natives in check, if nothing more.'

'Will all be well for the hatchlings if you stay here?' Ttomalss asked. 'I know Slomikk was considering sending females away, to reduce the risk of radiation damage to their eggs.'

'The risk is relatively small, and my work is important to me and to the Race,' Felless replied. 'I have considered, and have decided to stay.'

'Very well,' Ttomalss said. Few Tosevite females, he judged, would have made the same choice. Because of their biology and the unique helplessness of their hatchlings, their females developed stronger attachments for them than was usual among the Race. Ttomalss had discovered that after taking the female Liu Han's hatchling and beginning the attempt to raise it as a female of the Race. Her revenge still made him shudder after all these years. Perhaps most frightening of all was the knowledge that she could have done worse.

Felless came back to what was uppermost in her mind: 'How can we properly punish these Big Uglies when they flout our wishes?'

'If I knew that, I would deserve to be the fleetlord,' Ttomalss answered. 'No – I would deserve to be above the fleetlord, for no one has yet found any sure answer to that question.'

'There must be one,' Felless said. 'Perhaps we *should* start smuggling large quantities of drugs into the *Reich* and let the Deutsche see how they like that. I know Ambassador Veffani is considering the scheme.'

'I hope he decides wisely,' Ttomalss said, which let him avoid stating an opinion of the idea. Thinking of opinions made him ask one of Felless: 'Do you believe, Senior Researcher, that a Big Ugly could impersonate a male of the Race well enough to deceive other males and females on our computer network?'

Felless considered. 'I would doubt it,' she said at last. 'Surely a Tosevite in close electronic contact with the Race would betray himself before long.'

'This is my belief also,' Ttomalss said with considerable relief. 'I am glad to hear you confirm it.'

'Why do you ask?' Felless inquired. 'Have you any evidence such impersonation may be occurring?'

'Kassquit has found enough to be thought-provoking, at least,' Ttomalss replied.

'Oh, Kassquit,' Felless said dismissively. 'Being a Big Ugly herself, she doubtless looks to discover others, even if they are not there.'

'You could be right,' Ttomalss said. 'That had not occurred to me, but it may hold much truth.' For all his efforts to make

Kassquit as much a part of the Race as he could, biology dictated that she remained in some part a Tosevite, too. Would it be any wonder if she thought she found other Big Uglies on the computer network whether or not they were actually there? Yes, Felless' words must indeed hold a good deal of truth – he was sure of it. He assumed the posture of respect. 'I thank you, superior female. You have done much to ease my mind.'

Monique Dutourd wished with all her heart that the world would simply return to normal once more. The British Jew who'd been after her brother on behalf of his ginger-smuggling pals was gone. So were the Americans who'd been after Pierre on behalf of the Lizards.

And Pierre himself was out of the German jail and doing his best to set up his business again, even if he could no longer operate independent of the *Reich*. So far as Monique knew, the *Gestapo* wasn't particularly aggrieved with him at the moment. Everything should have been fine, or as fine as it could get in a France under the Germans' control for so long.

But Dieter Kuhn remained enrolled in her classes. As far as she was concerned, that in and of itself meant trouble hadn't yet disappeared. Monique wished the SS man gave her an excuse to fail him; that might have got him out of her hair. But he was – *he would be,* she thought with resigned anger – a good student, easily in the top quarter of the class.

Every so often, something inside her would snap. Once, she barked, 'Damn you, why can't you leave me alone?'

'Because, my dear, you know such . . . interesting people,' he answered. His grin might have been attractive, had she been able to stand him. 'You know smugglers, you know Jews, you know me.'

'My inscriptions are more interesting than you are,' Monique snapped, 'and they're dead.'

Too late to recall the words, she remembered that, at a nod from *Sturmbannführer* Kuhn, she could become as dead as any inscription praising Isis. He didn't order her arrested and tormented. But he could have. She knew he could have. These days, a lot of fear of the Nazis was based on what they had done and might do, not on what they usually did. That fear sufficed.

'You are still a key to your brother's good behavior,' Dieter Kuhn said imperturbably. Then something in his face changed. 'And you are also an intelligent, good-looking woman. If you think I do not find you attractive, you are mistaken.'

Monique looked around the empty lecture hall as if seeking a place to hide. She found none, of course. She hadn't been sure whether Kuhn was interested in her that way or not; she'd wondered if he preferred his own sex. Now that she knew the answer, she wished she didn't.

'It is not mutual,' she said sharply. 'And you could keep a perfectly good eye on me without my ever knowing you were doing it. I wish you would keep an eye on me without my knowing it. Then I wouldn't have to worry about you all the time.'

She hoped she hurt him. She wanted to hurt him. But if she did, he gave no sign. 'I do not suggest how you should conduct your research,' he said. 'In your area, you are the expert. Leave mine to me.'

She said something venomous in the Marseille dialect. It rocketed over Kuhn's head: the French he spoke was purely Parisian. Having vented her spleen, she asked, 'May I please go now?'

He looked innocent – not easy for an SS man. 'But of course,' he said. 'I am not holding you here by force. We are only having a conversation here, you and I.'

He wasn't holding her, but he could. He could do anything he wanted. Yes, the knowledge of his unlimited power was what made him fearsome. Monique said something else she hoped he would not understand before stalking past her. He didn't interfere. He didn't follow her as she rode home. But, again, he could have.

A crane with a wrecking ball was demolishing the synagogue

on Rue Breteuil. Monique wondered what sort of Teutonic thoroughness that implied. Had the Germans decided to knock the place down because it was on their list of Jewish monuments or to keep any other would-be independent ginger smugglers from meeting behind it? Only they would know, and they would assume it was no one else's business.

Monique carried her bicycle upstairs and sautéed some mullet in white wine – the Romans would surely have approved – for supper. She kept eyeing the telephone as she did the dishes afterwards, and then as she got to work on her inscriptions. It stayed quiet. She gave it a suspicious look. Why wasn't Dieter Kuhn calling her to complain about this, that, or the other thing? Or why wasn't her brother on the line to complain about whatever made Kuhn happy?

The telephone did not ring for four days, which, lately, came close to being a record. When at last it did, it was neither Kuhn nor Monique's brother, but Lucie, Pierre's friend with the boudoir voice. The rest of her, Monique knew, was dumpy, and she was acquiring a mustache, but on the phone she might have been Aphrodite.

'He's back,' she said happily. 'He's made it all up with them.'

'Back where?' Monique asked. By the way Lucie sounded, she meant back in her arms, but she always sounded that way. And it didn't fit the rest of what she'd said. 'Made it up with whom? The Germans?'

'No, no, no,' Lucie said, and Monique could almost see her wagging a forefinger. 'With the Lizards, of course.'

'He has?' Monique exclaimed. The Nazis were sure to be listening. She wondered what they'd make of that. She wondered what to make of it herself. 'I thought they wanted something bad to happen to him.'

'Oh, they did,' Lucie said airily, 'but not any more. Now they're glad he's free. Some of them are glad because he'll deal in ginger again, others because they can use him to smuggle drugs for people into the *Reich*. Many important Lizards want him to do just that.'

Lucie was no fool. She had to know the Germans were listening to Monique's telephone. That meant she wanted them to hear what she was saying. If she wasn't thumbing her nose at the Nazis, Monique didn't know what she was doing.

Monique also didn't know how she felt about the news Lucie gave her. She had taken Pierre's ginger-smuggling more or less in stride. She didn't mind his selling drugs to the Lizards, no matter what those drugs ended up doing to them. In principle, then, she didn't suppose she ought to mind if the shoe went on the other foot. Principle, she discovered, went only so far.

'What will the Germans do when they find out Pierre is working for the Lizards again?' she asked, and then answered her own question: 'They will kill him, that's what.'

'They can try,' Lucie said airily – yes, she had to be expecting, and hoping, the *Gestapo* was tapping the telephone line. 'They have been trying for a long time. They haven't done it yet. I don't think they can, not with the Lizards helping us. Your brother will call you soon.' With a last breathy chuckle, Lucie hung up.

My brother, Monique thought. *The brother I thought was dead. The brother who smuggles drugs.* If Pierre didn't care about the difference between selling drugs to Lizards and selling them to human beings . . . what did that prove? That he was generous enough to treat everyone alike? Or that he simply didn't care where he made his money, so long as he made it? After growing reacquainted with him, Monique feared she knew the answer.

She returned to her inscriptions with a heavy heart. Aside from everything else, this had to mean the Nazis would stay on her brother's tail. And it had to mean Dieter Kuhn would stay on her tail. Not for the first time, she wished her tail were the main thing he was after. Even if he'd ended up in bed with her, she wouldn't have felt so oppressed as she did now.

When the telephone rang again a few minutes later, she ignored it. She had the feeling she knew who it would be, and she didn't want to talk to him. But he, or whoever was on the other end, wanted to talk to her. The telephone rang and rang and rang. At last, its endless clanging wore her down. Cursing under her breath, she picked it up. *'Allô?'*

'Good evening, Monique.' Sure enough, it was Kuhn. 'I suppose you know why I'm calling you.'

'No, I haven't the faintest idea,' she answered.

The SS officer ignored her. 'You may tell your brother that the *Reich* showed him mercy once by not turning him over to the Lizards when they demanded that we do so. Instead, we released him from prison—'

'So he could do exactly what you told him,' Monique broke in.

Kuhn went on ignoring her, except that he had to repeat, 'We released him from prison. And how does he repay us? By going back to his old ways, as a dog returns to its vomit.' Monique hadn't expected him to allude to Scripture. If he knew any verse, though, she supposed that would be the one. He went on, 'You are to tell him that, when we take him again, we will give him justice, not mercy.'

'I don't think he would expect mercy from you,' Monique said. 'I don't suppose he expected it from you the first time.' That was a dangerous comment, but she knew Kuhn was short on irony.

'And if the Lizards call you,' he went on, 'you can tell them what we have told them before: if they want to have a war of drugs, we will fight it. We can hurt them worse than they can hurt us.'

'No Lizard has ever called me,' Monique exclaimed. 'I hope to heaven no Lizard ever does call.'

'Your brother is conspiring with them against the Greater German *Reich*,' Kuhn said, sounding every centimeter the *Sturmbannführer*. 'Therefore, we must also believe you may be conspiring against the *Reich*. You are on thin ice, Professor Dutourd. If you break it and fall in, you will be sorry afterwards – but that will be too late to do you much good.'

600

Monique had thought she'd been alarmed when the SS man said he found her attractive. This inhuman drone of warning was infinitely worse. 'Why can't you just leave me alone?' she demanded. 'If you hadn't told me Pierre was alive, I never would have known it. I–I wish I didn't.' She wasn't sure that was true, but she wasn't sure it wasn't, either.

'I have said what I have to say,' Kuhn told her. 'I will see you in class tomorrow. And if I ask you out with me, you would be wise to say yes. Believe me, you would find other watchers less desirable than me – and you may take that however you like. Good night.' He hung up.

'Damn you,' Monique snarled. She wasn't sure if she meant Kuhn or Pierre or both at once. Both at once, probably.

She returned to the inscriptions – a forlorn hope, and she knew it. Latin seemed spectacularly meaningless tonight. She almost screamed when the telephone rang again. 'Hello, little sister,' Pierre Dutourd said in her ear. 'By God, it feels good to be on my own again.'

'I'm glad you think so,' Monique said, sounding anything but glad. 'I'm on my own, too, but not the way you mean.'

As Dieter Kuhn had, her brother ignored her. 'I had to play both ends against the middle,' he boasted, 'but I pulled it off.'

'How lucky for you.' This time, Monique got the last word and hung up. But it did her little good. Thanks to Pierre, she was stuck between the Nazis and the Lizards, too, and the only thing to which she could look forward was getting crushed when they collided.

Vyacheslav Molotov wished for eyes in the back of his head. They might not have done him any good; plotters were generally too subtle to show up under even the most vigilant inspection. But that didn't mean the plotters weren't there. On the contrary. He'd found that out, and counted himself lucky to have survived the lesson.

Stalin, now, Stalin had seen plotters everywhere, whether they were really there or not. He'd killed a lot of people on the off chance they were plotters, or in the hope that their deaths would frighten others out of plotting. At the time, Molotov had thought him not just wasteful but more than a little crazy.

Now he wasn't so sure. Stalin had died in bed, without anyone having seriously tried to overthrow him. That was no mean achievement. Molotov admired it much more now that he'd weathered an attempted coup.

His secretary poked his head into the office. 'Comrade General Secretary, Comrade Nussboym is here to see you.'

'Yes, I was expecting him,' Molotov said. 'Send him in.'

In came David Nussboym: Jewish, skinny, nondescript – except for the golden star of the Order of Lenin pinned to his breast pocket. He nodded to Molotov. 'Good morning, Comrade General Secretary.'

'Good morning, David Aronovich,' Molotov answered. 'What can I do for you today? You have asked for so little since the day of the coup, it rather makes me nervous.' From another man, that might have been a joke, or at least sounded like one. From Molotov, it sounded like what it was: a statement of curiosity tinged with suspicion.

'Comrade General Secretary, I can tell you what I want,' Nussboym said. 'I want revenge.'

'Ah.' Molotov nodded; Nussboym had picked a motivation he understood. 'Revenge against whom? Whoever it is, you shall have it.' He made a sour face, then had to amend his words: 'Unless it is Marshal Zhukov. I am also in his debt.' *And if I try to move against him, he will move against me, and the outcome of that would be . . . unfortunate.*

'I have nothing against the marshal,' Nussboym said. 'He could have quietly disposed of me after we came out of NKVD headquarters, but he didn't.'

He could have quietly disposed of me, too, Molotov thought. *Maybe it is that he is like a German general – too well trained to meddle in politics.* In the USSR, that made Zhukov a rarity. 'All right, then,' Molotov said. 'I asked you once; now I ask you again: revenge against whom?'

He thought he knew what Nussboym would say, and the Polish Jew proved him right: 'Against the people who sent me to the Soviet Union against my will twenty years ago.'

'I cannot order the Jews of Warsaw punished, you know, as I could with citizens of the Soviet Union,' Molotov reminded him.

'I understand that, Comrade General Secretary,' Nussboym said. 'I have in mind the Jews of Lodz, not Warsaw.'

'That will make it harder still: Lodz is closer to the borders of the *Reich* than it is to us,' Molotov said. 'Had you said Minsk, life would be simple. Infiltrating Minsk is child's play.'

'I know. I have done it,' David Nussboym replied. 'But I come from the western part of Poland, and that is where my enemies live.'

'As you wish. I keep my promises,' Molotov said, conveniently forgetting how many he had broken. 'I give you a free hand against your enemies there in Lodz. Whatever resources you require, you have my authorization to utilize. The only thing you may not do is embarrass the Soviet Union's relations with the Lizards. If you do that, I will throw you to the wolves. Is it agreeable? Do we have a bargain?'

'It is agreeable, and we do have a bargain,' Nussboym said. 'Thank you, Comrade General Secretary.' Despite having saved Molotov's life, he did not presume to address him by first name and patronymic. The USSR was officially a classless society, but that did not change who was on top and who below.

'Good enough, then, David Aronovich,' Molotov said. 'So long as you do not embroil us with the Race, do what you will.' He realized he sounded rather like God sending Satan out to afflict Job. The conceit amused him – not enough for him to let it show on the outside, true, but he found very few things that amusing.

Nussboym also knew better than to linger. Having got what he wanted from Molotov, he rose, nodded, and took his leave. After he was gone – but only after he was gone – Molotov nodded approval.

Half an hour till his next appointment. Those thirty minutes might stretch, too; Khrushchev had the time sense of the Ukrainian peasant he'd been born, not of the West. He came and went when he thought it right and fitting, not according to the bidding of any clock. Molotov pulled a report from the pile awaiting his attention, donned his spectacles, and began to read.

He remembered memoranda wondering what the United States was doing with its space station. From the report in his hands, it appeared that the *Reich* and the Lizards were wondering, too. He scratched his head. Such aggressive work seemed more likely the province of the *Reich* than of the USA. President Warren had always struck him as a cautious and capable reactionary. He hoped the man would be reelected in 1964.

But what were the Americans doing up there? From the report in front of him, even some of them were wondering – wondering and not finding out. Molotov frowned. Secrecy was unlike the Americans, too, at least for anything less vital than their nuclear-explosives project.

He scribbled a note to spur further investigation. Most of that would have to be on the ground. The Soviet Union had forced itself into space along with the Germans and the Americans, but it was not the player there that the other two independent human powers were.

On the ground . . . 'Damm you, Lavrenti Pavlovich,' Molotov murmured. In the wake of Beria's failed coup, the NKVD was being purged. That had to happen; the fallen chief's backers had to go. But Molotov wished they didn't have to go now. With the NKVD in disarray, he had to rely more on the GRU, the Red Army's intelligence operation, which – again – made him more dependent on Georgi Zhukov. With two agencies doing the same job, he could play one off against the other. For the time being, he'd lost that option.

Muttering balefully under his breath, he reached out for the next report. It gave him good news: several caravans of arms

604

had crossed the border into Lizard-occupied China and reached the People's Liberation Army. Mao would keep the Race hopping like fleas on a griddle; Molotov was confident of that.

He worked his way through the whole report instead of contenting himself with the one-page summary stapled to the front. An eyebrow rose – with him, a sign of considerable emotion. Someone had tried to sneak something past him. The report mentioned that a shipment of U.S. arms had reached the People's Liberation Army despite the best efforts of the Kuomintang, the Lizards, and, ever so secretly, the GRU. The report mentioned that – but the summary didn't.

In future, he wrote, *I expect summaries to conform more closely to the documents they are supposed to summarize. Failure in this regard will not be tolerated.* If that didn't make some *apparatchik's* ulcer twinge, he didn't know what would.

Before he could reach for the next report in the stack, his secretary said, 'Comrade Khrushchev is here to see you.'

Molotov glanced at his watch. Khrushchev was fifteen minutes late – not bad at all, by his standards. 'Send him in,' Molotov said.

'Good day, Comrade General Secretary,' Khrushchev said, shaking hands with Molotov. He spoke Russian with a strong Ukrainian accent, turning g's into h's, and had a peasant drawl to boot.

'Good day, Comrade General Secretary,' Molotov echoed with a wintry smile. The rank he held in the Communist Party of the Soviet Union, Khrushchev held in the Communist Party of the Ukrainian Soviet Socialist Republic. 'And how are the pacification efforts progressing?'

Khrushchev made a remarkably sour face. He was ugly as sin to begin with: squat, bullet-headed, snaggle-toothed, with a couple of prominent warts. When he got angry, he got uglier. 'Not so good,' he answered. 'The *Reich* keeps shipping the robbers arms across the Romanian border. You ought to call the sons of bitches on it.'

'I have done so, Nikita Sergeyevich,' Molotov answered. 'The *Reich* states that Romania is an independent nation pursuing an independent foreign policy.' He held up a hand. 'And I have protested to the Romanians, who say they are helpless to keep the Germans from shipping arms through their territory.'

'Fuck 'em,' Khrushchev said. 'Fuck 'em all. The Lizards are sneaking shit in from Poland, too. We hold things down, but it's a damn pain in the arse.'

'So long as you do hold things down,' Molotov said. 'That is why you have your job, after all.'

'Don't I know it,' Khrushchev said. 'Stinking nationalist bandits. As soon as we pull one band up by the roots, another one sprouts.' He raised an eyebrow. 'Anybody would think they didn't fancy taking orders from Moscow.'

'Too bad,' Molotov said coldly. Khrushchev laughed out loud. They didn't always agree on means, but they stood together on keeping the Ukraine a part of the USSR. Molotov asked, 'You can document the fact that some of the bandits' weapons come from the Lizards and not the fascists?'

'Oh, hell, yes, Vyacheslav Mikhailovich,' Khrushchev exclaimed.

'Good. Give me your evidence, and I will protest to the Lizards,' Molotov said. Khrushchev nodded. Molotov went on, 'When confronted with evidence, the Lizards often draw back – unlike the fascists, who are strangers to shame.'

'Unlike us, too,' Khrushchev said with a grin. 'But we have the dialectic on our side, and the goddamn Nazis don't.'

'Neither do the Lizards,' Molotov said. *And a good thing, too, or they would surely beat us,* he thought somewhere down deep.

Khrushchev departed in due course, loudly and profanely promising to give Molotov the evidence he needed to protest to the Lizards. Based on his previous performance, Molotov figured the chances he would were a little better than even money. Molotov was reaching for another report when the telephone rang. His secretary said, 'Comrade General Secretary, Marshal Zhukov wishes to speak with you.'

'Put him through,' Molotov said at once, and then, 'Good day, Georgi Konstantinovich.'

'Good day, Comrade General Secretary,' Zhukov said politely. 'I wonder if you might be able to stop by my office some time today, to review the revised projections for the military budget in the upcoming Five-Year Plan.'

Revised upwards, he meant – revised sharply upwards. Zhukov might not want to rule the USSR, but he was taking his pound of flesh for suppressing Beria. And Molotov could not – did not dare – do anything about it. Things could have been worse, and he knew as much, but they also could have been a great deal better. With the resigned sigh of an animal in a cage too small, he answered,' I will be there directly, Marshal,' and took a petty revenge by hanging up the phone very hard.

Of all the Lizards Rance Auerbach had hoped never to see again, Hesskett topped the list. The interrogator had threatened to lock him and Penny Summers in jail and lose the key if they didn't put that French ginger smuggler out of business for good. Rance would have liked his trip to the south of France a hell of a lot better if it hadn't ended up in a Nazi jail.

He still didn't think that was his fault. Hesskett took a different view of things, though, and his would be the one that counted. He turned one eye turret toward Rance, the other toward Penny. 'You failed,' he said in a voice that somehow held echoes of slamming metal doors.

Penny spoke quickly: 'We didn't fail all the way, superior sir. The Germans still have that Dutourd in jail, or they did when they let us go. That puts him out of business, doesn't it?'

'It does not,' Hesskett said, and Auerbach imagined he heard more slamming doors. 'The Deutsche released him some time ago. No doubt he will soon be selling the Race ginger again.'

'That's not our fault, dammit!' Rance said. 'Now that you flew us back here to Mexico, we can't do anything about what happens on the other side of the ocean, and you can't hold it against us.'

'Who says I cannot?' Hesskett returned. His English wasn't usually idiomatic. He probably didn't intend it to be idiomatic here. 'Who says I cannot?' he repeated. 'The agreement was to reduce your punishment if you acted to further the interests of the Race. Can you say you have furthered the interests of the Race?'

'The agreement was to reward us if we did that,' Penny said. 'You told us we'd get a big reward if we did it. Well, we did some of it – maybe not as much as you wanted, but some. So we deserve some reward, anyway.'

'That's right,' Auerbach said. Whether it was right or not, though, he didn't expect it to do him a plugged nickel's worth of good.

Hesskett took him by surprise, then, by saying, 'Perhaps. This Big Ugly will now also be selling drugs we supply to the Tosevites of the *Reich*. So your mission may have accomplished something, even if it was something small.'

'In that case, why are you saying we failed?' Penny demanded. 'Okay, we don't deserve the whole great big reward, but you've got no business keeping us locked up like this.'

'Your efforts did not bring Dutourd over to the side of the Race,' Hesskett answered. 'The Deutsche released him to continue his role as a destructive menace. They did not know we would be able to turn him – to turn him to some partial degree – to our own purposes.'

'Well, what are you going to do with us, then?' Auerbach asked. 'This teasing gets stale.'

'What to do with you is a puzzlement,' the Lizard said. 'You did not completely fail, but you were far from complete success. And, if you are set at liberty, you are only too likely to return to your own noxious habit of ginger-smuggling.'

I wouldn't! Rance almost shouted it. He hadn't had anything to do with smuggling ginger for years till Penny came back into his life. If they let him go and kept her in the calaboose, they wouldn't hurt themselves one bit.

Without turning his head to look at her, he felt Penny's eyes on him. She had to know what was going through his mind. She also had to know he hadn't asked her to come back to him. She'd done it on her own, because she couldn't find any other choice. If he walked away and sold her down the river, how much guilt would he have on his conscience?

He asked himself the same question. *Just how big a son of a bitch are you, Rance? How low have you fallen?* The clean-cut West Point cavalry officer he'd been once upon a time wouldn't have let a pal down for anything. But he hadn't been that fellow for a lot of years. A couple of Lizard bullets had made sure he'd never be that fellow again. And afterwards, he hadn't even been able to make a go of it as a ginger smuggler after Penny left him the first time, even if some of his buddies had stayed in touch with him on the off chance he might be able to do something for them. He'd turned into a petty grifter, a loser, a drunk. Christ, what else had he turned into on the way down? A Judas?

He sat quietly. Over in the other chair in the interrogation chamber, too far away to touch, Penny let out a soft sigh of relief. He wondered what she would have done had their positions been reversed. Odds were he was better off not knowing.

Penny said, 'Superior sir, if you do let me go, I don't want to go back to the United States. Too many people there want me dead.'

'This is a perspective with which I have some sympathy,' Hesskett said. 'It is also, you realize, an argument for keeping you imprisoned.'

'If that's what you want to do, go ahead – go ahead for both of us.' Now Auerbach spoke before Penny could. 'If you don't care about going back on the bargain you made, go ahead and do that.'

Against a human being, he wouldn't have had a prayer. Had he been stupid enough to try that argument on his Nazi interrogators, they might have burst a blood vessel laughing. But Lizards, whatever else you said about them, were more honest than people. They didn't always make bargains in a hurry. When they did make them, they commonly kept them.

Hesskett didn't show what he was thinking. Lizards rarely did, at least not in ways people could recognize. 'Not spending all your lives in prison would be a reward, thinking of how much ginger the two of you had when we caught you,' he said.

Rance tried not to show what he was thinking, either, but couldn't help leaning forward a little. He knew the start of a dicker when he heard one. 'Hey, we did the best we could for you,' he said.

'That's right,' Penny said. 'It's not our fault all the Nazis in the goddamn world came busting out of that building. And how come your fancy gadgets didn't tell us they were there?'

'They must not have been using electronics to monitor their surroundings,' Hesskett said. 'Had they been using electronics, you would have been warned.'

'Well, they weren't, and we weren't, and now you're trying to blame us for it,' Auerbach said. If he had the Lizard on the defensive, and he thought he did, he'd push him hard.

'What do you think a fitting reward would be?' Hesskett asked.

'Letting us go free, that's what,' Penny said at once.

'Let us go free someplace where they speak English,' Rance added. He didn't want to get turned loose in Mexico, not when he knew maybe a dozen words of Spanish, and most of them swear words. He wasn't jumping up and down at the idea of going back to the USA, either, not after he'd ventilated those goons. Their bosses wouldn't remember him fondly.

'We do not want you going back to your friends. That would mean going back to smuggling ginger,' Hesskett said. 'Where in the lands the Race rules do Big Uglies speak English? I cannot be bothered keeping track of your languages. You should have only one, like us.'

'Austr—' Penny began, but Auerbach gave her such a sharp look, she didn't finish. Australia was going to be a place where Lizards outnumbered people, if it wasn't already. Rance didn't want that.

Hesskett was checking a computer screen. Turning one eye turret away from it and toward Rance and Penny, he said, 'Your choices are fewer than I thought. Most of the Tosevites who speak your language are not under the rule of the Race. I do not want to add more Big Uglies to the population of Australia. That is to be our land, in particular.' Auerbach gave Penny a told-you-so look. The Lizard went on, 'Perhaps South Africa. It is isolated. You would have a hard time causing the Race great trouble there – and we would be able to keep an eye turret aimed in your direction.'

'Can we think about it?' Auerbach asked. 'Can we talk it over, just the two of us?'

Hesskett used the hand gesture that was his equivalent of a headshake. 'No. We do not have to give you anything at all. You may say that you tried to aid us, but you failed. You may have South Africa, or you may have a cell each.'

'Not much choice there,' Penny said, and Rance nodded. She looked a question at him. He nodded again. She spoke for both of them: 'We'll take South Africa.'

'You shall be sent there,' Hesskett said. 'You shall live out the rest of your days there. You shall not leave, unless by order of the Race. Do you understand this?'

'Exile,' Auerbach said.

'Exile, yes,' Hesskett agreed. 'I have heard this word in your language before, but I did not remember it. Now I shall.'

Auerbach tried to remember what he knew of South Africa. Not much, he discovered. Gold and diamonds came to mind. So did the Boer War. Before the Lizards arrived, the South Africans had been on the Allies' side, but a good many of them wished they'd lined up with the Nazis instead. Whites lorded it over blacks who enormously outnumbered them. It was sort of like the American South, only more so.

He looked down at his arm. Sure as hell, he was the right color to go there. He hadn't heard much about the place since the fighting ended. Every now and then, there'd been stories about a low-grade guerrilla war. Those had mostly disappeared from the newspapers in the past few years. That probably meant most of the guerrillas had gone to their heavenly reward.

Still, it didn't seem too bad, especially for a white man – and a white woman. 'South Africa,' he said in musing tones. 'I think we can make the best of it.'

'Me, too,' Penny said. Auerbach wasn't altogether comfortable with her expression. What it seemed to say was, *If I find something good, I can always dump this guy*. She'd done it before.

Of course, he would have been better off if she'd stayed out of his life once she dumped him. Still, getting laid regularly had its points.

Hesskett said, 'Once you are there, we do not provide for you. You will have to make your own way.'

How the hell am I supposed to do that, crippled up like I am? Rance wondered. If the other choice was a cell, though, he supposed he could try. The Lizards' jail hadn't been so bad as he'd expected, but he didn't want to live there the rest of his life.

Penny said, 'You can't just drop us there without a dime in our pockets. We need enough money to keep us going till we can get on our feet.'

That started the haggling again. Auerbach wondered if he could arrange to have his government pension sent to him in Cape Town or wherever the hell he ended up. He didn't mention that to Hesskett. He did point out his injuries, adding, 'These are your fault, too.'

Hesskett wasn't the best bargainer who ever came down the pike. Few Lizards were good bargainers, not by human standards. By the time Rance and Penny got done with him, he'd promised the Race would support them for six months, with another six months' help forthcoming if they were still having trouble after that.

'Beats the hell out of jail,' Penny said as the Lizard airplane on which they would fly took off from Mexico City.

'Jail, nothing – beats the hell out of whatever we could think of,' Auerbach said. 'Talk about coming up smelling like a rose.' He leaned over and gave Penny a kiss. Maybe she'd dump him, maybe she wouldn't. Meanwhile, he'd enjoy what he had while it lasted.

Straha would never have got interested in the U.S. space station if it hadn't been for Sam Yeager. The ex-shiplord knew as much. He'd agreed to stick out his tongue in the station's direction not so much because he thought anything about it was particularly odd as because his Tosevite friend – a notion he was still getting used to – had asked it of him.

He'd always known Yeager was a clever Big Ugly. Now he was seeing just how good the American officer's instincts were. He still hadn't the faintest idea what the USA was doing with its station. As far as he could tell, not a male or female of the Race knew the answer to that. But something strange – which presumably meant something illicit – was going on up there.

He wondered how many American Big Uglies knew what was going on at the space station. Not many, surely, or Yeager would have been one of them. That he wasn't anyhow puzzled Straha. He'd been entrusted with important secrets before. Straha knew of some of them. For that matter, Straha *was* one of the important secrets with which Yeager had been entrusted. That a secret should be so much more important than he had been during the fighting wounded his vanity.

He would have asked more questions among the humans of his acquaintance had it not been for his driver. He feared that, whatever the formidable male heard, the U.S. government would hear in short order. His driver no doubt knew a good many secrets of his own. He might even know what the Americans were doing up at the space station. Straha did not have the nerve to ask him.

At the moment, Straha was catching up on the Race's computer discussion about the station. A female named Kassquit kept asking leading questions, good ones. She showed unusual understanding of the Big Uglies. The experience Straha had gained in twenty long Tosevite years of living among them made him able to see that.

'Psychologist's apprentice,' he muttered, looking at the way she described herself. 'She ought to be an intermediate researcher by now, heading toward senior. By the Emperor, she would if *I* were in charge. But those fools up there are dim themselves, so they think everyone else must be, too.'

If I were in charge. Even now, after all these years of exile, the words still leapt to his mind. Atvar had bumbled along, doing the safe, doing the cautious, occasionally doing the stupid. And the Race had got by, as it had got by on Home for a hundred thousand years. Even snout-to-snout with the Big Uglies, the Race had got by. Atvar had made his share – more than his share – of mistakes, but the Tosevites had made their share, too, and disaster hadn't come. Quite.

'Still,' Straha said, 'I would have done better.' His pride was enormous. If only a few more males had gone with him at that climactic meeting after the Soviet Union touched off its first explosive-metal bomb. He would have ousted Atvar, and Tosev 3 would have looked . . . different.

The telephone rang, distracting him. Tosevite telephones were simple-minded machines, without screens and with only the most limited facilities for anything but voice transmission. Straha often missed the versatile phone he'd had before he defected. So many things he'd taken for granted . . .

'Hello?' he said in English, and then gave his name.

'I greet you, Shiplord,' a male said. 'Ristin speaking. Ullhass and I will be holding another party on Saturday night' – the

614

name of the day was in English – 'and hoped you might join us.'

Straha started to decline; he hadn't had that good a time at Ristin's earlier gathering. Then he thought that he might meet interesting males there – former prisoners who had thrown in their lot with the American Big Uglies, perhaps even visitors from areas of Tosev 3 the Race ruled. Who could tell what he might learn from them?

And so he said, 'I thank you. I believe I will come, yes.'

'I thank *you*, Shiplord.' Ristin sounded surprised and pleased. 'I look forward to seeing you there.'

'I will see you then,' Straha said, and hung up. He didn't particularly look forward to it. Having committed himself, though, he would go.

His driver greeted the news with something less than rapture. 'A party?' the Tosevite said when Straha told him. 'I was hoping to watch television that night.'

'You Tosevites did not even have television when you were a hatchling,' Straha told him. 'You cannot find it as necessary as the Race does.'

'Who said anything about necessary?' the driver returned. 'I enjoy it.' Straha said nothing. He stood and waited and looked at the driver with both eye turrets. The Big Ugly sighed. 'It shall be done, Shiplord.'

'Of course it shall,' Straha said smugly. The driver gave him more trouble than a male of the Race with a similar job would have done. Big Uglies – especially American Big Uglies – did not understand the first thing about subordination. But the driver, having made his complaints, would now do what was required of him.

Body paint perfect – he had spent considerable time touching it up – Straha went off to the gathering with something approaching eagerness. Ristin and Ullhass had had good ginger at their house. If nothing else came of the evening, he could always taste till he'd sated himself. He could do that here, too, but the experience was different in company.

'Have a good time,' the driver said as he halted the motorcar in front of the house Ristin and Ullhass shared. 'I will keep an eye turret on things out here.' The Race's idiom sounded grotesque in his mouth, but *keep an eye on things*, the English usage, would have been equally strange in Straha's language.

As at the last gathering, Ristin met him in front of the door. The ex-infantrymale's red-white-and-blue prisoner-of-war body paint was as carefully tended as Straha's official coat. (Straha chose not to dwell on the fact that, having deserted, he wasn't entitled to the fancy body paint he still wore.) 'I greet you, Shiplord,' Ristin said. 'Alcohol and ginger in the kitchen, as before. Help yourself to anything you fancy. Plenty of food, too. Make yourself at home; you are one of the first ones here.'

'I thank you.' Straha went into the kitchen and poured himself a small glass of vodka. Ginger could wait for the time being. He also took some thinly sliced ham, some potato chips, and some of the little, highly salted fish the Big Uglies used to spice up dishes. Like most males of the Race, Straha found them delicious by themselves. And Ullhass and Ristin had laid in another delicacy he did not see often enough: Greek olives. He let out a small, happy hiss. Regardless of what sort of company the night yielded, the food was good.

He carried his plate and glass out into the main room, where Ullhass, who'd been talking with a couple of other males, greeted him. Like Ristin, Ullhass wore American-style body paint instead of what the Race authorized. The other guests were more conventional. They also seemed astonished to see a shiplord there. Then they realized *which* shiplord Straha had to be, and were astonished again in a different way. Straha had seen that before. He'd heard the whispered, 'There is *the* traitor,' before, too. He sat down and relaxed. In a while, with alcohol and ginger in them, they'd grow less shy of him.

His eye turrets scanned the shelves of books and videos along the walls of the main room. 'Some of these are new, are they not?' he asked Ullhass. 'New since the conquest fleet left Home, I mean?'

'Yes, Shiplord,' the male answered. 'We have had visitors from the colonization fleet here before. We expect some tonight, in fact.'

'I thought you might,' Straha said. 'I wonder if, some time or another, I might borrow some of these, to see what they were doing on Home after we went into cold sleep.'

'I would be pleased if you did,' Ullhass told him. That might be more polite than sincere, but Straha intended to take him up on it.

Sure enough, some males and a couple of females from the colonization fleet, in Los Angeles on a trade mission, joined the gathering. They exclaimed in pleasure at the delicacies. Seeing Straha's body paint, they began to fawn on him till Ristin took one of them aside and spoke quietly. After that, they didn't seem to know what to make of the self-exiled shiplord.

After a while, he did get into a conversation with one of them, a male whose body paint proclaimed him a foods dealer. 'It must be strange living here,' the fellow remarked.

'It is,' Straha agreed. 'At times, I feel as out of place as the American space station in orbit not far from the ships of the colonization fleet.'

He threw out the comparison to see if the foods dealer would rise to it. 'That thing!' the male said with an indignant hiss. 'A big, ugly construction from the Big Uglies.' His mouth fell open in appreciation of his own wit. He went on, 'I hear they are building a separate section onto it, well removed from the main body. It will be even uglier than it is now.'

'That is difficult to imagine,' Straha said. It was also something he had not heard before. He wondered if Sam Yeager knew about it. He would have to remember to pass it on to the Tosevite. Maybe Yeager would have some better idea of what it meant than he did.

After drinking some more vodka, he went back into the kitchen to get his first taste of ginger. One of the females from the trade delegation was in there. She had an almost empty glass of vodka or rum in her hand, and was laughing a wide-mouthed, foolish laugh. Pointing to the bowl of ginger on the counter, she said, 'In any proper land' – by which she meant any land the Race ruled – 'I would be punished for standing even this close to that herb.'

'It is not against the law in this not-empire,' Ristin said. 'If you want to taste, go ahead.' He gestured invitingly.

'It smells good.' The female laughed again, even more foolishly than before. 'I think I will.' She scooped up about four tastes' worth. Her tongue flicked in and out, in and out, till the herb was gone. 'Oh.' Her voice went soft with wonder. 'I did not think it would be like *this*.'

Remembering his own first taste of ginger, Straha empathized with her – and his hadn't been nearly so monumental as this one. But then, a moment later, he almost stopped thinking altogether as his scent receptors caught the pheromones the ginger released in the female. Sam Yeager had offered to get him a female who'd tasted ginger. He'd turned the Big Ugly down. What an addled egg he'd been! The long scales of his crest rose.

He straightened into his mating posture as the female bent into hers. Ristin started for her, too, but Straha's display of crest, outspread fingerclaws, and colorful body paint made the other male yield to him. He took his place behind the female. Their bodies joined. Not much later, he let out a loud, ecstatic hiss.

When he stepped back from the female, Ristin took his place. Other males crowded the kitchen, drawn by the female's pheromones as surely as Tosevite flying pests were drawn by light. A couple of males got clawed; one got bitten badly enough to draw blood. Straha, satiated, withdrew. He knew he was supposed to tell Sam Yeager something, but for the life of him couldn't remember what.

Felless was glad she was in the Race's embassy in Nuremberg when the urge to lay her eggs became overwhelming. She and

618

the Race would have been embarrassed if the urge had struck her while she was interviewing some Deutsch functionary with preposterous ideas. And she might not have – she probably would not have – found a proper place in which to lay had she been out among the Big Uglies.

Inside the embassy, though, Slomikk the science officer had prepared a chamber to which gravid females could go when their time came. It had a deep layer of sand on the floor, and plenty of rocks and dry branches the females could use to conceal their clutches. In the chamber, of course, such concealment didn't matter. But it would have mattered very much to the Race's primitive ancestors, and the urge to conceal remained strong.

Slomikk had also given the chamber extra shielding against local background radiation. That wouldn't have mattered to Felless' primitive ancestors, but she was glad of it.

When she went inside, she looked around warily to make sure she was alone – another triumph of instinct over reason. The door to the laying chamber clicked shut behind her. She was, as far as she knew, the first female to use it. Few others, here or anywhere, had tasted ginger as early as she had. Few others had mated as early as she had. And few others had become gravid as early as she had.

She scurried over to a corner of the chamber half screened from the doorway by branches and rocks. All her instincts shouted *This is the place!* to her. She could not have found anywhere better to lay her eggs. She was sure of it, sure in a way that transcended reason. This place felt *right*.

Splaying her legs apart, she bent forward and scooped a hollow in the sand. No one had ever told her how deep to make the hollow, but she knew: the knowledge was printed on her genes. Had the sand been warmer, she would have dug deeper; had it been cooler, the hole would have been shallower. Again, she knew that at a level far below the conscious.

With an effort, Felless straightened up enough to take a couple of short, spraddle-legged steps. That positioned her cloaca just above the hollow she'd dug. She bore down hard – and in absolute silence. At any other time, in any other place, she would have grunted and hissed with the effort she was making. Not here, not now. Grunts and hisses might have drawn predators to her, and to her clutch.

Her two eggs were far bigger than the waste that usually passed through her cloaca. At first, she did not think they wanted to come at all. She was sure the leading one had got stuck inside her body, and would obstruct everything behind it till she perished. Logically, she knew that was unlikely, but she wasn't thinking logically at the moment.

Still silent, she bore down again. The pain of making that first egg move inside her threatened to tear her in two from the inside out. And the egg would not move. Maybe it really was impacted. After every mating season back on Home, a handful of females needed surgery to remove impacted eggs. Wouldn't that be just her luck, to have a medical emergency here in the middle of the *Reich*? They'd have to take her away then.

I'll try once more, she thought, *and then I'll shout for a physician.* Unlike the arid plains on which the Race had evolved, the laying chamber was equipped with a telephone on the far wall. If Felless needed help, she could get it.

She took a deep, deep breath, as if filling her lung with air could somehow help force the egg out of her and into the sand. And maybe it did, for she felt the accursed thing shift inside her. That made her redouble her effort to force it out. It also redoubled her pain, but somehow she hardly noticed.

The egg came forth and dropped into the sand. With it came a sense of relief and determination that surely sprang from some hormonal source, not the reason on which she usually relied. Still straddling the hollow in the sand, she bore down again.

She had an easier time with the second egg than she'd had with the first. Maybe the first had helped stretch the way for the one that came after it. Before long, two yellowish, speckled eggs – colored to match the sand in which her ancestors laid them – rested in the hollow.

She covered them with the sand she'd scooped aside. Her motions were sure and deft; her body knew how much sand to put over them. Then, on top of the sand, she voided a little. That was as instinctive as the rest of her laying behavior.

As soon as she'd done it, she took several quick steps away from the place where her eggs rested. Any other female of the Race who sought to lay in that spot would be similarly repulsed by the pheromones in the dropping. So would the females of several species of predators back on Home. Females of the Race rarely had to worry about them these days, but evolution didn't know that.

Felless made her way out toward the door of the laying chamber. Those first few voluntary steps told her how worn she was: her legs didn't want to bear her weight. She felt empty inside; the eggs growing within her had compressed the rest of the innards, which now seemed to have more room than they knew what to do with.

She wanted to hurry to the refectory, but could not – she couldn't hurry anywhere. She could only walk slowly, her legs still wide apart. Her cloaca smarted – worse than smarted – from having been stretched far more than it had to open at any other time in her life.

There was ham in the refectory. Felless approved of ham. It was one of the few Tosevite foods of which she did approve. She ate several slices, went back, and ate several more. It seemed to give her ballast. When she came back again for a third helping, the server gave her a dubious look. Voice sardonic, he inquired, 'What did you do, just lay four eggs?'

'No, only two,' Felless answered, which made the would-be wit retreat in as much embarrassment as the Race had known in retreating from England.

After she'd eaten, Felless went to her quarters. She knew what she wanted to do there, and she did it: she lay down and fell asleep. When at last she woke, she was ravenously hungry. A glance at the chronometer showed why: she'd been asleep for a day and a half.

Still feeling logy and slow, she checked her messages. Only one mattered enough to answer right away. *Since I am a male, I had to do my best in preparing the laying chamber,* Slomikk had written. *Was it satisfactory?*

In every respect, she wrote back, and sent the message. The science officer had done as well as any female might have.

After the message went out, one of Felless' eye turrets slid down to a locked drawer in her desk. In that drawer, Veffani's warnings notwithstanding, rested a vial with several tastes of ginger. She wanted a taste. She was sure the herb would help ease her post-laying exhaustion. As far as she was concerned, ginger eased everything.

But, with a small hiss of regret, she made herself move away from her desk. She couldn't be tasting ginger if she was going out in public – and she was going out in public, because she was starving again. She didn't want to have to pause to mate on the way to the refectory. She didn't want to pause at all on the way to the refectory, and she didn't want to get in trouble for using ginger. Most of all, she didn't want anything, even something so small as a male's reproductive organ, entering her cloaca.

She hissed again. No matter what common sense told her, she still craved ginger. She had far fewer chances to taste these days than she would have liked. For a while, she'd hoped her craving would ebb because she could safely taste but seldom. That hadn't happened. If anything, her desire for the herb grew stronger because she had so few chances to satisfy it.

Out into the uncaring world of the embassy she went. Ttomalss was just coming out of his quarters, too – as well she hadn't tasted. 'I greet you, superior female,' he said.

'I greet you, Senior Researcher.' Felless' voice was a scratchy parody of the way she usually sounded.

Ttomalss noticed. His eyes turrets went up and down her, noting the way she stood. 'You have laid!' he exclaimed.

'Truth,' Felless said. 'It is over. It is done.' She amended that: 'Until the hatchlings break out of their shells, it is done. Then begins the task of civilizing them, which is never easy.'

'Yes, I know of this, although with a hatchling of a different sort,' Ttomalss said.

'Why, so you do,' Felless said. 'In that, you are an unusual male. But now, if you want to keep talking with me, come along to the refectory.' She started that way herself.

'It shall be done.' Ttomalss fell into stride beside her.

'How does it feel to bear the burden of rearing a hatchling?' Felless asked. 'Even if Kassquit is a hatchling of a very different sort, you are to be commended for your diligence. On Home, that is the work of females.'

'Kassquit is indeed a hatchling of a different sort,' Ttomalss said, 'and she truly may have discovered a male of the Race of a different sort.' He told her more about Regeya, and about the cryptic message he'd had from Security.

'She still thinks he may be a Big Ugly masquerading as a male of the Race?' Felless said. 'As I told you before, I find that very hard to believe.'

'The more I think about it, the more plausible I find it,' Ttomalss said. 'Underestimating the Tosevites' cleverness has hurt us countless times before.'

Felless said, 'They are what they are. They cannot be what we are. They *cannot*.' She added an emphatic cough, then continued, 'Can you imagine one of these Deutsch males with whom we have to deal carrying off such an imposture for even the time light takes to cross an atomic nucleus? The *Reichs* minister of justice, for instance – this Sepp Dietrich. I doubt he can even use a computer, let alone pretend he belongs to the Race on one.'

She snorted at the absurdity of the notion. But then she remembered Dietrich's secretary. That male had spoken the language of the Race well, for a Tosevite. If he could somehow sneak onto the computer network, could he pass himself off as a male of the Race? She made the negative hand gesture. She couldn't believe it.

Ttomalss said, 'Kassquit has had trouble making anyone in authority think Regeya might be a Big Ugly. Investigators believe him more likely to be some sort of swindler, but analysis of his messages shows no attempt to defraud. Real interest in the question is minimal.'

'If the authorities do not believe Regeya is a Tosevite, how can Kassquit persist in opposing them?' Felless said. She was typical of the Race in that she trusted and followed those above her till they gave her some overwhelming reason not to.

'Perhaps, as you said, like calls to like,' Ttomalss suggested.

'I said she wished like called to like,' Felless pointed out.

He thought about it. 'Truth: you did,' he admitted.

'Yes, I did,' Felless said. 'And now, very loudly, food calls to me.' She hurried on toward the refectory, not caring in the least whether Ttomalss came along.

19

Little by little, Nesseref was getting used to her flat in the new town that had gone up east of the Tosevite hamlet called Jezow. The flat itself boasted all the conveniences she'd enjoyed back on Home. She had access to the Race's computer network, which put her in touch with all of Tosev 3. Telephone and television service were also as good as they would have been on the world she'd left behind. She could find entertainment programs at the touch of a fingerclaw. They were all recordings, of course, but that mattered little to her. Over the course of a hundred thousand years, the Race had produced so much that one lifetime's viewing couldn't give a female even a smattering of it.

Only her furnishings told her she dwelt on Tosev 3. The pieces that had come from Home with the colonization fleet were of the lightest and most austere manufacture, nothing she would have had in her apartment there. The tables and chairs made locally did not look like work the Race would do. Even the ones that weren't too tall and too large were . . . not so much wrong but alien in style and decoration. The very grains of the woods were strange, as were the gaudy fabrics the Polish Tosevites reckoned the height of style.

Also strange was the view out her window. *It is all far too green,* she kept thinking. The trees sprouted great profusions of leaves. Grass and shrubs grew lavishly, far more lavishly than most places on Home. Having rain drum against that window almost every other day also felt unnatural.

Going to the shuttlecraft port was always a relief. The facilities there were full of the Race's gear, even if Big Uglies had erected them. Taking a shuttlecraft up into orbit was an even greater relief. The craft and the starships they served were pure products of the Race. Aboard them, she could almost forget she wasn't orbiting Home.

Almost. For one thing, the world beneath her looked different. *Waterlogged* was the word that most readily came to mind. Those vast expanses of ocean seemed as wrong as the frequent rain. And, for another, the Race had to share orbital space with the Big Uglies. Their mushy voices, chattering in their languages and in hers, crowded the radio bands even worse than their hardware crowded space.

One piece of hardware in particular stood out. 'What *are* the Big Uglies doing?' she asked as she floated weightless at the central docking hub of the *27th Emperor Korfass*. 'Are they building a starship of their own?'

'Do not be absurd,' answered the male she had come to ferry down to the surface of Tosev 3, a chemical engineer named Warraff. 'They cannot hope to fly between the stars. They did not even travel beyond their own atmosphere until after the fighting stopped. That is only the space station of the not-empire called the Confederated – no, excuse me, the United – States.'

'Why is it so large?' Nesseref asked. 'I am certain the Tosevites had nothing of that size in orbit when we first came to Tosev 3.'

'No one knows the answer to that,' Warraff replied. 'No one of the Race, at any rate. The American Tosevites are doing something peculiar there; I would be the last to deny it. Keep an eye turret on the computer network to stay up with the latest gossip, but bear in mind it is only gossip.'

'I thought you told me it belonged to the United States,' Nesseref said. 'Who are the Americans?'

Straightening out that misunderstanding took a little while. Nesseref had paid little attention to the lesser continental mass. She knew about the SSSR and the *Reich* because Poland lay sandwiched between them. But she'd had only radio contact with U.S. spacefliers and ground stations, and had forgotten those Big Uglies had an alternative name for themselves.

Several officials were waiting for Warraff when she brought him down to the shuttlecraft port outside the new Australian cities; he was, evidently, good at what he did. No one was waiting for Nesseref, no matter how good she was at what she did. She found transportation from the shuttlecraft port to the airfield not far away. Then she had to wait for the next flight to Poland, and then she had to endure the journey halfway round the planet.

By the time she walked into her flat, her body had no idea whether it was supposed to be day or night. Locally, it was late afternoon. She did know that felt wrong. Uncertain whether to eat breakfast or go to sleep, she chose the latter. When she woke up, it was the middle of the night, but she could not go back to sleep no matter how hard she tried.

She felt caged inside the flat. She'd spent too much time inside her shuttlecraft and inside the airplane that had brought her home. She rode the elevator down to the lobby of her building and then strode out into the street. This sort of thing had happened to her after other missions, too. Once more was an annoyance, not a catastrophe.

Few other males or females of the Race were on the street. Nesseref eyed the ones who walked or motored past with a certain amount of wariness, but only a certain amount. The Race was generally more law-abiding than the Big Uglies, and males and females chosen as colonists were generally law-abiding even by the standards of the Race. Still, every hatching ground held a few addled eggs.

Tosev 3 could do some addling of its own. A male sidled up to Nesseref, saying, 'I greet you. How would you like to greet something nice for your tongue?'

'No,' Nesseref said sharply – all the more sharply because she did crave ginger. 'Go away.' When the male did not move off fast enough to suit her, she added, 'Very well, then, I will call the authorities,' and reached for her telephone.

That got the fellow moving at a better clip. Nesseref felt more regret and anger than satisfaction. She walked along the quiet streets. Loud metallic crashes sent her skittering forward to investigate. She found a couple of Big Uglies loading trash cans into a ramshackle truck of Tosevite design.

'We greet you, superior sir,' they said, lifting cloth caps from their heads in unison. Their accents were even worse than the foremale Casimir's, and they couldn't tell Nesseref was a female. But they acted as if they had every right to be where they were and do what they were doing.

'What is going on here?' Nesseref asked.

She had little experience in judging Tosevite expressions, but needed little to realize they found the question stupid. So did she, once she thought about it. One of the Tosevites said, 'Taking trashes away, superior sir. Race not wanting to do. Paying us to doing instead.'

'Very well,' Nesseref said, and the Big Uglies resumed their noisy, smelly work. Indeed, it was labor no male or female of the Race would want to perform. Paying the Tosevites to do it made perfect sense.

The truck rumbled off down the street, leaving a cloud of noxious fumes in its wake. Nesseref coughed a couple of times, and did her best not to breathe till the cloud dispersed. Yes, paying Big Uglies to haul trash made sense. But Big Uglies also made trucks. If they did that more cheaply than members of the Race could, would paying them for such manufacturing also make sense? Nesseref didn't know. She did know some of the colonists were industrial workers. If they didn't manufacture, say, trucks, what would they do?

If the trucks they did make were better but at the same time more expensive than those of the Big Uglies, what would the

Race do? What should the Race do? She was glad she didn't have to decide things like that.

She prowled the streets of the new town, now and then looking up through the scattered clouds at the stars. She knew the constellations well; they didn't look a great deal different from the way they would have in the northern hemisphere back on Home, though of course they rotated about a different imaginary axis.

Little by little, the eastern sky turned pale with the approach of day. Before the star Tosev came up, a mist rose on the fields and meadows around the settlement the Race had built. Tendrils flowed through the streets, leaving the air damp and clammy. Despite that and despite the unpleasant chill, Nesseref stayed out, watching in fascination. Such mists occurred in only a few places back on Home, and then but seldom; the air usually stayed too dry to support them. They seemed common enough here in Poland, but still intrigued her.

This one, like most, hugged the ground. When Nesseref looked up through it, she had no trouble seeing the tops of taller buildings. But when she turned her eye turrets down to street level, so that she peered along the layer of water droplets, the lower stories of nearby structures blurred, while those farther away – and not much farther away, at that – disappeared altogether. She might have been alone in the center of a small, clear circle, the rest of the planet (for all she could prove, the rest of the universe) shrouded in fog. Even the sounds that reached her hearing diaphragms were distant, muffled, attenuated.

When Tosev rose, the mist let her look at it without protection. That seemed even stranger to her than the fog itself. As a shuttlecraft pilot, she'd grown used to harsh, raw sunlight, unfiltered even by atmosphere, let alone by these billions of droplets. Even a glimpse of a sun should have been enough to make her automatically turn her eye turrets away. But no, not here. She could look at Tosev with impunity – and she did.

With sunrise, the town began to come to life around her. Males and females trooped out of their apartment buildings. Off they went, to whatever work they had. A couple of them turned curious eye turrets in her direction. She wasn't going anywhere. She was only standing and watching. That made her not fit in. She kept on doing nothing but standing and watching, too, which left the curious no excuse to ask her any questions. That suited her fine.

Now she didn't know that she felt like breakfast, but she didn't know that she felt like any different meal, either. She did feel like something, and breakfast would do. She had to look around to see where she was; she'd walked through the night almost at random. But the new town wasn't large enough to make getting lost easy. Before long, she found herself in an eatery she'd already visited several times.

'Ham and eggs,' she told the male behind the counter. Ham she esteemed, as did most of the Race; the only thing better she'd found on Tosev 3 was ginger, and ginger she stubbornly refused. The local eggs tasted different from those of Home – rather more sulfurous – but weren't bad when flavored with enough salt.

As the male gave her the meal, he remarked, 'Before long, they will start bringing down our own domestic animals. Then we shall have proper eggs and more kinds of meat worth eating.'

'Good,' Nesseref said, handing him her identification card so he could charge her credit balance. 'Yes, that will be very good indeed. Little by little, we may be putting down roots on this world after all. Perhaps our settlement here will work out, even if not in the way we thought it would before leaving Home.'

'This is not such a bad place,' the male answered. 'Cold and wet, but we already knew that. If only there were fewer Big Uglies running around loose with weapons.'

'Truth,' Nesseref said. *Did* the Tosevite called Anielewicz have an explosive-metal bomb? Even if he didn't, did it matter?

The *Reich* and the SSSR and the United States had them. She was sure the countermale had meant Tosevites with rifles and submachine guns. They were the visible danger. But the ones with bombs were worse.

Atvar was feeling harassed. He should have been used to the feeling, after so much time on Tosev 3. In fact, he was used to the feeling. But he had less chance than usual to make the male addressing him regret it, because Reffet was every bit as much a fleetlord as he was.

'By the Emperor, Atvar,' Reffet snarled now, looking most unhappy indeed on Atvar's screen, 'what are these accursed American Big Uglies playing at with their preposterous space station? The miserable thing bloats like a tumor.'

'I do not know what they are doing,' Atvar answered. What he was doing was trying to hold his temper. Being an equal, Reffet was entitled to use his unadorned name. Equal or not, the fleetlord of the colonization fleet wasn't entitled to use his name in that tone of voice. 'Whatever it is, I doubt it means danger to us. When Big Uglies plan something dangerous, they rarely let us see any of it beforehand.'

'They have no business planning anything we do not know about in advance,' Reffet said. 'They have no business being in space at all. It is preposterous' – he liked that word – 'that we have to endure their presumption.'

'You must adapt,' Atvar said, knowing full well he could give no more infuriating advice to a male of the Race, especially one newly come to Tosev 3. 'We have been over this ground before. They were on the point of developing this technology themselves when we arrived. Much of what they use is independently invented.'

'Much also is stolen from the Race.' Reffet's tone suggested Atvar had personally handed over the engineering drawings.

'They developed rockets on their own. They were in the process of developing explosive-metal bombs when the conquest fleet came,' Atvar said. 'They made it plain they would go to war and wreck this planet if we sought to keep them from doing what they had the ability to do. The colonization fleet would have had a thin time of it then.'

'Had the conquest fleet done its job properly, we would not be having this discussion now,' Reffet snapped.

Atvar wanted to bite him. All at once, he understood how Straha must have felt when he, as fleetlord, rejected the ambitious shiplord's schemes one after another. For the first time, he even got some inkling of understanding why Straha had defected to the Big Uglies. At the moment, he felt rather like defecting himself. Then he wouldn't have to deal with fools like Reffet, too hidebound to shed his own skin.

'You were not here at the time,' he said. 'No doubt we could have benefited from your wisdom.'

'Truth,' Reffet said, not recognizing sarcasm. 'Now we have to make the best of this bad situation. And I tell you this: even some from the conquest fleet are growing alarmed. My Security personnel and I have been bombarded with messages from a female named Kassquit, urging some sort of action against this space station.'

'Have you been tasting ginger, Reffet?' Atvar demanded. 'You know perfectly well that the conquest fleet had no females.' Yet the name Kassquit was familiar to him. He checked the computer records, then started to laugh. By the time it was through, that laugh was so enormous, it looked as if he were taking the bite he so desired out of the other fleetlord.

'That is an offensive expression on your face,' Reffet said angrily, 'and I will have you know for a fact, Atvar – for a fact, do you hear? – that no Kassquit with that identity number came from Home aboard the colonization fleet. Therefore, she must have come with you. I do not know how she did it, but I do know that she did it.'

Atvar laughed harder and wider than ever. Almost shaking with mirth, he said, 'I will have you know for a fact – for a fact, Reffet, do you hear? – that you are an idiot, addled in your eggshell before you hatched. Do you have any notion who this Kassquit is?'

'One of yours,' Reffet answered. 'One of yours, by the Emperor, which is all that matters to me. Try to evade it as you will, you—'

'Oh, shut up,' Atvar told him. 'Truth: Kassquit is one of mine, in a manner of speaking – but only in a manner of speaking. She is a female Big Ugly hatchling one of my research psychologists obtained not long after the fighting stopped. He has been raising her as nearly as possible as a female of the Race ever since. And because of *her* word you are jumping around as if you had parasites sticking their pointed little snouts between your scales and sucking your blood.'

Reffet looked as if his eyes were about to pop out of the turrets that housed them. Atvar rather wished they would. At last, the fleetlord of the colonization fleet wheezed, 'A Big Ugly? I have been taken in by a Big Ugly?'

'Again, in a manner of speaking,' Atvar said. He had the computer file he needed on the screen beside Reffet's reduced but still furious image. That gave him all the advantage over the other fleetlord he needed. 'She is, however, a Big Ugly in biology only. In culture, she is a citizen of the Empire, as much as a Rabotev or one of the Hallessi.'

'A Big Ugly,' Reffet repeated. He still sounded so disbelieving, Atvar wondered if he'd heard a word other than that. Reffet went on, 'Well, if one can do it, maybe more than one can do it, too.'

'And what are you maundering about now?' Atvar inquired sweetly. He hadn't liked Reffet since the colonization fleet arrived. The more he got to know his opposite number, the more he despised him, too.

But then Reffet brought him up short. 'One of the things this Kassquit keeps complaining about is possible – she says probable – Tosevite penetration of our computer network. I thought that even more ridiculous than everything else the female was saying. But if she herself is a Big Ugly and tricked me into believing her a female of the Race, other Tosevites may be practicing similar deceptions.'

'I find that unlikely,' Atvar said, but it disquieted him just the same. 'What do your Security males and females think of the notion?'

'They reckoned it nothing more than the glow that comes from rotten meat – till now,' Reffet said. 'With this new information, they may take the idea more seriously. With this new information, I know I take it more seriously.'

'Have them transmit Kassquit's allegations to my males in Security,' Atvar said. 'They do have more experience of Tosevites than is true of your personnel. I shall be interested to learn if they, too, revise their opinion.'

'So shall I.' Reffet used the affirmative hand gesture. 'All right, Atvar, I will do that.' No *Exalted Fleetlord* from him, no. No *It shall be done,* either. Unique among all the members of the Race on and around Tosev 3, he was not Atvar's subordinate. That was one of the reasons Atvar disliked him, even if Atvar might not fully realize as much himself. He had to hope Reffet would do as he asked; he could not insist on it. This time, Reffet had chosen to oblige him. He had to be grateful, which irked him, too.

'I thank you,' he said, hoping he sounded as if he meant it.

'And I will thank your Security males for their analysis,' Reffet replied. Now that they had found something to worry them both, they could be civil to each other. Reffet continued, 'Having Tosevites pawing through our files is the last thing we need.'

'That is another truth.' Atvar meant it. 'Leaks of intelligence can prove disastrous, as our military history before Home was unified proves.'

'Does it?' Reffet said. 'I would not be surprised, but I am not the male who could prove it. You who were brought up in a Soldiers' Time have a training different from mine.'

Then why do you endlessly criticize what I did and did not do? You do not understand it. But Atvar did not drop that on Reffet's

634

snout, as he would have a little while before. All he said was, 'I am sure the data will be valuable to us. On behalf of my Security force, I look forward to receiving them for analysis.'

'I will send them,' Reffet said, and blanked the screen.

Atvar promptly telephoned Security and warned them of what was coming. 'Whatever you learn from these data, inform me before transmitting your analysis to Reffet,' he told the chief of the service, a male name Laraxx.

'It shall be done, Exalted Fleetlord,' Laraxx said. Unlike Reffet, he had to show Atvar proper deference.

'I look forward to hearing from you,' Atvar said, and tried to pick up the threads of what he'd been doing before Reffet telephoned.

Laraxx telephoned back much sooner than he had expected – soon enough to distract him from the work he had begun to gather into his hands once more. 'Exalted Fleetlord, we have seen this material before. There is nothing new here,' the Security chief said.

'You have?' Atvar said in surprise. 'Why was I not informed of it?'

'Why?' Laraxx sounded surprised, too. 'Because we paid very little attention to it, is why. That Big Ugly the researcher – Ttomalss, his name is – keeps for a pet is utterly mad, you know. She cannot be blamed, of course, but still . . . In any case, we most assuredly did not think we should waste our time or yours with this.'

'I see,' Atvar said slowly. And Laraxx did make some sense. How could Kassquit, hatched (no, born; revoltingly born) one thing, raised another, be anything but addled? As the Security male said, no blame could attach to her. But, as the saying went, being addled wasn't always the same thing as being wrong. The fleetlord said, 'She may have found something interesting after all. Do a thorough analysis, as if this were new data.'

Laraxx's sigh was quite audible. So was the resignation in his voice as he said, 'It shall be done.'

Over the next two days, Atvar forgot all about Kassquit. Irrefutable evidence reached him that the agitator Liu Han had succeeded in reaching Peking, the leading city in the Chinese subregion of the main continental mass. He had hoped the accursed female would not succeed in returning from the United States. The Japanese Empire had let him down. So had the Chinese working for the Race along the coast of China. He wondered whether that was treason or ineptitude, then wondered which he dreaded more.

He was still trying – without much hope of success – to straighten out that situation when Laraxx called again. 'Well?' Atvar demanded testily.

'I have the analysis you requested, Exalted Fleetlord.' Laraxx sounded much more subdued than he had before.

By the Emperor, he has found something, Atvar thought. 'Well?' he said again.

Laraxx said, 'Analysis of the messages issued by the male calling himself Regeya shows traces of syntax and idiom from the Tosevite language called English, Exalted Fleetlord.'

'He *is* a Big Ugly!' Atvar exclaimed.

'So it would seem, our previous belief to the contrary notwithstanding,' Laraxx agreed. 'Investigation of how a Tosevite has penetrated our networks and how deeply he has penetrated them is now ongoing.'

'You had also better investigate how many other Big Uglies, as yet undetected, are doing the same thing,' Atvar snapped.

Laraxx looked startled all over again. That evidently hadn't occurred to him. The fleetlord wondered what else hadn't occurred to him. 'It shall be done,' Laraxx said.

'Good,' Atvar said, in lieu of something harsher. The Security chief vanished from his computer screen.

Before Atvar could get any useful work done, Pshing rushed in, exclaiming, 'Exalted Fleetlord!'

That always meant trouble. 'What has managed to go wrong now?' Atvar asked his adjutant.

'Exalted Fleetlord, one of our reconnaissance satellites, one of those with a near approach to the U.S. space station at apogee, reports a sudden sharp increase in radioactive emissions from the station,' Pshing replied. 'The significance of the increase cannot yet be established, but it is most unlikely to be beneficial to us.'

Lieutenant Colonel Glen Johnson felt like whistling with glee as he eyed the *Peregrine*'s radar screen. Things couldn't have been better if he'd scripted them himself. Since he wasn't over the United States, he called down to a relay ship: 'Requesting permission to visually evaluate Lizard satellite 2247, and to make orbital changes required for prolonged visual inspection.'

'Have to check with Kitty Hawk on that one, *Peregrine*,' the radio operator answered. 'Monitor this frequency. Somebody will get back to you.'

'Roger,' Johnson said, and then, under his breath, 'What the hell else would I do but monitor this frequency?'

Kitty Hawk might remember he'd been too nosy about the American space station and refuse him permission to eyeball the Lizard satellite. Somehow, though, he didn't think that would happen. Satellite 2247 and several others with similar orbits had been launched so the Lizards could keep an eye – or an eye turret – on the space station themselves. They were curious about it, too. He knew that from intelligence intercepts, from his conversations with their radio operators, and from his conversations with Major Sam Yeager.

But were satellite 2247 and the others like it just designed to keep an eye on the space station, or could they also harm it? The Lizards said no. Johnson wouldn't have wanted to take their unsupported word on anything that important. He didn't think the people in charge of the space station would, either.

After about five minutes, the word came back: '*Peregrine*, you are clear to change your orbit to inspect 2247. Burn parameters follow . . .'

Johnson listened carefully, read the parameters back, and

smiled to himself. They were very close to the ones he'd calculated for himself. They would put him up near 2247 when the Lizards' satellite was close to the space station. He was glad he was flying *Peregrine* and not a Russian tin can. In one of those, he wouldn't have been able to make such a large orbital change or to do so much of his own calculating. The Lizards might look down their snouts at *Peregrine*, but he thought he was flying a pretty fine bird.

He made the burn on schedule, kicking himself up into a more elliptical orbit that would let him pass within a mile or so of satellite 2247's path and within about ten miles of the space station. He actually was curious about the reconnaissance satellite. He was even more curious about the space station. His smile got wider. With a little luck, he'd be able to satisfy himself twice in a few minutes, which wasn't easy for a man his age.

'U.S. spacecraft! Attention, U.S. spacecraft!' That wasn't an American relay ship. It was a Lizard, using his own language. 'You are not to damage the satellite with which you are closing. Damage to this satellite will be taken as a hostile act. You have been warned. Acknowledge immediately!'

'Acknowledged,' Johnson answered in the same language, thinking, *You arrogant bastard*. 'No damage intended – inspection only.'

'See that action matches intent,' the Lizard said coldly. 'Out.'

As he drew near the satellite, Johnson photographed it with a long lens and studied it through binoculars. It didn't look as if it could launch a missile; he saw no rocket motors. But that didn't necessarily signify. The Lizards were as good at camouflage as any humans around. The satellite wasn't very big. But that didn't necessarily signify, either. These days, nuclear bombs didn't have to be very big, not even human-made ones. If the Lizards couldn't build them smaller still, Johnson would have been surprised.

Still, 2247 had the look of a reconnaissance satellite. It

bristled with sensors and dishes, almost all of them aimed at the space station. A few swung from the station toward *Peregrine* as Johnson neared. What those said in electronic language was, *If you do anything nasty to me, I'll know about it.* And what the satellite knew, the Lizards would learn at the speed of light.

But Johnson didn't aim to do anything nasty to it. He took a couple of rolls of photographs as *Peregrine* reached its nearest approach to 2247. That done, he set down the camera and took out a screwdriver. He used it to undo a piece of sheet aluminum not far below his instrument panel. That done, he reached in and detached a length of wiring. The wire with which he replaced it was almost identical, but had bad insulation. Whistling, he plucked the panel out of the air and screwed it back into place. One of the screws had drifted farther away than he'd expected, which gave him an anxious moment, but he found it.

He waited till it was time to make the burn that would take him back into his lower orbit. When he flicked the switch, nothing happened. 'Oh, damn,' he said archly, and turned his radio to the frequency the space station used. 'Station, this is *Peregrine*. Repeat: station, this is *Peregrine*. I have had a main motor malfunction. My attempted burn just failed. I have to tell you, I'm glad you're in the neighborhood.'

'This isn't a gas station, *Peregrine*,' the space-station radio operator said, his voice friendly as vacuum.

'Christ!' Johnson hadn't expected to be welcomed with open arms, but this went above and beyond, or maybe below and beneath. 'What the hell do you want me to do, get out and walk?'

The silence that followed suggested the radioman would have liked nothing better. But Johnson wasn't the only one listening out there. The fellow couldn't very well tell his own countryman to get lost, not unless he wanted to create an enormous stink and raise enormous suspicions. And so, slower than he should have, he asked, 'Can you make it here on your maneuvering jets, *Peregrine*?'

'I think so,' answered Johnson, who was sure he could: he'd done a lot of calculations before he requested permission to change orbit.

'All right,' the operator in the space station said. 'You have permission to approach and suit up and come aboard. Do not – repeat, do not – approach by way of the unit on the end of the long boom there.'

'Why not?' Johnson asked. He wanted to find out what was on the end of that boom.

'Because you'll regret it for the rest of your days if you do,' the radioman answered. 'You want to be a damn fool, go ahead. No skin off my nose, but it will be off yours.' He had a very unpleasant laugh.

Johnson thought it over. He didn't much care for the sound of it. 'Roger,' he said, and picked a course that took him over toward the space station's enormous, untidy main structure, giving the smaller, newer section on the end of the boom a wide berth.

'Smart fellow,' the radio operator said: he had to be tracking *Peregrine*'s slow, cautious approach either by radar or by eyeball. Did he sound disappointed that Johnson had listened to him, or was that just the tinny speaker inside *Peregrine*? Johnson didn't know, and wasn't sure he wanted to find out.

He didn't have much of a chance to worry about it, anyhow. He was busy making sure his pressure suit – a distant, a very distant, descendant of the suits high-altitude pilots had started wearing around the time the Lizards came – was tight. If it failed, he had nobody to blame but himself . . . and he wouldn't be blaming himself for long.

'You want to kill as much relative motion as you can there,' the radioman said. 'A quarter mile is plenty close enough.'

'Roger,' Johnson said again, and then, with his transmitter off, 'Yes, Mother.' Didn't the fellow think he could figure all that out for himself? Maybe he wasn't so glad to be visiting this place after all. It looked to be full of Nervous Nellies.

He bled his cabin air out through the escape vents, then opened the canopy and stepped out. He had more time here than he would have had trying to bail out of a burning fighter plane. An air lock opened in the space station. Tiny in the distance, a spacesuited man waved in the lock.

His jump took him in the general direction of the lock, but not straight toward it. To correct his path, he had a pistol that looked as if it should have come from a Flash Gordon serial but fired nothing more lethal than compressed air. Before he used it, he let that length of good wire go drifting off into space. Then he fixed his aim with it and slowed himself as he neared the air lock.

The other suited figure reached out, snagged him, and touched helmets to say something without using the radio: 'That's real smooth, sir.'

Looking at the face bare inches from his, Johnson recognized Captain Alan Stahl. He puckered up, as if to kiss the younger man. Stahl laughed. Johnson said, 'I didn't plan on coming up here, but here I am. Can you show me around?' Lying to somebody he knew was harder than holding off a stranger would have been, but he did it anyway.

Stahl didn't laugh this time. He said, 'I don't know about that. We'll have to see what Brigadier General Healey thinks.'

'Take me to him,' Johnson said as the outer air-lock door swung shut.

But, once he got a good look at Charles Healey, he wasn't sure he was glad to have it. Despite looking nothing like Curtis LeMay, Healey had the same clenched-fist combativeness stamped on his face. And he knew about Johnson, growling, 'You are the damned snoop who tried talking his way aboard this spacecraft before. You should have let well enough alone, Lieutenant Colonel.'

'I didn't have much choice, sir,' Johnson answered with as good a show of innocence as he could muster. 'My main motor wouldn't fire.'

Save for having rubber bands holding down papers to keep them from floating away, Healey's office might almost have belonged back on Earth. He picked up a telephone and barked into it: 'Steve, go check out *Peregrine*. You find anything fishy, let me know.' He turned his glare back toward Johnson. 'If he finds anything fishy, you're history, just in case you were wondering.'

Johnson didn't say anything to that. He simply nodded and waited. He had a considerable wait. Steve seemed thorough.

Presently, the telephone rang. Healey snatched it up, listened, and said, 'Bad wiring, eh? All right. Can you fix it? You can? How long? Okay, that's good enough. Stahl will take it downstairs again. We'll say Johnson got sick up here and couldn't.'

'What?' Glen Johnson yelped.

Brigadier General Healey glared at him. 'You wanted to know so goddamn bad, didn't you, Lieutenant Colonel? Well, now you're going to know, by God. You've heard too much, you've probably seen too much, and you're not going downstairs to run your mouth to anybody.' That hard face yielded a meager, a very meager, smile. 'You're part of the team now, whether you like it or not. Good thing you don't have much in the way of family. That makes things easier. Welcome aboard, Johnson.'

'Christ!' Johnson said. 'You're shanghaiing me.'

'In a word, yes.' Healey had no budge in him, none at all. 'You just signed up for the duration, soldier. You're here permanently now, same as everybody else.'

'Permanently?' Johnson spoke the word as if he'd never heard it before. What the *hell* had he blundered into?

'That's right, pal.' The general smiled again, this time with an odd sort of pride. He tapped his chest with his thumb. 'That's what you just bought. I don't expect to set foot on Earth again, not ever. And neither should you.'

Sam Yeager had no trouble understanding why the Lizards had given him access to some parts of their computer network.

'These are the sections that don't tell me anything much,' he muttered. That wasn't strictly true. But it was a red-letter day when he learned anything in those areas that he couldn't have learned from the Race's radio or television transmissions. The stretch of the network he was allowed to roam was the stretch where the Lizards presented the world their public face.

Even though he didn't learn much, he dutifully skittered through it every day, so the Race could see how glad he was to have even that limited access to their computer network. But when he left, it was always with a sense of relief and anticipation, for his real work on the network started then.

After signing off as Yeager, he signed on as Regeya. Going from himself to the artificial male of the Race he'd created was like going from Clark Kent to Superman. Regeya leapt over all the obstacles that held Yeager back on the network. He could go anywhere, do anything a real male of the Race could go and do. Yeager's Lizard friends had done a terrific job of creating a new identity for him.

And Yeager himself had done everything he could to make his scaly alter ego seem real to the males and females he'd met only as names and numbers on the computer screen. He'd fooled every damn one of them, as far as he could tell. To be accepted as a Lizard among Lizards . . . If that didn't mean he'd done his homework, what could?

Sometimes Regeya seemed real to him, too. The fictitious male of the Race was fussier and more precise than he was himself. Yeager really did think differently when he assumed that identity. Things that wouldn't have upset him as himself became infuriating while he looked down the snout he didn't have at the innumerable follies of the Big Uglies.

Today, feeling very Lizardy indeed, he typed in Regeya's name, identification number, and password (he'd chosen *Rabotev 2* for a password – it was easy to remember, but did nothing to suggest Tosev or the Tosevites). He wondered if he could learn any more about Kassquit. Sometimes he thought she was another Big Ugly masquerading as a Lizard. He doubted it, though. His best guess was that she was his opposite number among the Race: a Lizard who somehow had the knack for thinking like a human being.

He waited for the network's road map to come up onto the screen. He admired that road map; it let a Lizard, or even a sneaky Tosevite, find his way around the whole complex structure with the greatest of ease. *A telephone book with a zillion cross references* was the way he'd explained it to Barbara, but that didn't begin to convey its intricacy.

But when the screen lit up, he didn't see the road map. Instead, three words appeared on it in large, glowing characters: ACCESS PERMANENTLY DENIED. And then the screen went dark again, as if a Lizard had reached out and pulled the plug.

'Oh, dear,' Sam said, or words to that effect. Wondering if the network had hiccuped, he tried again. This time, he didn't even get the forbidding three-word message. The screen just stayed dark. 'Oh, dear,' he said again, rather more pungently than before.

He felt like kicking the Lizard computer. What the devil had gone wrong? One possibility leapt to mind: if Kassquit was a female who had a knack for understanding people, maybe she'd recognized him for what he was. That hurt his pride, but he supposed he'd live through it.

He didn't want to have to live through it for long, though. He telephoned Sorviss, the male who'd done most to arrange his extended access in the first place, and explained what had gone wrong.

'I shall see what I can do,' Sorviss said – in English; he enjoyed his life among people as much as Yeager enjoyed pretending to be a Lizard. 'I will call you back when I discover what the problem is.'

'Thanks, Sorviss,' Yeager said. 'Maybe we'll have to come up with a new name for me, or something like that.' Whatever they had to do, he wanted it taken care of. He couldn't begin to do his job without the fullest possible access to what the Lizards were thinking and saying.

When the phone rang half an hour later, Sam sprang on it like a cat onto a mouse. It was Sorviss, all right, but he didn't sound happy. 'Restoring your access will not be easy or quick,' he said. 'The Race has installed new security filters on the lines leading into the consulate here. I am not certain I will be able to find a way around them: they are well made.'

'Then Straha is liable to be cut off from the network, too, isn't he?' Yeager asked.

'He is,' Sorviss agreed.

'He won't like that,' Sam predicted.

'I think you are right,' the Lizard said. 'I also think this is not something I can control. If the shiplord starts biting his arms' – a Lizard idiom translated literally into English, a sin whose reverse Yeager sometimes committed – 'I can only say, "Oh, what a pity." '

'Is that all you can say?' Yeager chuckled. A good many of the Lizards who'd chosen to stay in the USA after the fighting stopped had turned into confirmed democrats. They wanted nothing to do with the multilayered society in which they'd grown up, not any more they didn't. Ristin and Ullhass, the males he'd known longest, were like that, too, though they stayed polite when dealing with their own kind.

'No, I could say some other things,' Sorviss answered. 'But Straha would not be happy if they got back to his hearing diaphragms.'

'You're right about that, I bet,' Sam said. 'But I sure hope you can put me back on the network before too long. Without it, I'm like a man trying to do his job half blind. That's not good.'

'I understand,' Sorviss said. 'But you must understand that I will have to evade many traps to restore you without drawing the notice of the Race. Maybe this can be done; I am a male of skill. But I cannot say, "It shall be done." ' The last phrase was in the Lizards' language.

'Okay, Sorviss. Please do everything you can. So long.' Yeager hung up, deeply discontented. He'd got along without the computer network for years. He supposed he could get along without it again for however long Sorviss needed to restore his access. That didn't mean he was happy about it, any more than he would have been happy about having to write everything out by hand because his typewriter broke down.

He went back and entered the network in his own proper persona once more. As long as he was recognized as a Big Ugly – and restricted because he was recognized – everything went fine. The only problem was, he couldn't find out even a quarter of the things he wanted to know. The Lizards didn't talk about the American space station, for instance, in any discussion area to which Sam Yeager, Tosevite, had access.

'Dammit, they know more about what's going on than we do,' he grumbled.

He wondered if he ought to call Kitty Hawk again. If he did, Lieutenant General LeMay was liable to come down on him like a ton of bricks. But if he didn't, he'd stay altogether in the dark. A Lizard would have had better sense than to bring LeMay down on him in the first place, and would have obeyed without question after getting in trouble. 'Hell with that,' Yeager muttered. 'I ain't no Lizard.' Barbara, fortunately, couldn't hear him.

He picked up the phone and dialed the Kitty Hawk BOQ. If anybody had any good notions of what was going on up there, Glen Johnson would be the man. Sam nodded to himself as the telephone rang on the other side of the country. Back in the old days, he'd have had to go through an operator and give her Johnson's name. Now he could just call, and leave no trace of himself behind.

Somebody picked up the phone. 'Hello?'

'I'd like to speak to Lieutenant Colonel Johnson, please,' Yeager answered. Whoever that was over there in Kitty Hawk, it wasn't Glen Johnson. This fellow had a drawl thick enough to slice, one that turned *hello* into a three-syllable word.

After a couple of seconds' pause, the Southerner said, 'Afraid you can't do that, sir. He's up in space right now. Who's calling, please? I'll leave a message.'

He sounded very helpful – too helpful, after that little pause. Maybe, maybe not, but Sam wasn't inclined to take chances, not after the trouble he'd just had from the Lizards. He didn't give his name, but said, 'Really? I thought he'd be down by now.' From what Johnson had told him, he knew damn well that the Marine was supposed to be down by now. 'Is he all right?'

'Oh, yes, sir, he's fine,' the man back in North Carolina answered. 'You want to leave your name and a number where he can get hold of you, I reckon he'd be right glad to have 'em. I'm sure he'll get back to you as soon as he can.'

Very gently, Yeager laid the telephone handset back in its cradle. Sure as hell, alarm bells were going off in the back of his mind. He didn't think this fellow would have been so eager to get his name and number if they were tracing his call (and, thanks to Sorviss, his calls were hard, maybe impossible, for anyone with merely human equipment to trace), but he didn't want to find out he was wrong the hard way.

He sat at his desk scratching his head, wondering what the devil to do next. He wondered if there was anything he *could* do next. The Lizards had shut him off from whatever they knew about the space station, and his best – Jesus, his only – American source had just fallen off the map, too.

'What the hell *is* going on up there?' he said, and leaned back in his chair as if he could stare through the ceiling and see not only the space station but Glen Johnson, too.

He hoped that fellow with the Southern accent had been telling the truth when he said Johnson was okay. Sam knew people didn't stay in space longer than they were supposed to without some pretty important reason. If the man had said the weather in Kitty Hawk was lousy so *Peregrine* couldn't come down on schedule, that would have been something else. But he hadn't. He'd made it sound as if everything were routine. That worried Sam, who knew better.

After some thought, he fired up the U.S.-made computer on his desk. If he used it to ask questions about the space station, he'd trigger alarms. General LeMay's visit had proved that. But if his security clearance wasn't good enough to let him find out what was going on with *Peregrine*, he saw no point to having the miserable thing.

No, sure enough, nothing tried to keep him out of these records. But what he found there made him scratch his head all over again. Unless somebody was doing still more lying, *Peregrine* had landed right on schedule.

'Now what the hell does that mean?' he asked the computer. It didn't answer. Facts it could handle. Meaning? He had to supply his own.

Was the screen lying to him? Or had *Peregrine* come down while Glen Johnson stayed up? If it had, how? Space wasn't a good place for one driver to get out of a truck and another to hop in and take it on down the line.

'Space isn't,' Sam said slowly. 'But the space station is.' He looked up at and, in his mind's eye, through the ceiling again. Some things he saw, or thought he saw, very clearly. Others still made no sense at all.

One evening, after Heinrich had gone to the cinema and the younger children were asleep, Käthe Drucker asked, 'How long will you go on flying into space, Hans?'

Johannes Drucker looked at his wife in some surprise. 'You never asked me that before, love,' he said. 'Until they don't want me to do it any more, I suppose, or . . .'

Or until I blow up, he'd started to say. He would have said it lightheartedly. Somehow, he didn't think he could have said it lightheartedly enough to make Käthe appreciate it. Peenemünde already had too many monuments to fallen (or, more often, vaporized) heroes for that. He didn't dwell on it. He couldn't dwell on it and do his job. If he did go, he'd probably be dead before he knew it. That consoled him. It was unlikely to console his wife.

'Don't you think you've given the *Reich* enough of your life?' she asked. By the look in her eye, the fallen heroes of Peenemünde were on her mind, sure enough.

'If I didn't like what I was doing, I would say yes,' Drucker answered truthfully. 'But since I do—'

Käthe sighed. 'Since you do, I have to watch you go off and be unfaithful to me, and I have to hope your mistress decides to let you come back to my arms.'

'That's not fair,' Drucker said, but he couldn't have told her how it wasn't. He *did* love – he dearly loved – riding an A-45 hundreds of kilometers into the sky. He did forsake his wife whenever he went into space. And an A-45 could indeed keep him from coming home to Käthe.

She sighed again. 'Never mind. Forget I said anything.' The corners of her mouth turned down. 'You will anyhow.'

'Let's go to bed,' Drucker said. 'Things will look better in the morning.'

After telling her no, he wondered if she'd want to have anything to do with him once they got under the covers together. But if he was willing to take chances every time he rode a pillar of fire up from Peenemünde, he was also willing to take them in the dark quiet of his own bedroom. And when in an experimental way, he set a hand on Käthe's hip, she turned toward him and slid out of her flannel nightgown faster than he'd imagined possible. She might have been so urgent on their honeymoon in the south of France; he wasn't sure he could remember any time since to match this one.

'Whew!' he panted afterwards. 'Call the ambulance. I think I need to go to the hospital – I'm all worn out.'

'To have your head examined, *I* think,' Käthe said, pressing her warm, soft length against him. 'But then, you fly rocket ships, so I should have known that already.' She took him in hand. 'Maybe I really can make you too tired to be able to fly. Shall I find out?'

He wasn't sure he would rise to the occasion, but he managed. This time, he didn't need to feign exhaustion when

649

they finished. As he sank toward slumber, he remembered screwing himself silly in military brothels before dangerous missions against the Russians or the Lizards. Maybe Käthe was doing the same sort of thing, only worrying about his mission, not something she had to face herself.

He'd almost drifted off when he remembered something he would sooner have forgotten: a lot of the women drafted into these military brothels had been Jewesses. That hadn't meant anything to him during his visits; they'd just been warm, available flesh back then. Once he'd buttoned his trousers and left, he hadn't given them a second thought. Now, looking back over twenty years, he wondered how long they'd lasted in the brothels and what happened to them when they couldn't go on any more. Nothing good – he was sure of that.

He didn't fall asleep right away after all.

For all his doubts, for all its horrors, he still served the *Reich*. A few days after Käthe failed to persuade him to stop going into space, he sat in a briefing room at the Peenemünde rocket base, learning what the powers that be particularly wanted to learn from his latest missions.

'You will pay special attention to the American space station,' said Major Thomas Ehrhardt, the briefing officer: a fussily precise little man with a bright red Hitler-style mustache. 'You are authorized to change your orbit for a close inspection, if you deem that appropriate.'

'Really?' Drucker raised an eyebrow. 'I would love to do it – I will do it – but I have never had this sort of authorization before. Why have things changed?'

He wondered if Ehrhardt would invoke the great god Security and tell him that was none of his business. But the briefing officer answered candidly: 'I will tell you why, Lieutenant Colonel. There has been unusual emission of radio-activity from the station over the past few weeks. We are still trying to learn the reasons behind this emission. As yet, we have not succeeded. Perhaps yours will be the mission that finds out what we need to know.'

'I hope so,' Drucker said. 'I'll do everything I can.' He got to his feet and shot out his right forearm. '*Heil* Himmler!'

'*Heil!*' Ehrhardt returned the salute.

The A-45 on which Drucker rode into space carried strap-on motors attached to either side of the main rocket's first stage. They boosted him into a higher orbit than the A-45 could have achieved by itself. Any deviation from the norm was bound to make the Lizards and the Americans suspicious (the Bolsheviks, he assumed, were always suspicious). But the Rocket Force Command must have warned the other spacefarers that he would be taking an unusual path, because the questions he got were curious, not hostile.

He enjoyed the new perspective he got on the world from a couple of hundred kilometers higher than usual. He'd seen nearly everything there was to see from the orbit *Käthe* normally took. The wider view was interesting. It made him feel almost godlike.

And he enjoyed the better view of the U.S. space station he got from this higher orbit. Even before he tried to approach it, his Zeiss binoculars gave him a closer look than he'd ever had. The only drawback to the situation was that, because he moved more slowly than he would have in a closer orbit, he didn't come up to the station as often as he would have otherwise.

'Having fun, snoop?' the space station's radioman asked as he did approach from behind.

'Of course,' Drucker answered easily. 'I would even more fun have if you had pretty girls at every window undressing.'

'Don't I wish!' the American said. 'It's supposed to be something special when you're weightless, too, you know what I mean?'

'I have heard this, yes,' Drucker said. 'I do not about it know in person.'

'Neither do I,' the radio operator said. 'This is something that needs research, dammit!'

Drucker tried to imagine such goings-on at the *Reich's* space station. Try as he would, he couldn't. Had Göring become *Führer* after Hitler died . . . then, maybe. No – then, certainly. Göring would have had himself flown up there to make the first experiment. But the Fat Boy had disgraced himself instead, and gray, cold Himmler frowned on fooling around for its own sake – all he thought it was good for was making more Germans. With a small mental sigh, Drucker swung back from sex to espionage: 'With so much room, you Americans should try to find out.'

'Not enough gals up here,' the radioman said in disgusted tones.

That was interesting. Drucker hadn't known the American space station held any women at all. He wasn't sure anyone in the Greater German *Reich* knew the Americans were sending women into space. The Russians had done it a couple of times, but Drucker didn't much care what the Russians did. Their pilots were just along to push buttons; ground control did all the real work. Unless war suddenly broke out, a well-trained dog could handle a Russian spacecraft.

'Maybe your women don't like the radiation,' Drucker said. American radiomen liked to run their mouths; maybe he could get this one to talk out of turn.

He couldn't. The fellow not only didn't say anything about radiation, he clammed up altogether. After a while, Drucker passed out of radio range. He muttered in frustration. He'd learned something that might be important, but it wasn't what he'd come upstairs to learn.

He made some calculations, then radioed down to the ground to make sure he – and *Käthe's* computer – hadn't dropped a decimal point anywhere. Once satisfied he had everything straight, he waited till the calculated time, then fired up the motor on the upper stage of the A-45 for a burn that would change his orbit to one passing close to the American space station.

When he came into radar range of the station, the radio operator jeered at him: 'Not just a snoop, a goddamn Peeping Tom.'

'I want to know what you are doing,' Drucker answered stolidly. 'For my country's sake, it is my business to learn what you are doing.'

'It's not your business,' the American said. 'It never was, and it never will be.' He hesitated, then went on, 'Looks like you're going to pass about half a mile astern of our boom.'

'Yes,' Drucker said. 'I will not to you lie. I want to see what you are at the end of it there making.'

'I noticed.' The radioman's voice was dry. He hesitated again. 'Listen, pal, if you're smart, you'll change your trajectory a bit, on account of if you don't it won't be healthy for you. You know what I'm saying? You don't want to pass right astern of that boom, not unless you don't have any family you care about.'

'Radiation?' Drucker asked. The radioman didn't answer, as he hadn't answered his last question about radiation. Drucker thought it over. Was he being bluffed? If it weren't for radiation, he wouldn't have been up here this far. 'Thank you,' he said, and used his attitude jets to change course.

What the devil were the Americans doing? He couldn't see as well as he would have liked, not even through the viewfinder of his camera with the long lens attached. One thing he did see: the boom looked very stiff and strong. He didn't know what that meant, but he noted it – in space, nobody built any stronger, any heavier, than he had to.

The Geiger counter Drucker had along started chattering. He listened to it with pursed lips. Here he was off-axis to the unit at the end of the boom, and he was still picking up this much radiation? How much would he have taken had he gone right behind it, as he'd planned? More. A lot more. He owed the U.S. radio operator a good turn. So did Käthe. He had the bad feeling Peenemünde's memorial would have got a new name on it had the American kept quiet.

He wasn't sorry when his orbit took him away from the space station, but he did some furious calculating for a burn that would bring him back to its neighborhood as fast as possible. Spaceflight was like the rest of the *Werhmacht* in some ways. Hurry up and wait was one of them. He had to wait till the proper time to make the burn, and then again till his changed trajectory brought him toward the space station.

And, as he began the approach, he stared first at his radar and then out the window of the A-45's upper stage – for the space station, far and away the biggest and heaviest human-made object in Earth orbit, was nowhere near where it was supposed to be.

To her surprise, Kassquit discovered she missed Regeya. No one came right out and told her, but she gathered he really was a Big Ugly. Because he was one, he had no place on the Race's computer network. But the chatter about the American space station was less interesting without him. He'd known a lot, and he'd had a knack for asking interesting questions. After he was purged from the network, discussion faltered.

Not long after Regeya vanished, Kassquit got an electronic message relayed through the Race's consulate in some city or another in the Tosevite not-empire known as the United States. *I greet you,* it read. *I do not know that I much like you, but I greet you anyhow. Unless I am wrong, you are the one who figured out I was nothing but a miserable Big Ugly looking where he should not. Congratulations, I suppose. Even as a Big Ugly, I do have access to some of your network, which is how I am sending you this. Best regards, Sam Yeager.*

She read the message through several times. Then, slowly, she made the affirmative hand gesture. Sam Yeager the To-sevite sounded exactly like Regeya, the purported male of the Race.

He still took her for a female of the Race. That gave her a certain amount – a large amount – of pleasure, pleasure of the same sort she'd known when she made the hateful researcher Tessrek back down. In those moments, life looked like a game, a game in which she'd just won a turn.

'How do I answer?' she murmured to herself. It wasn't an

easy question. She'd never exchanged words with a wild Tosevite before, not knowingly. If she kept doing it, would he realize she was a Tosevite, too? He was a clever male; she'd seen that. Could she stand being discovered? What would he think of her?

I greet you, she wrote in reply. Her back straightened. She stuck out her chin. No matter what the Tosevite thought of her, she was proud of herself. No, she wouldn't let him know she was anything but a female of the Race. He wouldn't find out anything different. She'd make sure he didn't, by the Emperor. *Your spying was doomed to fail,* she went on. *You cannot pretend to be what you are not.* Her mouth fell open in amusement – here she was, pretending to be what she was not. *Now that you openly admit to being what you are, perhaps we shall become friends, as much as two so different can.*

She studied that, then decided to transmit it. She did not think the wild Big Ugly would take it for undue familiarity. He might not belong to the Race, but he did show considerable understanding of it. He had, in fact, fooled males and females who truly came from eggs.

I hope we shall become friends, you and I, Yeager responded. *Tosevites and the Race are going to be sharing this planet for a long time. I have said it before – we need to get along with each other.* Kassquit made the affirmative gesture again. Then the Tosevite wrote, *I have a question for you: why, when you thought I was Regeya, did you say you would not talk with me on the telephone?*

Kassquit studied those words with dismay. No, this Tosevite was anything but a fool. He noticed discrepancies and put them together. And he knew she was a female, even if not of which species. She couldn't say, for instance, that she was a veteran with a horrible scar she didn't like to display on the screen.

Yeager sent another message while waiting for her reply. *You would have found out for sure I was a Tosevite if we had talked on the telephone,* he wrote. *I speak the language of the*

Race pretty well, but there are some sounds I cannot make quite right no matter how hard I try, because my mouth is the wrong shape.

'I know,' Kassquit whispered. 'Oh, I know.' The language of the Race was the only one she knew, but she spoke it mushily, too. She couldn't help it. Like this Yeager's, her mouth was the wrong shape.

Again, she asked herself how she was supposed to answer that. *Telephones are too spontaneous,* she wrote at last. *I might have given away something I should not have.* And that was true – she'd have given away that she was a Big Ugly by birth. But Yeager would think (she hoped he'd think) she was talking about security.

All right, then, he replied. *I hope whatever it is you cannot talk about goes well for you.* He was friendlier than most males of the Race. Of course, they looked down their snouts at her because she was a Tosevite. This Sam Yeager – she wondered why he had two names – wouldn't do that, anyhow.

She was pondering her reply when a flashing red star appeared in the lower right-hand corner of her computer screen. That meant an urgent news flash. She gave up on her message – the Tosevite could wait. She wanted to find out what was going on.

The image that appeared on her screen when she switched to the news feed made her exclaim in surprise. She'd seen video of the American Big Uglies' space station before, and had spent a lot of time discussing it on the network. Now here it was – and it was moving. She saw a faint glowing stream of expelled reaction mass emerging from the lump at the end of the new boom.

A commentator from the Race was saying, '– is the first known use by the Big Uglies of a motor powered by atomic energy. It appears to be a fission motor, not the far more efficient and energetic fusion reactors we have used for so long. Acceleration is feeble, hardly more than one part of gravity per hundred. Nevertheless, as you see, it moves.'

656

Kassquit watched the American ship – space station no longer. But for the exhaust, she could not have proved it moved. The motion she saw might as easily have come from the camera.

'We have sent urgent queries to President Warren, leader of the not-empire known as the United States,' the commentator said. 'Fine details of his reply are still being translated, but he asserts that the ship was built for no warlike purpose, but solely for the exploration of this solar system.'

'How can we trust that?' Kassquit said, as if someone were standing beside her insisting that she trust it. 'They built the ugly thing without telling us what they were up to.'

'Their ship is too slow and ungainly to make a likely weapons platform.' The commentator might have been answering her. 'It is also moving away from Tosev 3. But investigation will continue until its nature may be precisely ascertained.'

'Its nature should have been ascertained a long time ago,' Kassquit said. 'Security has done a slipshod job.'

Again, she was arguing with the commentator. This time, he did not even seem to pay attention to her. He said, 'Fleetlord Atvar of the conquest fleet and Fleetlord Reffet of the colonization fleet have issued a joint statement affirming that there is no cause for alarm in this new development, and expressing relief that this ship does appear to be no more than an oversized exploration vessel, as the ruler of the not-empire known as the United States has declared.'

'And if we start blindly accepting a Big Ugly's word, where will we be?' Kassquit answered her own question: 'In trouble, nowhere else.'

But the commentator sounded convinced everything was fine. 'The subject of the American space station has been on the minds of males and females in recent times, as the computer discussion areas show,' he said. 'Now we see that much of the anxious speculation was misinformed, as anxious speculation commonly is.'

'How do you know we see anything of the sort?' Kassquit demanded, as if the male could hear her.

The U.S. spacecraft disappeared from the screen, to be replaced by a graphic showing its projected course. 'As you can observe, the craft is headed for none of the major planets of this solar system. It is not heading toward Home or any other world of the Empire. And, with its feeble acceleration, it must lack the fuel capacity to be a starship. Its most likely destination appears to be one of the many useless and insignificant rocks orbiting between Tosev 4, a small world, and Tosev 5, a gas giant larger than any in Home's system. The American Big Uglies have previously sent chemically powered exploration rockets out among these minor planets, as the Tosevites term them. Now it appears they are visiting them on a larger scale. As far as the Race is concerned, they are welcome to them.'

There, for once, Kassquit agreed with the noisy male. Here as in so many other ways, the star Tosev's solar system was different from those of other stars in the Empire: it held far more such debris. No one was sure why; speculation centered on Tosev's greater mass.

How typical of Big Uglies, she thought, *to spend so much time and so many resources going off to examine what is not worth examining in the first place.* Feeling obstreperous (and hoping that feeling was not a product of her own Tosevite heritage), she decided to send Sam Yeager a message. *So this, then, is what so concerned you,* she wrote. *A large, clumsy spaceship that was not worth being kept secret.*

I agree, he wrote back a little later. *It was not worth being kept secret. In that case, why was it?*

Who can tell, with Tosevites? Kassquit answered.

This time, Yeager did not reply. She wondered if she'd insulted him. She didn't want to do that by accident. When she offended, she aimed to get full value from it.

Then she began to wonder if he'd been trying to tell her something else, something she would miss if she weren't paying attention. If the American space station or spaceship or whatever it turned out to be had been kept so secret without there being any need for that, all that implied was that Big Uglies were fools, a notion Kassquit was prepared to take on faith.

But not all Big Uglies were fools all the time. She didn't like believing that so well, but the conclusion was inescapable. Tosev 3, or some parts of Tosev 3, had come too far too fast for her to doubt it. Suppose the American Tosevites had had good reason to keep their project secret. What then?

Then, by logic inescapable as that of geometry, their spacecraft wasn't so harmless as it now seemed. They had to have something in mind beyond what the Race was seeing.

'But what?' Kassquit wondered aloud. 'Their atomic motor?'

Maybe. The idea appealed to her. Having fought the Race with explosive-metal bombs, the American Tosevites had to know the Race would be less than delighted at their using nuclear energy in space. Before the space station turned into a ship, the United States could have shouted its peaceful intentions as often as it liked, but it would have had a hard time convincing the Race it was telling the truth.

Was the United States telling the truth now? Had the Big Ugly named Sam Yeager, the Big Ugly who was and was not Regeya, hinted otherwise? Or was Kassquit reading too much into what he had written? And even if she read him aright, was he really in any position to know?

Those were good questions. Kassquit wished she knew the answers to all of them. As things were, she didn't know the answer to any of them. She sighed. As she came into adulthood, she was discovering that such frustrations were part of life.

20

Fotsev's head came up sharply. His eye turrets swung now this way, now that, as he prowled through the streets of Basra. 'Something is wrong here,' he said in a voice that came out flat because he forced all the nervousness from it. 'Something does not taste the way it should.'

'Truth,' Gorppet said. His eye turrets were moving unnaturally fast, too. That he thought something wasn't the way it should be helped ease Fotsev's mind. With the combat Gorppet had seen, he ought to have a knack for recognizing trouble before it became obvious.

'Everything seems quiet to me,' Betvoss said.

'I wish you seemed quiet to me,' Gorppet told him.

Betvoss liked to contradict for the fun of contradicting. Fotsev had seen that before. But, this time, the other male's words helped Fotsev see where the trouble lay. 'Everything does seem quiet,' he said. Gorppet gave him a reproachful look till he went on, 'Everything seems too quiet.'

'Yes, it does.' Gorppet used an emphatic cough. 'That is it exactly! Not many Big Uglies on the street, not even many of the cursed yapping creatures they use for pets.'

'Not many weapons, either.' Betvoss kept right on contradicting. 'Usually the local Tosevites have about as much firepower as we do. If anyone thinks I am sorry to see something different for once, he is an addled egg.'

'If something is different, that is likely to mean something is wrong,' Fotsev said. His opinion sprang partly from the innate conservatism of the Race, partly from his own experience on Tosev 3.

Gorppet made the affirmative hand gesture. 'If things go quiet all of a sudden, you always wonder what the Big Uglies are hiding. Or you should.'

'And it could be anything,' Fotsev said gloomily. 'It could be anything at all. Remember the riots we had to put down when the colonization fleet started landing? If I never hear one more Big Ugly wrapped in rags screaming *'Allahu akbar!'* I will be the happiest male on the face of this planet.'

Betvoss didn't argue with that. Fotsev didn't see how even Betvoss could have argued with that. Another male on patrol said, 'Hardly any of the little half-grown beggars around today. And if that does not prove something is wrong, what would?'

'Truth,' Fotsev said. 'They act like parasites – or they do most of the time. But where are they this morning?'

'Not at their lessons, that is certain,' Gorppet said with a nasty laugh. Most of the local Tosevite hatchlings had no lessons to attend. The ones who did receive what the locals considered an education learned to add and subtract a little, to write in their language, and to read from the manual of the superstition dominant hereabouts. Maybe that was better than nothing. Fotsev would not have bet anything he cared to lose on it.

When the patrol came into the central market square, he saw for himself that things were not right. On almost every day, the pandemonium in the market square outdid the rest of Basra put together. Not today. Today, hardly any merchants displayed food or cloth or brasswork or the other things they made. Today, males and females of the Race from the new towns out in the desert outnumbered Tosevites as customers.

'Too quiet,' Gorppet said.

'Much too quiet,' Fotsev agreed. He waited for Betvoss to

weigh in on the opposite side, but the other male said not a word.

Horrible electrified squawkings burst from the towers attached to the buildings where the local Big Uglies practiced their superstition. 'The call to prayer,' Gorppet said, and Fotsev made the affirmative gesture. 'Now we shall see how many of them come out,' Gorppet went on. 'If they stay home for this . . . well, they never have, not in all the time I have been here.'

Sure enough, robed Big Uglies emerged from houses and shops and streamed toward the mosques of Basra. 'Praying is not the only thing they do in those buildings,' Fotsev said worriedly. 'The males who lead them in prayer are also known to lead them in rebellion against the Empire.'

'We ought to go in there and make sure they say only things that have to do with their foolish beliefs,' Betvoss said. 'Those males have no business meddling in politics. They should be punished if they try.'

'We have punished some of them,' Fotsev said. 'Others keep popping up.'

'The other fork of the tongue is, they have no notion where their superstition ends and politics begins,' Gorppet added. 'For them, the two are not to be separated.'

'We should instruct them, then.' Betvoss flourished his rifle to show what kind of instruction he had in mind. 'We should go into those houses of superstition and kill the Big Uglies who preach against us, kill them or at least take them away and imprison them so they cannot inflame the others.'

'We tried that, not long after we occupied these parts,' Gorppet said. 'It did not work: it created more turbulence than it suppressed. And so many of these Tosevites are experts in the fine points of their foolish belief that new leaders arose almost at once to replace the ones we captured.'

'Too bad,' Betvoss said, and there, for once, Fotsev couldn't disagree with him.

With most of the Big Uglies worshiping, the patrol prowled

down streets even more deserted than before. 'Too easy,' Fotsev muttered under his breath. 'Too easy, too quiet.'

His eye turrets kept on sliding now this way, now that, looking for places from which the Tosevites might ambush the patrol, and also for good defensive positions in case of trouble. That there was no sign of trouble except for things being calmer than usual did nothing to deter him. He felt like a hatchling still in the egg that trembled when it heard a predator's footsteps. It could not see danger, but knew danger was there nonetheless. Fotsev thought it was here, too.

His telephone hissed. The sound, designed to get his attention, made him start with alarm, though danger on Tosev 3 was likelier to start with angry shouts from Big Uglies or with the frightened yappings of their animals. He put the phone to a hearing diaphragm, listened, said, 'It shall be done, superior sir,' and set the instrument back on his belt.

'What shall be done?' Gorppet asked.

'I knew trouble was stirring somewhere,' Fotsev answered. 'The Big Uglies have captured a bus on its way into Basra from one of the new towns and kidnapped all the females who were riding in it. The suspicion is that they intend to hold them for ransom.'

'Clever of the authorities to figure that out,' Gorppet said with heavy sarcasm. 'Lesser minds would have been incapable of it.'

'Why kidnap only females?' Betvoss said. 'Males are more dangerous to them, for there are no female soldiers.'

'That is not how the Big Uglies think,' Gorppet said. 'Females matter more to them, because they are always in season. And besides, females do not know how to fight back. If they captured males, they might capture a trained soldier, one who could harm them.'

'That makes sense,' Betvoss said – he was being unusually reasonable today. 'If we can find them, we can probably earn promotions.'

'If we see some evidence that we are near these kidnapped

females, of course we shall try to rescue them,' Fotsev said. 'But we must not forget everything else while we search for them.'

'Truth,' Gorppet said. 'Otherwise, the Tosevites will make us regret it.'

'Onward, then,' Fotsev said.

Onward they went, through the narrow, winding streets of Basra. A breeze sprang up, sending new and different stinks onto their scent receptors. After a while, the Big Uglies came out of their houses of worship. Gorppet, who spoke their language, called out to some of them. A few – only a few – answered. 'They deny knowing anything about these females,' he said.

'Did you expect anything different?' Fotsev asked.

'Expect? No,' Gorppet answered. 'But you never can tell. I might have been lucky. The Tosevites have feuds among themselves. Had I found a male at feud with the kidnappers, he might have told us what we need to know.'

For a small stretch of time, the Big Uglies returning from their worship filled the streets. Then they might have disappeared off the face of Tosev 3. Everything grew quiet again – much too quiet, as far as Fotsev was concerned. Something simmered under the surface, though he couldn't tell what. That sense of walking on uncertain ground gnawed at him.

The breeze picked up and swirled dust into his face. His nictitating membranes flicked back and forth, back and forth, protecting his eyes from the grit. 'Weather reminds me of a windy day back on Home,' he remarked, and a couple of the other males made the affirmative hand gesture.

Then, all at once, the breeze blew him a scent that also reminded him of Home. 'By the Emperor!' he said softly. He was not the only male in the patrol to smell those pheromones, of course. Everyone else started standing more nearly erect, too.

'She's close,' Betvoss said hoarsely. 'She's very close.'

'She . . . maybe they,' Gorppet said. 'The scent is *strong*.'

His voice was hot and hungry, and he added an emphatic cough.

'I wonder if these are the kidnapped females.' Fotsev reluctantly reached for his telephone to report the possibility.

'Investigate with caution,' a male back at the barracks told him.

'It shall be done,' Fotsev replied. But that other male, that distant male, did not have a cloud of pheromones blowing into his face. When Fotsev relayed the order to the rest of the patrol, what he said was, 'We have permission to go forward.'

A couple of males exclaimed in delight. Betvoss said, 'It will probably be a couple of ginger-addled females from the new towns. But if they are ginger-addled, they will want to mate, and smelling them certainly makes me want to mate. And so . . .' He hurried in the direction the delicious scent led him. So did Fotsev. So did the whole patrol. They were investigating, but had forgotten all about caution.

Rounding a corner, Fotsev saw a couple of females at the dark dead end of an alleyway. The pheromones came off them in waves. He and his comrades rushed toward them. Only when he got very near did his lust-impaired senses note they were bound and gagged.

He tried to make himself stop. 'It is a trap!' he shouted. The realization came just too late for him. Big Uglies concealed in houses on either side of the alley had already opened up with rifles and automatic weapons. Males fell as if scythed down. Fotsev screamed for help into his telephone. Then something struck him a heavy blow in the flank. He found himself on the ground without knowing how he'd got there. It didn't hurt – yet.

The Tosevites swarmed out of their hiding places to try to finish off the patrol. *'Allahu akbar!'* they shouted. A male fired at them, and some fell. The rest kept shouting, *'Allahu akbar!'* It was the last thing Fotsev ever heard.

*   *   *

'*Allahu akbar!*' The cry echoed through Jerusalem once more. Reuven Russie hated it. It meant horror and terror and death. He'd seen that before. Now he and the city he loved – the only city he'd ever loved – were seeing it again.

In the most hackneyed, clichéd fashion possible, he wished he'd listened to his mother. If he hadn't gone in to the Russie Medical College this morning, he wouldn't be worrying now about how he was going to get home in one piece. Things hadn't been so bad this morning. He hadn't wanted to miss the day's lectures or the biochemistry lab – especially not the latter, whose equipment and techniques far outdid anything human technology could offer.

And so he'd come, and he hadn't had too hard a time doing it. People had been shouting '*Allahu akbar!*' even then, and there were occasional spatters of gunfire, the *pop-pop-pops* sounding like fireworks. But Reuven had gone through the empty market square without so much as seeing a man with a rifle or a submachine gun. The shopkeepers who'd stayed home and merchants who hadn't set up their stalls, though, had known something he hadn't.

The Race, as a matter of course, efficiently soundproofed the buildings it put up. Reuven approved; distractions were the last thing he needed when trying to keep up with a Lizard physician lecturing as quickly as he would have for students of his own species. He and his fellows never heard Jerusalem's ordinary street noise, which could be pretty raucous.

But the noise outside today was anything but ordinary. Nearby smallarms fire and helicopters roaring low overhead provided constant background racket, now louder, now softer. Even the most efficient soundproofing in the world couldn't keep out the deep, thunderous roars of exploding bombs. And some of those bombs burst close enough to shake the whole building, as if from an earthquake. Reuven had been through a few quakes. The shaking here wasn't so strong as in a bad one, but he kept wondering what would happen if a bomb happened to hit the medical college square. It wasn't the sort of thought that helped him pay attention to Shpaaka, the male of the Race who went on lecturing as if it were an ordinary day.

After a miss that sounded and felt nearer than any of the others, Jane Archibald leaned toward him and whispered, 'This is bloody awful.'

'Oh, good,' he whispered back. 'I thought I was the only one scared out of my wits.'

Blond curls flipped back and forth as she shook her head. 'I don't know how anybody stands it,' she said. 'It takes me back to the days when I was a tiny little girl and the Lizards were mopping up Australia after they'd bombed Sydney and Melbourne.'

Reuven nodded. 'I remember the fighting in Poland and in England and here, too.'

He might have known that Shpaaka would notice he wasn't paying so much attention as he should. 'Student Russie,' the Lizard said, 'are you prepared to repeat back to me my remarks on hormonal function?'

Before Reuven could answer, another bomb burst even closer to the building. It almost threw him out of his seat. He had to fight the urge to dive for cover. In a shaky voice, he answered, 'No, superior sir. I am sorry.'

He waited for Shpaaka to read him the riot act about insolence and insubordination. Instead, the male let out a very human-sounding sigh and said, 'Perhaps, under the circumstances, this is forgivable. I must note, I find these circumstances unfortunate.'

No one argued with him. People who were liable to stand up and scream *'Allahu akbar!'* or even 'Lizards go home!' were unlikely to enroll in the Moishe Russie Medical College. As far as Reuven was concerned, the Race did a better job of ruling its territory than the *Reich* or the Soviet Union did theirs. He glanced over toward Jane, which he enjoyed doing every so often any day of the week. She had a different opinion of the Lizards' rule, but she couldn't enjoy watching – or rather, listening to – Jerusalem going up in flames.

Shpaaka said, 'I hope you will forgive me, but I really feel I must speak on something other than the assigned lecture topic for a little while. I trust I hear no objections?' His eye turrets swiveled so he could look at all of his students. Again, no one said anything. 'I thank you,' he told them. 'I merely wanted to state my opinion that, in view of the factional strife so prevalent among you Tosevites, the coming of the Race to Tosev 3 may well prove a boon to you, not the disaster so many of your kind perceive it to be.'

Reuven started to nod, then checked himself. It wasn't so much that he didn't agree: much more that he didn't want Jane seeing him agree. He knew she wouldn't, no matter how eloquently Shpaaka spoke. He didn't blame her for having a view different from his, but wished she wouldn't.

'I say this even if the Race should eventually incorporate all Tosevites into the Empire,' Shpaaka continued. 'You value independence very highly: more so than any other species we know. But unity and security also have their value, and in the long run – a concept I admit seems alien to Tosev 3 – that value may well prove greater. We have found it so, at any rate.'

Now Reuven wasn't so sure he agreed. He was content to live under the Lizards' rule because all other choices for Palestine looked worse. He didn't think that was true all over the world, nor even in all parts of the world where the Race presently ruled.

He glanced over toward Jane again. She surely didn't think that was true all over the world, either.

'Let us live in peace together, as far as we can,' Shpaaka said. 'Let us learn in settings like this one to extend the boundaries of peaceful living, and let us—' He had to break off, for the lights flickered and the floor shook from another near miss.

'So much for peaceful living,' somebody behind Reuven said.

A telephone on the wall behind Shpaaka hissed for attention. He answered it, spoke briefly, and then hung up. Turning back to the class, he said, 'I am told to dismiss you early. Armored vehicles are on the way to take you all back to the dormitory, which has a strong perimeter around it.'

Reuven threw up his hand. When Shpaaka recognized him, he said, 'But, superior sir, I do not live in the dormitory.'

'You might be well advised to go there in any case,' the Lizard said. 'Doing so will be far safer for you than attempting to traverse the city while it is in such a state of disarray. Assuming the telephone system is still operational, you may contact whomever you require from there.' He paused, then went on, 'I do not have so many students as to be able to contemplate with equanimity the loss of any of them.'

'But my family . . .' Reuven began.

'Don't be silly,' Jane hissed at him. 'Your father advises the fleetlord. Do you think the Race will let anything happen to him?'

He started to answer that, then realized he couldn't – she was right. The Lizards took such obligations far more seriously than most people did. And so, instead, he spoke to Shpaaka: 'I thank you, superior sir. I will go to the dormitory with my fellow students.'

'It is good,' the male said. 'And now, until the vehicles arrive, I resume my remarks on hormone functions . . .'

He did not get to lecture long. A male wearing the body paint of a mechanized combat vehicle commander burst into the chamber and called, 'You Tosevites going to the dormitory, come with me at once.'

Along with everyone else, Reuven rose and hurried out to the entrance-way. The air outside was thick with smoke, smoke nasty with the scents of burning paint and burning rubber and burning meat. He plunged into one of the waiting combat vehicles – not altogether by accident, the one Jane Archibald also chose. The seats in the back were made for Lizards, which meant they were cramped for humans. He didn't mind being knee to knee with her, not at all.

A male scrambled in after them and slammed the rear doors

669

shut. The mechanized combat vehicle rattled forward on its treads. It hadn't gone far before bullets started slamming into it. Its own machine gun and males at the firing ports shot back. The noise inside was deafening.

Rioters kept shooting at the mechanized combat vehicle all through the short trip from the college to the dormitory. None of the hits penetrated, which Reuven took as a tribute to the Race's engineering. One of the Lizards inside with him and Jane turned an eye turret their way and said, 'We make them pay.'

He was talking about human beings, people like Reuven. They were, unfortunately, also people doing their best to kill him. He couldn't work up much sympathy for them. What came out of his mouth was, 'Good.'

The mechanized combat vehicle spun, backed, and stopped. The Lizard, who could see out, said, 'We are just in front of your building. I will open the doors. When I do, you run inside.'

'It shall be done,' Reuven and Jane said together. The doors flew open. Ducking low to keep from banging their heads on a roof made for shorter beings, they jumped out and ran. No bullets smote them. As soon as they were inside the dormitory, students who'd got there before them slammed the building's doors shut again.

'Are the telephones working?' Reuven asked. When somebody told him they were, he called his parents' house. He got one of his twin sisters. 'I'm at the dormitory. I'm going to spend the night here,' he said. 'How are things around the house?'

'Quieter here than last time,' Esther or Judith – he thought it was Judith – answered. 'Getting home wouldn't have been easy for you, though, I don't suppose. I'm glad you're all right.' She said that last with the air of someone granting a great concession.

'I'm glad all of you are safe, too,' Reuven answered. 'I'll be home as soon as I can. Take care.' He hung up.

'We have no vacant bedrooms,' one of the dormitory workers told him. 'I will set up a cot for you in the hall.'

Reuven hadn't thought there would be any empty rooms. He'd dreamt of sharing a bedroom with Jane Archibald. By the way she'd kissed him every now and then, he'd dared hope he wasn't the only one dreaming of such things. Whether he was or not, he wouldn't find out tonight.

She handed him a chicken sandwich and a bottle of Coca-Cola. She had a sandwich and a soda of her own, too. 'Thanks,' he said, realizing how hungry he was. He gulped down an enormous bite, then went on, 'That's . . . almost as good as what I hoped for.'

Her eyes widened a little; she could hardly misunderstand him. Then she said, 'Not tonight, Reuven.' He nodded – he'd already figured that out for himself. But she was smiling, she wasn't angry, and she didn't say anything more. All of a sudden, the whole hellish day didn't look so bad.

Nieh Ho-T'ing was normally perhaps the most self-contained man Liu Han knew. Today, though, he seemed as bouncy as a sixteen-year-old who imagined himself in love for the first time. 'We have more weapons than we know what to do with,' he said jubilantly. 'We have weapons from the Americans – thanks to you, Comrade.' He grinned at Liu Han. They weren't lovers any more, but seeing that grin reminded her of why they had been.

'Thanks to the Americans, too, for trying till they got a shipment past the Japanese and the little scaly devils and their Chinese lackeys at the customs houses,' Liu Han said.

Nieh brushed that aside. His mind was on other things. 'And we have weapons from our Socialist brethren in the Soviet Union,' he burbled. 'Theirs got through, too' – which might have meant he'd been listening to her after all. 'And with all these toys in our hands, we ought to find something worthwhile to do with them.'

'Something that will make the little scaly devils wish they'd never been hatched, you mean,' Liu Han said.

'Well, of course,' Nieh Ho-T'ing replied in some surprise. 'What other worthwhile use for weapons is there?'

'The Kuomintang,' she said.

'They are a small enemy,' Nieh said with a scornful wave. 'The scaly devils are the great enemy. So it was before the scaly devils came: the Japanese were the great enemy, the Kuomintang the small. They cannot destroy us. The scaly devils might, if they had the will and the skill.'

'Their will is considerable,' Liu Han said. 'Never think too little of them.'

'They have not the dialectic, which means their will won't endure,' Nieh said sharply. 'And they have little in the way of skill.'

Liu Han could not disagree with that. Talking quietly over a couple of bowls of noodles in a neighborhood eatery on the west side of Peking, she and Nieh Ho-T'ing might have been deciding when to hold a party for a neighbor, not how best to visit death and destruction on the imperialist little devils. 'What have you got in mind?' she asked.

He slurped up another mouthful of noodles with his chopsticks before answering, 'The Forbidden City. I think we have a chance to take it, or at least to wreck it so the little scaly devils cannot use it any more.'

'Eee, wouldn't that be something!' Liu Han exclaimed. 'The Chinese Emperors kept the people out of it, and now the little devils do the same.' She'd seen some of the marvels at the heart of Peking when serving as an emissary to the little devils. Thinking of them in ruins hurt, but thinking of striking a blow against the little scaly devils made the hurt go away. She turned practical: 'We should strike the little devils somewhere else first, so they will not be thinking about an assault on the Forbidden City.'

Nieh Ho-T'ing nodded respectfully. 'That is part of the plan, yes. You see things the way a general would.' As he was a general himself, that was not the sort of compliment he gave lightly.

'Good.' Liu Han nodded, too. 'Now, you have talked the Muslims into joining the first attack, the one that won't go anywhere?'

This time, Nieh stopped with a load of noodles halfway to his mouth. 'I've dealt with the Muslims of Peking every now and then – you know that,' he said slowly, and waited for Liu Han to nod. When she did, he went on, 'Why would you want me – why would you want us – to involve them now?'

'Ah.' Liu Han smiled. She'd seen something he hadn't – she'd seen something the rest of the Central Committee hadn't. 'Because the Muslims farther west are rebelling against the scaly devils. If we have an uprising here, why shouldn't our Muslims get the blame, or part of it?'

Nieh stared at her. The noodles, forgotten on the chopsticks, dripped broth down onto the tabletop. After a moment, he shook his head and started to laugh. 'Do you know what a terror you would have been if you'd stayed a peasant in a little village?' he said. 'You would be running that village by now – no one would dare sell a duck, let alone a pig, without asking what you thought first. And if you had daughters-in-law . . . Eee, if you had daughters-in-law, they wouldn't dare breathe without asking you first.'

Liu Han thought about it. After a moment, she laughed, too. 'Maybe you're right. That's what mothers-in-law are for – making life miserable for daughters-in-law, I mean. Mine did. But it hasn't got anything to do with anything now. Will you talk to the Muslims, or won't you?'

'Oh, I will – you've convinced me,' Nieh said. 'I wish I'd thought of it myself, as a matter of fact. It's good to have you back in China.'

'It's good to be back,' Liu Han said from the bottom of her heart. 'If you know some of the things they eat in the United States . . . But never mind that. Why wasn't I involved in planning the attack on the Forbidden City as soon as someone got the idea?'

Suddenly, Nieh Ho-T'ing looked uncomfortable. 'Oh, you know how Mao is about these things,' he said at last.

'Ah.' Liu Han did indeed. 'He thinks women are better in bed than at the council table. Hsia Shou-Tao thinks the same way. How much self-criticism has he had to give over the years because of it? Maybe Mao should criticize himself, too.'

'Maybe he should – but don't hold your breath,' Nieh said. 'Now you have shown you deserve to help plan the attack. Isn't that enough?'

'It will do, for now.' Liu Han leaned forward. 'Let's talk.'

Theirs was not the only talk that went into the plan, of course. They met with leading officials from the Party and the People's Liberation Army, hammering out what they wanted to do and also how to keep both the little scaly devils and the Kuomintang from getting wind of it before the attacks went on. Liu Han helped organize a disinformation campaign: not one that claimed there would be no attack, but one that said it was aimed at a different part of Peking a week later than the real assault would be launched.

Nieh Ho-T'ing went several times to the Muslim quarter in the south-western part of the Chinese city of Peking. He came back from one trip laughing. 'I met with a mutton merchant,' he told Liu Han. 'Across the street, an ordinary Chinese has set up as a pig butcher. The fellow painted a tiger in the front window of his shop, to frighten the Muslim's sheep. The Muslim put a mirror in front of his own place, to make the tiger turn on the pigs, which the Muslim cannot eat himself. I thought it was a good joke.'

'It is a good joke,' Liu Han agreed. 'Now, will the Muslims make their diversion?'

'I think they will,' Nieh answered. 'The scaly devils oppress them because Muslims cause so much trouble in the west – you had a good notion there. That pig butcher is an example of this oppression: pigs offend Muslims, but the little devils let him open his shop in that district even so.'

'If they are fools, they will pay for being fools,' Liu Han

said. 'A pity we have to give the Muslims weapons to help them rise up. The ones who live may end up turning some of those weapons against us.'

'It can't be helped,' Nieh said.

'I suppose not,' Liu Han admitted. 'I wish it could. But the Muslims are less dangerous to us than the Kuomintang, much less than the little scaly devils.'

The chosen day dawned clear and cold, with a strong wind blowing out of the west. The wind brought with it yellow dust from the Mongolian desert; a thin coating of dust got everywhere, including between Liu Han's teeth. That gritty feeling in the mouth and in the eyes was part of living in Peking. Liu Han quickly got used to it again, though she hadn't missed it when she and Liu Mei went to America.

She stayed in her roominghouse with her daughter, waiting for things to happen. In a way, she wished she were carrying an American tommy gun or a Russian PPSh submachine gun, but she wasn't an ordinary soldier any more. She was of more use to the cause of popular revolution setting others in motion than moving herself.

Right at the appointed hour, gunfire broke out south of the rooming-house. 'It begins,' Liu Mei said.

'Not yet, not for us,' Liu Han replied. 'If the Muslims do not draw enough scaly devils away from the Forbidden City, our fighters will sit on their hands and let the little devils crush this uprising. That will be hard on the Muslims, but it will save our men for another time when we can get better use from them.'

'We will give the Muslims to the Kuomintang if that happens,' Liu Mei said.

'Truth,' Liu Han answered in the scaly devils' language. Returning to Chinese, she went on, 'It cannot be helped, though. If we waste the substance of the People's Liberation Army, we have nothing left.'

Before long, her practiced ear caught the rattle of the little scaly devils' automatic weapons, a sound different from the one the Muslims' rifles and submachine guns made. When she caught the rumble of tanks rolling through the narrow streets of Peking, she grinned at her daughter. Things were unfolding just as Nieh Ho-T'ing had planned them. Liu Mei didn't grin back; that was not her way. But her eyes sparkled in an otherwise expressionless face, and Liu Han knew she was pleased.

Had the People's Liberation Army been fighting the Kuomintang, the attack on the Forbidden City would have come after sunset. But the Chinese Communists had learned to their sorrow that the scaly devils had devices allowing them to see in the dark like owls. And so the assault on the moated walls surrounding the rectangle of the Forbidden City began in the early afternoon. American submachine guns smuggled one by one into the surrounding Imperial City opened up on the walls. So did heavy Russian mortars. The gates into the Forbidden City – especially the *Wu Mên*, the Meridian Gate, at the south – would already be open, to let the soldiers of the little scaly devils and their fighting vehicles go forth to put down the Muslims. Teams of picked Chinese fighters were to rush in through them, to make sure they stayed open so more human beings could follow.

'If we take the Forbidden City, can we keep it?' Liu Mei asked.

'I don't know,' Liu Han answered. 'We can do a lot of damage. We can kill a lot of their officials and a lot of running dogs. And we can embarrass them, make them look like fools all over the world. It's worth the price we'll pay.'

'They do fight hard,' her daughter remarked. 'They will slay more of ours than we slay of theirs.'

'I know that.' Liu Han's shrug was not so much callous as calculating. 'Mao is right when he says they can slay hundreds of millions of Chinese and still leave us with hundreds of millions to resist them. They cannot afford losses that match ours. They cannot afford losses that are the tenth part of ours. That is what this attack is supposed to tell them.'

Someone pounded on her door. She opened it. A runner, a

man she recognized as one of Nieh Ho-T'ing's junior officers, stood panting in the hallway. Half his left ear had been shot away; blood dripped down onto his tunic. He didn't seem to notice. 'Comrade – Comrades' – he corrected himself, catching sight of Liu Mei behind Liu Han – 'I am to tell you that the *Tai Ho Tien*, the Hall of Supreme Harmony, at the heart of the Forbidden City is in the hands of the People's Liberation Army.'

'So soon?' Liu Han exclaimed. The runner nodded. She shook her head in slow wonder. 'I think we will conquer – I think we have conquered – after all.'

Except on the days when he felt worse, Mordechai Anielewicz bicycled through the streets of Lodz. It was defiance as much as anything else, a refusal to let the nerve gas he'd breathed twenty years before do anything more to his life than he could help.

When he saw Ludmila Jäger hobbling along on a stick, he pulled to a stop beside her. Her broad Russian face bore a look of intense concentration; she was fighting pain as best she could, too. 'How is it today?' Mordechai called to her.

She shrugged. 'Today, not so good,' she answered. 'When the weather is cold and wet, it hurts more,' she went on in her Russian-accented Polish. Then she eyed him. 'But you know this for yourself.'

'I suppose so,' he answered, again feeling oddly guilty that the gas had done worse to her than it had to him.

She snapped her fingers. 'Something I meant to tell you. Someone asked me yesterday where you live.'

'*Nu?* Did you tell him?' Mordechai asked.

Ludmila frowned. 'I did, and now I wonder if I should have. That's why I wanted to let you know: in case I was stupid.'

Anielewicz grew alert. 'Why? Do you think he was a Polish nationalist? Or did he like a Nazi talk?' He smiled as he put on the German accent, but the expression didn't reach his eyes. He'd done the Greater German *Reich* a few favors during the fighting, but he'd done the Nazis any number of unfavors during it and since, not least refusing to let himself and Lodz go up in fire when the SS smuggled what was now the Jews' explosive-metal bomb into the city.

'No.' Ludmila shook her head. 'And no again. As a matter of fact, he spoke Polish the same way I do. Not as well, I don't think.'

'A Russian?' Mordechai asked, and she nodded. Now he frowned. 'What would a Russian want with me? I haven't had anything to do with Russians . . . for a while.' Ludmila was his dear friend, but that didn't mean she needed to know everything he did as one of the leaders of Poland's Jews. She nodded again, understanding as much. He shrugged. 'Isn't that interesting? All right, I'll keep an eye open for Russians. Can't trust those Reds, after all. You never know what they might do.'

'No, you never know.' Ludmila, former Red Air Force senior lieutenant, smiled at him. 'Reds are liable to do all sorts of foolish things. They might even decide they like living in Poland.'

'Oh, I doubt that,' Mordechai said. They both laughed. He went on, 'I wonder what the fellow wants with me. I know some Russians – some Russians in Russia, I mean – but if they need to get hold of me, they know how.'

Ludmila looked troubled. 'Maybe I shouldn't have told him anything. But I didn't think it could do any harm.'

'It probably won't,' Anielewicz said. 'Don't worry about it. I don't intend to.' He brought his feet back up onto the bicycle pedals and rode off. When he looked back over his shoulder – not the safest thing to do in the narrow, crowded, winding streets of Lodz – he saw Ludmila walking along with the same limping determination she'd shown ever since coming to the city. She never said anything more about the nerve gas that still tormented her than *nichevo* – it can't be helped. Heinrich Jäger had been the same way till the aftereffects of the gas helped put him in an early grave.

As Mordechai pedaled back toward his flat, he kept on pondering what Ludmila had told him. He couldn't make heads or tails of it. Russians who dealt with him in official ways necessarily knew how to reach him. Those who dealt with him in unofficial ways, as David Nussboym had, could also get hold of him whenever they needed to. But he didn't think he'd be seeing Nussboym, officially or unofficially, for a long time, if ever. By the word that filtered out of the Soviet Union, the NKVD was still being purged. Odds of Nussboym's survival didn't strike Mordechai as good.

'And I won't miss him a bit,' he muttered as he stopped in front of his block of flats. But what did that leave? After a little while, he realized it might leave a Russian who had nothing to do with the government of the Soviet Union. That government was so all-embracing inside the USSR, it was no wonder the thought had taken so long to occur to him. The wonder was, he'd come up with it at all.

When he got up to the flat, he asked his wife if anybody speaking Polish with a Russian accent had come around looking for him. 'Not that I know of,' Bertha answered. She turned to their children, who were doing homework at the kitchen table. 'Has anyone with a funny accent been asking for your father?'

Heinrich Anielewicz shook his head. So did his older brother David and their older sister Miriam. 'Isn't that peculiar?' Mordechai said. 'I wonder who the fellow is and what he wants.' He shrugged. 'Maybe I'll find out, maybe I won't.' He started to shrug again, then paused and sniffed instead. 'What smells good?'

'Lamb tongues,' Bertha answered. 'They're usually more trouble than they're worth, because it's so hard to peel off the membrane – it comes away in little pieces, not in big chunks like a cow's – but the butcher had such a good price on them that I bought them anyhow.'

David said, 'I hear the Lizards have such sharp teeth, they can eat tongues and things like that without peeling them.'

Heinrich and Miriam both looked disgusted, which had to be part of what he'd had in mind when he spoke up.

'If you remembered your Hebrew half as well as the things you hear on the street, you wouldn't have to worry so much about your *bar mitzvah* next month,' Mordechai said.

'I'm not worried, Father,' David answered. That was probably true; he had an easygoing disposition much like his mother's. Mordechai was worried, though. So was Bertha, even if she did her best not to let it show. They would go right on worrying till the momentous day had passed, too. Having a son who excelled at his *bar mitzvah* was a matter of no small pride among the Jews of Lodz.

Over the supper table, in between bites of flavorsome tongue (the lamb tongues might have been a lot of trouble to make, but turned out to be worth it), Heinrich asked, 'Father, what's an irrational number?'

'A number that drives you crazy,' David put in before his father could answer. 'The way you do arithmetic, that's most of them.'

Mordechai gave him a severe look and Heinrich a curious one. Mordechai knew something about irrational numbers; he'd studied engineering before the Germans invaded Poland and turned his life upside down. 'You're just barely nine years old,' he said to his younger son. 'Where did you hear about irrational numbers?'

'A couple of my teachers were talking about them,' Heinrich answered. 'I thought they sounded funny. Are they crazy numbers, or numbers that make you crazy, the way David said?'

'Well, they call them that because they used to drive people crazy,' Mordechai said. 'They go on forever without repeating themselves. Three is just three, right? And a quarter is just .25. And a third is .33333 . . . as far as you want to take it. But pi – you know about pi, don't you?'

'Sure,' David answered. 'They have us use three and a seventh when we figure with it.'

'All right.' Anielewicz nodded. 'But that's just close – you know what an approximation is, too, right?' He waited for his son to nod, then went on, 'What pi really is, at least the start of it, is 3.1415926535897932 . . . and it'll go on forever like that, not repeating itself at all. The square root of two is the same kind of number. It's the first one that was ever discovered. The ancient Greeks who found it kept it a secret for a while, because they didn't think there should be numbers like that.'

'How did you remember all those decimal places for pi?' Miriam asked.

'I don't know. I just did. I used to know a lot more, even though they're pretty much useless after the first ten or so,' Anielewicz answered.

'I could never remember so many numbers all in a row,' his daughter said.

He shrugged. 'When you play the violin, you remember which note goes after which even when you haven't got the music in front of you. I couldn't do that to save my life.'

'I know.' Miriam sniffed. 'You can't carry a tune in a pail.'

He would have been more offended if she'd been lying. 'I can remember numbers, though,' he said. Miriam sniffed again. He could hardly blame her; set against musical talent, that didn't seem like much. 'Every once in a while, it comes in handy.' Having said that, he'd said everything he could for it.

After supper, the children went back to their books. Then Miriam practiced the violin for a while. David and Heinrich played chess; David had taught his brother how the pieces moved a few weeks before, and took no small pleasure in beating him like a drum. Tonight, though, he let out an anguished howl as Heinrich forked his king and a rook with a knight.

'Serves you right,' Mordechai told him. 'Now you've got somebody you can play against, not somebody you can trample.' By David's expression, he preferred trampling. He couldn't unteach Heinrich, though. He was more than usually willing to go to bed that night.

'I'm not going to stay up, either,' Bertha said less than half an hour later. 'I'm going shopping with Yetta Feldman tomorrow morning, and Yetta likes to get up at the crack of dawn.'

'All right.' Mordechai stayed put by the lamp in the front room. 'I'll finish the newspaper, then I'll come to bed, too.' If the children were asleep and Bertha still awake, who could say what might happen then?

Before he'd finished the paper, though, someone knocked on the door. He was frowning as he went to answer it; ten past ten was late for visitors. 'Who's there?' he asked, not opening the door.

'Is this the flat of Mordechai Anielewicz?' It was a man's voice, speaking Polish with a palatal Russian accent.

'Yes. Who's there?' Mordechai asked again, his hand on the doorknob but still not turning it – this was an especially odd time to be receiving strangers. His eyes went to the pistol on the table by the door.

After a moment's silence out in the hallway, he heard a faint click. His body identified the sound before his mind could – it was a safety coming off. He threw himself to the floor an instant before a burst of submachine-gun fire tore through the door at chest to head height.

Behind him, windows and a vase on the table shattered. Through and after the roar of gunfire, he heard people shouting and screaming. He waited till bullets stopped flying over him, then grabbed the pistol and pulled the door open. If the assassin was waiting around out there, he'd get an unpleasant surprise.

But the hall stood empty – for a moment. Then people poured out, many of them also carrying pistols and rifles. Behind him, Bertha exclaimed in horror at what the gunfire had done to the flat, and then in relief that it hadn't done anything to Mordechai.

'Why would anybody start shooting at you, Anielewicz?' asked a fellow who lived across the hall from him.

He laughed. He couldn't remember the last time he'd heard such a stupid question. 'Why? I'm a Jew. I'm a prominent Jew. Poles don't like me. The Lizards don't like me. The Nazis don't like me. The Russians don't like me.' He ticked the answers off on his fingers as he spoke them. 'How many other reasons do you need? I can probably find some more.' His neighbor didn't ask for them. Anielewicz shivered. Why somebody had started shooting didn't worry him so much. Who, now, who'd started shooting was a different story.

As he walked along High Street, Little Rock's Embassy Row, Sam Yeager paused and gave a colored kid a nickel for a copy of the *Arkansas Gazette*. 'Thank you, Major,' the kid said.

'You're welcome.' Sam tossed him a dime. 'You didn't see that.'

The kid grinned at him. 'Didn't see what, suh?' He stuck the dime in a back pocket of his faded blue jeans, where it wouldn't get mixed up with the money his boss had to know about.

Yeager went on down the street reading the paper. The *Lewis and Clark* was still front-page news, but it wasn't the banner headline it had been a couple of days before. Everything seemed to be going just the way it should; the space-station-turned-spaceship would reach the asteroid belt faster than seemed possible. An acceleration of .01 g didn't sound like much, but it added up.

'Acceleration adds up,' Yeager muttered to himself. 'It's about the only thing that does.' He still couldn't figure out why his own government had kept the *Lewis and Clark* so secret for so long. Sure, it had an atomic engine. But there were a lot more untamed atoms running around loose up in orbit than the ones that were pushing the enormous ship out toward the asteroids. The Lizards wouldn't have pitched a fit if President Warren had told them what the USA was up to. They thought people were out of their minds for wanting to explore the rockpile that was the rest of the solar system, but they didn't think it made people dangerous to them.

He sighed. Nobody'd asked his opinion. Somebody should have. If he didn't know about the Race, who did? He sighed again. Whoever'd been in charge of that project had decided secrecy was a better way to go. Secrecy so blatant it put everybody's backs up, Lizards and Nazis and Reds? Evidently. It made no sense to Sam.

Still chewing on it – he wasn't particularly quick-witted, but was as stubborn a man as was ever born (if eighteen years in the low and middle minors didn't prove that, what would?) – he walked past the Arkansas State Capitol and on toward what newspapers called the White House, even if it was built of golden local sandstone. President Warren hadn't given him any details about why he'd been ordered out of California. If it didn't turn out to have something to do with the Lizards, though, he'd be surprised.

The president wants to know what I think, Sam thought. *But some damnfool general doesn't care.* He wondered if he could get Curtis LeMay and whoever LeMay's boss was in trouble. He rather hoped so.

At President Warren's official residence, a guard checked his ID and passed him on to a secretary. The secretary said, 'The president's running a few minutes late. Why don't you just sit down here and make yourself comfortable? He'll see you as soon as he's free, Major.'

'All right,' Sam said – he could hardly say no. A few minutes turned into three-quarters of an hour. He would have been more annoyed if he'd been more surprised.

In due course, the flunky did escort him into the president's office. 'Hello, Major,' Earl Warren said as they shook hands. 'I'm sorry to keep you waiting.'

'It's all right, sir,' Yeager answered. He'd long since learned not to pick fights where it couldn't do him any good.

'Sit down, sit down,' Warren said. 'Would you like coffee or tea?' After Sam shook his head, the president went on, 'I suppose you're wondering why I asked you to hop on an airplane and pay me a call.'

'Well, yes, sir, a little bit,' Yeager agreed. 'I suppose it has to do with settling the Lizards' feathers after the *Lewis and Clark* got moving, though.'

'As a matter of fact, it doesn't,' the president said. 'It hasn't got a single, solitary thing to do with that. From what I hear, you kept looking in that direction till you got your ears pinned back for you.'

'Uh, yes, Mr. President.' Sam had kept looking in that direction after he'd got his ears pinned back, too. President Warren didn't seem to know that. *A good thing, too,* Sam thought. No, he wouldn't get LeMay into hot water. He was lucky not to be in hot water himself.

'All right, then. We'll say no more about it.' Warren sounded like the prosecutor he'd once been letting some petty criminal off with a warning because taking him to court would be more trouble than it was worth. 'Now, then: are you even the least bit curious why I did ask you to come back East?'

Presidents didn't ask; they ordered. But Sam could only answer, 'Yes, sir. I sure am.' And that was the truth. He was even more curious now than he had been before. While he was coming out from California, he'd thought he knew what Warren had on his mind. Discovering he'd been wrong piqued his curiosity.

'Okay. I can take care of that.' Warren flicked the switch on an intercom, then bent low to speak into it: 'Willy, would you bring the crate in, please?'

'Yes, sir,' answered someone on the other end of the line. *The crate?* Sam wondered. He didn't ask. He simply waited, as he'd sat in the dugout and waited out any number of rain delays.

A side door to President Warren's office opened. In came a blocky little man – Willy? – pushing what looked like a metal box on wheels. An electric cord trailed after it. As soon as the fellow stopped, he plugged the cord into the nearest outlet. At that point, Sam's curiosity got the better of him. 'Mr. President, what the he – uh, heck – is that thing?'

Warren smiled. Instead of answering directly, he turned to the man who'd brought in the box. 'Open the lid.' As the assistant obeyed, Warren gestured to Sam. 'Go on over and have a look.'

'I sure will.' When Yeager stepped up and peered into the box, he had to blink because he was looking at a couple of bare lightbulbs that put out a good deal of light and heat. They illuminated a pair of large eggs with speckled yellow shells. Sam looked back at the president. 'It's an incubator.'

'That's right.' Earl Warren nodded.

Sam started to ask a question, then stopped. His mouth fell open. He came closer to losing his upper plate in public than he had for many years. Only one kind of egg could account for his being summoned from Los Angeles to Little Rock. 'Those . . . came from a Lizard, didn't they?' he asked hoarsely.

President Warren nodded again. 'That's right,' he repeated.

'My God.' Yeager stared at the eggs. 'How did we ever manage to get our hands on them?'

'*How* doesn't concern you,' the president said crisply. 'I am only going to tell you that once, and you had better get it through your head. It is none of your business. I hope you've learned your lesson about things that are none of your business.' He gave Sam a severe look.

'Yes, sir.' Sam wasn't looking at the president as he spoke. His eyes kept going back to those incredible, sand-colored . . .

'All right,' Warren said. 'How would you like to take those eggs back to California with you and raise the babies when they hatch? Raise them up like people, I mean, or as much like people as you can. Finding out just how much alike we and the Lizards are and how and where we differ will be very important as time passes, don't you think?'

'Yes, sir!' Sam said – no polite acquiescence now but hearty, delighted agreement. 'And thank you, sir! Thank you from the bottom of my heart!'

'You're welcome, Lieutenant Colonel Yeager,' President Warren said, chuckling at his enthusiasm.

'Lieut—' Yeager stared, then snapped to attention and saluted. 'Thank you again, sir!' He felt like turning handsprings. He hadn't thought he'd ever see the oak leaves on his shoulder straps go from gold to silver. For somebody who'd started out as a thirty-five-year-old buck private, he'd turned out to have a pretty fair career.

'And you're welcome again,' Warren answered. 'You've done very well for us, and now you're taking on another assignment that won't be easy. You deserve this promotion, and I'm pleased to be able to give it to you. As a matter of fact . . .' He reached into a desk drawer and took out a jewelry box. 'Here are your new insignia.'

Sam wondered how many lieutenant colonels had got their rank badges from the hand of the president of the United States. Not a whole lot, or else he was Babe Ruth. He paused, bemused. When it came to Lizards, he pretty much *was* Babe Ruth. His eyes slid back to the incubator. 'How long till those eggs hatch, sir?'

Willy answered for President Warren: 'We think about three weeks, Lieutenant Colonel, but we might be off ten days or so either way.'

'Okay.' Yeager knew a different sort of bemusement. 'It'll feel funny, being a new father again at my age.' President Warren and Willy both laughed. Then something else occurred to Sam. 'Lord! I wonder what Barbara's going to think of becoming a new mother again.' That was liable to be more interesting than he cared for.

But the president said, 'This is for the country. She'll do her duty.' He rubbed his chin. 'And we'll give her a civil-service promotion, too. You're right – she'll earn it.'

'That's fair.' And Yeager thought Warren was right. Barbara would pitch in and help. Chances to learn about the Race like this didn't grow on trees. Sam suddenly grinned. Jonathan would pitch in, too. He'd leap at the chance, where he'd run screaming from the idea of taking care of a human baby.

'You should have some fascinating times ahead of you – and

busy ones, too,' Warren said. 'In a way, I envy you. You'll be doing something no one has ever done before, not in all the history of the world.'

'Yeah,' Sam said dreamily. But this time, when his gaze went back to the incubator, he turned practical again. 'You'll either need to fly that out to L.A. in a pressurized cabin or ship it by train. We don't want to take any chances with those eggs.'

'No, indeed,' President Warren agreed. 'And that has been taken care of. A military charter will get into Los Angeles an hour after your return flight. That should give you time enough to meet it and accompany the truck that will bring the incubator to your home.'

'Sounds good, sir,' Yeager said. 'Sounds great, in fact. You're a couple of steps ahead of me. Better that way than to find out you're a couple of steps behind.'

'I don't think anyone who serves the United States can care to an excessive degree about details – that is, there is no degree of care that could be too large,' the president said, with a precision of which Barbara would have approved.

'All right.' Sam didn't want to leave the incubator even for a moment. He laughed at himself. After the eggs hatched, he'd be praying for free time. He remembered that from the days when Jonathan was a baby. He didn't think two Lizards would be less demanding than one human had been.

After President Warren dismissed him, he left the new, not so white White House with so much spring in his step, he might have been walking six inches off the ground. A promotion, a new assignment that would keep him busy and fascinated the rest of his career if not the rest of his life . . . What more could a man want?

One thing looked pretty clear: once he got those eggs home, he wouldn't have time to worry about the *Lewis and Clark* or much of anything else for quite a while. He paused and looked back toward the president's residence. Could Warren have . . . ? Sam shook his head and walked on down High Street, a happy man.

* * *

Glen Johnson had never gone to the moon. He'd never got out of close orbit around the Earth till he went up to have a look at the Lizard reconnaissance satellite and, not so coincidentally, the space station that had turned into the *Lewis and Clark*. Now, peering out one of the windows of the enormous, ungainly ship, he saw Earth and moon together in the blackness of space: matching crescents, one large, one small.

He couldn't just float weightless by the window and gape to his heart's content, as he might have done aboard *Peregrine*. Acceleration was ghostly; he couldn't feel his effective weight of a bit over a pound and a half. But if he tried to hang in the air, he moved back toward the *Lewis and Clark*'s distant motor – four inches the first second, eight the next, a whole foot the third, and so on. Up and down had meaning here, even if they didn't have much. Papers needed to be clipped or held with rubber bands on any surface that wasn't *down* in respect to the axis of acceleration . . . and on any surface that was, because air currents were plenty to send them fluttering off desktops under .01 g.

The crew of the *Lewis and Clark* had already started inventing games suited to their unique environment. One involved spilling a stream of water at the top of a chamber, then hurrying down to the bottom to drink it when it finally got there. It took more skill than it looked; an error in judgment sent water droplets flying every which way, some in slow motion, others not.

One of those errors in judgment had sent water droplets flying into the *Lewis and Clark*'s wiring. It had also sent a spate of orders flying from Brigadier General Healey. Their gist was that anybody who tried such a damnfool stunt again could see how he liked trying to breathe outside without a spacesuit. That hadn't stopped the games, but it had made people more careful where and with whom they played them.

Somebody stuck his head into the compartment where Johnson was rubbernecking: Danny Perez, one of the radiomen who'd helped show the world a sardonic face while the space station stayed in orbit. 'It's pretty, all right,' he said now, 'but I wouldn't get real excited about it. It's not like we're going back.'

'Yeah, I know. That's what everybody's been saying since we left,' Johnson answered. 'I'll be damned if I signed up to go rock-hunting a couple of hundred million miles from home, though.'

'Sir, when you came looking around, you signed up,' Perez said, snotty and deferential at the same time. 'Now you're here for the duration, just like the rest of us who really did volunteer.'

'Thanks a lot,' Johnson said, which only made the radioman laugh. 'Christ, I still don't see why you guys had to keep this place as secret as you did.'

'Don't look at me. I just work here.' Perez grinned, his teeth very white in his swarthy face. 'You want to know that kind of stuff, the only one who can tell you is General Healey.'

'I don't think I want to know that bad,' Johnson muttered, at which Perez laughed again and zoomed away.

But, less than an hour later, the intercom blared forth the news that Healey wanted to see Johnson. One thing the crews that built the *Lewis and Clark* had done: they'd put handholds everywhere. Johnson swung along corridors the way Tarzan dreamt of swinging through the trees. And if he missed one hold, he didn't have to worry about falling into a river full of crocodiles. All he had to do was let momentum carry him along till he latched onto another.

And so, much sooner than he wanted, he found himself back in the office to which Alan Stahl had guided him. Brigadier General Charles Healey, belted into a chair, looked no friendlier now than he had then. Fixing Johnson with a cold, gray-eyed glare, he said, 'How are we going to make you useful, Johnson?'

'Sir, you already know I've got a lot of time in space,' Johnson began.

'So does everyone else aboard the *Lewis and Clark*,' Healey said.

'Yes, sir, but I've got piloting experience,' Johnson answered. 'Most people' – *including you, you son of a bitch* – 'are just passengers.'

Healey's scowl got even chillier. 'You have piloting experience with rockets, not under continuous acceleration.'

'Sir, I have piloting experience with aircraft under continuous acceleration – everything from a Stearman trainer up to an F-83 – and on *Peregrine*, too,' Johnson said. 'One more kind of piloting won't faze me, not after better than twenty years of flying.' He fiddled with the belt on his own chair, across the desk from Healey's.

'Lieutenant Colonel, I only wish there were some way I could make you spend your whole tour aboard the *Lewis and Clark* breaking rocks,' Healey said. 'As best I can see, you came aboard this ship with the deliberate intention of spying on it. You had already attempted to gather information you were not authorized to have, and your visit was most likely more of the same.'

He was right, of course. Johnson was damned if he'd admit as much, though. 'Sir, I can't help it if *Peregrine*'s motor picked exactly the wrong minute to go on the blink.' He'd said the same thing so many times, he needed a distinct effort of will to recall that he'd made the motor go on the blink.

'You're a liar. Coincidences are never that convenient, not unless they're arranged,' Brigadier General Healey said. Johnson said nothing at all. With any luck, Healey would have a stroke on the spot. He was certainly turning purple. Fixing Johnson with the evil eye again, he went on, 'If I could prove you're a liar, you'd go out the air lock, Lieutenant Colonel, and your next of kin would get your death benefits.'

He wasn't joking. A chill went up Johnson's spine. Maybe Healey would have been able to get authorization from Kitty Hawk or Little Rock for an unfortunate accident. Maybe he wouldn't have bothered with authorization. Maybe he would have just . . . taken care of things.

He kept on looking at Johnson with deep discontent. 'But I

can't prove that, dammit – so you get to keep breathing. And, since you get to keep breathing, you're going to have to make yourself useful. Maybe you will end up in pilot training. I can't say for sure yet. I still have to do some more checking on you.' By the way he said it, he'd end up knowing what Johnson had thought of his fourth-grade teacher.

'May I ask a question, sir?' Johnson asked.

'You may ask. I don't promise to answer,' Healey said. 'A lot of questions you're probably thinking about, I almost promise not to answer.'

I won't lose my temper, Johnson told himself. And he didn't, though holding it wasn't easy. He said, 'Sir, all I want to know is, what are we really going to be doing out in the asteroid belt for the rest of our lives? Going out there is one thing. Staying out there . . . that's something else.'

'Have you asked other people?' Healey demanded. 'What have they said?'

'They've said to ask you,' Johnson answered, 'and so that's what I'm doing.'

For the first time in their brief, stormy acquaintance, Healey looked pleased. 'Good,' he said. 'You can see by this that no one here is much inclined to trust you any further than I do.'

'Yes, sir,' Johnson said with a sigh. He *had* seen that. He didn't like it for beans. Again, he managed to forget almost completely that he had approached and boarded the *Lewis and Clark* intending to snoop. 'And so, sir, I am asking you,' he repeated. 'I'm not going anywhere now – it's an awfully long walk home.' The images of crescent Earth and moon hanging together in space sprang into his mind again. How soon would they stop being crescents and turn into nothing but stars?

'We are going out to become a base for American prospectors, you might say, in the asteroid belt,' Healey told him. 'You'll have gathered that for yourself, I shouldn't wonder. All sorts of useful minerals among the asteroids – all we have to do is find them. Ice, too, or so it seems, and where there's ice, there's hydrogen and oxygen – rocket fuel and stuff we can breathe. Doesn't that make sense to you?'

'Yes and no, sir,' Johnson answered. 'Yes because I want us to go out into space as much as the next guy does. We need to be there, and this is an important step. I understand that. I don't understand why we're never going home, and I don't understand why we kept the *Lewis and Clark* secret for so long. We could have told the Lizards what we were up to. They wouldn't have tried to stop us. They would have just laughed. They're not interested in anything but Earth.'

'You have a touching faith in them, Johnson,' Healey said. 'Some of us are less trusting – of them, of you, of things in general.'

'I've noticed that,' Johnson said, as dryly as he dared. 'Trouble is, the Lizards noticed it, too. So did the Germans and the Russians.'

'Hell with 'em,' Healey said. 'Where we're going, they'll have the devil's own time spying on us. As far as the Russians are concerned, we're gone – they don't have the capacity to come after us and look. The Lizards can, of course, but they won't bother. You said it yourself: they think we're nuts for going out there.'

Johnson wasn't so sure he didn't think the *Lewis and Clark* and her crew weren't nuts for going out into deep space the way they were doing it, but he didn't mention that. He did say, 'The Lizards probably won't send a piloted ship out to look at us, sir, but they could easily send a reconnaissance probe like the one I was looking over when my motor failed – I *was* in the neighborhood for a reason, you know.' He'd set it up that way. If he hadn't set it up that way . . . *If I hadn't set it up that way, I'd probably be dead,* he thought, and another chill went through him.

Brigadier General Charles Healey gave him a most unpleasant look. But this one, he judged, was aimed at what he'd said, not at him personally. 'You have a nasty mind, don't you, Lieutenant Colonel?' Healey said. 'But you may have a point, too. We will have to keep an eye on outbound launches. And we'll have to keep an eye on the *Reich*. The Germans could do something like this if they set their minds to it.'

'It wouldn't be the end of the world if they did, would it, sir?' Johnson said. 'If there aren't enough asteroids to go around, we're all in a lot of trouble, right?'

'I suppose so,' Healey said peevishly. 'Asteroids.' Just for a moment, Johnson wondered if he cared so much about them as he'd seemed to a little while earlier. Then the commander of the *Lewis and Clark* said, 'Well, the odds are the Nazis will worry about things closer to home. They have more to worry about than we do, and that's the truth.' He pointed at Johnson. 'Now – about you.'

'Yes, sir?' Johnson tensed and tried not to show it. The name-calling was over; he could feel as much. Whatever Healey was going to do with him or to him, he'd find out now.

'Pilot training.' The sour-faced brigadier general spoke as if the words tasted bad. 'We're already redundant there, but we can't have too many backups. If the latest checks come back all right, maybe you can learn it. You have to learn something, that's for damn sure. No drones here.'

'I don't want to be a drone,' Johnson answered. 'I've said that ever since I came aboard.'

'Talk is cheap,' General Healey said, and Johnson discovered the name-calling wasn't over after all. But then Healey relented, ever so slightly: 'If you work as hard now that you are aboard as you did to get aboard, maybe we'll get some use out of you after all. Dismissed.'

Johnson saluted, unbelted, and flew out of the office – metaphor back on Earth, literal truth here. Healey would give him at least some of what he wanted, not least because he had no true choice . . . except putting him out the air lock. *I'll learn all I can,* Johnson thought. *Maybe I'll even learn what the* Lewis and Clark *is really for.*